Han Suyin is the daughter  her who, a Mandarin and scho ny, had chosen instead at the ip to Europe.

She was moved by the ound her to take up medicine. She s classics and mathematics while waiting for a place at Yenching University. Then, after completing her pre-medical education, she travelled across Siberia to Europe on a scholarship and continued her studies at the University of Brussels. In 1938 she returned to China, married an ex-Sandhurst Chinese officer, who later became a general in Chiang Kai Shek's army, and practised midwifery in the interior during the Sino-Japanese War. From this experience she wrote her first book, *Destination Chungking*, in 1940. In 1942 she came to London, where her husband had been appointed military attache. Three years later he returned to active service in China, leaving Han Suyin to complete her medical studies in London. After her husband was killed in 1947, she spent a year as a house surgeon at the Royal Free Hospital before accepting a doctor's post in Hong Kong. There she wrote the Eurasian love story (her own) that brought her international acclaim and success as a writer. The Sunday Times described *A Many-Splendoured Thing* as 'an astounding love story . . . brilliantly topical, but far more than that, for she handles an eternal theme with power, insight and unfailing artistry.'

Since that time she has written numerous books, both novels and non-fiction. Her combined autobiography and history of China in five volumes, has been hailed as an important contribution to international understanding. Bertrand Russell said of the first volume, *The Crippled Tree*, 'during the many hours I spent reading it, I learnt more about China than I did in a whole year spent in that country'.

'A love story in which the magic of the background, Khatmandu, its mountains, people and customs, is all vividly brought to life . . . the contrast between the Nepalese and the precisely defined European colony is skilfully achieved.'   *Sunday Times*

' . . . this lovely and moving book . . . It is difficult briefly to convey the flavour of this rare novel . . . in which wit and humour are combined with a wise tolerance.'   *Daily Telegraph*

'The ceremonies of the coronation provide colour, humour and eroticism enough to give rare background for a powerful novel, and Han Suyin has dealt magnificently with the background.'   *Punch*

By the same author

Autobiography, History

The Crippled Tree
A Mortal Flower
Birdless Summer
My House Has Two Doors
Phoenix Harvest

Novels

A Many-Splendoured Thing
Destination Chungking
. . . And the Rain My Drink
Cast But One Shadow and *Winter Love*
Two Loves
The Four Faces
Till Morning Comes

Non-Fiction

China in the Year 2001
Asia Today
Lhasa, The Open City
*The Morning Deluge: Mao Tsetung and the
    Chinese Revolution 1893–1953*
*Wind in the Tower: Mao Tsetung and the
    Chinese Revolution 1949–1975*

HAN SUYIN

The Mountain is Young

TRIAD
PANTHER

Triad/Panther Books
Granada Publishing Ltd
8 Grafton Street, London W1X 3LA

Published by Triad/Panther Books 1973
Reprinted 1976, 1982, 1984, 1985

Triad Paperbacks Ltd is an imprint of
Chatto, Bodley Head & Jonathan Cape Ltd and
Granada Publishing Ltd

First published in Great Britain by
Jonathan Cape Ltd 1958
Copyright © Han Suyin 1958

ISBN 0-586-03816-7

Printed and bound in Great Britain by
Collins, Glasgow

Set in Monotype Bembo

Contents

Some of the Characters

John Ford – *a retired Colonial Civil Servant.*
Anne Ford – *a beautiful English girl, a wayward writer in search of herself.*
Leo Bielfeld – *UNO expert in International Goodwill.*
François Luneville – *a reporter-photographer.*
Unni Menon – *a modern incarnation of the Lord Krishna.*
Paul Redworth – *British Resident in Khatmandu.*
Martha Redworth – *an expert on sweetpeas.*
Vassili – *Manager of the Royal Hotel.*
Hilde – *a Nordic goddess.*
General Kumar – *a natural Lifeman.*
His Maharani – *the most serene woman in the world.*
Deepah – *the General's son.*
Lakshmi – *the General's daughter.*
Sri Ranchit – *a handsome, matt-complexioned villain.*
Rukmini – *his Maharani, the second most beautiful woman in the world.*
The Field Marshal – *a philosopher.*
His Maharani – *the most beautiful woman in the world.*
Father MacCullough – *the inevitable, indestructible, knowledgeable priest.*
Isobel Maupratt – *Superintendent of the Girls' Institute, Khatmandu.*
History – Miss Newell – *teaches history.*
Geography – Miss Potter – *teaches geography.*
Suragamy McIntyre – *teaches gym.*
Mutti Aruvayachelivaramgapathy – *Suragamy's fiancé, a Christian business man.*
Dr. Frederic Maltby – *Chief Medical Officer of the Hospital, Khatmandu.*
Eudora Maltby – *a writer of inspirational music.*
His Preciousness the Rampoche of Bongsor – *the biggest crook of the Himalayas.*
Dearest – *the Rampoche's daughter.*

Mariette Valport – *a French woman who wrote* Men of Five Continents.

Colonel Jaganathan – *an engineeer on the road to Khatmandu.*

Major Pemberton – *of The Gurkhas.*

Enoch P. Bowers – *President of the Valley Club.*

Mike Young – *an American engineer.*

Michael Toast – *an English impresario.*

Sharma – *a Nepalese revolutionist.*

The Hindu Poet – *a poet.*

Pat – *an American artist with dirty finger nails.*

Dr. Korla – '*diplomied at stitch and cut*'.

Mita
Regmi } – *servants of the General, on loan to Anne.*

Prof. Rimskov – *an expert on Tibet.*

Suriyah – *a whore of Khatmandu.*

The Swami of Bidahari – *who does not say anything.*

Preface

THIS book is fiction, which means that it endeavours to give as exact a picture as possible of the time, the place, the manners and the people concerned as is compatible with imaginary characters and situations.

There is no British Residency nor Girls' Institute nor Valley Club in Khatmandu; Bongsor, its Monastery, its Rampoche and its dam, do not exist; and, apart from the gods and the goddesses, the beings in this book are illusions of the mind.

PART ONE Plain

And tomorrow weeps in a blind cage
••• ••• •••
But dark is a long way.
DYLAN THOMAS

Chapter 1

'ONE moment please sar! Madam, if you please! Sahib, sahib!'

The fortune-teller was pursuing them. He ran jerkily, puffs of dust spurted from the soles of his brown sandals. His cane gleamed, as the sweat on his bearded face. His full mouth was fresh, red, and smiling, outlined by the surrounding black hair.

'What is it now?' asked John Ford, not stopping after a backward look. 'What does that ass want, d'you know?'

Anne said: 'You saw him last night.'

'I saw him last night? *I* did? What on earth are you talking about?'

John's voice was as tritely astonished as a pair of raised eyebrows, the intonation of surprise employed when, knowing what Anne did mean, he would yet exact from her, to make her acknowledge his existence, monosyllabic replies, reluctant explanations, sentences as brief as she could keep them. He thus extracted, from her taciturnity like a blank back turned upon him, a reassurance of their relationship. He strove to reach her by a bridge of syllables, forcing her to break with speech the solitude she imposed by her presence at his side.

He wanted Anne to say: 'This is the Sikh fortune-teller who waddled up to us last night as we sat on the hotel verandah under the fan after dinner.' But she vanished in wordlessness as a stone under water. It angered and frightened him. It left him alone with unworded, for ever unmentioned episodes, such as their bedroom that morning. He could only escape in rancorous questioning, picking up the daily trivia of their outward lives in words thrown at Anne as gravel at a closed window.

'When am I supposed to have seen this chap, and where?'

If only Anne would be as in their first year together, soon after their marriage. Then, to his 'What, what's that? What d'you mean!' (always abrupt, delivered with a jerk of the head to emphasize the virile precision, and a flash of the eyes, employed for fifteen years of administratorship in a colony now become self-governing) she had responded with laughter verging on a giggle, a puzzled, girlish, unassured mirth which was her reflex to jokes she did not understand.

He had known this timidity in her, an uncertain apprehension of causing offence, and it had pleased him, as it pleases some men to keep their marriage partner in simpering placation as they expect their dogs to wag tails when they come home. He loved to make her jump with a sudden bark of questions, and see her startled, because loud noises, abrupt voices, banging doors, products of human violence, always frightened her inordinately. Yet she was not afraid of thunder. She had uttered little apologetic laughs which he had liked. Later the laughs diminished; dwindled, finally disappeared, replaced by a gritty annoyance, like a sheath of dust hardening upon a mirror, obliterating its sheen.

'Please don't ask me again. You know this as well as I do.'

Still later, in the third year of their married life, she had begun to lose her temper, clasping her hands behind her back to hide their tension, her eyes dilated, her jawbone sharp. This had fascinated him, given him a lift of pleasure, almost made him feel potently excited. 'Now don't shout. Just now you were shouting. Well, I call that shouting. Your voice was going higher and higher. Oh but you were. My dear girl, you're getting very emotional. Really should take yourself in hand. You may be an artist and all that but there's no excuse for being so high-strung. Age and background, I suppose. You're looking quite run down.'

A few times he added: 'After all, I'm your husband, you know.'

Within the past year she had begun what he considered a technique devised to annoy him. Silence.

Now he waited for an answer, waited with an acuteness which made him sweat. A moistening of the lips, slight quiver of the throat muscles preparing words. But there was no alteration of the blank evading face. Nothing. And now the fortune-teller had caught up with them, his hand with the cane raised as if halting a taxi, a thin iron bangle circling his wrist, his turban a clear, cool lime green.

John stopped, turned upon the Sikh, fists slightly doubled, feet braced in his shoes, lower lip thrust out, head forward, large blue eyes upon the velvet brown ones. And just as suddenly as he had assumed it he let go of the pugilistic stance, mimicked a recognition; his brow smoothed, he extended a hand, beginning another game in front of Anne, feeling that Anne resented this clowning yet unable to stop himself from listening to his own voice in front of her.

'Indeed and it is you, master.' (John prided himself on being able to speak to any native in the proper way. 'I could always talk with them, never had any trouble.') 'I did not recognize you at first,' and turning to Anne, 'This gentleman is the fortune-teller we saw last night, dear.'

The Sikh saluted as a soldier, solemn at the mention of his craft.

'Yes sar, but I am more than tell your future. I am also Yogi, wise-man. See here.'

He drew from a side pocket a rosary of brown beads, fingered them rapidly, uttering what sounded like a whine and was a prayer, and dropped them back.

'And this.'

From another pocket appeared the frayed photograph of an old man with long white beard, the Jesus-like forehead and nose of the Indian ascetic, haloed with fine-spun curly white hair, sitting in the lotus pose of meditation among vases containing what looked like paper zinnias.

'That, sar, Swami Narayanda, my teacher, Great Guru, Gurudev ... famous holy man, all countries know about Swami Narayanda.'

And now, most precious, from inside his coat he extracted much thumbed notepaper, some blue, some white, a packet of letters.

'This letter from British general, very famous, great man, a, d, and c to the last British Viceroy of India. Please read him.'

' "The gentlemen certainly seems to trust his own predictions," ' read John. 'Ha, haha.'

'Trust his predictions,' repeated the fortune-teller, beaming with perspiration and pride. 'British generals don't lie, all in world know that. The word of an Englishman. And now sar, madam, I want help you, yes you, not make money, money never mind, don't give money, I only want help. Your right hand, excuse me, madam, aaaaaaaah.'

He seized Anne's right hand in his right, contemplated the palm with prodigious attention, then shut his eyes so tight that the brown skin folded over at the outer corners.

'I tell you ...' (his free hand enclosed a wide half-circle of space) 'everything, something for your whole life make it change; just for twenty rupees,' he ended, opening his eyes and dropping her hand.

'Twenty rupees, did you say twenty, master? Oh that is too much, too much.' With the replete, derisive bonhomie often employed in the last days of colonial administration, John parleyed with the Sikh, happy because while being called 'sar' he was putting the fortune-teller through tricks of smiles and speech and expostulation ('But sar, it is cheap ... everything true ... no sar, I never cheat, can ask the Swami ... the General ...'), and gradually, slowly making him come down in price, rupee by rupee. At his back he felt Anne standing still, and hoped her attentive, held to the scene. But she moved, walked a few paces to a tree along the roadside, leaned against the trunk, and looked into the foliage: the leaves were pointed like attentive listening ears. She was aware of them as if someone said in a precise, dry voice by her ear: 'This is a tree with leaves. You asked the name and now you have forgotten it. The Indians use the juice of its twigs, mixed with salt, to clean their teeth.' She no longer saw green succulent tree-flesh taut within the leafskin, alive, cool inside the green skin. This is a something tree, her mind said. Arid words. Information. The Indians use its twigs ...

'Anne, Anne, for God's sake, will you answer when you're spoken to.'

John was looking at her furiously. She turned her face towards him and then away and his tone changed and he said: 'I've now bargained him down to six rupees for you. D'you want him to tell your fortune or not?'

She came back to the men, stretched her right hand palm upwards to the fortune-teller, while John strode to the same tree under which she had stood. The fortune-teller bent his turban over her hand, gazing. Anne smelt his stocky body, chicken and ghee and sweat, just that. He might have been a tree too. She was not more nor less aware of him. This is a Sikh. This is a turban. Lime green. There is a man's head inside the turban. She was so tired she wanted to close her eyes and sleep, standing up.

'Aaaah,' said the Sikh furtively, not looking at John ten yards away. 'Your heart, memsahib, your heart, like butterfly. People think you nice, sensible lady, always good, always right, but you not like that. You like running water, like butterfly looking for flower, looking, and wanting.'

'You're quite wrong,' said Anne, believing every word she spoke, 'I'm not looking, and I don't want anything.'

'That's what you want think, yourself make you think,' said the relentless Sikh. 'You want: I don't feel, I quite okay, I happy. But is not true. Is not real woman. One day you find. You now have eyes, not see yourself, ears, not listen to own heart, see other things, look other people and listen everybody else, always very clever, but not your own self. But this year you will see and hear. Some time this year,' he repeated loudly.

The Fords walked back to the hotel, choosing the shade under the banyans and gold mohurs. This had once been a cantonment in Agra, and there were fairly large, slightly dilapidated bungalows and gardens on both sides of the road. They turned to the right and were in the street leading to their hotel, with jewellers' shops and sari and leathercraft shops for tourists. Outside each stood salesmen, thin and brown, with scrutinizing eyes and soft voices, in western style jackets with white dhotis round their legs.

'Sahib, memsahib, come, come in, you have nothing to lose. Come, take a look. I have here rubies, sapphires, diamonds, topaz, come in and find what your heart desires.'

On the verandah of the hotel, with potted palms in brass receptacles and cane chairs and dusty fly-blown oleographs of angels and Swiss landscapes, another contingent of tourists had arrived: the usual, all-American, past middle age, round-the-world-by-air party, over-clothed and burdened with extra travel rugs, coats, mackintoshes, hold-alls, umbrellas, their feet swollen in sensible shoes for hiking, the women in straw hats with voilettes and flowers. They sat, glazed with fatigue, stiff with sitting, perspiring under the creaking fans going full blast. Most drank Coca-Cola, the more enterprising had orange juice, asking if it were safe, could they have ice, had the glasses been sterilized, was it true that there was cholera in Agra? 'Oh no madam, there is cholera ONLY in Calcutta and maybe Delhi, but not in Agra, here we have smallpox,' replied the hotel clerk.

'Drink your orange juice without putting your lips to the rim, dear,' said a white-haired old lady to her husband, who wore a hearing aid.

On the floor along one side of the verandah, facing the tourists and gradually advancing upon them by edging forward upon crossed legs, squatted a small battalion of sellers of painted glass and wood bangles, brass gongs and trays and bells, cigarette boxes inlaid with mother of pearl Taj Mahals, ivory miniatures of peacocks and elephants and the Taj, statuettes of dancing girls with naked busts and painted eyes. In

17

the garden, glancing yearningly upward towards the Americans and blowing their flutes as enticement, stood snake-charmers and fortune-tellers, the latter calling with their hands in the Asian manner, palm forward, with a downward movement of the fingers. On tables piled with silks and brocades two fat Bengalis exploded in the air yards of flashing blue and green and tawny gold saris.

Anne and John sat in the cane chairs at a small table, on the rim of the tourists and their talk.

'Where *were* we last night?'

'Was it Karachi or Colombo we bought that Chinese blouse?'

'It says on the schedule: morning view of Taj Mahal, lunch at the hotel, afternoon shopping, and Delhi tonight.'

'Benares … Is that where we saw the cow, Father?'

'Is it handmade?'

'Even the ice cubes are hot in this dump.'

'I must have it handmade.'

'Well, burn me up, they're cheaper in New York.'

'Third batch of blasted tourists in two days,' said John. 'Phew, it's hot.' He slumped back in the chair, pathetically sulky, posturing exhaustion. Behind the narrow forehead, the handsome, petulant features, there was something like pain. In Anne began the familiar compassion and nausea, assailing her together, inveterate mixture of remorse and repulsion which now made her put a hand upon his arm.

'Not here, with all those people round us.' Irritably he withdrew the arm.

Anne's hand came back to her. It was just one more time. In their first year together she bought a new dress. 'How do I look?' she still heard herself gaily calling out (for she was still gay then) to him as he had returned at noon from his office, and put her hands upon his shoulders and danced him round. 'Oh, not now, not in front of *people*,' he had said, frowning and throwing off her hands. Only then had she noticed the two colleagues with him. And now she had nothing to say to him at all.

Her hand back upon her lap, self-immured and relieved of guilt, it was possible for Anne to go back to the morning, to *know* it, with silent words. Débâcle. Her fault. Of course it was her fault. Well, it was. She could not help the way she was made. Frigidity. John had said it. The doctor had said it. There were a lot of women like her.

Sex meant nothing to them. Cold, frigid, she had no sex urge or whatever it was one was supposed to have. Maybe she was getting old.

That too had started long ago. Going to bed together less and less, once a month, once every six weeks, two months, three. This morning in Agra the first time after nearly five months. And still she didn't want it. Tranquil, she accepted that she didn't want it. So it was her fault, as John said. But it wasn't anything she'd want to do anything about. Somehow she felt a little pleased when the doctor had spoken of frigidity. It was a defensive virtue.

This morning John had wakened in the twin bed, next to hers. She had wakened also, seen his face looking at her; he then rolled over and was in her bed with the usual giggle, under the sheet next to her body. Then had come the fumbling at her chest, insentient touch, undelighting, mechanical, which by obvious perfunctoriness always made her feel that her breasts were too small. Then his words, always the same, 'Naughty, naughty,' then his getting up to make sure the door was locked, to adjust the window curtain, and to the bathroom to pass water, and then returning to her, and she waiting, waiting, body waiting, clamped stiff, tight, cold, full of silent shrieking. A little more fumbling with pyjamas, her face turned away to avoid his mouth, his knees pressed between her thighs, opening her legs, and the pain.

There had been times before when he had tried to enter, and could not, and after a few seconds she had felt him go soft, sag, and then he had gone back into his own bed. This morning he had succeeded in forcing his way inside her. It was a long time since she had done what wives did in their stale marriages, what prostitutes do with their clients, with the same intent, to lessen the work: pretend, beating mechanically with their fists on the bed, say ha ha, utterly bored, wondering when the swinging body above them would stop. This time he had come, his mouth pouring saliva upon her hair as well, and she had got up quickly and gone to the bathroom and washed herself completely, hair too.

But the explanation that she was frigid, and did not like it, was acceptable, even vaguely satisfying. It made John feel secure. After all, Anne wasn't the kind that would open her legs to anybody. She'd got over that young affair of hers years ago. Her coldness made John feel safe.

They were now back in the faintly Lysol-flavoured dampness of the hotel bedroom, the morning's enactment erased by the striped counterpanes upon the twin beds.

'God, it's stifling, even here.' John turned on the fan, sighing loudly. Mosquitoes sang, even by day, in the moist dark corners.

Anne sat on a chair.

'You look worn out, as if you had a headache or a backache,' John said. He was solicitous at once, pulling out both pillows of the beds, making her lie down, put up her feet. He bustled about, urged Anne to have an Aspro, rang the bell for the bearer to bring some water in a glass.

'There's water in the Thermos flask,' said Anne.

He is always happier when I am unwell, she thought.

'I think I'll have a shower before lunch,' John said. He proceeded to remove his clothes. When he sat to undo his shoes there was a trickle of sweat between his breasts, white, planted with darkish hair. He raised his arms, flexing his muscles in front of the mirror. His legs were hairy and his belly pale and his buttocks; once upon a time he had been lean and good at games, and when he looked at himself it was the image of the husky athlete and not the flabby man of forty-three that he saw in the mirror.

From his armpits came a sweetish smell, quite different from the fortune-teller's.

'I'm going to have a shower,' he repeated loudly. He walked to the bathroom, the door creaked, the water started its blubber with detonations in the plumbing, his smell remained behind, whirled about under the fan.

I don't think I can stand all this much longer, thought Anne. She saw the words, as if typed on a white sheet of paper. They looked theatrical, empty of meaning. What was it she could not stand? She closed her eyes. What had the fortune-teller said? She wasn't quite sure.

They went that night to see the Taj Mahal, by full moon, with Leo Bielfeld, their great friend.

Leo Bielfeld made them laugh. They laughed at the same time when Leo joked, and it sounded as if they were laughing together.

John could sit late at night with Leo, drinking whisky and laughing.

Leo's narrow face twisted, his hands gestured, he acted out amusing anecdotes, his voice taking on accents, intonations, from the arrogantly nasal dulcet of a Daughter of the American Revolution to the high-pitched gesturing incomprehensibility of an English-speaking Ceylonese.

Leo was a UNO man in a well-paid job, which allotted him besides money large portions of space and time to do with as he pleased. His title was Technical Adviser in International Goodwill, and this was printed in full upon his cards:

LEO BIELFELD
United Nations Organization
Technical Adviser in
International Goodwill
New York, London, Rome, and Asia

Leo travelled about the world, stopping for weeks, months, where he chose, and producing reports of phenomenal bulk. These compilations were peppered with charts showing rising curves of goodwill, plotted in decimals per unit of i.g.w. (a measure patented by Leo ten years ago). He had once done a survey showing an increase of 0·4 i.g.w. per capita among 38,796 untouchables in 21 communities in Cochin and Travancore in South India. His statistics based on figures showing harmonizational kinetrends versus dysnoiac fissional evolutives were regarded as significant. Thus a noticeable increase, among other data, in the purchase of locally supplied toilet paper in seven large Calcutta hotels had led him to inference of a definite increase in the number of American tourists who trusted their bodies to Indian products, since Indians were not addicted to toilet paper, sluicing themselves with water instead. 'Goodwill is Increasing in the World', an exclusive interview given by Leo Bielfeld to the *New York Times*, had provoked controversy; two senators denounced Leo as a fellow-traveller; the Afro-Asian group hailed him a contributor to world stability. Now Leo was in Agra with Anne and John Ford.

The Fords had met Leo four months previously, when he had landed at Dumdum Airport, Calcutta, at three o'clock of a sweltering November morning, and approached them, a vague object whose outline was blurred by clouds of night insects whirling about him and about the neon lights.

'Mr Ford, Mrs Ford ... but I am delighted, enchanted ... so kind of you to come and meet me.' Leo had a prepossessing Austrian accent. 'Yes, your friend François, François Luneville, told me all about you ... but you shouldn't have troubled to meet me ... it is so late, I mean so early.'

His bouncing cheerfulness at three a.m. made them feel light, easier, amiable. Leo blinked, clapped a hand to his eye. An insect had flown into it. He sneezed. Anne smiled, her lips curving gently. 'Those green flies are a pest. Here's a handkerchief, let me get it out.'

'Green flies, green flies, that's the first time I've heard flying ants called green flies,' said John. His tone was benign.

Leo talked all the way as the taxi drove into Calcutta to the Fords' comfortable flat where he would stay as their paying guest. Voluble, amusing, he dazed them with the loquacity of his hands and the kaleidoscopic tumble of his voice. The next morning he tried to make love to Anne.

Anne sat at her desk in the large living-room, her typewriter with a blank sheet of paper in it in front of her. Through the french windows with their small balconies giving on to one of Calcutta's larger avenues, rose steamy noisiness, a perpetual stomach rumble, traffic of the sprawling, unkempt city.

' "Only thirty-four cases of cholera last week, no epidemic yet, declares Health Minister," ' read Leo, bringing the *Times of India* and sitting at Anne's feet on a round leather stool. '*Et cette paisible rumeur*, how can you work, Anne, with this noise?'

'I like it,' said Anne.

'Surely that lovely prose of yours deserves all the amenities,' said Leo, who though Gallic in aspiration had a touch of Germanic wit.

Anne winced, and Leo felt as if he had struck a child.

'I didn't mean to hurt you, Anne.'

'You haven't. It's just that I know I can't write.'

'Oh nonsense, Anne, your book ...'

'That was six years ago. I've done nothing but magazine articles since then.'

'But Anne, short stories have their own genius.'

'Please,' she said.

Leo's arms were now round her, and yet, for once, he felt it an unplanned move. 'Anne dear, please, don't speak like that. I adored your book. I love your stories too. Please don't cry.'

She was not crying. Her face was embarrassed and stubborn and surprised. Leo's protectiveness was aroused and with it his amorous urge. It was always so: women went in for self-pity and it ended in bed. And then everything got better.

He tried to cover her face with kisses, a thing some of his women had liked. Women liked their tears kissed away; but since Anne was not crying, he directed his kisses towards her mouth, and then found her hand covering her lips. He kissed her hand, and she rose. His arms went round her waist, and he rubbed his face on her dress over her belly. He noted it was flat, her thighs long, firm, neither thin nor fat. Simulating a passion half felt he rose. Keeping one hand round her waist his other went to her breasts, small, high, and somehow virginal. Why, he thought, the woman's got a darn good body. No showy curves, probably grand in bed.

'Darling,' he murmured, 'oh darling.'

'No,' she said.

Leo found himself back upon the leather stool and wiping his hands on his handkerchief.

She handed him one cigarette. He took it, lit it, blew a ring of smoke, felt comical. 'Damn it, Anne, you do make a fellow go you know.'

'I'm sorry.' Her voice was infuriatingly colourless.

'You're so damn attractive.'

'Thank you.'

Leo bent forward, trying once more, dilating his eyes and curving his lips in the semblance of a kiss. 'Darling, darling, a kiss, just one.'

'You don't seem to understand,' Anne said, incredulously. 'I'm not angry. Not at all. It's only natural, I suppose, but I don't believe you.'

'Don't believe what? That I love you?'

Her hand waved the words away. 'Please not that, don't let's even begin to say the word love. That's another dimension altogether. I just, you see, I can't believe ...' She hesitated. 'I cannot believe that any man should really want me, as a woman. I mean, feel attracted to me.'

'But how ridiculous, Anne. Why, you're beautiful,' said Leo. 'Not pretty, but beautiful.'

'I don't know. I don't know anything. I just don't believe. I don't want anything. Don't want anybody to touch me. Please don't misunderstand. It's not personal. Not you, because it's you. It's me. I guess I have no sex feeling ... no sex feeling,' she repeated. 'I'm not made that way.'

If she had gone then, he would have pursued her, feeling that it was but another coquetry. (Women had so many ways of expressing what they wanted. He'd had them, coming to him, saying they had no feelings, saying: 'I warn you, I'm frigid,' in the very act of sidling into bed with him. It excited him to greater prowess ... it worked all right.) But there was so much conviction in her quietness. She did not go, she remained on her chair, smoking and looking vaguely across at the balcony, at ease, as if nothing had happened.

He tried again; living in their flat, it was easy. Not that John was working, but he gave himself jobs. 'Got to post this letter,' he would say. 'Must go to the G.P.O. for it, or something's bound to go wrong. Coming, Leo?' 'Sorry, got to rush, I'm interviewing the Mayor,' Leo would lie. That Anne repulsed him, with a kind of weary indifference, neither annoyed nor pleased, not avoiding him afterwards, did not abate his desire to conquer her. For he was a combative little man, more than ordinarily promiscuous through vanity more than uxoriousness. He could not altogether believe at first that hers was not a pose, and tried to change her by redoubled assaults, verbal and physical, only to meet with the same half apologetic denial. I know you're trying to please me, to convince me that I am attractive by making these passes at me, she seemed to say as she pushed him back and then forgot him instantly, and went back into a frozen, slightly staring dream, leaning on the balcony looking at the distance.

'Damn it Anne, don't you ever want a man?'

'No.'

'What about John?'

'John is my husband.'

'From what I can guess he can't be much good at it,' said Leo one day.

'I'm very fond of John,' she replied, her voice like a grey stone.

'Does John like it this way too?'

Her silence forgot he was there.

In Freudian and Jungian terms it was all explainable, and Leo explained at length. She listened and looked polite and then vague. He lent her books. 'Didn't you like it on page twenty-three, Anne, when he ...'

'I don't understand.'

'D'you mean you don't understand what they're doing?'

'No, I mean I don't understand what all the fuss is about.'

One day he nearly shouted: 'But Anne, it's not normal.'

'Maybe I'm not normal,' said Anne, relief in her voice. That's what the doctor and John had said, and now Leo. 'I'm nicely dead,' she told Leo, and it was his turn to find nothing to say.

It was François Luneville, the French photographer, who had told Leo, passing through Paris on his way to India, about the Fords.

'You must stay with them in Calcutta. If their spare bedroom is free. They've got a nice flat, far more comfortable than the hotels and cheaper. Anne Ford is nice.'

They had discussed Anne; for Leo would not, as he said, put his head in a noose or his hostess to bed for courtesy's sake only.

'Nothing doing,' said François. 'Good figure, slight, no sex appeal. And yet there's something ... fire in ice, *un je ne sais quoi*. We professional photographers, whizzing round the world taking pictures, so busy producing sensations of living for our readers (and more people read photographs than the words written round them), we don't have time to live out anything for ourselves, to follow any private event to its consummation in our own existence. So I still didn't know, after two months with them.'

'What's the husband like?'

'Quite all right. What the English call a decent chap. I think an early-retired colonial civil servant. The flat belongs to his brother, who, John gives me to understand, is a baronet or something, living on an estate in Surrey crippled by taxation. John doesn't do anything except get his pension, which I feel isn't very big. He is devoted to Anne, in the English manner, tries to catch her attention, talks loudly, listens to his own voice, and nothing he does or says looks quite real and it all falls flat because she is away dreaming, and doesn't look at him or talk to him.'

'Do they sleep together?' asked Leo.

François's hands rose in the usual French gesture. 'Who knows, *mon cher, les mystères d'un couple marié*? The legitimate bedroom, who can know what goes on there? *Terriblement morne et terne*, probably; but I did not study their bed habits.'

As an afterthought he had added: 'Anne has a beautiful mouth. Always look at a picture upside down, you see the harmony in the composition. And so for her lips, it is not obvious unless she is lying down and you look from above. No, no, Leo, all *parfaitement comme il faut* ... we were at a picnic, quite a lot of people, and she lay flat on the grass and crossed her hands over her eyes. That is why I say, *un je ne sais quoi.*'

Leo spent November and December with the Fords in Calcutta, alternating between studying what he called 'Anne's case' in psychological terms, and bouts of fun obtained, with more or less satisfaction, in swift encounters with the more willing members of the cosmopolitan set of the city. He told Anne about his successes with complete candour. Between spasms of wanting to make love to her, he talked to her unembarrassed for long hours about himself. She listened, and never told him anything in return.

'I must have had nearly one thousand women in my life, Anne. I was counting them up the other night. Last year, for instance, eight in New York in about six weeks, about twelve in London, and I've just had my seventeenth here. I made it altogether nine hundred and sixty-nine and some I've forgotten.'

Now at Agra, meeting the Fords by arrangement on a holiday after two months' absence in South India, he walked with Anne along the marble edge of the Taj Mahal pool; a black mirror in which, pale and bulbous, the Narcissistic monument glistened back at itself. It reminded him, he said, of a Swedish girl with very full white breasts. 'Literally white as snow. And after a while it became quite unbearable. I had the sensation of embracing twin igloos.'

Anne leaned on the marble parapet. Under the high round moon riding absolute overhead, the central dome of the Taj Mahal emitted a livid, glow-worm brilliance. In the blue shadows at its base stood small groups of veiled prostitutes, tinkling silver anklets and bangles. Up and down the terrace strolled Indian men, full of male consciousness, glistening hair damp with brilliantine, very shining whites to their eyes. Behind the Taj, below the place where Anne was, the river, winter-low, trickled between sandbanks. The other shore was pale, unkempt wilderness.

Leo, as John lingered round the shadows full of women's titter, put a sudden arm round Anne.

'Oh please,' she said, suddenly pushing him back with more violence than she had ever done.

'My God, is it that unpleasant?'

They looked at each other, their faces drawn with anger and near-hate.

'All right, I won't bother you again,' he said, as he had said many times before. She's not even my type, he thought, raging, for his taste ran to the full-fleshed, the pictorially sumptuous, a news-stand parade as at the airports he flew in and out of in his wanders. Damn that cow, she's just plain stupid, not a spark in that body. Nothing, except that memory of an occasional softness in the way she spoke.

John came near and announced that it was getting late, and turning their backs upon the frigid splendour they had come to see, they went back in the taxi in the powdery moonlight to the hotel and to a late dinner in the hideous dining-room, a well-like structure with columns, fans, tables, and bearers, all the same colour, a grey, dusty off-white.

'Mountain lamb with green peas,' read Leo on the menu. 'It was wild sheep with cabbage for lunch, wasn't it? The food's certainly a relic of British colonialism, if nothing else is. What's the difference between mountain lamb and wild sheep?' he asked the head waiter.

'Sar, it's the same, Australian frozen mutton.'

'Registered letter for you, sahib.' A bearer was by John's elbow with a letter on his tray.

'Mrs John Ford, 134 Hoogly Avenue, Calcutta, redirected here,' said John, and was going to open it when Anne's hand reached across the table.

'Mine, I think.'

He avoided looking at her as she opened the envelope. Leo, covering awkwardness with verbiage, discussed Indian colour consciousness.

'Just as aware of pigments as we are, old boy. Look at their marriage adverts in the newspapers: Wanted, girl of good family, must be fair skinned. All over this emphasis on fairness: even in government departments, I'm told, they don't like the South Indians taking over so many posts. They're cleverer, better educated, but above all, they're dark.'

'Dear Mrs Ford,' Anne read, 'Your application for the post of

Lecturer in English at the Girls' Institute of Khatmandu, Nepal, has been considered by the Board and we have great pleasure in informing you that you have been selected, on the recommendation of the Principal, Miss Isobel Maupratt, who we believe was once a schoolmate of yours in Shanghai.

'Miss Maupratt has told us about your book, and we are pleased to have a genuine author on our staff.

'The contract is for six months from 15 March, renewable at the end of the term. We are not in a position to offer a longer contract because this is against the policy of the Nepalese Government.

'The salary ...'

'Well,' said John, 'that's a long letter. Your soup's getting cold.'

Now was the time to speak. Leo was here. Once in the bedroom, the two of them alone, it would be impossible.

'I've got myself a job.' Anne's eyes bent to the soup, she picked up the spoon and started eating. She did not look at the men.

'A job?' Not believing it, John put his spoon down, his face arranging itself slowly into profound surprise.

'A job.' Leo seemed puzzled, then quickly recovering himself, laughed richly. 'My dear dear Anne, how sweet and too fantastic. What kind of a job?'

'As Lecturer in English at the Girls' Institute, Khatmandu.'

'What's this, what? What did you say: Lecturer? In Khatmandu? Where the hell is Khatmandu? I don't believe it. How did this happen? This is the first time I've heard about all this.'

'Naturally,' said Anne, suddenly violent again, a smothered, low-spoken violence as on the moonlit terrace of the Taj Mahal, 'I did not mention it.'

'Will you please explain yourself,' ordered John.

'I wrote and asked them. There is nothing to explain.'

'You mean you wrote and applied for a job, in Khatmandu, and you never told *me* about it? Khatmandu? Where is it, by the way, Leo? Nepal? Nepal, in the Himalayas? Next to Tibet?'

As if diving for a drowning body, Leo plunged:

'John, this is too wonderful and enchanting. Of course Anne wished to surprise you, it is a joke, a splendid joke. She wrote to apply for a job and she's got it, ha ha, how utterly lovely and feminine, ha ha ha.'

'It's not a joke,' said Anne. 'I applied, and I'm going to Khatmandu. Khatmandu ...' she repeated.

'Well, I must say,' began John. Then he stopped. John looked at Leo. Leo looked at Anne. Anne's eyes were on her soup, mechanically she was carrying the spoon to her mouth, and back to the plate. Her hand lay on the table, clenching the envelope. *Himmel*, thought Leo, fire in ice. There it is. He remembered the sudden hate on the terrace, the tense, pent-up violence. Suddenly he was a little afraid of her. 'Well, Anne,' he said, lamely, 'I wish you all the best in Khatmandu.'

'Thank you. Leo, how does one get to Khatmandu, d'you know?' asked Anne.

PART TWO Valley

Along the slopes of the Himalayas, between Tibet and India, lies the Kingdom of Nepal. Landlocked and cut off from the rest of the world by its mighty mountains, Nepal remained a territory whose rulers actively discouraged foreign visitors and foreign ways.

Since 1951 all this has changed. Until then Nepal was a despotism. From 1850 to 1950 the hereditary Prime Ministers of the Rana family wielded supreme power under the aegis of titular kings. As a result of a palace revolt in 1950 the King regained his position of authority, a popular ministry was formed, and Rana rule was abolished.

Nepal can roughly be divided into three regions: the high Himalaya country, the foothills, and the low, swampy, malarial jungle of the Terai, famous for its tiger and rhinoceros hunts.

The foothills which contain the bulk of the population form several fertile valleys, of which the largest is Khatmandu Valley, at an altitude of 4,500 feet. It is the administrative, economic, and cultural centre of the kingdom. It is about 20 by 18 miles in area, and inhabited mainly by the Newaris, highly skilled craftsmen. The valley's three main towns, Khatmandu, Patan, and Bhadgaon, have a very old and glorious history. Their art and architecture have influenced Chinese craftsmen and it was Nepalese architects who are said to have built the temples and monasteries of Lhasa in Tibet.

Until 1951 there were no ways into Nepal except narrow bridle paths often too steep for horses across the southern ranges from India, or north into Tibet. Today a motorable road built by Indian Army engineers links Khatmandu Valley with India. Until the road was completed, at the end of 1956, the only efficient and quick means of transport within Nepal was by air.

In 1955 the tourist age came to Nepal in the form of ten American and two Brazilian visitors shepherded by Thomas Cook & Son. In 1955 Nepal became a member of the United Nations.

In May 1956 the King was crowned in a fabulous ceremony which was filmed by Cinerama and attended by sixty foreign correspondents.

(Excerpt from Focus, published by the American Geographical Society.)

Chapter 1

ISOBEL MAUPRATT craned forward, scanning the sky. Above her arms, pillowed on the cylindrical railing which enclosed the airfield landing apron, her heavy breasts dipped forward, rolling over her wrists, a pleasing sensation. She lowered her head and peered at the cleft between them. Like twin doves, resting twin doves. The words, cooing, hovered in that nebulous twilit region of self where Isobel, spinster, thirty-seven, was a different person from Miss I. Maupratt, B.A., daughter of missionaries and Superintendent of the Girl's Institute, Khatmandu.

Doves. The words went unrebuked, hallowed by the large, black, grandfather Bible brought with Miss Maupratt two years ago to do the Lord's work in Khatmandu.

At two-thirty every day except Saturday – the Nepalese day of rest – a Dakota, carrying passengers, freight, and the mail, took off from Patna, in the Indian plain, and winged over the southern hill ranges and valleys of Nepal to land on the new airfield of the capital, Gaucher Airport, Khatmandu. The trip took fifty minutes. Today there were billowy clouds like bulging sails, silky with reflected sunlight, above the lower hills, masking the higher ranges and the snow mountains behind them. The sky above the Valley itself was a jagged blue opening. The airplane might be there, in the cloud mass, the pilot trying to find the Valley, circling until a rent would show him Khatmandu, its golden spires and many-roofed pagodas flashing and the white tower called Bhim Seng's Folly like an admonishing finger raised to the blue sky.

'Anne,' muttered Isobel Maupratt half aloud. 'After all these years, Anne.'

Round her lay the beautiful Valley of Khatmandu, suspended in golden sunlight, a Cézanne landscape spreading clear with blues and greens, pinks and yellows of the Himalayan spring. The soft splayed-out hills which delimited the Valley undulated tree-feathered crests, the hedges were heavy with blossom, the air held a lucid, apple freshness, of new sap and young grass and swelling bud, and the deep down freshness of mountain snow. Across the green fields which led to the holy temple of Pashupatinath, not far from the airfield, walked an endless file of Nepalese men and women, with flowers in their hair or above the ear, going to worship; two Tibetans with hanging moustaches, crew-cuts, and ciné cameras, with thick purple dresses, one sleeve of which hung empty down their backs, scarlet and yellow sashes round their waists and high-to-the-knee boots, leaned on the railing a few yards away from Isobel, waiting for the airplane. A few beggar children, grey with dirt, their soft homespun Nepalese caps jauntily askew (as are all caps in Nepal) upon their lice-sprinkled hair, watched Miss Maupratt from behind and from the side and commented with mirth and precision. Miss Maupratt caught a word and crossed her arms more firmly. Horrid, nasty brats. All Nepalese were the same. Only *one* thing in their minds, all the time. Even the children. You had to watch those girls at the Institute like a hawk, or they'd be whispering in corners, caressing the bangles of marriage upon their arms, laughing that tinkling relentless laughter so pointless to her ... as if life were really wonderful all the time, as if there were no such things as saving souls, and sin, and suffering for one's own good. It was those ... those frightful carvings and paintings everywhere, thought Isobel Maupratt, agitated again by that strange tremor when she thought about them. Horrid, horrid things. One tried hard *never* to look at them. Whenever Miss Maupratt passed a temple at Khatmandu, she adjusted her sunglasses on her face, firmly, and walked on. It wouldn't do to glance up. 'Nasty, nasty,' she said aloud, her voice shaking.

There was a trembling of the earth around her, and it was a little while before Miss Maupratt realized it was no longer due to her thoughts, but a vibration external, of the ground and air, the airplane, closing in now upon the Valley, and loud though still unseen. The two flimsy tents pitched upon the apron which served as Customs and passport offices seemed to shake; out of the open flaps came two handsome Nepalese youths in the soft black caps, buttoned black coats, and white jodhpurs of officials. They looked meditatively at the sky, where like a slow, large bird-god, a silver Garuda, the plane now came into view, and the Tibetans exclaimed and waved their hands and pointed it out to each other. The Dakota circled the airfield, losing height in a wide loop, and suddenly was down, swallowing up the stretch of tarmac with its long white streak, running swiftly towards Miss Maupratt. For a wild moment Isobel Maupratt dreamed herself hurled to the ground on her back by the impact of that enormous winged body rolling over her.

The plane stopped, turned, slow, clumsy, its propellers appeared to reverse their motion. Miss Maupratt straightened herself. 'I wonder if I'll know her.' Nepalese workmen in grey homespun with legs bare to the buttocks pushed a ladder towards the opening plane door, a feat they accomplished with laughter and ribald jests. Indian airlines men, tall and dark in navy trousers and white shirts, strolled up the ladder with the nonchalant lope of men who know themselves male and therefore desirable; they came down again, and the passengers one by one behind them; five Nepalese women, pea-green, sweating with airsickness and trampling the hems of their saris; a Tibetan woman with copper face, splendidly heavy thick braids, and large gold ornaments encrusted with turquoises, carrying a baby, a large plastic hold-all, and an electric fan, and surrounded by a small crowd of teenage Tibetan girls in convent uniforms and boys in emerald velvet wind-cheaters; the two men who were waiting for her now called gutturally, and the teenagers waved and shouted; a British Gurkha officer with thick handlebar moustache and a corpulent brief-case came next, followed by two Nepalese officials with black umbrellas hooked into the collar of their coats at the back, and fourteen American tourists with coats and bags and cameras and canes and Homburgs and flowered hats.

'Americans.' Reverently the murmur rose and floated among the beggars, now multiplied into a crowd of all ages and sexes. And like a sudden wind they rippled forward, a foaming crest of hands upraised to claw at the wealth coming down the plane ladder.

'Twenty years, I wonder if I'll know her.' Twenty years ago Isobel's parents had run a mission boarding school in Shanghai. Anne had been a boarder, one of that small handful of Eurasians and White Russians and illegitimates who never went home for holidays. Isobel still felt her mother's pursed mouth and heard her voice: 'We *must* be kind to Anne, dear, her mother's an actress.'

One day Anne's mother had come to see Anne, and Isobel remembered the pink silk dress, the scarf of pale grey feathers, the shoes with buckles, and the rickshaw that she came in stopping in front of the gate, at recreation time, and Anne running, running *away*, and Isobel staring at the thin brown legs and then back to the woman in pink staggering out of the rickshaw with four boxes of chocolates (Isobel saw still the bright silver and gold ribbons round them) in her arms.

And now here was Isobel, of all places in Khatmandu, and Anne … here was Anne now, coming down the ladder, in a pale tan dress fitted to her slim body, bare brown legs in sandals, windblown dark hair, looking exactly the same, walking with that extraordinary look of outward pliability, docile Anne with the sudden furies and the long silences, coming straight down towards Isobel.

'Anne,' shouted Isobel. 'Yoohoo Anne, A-anne!' And then she was hugging Anne, who had stretched out her hand, and she heard herself, a high-pitched voice, saying, 'My dear, how nice, how absolutely too too wonderful after all these years, I'd never have dreamed … Did you get my letter? Oh but of course you did, you wrote back, how silly of me. But you haven't changed a bit … too wonderful, mmm …'

'You have not changed much, either, Isobel.' Anne still had her quaint way of articulating each word, exactly, making even the punctuation felt, as if she were typing, and thus establishing a distance. She did not look at Isobel, she looked round her at the Valley, turning her eyes and her head, following the line of the hills, squinting against the gold puddle of the sun.

'Khatmandu,' she said, and gulped a little, and opened her mouth as if she found it hard to breathe.

'My dear, it's the height, we're over four thousand here, one does find it a bit strenuous at first. Is your heart all right? Mine isn't quite, you know, I had rheumatic fever in Shanghai, in our last year, remember?'

Anne nodded and suddenly her face shut again as Isobel Maupratt, affectionately, gave her arm a little squeeze.

'I feel quite all right, I just thought it was so lovely.'

'I knew you'd say that, bless you for finding it so charming. It's *quite* a pretty valley of course, and in winter you can see the snow peaks all day, but it tends to cloud over after lunch. But the *people*,' she added in a low voice, 'my dear, you'll find it so different here, they're so *ignorant*, one does try to help them … they don't help themselves *one* little bit.'

'This is my husband, John,' said Anne. John had been held up by a Sikh couple with a seven-year-old son who screamed and refused to go down the ladder. Like all spoilt Asian children he had been cajoled and caressed and pleaded with, until he had consented to walk down, step by step, his enormous bearded father meanwhile blocking the ladder and applauding each step. Isobel shook hands with John, and John saw a tall woman, full-bodied, an imperious expression, a Roman chin.

'This is Isobel Maupratt,' said Anne. To John Isobel looked capable, solid, and sensible. The kind one met in the colonies, in social welfare departments, matrons in charge of hospitals.

'Well, we mustn't stand here all day,' said John amiably. 'Let's rescue the luggage, if these types haven't loaded it on to the wrong plane at Patna. I never saw such chaos as Patna, how anything ever gets done there beats me. Let me see, passports. Where does one go for passport check? Those tents? My God, it's rather primitive here, isn't it? Now where are the passports, Anne? I've got them? Not yours, I'm positive I haven't ... oh here it is, well, must keep all papers together.'

And now the simple process of waiting for the luggage to be disentangled was made complicated by the efficient and the impatient. John and the tourists hovered, walked up and down the airfield, loudly demanding their luggage, asking for their passports to be checked, breaking the broad sweep of arrival into minute particles of apprehensions, anxieties, and inquiries, until the sharp-edged moment of change, the swift ascent from the hot plain to the cool valley became like chewed gum, an amorphous and savourless mass. Anne stood, doing nothing, and this irritated John and Isobel, for she had now withdrawn from them, she stood gone from them. She was looking at the hills, the fields, the beggars. John strode with camera clinking and batting against his chest, marching into the tents, then out again. No luggage had as yet been unloaded. The passports were still clutched, in a perilous pile, against the bosom of the air hostess, a tall girl in a sari wind-swept about her with sculptured effects.

'Everything's always so disorganized round here,' said Isobel. 'I can see John's efficient. Thank goodness there is a man around to bring some sort of order into this place, or we'll be waiting here all night.'

Isobel then noticed that Anne had put her typewriter and handbag on the ground.

'Oh, do be careful dear. Here, let *me* hold them for you. They're so light-fingered here, never never leave anything lying around, always lock everything up.'

'I never lock up anything,' said Anne, hostile.

'Well, you'll have to in Khatmandu. Why, even at the Royal Hotel, where the bearers are all vetted, a tourist lost a diamond ring she had left in her room. Went out without locking the door. It was gone in a few moments.'

'She probably found it later in her bag,' said Anne.

Isobel looked at her sharply. Anne had not changed. Docile, demure, even obedient, then the sudden flare-up, thunderbolt out of the blue. Twenty years ago. Odd, it still felt odd, hurting yet pleasant, thinking back to the school, and Anne punished, Anne behind the blackboard, standing with a cap on her head on which was written The Devil is in Me. 'I can't understand that child,' Mrs Maupratt's voice, prim, dragging through twenty years. 'I've prayed and prayed *for* her, and *with* her. And I *know* my prayers are heard. Only last week she was awfully sorry for having been so wicked, and then she goes and sins all over again. I've told her about hurting Jesus with her sinning, and do you know she said she didn't care? Satan, speaking clearly through a child. Oh Isobel, we *must* pray for her, hard.'

And Isobel had prayed, hard, for Anne. Though now she could not remember Anne's sins, she remembered clearly her own prayers, the ache in her knees, the feeling of elation praying for Anne.

John was back, important, harassed, and happy. 'It's all lined up,' he announced, 'luggage is coming out at last. God, what a mix-up. Nobody knows anything in this place.'

Outside the tents two small tables had been set up and the Nepalese officials sat at them. They were gentle slim youths, about nineteen by their looks, with sleek curly hair, long Nepalese eyes slightly tilted at the outer corners. Their features were a mixture of Indian and Mongol, oval faces, straight noses with arched eyebrows, admirable teeth and complexion.

'These are Newaris, the original inhabitants of the Valley of Khatmandu,' explained Isobel to John. 'Quite good-looking. Some say they're the most artistic people in the world. Well, you'll see their temples and pagodas and houses. You can't *miss* them out here, the place is just littered with carvings. Personally I don't care for them, it's rather a pity that such a nice-looking people should produce such revolting things. *I* can't see anything beautiful in them, but then, I mustn't put you off now you've only just come.'

John looked at her admiringly. 'That's very interesting,' he said, nodding his head as if some weighty matter was in debate, and eyeing the youths. 'I should have said myself these people hadn't any backbone, inbred probably.' Isobel nodded vigorously. 'Funny to think that *we've* made such good soldiers out of them ... the Gurkhas come from out here, don't they?'

'But the Gurkhas are quite a different race. They're hill people from the west of Nepal, lots of them have never even been to Khatmandu,' said Isobel. 'Nepal really has lots of different ethnic groups, Tibetans, Botthyas, Gurungs, Limbus, all very different from each other. In Khatmandu Valley the Newaris are the original people. They are, of course, a subject race, they've been ruled for decades now by the Ranas. The Ranas are really one big family, descended from the warlike Rajputs of India. They're not ruling now, but they're still quite powerful.'

'No guts,' repeated John. 'Now I can see that these Newaris look different from *our* Gurkhas, who're little strapping fellows, tough as they make 'em. Very interesting indeed,' he repeated.

The youths, inexhaustibly serene, went on filling forms in quadruplicate. The American tourists rampaged up and down in front of them like caged tigers. A crowd of porters, ragged as beggars except that they wore no trousers at all, filled the air with whoops of laughter as they ran back and forth from the plane, bringing boxes and crates, suitcases and bags, and dropping them haphazardly round the two officials. Angry yells from the tourists served only to exalt them in their game of pitch and toss from plane to ground. 'Cussedtoms, Cussed-toms,' laughed the porters, running for yet another load. Between their tight, slim buttocks was a cord holding fast a piece of cloth over the crotch, like a diaper with only a front to it. Unmoved as their own stone gods, the young Customs officials wrote on, nodding gently as each passport was inspected and then returned, throwing a cursory glance at the contents of the luggage round them.

'My bag, oh my bag,' cried a shrill voice. A small round woman, neatly encased in a light blue coat, a hat with a spray of feathers upon her dyed blonde hair, was wrestling with a bare-legged Nepalese, small as a boy of twelve, who was trying to carry away a large bag.

John transfixed the boy with a suddenly powerful index finger and a commanding voice: 'Put it down ... put it down I say!'

The boy grinned, let the bag drop suddenly at Anne's feet, and sauntered away, laughing, cheered by all his friends. Anne stooped to pick it up for its owner. Upon it was tooled in black in the leather: Eudora Maltby, Lecturer in Inspirational Music, New York and London.

'Oh thank you, thank you,' wailed Eudora Maltby. 'Oh dear, this is *such* a bad beginning. I just don't know how I'm going to concentrate on all the beauty that I know I've come to give to these people here, after the way they've treated my bags.'

Isobel eyed her. 'One does one's best,' she remarked. 'Of course one can't expect to have everything quite up to scratch. We're all roughing it out here in the Himalayas. We've got Tibet and Red China next door.'

'I do hope the hotel's clean. I can't stand a place that isn't clean. I cabled specially to make sure there was modern sanitation. I couldn't have come otherwise.'

And now all was falling into place. The porters pushed John's and Anne's luggage into Isobel's waiting jeep. Other jeeps, the taxis and private vehicles of Khatmandu, carried the tourists to the Royal Hotel. Solicitously, Isobel threw her overcoat round Anne's shoulders. 'It's cold here dear, freezing as soon as the sun is down ... and you've only got a dress on, where's your coat?'

'In the luggage somewhere,' said Anne. 'I forgot to take it out.'

'That's Anne all over,' said John. 'She'd forget her own head if it weren't screwed on. I don't know what she'd do if she had to travel alone. Was she like that in school, Miss Maupratt?'

'Oh no, Anne never forgot *anything*, did you, Anne?' said Isobel, loyally.

'I say, where's Mount Everest?' said John. 'Had a peek from the plane window on our way over the southern ranges, couldn't see a thing. Most disappointing.'

'You can't see Mount Everest from the Valley of Khatmandu,' said Isobel. 'Other mountains yes, but not Everest.'

'Too bad,' said John, 'I'd looked forward to seeing Everest from here, and maybe doing a few treks myself. I was quite a climber in my time, you know.'

With much grinding of gears the jeep drove off, along the six mile dirt road from Gaucher Airport to the city of Khatmandu. The sun was now falling behind the hills and swiftly the light narrowed and drained out of everything, and it was very cold.

Chapter 2

Anne wrote:

KHATMANDU, word, peel of bells, sweet and grave bronze bells with a prodigious echo, calling among mountains. I heard it first at a cocktail party in Calcutta given by the French Consul for François Luneville, a photographer who happened to be our paying guest.

'Khatmandu,' said the French Consul.

'What did you say?' Something, breeze of premonition, tingled among my hair, my skin pricked with unfamiliar gooseflesh.

'Khatmandu,' he repeated.

'Where is that?'

'In Nepal, land of the gods. You should go there, madame. There it is still Shangri-la. Snow peaks and temples, tigers and roses, palaces and gods gods gods. Everyone is a god there, men and beasts, stones and trees.'

Khatmandu. Echo of mountain bells, calling, lingering, tolling, reflected from slope to slope. A few days later echo made word, in print, advertised in *The Statesman* of Calcutta: 'Situation vacant, English lecturer (lady) for Girls' Institute, Khatmandu, Nepal.' I could not resist Khatmandu. I wrote and applied. I did not tell John. François left us to go to Indo-China on a photographic assignment; his friend Leo Bielfeld came and stayed with us. We went to Agra, and there the letter caught up with me. Until then I had believed in Khatmandu as in Father Christmas when I was six: knowing that there was no such person, yet mightily praying and hoping there was, reindeer and sledge, sack of toys and all, and looking for a sign. If I see a white horse today, it is true, Father Christmas is. I played this game, in Agra, with Leo. If Leo makes no pass at me today, Khatmandu is, Leo made a pass but the letter came, all the same. In the drifting weeks it had merely receded, a dream of bells ... and now suddenly the bells were here, calling, deep and sweet. Khatmandu existed, wasn't one of those things grown-ups pretend and children are not allowed to call lies, one of those things we are made to believe until they are part of us, and then grown-ups chip them off us ('A big girl like you, still believing in Father Christmas!'), and jagged bits, like the edges of a broken glass, hurt when touched.

I could not tell John and Leo that I had written *because* of the word, that I wanted to go to a place *because* of its name. Leo wouldn't have understood, and neither would John. Of course, John is my husband, and I am fond of him and I suppose he is fond of me, and we have now been married six years, and oh, what's the use? I don't know why I should lie to myself, even in writing. Anyway, I was frightened, after I had done it, that John would start talking, in that way he has which I cannot stand very much longer (I go on saying it, yet at the same time I go on standing it – how odd). I prepared some arguments. The salary seemed ample, I needed to do something, and there might be some good stories to write about Khatmandu, I could make some money, and Calcutta was so hot in the summer, why not Khatmandu? We could always go back to Calcutta.

When we said good night to Leo I went quickly to the bathroom and shut myself in, gathering courage. When I came out John had already undressed. We went to bed without a word, as is usual in our dull, discourteous life together. I mustn't say that but I cannot lie any more, or I shall again go dead as I have been dead for so long, in fact, until I heard the word Khatmandu. I mustn't dramatize myself. Only it is true, that suddenly I want to write and write, and I have spent months sitting, staring at my typewriter, squeezing out profitable, stale words for magazines, words forespent, stories which are no good, and pretending thus, like a shadow play posturing, that I was still a writer.

And now I who have not written a line I wanted to write for nearly three years, suddenly I am writing for pleasure again, for myself, a diary to record myself. I have become a little stiff, unused to communicate with myself, to talk to me, and yet I want, I must do it now, I want to grope and find the me again that I had lost, and put it on paper while it slips away from me as I am writing it down. Hurry hurry, suddenly I want to watch me live, I want to know, I want … for nothing is real, nothing is true, nothing happens, until it has been observed and noted and put down in words like bells, ringing the changes of love and hate, beauty and happiness and misery. Without words, how much of us really does exist? Perhaps all living is thus only echo, prolongation of sound into symbol, when the original the primal fault, the stroke which began the lovely sound, is no more. Hurry hurry, suddenly in this short half day, so much has happened that it seems I shall spend all night writing it down and not be done. And I must catch it all, strain it and gather it all into one scrawl, for it is terribly important, and why it is I do not know. For with names, with words, is the world as we know it called out of empty air. In words written in dust and upon the worm and upon the stars, can they all claim the same immortality; immortality, a reverberation ... an echo, echo.

I know that in this half day, ever since leaving the plain at two o'clock this afternoon to come to the Valley, so much has happened, or rather, whatever has happened has become so significant, so full of life and meaning, which is joy and pain mixed, that I cannot wait to write it all down. It is intense exhilaration, and I feel like exploding sitting here and writing after barely five hours in Khatmandu, and I don't know where to begin, except, as a child, to describe the space where I sit, the laughing parakeets green and pink on the wall among the painted gold sunflowers ... but I anticipate.

Patna of the plains, flat and yellow with the great Ganges drifting its heavy waters past, and the flat airfield with the eternal confusion on its verandah where, upon two tables, passengers have their passports and luggage examined together; and the Indian Airline officials, harassed and temperamental, and the telephone eternally ringing, and the hot March wind, spiked with sand ... Patna is really the beginning.

'Are you sure we go to Khatmandu?' I asked the Indian air hostess as we filed across the tarmac to the waiting airplane.

'Oh, quite sure,' she replied laughing, 'and next year we may be going to Lhasa. Who knows?'

As if to confirm this, in front of me walked a Tibetan woman, with burnished bright face and gold and turquoise in thick shining hair, surrounded by five children and carrying an electric fan and a baby. On the plane she sat across the aisle from me. She told me that her daughters studied at the convent in Darjeeling. 'My biggest one has just passed her Cambridge,' she said proudly.

'You live in Tibet?' I asked.

'Oh, part of the year in Lhasa, but we often drop into Calcutta for some shopping, and Khatmandu to visit friends,' she said, as if dropping in at a neighbour's for tea.

It was fifty minutes in the sky from Patna to Khatmandu. The other passengers crowded at the window panes to glimpse the snow peaks, but there was cloud about us, a confectioner's dream of spun sugar drifts, whipped cream and icing, as for a lavish Olympian birthday party, and the snow peaks could not be seen. And then the clouds parted, and down below lay a tumultuous land, no longer the flat, chequer board, limitless Indian plain, but narrow-crested hills strung as a tangle of beads, in coils, in knots, dovetailing and twisting, pushing and plunging, melting into each other, bewildered crests and contorted gullies and narrow valleys, a heaving and restless landscape, as if these mountains were still moving, like waves of the sea flocking forward and back in some gigantic turmoil, as if they hadn't finished pushing each other into place. Cloud again, and the airplane shadow rainbowed upon them; another gap and below us, green and gold, gold and green, circled by hills, lovely, a spreading valley, in its middle a clear cord of water, and a city, a city with flashing gold spires and roofs, jewelled like a sword hilt.

'Khatmandu!' yelled the Tibetan woman, leaning to my ear.

'I know,' I yelled back.

We went lower. Green and yellow fields, like a pattern upon a bee's wing, little ochre farmhouses, many-roofed pagodas, pink brick houses in clusters, large white colonnaded mansions with formal gardens. It was so incongruous, to go to the Himalayas in an airplane and find a golden valley like Switzerland or northern Italy and a city in its middle that was a Hollywood dream of Cathay. Only the clichés of tourism could describe it: smiling Khatmandu, sunlit Nepal, and of course Shangri-la, Shangri-la.

The airfield spread below us, we came down upon it, the door opened, we walked out, there at the barrier was Isobel Maupratt, looking as if she could not be anywhere else but waiting here to meet me in Khatmandu. Her frame was larger than I remembered, a bulk achieved and permanent, imposing and imperious, straight and firm and solid in brown, with the Nepalese so small in homespun grey about her; Boadicea with her arms crossed and the wind plastering her dress upon her with an armour sheen. But as I walked towards her I saw her eyes under the dry brown hair parted in the middle and neatly curled; desperate eyes coming out at one from her massive face, as if she were waiting for something, something that had not happened, would never happen unless she kept staring with those hungry, hopeless eyes.

She spoke before I did. 'Yoohoo, Anne!', then clung to me strongly, a fervour only half recognizable as due to the occasion. And the usual lies, that we had not changed. And then she became I suppose herself, dogmatic and certain, and I was weary and looked round. Khatmandu ...

This is real. They do say that there is a thing called mountain exhilaration, that when in the high places a strange elation seizes one; akin to ecstasy or madness. We are up four thousand feet in the Valley of Khatmandu. But I was mad already through echo of the name; and to find that one really arrives, and here it is, the heart of spring itself, golden sunlight spilling off the tops of dark hills, softness in the air, as of petals much compounded, crushed within substance of air; like burning bushes the pink fire-brands of almond and plum blossom, more luminous as evening grows blue and dark. A dusty road, untarred, honking jeeps going honk honk, honking away, veering at whim and overfilled. Small proud people with beautiful faces and elongated tip-tilted eyes, wrapped in white or grey shawls, self-contained and poor; suddenly trumpets blowing and a company of toy soldiers with gold braid epaulettes and red coats, marching. ... Houses carved from roof to door-step, a street between two pink brick walls imprisoning at the other end an enormous orange, the sun. And joy, joy in being, merely being alive.

I think Isobel worried because I did not speak on the six mile road to the Girls' Institute, and I could not for in this half-hour of beginning obscurity I was learning to see and to hear again.

We were to stay with Isobel for a few days at the Institute; then a room would become available at the Royal Hotel. 'It's the only hotel one *can* live at,' said Isobel. At the moment it was full of American tourists. 'And it will be worse in about two months' time, at the Coronation of the King of Nepal, in May.'

It was difficult to look because Isobel and John kept on talking; about how bad things were, how difficult because everything had to come by airplane.

'It's the Indians who've built the airfield, and now they're building a road for the Nepalese. A road to India. Everything has to come to Nepal through India. There is no other way, except Tibet. The road will be finished at the end of the year and things may be cheaper then.'

Isobel then started a do-you-remember series, wanted to know what had happened 'all these twenty years'. John told her of our marriage, how we'd met in Hongkong. 'I *must* get your book,' said Isobel with great conviction of enthusiasm, 'I'm *sure* I shall enjoy it.' Once she threw another of her spaniel looks at me, and the next moment turned her shoulders, statuesque, brusque Boadicea in a jeep, telling us how ungrateful the Nepalese were, making me feel that it was my ingratitude, my silence she reproached. 'It's that beastly religion of theirs, we haven't made one convert in nearly three years here.'

The light had gone out of everything by the time we reached the Ruby Palace, as the Girls' Institute of Khatmandu is called. Like many another public institution, it is a converted Rana palace. Monumental steps of veined marble, leading into a hall all ogival windows, ceiling of tin plates lit by half a dozen enormous chandeliers with electric bulbs inserted among the lustres diffusing a brown refracted glare; bronze busts of the Ranas, oil paintings of the Ranas, in uniforms of red with gold braid and medals and whiskers and jewelled swords and upon their heads those fabulous Rana helmets (constructed entirely of precious stones with a spray of bird of paradise feathers to crown the top), said to have been fashioned out of the plundered store of jewels of Nana Sahib, who after the Indian Mutiny of 1857 escaped to Nepal and was never heard of again. Up the marble stairs overhead a pattern of shadows, dark heads picked out against the lurking colours of the stained glass windows, a young giggle.

Isobel clapped, shouting, unnecessarily high: 'Now girls, girls, stop this noise AT ONCE!' Diminuendo, the giggles ebbed like bird-song at nightfall, a great pity.

We had tea in Isobel's living-room, nondescript as any living-room in England, sofas and chairs draped in cream shade with pale stamps of flowers; only the columns, spiralling between each window, the tin plate ceiling, painted with white lilies upon a green background, with holes punched along the sides haphazardly (which Isobel explained was done for ventilation), a monumental steel and marble

47

fireplace, two enormous Brussels mirrors, hinted at the Ranas, their hereditary wealth, and their Victorian acquisitions.

'You'll see some of the other palaces, they're a scream,' said Isobel, poking the logs of the fire. 'Everything here, of course, the Ranas brought back from their tours in Europe in the last century and the early twenties of ours, chandeliers and mirrors and grand pianos, billiard tables, and Greek statuary. All on the backs of men porters up the steep mountain paths. They even brought in Rolls Royces when there were no roads to drive on. They had sixty men carrying the body across the mountains on a platform of bamboo. I'll say one good thing for the Ranas though, they wouldn't have those Newari carvings. Some of them, thank God, think they're just as obscene as we do.' And she flushed down her forearms and the V of her dress.

After tea Isobel took us to our temporary bedroom, Rana furnished: mirrors on *all* the walls, two chandeliers, embroidered footstools, and a monumental carved bed, a four-poster, with a canopy of purple satin with gilt tassels, and two enormous gilded dragons playing ball at the head.

'We can't afford to refurnish the whole place, so we've got to use what there is. We're only using the first floor, the second and third floor rooms are shut.' Suddenly Isobel turned to me: 'Come with me. I've got something to show you.'

I followed her, leaving John in the bedroom.

'Power's very poor,' said Isobel over her shoulder, as we proceeded from the stone corridor and towards the back of the palace. I could see the filaments just glowing in the bulbs swinging fifteen feet from each other. 'They're installing a brand new electric plant, Diesel run, for the Coronation. Light'll be better then.' We groped down a staircase and out through a back door.

'This part used to be the back garden, used by the women only,' said Isobel. Swathed in blue evening light, it was a sunken Elizabethan garden: a fountain, an arbour of climbing plants, roses by the scent, a lawn, and at the end a whitewashed small building like a pavilion. We went in.

'It isn't wired but there are candles upstairs,' said Isobel. The stairs were wood and her heels rang on the boards; she pushed a door and walked in, sure of the way. She lit one, two, three candles, the flames at first small then leaping higher, illuminating the room.

'Oh Isobel,' I said. I think these were my first words since getting out of the jeep.

This the miracle. A small room, with two large french windows with narrow balconies of wrought iron and balcony seats. A child's desk and a wooden chair, a couch covered with a glowing patch-work quilt in orange and blue. The walls painted a deep, sun-lingering orange. Above the windows two childish suns, circles of chalk with a few thick white rays; the door brown wood covered with a pattern of shining copper nail-heads. A pair of eyes, the whites chalked in, dark blue irises, long black lashes, painted on either side of the door and on the wall opposite to the windows, two large painted parakeets, green and pink, with red beaks open as if laughing, among yellow sunflowers big as life.

'It's yours,' said Isobel. 'I thought you'd like it, Anne. I used to come here sometimes, but it's yours now.'

'Oh, Isobel,' I said stupidly. 'It's beautiful.'

I don't understand. Why does Isobel give me this marvel? What impulse made her stalk in front of me, far from the surfeit of ugliness which is the palace, to this Eden, glowing like a small sun on its own, alone in its separate garden, looking into the night towards – I think – the mountains?

Who painted the parakeets, the eyes, the suns? What does it mean? I did not ask Isobel. I was afraid. We went out, and in sign of posses-sion I closed the door behind me, I took the matchbox, I snuffed the candles. Never will I give back to her this room. It is mine.

Here I sit, solitary child awake in a rage of gladness, light-headed mirth of the high places. I am caught home in the unfamiliar, the new. My body falls into the folds and slopes of the guessed hills in the dark-ness there. I am alive after a long-drawn discontented death.

This child in me knows that something prodigious is happening, if wanting to write again, if feeling alive again is prodigious. Perhaps it is the altitude's oxygen lack; that rather nice doctor whom Isobel asked over to coffee, after dinner, said: 'Everything becomes colour-ful, significant, charged with emotional meaning when you're up four thousand feet. Everyone here becomes more exuberantly them-selves.'

It is true. Isobel was nearly a caricature of Isobel, even when that famished look came into her eyes and she was also someone else. The

49

doctor, too, seemed a little grotesque, overdoing the physician-cum-philosopher. 'The Nepalese seem to us to be very happy, always laughing or singing or telling ribald stories. They appear an uninhibited people, you'll find that out, Mrs Ford. I think some of their euphoria may be due to malnutrition. The less protein one eats, the greater the pot belly and the light-headed feeling of being gay.'

Isobel disagreed violently, put it all down to native character 'like children, no thought for the future', etc. etc. But deprivation of protein or mountain ecstasy, I find myself different, and the world new. The muffled ragged people shuffling along bad roads; the small dungeon-like hovels scooped within pink brick houses; a flare of oil lamp gilding a slant-eyed face; an ear encrusted with brass coins ... one jeep ride is enough to know that this is by no means Shangri-la, but merely another under-developed Asian country, possibly worse off than many another one, with horribly poor people, great wealth for a handful of aristocrats, misery for most of the population, sanitation non-existent, disease rife, pi-dogs and filth, sacred fat cows, and hungry children. All this I know, and that I, too, am entrapped in the work of 'progress', trying to do something to change all this by coming here to teach English to a bevy of Nepalese girls. But at the moment I only know that I'm in touch with myself again, myself alive, aware, and wanting to write.

The candles are going fast. I must go back to the bedroom, where the sporting dragons grin and cavort about us as we lie in the double bed.

Chapter 3

DR FREDERIC MALTBY did not like to walk with other people. People meant talk, their tongues moving as their legs scissored the ground, and the doctor suffered acutely from their logomachia which interfered with his daily happiness. Walking in the morning in the Valley of Khatmandu was a pleasure whose recollection, during the day, lifted him on a crest of remembered delight above the weariness and frustrations of his work. There was the early light, cool and frosty, delicate like a bubble, the nourishing air, heady with the smell of rising sun and the sharpness of all stirring things. It made him want to sing and run on the road still crackling with the nimble hoar of frost. Thousands of cobwebs, glistening like spun diamonds, were on the hedges and filled the cracks on top of the pink brick walls of the Rana palaces and the Newari houses. The marvellous prodigal sun threw his light about, and in the trees with their close-cupped, half-budded spring leaves, orioles and finches and sunbirds blossomed and sang their hearts out.

Even at grey dawn there would be people about, porters in long grey files with their oval wickerwork baskets slung by a fibre belt across their foreheads. With the first light the houses stirred; from their first floors the fuchsia came flowering down in a cascade of carmine; on the lower floors, between carved and delicate wooden pillars, women could be seen combing each other's hair. More women would be walking to the shrines, ringing bells to call the gods to notice. They would have flowers on their heads, beads round their necks, bangles on their wrists, and in their hands trays with the offerings for the gods. They walked, tranquil and absorbed with worship, throwing grain and placing flowers upon the deities and the lingams, then washing the offering away with water.

Frederic Maltby knew the bend of the road where he would suddenly see, and always with the same shock of happiness, the snow peaks, rosy in the early light, emerging above the near hills. Although from his bedroom window he could see them just as well, yet it was pleasure redoubled to meet them just at that corner, to see the lords of the snows towering incandescent pink in the early sky. I shall see them here again tomorrow, he thought, and felt himself fulfilled. He had been five years in the Valley. He would never leave it. Never would he go back to the plains. He would remain here till he died, lifting his eyes to the mountains in the morning and many times during the day. 'For the chief things of the ancient mountains, and for the precious things of the lasting hills, ...' These words were in him as he walked, knowing himself the happiest man on earth, forgetting all but the joy and beauty of life in the trance of all his senses: sun warmth and snow tang; the happy cries of birds; and the vision of the lords, the Himalayas, standing in absolute rule, gods with wonderful names, Annapurna and Manaslu, Dhaulaghiri and Himalchuli, and Gosainthan so tall and grave, first one to come back to the Valley's sight after the summer monsoon. He had gone trekking among their lower reaches but had never attempted to climb them to the summit: it seemed to him a sacrilege. And though he knew of the expeditions to conquer this or that mountain, and spoke to the climbers, and met the mountaineers who camped in the grounds of the Royal Hotel, Khatmandu, on their way up to tame this or that famous peak, yet he felt sometimes like begging forgiveness for their manlike desecration, a feeling only communicated to Nepalese friends. His own kind would have smiled, they were men with little reverence for the earth they lived upon, who wanted to dominate and to reign over all Creation, and certainly over the last strongholds of the gods, the accessible Himalayas.

Once upon a time Frederic Maltby had been a married man, a state terminated by flight nearly eighteen years ago. After wandering for many years, he had settled in Khatmandu, and from the first day of mountain madness felt safe, unpursued, and happy. He was now the Chief Medical Officer of the hospital recently established in one of the Khatmandu palaces. Since the airfield had come into being, in 1952, his medical supplies and his books had been flown in with little delay, if at some expense. Occasionally he went to Delhi or to Calcutta to meet colleagues at medical conferences, or to purchase new equipment, but he felt nervous and irritable in the plains, and kept looking over his shoulder when walking a civilized street as if someone were staring at his back.

For five years, since his arrival in 1951, he had taken a morning walk almost daily. Isobel Maupratt, arriving in 1954 to organize the Girls' Institute, had launched herself upon him one day at tea at the Royal Hotel, breasting forward in sprightly warrioress fashion, and declared it so jolly to take a trot together in the early morning. 'I just don't dare to go out alone on the roads in this place, Dr Maltby. You know what these people are like.' Her nostrils dilated, her frame heaved. Dr Maltby knew the rumour in the market place (and rumour in Khatmandu often proved accurate): she had been pinched in the right buttock while bending over to admire some of the clay pots in the main square, clay pots turned by hand on a stone wheel, ordinary clay pots which tourists always admired, much to the surprise of the Nepalese potters. Rumour added embellishments: Isobel had complained to Paul Redworth, the British Resident. The latter, suavely inured to the ways of the Valley and its recuperative sensuality, had quoted Kipling to her:

> Still the world is wondrous large, – seven seas from marge to marge –
>   And it holds a vast of various kinds of man;
> And the wildest dreams of Kew are the facts of Khatmandu,
>   And the crimes of Clapham chaste in Martaban.

'But it's an insult, I want something done about it!' Isobel had said.

'My pet, it's not an insult, out here it's a compliment to you,' Mr Redworth had replied.

When Isobel accosted him and suggested a trot, Fred Maltby was seized with familiar terror recognized, clinically, as the same symptom with which he became paralysed in the presence of his wife. 'I just dawdle along, y'know, you'd find it all rather pointless,' he said lamely, in the grip of a helplessness which had made flight the only possible way out so many years ago.

But Isobel, clad in grey flannel and holding an alpenstock, lay in wait for him very early one morning at the armorial gate of the Girls' Institute, her face turned towards the Serene Palace, now become the Hospital, on the opposite side of the road. Absent-minded with anticipatory pleasure, clad in a Tibetan yellow-grey sweater and an Indian woven silk scarf (presents from Amrita, his Nepalese wife, who had soothed him and taught him so much happiness, and then had died), it was too late for Fred to turn back when he caught sight of

53

her, and Isobel had pranced up to him, tossing her head and saying, 'Ah! There you are!' in the neighing tone of a joyful mare.

In vain did Fred at that moment pray to all the gods of Khatmandu for sudden rain, to the Lord of Thunder and the Goddess of Lightning herself for an instantaneous monsoon; the sun was shining in insolent heaping of light. In the long pause, minuteless like death, when Isobel and her alpenstock installed themselves into a walk by his side, he had known despair. Trudging an endless road, he had seen, but without knowledge, without this dark wordless merging into himself which was true knowledge and the strength thereby, the spurts of green burning like tongues of green fire on the tips of the walnut trees; and the long stiff whips of the plumeria with their knobby pink buds, the gold little knobs on the Nimm trees, and all the greens and blues and pinks of the soft valley, tilted and round, soft and feathery and brilliant, as lit from inside; and the soft stubble in the fields, like children's hair, had passed him by, with the women hoeing, their burnished faces, their feet treading naked and happy with the snakes and the lotuses tattooed upon them in blue, their heavy dark skirts with the red hem swinging about them like bells. Isobel had walked with him and drained it all of sense, she had spun round him, indefatigable as a morning spider, a shroud of talk, hiding the meaning of things by calling attention to them, saying, 'Oh, look at this *darling* little bird there, *what* is it?' from time to time exclaiming about the Nepalese, expressing her inquisitive disgust at the shrines, with their lingams crowned with flowers, their gods with faces so weathered and worn with fondling and rubbing with vermilion powder, they had become featureless red daubs. 'How horrible, like great big wounds, how can anyone worship these horrors?'

He had even missed the lords of the snows because Isobel had exclaimed about what she called 'their admirable contours' and urged him to look up, to watch. Returning leaden-footed, he fled to his Nepalese friends, and the next day Isobel had received a letter in which Frederic Maltby said that he preferred walking by himself.

Isobel had not spoken to him for three months. She cut him dead at the British Resident's teas, and he, only afraid that she would talk to him, was much relieved. Strong and able as a physician, powerful when armoured in white gown and stethoscope, he was a meek and timid man, and in the self-humbleness of the good craftsman, if anyone paid attention to him, felt it undeserved. Exonerated by his in-attention he spoke to her quite naturally one day, which had allowed her to forgive him, in a Christian spirit, his rudeness, though she did not forgive him what she called his 'private life'.

The day after the Fords' arrival, as Fred Maltby came out of the Hospital that morning, he saw a woman standing at the gate of the Ruby Palace; thinking it Isobel he stopped, half-turned on his heel, ready to run back. But in that hesitation his eyes knew the woman not as Isobel but as Anne Ford, wearing slacks and shirt with a pink cardigan. She'll tack on, he thought terrified, all these blasted women try to tack on, and already saw her, as he saw the women of his kind, breathless and bravely chatting, stumping after him with that queer, jerky walk of sportswomen and Siamese cats, her tongue restless and her feet padding the earth without love, and asking questions. All women asked questions, and remarked upon things, instead of just letting them be, flowers and birds and mountains, quietly and peacefully, letting things and the deep and tender knowledge of them which comes with reverence, courtesy towards life in all its shapes, seep into them in the lovely silence.

Anne turned to the right and went down the road, and Dr Maltby was relieved. He turned in the opposite direction, to make sure he would neither catch up with her nor meet her. The day was Saturday, the Nepalese day of rest, and he was off duty. He planned to go on to the market place, the Temple Square, stand and loiter there watching the bustle, and then on to Pashupatinath, the great Siva temple of Khatmandu, renowned and visited by Hindus from all over India.

Dr Maltby had met the Fords the night before, Isobel having sent a note round saying he must come for a cup of coffee to meet them. 'You'll like them,' she had prophesied. Knowing he would not like them, he had come and acted the busy, unapproachable doctor at the end of a long day. He remembered under the light, worse than usual, the woman Anne mute, quite stupid, thin, and drained looking. Isobel talked, and John Ford. Talk about the Nepalese. Isobel and her usual missionary nonsense. Irritated, he had shut his ears to them. A good, dull, placid fellow, with the usual nervous, egocentric, high-strung, tense wife. Wrapped up in herself, said to write. Probably thought her writing the most important thing in the world. Lots of people like that came to Khatmandu for a week or two to 'write a book' about it. He had defended the Nepalese against Isobel, said that here, more than anywhere else, human contact, touching a human hand, looking into human eyes, made one believe in God, or the gods.

'Really?' John said, profoundly serious and a little like a judge about to censure a witness. 'I don't quite get what you mean. Please explain. There's nothing godlike in all this, I'm afraid. It seems to me pretty indecent.'

Then they'd all had a spot of brandy, Isobel saying that it was cold in the Valley, and such a strain for the heart, four thousand feet. She'd had rheumatic fever when young, she sometimes did have a tiny wee drop of brandy at night. As if, thought the doctor, I didn't know about the brandy.

Bored, muddled, constrained, they had talked of the poverty and malnutrition of the Valley. People always seemed so cheerful talking of famine after they had fed. Fred Maltby, exasperated and truculent, had maintained that there was no relationship between misery mental and misery physical, a theme which he debated in the abstract because, as a doctor, he became so indignant at concrete poverty and disease. It made him sound a cynic and shocked himself to maintain that the pot-bellied, red-haired babies with enormously long lashes, who squatted on diminutive legs, passive, their skins a coppery brown (a recognized disease entity due to protein deficiency), under the carved snakes and peacocks and gods of the dark, medieval houses, were not really feeling unhappy; that when one saw the hill people half-naked in the biting cold wind, laughing and singing though blue with cold, this euphoria was due to the fact that in a state of chronic malnutrition their feelings of pain were blunted. He remembered Anne staring at him as he spoke, but she had neither exclaimed nor contradicted. What a fool I made of myself last night, he thought, unworried.

He had now passed the British Residency, and the new Royal Palace where the King now lived, and was walking by the Rana Pokhra, a large rectangular pond in the middle of Khatmandu where before 1951, when the Rana rule was abolished, people had been totally immersed to find out whether they were innocent or guilty. It was just as illogical, and just as sound, as the medieval trials by fire.

Some of his Nepalese friends maintained that it was a much better way to find out who was lying and who was not than the new, democratic courts of law, which were inefficient and corrupt. A guilty conscience was a terrible weight upon the breast, and increased the choking sensation produced by submerging. Inevitably the guilty man would come surfacing up first, gasping for air, while the innocent, with the help of the gods, could hold his breath much longer under water.

The street of pink shards, fragments of the bricks that built the walls and houses of Khatmandu, and which could be seen in the grey, primal state, drying in the fields around the city, felt elastic and springy to his feet. He passed along more waking streets lined with carved two-storeyed houses; the upper storeys had overhanging wood balconies which were one solid mass of carving; windows, round or square glassless apertures, framed in carved wood like portrait frames.

The market place and Temple Square of Khatmandu was an agglomeration of temples, shrines, gods, animals, and open-air stalls. It was lined by the Buddhist priests' houses of Tibetan architecture: white walls, black mass of carved pillars and beams, carved windows with projecting latticed balconies, and central courtyards. On the right was the Hanuman Dhoka, the ancient great palace of the kings, now in a ruinous condition. At its gilt copper gates women were putting a new mantle upon the stone figure of the Monkey God Hanuman, holding a trident, his face worn to a scarlet gash. Big and small, many-roofed, rose the pagodas, temples, and shrines; the pagodas had rows of beams slanted forward and upward supporting roofs superimposed one upon another, each beam carved with many-headed, many-armed gods. At the foot of each god, on a slab of wood, were carved humans in the act of love in all its manifold and various attitudes. It was strange, thought Dr Maltby, looking at them without shame or excitement (the Valley having cured him both of prudery and of smut), that the Europeans of Khatmandu NEVER mentioned these carvings at all, except to condemn this beautifully ribald and accurate observation of human behaviour with a tedious and, in Khatmandu, a silly word: obscene. The Nepalese themselves did not pay any attention to them. For them they were, as everything else, sacred, they served a ritual function: they prevented lightning from striking the buildings. For the Goddess of Lightning was a virgin, and fled before such depictions. And the act of love was as everything that was, holy and of God, who found Himself in creation.

Round the temples, the shrines, along the narrow street, were spread out vegetables, grain, pots and pans, clay pots, in a medley of hawkers, cows, pi-dogs, and children. Enthroned in the middle of the Square stood the large black stone effigy of Kala Durga, the terrible goddess vanquisher of demons. Kala Durga was another incarnation, the obverse personality of the goddess Parvati, the smiling, the bounteous and good deity of love and plenty. For like humans, the gods had many natures, personalities, and manifestations, some good, generating, creative, and others terrible, destructive, and evil.

'Schizophrenia isn't a disease, it's a natural state with gods and men, after all,' the doctor had said to Father MacCullough, the Roman Catholic priest of the Valley. 'Even you, Father, believe in God and the Devil.'

'But that's quite different,' Father MacCullough had said. 'We don't make effigies of the Devil.'

Anyway here she was, Kala Durga, destroyer of demons and Lady of Death, black and fierce with a chaplet of skulls and a demon underfoot and a sword in her hand, and many worshippers already offering milk and grain, and a garland of blue-black anemones which a child with a heavy load of wood upon her back placed round the statue's upraised foot.

'Let's go and see what my friend Doc Korla is up to,' said Dr Maltby to himself, crossing the Temple Square.

Two hundred yards, fifty shrines, a dozen Garuda bird-gods and three score of lingams away from Kala Durga, down a busy street of carved houses with projecting first storeys and filthy inner courtyards (which served as sewers and cesspools), Doc Korla, the Nepalese whom Fred Maltby had now adopted as his other self, Kala Durga to his Parvati, Hyde to his Jekyll, lived in a house inside a temple. At the entrance was a graceful Buddhist pillar carved as a single lotus, leaf, stem, and flower; two hierogryphs of bronze, half lion, half dog, flanked the doors. This morning they were draped with laundry put out to dry by some women now washing themselves at a bronze water spout carved in the shape of a seven-headed naga snake.

Dr Maltby walked into the paved courtyard, in the middle of

which rose the temple, a three-roofed structure, half Buddhist, half Hindu, with Buddhist flags and bells hanging from the eaves, and a hundred and twelve carved beams. At the four corners of the lowest and largest roof the massive upthrust beams were Biblical rams in full rut with erect and painted phalluses. The courtyard was crammed with innumerable small Buddhist stupas, lingams, children, a Greek statue of a naiad, a large white stone, reputedly an incarnation of Ganesh, the Elephant-God of Wisdom, with a silver umbrella above it to shield it from rain, crows, goats, cows, pigeons, worshippers, and the Nepalese doctor operating on a patient held down by half a dozen friends.

'Hi, Doc,' said Korla gaily, with a genuine American accent.

'Hi,' said Frederic Maltby.

Doc Korla was a slim, handsome youth with black, curly hair under his rakish cap, luminous eyes, and a burning cigarette at the corner of his mouth. His victim, laid at his feet as the demons under the Black Goddess, was a trouserless porter with a huge abscess in one buttock pouring pus and blood from a large incision. Korla was packing it with gauze steeped in iodine. The operatee raised his head and made a joke, there were roars of laughter, Korla capped it with a more piquant remark, and the human blend of the courtyard was convulsed with mirth. Pigeons whirred about, pi-dogs snuffed at the wound, bells rang, a bull walked by, worshippers went clockwise round the temple, their hands spinning the Tibetan prayer mills, some children flew kites, and Fred Maltby stood looking, outwardly smiling, inwardly groaning.

'My patient has to walk across the hills to Lamidanda to pacify his wife, so I operated although it was Saturday,' said Doc Korla, slightly on the defensive.

'Tough,' said Dr Maltby. 'I shouldn't pad too much stuff in that gash though, or he won't be able to walk the thirty miles to Lamidanda.'

Korla shook the ash from his cigarette, took another long roll of gauze which was in a wicker basket, cut off a piece, and wound it round the porter's buttocks.

'Well,' said Dr Maltby, 'I'll be going.'

'Good-bye, Doc,' said the Newari warmly. 'And thanks,' he added. Above the front door of his pretty house, beautifully carved and totally filthy, hung a sign in English: 'Diplomied in able stitching and cutting is committed here by Western schooled man of science.'

That boy's a menace, thought Dr Maltby for the hundredth time. Why on earth did I ever train him? Korla was one of several former hospital assistants who after a few months with Maltby had set themselves up as 'Western medical scientists, able at stitch and cut'. Dr Maltby had exhausted himself denouncing to charming, elusive, and witty Nepalese officials the public danger these 'doctors' could be. In vain. Now, after four years, he made friends with them, or at least with the best of them like Korla, who never attempted anything more than an abscess in the buttock. They, in return, had begun to send him their worst cases and even came occasionally for advice. It was co-existence, unsatisfactory but better than nothing. Thank God, they never went near a woman in childbirth, so it was slightly better than medieval Europe. But they gave insufficient penicillin injections to the Gurkha soldiers on leave through Khatmandu, returning from the British regiments in Malaya and Hongkong via the brothels of Singapore and Calcutta. 'If you shut your door to all errors, truth is also shut out.' Dr Maltby repeated the Nepalese proverb to himself and felt better. He must not get indignant because Doc Korla did not wash his hands or sterilize his scalpel, and operated with a cigarette in his mouth. Nepal still had a long way to go, from the eleventh century to the twentieth.

He walked out of the temple through more streets, jostling the money changers squatting with neat piles of Indian and Nepalese rupees in front of them; the copper and brass workers with marvellous glinting dragons and tangled snakes upon ewers and plates, the street intersections with sacred peepul trees, lingams, and water spouts, and thus came to the river, the holy Bhagmati, flowing in winter shallowness between leaf-shaped sandbanks of white gravel. In the runnels of the stream lay radishes in serried bunches like a pink and white carpet, sluiced by the holy waters. In the middle of the river stood saddhus, holy men, gleaming brown, pouring water over their shoulders with round copper vessels.

He neared Pashupatinath, the holiest and greatest temple of Siva, not only in Nepal but in the whole of India. Cobbled streets ran unevenly among tree-shaded meadows and houses with geraniums on the balconies and cauliflowers in baskets on the front door steps drying in the sun. The temple sprawled along the river edge, a huge assemblage of buildings big and small composed of many shrines, pavilions, shaded cloister-like galleries for pilgrims, bathing ghats, and burning ghats. The river narrowed here as it flowed between the stone banks which formed the ghats. It was crossed by a small bridge, and on the opposite bank was the sacred hill of Pashupati, a gentle promontory climbed by slabs of hewn stone. The slope facing the river and the temple was covered with hundreds of lingam shrines.

Fred now approached the main temple. White and a Christian, he was not allowed to cross the gate, he could only stop at the entrance, look from the threshold at the courtyard to see whatever was not blocked from view by the golden backside of the eight-foot bull on its pedestal, the steed of Lord Siva. It was Siva's great carved lingam, hidden within the great middle structure with its flashing roofs, gilt copper finials, and large golden doors, which was the reason for Pashupatinath's exceeding holiness.

And this is where Frederic Maltby was jolted back into his former life. For as he stood outside the main gate he heard a jeep, and saw a vehicle coming up from a side alley in which it had been parked. It was now climbing the slightly tilted road towards him. He was on the point of hailing it, for he had recognized Father MacCullough's transport, and he was smiling, thinking he would ask Father MacCullough what on earth he, a Roman Catholic priest, was doing at this hour at the Hindu temple, when he saw the other person with the priest: a corpulent little woman with a flowered hat perched upon her blonde hair as a bird on a golden bush.

The jeep was a left-hand drive, and Father MacCullough, guiding it in first gear to take the upgoing slope, his glasses gleaming with the sun upon them, espied the doctor standing there, and the greeting he was about to shout, 'Top of the morning to you, sir,' stopped in his throat as he saw Frederic Maltby lift his Tibetan sweater by the collar over his chin and nose and run, pelting through the archway, on to the terrace of the ghats where only the feet of a corpse remained to be consumed, across the bridge, and up the steps of the sacred hill.

'What was that?' asked the woman, as the jeep jerked to a stop when Father MacCullough turned his head to follow the flight of his friend.

'Well, now ...' said Father MacCullough. Then his Jesuit training took him in hand. Obviously if Fred ran away at sight, it was serious. Human perceptions were quick in Khatmandu, even if one's moral sense and principles went a bit haywire. 'Oh, just a chap with an errand,' he said cheerfully, and started the jeep again.

Chapter 4

LEAPING up the sacred hill Dr Maltby felt exposed to view, and half way up bounded sideways on to the slope and ran among the huddled fifteen hundred shrines which in serried ranks covered it to the river. 'The forest of lingams,' Dr Maltby had called them, and as he hurtled between these ornamented sentry boxes of brick and carved stone, each one with an adoring stone bull in front of it, he obliqued to avoid a large bell with a frieze of Garudas and naga snakes upon its rim, and collided with someone who stood there, unexpected, quiet as another stone. Both fell down.

'Oh, I do beg your pardon. I say, I'm terribly sorry,' said Dr Maltby, picking himself up and then helping the other person to get up.

'It's all right. Hope you're not hurt?' said Anne. They stood, slapping their legs free of the grass dew, and looked at each other.

'I'm not hurt. I say, *I* ought to ask you that question.'

Anne smiled. Behind her head was the bronze lattice small door, which worshippers opened to throw their offerings upon the gleaming cylinder of black stone, crowned with a chaplet of flowers, lubrescent with smeared oil and water, upright within the shrine.

Dr Maltby was quite breathless, but trying to explain. 'You see,' he gasped, controlling the tremor of his voice and his body, 'I've just had a terrible shock. I've seen Eudora.'

'Eudora?'

'My wife,' he explained.

'Oh,' said Anne. And began to laugh.

'Seventeen, no eighteen years. I recognized her immediately, although she's a bit fatter now, of course.'

'Of course.' She laughed again. Silence came between them. A Newari woman padded up, hibiscus in her hair, a laden tray in right hand, opened the lattice door, threw flowers and grain upon the lingam, stood with mouth moving inaudibly, took a small pewter jug with milk and poured a little upon the cylinder, then another small jug with pure water and washed the milk off, closed the lattice door, and went on to the next shrine after having rung the bell.

'It's nice here,' said Anne.

'It is,' said the doctor. He could speak more easily. 'I left Eudora in London, ages ago. I don't know why I got so frightened, I just ran when I saw her in the jeep. She was with Father MacCullough. You haven't met him yet. You will.'

'Now I know who she is. Eudora Maltby, writer of Inspirational Music. I saw her bag at the airport.'

'Then she's still my wife, I suppose. Hasn't bothered to divorce me. I wonder how long she's staying in Khatmandu?'

'Why are you so afraid of her?' asked Anne. She added: 'I'm sorry,' as she saw the doctor's stricken face.

'It doesn't matter,' said Frederic Maltby. 'I don't mind telling you, in fact it might be good for me, psychologically I mean.'

Anne laughed again, and the doctor also laughed. Last night they had been other people; her strained face, his irritability, did not belong here among the lingams in the spendthrift morning. They had collided into each other and found themselves companionable.

Frederic Maltby drew his cigarette case and offered Anne a cigarette. They sat on the damp grass.

'I don't know why I should talk to you. Sure I won't bore you? All right then. Eudora and I. We should never have married. I suppose everyone says that of their marriage when it goes wrong. I'd just finished a stiff job as surgical registrar and thought I was in love with a nurse until I found her in bed with my boss – fat little fellow, the consultant, used to go round the hospital and bark at us. Then Eudora came along, and she quite dazzled me. Dabbled in politics and art and had some money of her own, very woman of the world to me. (I was very crude then; the raw overgrown medical student.) We got married.

'It sounds ridiculous, in the sun here. But that woman absolutely broke me,' said Maltby cosily. 'Not all at once, mind you. In steps. Can't even describe how it was done. It was a kind of perpetual nervous state. I couldn't do anything right. I felt a boor all the time. Didn't know which fork to use. When I made love to her, and very clumsy I was, she called it unspiritual, and when I didn't she snapped and nagged. She demanded from me a constant attention to herself, her music, her friends. I did my best, but I was busy, trying to get a higher degree as well as working at my practice. I came home with more work to do to find the house full of strange girls with Bohemian earrings and lots of talk and languid clever young men who wrote books or plays or music. And then Eudora took up fads. For a time we went vegetarian, and when I asked for meat I was called a cannibal.

'By and by I became terrified of her. She was always so *right*. I was so unspiritual (that was her word), so boorish, I hurt her. She, the creative one, the artist, was trammelled by me. I tried not to believe it but it corroded me. And when the war came I was happy, as I think many people were happy. Relief from so many things. From futility, the blackmail of daily living, from for me this chain, the conjugal chain, the longest journey, the dreariest friend ...

'I was in Burma, and a prisoner of the Japanese. Those years were supposed to be hell, but I was happy. No Eudora. My terror of her did not abate. It grew. After the war I couldn't face going back. I disappeared. Stayed in India, travelled about a bit, came here. I've been happy here,' he repeated. 'I'd even forgotten about Eudora. Now up she pops, after so many years. It was extraordinary, clinically speaking I mean, watching the terror spring up in me, vigorous as before, so that I ran without thinking. I can't understand it, it's crazy. What would my nurses say, my patients say, if they'd seen me, me, run away like that?'

In front of them, on the ghats, another corpse was being brought, swinging lightly on a small stretcher, covered with a grey veil for burning. A woman who had lain for hours in one of the temple courtyards, waiting for death with joy, for to die in Pashupatinath and to be burnt upon its ghats was to be for ever gathered to the One who expresses Himself through the Many, to be freed from the weary immortal journey of eternal rebirth. Now she lay stiff, with covered face and feet protruding from the wood pyre heaping round her, while her relatives sang a dirge only half-sad.

A little further down the river some women were washing their clothes, slapping them flat on the flat stones, and at each slap their red beads danced round their necks.

'I saw radishes in the river this morning,' said Anne. 'Like a Bokhara rug being washed under the sun.'

'I saw them too,' said the doctor. There was a scent of smoke and grass in the air about them. He looked at Anne. The light *must* have been bad last night. She was small boned and light like a Nepalese girl, and with dark hair, softly wavy, and smooth skin upon her arms. But there were small wrinkles at both corners of her mouth, two drooping lines, and some at the outer corners of her eyes, and something thin, pathetic, tired in her neck, eliciting his compassion.

'D'you know, I saw you this morning.'

'I did too,' said Anne. 'It's all right, I wanted to walk alone. I guess you felt the same.'

'It's the talk,' said the doctor. 'I can't stand people plastering their voices all over this ... this wonder, the Valley, and making it stale and unprofitable.'

'Khatmandu,' said Anne. 'A lovely and harsh word.'

Frederic Maltby again felt stirred by a delicate, wispy pity. Now he wanted to tell Anne about Amrita.

'Would you like to come back with me, we can have some morning coffee? I'd like my friend General Kumar to meet you.'

'I must get back,' said Anne. 'My husband and Isobel might worry.'

'Oh, we'll send a chit round by a bearer, let them join us for morning coffee later. But do come and meet the General. He owns the palace where I live. Some of it is my Hospital now, but he keeps the rest to live in, with his family. You'll like him. He's a Rana and a gentleman. Besides,' he said, relapsing in gloom again, 'I must tell him about Eudora. In case she comes hunting for me. Maybe the General will think up a way of keeping her off. He knows all about women, he's had so many.'

Chapter 5

THE Serene Palace, housing the Hospital, was even larger than the Ruby Palace, now the Girls' Institute. It had more porticoes, pillars, naiads sorrowing over decrepit fountains; it was set in more acres of land, half fields of unkempt rice and maize, half unweeded garden. Its grounds were dotted with small bungalows and ochre and white thatched farmhouses, and the whole was enclosed by a low wall of pink brick, frittered in places, which crept down declivities and ascended gentle slopes in its sinuous course.

The Hospital occupied one quadrangle; another was in possession of the owner, General Kumar Sham Sher Bahadur Rana, and his family, guests, relatives, and friends were lodged in it; one of the haphazard small bungalows built about the main edifice was Dr Maltby's abode, in another resided two missionary nurses. The Serene Palace had manorial gates of wrought iron imported from England in the last century; hierogryphs of bronze, roofs of rolled tin sheets above splendidly carved wooden eaves depicting greyhounds and stags and dotted with painted marigolds; stairs of the pinkish veined marble so beloved of the Ranas; rotund pillars with clusters of grapes and cherubs upon their capitals; corridors; immense rooms, with walls panelled in mirrors and ceilings made of tin plaques with flowered designs, imported from Italy, with those ubiquitously haphazard holes punched with a chisel along the sides, for the passage of air. Furniture of vast dimensions and depraved taste appeared as Anne and the doctor made their way to the main drawing-room.

'The family like to receive guests in there,' said Dr Maltby. 'Isn't it odd, when the Newaris are such artists and craftsmen, to find that their rulers, the Ranas, had no taste at all?'

They traversed a gallery where, between fluted columns with capitals moulded with bird-gods and snakes, were suspended, in frames of sandalwood carved with peacocks and deer in a landscape of leaves and lotuses or in frames of massive wrought silver, oil portraits of the Ranas. They loomed upon the multi-coloured walls, prosperous Edwardian gentlemen with protruding brown eyes out of pink faces, brown moustaches, sideburns, and beards, clad in scarlet uniforms with a smother of medals and gold braid, manicured hands on identically jewelled hilts of swords. When their wives, the Maharanis, appeared they wore bustle gowns, diamond tiaras, five or six necklaces of emeralds and rubies, and a few brooches of the dimensions of saucers.

'These are the ancestors and contemporaries of my host, General Kumar,' said Dr Maltby. 'As Isobel might have told you, all the Ranas are related to each other. They ruled Nepal as their private domain for a hundred years, from 1850 to 1951, to be exact. The title of General is hereditary with them, as was the office of Prime Minister. Now here's the grand salon. I hope you don't mind if I leave you alone for a few minutes while I hunt up the General. He may be at his prayers still.'

Anne remained alone in a vast room like an audience hall, with eleven mirrors, an enormous settee covered in pink brocade; a chaperoned love seat for three, each stool facing a different way; six padded armchairs, four marble-topped tables, two grand pianos, and five chandeliers drooping tremolos of pear-shaped lustres. Four large french windows opened on to the balcony, and the sun streamed on the tiger skins and bear skins upon the varicose floor.

General Kumar entered the grand salon and bowed to Anne, who rose. He put his hands together in the Indian salutation, and Anne did the same. He was a beautiful old man, extraordinarily tall and thin, with young brown eyes in a face like a Goya Christ, topped by a shock of pure white hair, wildly streaming in all directions under his soft Nepalese cap. He wore jodhpurs and a Nepalese tunic, on the old Chinese pattern, and a western style hunting jacket of Harris tweed on top. His naked feet were encased in brown and white co-respondent shoes.

He sat in one of the padded armchairs, extracted a packet of Lucky Strike cigarettes, and offered one to Anne. Being an orthodox Hindu he inhaled, not holding the cigarette end in his mouth, but through his hand closed upon itself to form a hollow tube; the cigarette was held between the palm and the little finger and he sucked the smoke at the thumb end. Thus his lips remained undefiled by contact with the tobacco.

General Kumar said in his courteous Nepalese English: 'You are welcome in my home, madam.'

'It is a great honour for me, General.'

The General continued: 'We heard of your coming through Miss Maupratt. My cousin the Field Marshal looked in his library and found your book there. We were delighted that a lady of sense and sensibility should come to teach our daughters. Miss Maupratt is an energetic lady, but her mind is much wrapped in Christian superstitions.' He took another puff and added: 'A very energetic lady. It is not ungood to be energetic when a spinster, otherwise insanity hovers.'

Anne was groping for something to say, but the General added reflectively: 'Activity dispels sexual humours into hot air.'

A maidservant of about fourteen, a girl from the hill tribes of the north, with stolid Tibetan features, thick braids of coarse black hair, and gold in her nose and ears, brought a coffee pot, a tin tea strainer, two cups, some not very clean sugar on a small plate, and condensed milk in a milk jug, and a bottle of Black and White whisky and a glass. Anne poured the coffee while the General gave himself half a glass of neat whisky and spoke again:

'You are possessed by a husband, madam? He is here too?'

'Yes, General.'

'Good heavens,' said Dr Maltby, 'I forgot all about him. I'll send a bearer with a chit immediately.'

'Why, my friend, do you wish to alert this lady's husband to come here? She is not unsafe with us?'

'Not a bit, General, but I left very early this morning for a walk, and my husband might be worried,' said Anne.

'In that juncture, I shall not oppose your sending immediately for him,' said the General, and spoke to the maidservant, who disappeared to return with a barefoot bearer who crept into the room with bent back and approached the Rana aristocrat with hand cupped to mouth, making the gesture of eating rust out of his hand, the old serf salutation to a Rana.

'He will take your message,' said the General to Dr Maltby, who scribbled on a piece of notepaper.

Anne suddenly found herself talking to the General about her room. 'I don't know why Miss Maupratt gave me this room. Perhaps there is no reason.' It's just that every little thing is significant, she wanted to add, but did not.

'She has given you Unni Menon's room,' said the General.

'And who is Unni Menon?'

'A beautiful man,' said the General, 'a cool head above an under-standing heart. You will meet him. Did you know that madam had Unni's room?' he asked Maltby.

'I wonder why Isobel gave it to you?' said Frederic Maltby. 'I always thought she'd have it burnt down, or whitewashed, or something.'

'I believe Miss Maupratt is still enamoured of him,' said the General. 'That is the rumour. And rumour is always true in our Valley.'

'There are suns and parakeets and sunflowers, and wonderful eyes on each side of the door.'

'Blossom-headed parakeets, madam, painted by my niece Ruk-mini,' said General Kumar. 'A very unfortunate girl. Beautiful and unhappy, and sweet as the moon. She is truly in love with Unni, though she does not throw herself at him, as some of the foreign women do. But her father did not agree, and now she is married to someone who is a proper fool.'

'Rukmini is a most beautiful child,' said Maltby regretfully. 'She has a strange helplessness about her, an utter lack of defence. That is the trouble. She is too kind, too generous, and too beautiful.'

'All the Nepalese women I have seen are beautiful,' said Anne.

'It's because they live in harmony with our valleys and our moun-tains,' said the General. 'And because they are virtuous and early wedded. Our maidens and our mountains are young and active; and twelve is not too soon for marriage in our land.'

'Your country, General,' said the doctor, 'is wonderfully medieval. Boys married at fourteen, girls at twelve; generals and statesmen at nineteen.'

The General smiled, as if complimented. 'Would you like to see a Rana wedding?' he asked Anne. 'March to April is *Chait*, the month of our weddings in Nepal. You have seen some of the wedding pro-cessions on the roads, perhaps it might not be unpleasant to attend one, tomorrow afternoon?'

'I'd like to very much.'

'Allow me to arrange it then,' said General Kumar. 'I shall obtain an invitation for you and your husband. My niece is getting married tomorrow. She was a student at your Institute for two months.'

'She is the Commander-in-Chief's daughter,' said Dr Maltby. 'It will be a public holiday. All the diplomatic corps will be there.'

'You will see Unni Menon there,' said General Kumar. 'He is in the mountains still, but he will be back tomorrow for the wedding.'

Dr Maltby put his coffee cup down and cleared his throat. 'By the way, General, I saw my wife this morning. She's in Khatmandu.'

'In Khatmandu?' said the General. 'This may not be unserious for your soul, my friend.'

'I felt so frightened I ran,' said Maltby. 'I ran straight into Mrs Ford actually. My wife was with Father MacCullough, in his jeep. He was taking her round.'

'If she is with the man in swaddling clothes,' said the General, 'then she will be at the wedding tomorrow. The man in swaddling clothes is a busybody, always showing people things, telling them about our Valley as if he was a masterly one-man tourist agency. Perhaps in his country he will be invited to talk about our Valley as an expert. All experts are busybodies. He will get her an invitation, to show his power with us.'

'Sooner or later she'll know about me. Everybody knows every-thing about everyone else in Khatmandu. It's a wonder someone hasn't already popped up to her: Maltby, *Mrs* Maltby? Are you a relative of *our* Dr Maltby? And the next thing we'll see her coming up the driveway ...'

'I will protect you, my friend,' said the General. 'She will not set foot in my house. I remember your suffering when Miss Maupratt wounded your spirit on a walk. Do you wish your wife to be put on the next airplane back to Patna? I could see the Foreign Secretary about it. He is my nephew.'

'I doubt if that can be done *now*,' said Dr Maltby.

'You are right,' said the General, shaking his head. 'We are, alas, a damn-ocracy now, madam, so fools have their way, and we Ranas have no power. I cannot help my good friend as I would wish. Five years ago, one word from me' – he snapped his fingers – 'but we are a damn-ocracy now.'

At that moment the bearer reappeared and said something in Nepalese to the General.

'Your husband and Isobel have gone to call at the British Resi-dency,' said Dr Maltby, 'so they won't be here for coffee. But you can stay on a bit, can't you? I'd like to show you over the Hospital.'

'Perhaps I'd better go back,' said Anne, suddenly nervous, unhappy. 'Isobel did say something about our going to sign the book at the Residency this morning, and I forgot. Oh dear.'

'Your husband will sign for you if he can write,' said General Kumar. 'Stay with us, madam, and let us think of a way of preventing that terrible woman from torturing my friend's soul with inhumanity.'

Maltby smiled. 'Oh, it's not that bad, General. I'd better make up my mind to meet her some time or other. It's bound to happen.'

'I have an idea,' said the General. 'Let us ask Unni when he comes back what to do. Perhaps he will think of a plan. He has a cool head above his heart.'

'What can Unni do?' asked Anne.

'I don't know,' said the General. 'But he has a way with him, for men and also for women, even those he does not wish to make love to. Perhaps he will talk to her, and change her heart. Let us wait, my friend, till Unni comes back.'

Chapter 6

ANNE'S my wife, I love Anne, love her, in spite of everything. John was soaking himself in two pails of boiling water and two pails of cold, brought by the room bearer and poured into the concrete tub. The plumbing at the Ruby Palace was rudimentary, though Isobel last night had said that fixtures would be installed soon. 'At least before the Coronation in May. But they've all got to be flown in. It will be better when the road is finished. We'll get things more easily. At the moment even the steam-rollers and the barrels of tar that go to build the road and the airfield are flown in from India.'

The concrete tub was large and John immersed gratefully in the soft water with its easy soap lather. The water covered all but his head. From his chest just under the surface the hair floated, like small weeds. He kneaded his abdomen vigorously. Since travelling from Calcutta the previous morning he had been constipated. Like so many people used to modern conveniences, he was inhibited when faced with primitive apparatus. Perhaps after a hot bath and a good breakfast his insides would start working by themselves.

His bad temper at Anne last night returned, tinged with self-gratification, floating in upon him lightly, not unpleasantly, lapping at him as the soapy water. He had told her what was what, yet remained dignified. He hadn't broken down. It was her fault, so obviously her fault. Always doing a disappearing act. And he loved her, he really did. First there had been dinner with Isobel. He'd been hungry, it wasn't too bad a dinner. Talked of the weather, a cosy topic, always making one feel secure and able to go on. Temperatures dropped suddenly here. Had to wear a pullover, asked Isobel for hot water bottles for the bed. Anne, of course, hadn't thought about them. Then that doctor chap had come, absent-minded fellow, rambling a bit; John had shaken him up a bit, of course, pulled him up, and Isobel had supported him. They'd said good night, gone to their bedroom and, while he'd been in the bathroom trying hard, Anne had disappeared, to return a good forty-five minutes later, carrying her typewriter.

'Where on earth have you been at this hour?' he'd asked.

'Oh, just in the garden,' she had answered, lying, and gone to the bathroom to undress, taking her pyjamas and dressing-gown.

He'd given her hell when she came back. He wasn't going to put up with double-crossing. She'd probably gone down to Isobel to make some more of her bloody plans about staying in Khatmandu. Well, they weren't going to stay. Filthy place this, cold and mucky, no light, no running water, and Elsans. Absolute scum these people were anyway, look at them sidling about round the jeep, with the dogs and the cows. Calcutta was bad enough. And it was her fault if they were in Calcutta. If he hadn't listened to her, he'd have another five thousand pounds. 'Five thousand pounds,' he shouted at her as she lay on her side of the bed, rigid, turned away from him. And coming here was another of her bright ideas that he'd have to pay for. He had fallen asleep.

He had wakened to find himself alone in bed, sat up to see himself in the large tall Brussels mirror opposite, startled by the mosquito net, green, hanging by a string under the baldaquin of purple satin with tassels, the dragons twisting at his back, himself hirsute, waxy creases of sleep down both sides of his face.

At first he had not worried too much. Anne might be downstairs with Isobel. He felt a little guilty after last night, she had lain so rigid there. But then it *was* her fault. He got up and pressed the bell and the little bearer came in.

'Hot water, lots of it, quick!' He heard his own voice, masculine, squaring his shoulders. Then he'd gone back to bed for a bit. 'Cuddle me,' he whispered to himself, 'cuddle me.' He rounded his back towards an imaginary Anne. As he used to do, in the first year or two, when she was nice to him, before she had started destroying him. Sapping the marrow of his bones, making him half impotent. No, it wasn't true, he wasn't impotent, though she'd tried her best to castrate him, emotionally. He was all right with others. He was a very sensual man, he must remember, and he'd kept quite a stable at one time, in that colony where he'd been. Quite a stable, thinking back with satisfaction to his bachelor days. At least two or three, native girls too, and one or two white girls. Off and on, here and there, some had been quite fond of him. But Anne ... well, it was her fault. Cold fish. 'Cuddle me, cuddle me,' he had whispered, replacing his absent virility towards her with other needs. She had cuddled him, wrapping her body round his back, and he had gone to sleep in her arms, embryo wrapped, her body fitting his, her legs under his bent legs, back against her, protected as in the wall of the maternal womb. It had been wonderful. She had loved him then, he felt, the way he wanted to be loved. She was nice and wifely to him then. He remembered his deep sleep, a dreamless saturation. And though even then he seldom made love to her, preferring this sleep, security, now he felt he had loved her more than anything else he had ever had. And then one day she had put her hands behind her head, stared at the ceiling, and said: 'I'm tired,' in that flat dull voice, as he had been fumbling at her breasts, whispering the mechanical and stirring words which to him were inevitable prelude to the sex act. 'You're not nice to me,' he had said, reproachfully. Always that had brought her round. 'I'm sorry, darling. I'm just irritable, that's all.' And then one day she had not answered at all.

'Is it your writing that's bothering you?' he had said, knowing she hated to talk about her writing. And she had stared at him, and after that he had wished he could have said something different. But Anne paralysed him, so that with her he fell back into the same words, the same pattern, knowing it made things worse. 'You're cold, you're not normal.' He had found this formula, this explanation. It was the truth. How simple. No fault of his. She was just made cold. It absolved them both ... and though sometimes he could still hear her voice, flat, saying: 'I'm tired,' he withdrew hastily from this memory, ran on to his grievances, her coldness, her painful physical tightness. Of course it was abnormal of her. He was quite all right. And very considerate really, never bothering her much that way now.

The bearer came back with the hot water and he went to the bathroom. In the bath, in the gentle water, he resolved to be nice to her when he saw her at breakfast. He hoped Isobel would be there. With Isobel there, it might be different. It would be easier. It was always easier with other people about them.

He heard a noise in the bedroom, and his heart lifted with joy and he bounded out of the bathtub and started rubbing himself vigorously. She was back, there, moving about. But she had no right to go off like that leaving him, first day in a new place. When they could have had a new start. When, perhaps, he might have made love to her ...

He threw the towel on the floor, and flooded with resentment, sudden as a blindness, he walked out of the bathroom, prepared for the slight quiver on her face going stock still with the shock of his nakedness, prepared for his own words: 'What's the matter, what's wrong? One would think you'd never seen your husband without his clothes on.' ('Nothing,' she would say, looking away, and he might walk up and down a little, flexing his muscles, while she kept her head down and a small vein she had on one temple stood out.)

But it was not Anne, it was the bearer, making up the bed; whose eyes went round then slanted into closure as he turned and walked out on bare feet and closed the door softly behind him.

John was alone again.

It was then that he saw the white piece of paper upon the marble-topped table in the middle of the room, against the gold ormolu clock with the cupids.

'Have gone for a walk. Anne.'

He sat down on the ornate armchair with its cross-stitch embroidered seat, suddenly felt cold, put on his dressing-gown again. Upon the wall the mirror showed him tying up his belt, looking at himself. He wanted to cry, but his eyes only got red-rimmed. 'Anne,' he whispered, 'Anne.' She wasn't there. She always left him alone, when he hated being alone. But do what he might, try what he could, she always evaded him, ran away from him. Always.

'God almighty, the f— bitch.'

It had always been like that. Years now. 'I haven't been happy,' he said aloud. It was her fault. A grievance of every hour, against Anne. He went back to the first day, when he had met her, and been fascinated by something glowing in her, a gaiety, and the fact that she wrote, and was different from all the women he had known; and then she looked so distinguished, slim, and not big-boned. He loved her and wanted her to pay attention to him, laugh, and cuddle him (couldn't she see, couldn't she hear, how much he wanted her to?) and she would not. It was her fault, her fault, her fault. Often he had said so, coming upon her as she sat at her typewriter, staring into space, and he planted himself in front of her, and began to talk, as he did, trying to capture her attention even if it made her angry. And now she always left him alone, ran away, inside herself or somewhere else, leaving him, alone.

The note crumbled in his hand, the sun came pouring in, he could see the inner quadrangle of the palace. There was a tennis court there, and the cement court looked slippery. A whirr of pigeons came flying in and out again.

'Have gone for a walk. Anne.'

Alone, without him, when he was so looking forward to a walk with her. When he'd made plans for a new start. Together. She went by herself. Purposely. She was always destroying him, in big ways and small ones.

He dressed automatically, taking clothes from the wardrobe of solid oak where Anne had hung them up last night. He slammed the bedroom door, going out, slapped his shoes hard on the corridor stones as he walked, stiff, with an exaggerated swagger, hands swinging, as he always did when he had been hurt. He went down the corridor, down the steps, crossed the verandah now full of sun, and entered the staff dining-room where they had eaten the night before.

Besides Isobel Maupratt the staff of the Institute consisted of two pale spinsters in their thirties, who looked perpetually powdered over with a fine layer of some soapflaky material, so pale, dry, and fine were their hair, eyebrows, and lashes. Their skins were dusted over with pale freckles. They had been at dinner the previous night, escaped afterwards to attend a prayer meeting, and John realized that he had forgotten which one of them was Miss Potter and which Miss Newell. They taught history and geography, and were now eating kippers, seated together along one side of the oblong table where Isobel presided over the morning tea and coffee and two bunches of sweetpeas in orange glass vases.

'Good morning, good morning,' cried Isobel with her heartiest booming. 'I see you're up bright and early. Hope you had a good night's rest? It wasn't too cold, was it, we gave you the warmest *razas* we had? (That's the local patchwork quilts, you know.) I expect Anne's still resting, poor thing, she must have been tired out after the journey.'

John sat down, facing History and Geography, and slowly unrolled his napkin. Tomato sauce, dry from last night's macaroni. He said: 'Anne appears to have gone out for a walk.'

'For a walk, alone,' boomed Isobel.

'Dear me, alone,' repeated History (or Geography).

'Alone, for a walk, how extraordinary,' said the other.

Their voices were similar, their pale lips remained slightly open. Their tongues were pale, their moist pale teeth appeared unreal, as if false. And yet there was a strange fascination. He imagined himself in contact with those pale-lipped mouths, dry, slightly cold, with the slight white streak of saliva along the nether lip, then he remembered how Anne turned her head away so that he could never kiss her. She hadn't always done that; she'd started that after the baby.

He buttered some very limp toast which lay covering with its dewy imprint a small plate. The bearer poured boiling water over the Nescafé powder in his cup. 'I can't think where she can have gone. I hope it's quite safe out here?'

'Oh, I do hope nothing will happen, but one can never tell out here,' said History.

'She might have gone for a walk with Dr Maltby,' added Geography.

Isobel's glare flashed across the sweetpeas like mild lightning, and with a simultaneous movement they raised their cups to their mouths, passed each other toast and the white-greyish butter which Isobel pronounced such a boon – a Swiss dairy farm expert was making it for the Royal Hotel, and all the diplomats, and the American Point Four Program people, and the Girls' Institute, and Father MacCullough, all of them were getting Swiss butter.

The conversational bus rolled off to the weather.

'March is still cold in the Valley.'

'But it gets quite warm round noon.'

'Did you know that March was the month of weddings in Nepal?'

'Everybody gets married about this time of the year.'

'You'll see wedding processions all the time, day and night.'

'In fact, there's a big Rana wedding on tomorrow. Too bad I couldn't get an invitation for you,' said Isobel. 'If you'd only been here a few days earlier Mr Redworth, our Resident, might have done something about it. By the way, we've *got* to go and call on him this morning. I hope Anne will be back in time. We're due there at ten.'

'She can't have got very far.'

'We might see a procession on the way to the Residency.'

'I saw one yesterday. The girl was tiny, a child like a little doll.'

'They do get married so young out here.'

'At twelve,' said History and Geography in shocked chorus. 'It's really terrible.'

The conversation proceeded safely on the depravities of Nepalese life and food, which Isobel pronounced 'absolute poison', while the bearers brought eggs and bacon, more kippers, and more wet toast.

After breakfast History and Geography, skipping like little girls, announced that they were going to visit the Americans at the Point Four Palace. 'It looks so nice there, not a bit like Khatmandu.'

'It's like being in America, everything's been imported.'

'Yes, they've got the money to do it,' said Isobel rising. 'They've got wonderful bathrooms.'

John followed her to the verandah, with its rattan chairs and tables.

'My, the sun is warm,' said Isobel sitting down. Below them the garden, geometrically French, went round one side. At the further end, behind some trees with a shiver of green leaves, was the white bungalow where Isobel had taken Anne the night before. It was not the only one. Here and there could be seen similar small buildings of vaguely no style, some in disrepair. Round the garden was the usual meandering wall of pink brick enclosing the Ruby Palace and grounds, and beyond was the street, along which now passed a wedding procession, a sound of flutes and drums and small trumpets, four or five men in caps, short tunics and jodhpurs, and behind them the bridegroom of fourteen carried in a chair swung on two poles with a red silk umbrella held over his head by a third.

'That's a poor man's wedding,' said Isobel. 'Most of the girls at our Institute are married already, and the others are only waiting to get married.' She looked at her watch. 'Well, we can't wait for Anne much longer.'

'I wonder whether one ought to go out and search for her?'

'It was rather rash of her to go off by herself, there's very little respect for a woman out here.'

'Do you think anything serious might happen?' John's voice was anxious.

'I hope not. After all, Anne isn't all that young, is she? I don't think she'll be kidnapped or anything like that, and she can't have got very far, doesn't know the way anywhere. Anne was always a bit headstrong you know. At school I mean. Of course we were *such* good friends. I meant to have a long quiet chat with her this morning after seeing the Resident, about old times in Shanghai. My mother was *so* very fond of her. We looked after her, you know. She used to spend her holidays with us.'

'I know,' said John ponderously. 'You've been very very good to her. I'm sure she must be very grateful to you. For all you did to help her, when she was a child.'

'Oh,' said Isobel, 'I'm sure Mother would be happy, seeing Anne *now*, how well it's all turned out, and the way she's got on with her writing and all that. What a comfort to know her safely married, a safe anchorage for her troubled spirit. I mean, Anne *does* need someone to look after her. And I'm glad she came here. She looked quite tired and pale last night. Hasn't got much vitality, has she? We'll try to build her up. The essential thing of course is to keep *fit* and to keep *healthy*, both mentally and physically. We've got some fine people here, Miss Potter and Miss Newell lead a Bible study group. I myself am a little too busy to go to all the meetings, but I'm sure Anne would enjoy them. They're essential out here, they make you see things in the right way, keep up one's faith. Goodness, it's almost half past nine,' she said, again looking at her watch.

John watched her with a kind of pleasurable anxiety. Her hair glowed, her body was solid, altogether a fine woman, energetic and full of common sense.

He waited for her to say something more about Anne. But she did not. Her eyes went over to the road, swept the landscape.

'I hope she turns up soon, we're due at the Residency at ten at the latest. And out here, you know, one tries to be punctual, it's such a good habit, isn't it? The Ranas are awfully sticky about these things. Of course, *they* never send one invitation cards until the very day of the function, and sometimes the notices don't reach one until after the function is over, but one always knows ... one keeps in touch somehow ... one's told things. You'll find that Khatmandu is quite a place for keeping in touch with people. There's a kind of grapevine. That's why one's got to be careful about the way one behaves out here.'

She seized some knitting which lay in a bag on a chair and applied herself to it. She was knitting for flood relief. Floods were disastrous in Nepal, the monsoon rains so heavy in the summer. Each purl on the needle, each glance at her watch, added reproof at Anne's flight from them, her disappearance into the Valley, the otherness round them from which they kept away sitting on the verandah as in a be-leaguered fortress: from the melting insidious echoes of the too soft air, the mocking pipes of the melodic wedding processions, the little boys in their chairs with their red umbrellas, the morning upon them, a morning that they received, in unctuous approval of its sun, but which went on to hint at other things, lascivious things, gooseflesh-making disagreeable things, from which they kept themselves by their buttressed approval and agreement of each other, a companioned security enhanced by Isobel's recital of floods and famines in the Valley, somehow just retribution for a feckless, godless people (though one did love their childishness, 'they're always laughing'). And it was Anne, Anne that John heard castigated, waywardness deplored, fecklessness chided.

'Well, we'll just *have* to go on without her, it's too late,' said Isobel suddenly.

At that moment the small bearer who brought John's bath water appeared, his eyes crinkled with laughter at the outer corners, and handed a letter to Isobel. Isobel read it and coloured.

'What's that, what's that?' said John.

'It's from Dr Maltby,' said Isobel. 'Your wife is having coffee with him, and he's asking us over. But I'm afraid we'll just have to go on to the Residency first and sign the book, I simply *daren't* make Mr Redworth wait for us and there's *no* telephone.'

The jeep drove along the main street of Khatmandu past the Serene Palace, Isobel and John looking straight ahead; past the statue of a Rana prime minister, bearded like Charlemagne, upon a horse, a bronze cast in a London foundry and brought on the backs of men across the mountain passes into the Valley; past the clock tower with its clock, which John checked with his watch and found kept exact time; past the Rana Pokhra, that piece of water once used for justice by ordeal, now a green mirror for the clock and the mountains behind it; round it grew irises and hyacinths, and a holy man on the steps washed his feet; past the Royal Hotel, also a palace. 'It's the only place one can really stay at, apart from the Residency and the Ameri-cans',' said Isobel. On in front of the King's palace, a major replica of Buckingham Palace, with white colonnades and fountains, and

Gurkha soldiers in khaki, one of them smoking, while little boys flying paper kites on short strings played round the armorial wrought gates.

'By Jove!' exclaimed John, moved to the depths of his self by the sight of a soldier smoking on duty, 'that kind of thing wouldn't have gone down at all well with Old Pickle (our last Governor, before we gave self-rule to the natives and they went and made a mess of things). Old Pickle knew all about the Gurkhas. Whole family was in the Gurkhas. Uncle colonel of the Fifth, jungle-bashing in Malaya against the Reds. Used to have quite a few kukris lying about Government House I remember.'

'You'll see some good ones at the Residency too,' said Isobel.

The Residency was a large white two-storeyed house with a comfortable look, a lawn of fine turf, and the largest and best flowers of Khatmandu. In all diplomatic enclaves of any capital city the British always own the best gardens.

'Martha Redworth's sweetpeas are really something, but the Americans at the Point Four Palace are getting quite close now.'

John gazed at their pastel display and for a moment was homesick. 'It's just like Kent.'

'Except that we're having snow blizzards in Kent,' said Isobel. 'My sister told me. Her letter took three days to get here, which is rather good. Planes've been punctual lately. When it's too cloudy we're cut off. It's dangerous flying into the Valley during the summer monsoon, it's so narrow and the mountains so near.'

The Resident himself opened the door. 'I saw your jeep drive up. Do come in.'

Paul Redworth was an affable portly man with a cherub pink face (his own description of it was: 'like a prize baby's bottom'). On the living-room wall were massive kukris, silver embossed, and portraits of Gurkha V.C.s. On both sides of the fireplace two rhinoceros feet held brass trays for calling cards. The furniture was restful and darkly quiet and very English, there were rhododendrons and plumeria blossom heaped in large bowls, and an antiquated Remington upon a desk.

'I've been typing,' said the Resident. 'It's quite hopeless to convince the Foreign Office that the volume of work in Khatmandu has increased considerably in the last few years. I keep on telling them that Nepal is turning into a modern state and has got a five year plan. No Asian country escapes a five year plan, these days. And they write back and say we didn't need a typist in 1945, and why should we need one now?'

'We've come to sign the book, sir,' said John.

'Oh, the book,' said Mr Redworth. 'It's here. We couldn't possibly leave it outside, as they do in other parts of the world. Although we've got a sentry it was constantly being scribbled on, most ingenious drawings, same tendency as those lightning protectors you see round the temples. Have you seen them? Not yet? Well, they're what a dear old American tourist described as intimate family scenes. Ha ha ha!'

'Mr and Mrs Ford only got here last night,' said Isobel stiffly.

'Oh well, you must get round to have a peek at them. I understand all the temples will soon be repainted for the Coronation, so you'll see a lot more of the minutiae than one does now,' said Mr Redworth amiably. 'The story goes that the virgin Goddess of Lightning gets a shock when she sees them and spares the building. Another theory is that it helps one's self-control. I mean, if one's a saint, or in the way of being a god (and everyone here, as in India, is a god or a saint, or will be one day), then one can look upon such things with perfect equanimity. Very fascinating theory, really. Anyway, we took the book away, its pages were unproducible, and the F.O. couldn't understand why we had to renew it so often, and we couldn't go into details with them. I mean, they'd have got *all* the wrong ideas about this place. As it is, we're getting some V.I.P. foisted upon us in a month or so. He's touring the world and we've got to entertain him, and keep him out of mischief in Khatmandu. I hope he won't want to ride an elephant, the last chap we had, we laid on an elephant for him, and the elephant just sat down and refused to budge. Bad show,' said Mr Redworth resignedly.

John explained, to restore his own equanimity in the face of this unconventional Resident, that his wife had found herself quite exhausted after the protracted plane journey, but Mr Redworth waved the halting words aside.

'Glad she's got into the spirit of this place already. Saw her strolling about this morning near Gaucher airfield when I drove down to see someone off. Recognized her from the picture on the dust cover of her

83

book, you know. Tell her I'm a fan of hers. I liked her last bit in the magazine too. But she ought to write a lot more than she does. When's her next book coming out?'

'For goodness' sake,' cried Isobel, 'to think that you had Anne's book all the time and I didn't know it. I *must* borrow it.'

'I haven't,' said Mr Redworth. 'Field Marshal lent it to me. We have a Rana Field Marshal who's got a marvellous collection of old manuscripts and quite a library of moderns too. You'll meet him one of these days. Sweet old boy. And if your wife cares for hikes, come with us one Sunday, we usually go up into the hills then. Martha would love it. She's rather cut up these days because our dear friend Sharma is in jail. He used to come with us, usually bare-footed, and spouting Eliot and Housman all the way. He's been cooped up for the past fortnight along with Vassili, the manager of the Royal Hotel. They're sharing a cell,' said Mr Redworth, throwing a look at his typewriter.

John was rather thoughtful as they climbed back in the jeep. 'The manager of the Royal Hotel, and this Nepalese who goes walking with the Resident ...' he began.

'It's all base intrigue, at least where Vassili is concerned,' said Isobel hotly. 'He's an absolute dear, and so's his wife. There'd be no tourists in Khatmandu without Vassili and his wife. They run the Royal Hotel, and it's the *only* hotel one can stay at.'

'What a place,' said John.

'Absolutely hopeless,' said Isobel. 'Everything in a mess, nothing gets done. And there's a Coronation in about seven weeks' time. Khatmandu packed with guests ... they'll have to be housed and fed, only one decent hotel and its manager is in jail, and nothing's been arranged. No one's doing anything about it. There won't be anything to eat and no water to drink or wash in. Mark my words,' said Isobel, 'it'll be a shambles.'

The jeep turned into the Ruby Palace gates, ground up the drive. On the front steps was Anne, with two men, a tall Nepalese with white hair and Dr Maltby. All three were laughing, and turned, laughter still in their eyes and upon their mouths, as the jeep stopped and from it Isobel and John stepped down.

*

Saturday, my second day in Khatmandu. Yesterday a day, a century ago. This is a different world, the world of the Mad March Hare, whose presence is as certain as the sunlit sensuality of the Valley, and I am Alice after the rabbit-hole, involved in madly sane tea-party dialogues. Here everything is true because it is, and not abstracted from reality by words, paled into symbols of what ought to be, should be, but is not. I have the same feeling as someone who has been in the dark looking at a film too long, and coming out everything leaps out brutal, real, solid, into sight, into being. The world, two-dimensional yesterday, is irrecoverably multi-dimensional, meaning within meaning, bizarre, fantastic, just-so, and somehow deeply satisfactory as if it really provided a clue to many puzzles. This is the world of Harvey and the Jumblies, the Abominable Snowman is not far, and I want to say 'Excuse me' when my foot kicks against a stone. I am quite certain that I shall go mad, but what a delicious madness. And what a certainty I have now that I am alive, where only yesterday I knew I was nicely dead.

'The magic words shall hold thee fast, Thou shalt not heed the raving blast. ...' It is not words, but the things they symbolize, which are real, at last at last, and in their impingement upon me produce words, only I am not sure that the words are right because they fall short. They can convey as a seismograph the scribbles which mean an earthquake, but they cannot give a picture of the landslides, the crevices, the crumbling destructions accomplished. They cannot paint, cannot set up this smouldering, electric, deep inside each cell feeling which Lawrence was perhaps talking about as darkness deep inside, living darkness, unworded trueness deep down things.

There was this mute getting up, not yet dawn, giving myself an icy cold shower, dressing and leaving the bedroom, and all the time John fast asleep, and I was not even concerned. I looked at his prone body and did not feel anything, not caring whether he should wake or not. And going down the corridor, the steps, out through the gates, the sleepy porter in the sentry-box opening them for me as if it were the most natural thing in the world, and walking out, a milky cold fog still upon the fields, and out of them the porters filing, heavy laden, their oval baskets swinging from the band across their foreheads, and they singing.

As dreams are more vivid than reality – perhaps because we have verbalized reality out of existence, or perhaps because our verbalizations create for us an unreal world, and below it, well below the slime of our talk, lies hidden all we do not wish to know about ourselves and our world – so this going out in the cold, alone, is something I shall never forget. I really owned myself then.

I walked, with the sun waking slowly, the birds waking noisily, the snow peaks appearing, splendid, rosy, cold, and awful. I wanted to pray. I didn't know where I was, it did not matter. A bridge, the river with the sun swimming in pink in it, and women putting radishes down in rows in the water. There were many people about now, and jeeps and cows, and it was all the same; I did not need to spring upon them with attention, tourist-voracious and greedy of strangeness, for I belonged with them, we were all part of each other. There was a road, I followed it. There was an airfield in front of me, the planes bestirred with men. I looked at them for a while as if I had never seen a plane, then I followed some women cutting across a field with rhododendrons in their hair and small trays for worship in their hands, and then we were among the lingam shrines, with men and women praying and making offering, and the sun was coming stronger, and I was on the slope among the shrines, and there was a great temple flashing golden roofs and golden gods on the other side of a river narrow and strong like a strong rope at the foot of the slope, and bellmetal striking the hour of a morning unfinishing, time everlasting.

I sat and looked, I could never look enough, and the sun was like a glory of giving upon us all, and a corpse was burning, and some people washed themselves on the white worn steps, and then Dr Maltby came hurtling into me, and that too was just as it should be. He told me about his wife. We went walking back, a jeep full of Nepalese gave us a lift, we all laughed together, without reason.

And then the General told me I had Unni Menon's room. Why did Isobel give me this bungalow, this room? Perhaps it is only explicable in terms of this light-headed madness which is the Valley. I should have thought that I, who have succumbed to it so quickly, could understand why. And Isobel, who seems so impervious to magic and blissful folly after two years or more here, is a mystery in the very fact that she could do a thing like that. And she does not like me. Perhaps she did yesterday, but today she no longer likes me. The door is shut between us now.

For Isobel and John will keep their perspective of feeling and language, they are in strong grip of themselves, their souls their own, moulded strongly and stonily, while I just lose myself, I *become* elsewhere, my consciousness growing with and into surroundings, altered by them, myself. ... But who am I?

Isobel knows this, thinks it terribly dangerous for me. She tried to warn me.

We were standing on the steps, Fred Maltby and General Kumar and I. It would have been worse had not Isobel started speech at once, forceful, imperious, as if clad in armour, a metal mask vizoring her hungry undefended eyes:

'Well, well, what a good time you're having, dear. We were rather worried about you, you know.'

'I went for a walk,' I said. The moment of a miracle is unending. Can one corner the sunlight or catch a star? I wanted to say: 'I went through the rabbit-hole,' but it would have been giving away a clue, exposing oneself, and I must be careful not to say too much to Isobel. Talking to some people is bringing them a ladybird, and the first thing they do is take it out of your hand and crush a foot upon it.

'How very very enterprising of you' (voice strewn with ground glass), 'I wouldn't do it myself. Your husband and I went to call on the Resident and sign the book. You may remember I mentioned it to you last night?'

'I forgot all about it.'

We stood, hesitant, uncomfortable, on the steps. Fred Maltby and the General said they must go. The General, like the sun, was above it all, a dusty, thin, and white-haired angel whose eyes remained far away. They had already walked off when the General came back and said: 'I will procure the cards for the wedding tomorrow,' and went away again.

'So you're going to the wedding too,' said Isobel. 'Of course the General can arrange it. It's his niece, all those Ranas are related to one another.'

'I hope I've been invited?' said John.

'Of course.'

'Thank you,' he said, sarcastic.

I followed John, walking ahead of me in that firm, high-stepping parade step which until now used to annoy me, that extravagant annoyance of marriage when small differences provoke a lasting sense of grievance. It did annoy me, for now I was again in their world, Isobel's and John's, empty and dust-tongued.

John turned upon me in the bedroom, and of course he said what I could have recited for him:

'I demand an explanation of your conduct, Anne.'

'My conduct?'

'You know what I mean. It was grossly selfish, not to call it ill-mannered. You never thought once of me, or of Isobel. I venture to suggest that you have created a very bad impression already. It's given us a bad start, and I feel very strongly about it. I don't wish to be personal but I am sure the Resident must have thought it extremely odd....'

'Oh, Tiddlywinks won't think anything,' I said. 'Fred Maltby says he's very intelligent and that we'll get on well together.'

'I don't care nor do I wish to hear what Dr Maltby thinks of the Resident. I may be old-fashioned, but I do not expect a wife, my wife, to disappear for hours on end with another man. I did not wish to make a scene, but I shall take up the matter with Dr Maltby and ask him what his intentions towards you are.'

'Oh, really, this is too silly,' I said.

But now John was shouting, winding up the windlass of his emotional bucket, to be poured into one of those storms of shouting which he practises occasionally. I watched, fascinated, telling myself that after the morning brightness I could never be frightened again, yet slowly invaded by fear, by nausea. I'd thought myself stronger, but it was not to be; unreleased the slave, even if the chain dangles. Frederic Maltby running at sight of Eudora; me, now shaking inside me, my soul pale, my preoccupation my face a gag upon me, the mounting sourness, myself my own appointed prisoner still.

'I won't tolerate it. I'm your husband. Yes, your husband, though you may not like it. I won't be ignored while you try to muck around with this doctor. Oh, I've no fears of your going to bed with him. If he tried you'd probably be sick. I've got a good mind to go over right after lunch to tell that f— bastard what I think of a man who tries to make someone else's wife and hasn't the decency to stand up to him.

I shall have to take measures to see that this won't be repeated.' He walked up and down a little. 'Maybe we shall leave Khatmandu by the next plane. You'd better start packing, I think.'

Why do I put up with it, I thought. I opened the wardrobe. I must change into a dress for lunch. I put it on my arm and walked to the bathroom, I wasn't going to run.

'Where are you going? Why can't you change in here? Anne, I'm talking to you, Anne ...'

The panting nausea, behind the closed door. It is a weakness John knows: emotion produces in me this hypermotility. It was the same when Jimmy died. I neither cried nor wept. Jimmy ... I haven't written his name in years. It seems so far now but very natural, nearly happy, here in this orange sun room, in Unni Menon's room, writing Jimmy.

Then washing my hands and face, changing, and facing John again, opening the door, calm, clenched so tight, from head to foot, that it hurts to walk.

John was sitting, having taken off his flannel slacks. He had his shirt over his underpants, his socks were held up by the maroon suspenders I had bought for him, and his knee caps were round and bald, like two skulls, above his hairy legs.

Nearly jocose, he asked me: 'Well, feel better now?'

Exactly in the same way he used to after making love.

He now crossed his legs to look at me do my hair, and this again is something I have lived with for years, and am dying to shout at him. John always crosses his legs too high, until he sits, his face above the barricade of his calf and knee, his body slumped sacklike behind, and his eyes abnormally observant and watchful, as if not a tremor, not a gesture, could get past their double-barrelled attention. I know, I know without ever having discussed it, that he does not observe anything, he is too busy creating an impression of massive attentiveness to see anything else but a picture of himself, a picture at once energetic and *désinvolte*, like a super-sleuth.

And as always when he crosses his legs thus, so high, thighs upwards, and is wearing shorts, the yawn between limb and cloth reveals the testicles, glabrous, a little bluish tinged skin. John is not alone in doing this: Old Pickle our ex-Governor did the same. It comes from wearing wide-cut shorts in the tropics, and it happens to a lot of Englishmen out East, sitting on those fairly low cane and rattan settees. But no one has ever said a word. I have never said anything about it either.

'Can't even change your dress in front of me now. My dear Anne, honestly, you're getting quite neurotic. Look at you, thin, dried up,' he laughed, 'I can't see you taking on Maltby. ... Ha, ha ha. Yes, look at me. I'm not dressed. What's wrong with that? Don't act as if you'd never seen me with my pants off.'

He was happy, an actor who's brought off a scene. At that moment our room bearer opened the door after a timid knock. 'Lunchong,' he said. He too looked at John. His eyes closed and his smile widened and he tiptoed out.

'I hope you'll have the patience to wait till I put on my trousers,' said John. So I waited, and we walked down the corridor together to lunch.

And now I have written it down. For the first time I have not lied about John and myself. I have put down in words the ugliness, the other side of me, and I taste a strange composure. It is nearly like revenge. My only revenge, the only way I can ever get even with whatever he or anyone else does to me: write it in words, give it shape, meaning, and some queer sort of life, in words.

Lunch was a bunched odious hour. Coffee on the verandah, and Isobel suggesting a drive later, which we took. We drove through crowded and pestilential streets, squalor abounding, peeping at un-walkable lanes which were cesspools – 'everything gets thrown into them from the top storeys, just as in eleventh-century England', said Isobel – to the white slim tower called Bhim Seng's Folly, built by a Rana prime minister with mixed intentions, and adorned with fanciful tales. It is said that Bhim Seng himself leapt from its top on horseback, escaping unhurt. Isobel had obtained permission to climb to the top, and from there we looked at the Valley. Both John and Isobel were showing me and each other with words the landscape, the hills, the clear air, the nearness of the snow mountains. It was I who saw nothing, felt nothing, while their words went clattering and thundering in their grooves near by me. Hoisted upon the small platform at the tower's top they showed me the world of the Valley and its glories and I pitied them and nodded.

I think Isobel knew I wanted no part of them, she knew in this nameless wordless way which things have of being known in this Valley. Is it the purity of the air, infectious transparency, which renders us so proximate, so visible to each other, or is it just my fancy? She now tried to win me back in the grand manner.

After tea John was amiable and said he'd leave us, we had a lot to talk about, and he'd go for a stroll with his camera. I went to Unni's room (since the General has said it, I think of it as Unni's room), and here Isobel cornered me, and I had to face her. She held an inchoate mass of knitting against her, a sweater with two white needles stuck into it. She sat on the couch, the bright orange and blue quilted raza lapping round her. Outside the sun lay in flat gold bars with bars of blue shadow between, and the vociferous crows, scolds of the air, were beginning their night trails home to the trees. Isobel spoke, she did not hear the crows outside; talked, desiring to approach me, knowing no other way of approach, of her work, the work to be done, the misery, how one must come to the Himalayas to teach the poor dear girls how to read and write and be clean and not smile too often at the boys. She would have them forget to put flowers in their hair and dance and live in their deep, lovely, unconscious way, their bodies in rhythm with the folds of the mountains and the laughter of the sun in their eyes.

In the golden web of the room she poured her fly-black energy and buzzed about medievalism, progress, and health. I felt as if she had said: Let us draw our chairs to the edge of the precipice, and fill it with our screams.

And suddenly she came to the point of all this: my conduct. She didn't blame me but it was so imprudent, people talked in Khatmandu, and John and I, our happy marriage ... Dr Maltby, excellent doctor, but I was a woman of the world and I would understand. He'd been living with a Nepalese girl, a maidservant, *given* him by the General, until she had died the year before, they said it was tuberculosis. And of course there was the mountain air. One is apt to get too emotional in the mountains, it's the altitude.

'For instance, one of our staff, I might as well tell you the story, you're bound to hear it ...'

A comical, lamentable story: old missionary couple, seasoned in puritanism and China, come to Nepal; he to conduct classes in Bible reading, she to teach literature. In three months he had gone completely 'stark, staring, raving mad' (Isobel's words), taken up Hinduism, made off with a hill woman, their servant. No one had seen or heard of them since. The wife had gone back home alone; hence the vacancy for me.

Of course, John was so sane, so balanced, she wasn't for a moment suggesting ... Everything would be fine, but there *was* gossip. And some day we must have a long long chat about our school days and all that's happened since. She got up. It was twilight. She looked out of the window and there was that terrible hunger upon her face.

She went and with her going I fell back into my state of acceptance, falling into the folds of the oncoming night and feeling the parakeets singing in the silence, and the ironic eyes, so much more wise than human eyes, watching me and making me safe. It was perfection, and I was very happy, and words came to me on paper, following each other, leading I don't know where.

Chapter 7

THE verandah of the Royal Hotel faced east. All morning the sun squandered itself upon the white cloth of the tables, and the seated tourists.

The Royal Hotel had been a Rana palace. In the entrance hall of marble with pillars, four crocodiles, stuffed, rampaged upon the marble floor, lifting voracious and many-toothed snouts towards tourist calves. Upon carved stools two rhinoceros heads showed decapitated necks, the backs of which, in papiermâché, reproduced the severed windpipes and muscles in most realistic fashion. Tiger skins up and downstairs hung snarls down upon the walls of the main rooms, and there were rugs made of deer skin and bear skin in most of the bedrooms. The usual oil paintings of the Ranas lined the walls in an upstairs gallery. Anne, passing them with Isobel and John, recognized several, having seen them at General Kumar's the day before. Solemnly General Kumar had introduced them: 'This is my second uncle, madam, a confused bastard whom God has punished with many no-good ugly daughters,' and 'My brother, now leader of a political party, the poor fool.' The uncle and the brother stared at her here also, in full panoply, but the frames were gilt wood decorated with crests.

There was the usual grand salon, with imitation *louis quinze* furniture covered in blue and silver brocade, with chandeliers, and side tables plated with mirrors. As always the mansion was a quadrangle built round a large centre courtyard, which had served as tennis court and was now green and slippery with weeds. There was a long procession of rooms, both up and downstairs, and a sound of hammering and sawing going on and dull thuds as if furniture was being thrown about.

'It is the bathroom fixtures,' explained Hilde, the wife of Vassili, the manager of the Royal Hotel who was at the moment in jail.

Twenty-seven bathroom sets, complete, had arrived by air, at a cost of seventeen thousand rupees per set, and were being installed. Soon the Royal Hotel would not have a room without a bathroom.

93

Already as if by instinct American tourists came flocking to it. 'We are booked up till June, and also from October all through next Christmas,' said Hilde. The only slack season was the monsoon season from June to September. 'But next winter I don't know *where* we'll put the tourists. And as for the guests and other people coming for the Coronation in May, I think most of them will have to sleep in tents.'

Hilde was beautiful. It was a natural adjective for her. There was no other word to describe her truly golden hair, naturally curly, a sunlit undulation bringing all the visions of van Gogh cornfields of a temperate Europe to mind as it cascaded down her back, a resurrected Chersonese for young men to dream of with passion as she walked up and down the verandah in the evening, the glory of her hair undimmed even by the smoky brown emanation misnamed electric light in Khatmandu.

In bright red corduroy slacks and a white sweater Hilde was calmly eating a four-egg omelette, while her large blue eyes raised with the tranquillity of supreme good health looked upon each face in turn. She was undoubtedly a young Scandinavian goddess, pagan as Khatmandu was pagan, and therefore at home in the valley of the gods.

Round her they clustered, breathless and adoring, young men and old, tourists of all ages, and sighed pleasurably and in vain.

'Vassili cannot sleep because it is spring and all the dogs are making love round the jail,' said Hilde in her childish voice.

'Oh dear,' said Martha Redworth, 'I'll bring him some of my sleeping tablets tomorrow.'

'No good,' replied Hilde. 'Vassili can't take sleeping tablets because of his liver. The Prince brought him some from Calcutta. "Try these, Vassili," he said, "they're very good with brandy." But Vassili isn't allowed to drink brandy because of his liver.'

'He can take them with water,' said Mrs Redworth, who was motherly.

'Vassili can't drink water,' said Hilde, lifting immense eyes fringed with dark lashes upon Martha Redworth.

Anne leant back in her chair, her fingers round the beer mug. Everyone was having beer, iced, sparkling, golden beer, to go with Hilde's golden hair. ... Martha and Paul Redworth, Isobel, John, and Major Pemberton, with the walrus moustache, who was in the Gurkhas. Upon all lay the sun, honeysuckle heavy. Anne felt like taking all her clothes off and lying down somewhere, away from all people, given up to the sun, and to sleep, fathomless sleep. Beyond the pink brick walls the soft pipes and drums of yet another wedding procession made her temples throb with pleasure.

On the verandah a bustle of tourists went by with cameras; an American artist in pony tail and too tight slacks, with crayons and drawing paper in her arms, followed by a handsome Nepalese of pale creamy complexion with a fatuous small moustache, obviously pleased with himself.

'That's Ranchit with Pat. He's a Rana. She paints him and beds him,' said Hilde, not too *sotto voce* to Anne. 'And he's got such a pretty wife. There is also Dr Maltby's wife, have you heard?'

'What's this I hear about Dr Maltby's wife?' said John. He sharpened his eyes, as if probing into the statements offered to him, and Hilde told him.

'Dr Maltby ran away from his wife a long time ago and now she has turned up in Khatmandu, and he is terrified of her, and we have to help them not to meet,' said Hilde.

'Thank you,' said John. 'At least someone here tells me what goes on.'

'She is a writer of inspirational music,' said Paul Redworth.

'I don't think I approve of this deception,' said John.

No one answered him.

'She's staying here,' said Hilde. 'Father MacCullough is taking her round because she is a socialist, or something like that.'

'And here they come now,' said Paul, glancing over the ironwork railing of the verandah. 'Hello, Father.'

Father MacCullough shook hands all round heartily, and introduced Eudora. 'Well, well, well! Still eating breakfast?' he asked, pointing to Hilde's omelette.

'It's my three little padlocks,' said Hilde mournfully. 'They took an age over theirs, so I'm having mine at beer time.'

'And how's my friend Vassili?' said Father MacCullough. 'I'm going to see him tomorrow and have a drink with him and Sharma.'

'Can't sleep because of the dogs making love all night round the jail,' said Hilde.

'Well now, ain't that just too bad?' said Father MacCullough. 'I'll have to think of something for that.'

Eudora wore slacks with a large sun-hat. She was full of vivacity. She and Isobel had given each other the measuring stare of Siamese boxers about to kick each other in the face.

'These poor poor wretched Nepalese people,' she exclaimed. 'It's dreadful, absolutely dreadful, their poverty. ... I saw an old woman this morning, she looked like a skeleton, yet there she was, throwing handfuls of rice on to one of those stone things. I tried to stop her. My dear, I said to her, hadn't you better keep it and eat it yourself? She just smiled, poor thing, then she took some milk out of a cup and poured it over the idol or whatever it is. I told Father MacCullough: and now you're capitalizing on their ignorance. You'll take away their old gods, merely replacing them with a new one, instead of teaching them to be *really* independent minded.'

Isobel's eyes flashed, her bosom heaved. 'How can you compare –?' she began, but the Resident, foreseeing a religious clash, intervened with the same tact he used when he went to see the Nepalese Foreign Ministry.

'I understand, Miss Maltby, that you are interested in music?'

'My name is Mrs Maltby. And I'm not merely interested. I create music.'

'I must introduce you to a friend of mine, a Nepalese singer, a very famous poet too. He's of course not really Nepalese, but South Indian. As you know, most of the sacred music of Nepal comes from South India.'

'How fascinating,' said Eudora. 'Let me get my notebook, I want to write his name down.'

'And then there are the Gurkha melodies,' said the Resident a trifle wildly, looking at Major Pemberton, who was dipping his moustaches in his third mug of beer. 'Major Pemberton here, who is in charge of the educational department for the Gurkhas (you know we recruit the chaps here in Nepal, don't you?), will tell you all about it.'

'Who, me!' said the Major, startled.

'He can tell me about the music,' said Eudora majestically, 'but I must make it quite clear that I disapprove totally, absolutely, of imperialism which takes these poor ignorant hillmen away from here and makes them fight colonial wars for the benefit of a clique of plutocrats abroad.'

'Plutocrats, madam,' said a voice behind her. 'Do you know that

Lenin was born in the Valley of Khatmandu? Were you in the conspiracy?'

A little Nepalese stood behind Eudora's chair, quivering from cap to shoes. He had a very thin, burning face with almond-shaped brown eyes, a rather dirty western coat upon his tunic and jodhpurs, and carried a large worn briefcase.

'Yes, Lenin and I were born here, we're twins,' he informed Eudora. 'It is no secret. Good evening, madam,' he added, turning towards Hilde. 'Is my friend Vassili still in jail?'

'He's still in jail, Your Excellency Prime Minister, thank you for inquiring.'

'Tell him,' said the Nepalese tapping his briefcase, 'I've got all the proofs of the plot against him here. I will give him the Order of Ganesh when he is released ... triumphantly released.'

'Thanks very much, Prime Minister,' said Hilde.

'This lady,' said the man, turning upon Eudora and shaking a thin finger, 'does she know about Lenin?'

'Do I know about Lenin?' said Eudora. 'Let me tell you, my dear fellow –'

'She's only just arrived,' interrupted the Resident. 'She's a tourist.'

'She is forgiven,' said the Nepalese. 'Good day to you.' And with a little bow he walked forward, and went to sit at another table. Placing the briefcase in front of him he sat, staring and moving his lips inaudibly.

'He thinks he is a Prime Minister,' said Hilde, wiping her mouth and seizing a mug of beer. 'He has been here ever since we opened. He thinks Lenin is his twin and Stalin his uncle. Both born in Khatmandu of a Rana family. Their real names General Ganesh and Field Marshal Indera Sham Sher Rana.'

'Oughtn't something to be done?' said Eudora indignantly. 'Surely you can't let a madman come here and mix with normal people; supposing he got violent?'

'The other tourists don't seem to mind,' said Isobel pointedly.

Eudora's bosom heaved, and her mouth opened, but at that moment appeared a bearer with a large envelope of the silky, corncoloured handmade local paper, which he handed unerringly to Eudora, and behind him, so tall that he seemed to hit the chandeliers, cap awry upon his white hair, General Kumar.

The Resident greeted him with joy not unmixed with relief, Father MacCullough jumped up and offered him a chair. He joined hands together in a respectful salute to Hilde: 'How is Vassili, Madame Hilde? And your three stalwart offspring?'

'Very well, General, except Vassili still cannot sleep because of the dogs.'

'Well now,' said Father MacCullough, 'wait a minute, I'm just thinking up something which might be of use against the dogs.'

Eudora gave an exclamation. 'Swami Bidahari is asking me to lunch,' she said. 'Right now. Oh dear. Do I know him, I wonder? Who can he be?'

'Swami means Wise Man, madam. Swami Bidahari is the greatest musician in Nepal,' said the General. 'He is my friend and mentioned to me how eager he is to be honoured by your visit.'

Eudora bridled a bit. 'Perhaps through my work in London, I think I do remember now, we must have met ...'

'The Swami is paralysed from the waist down,' said the General, 'and so he prays you to visit him.'

'But,' began Father MacCullough, bewildered, 'the Swami –' and then Paul Redworth kicked him under the table, and he plunged his face in his beer mug.

'I am to lunch at Bidahari Mahal. That means castle, doesn't it, Mahal? Where is it, I wonder?'

'Twelve miles from here,' said Major Pemberton, and he too suddenly appeared to have received a blow upon his shin for his moustaches disappeared in his beer.

'Twelve miles? I won't be able to make it in time and I'll miss the wedding this afternoon,' said Eudora.

'He means twelve Nepalese miles, which is three English, madam,' said the General. 'It's only a very little distance, at most half of an hour by jeep, and I have brought my personal jeep and my eldest son to escort you.' He pointed to a young man, very handsome, with the willowy eyes, tip-tilted at the corner, of the stone gods. 'This is my son Deepah, madam, who will escort you in my jeep to the Swami. He is eighteen years old and very strong and will protect you against all ravishments.'

Eudora got up, smiling broadly. 'In that case and if I can be back for the wedding I'll be very pleased to accept,' she said graciously.

'Goodness, I must go and dress, the invitation says one o'clock and it is nearly one.'

'The Swami eats at two,' said the General. 'You will fill his heart with delight.'

As Eudora disappeared Father MacCullough turned to the General: 'What's all this about old Bidahari, General? Holy Mother of God, I thought the man was deaf and gaga, and lived miles out.'

'He has recovered,' said the General gravely.

'Well, the General knows best,' said Paul Redworth.

'Madam Eudora will have a very pleasant drive, with my son to entertain her, and will admire the scenery which is particularly beautiful now in the spring,' added the General.

'I hope she will be in time for the wedding,' muttered Father Mac-Cullough.

'I am in full responsibility of her physique,' said the General with hauteur.

'If only Vassili could find a way to stop those dogs making love round the jail,' said Hilde to change the conversation.

'Don't worry,' answered Father MacCullough. 'I think I've got just what he needs.'

'Not a sleeping pill,' said Hilde, 'because that's got to be taken with water and Vassili doesn't drink water.'

'No, not that, but a catapult. The kind of thing that David used on Goliath. You know, ping ping ping. I'll get one for Vassili and give it to him when I go tomorrow.'

'You are a genius too, sir,' said the General. He sat next to Paul Redworth and whispered in his ear.

'I'll circulate it among my staff,' said Paul Redworth in a low voice under cover of the others' talk. 'Poor Fred. Is he really very worried?'

'He is transported with fear,' replied the General. 'But let us not be unheartened. She is only staying two weeks, my nephew tells me.'

'Two weeks ... I doubt we can keep the secret that long. Of course nothing will come from us. I'll pass the word round, but we can't keep it two weeks.'

'Just a few days,' said the General, 'while my friend prepares himself for his struggle.'

'All right then,' sighed Paul Redworth, as Eudora reappeared in dress and flowered hat, 'after the wedding, we'll see.'

Chapter 8

THE wedding would start at four that Sunday afternoon, an auspicious hour chosen by the chief astrologer; but since his calculations could be affected by last minute whimsies, such as a thunderclap without rain, the dead body of a bird in the garden, or other manifestations of maleficent intent, it was noon before Father MacCullough, installed on the verandah of the Royal Hotel, received a message that four o'clock was definite.

'I'll be going off now to round up a few more people,' he said, rising in the business-like way he had of doing things. 'Will be seeing you there. Anyone need a lift anywhere?'

Father MacCullough had had a pleasant lunch, surrounded by attentiveness. Not only the Fords, Isobel Maupratt, Major Pemberton, and the Redworths had been sitting at the next table, aware of him, but before and after that small groups of tourists had stopped by, to be introduced to him by Hilde. He had spoken at length on the history, the geography, the religions, the demography of Nepal, 'this once hermit kingdom, now striving to take a Himalayan leap from the eleventh to the twentieth century', was how he'd phrased it. Some of the visitors, impressed, had scribbled notes hastily on pads they carried with them.

'Isn't he wonderful?' they said to each other.

'Certainly knows all there is to know about this place. What he doesn't know isn't worth bothering about.'

'That *was* lucky, meeting him like that. I can send in my piece to *Gracious Living* now.'

'He sure gives one the dope about this burg.'

'No need going round trying to find out *what's* important, what isn't.'

'We wouldn't know where to begin, anyway.'

'Honest, this is the most guideless place.'

'Fancy a people not being interested in showing their temples and things.'

In spite of his priestly humility, Father MacCullough felt pleasantly important when imparting knowledgeableness. It induced him to verbal swagger, which the Nepalese received without a ruffle upon their smiling suave features, their luminous eyes fixed calmly upon the stranger in their midst who professed to know them so well. 'You must meet so-and-so. Used to be in jail. Now the King's right-hand man. Good pal of mine. Anything I say, he listens to.' Rumour in the bazaar would interpret: 'Ah, so-and-so is receiving money from the foreigners through the man in swaddling clothes.'

'Want to visit Bhim Seng's Folly?' Father MacCullough would call cheerfully in ringing Irish-American tones. 'Leave it to me, I'll fix it.'

And it was a great pity, for few men did more and better work in the Valley than Father MacCullough.

After the priest's leave-taking, Isobel and the Fords also prepared to go to dress for the wedding. The Redworths offered to take Hilde with them, but she refused.

'Unni Menon is coming to fetch me.'

'But he's not back yet,' said Paul Redworth.

'He will be,' said Hilde. 'He is driving me to see Vassili in the jail afterwards.'

'Well, we mustn't be late,' said Isobel. 'I think we'd better be there at quarter to four, don't you? If one's late *they* have a habit of lining up in full uniform, waiting for one on the doorstep. Most uncomfortable.'

The Commander's Palace was a little way out of the city. The road passed on either side succulent fields of black earth, covered with the fuzz of young growth, some bright yellow with the flower of the rape, others pinky-white or light green with blossoming peas and beans and barley. Here and there were modern bungalows with gardens, built in the last six years: hideous, whitewashed, utilitarian. John exclaimed at their ugliness. Everywhere in Asia people were losing their sense of beauty; filling their cities with these ugly new houses, with plastic lampshades, machine-turned tableware, nightmarish ashtrays, ornate radios, lace tablecloths made in Japan, and pin-ups cut out of American film magazines. 'They're too much in a hurry to get on, they're losing all their old traditions.'

And Isobel now bemoaned the lack of skilled handiwork. 'It's all dying out, all these people want now is machines, progress.'

'Well,' said Anne, almost shouting above the noise of the jeep, 'isn't that what we're bringing them, progress?' But the other two did not hear. Anne wanted to say: this abeyance of taste, sudden ignorance of beauty, is a temporary disarray, an alienated sense, not permanent token of ineptitude. And we've had the same aberrations; look at the Victoriana in the Ranas' palaces, that was *us*, fifty years ago. But she felt it a futile explanation for Isobel and John, and now the jeep turned up the dirt lane to the Commander's Palace.

On both sides of the lane poles hung fluttering small red flags, and in between were looped arches of cut green boughs. The usual iron gates led into grounds of modest dimensions and a 'palace' like a comfortable, Edwardian large country house in the South of England. An embroidered piece of satin hung across the top of the gate. On the lawn a squad of red-coated soldiers with trombone and drum and saxophone played a tune Anne was able to identify, gradually, as *A Bicycle Made for Two*.

On the front door step stood the Commander, with a hover of generals dressed in gold braid uniforms. The Commander was an extremely handsome man, tall, well proportioned, with fine masculine features, a creamy Nepalese complexion like a smooth blend of sandalwood soap, arched eyebrows, and lustrous eyes. He was not in uniform, but wore a broadcloth tail-coat cut in Savile Row and just getting tight under the armpits, pin-stripe trousers, and black shoes. Upon his chest gleamed a row of enormous medals studded with diamonds, emeralds, rubies, and sapphires. Upon his head he wore the Rana helmet, the casque of pearls and diamonds and rubies, fringed with a hundred and twenty-six oval emeralds, like small quail's eggs, round the entire rim. Above his forehead, in a crest of gold, a bird of gold and ruby plunged a diamond beak; its body was formed by yard-long sweeping feathers of the New Guinea bird of paradise. The Ranas round him, cousins, uncles, brothers, nephews, looked as if they had just stepped out of their family portraits. General Kumar was there too, but being the eccentric of the family he wore a lounge suit and his Nepalese cap. He smiled his tender, pensive, intellectual smile and came forward to guide Isobel and the Fords upstairs.

'You, sir,' he said gravely to John, 'I will introduce you to His Excellency the Minister for Economics, as I understand you are interested in many such questions.' He piloted John with flattering dexterity towards a small knot of men, Americans from the Point Four Mission, a Swiss geologist, and Nepalese officials in black caps and suits and white jodhpurs, holding glasses of whisky in their hands and looking round vaguely in need of a topic.

'I will take madam your wife to meet some ladies,' he told John, and guided Anne into a long oblong room, marble to mid-wall, with hanging skins of tigers and leopards topped by bristling antlers and horns on frames. Chairs, sofas, settees, and armchairs were drawn up in two rows on either side, leaving the centre empty as a church aisle up to the room end, where under the largest chandelier was placed a settee covered with a cloth of woven gold. Upon this the King and Queen would sit later, and next to them the bridegroom, who had not yet arrived. The guests were waiting for him, men in clusters in the hall, ante-rooms, and garden, the women mostly here, sitting together, their saris round them, iridescent silks shimmering softly as they moved and the folds changed and caught the light, and flashing jewellery in sudden fires, jewellery in chains, in chunks, emeralds and diamonds and rubies in strings and twists. The women's faces were powdered, their eyes outlined with kohl, and in their hair, long, oiled, dressed in upstanding loops, were flowers, pink camellias and scented jasmine. They varied greatly in looks; some totally Indian and others with distinctly Mongol features; many with the Valley mixture of Indian with Mongol, features delicate and fine, skins flawless and translucent, long slanting eyes.

The General took Anne to a settee to salute the wife of the Field Marshal, 'the most beautiful woman in the world doubtless, madam'. She had an oval, perfect face, beautifully arched eyebrows, a fine thin nose just big enough, a small mouth, the lips curved and slightly protruding and then the corners tucked in again, as on the stone goddesses, lips with a floating smile upon them. Her body was tall and slim and graceful. She smiled and turned her head to Anne with subtle grace, and made as if to give her a place by her on the settee, and it seemed to Anne that the line of the blue-black hair down to the fine long neck, and the curve of the cheek, were the loveliest things she had seen in a woman.

'And here, madam, is Rukmini my niece, the wife of Ranchit,' said the General.

Sitting by the side of the Field Marshal's wife, smaller, with a rounder face, was Rukmini. Where the Field Marshal's wife was like a camellia blossom, Rukmini was like a rose bud, a bud unfolding and perhaps in maturity not as compelling as now when there was still something reticent in her, half-dormancy in her face, changing as she moved, capricious and uncatchable as that heart-wringing moment in spring when the first green shiver goes through the trees, elusive like the slight wind of dawn. Rukmini had the same blue-black hair as the Field Marshal's wife, but it was cut short and curled softly round her face. Her eyes were tip-tilted and her pupils looked at one not straight but always a little from the side; they were shaded by long lashes curving extravagantly when her eyelids closed. She held innocence in all of her yet was full of the promises of love, and this duality was her compelling charm. Her sari was blue with silver stars, and she had sapphires and diamonds in her ears and round her neck.

Rukmini looked up at Anne quickly and shyly, and then her glance swept by and looked behind Anne, looked and there came upon her face such radiance that Anne also turned, but she saw only a good many men collected at the entrance, talking together, and then Hilde walked in with Mrs Redworth and the Commander. The General then introduced Anne to the Commander-in-Chief's wife, who, with the busy air of a bird, went in and out from the inner apartments where the bride was being dressed; then took her to his own wife, as round as he was thin, a woman of great dignity with a serene smile upon a Buddha-round face.

'My wife is a fine musician,' said the General proudly. 'She plays the sitar and is studying the *Bhagavad-Gita*, the Song of God, to improve the spirit of love in her music. For without love, nothing is beautiful.'

Hilde, then Mrs Redworth, came up, and they and Anne sat and smiled at the Nepalese ladies who smiled back. Rukmini appeared to dream and did not speak, and Anne did not know how to begin talking to her: obviously not about the parakeets. Two beautiful youths, the sons of the Commander, offered open boxes of heavy wrought silver containing sweetmeats and spices: dates, small pieces of rock sugar, cloves, cashew-nuts, cardamon big and small, skinned and unskinned almonds, betel nut and copra and coconut chips.

The room filled quickly with guests, men and women. Isobel now stood on the balcony in conversation with John, and with them the young man with the small moustache whose name was Ranchit, and the American artist whom everyone called Pat. She wore a dirndl skirt, off-the-shoulder blouse, and sandals, the same clothes as she had on before lunch.

'She looks as if she needed a good bath,' whispered Martha Redworth to Anne. 'Look at her nails. Dreadful. Poor Rukmini. I bet Ranchit will come over and introduce the girl to his wife. Yes, here he comes.'

And then Anne realized that Ranchit was the husband of Rukmini, and the 'proper fool' the General had spoken of.

Rukmini rose, gracefully, dutifully. Anne saw how young she was, with the small neck of a child under the heavy jewellery, little curls at the nape. The beautiful face was immobile, slightly frozen, yet Rukmini inclined her head, shook hands with the American girl, sat down again.

'She's only sixteen or seventeen,' whispered Martha Redworth, 'the age of my youngest daughter who's at school in Devon. Ah, good afternoon, Field Marshal.'

A small man, short and compact of body, in grey tunic and jodhpurs with the ubiquitous western jacket and cap, stood in front of them. He had a round, high-cheek-boned face creased with benevolence, round eyes which were shrewd and observant. Martha Redworth introduced him to Anne, and he said: 'Yes, I was just coming to say that I have known you for some years, Mrs Ford, through your book. And also to tell you that you look like Luise Rainer.'

'Thank you,' said Anne, smiling.

'She was my ideal for many years,' said the Field Marshal. 'I used to know the names of film stars from their pictures and also from my trips abroad, but now I don't get accustomed to the new names and faces. I have remained with those I loved, Luise Rainer, Greta Garbo, Carole Lombard.'

'But the youngsters don't know them any more,' said Martha Redworth. 'The stars of *our* youth ... when I said something about Greta Garbo to my youngest she turned round and said: "Mummy, *who* are you talking about?"'

'You must come to my humble house,' said the Field Marshal to Anne, 'my wife and I would be delighted to have your company. And I would like to show you my books.'

At that moment General Kumar floated near them and said: 'Come, madam, I want to take you the rounds,' and Anne followed him.

Outside the house the band, after a little silence, burst into more music.

'It's going to rain,' said the General sniffing the air. 'That is a good omen. I called you, madam, because I would like you to see Unni Menon, but did not wish to bring him near to Rukmini for fear of havoc. I think Ranchit is in quarrelsome mood today.'

They walked out of the room, across the hall, full of tusks and horns and rhinoceros heads, stuffed bears, and chairs covered in tiger skins, to another smaller room, where, leaning against a grand piano, a man stood talking with Fred Maltby.

'Unni,' said the General, and the man turned and Anne thought: how tall he is, and then: how dark he is. She shook hands, her hand disappeared into his.

'Oh hello,' said Fred Maltby, 'nice of you to come to us here. It's quieter than in the main room.'

The General said: 'Have you told Unni about your wife?'

'Not yet,' said Fred, looking harassed.

The General passed cigarettes round and they each had one, and Anne leaned back against the grand piano, and suddenly someone said in a sharp high voice: 'Ah, *there* you are!' and Isobel was there, and following her Ranchit and the American girl, who walked up to Unni with a quick swing of her skirt brushing past Anne, and a shrug of the shoulder shrugging a little more blouse off it, and put a hand on his arm and said: 'Darling,' looking up in his face with a pert grimace, 'you're back from your mountains? Why didn't you let me know?'

'Should I have let you know?' he said pleasantly. His voice was very deep, low pitched like the lowest tone of a bell. It's like dark honey, thought Anne. It's like being under the shade of an enormous tree in a hot noon. A dark voice. This voice can never shout. She looked down at her arm on the piano lid and wondered. There was fine gooseflesh upon it.

'Well,' said Ranchit, and in contrast he sounded ridiculously falsetto, 'how's the work going, Unni? I hear that you're killing a lot of our men at the dam.'

There was a clear peal of thunder, and the soft splash of rain outside, on the flags, on the sputtering gravel, on the cars and jeeps, on the soldiers. People standing on the balcony came into the room. The downward glitter of water lasted only a few minutes, freshness wafted in, the band played, the sun came through again.

'Rain before the bridegroom comes,' said Unni. 'It is a good omen.'

'It is,' agreed the General. 'Beautifully propitious the rain to lay the dust before the bridegroom's steps.'

'Shall we move to the balcony?' Unni asked Anne, and she moved forward, followed by Unni, the General, and Dr Maltby, to stand in an open french window above the garden. Along the road, winding and swaying from side to side, in a rumour of wind-swept music and laughter, came the bridegroom's procession like a short and colourful snake towards the house.

Paul Redworth joined them. 'Hello, Unni. How's the dam getting on?'

'Fine,' said Unni. 'Still the same trouble, but otherwise fine.'

'The Wayward One?'

'She keeps moving about. A week ago she suddenly gave a big scream, and split off a chunk down the left slope, and tumbled a good bit of embankment and some of the road a few thousand feet down. Nearly took a dozen workers, but they jumped clear in time. She's going to play up again during this year's monsoon.'

'Believe it or not, that's only a mountain he's talking about,' said Paul to Anne. 'It's been giving him more trouble than any woman, I think.'

'Only ...' said Unni. 'It's Mana Mani, the Wayward One. She's beautiful and young and doesn't like being tamed. But you must come up soon. The rhododendrons are beautiful on the slopes now.'

'I'd like to come with you and see your dam,' said the Resident.

'I fly back tomorrow,' said Unni.

'That's too early,' said Paul Redworth. 'You've also promised to take me over the new Indian Road next week, remember?' He turned to Anne. 'By the way, Anne, wouldn't you and your husband like to come on the road with us next week?'

'The rhododendrons are beautiful on the slopes,' repeated Unni, 'and all the birds have come back. When the Indian Army Engineers started blasting the mountain-side two years ago the birds went away. But now they are no longer afraid of the blast.'

The procession now came in through the gates, loud music first, on foot; the musicians, swaying, with drums and small trumpets and cymbals. As they approached, the band waiting on the lawn started a loud march, and all the Nepalese laughed at the duel of sound. Behind the musicians was the bridegroom's coach, a landau drawn by two bays.

'An Edwardian landau, joy of my adolescent days!' exclaimed Paul Redworth delighted. 'Martha! Where is the woman? We had one like that in Dublin for our honeymoon.' Off he went to fetch his wife.

On the back of the landau, upright, with gold epaulettes, shakos, and scarlet livery, two footmen held up over the seated occupants a large sunshade, as big as a beach umbrella, of red silk fringed with gold tassels. Behind the landau came a trail of male friends and relatives of the groom, some in Rajput turbans with coquettish gauze wings, dressed in gold and crimson tunics with sashes and jewelled short swords and white jodhpurs underneath. In the coach the groom glittered and shone in scarlet and cloth of gold with a twisted hat encrusted with jewels, and a sword in his belt. Slowly the procession went round the lawn. Out of the pillared hall, playing an old and classic tune of welcome, another band came tumbling down the steps with flutes and drums and cymbals. Happy laughter came from all the guests.

'Music unlimited,' shouted Father MacCullough, smiling from ear to ear in the general inebriation of mirth.

The three bands played together, clashing bravely, working to a crescendo volume. The coach stopped in front of the entrance, and the Commander and his relations proceeded to walk solemnly three times round it, scattering flower petals and throwing water from a gold ewer with a small spout upon the groom.

'Isn't it pretty and gay?' said Fred Maltby smiling, momentarily forgetting his wife. 'What are they doing now, Unni?'

'Welcoming and blessing the groom,' said Unni. 'And now the father of the bride puts upon his forehead the sign of welcome, the red *tika*.'

The groom now stood up in the coach ready to enter the house. He wore red cloth shoes with upturned toes. Father MacCullough explained the significance of the *tika*, and its composition: of red sandalwood and ash and holiness. 'The rest of the welcoming ceremony will be in the centre courtyard. Let's go down, shall we?' He walked with Anne down the stairs, explaining with gusto the heads along the walls. 'Hunting trophies ... the Ranas, great hunters as you know. The Field Marshal there, got the largest tiger skin you've ever seen, shot it in the Terai jungle, biggest hunting ground in the world. He'll show it to you some day maybe, if he likes you. Have you met his wife?'

Anne nodded, overwhelmed by his informativeness.

'Talking of wife,' said Father MacCullough uneasily, 'I didn't know about our friend the doctor. Of course, you were with him when it happened, I hear. Such a good thing I didn't open my mouth when she told me her name ... but you know, I'm a bit hard of hearing in one ear, I heard her say Maubrey, not Maltby, it didn't click till I saw old Fred leap off like a hare. My, how that boy can run. It's a shock for some of us, we didn't know the Doc was married. What a good thing General Kumar got her off elsewhere. It's only temporary, of course, a respite, give Fred time to prepare himself for the inevitable. .... I'll have to talk to him about it, see if I can help in any way.'

'I thought it was Mr Menon's idea to get her out of the way this afternoon,' said Anne.

'Unni? Oh no, it was the General's,' said Father MacCullough. 'Unni wasn't back. It's harmless, mind you, but it's a deception, and Unni is a good chap,' said Father MacCullough with defensive energy, 'a *very* good chap. Don't you believe all you hear about him. Lots of people are jealous. Anyway, he'd have tackled the job differently. I have great hopes that Unni may see the light one day and turn to us,' said Father MacCullough gravely. 'I think he's a rare soul. He likes mountains better than er ... you know. But people here are rather earthy, if you see what I mean, Mrs Ford. There's so little else to do round here ... no theatres, no place to go, not much cultivation of spiritual things, a small community ... it's a great temptation – though I will say that the Nepalese ladies are very virtuous and moral. Very. It's the tourists, really, that are the worst of the lot. They come here and they expect ...'

'What they get in London and Paris,' said Anne.

'Well, yes, let's put it that way. Every place is pretty much the same, isn't it? But they never really get to know the Nepalese, they don't stay long enough.'

By now Father MacCullough and Anne were standing in a gallery, round the centre courtyard (all Nepalese houses and palaces were built as a quadrangle, or a succession of quadrangles, with courtyards in the middle), which was in part lawn, with a cement tennis court in its middle now smoothed over with ochre clay upon which beautiful patterns of fruits and flowers in coloured powder had been poured by hand, Indian fashion. Arches of green boughs enclosed it. The groom stood inside, in the posture of a Mogul painting, hand upon his jewelled scabbard, his feet naked, while ceremonially relatives of the bride presented him with rice and corn, and water in a golden pitcher.

Near him stood the priest, a Newari, much shorter than the tall Rana, in a torn jacket whose lining hung to his thigh behind, faded jodhpurs, a thick muffler round his neck, and a cheerful sniffle with which he interspersed the half-chant half-talk prayer he read out of a thumbed yellow thin-leafed book. A woman, looking like a maid-servant, short and dumpy with flat broad Mongol face and a home-spun sari, earlobes elongated by heavy gold knobs ('That's a Gurung, another hill-tribe, look at those heavy gold ornaments,' informed Father MacCullough), now came up to the bridegroom. She had square feet with widely separated toes, prehensile like the barefooted field workers. She held in both hands what looked like a cap one pulls out of Christmas crackers; it was a triangle of red silk mounted upon some stiffener, profusely spangled with gold, with twisted red strings at two angles and a pompom at the third. She proceeded to bind this upon the bridegroom's head, above his hat, standing on the balls of her squat feet to do so, while he, like a stone statue, stood looking fixedly in front of him. With arms upraised her hands just reached his forehead, and as he did not bend his head she clung to him, like a woodpecker upon a tree, trying to bind the triangle on top of the crimson and gold hat he wore. Both his hands were occupied, a golden sceptre in one, a golden ewer filled with water in the other. The triangle slipped upon his face once or twice. He did not move. The woman pushed it up, it slipped again. Finally two men came to help her, but neither could adjust the triangle, and after ten minutes all three gave up. Laughing, the woman sauntered away, gaily flicking the strings and joking with the guests. Meanwhile rice in a sieve, cloth, grain, fruit heaped upon woven mats, had been offered to the bridegroom to show that all the house contained, precious and valuable, was given to him. All this time the Nepalese bands kept up a tune which sounded like something performed on Scottish bagpipes.

From the balconies above and from the open windows, women looked down upon the scene, but only women; the Nepalese men and the foreign community (nicknamed All-Khatmandu by Paul Redworth) were downstairs in the courtyard. Father MacCullough explained: 'In Nepal the women are not cowed and relegated to harems, as in the Muslim countries. Here they laugh and are happy and free, and no Nepalese widow has ever got burnt on a pyre either. The Nepalese are wonderfully tolerant and all the harshness and cruelty of Hinduism has come out of their festivals. At the festivals it's the women who sit upon the pyramidal tiers of the pagodas, step on step, until the pagoda looks like a living tower of women. The men stand below them, in the streets. And the women wash at open taps in the streets, but somehow they're always decently covered up, even then. I think they're an example of chastity and virtue to many of our ladies back home.'

The Commander now motioned his guests to come nearer to the enclosure to watch the ceremony. John and Isobel moved forward, John with his camera upon his chest. What a funny hat Isobel has, thought Anne. She had not noticed it before. It was bright red, shaped like an admiral's cocked hat, with two large pins in it, their knobs like an enormous fly's eyes. In the downgoing sunlight filtering above the courtyard it looked like a live animal perched on her head, staring with insect-multiple eyes. Suddenly it was cold, a cold layer of air descending as a mantle upon their shoulders, and Anne drew her wool stole round her. History and Geography were near, talking to each other and greeting people here and there, tossing their heads and laughing and glancing round. In a corner of the gallery Fred Maltby, paying no attention to the lengthy ceremony, stood talking earnestly to Unni, whose hand was playing with a coin, throwing it up and catching it without looking, his eyes fixed upon Fred. The groom left the enclosure and walked indoors, and the guests in the courtyard and gallery followed him.

Drinks were served, whisky, brandy, red grenadine, and Coca-Cola. People walked about, talking; John and Ranchit and Pat and Isobel were together again, Isobel's voice loud, her face flushed. She tossed off the contents of one glass and immediately a bearer brought another one on a tray. The lights were switched on and the brown, fumous emanation under the chandeliers made the shadows darker, the horns sinister along the walls. Of the Nepalese women, most were now in the inner rooms, a few remained, their saris lustrous about them. Some jeeps and cars were leaving, others arriving. Hilde came up to Anne.

'Would you like a drive, Anne? Unni is taking me to the jail and the Redworths are going off. Paul can't eat the food so they're going to have a snack at home and then come back. We've got a couple of hours to wait before His Majesty arrives, and the banquet won't be before midnight. It never is.'

'I'll come,' said Anne. She crossed the room to John. He started laughing hard, having watched her walk towards him, to show what a good time he was having.

'I'm going for a drive with Hilde, John. Be back soon.'

'Eh? Oh sure, sure,' said John, turning round. He was happy, telling stories of his early days. Pat listened, laughed at the right places. So did Isobel. He couldn't tell his stories so well with Anne around, that shut-inness of hers, the way she had of not being there, slamming the door of her attention shut in his face, made the funniest things unfunny. She had no sense of humour at all.

In the garden Tilley lights tilted upward threw visibility upon the house. Hilde and Anne came to the jeep and climbed in, swinging by the leather hand thong; Unni switched the motor on and they roared softly out of the garden, the jeep lights cantering up and down the fields and hedges, catching an occasional Newari, shoulders huddled in his blanket and legs bare, face grinning straight into the light. The cold early night was a new world, moonless dark. Turning a corner they came upon some pilgrims round a shrine, biblical in their folded garments, children's round heads nestled asleep upon laps; and a gaunt and naked saddhu, like the shaggy leader of a pack of wolves sat up to stare at the jeep, hands upon his legs, his matted hair a mane upon him.

'The Feast of Siva in ten days,' said Unni. 'These pilgrims have come from South India for it. Some walk hundreds of miles to the Festival at the Temple of Pashupatinath.'

'I hope Vassili will be out of jail by then,' said Hilde, a little forlorn.

They reached a dark massive building with high walls. Two soldiers in khaki with fixed bayonets, peering at the jeep, flashed torches upon Unni and the women, opened a small postern door, a square of light, into which Hilde, saying: 'Good-bye Anne, thanks Unni,' stepped without looking back. Her shoes sounded a run upon the stone flagging, the soldiers shut the door, and Unni, getting back into the jeep, gave Anne a cigarette before driving off.

'Shall we go to the Royal Hotel for a drink and some sandwiches? It will be more comfortable.'

'I'd like to.'

At the Royal Hotel some tourists were drinking at the bar, others were playing billiards. Anne went to the Ladies' to comb her hair and wash her hands. She found herself sighing with ease, walking back to the verandah, her body confident and relaxed. The lights went out suddenly. She stood blinded, took a groping step, and found Unni at her side, aware of him without a touch. In the background the bearers were calling for candles. Unni took her hand.

'Let me guide you to a table.'

He was a darkness sitting next to her, but for the white V of his shirt. He smiled and she saw his teeth.

'You make me think of the Cheshire cat,' she told him. 'The last thing to go of him was his grin.'

'It comes from being so dark,' he replied. 'All of me disappears at night, except my teeth.'

The candles came, throwing a burnished copper glow upon both their faces. Anne drank a sherry, sweeter than she liked it, they ate chicken sandwiches, then smoked in silence, contented, wholly self-contained, without unease, nearly unaware of each other in this new serenity, saying:

'It was a wonderful wedding, I liked everything I saw.'

'Here I remember everything I see.'

'So do I. I've been here four years, I'm always finding new things to look at.'

'You're not from Nepal then?'

'Not altogether. My father was Indian and my mother Nepalese.'

'You're building a dam?'

'We call it a dam, yes. There's a lot of trouble with floods, the river we're tackling does much damage to the land. But anything, dams, roads, is a difficult job in these mountains.'

'Why?'

'Because the mountains are so young. They're young and active, they're still moving about. Would you believe it, but the best site to locate our dam is also the epicentre of an earthquake region?'

'It sounds fascinating.'

'It's strenuous and sometimes dangerous work. But it's going to make so much difference to the people in a few years. Hydro-electric power, good roads, better crops, no floods. You must come and see our dam one day.'

'I'd love to!'

'I'll take you there. Meantime, why not come with Paul Redworth and myself next week and have a look at the road that's being built? That's part of the Indian Aid to Nepal programme. Everybody is so keen and eager to help Nepal ... The Americans have a special Point Four Aid Mission here, to build hospitals and schools, establish handicrafts, bee-keeping, sawmills, anything to get the people out of their poverty. They also plan to build a road and develop some valleys. Possibly the Chinese later may also offer to do things for Nepal. Nepal is like a woman with many suitors now, only too eager to please her with gifts.'

'The cold war?'

'Yes. Fear makes us generous. The cold war, pursued in Khatmandu as in every other capital of the world. Nepal is a backward underdeveloped country, and all underdeveloped areas are potential exploitation for communism; and so the idea is to plunge in and do something before the other side does it.'

'Does it work?'

'Not always. For various reasons, chiefly because Aid, as it is called, is often not suited in style and scope to the country for which it is aimed. Our friends the Americans are the worst offenders in that respect: they build a marvellously equipped hospital, and then leave it to fend for itself, and of course it goes to bits in no time; they draw up a programme for building a road which will cost millions, and send so many experts and tons of machinery, yet they fail to import also the ordinary, run-of-the-mill technician to keep the machinery in good order, and it'll rot – there are some wonderful bulldozers rotting here right now. They vote millions of dollars in Aid to foreign countries, but more than two-thirds of it goes in paying the enormous salaries and in building amenities for their own staffs – then they are surprised that the countries they help are not a bit grateful. But they'll learn to do better. They've got to.'

'The Chinese?'

'Oh, they will come, but they're not really competing, though the Americans always feel jittery about them. There will be a Chinese delegation at the Coronation. They've built some good roads in Tibet, and they are a serious-minded people. But they have enough on their hands. So far India has done most to help this country, but then India is more involved than anyone else, since Nepal is her northern bulwark. The road from India to Khatmandu is going to make all the difference to this Valley and to the other valleys it crosses. You ought to see it ... and also the rhododendrons and the birds, of course.'

'If John and I can make it,' said Anne. 'I'll have to ask Isobel. I'm lecturing in English at the Girls' Institute, you know.'

'I know,' said Unni smiling, 'and you've written a book, but I haven't read it.'

'Don't,' said Anne lazily, 'don't.' She felt a little light-headed on one glass of sherry. 'The sandwiches are good,' she said gravely.

'They are,' said Unni.

There was a flurry of footsteps and the anxious features and white hair of the General peered from the stairs. 'Ah, there you are,' he said, sat down at their table, and started talking in Nepalese. As he spoke Unni listened, then he laughed, tilting his chair backwards, and the General laughed too, but with an ironic shrug of his thin shoulders.

'I am sorry,' said Unni, turning to Anne. 'The General sometimes finds it easier not to speak in English. He tells me that Mrs Maltby has arrived at the wedding.'

'Oh dear, that may not be unserious,' said Anne, and the General, recognizing his own phrase, smiled then shook his head desperately and groaned and ran his fingers through his wild white hair.

'She's arrived with the Rampoche of Bongsor, whom she met on the way and whom I know quite well, he's quite one of the most charming and gifted crooks in the Himalayas,' said Unni. 'And she strode in saying: "I wish to speak to Dr Maltby." So the game's up. The General saw her come in, rushed to find Fred, but he wasn't there. Eudora is at the wedding now, talking about her right to see her husband to Paul and Martha. Their Majesties are due to arrive any moment. So far Martha is handling the situation.'

'So what do we do?'

'The General would like us to get back. He thinks we may talk her into a better mood.'

'*You* talk,' said the General. 'I shall pray. We can stop on the way at the Padmani Shrine. I would like to begin my prayer there.'

'Let's go and pray,' said Unni, 'and then talk to Eudora.'

Chapter 9

IT had been a little difficult to persuade Frederic Maltby to go to the wedding. About noon, while Anne and John, the Redworths, and Isobel were at the Royal Hotel, Fred, seized with panic, visited General Kumar in his rooms and declared he would not go to the wedding.

'Not go to the wedding?' The General, smoking, sipping his morning whisky, and playing with his seventeenth and youngest child, sat on the floor and stared at the doctor. 'My dear friend, you comprehend that you are one of the honoured guests of our democracy ... you cannot be unpresent.'

'I could be ill,' said Fred.

'Out of the question,' said the General. 'You are as strong as the bull of the Lord Siva, and have not been diseased one day since your arrival in the Valley five years ago. A sudden visitation of malady today would be a bad omen for the wedding. Doubtless the chief astrologer would have to postpone it while he verifies the stars again.'

'Oh, come, come,' said Fred.

'If not astrology, then courtesy,' said the General severely. 'Illness today would be ill-mannered of you, my friend. No, I am still waiting for Unni, who has a better head than you or I. But if he comes not within the half hour, I have a modest stratagem of my own.' He held out his empty glass, and the Tibetan handmaiden, who shuffled near by, filled it from a bottle of Vat 69 on the table. 'Vassili gave me thirty bottles just before he went to jail a month ago,' said the General sadly. 'This is the last.'

Fred paced up and down. 'I don't think ...' he began.

'Only a bad dancer blames the slope of his hill,' said the General. 'This woman is draining your spirit and you can only avoid her till you become, like the Lord Buddha, so detached that no appearance or devil can hurt you. But we are human, and even a dog takes shelter from the storm. Now I bestir my utmost energy for you, my friend. Call my son Deepah,' he said to the handmaid.

Fred had not liked the scheme of sending Eudora off to see the

Swami Bidahari. The last time he had seen the Swami three years before, the Swami was already senile. And Bidahari Mahal, the palace where he lived, was fully twelve miles away, half the length of the Valley of Khatmandu. Eudora would miss the wedding, but he was not sure that she would enjoy the Swami.

'The Swami was a great musician once,' said the General.

'Twenty-five years ago, when he could still talk,' replied Fred Maltby. 'He was completely gaga when I saw him last.'

'My son Deepah is resourceful and will interpret,' said the General with finality.

Fred Maltby shrugged his shoulders and then laughed. Why become so upset? After all, Eudora would be looked after, even if she would miss lunch, and a wedding ... suddenly, with a shock, he realized that he still felt protective towards her ... it hurt him to do this to her. He felt ashamed. But things had gone too far now. It was his fault for being a coward. 'I must try to meet her, of my own volition, tomorrow.'

The wedding relaxed him. He had seen Unni arrive, bringing Hilde; he had got Unni alone in a corner of the gallery, poured out the story of Eudora. Fred loved the General, and many another man in Khatmandu was his friend, but there was a closer bond between him and Unni than the others. Perhaps because, like himself, Unni was a builder, one of those people who changed the world and were unknown. Unni built bridges and roads and dams and moved mountains, and Fred Maltby performed medical miracles, both of them making time run, transporting an eleventh-century country into the twentieth in a decade, compacting nine hundred years into two five year plans. Unni stayed with Fred when he came to Khatmandu, once or twice a month. They had drinks together, listened to Fred Maltby's long-playing records, smoked, talked. It was a male friendship, undescribed, unquestioning, needing nothing, unalterable.

He felt happier now, lighter, after talking to Unni, who heard him in silence, tossing a coin soundlessly up and down, while round them the guests surged back into the rooms for drinks. He was ready, he felt, to cope with Eudora. He would not deliberately seek her out, that would be childish, but he would see her if she asked to see him. He would be polite and natural, say 'Hello, Eudora,' as if it were the most obvious thing in the world for a husband and wife to meet in

Khatmandu after eighteen years apart. In the dimness of the evening, while the wedding settled to a shadowed, patient waiting for the King to arrive, he walked about from group to group, a drink in his hand which he kept there untouched, but which protected him from the attentive bearers, always ready to pounce upon empty glasses for a refill.

The bride's father, the Commander, had now changed into full dress uniform. A suave, accomplished host, faultlessly good-mannered, he bent his creamy complexion and serene Buddha contemplation over each group in turn: the Americans from the Point Four Palace, formally dressed, the ladies with hats and gloves; the nice English redheaded woman doctor from Pokhra Valley, two weeks' trek and twenty minutes by air from Khatmandu; History and Geography, giggling and coyly protesting they couldn't drink; Martha Redworth, installed near some silent smiling Nepalese women, munching coconut shreds. Isobel was still with John Ford and Ranchit and the American artist. How funny that hat of Isobel's, thought Fred Maltby, with the pins stuck on both sides, like a sacrificial bullock's head upon an altar, or like the neck of a bull he'd seen in Spain stuck with banderillas. Isobel was talking loudly, and panting, all authority shed, as if she had not time enough to draw breath, as if there was something excruciatingly important that she wanted to say and never said; above her for a moment hovered the Commander's handsomeness, an amber and wax attention, dissolving in an agreeable laugh, while his eyes estimated shrewdly the moment when, like some of the other guests, she would have to be removed to an inner room to be sick.

Fred Maltby chuckled as he saw Major Pemberton lurch gravely into a discussion of the merits of the Gurkhas with the Commander. The Field Marshal passed, deep in conversation with the Curator of the Museum and the Minister for Education. He watched the Redworths leave quietly for their snack. He saw Hilde and Anne going out with Unni, and Rukmini, resigned and beautiful and playing with her jewels, following them with her eyes. What a fool Ranchit is, thought Fred, runs around with any tramp that comes to Khatmandu because it's a tourist and a 'white woman' and Ranchit thinks that to go to bed with a white woman is a kind of superiority, a revenge of the coloured male, boomerang for those days when the whites lorded it in Asia and took coloured women for pleasure and kept their own women unattainable. There was still a lot of this kind of twisted emotion in Asia as well as in the West. But the world had now changed: new wealth in Asia, new poverty in Europe, and women, more swift to respond to change than men, gravitated to wealth. In the night-clubs of Calcutta and Singapore and Saigon, white women stripped bare and danced while the coloured man, brown and yellow and black, looked on and clapped the show. Ranchit thought himself a 'modern' sophisticated Don Juan. He kept lists, a 'Hunting Record', recounted his prowesses openly. Rukmini should have married someone like Unni, thought the doctor. Well, Ranchit would have it coming to him one day. Rukmini was sixteen and still a child in so many ways, but one day she'd take a lover, and pay him back. Only it wouldn't be Unni, it would be probably some good-for-nothing wastrel, or a tourist-artist who would break her heart and leave her. She was too docile, pliable, and sweet, tried to please too much. And then someone came walking across the room to talk to Rukmini, a tall blond American with a frank, open face.

'Mike Young. From the Point Four Mission. An engineer,' said the voice of the Field Marshal, suddenly next to Maltby. 'A jolly good chap, *very* young.' Nothing escaped the Field Marshal. Seated in his library among his books, his Nepalese and Tibetan manuscripts, his French and German and English first editions, his old bronzes and the paintings of himself hunting in the Terai jungle, he knew the desires and thoughts of the people of the Valley. Often enough Fred, who borrowed books from him, had been startled by a casual remark of the Field Marshal's which with an ingenious twist of phrase made one of the many complicated political intrigues of the Valley clear to him.

The Field Marshal said with a bland expression: 'My dear doctor, you seemed a little discomforted when you arrived. I hoped that the remedy was close at hand.'

'It always makes one feel discomforted to be faced with an unpleasant situation,' replied the doctor.

'Ah,' said the Field Marshal reminiscently, 'yes, yes, it does. Similar situations have arisen before, among some friends of mine ... is not much of their unpleasantness because we live historically with people? Building mental images of them to which we respond with irritation, pain, or disgust? When they and we have changed we conceive it not, but retain them in our memory's grasp as they were, with their failings which bore us and their virtues which bore us even more, both of which may no longer exist. I was wondering ... merely wondering, mind you ... if the lady you remembered is the same lady as the one you saw yesterday; and whether, even if it were possible by a dispensation of the gods to alter her to the most beautiful and virtuous woman in the land (say something approaching my own wife, who, as you know, is to me the paragon of all beauty, rapture, and womanliness), whether you *would* be satisfied and happy to meet her again, and not still prefer to think of her as repellent, as you have done for many years?'

'I don't know,' said Maltby. 'It's an interesting question, psychologically, but somehow I don't believe people change so much as all that. I think they remain essentially the same.'

'But even so you ran away from an image of her, not from herself,' persisted the Field Marshal, 'because you do not really know what she is like now.'

'Yes ...' said Fred Maltby, 'but I'm afraid the original will be very much like what I ran away from. Still, I'm quite willing to meet her. The whole thing is ridiculous, of course ... how you must laugh at me, Field Marshal, really.'

'On the contrary, my friend, I understand very well indeed,' said the Field Marshal gravely, 'and I shall watch developments.' His glance returned to Rukmini. Two more young men had joined Mike Young in a court round Rukmini: an Indian officer from Indian Aid, resplendent in uniform; and a young Englishman, Michael Toast, who had announced that he was an impresario writing a great novel about Nepal. It would be filmed, he explained, and he had offered the star role to several Nepalese ladies he had met at parties, the only minor condition being that they should sleep with him. But so far there had been no takers, his offer having been uniformly received with so much laughter that he had gone back rather puzzled, wondering if they'd quite understood his: 'How about bed, old girl? We'd have some fun together,' approach. Whenever thus refused, he would say to Hilde (whom he had made his confidante), in his quaint Oxford accent which sounded strange in the Valley: 'She can't be quite normal, you know. ... I'm afraid she must be a lesbian.'

'Like moths round a lovely flame,' murmured the Field Marshal, looking at Rukmini. 'Ah, well ...' he drifted away.

Fred then joined the group formed by the Curator of the Museum, a tiny Newari many years in prison during the despotic Rana reign, a Hindu poet, and some Ministers of the Government. They were listening to the Hindu poet's recitation of Tagore:

'O beauty, find thyself in love, not in the flattery of the mirror ...'

'Now, isn't that pretty?' said Father MacCullough, who had been stuck with History and Geography for a while and longed to talk to someone else.

The poet did not look at them, but started in Hindi his translation of Blake:

'Abstinence sows sand all over
The ruddy limbs and flaming hair ...'

'Doctor, doctor,' someone was pulling at Maltby's sleeve. It was a maidservant. 'The Maharanis wish you to come.'

He followed her, wondering which Maharanis, a title applicable to any married woman there. The maidservant led him into one of the smaller private rooms. There, on the sofa, heavy, sacklike, mouth open, flat on her back, was Isobel.

'She came through here, she was looking for the toilet,' said the Field Marshal's wife, who was standing near the sofa. 'Then she suddenly fell on the floor. We put her on the sofa and sent for you.'

Isobel's eyes were glazed, fixed, her breath stertorous. Dr Maltby shook her and she did not move. He began to feel a little disturbed. 'I think she'll be rather ill if I don't do something now,' he said.

'It's the first time she's been so bad, isn't it?' said the General's wife.

The other times, few and far between, she had just talked nonsense, drinking with that amplitude of movement, that masculine exaggeration which could be transformed into such heavy authority. Always someone, Paul Redworth, or Vassili, or Maltby himself, had been there to stop her in time. This time she'd passed out cold.

'I think I'd better take her to the Hospital,' said Dr Maltby, 'and pump her out and put her to bed in a ward. Here, with everyone coming and going, it won't be very good for her.'

'We'll help you to carry her,' said the Commander's wife. She now showed uncommon strength and resourcefulness, first adjusting her sari and her rubies and emeralds, then securing the flowers in her hair, and then lifting the heavy arms, while the General's wife arranged the sagging legs of Isobel Maupratt, and with the help of four maid-servants, they staggered their burden through the door, groped down a corridor to the back of the house.

'Bring your jeep round here to the back,' they whispered to Fred.

Fred knew that nothing had escaped the attention of the Field Marshal, who smiled affably and nodded as he passed through the hall muttering to guests who stopped him that he was going to an emergency and would be back.

They put Isobel in the back of the jeep and her head hung, her breath smelt acid, she was snoring a little. The Field Marshal's wife had brought a quilt and tucked it round her.

'Gee,' said Dr Maltby admiringly, 'you're wonderful, Maharani. Think of everything. What a good nurse you'd make.'

All the Maharanis smiled, and then became timid and shy again, but they did not relax their grip on Isobel until she was ensconced at the back of the jeep and had stopped rolling as if her neck were broken.

And that is how Fred Maltby escaped Eudora, for as the jeep rounded the house to the back, Eudora had been driven to the front entrance in the jeep of His Preciousness the Rampoche of Bongsor. The General saw her, nearly dropped his whisky, and ran to warn Fred Maltby, to find that he had gone.

Chapter 10

'PRETTY, pretty,' whispered Eudora. The jeep rode the Bidahari road, as a cork bobbing upon waves. The Bidahari road was a quagmire in the rain. In the dry season it had pot-holes the size of small cars. The General's personal jeep driver favoured a direct assault upon obstacles, and it went hard for Eudora, who believed in keeping her thoughts beautiful. The invocation 'Pretty, pretty', addressed to the landscape, did help. As they bounced the hedges distilled upon their passage the scents of jasmine and roses; the lovely brilliant spring swayed and fell about them in sudden bright pink fires of almond trees, flights of swallows, volleys of parakeets. Above the near circle of hills spread the immense arc of the snow peaks in a pure blue sky. 'Lovely, lovely,' sighed Eudora, and wished the jeep would not bounce so much. Something seemed to move in her as she looked at the snows. Something new, which had no name, was uneasy. She had been prepared verbally for the Himalayas, the snow peaks; but for this all words were trite. She could only look, as she rose and sank abruptly with the jolting vehicle.

The soft air combed back her hair, pressed the little voilette of her hat against her face; she wanted to take off her hat, wave it, sing. There was a hill in front of her, mild looking, like a girl sitting in the folds of a blue-green skirt. And next to Eudora sat Deepah, slim, elegant, with those wonderful eyes, a beautiful faun of the Valley. Eudora felt stirred, restless yet dreamy. She'd washed her hair, and rinsed it with the blonde shampoo she used. The water here was soft, so soft. Mountain water. I like it here, she discovered suddenly. Last night at the hotel, coming out of her bath she'd turned round to find, through the frosted glass pane of the half-door from bathroom to corridor, the shadow of a tilted cap and a black eye applied to a small translucent patch. She had shrieked, seized the towel, later complained to Hilde. Afterwards she had looked at herself in the long mirror. Eudora, forty, Eudora, forty ... she wasn't bad really, a little plump perhaps, she had felt her thighs and hips, squeezing them. That's where all women went first. Sagging flesh on the thighs, the fat pursing up in little molehills between the tighter tissue.

The fact that at fifteen, on a holiday in France with her wealthy parents, Eudora had been tumbled in the bedroom of the expensive hotel where they stayed, had been the start of her spirituality. He was an elegant boy, precocious and slim, the son of the couple in the next suite. He had come in while her parents had been out visiting a museum. He must have watched their going. They had not talked, for she knew no French and he no English. There were those slim dark hands suddenly upon her, and the pleasant forcing, upon the carpet by the bed. She had said 'No, no!', put her hands over her face a little while. Now in the jeep she remembered the hands, the floral design on the carpet, and the hard slim thighs pressing hers. How strange she remembered NOW. She caught herself with a start. How TERRIBLE.

A bigger jolt sent a quiver through her and brought her back to the present. She glanced at her watch. It was two o'clock. 'Where are we *now*? Aren't we getting there quite soon?'

Deepah smiled, showing a row of girl's white teeth. He moved his head from side to side in that perfect indeterminate which is the Indian yes. 'Soon,' he said.

Up and down went the jeep, bumping, twisting, and turning. It finally went clattering on a slope. Above was a heap of pink houses, streets, a ruined market place encumbered with the ruins of shrines and temples. 'Kirtipur,' said Deepah triumphantly.

'Is that Bidahari?'

'No, Kirtipur. Here, madam, to contemplate the Emperor Asoka stupas, erected by him on a visit to Nepal, many years before B.C.'

'Oh, how interesting,' said Eudora, who was getting hungry.

'And here, madam, much better than old stupas, the new police station,' said Deepah, who as all Asian teenagers only liked new things.

'Oh yes,' said Eudora. 'Where *is* Bidahari?'

'We stop here, madam, few moments. We have repast here, I brought from my home,' said Deepah as the jeep stopped by the edge of a meadow with an enormous peepul tree. 'Here, madam, we rest and admire scenery.'

'But the Swami and his lunch?'

'The Swami old, madam, cannot eat much, only at sunrise and milk at sundown.' Deepah lowered his lids upon his wonderful eyes and then raised them and looked full at Eudora, who felt her indignation ebb.

'Oh,' she said weakly, 'I didn't know. Well, let's have lunch first.'

Out of the jeep were suddenly produced those cylindrical tins superimposed on each other, invented in China and now used all over Asia. Each held a different dish: roast chicken, a vegetable curry, breadfruit soaked in curry sauce, broccoli and cauliflower, radishes in salad with chives and tomatoes, rice, French beans. The cooking at the General's house was renowned. There were plates, forks and knives, white napkins, coffee and iced water in Thermos flasks. 'Vegetarian curry, if you wish, madam,' said Deepah.

'How nice,' said Eudora. 'But how did you know that I'd been a vegetarian? I've given it up now, I'll have some roast chicken.'

'One guesses,' said Deepah, shaking his head from side to side.

All the children of Kirtipur were round them at once, or so it seemed to Eudora. Little boys in rags, but all with caps on, pressing forward to touch her, stare at her, run in front of her. The Temple Square of Kirtipur (all the cities of the Valley had a Temple Square) was sunsprayed and cobbled, happy with birds swooping everywhere and pilgrims squatting on the pyramidal steps of the shrines, eating out of great round copper bowls in a medley of glitter and dust. Many had three horizontal grey bars drawn with ash upon their foreheads. 'The sign of Siva, madam, for in ten days there is the great Siva Festival.'

They had lunch under a peepul tree. To the little boys were now added little girls, some with pigtails. They stood looking at Eudora and giggling. A few carried puny babies on their backs. One of those tiny infants began to cry, and the little girl swung him forward, opened her tunic, and flinging the beads round her neck over her shoulder gave him her breast.

'Oh,' cried Eudora, confused.

'The child's mother. Some of these Newaris are very small. She is fully thirteen, I am positive, madam,' said Deepah, helpfully.

The little girl smiled, holding her baby proudly. Her nostril was pierced with a small brass ornament. She had a lovely dirty face with enormous almond eyes.

After lunch Deepah lay on the grass under the peepul. His head rested at the foot of one of several statues and lingams planted below the tree. This statue was about a foot tall, a phallic god, erect, organs delineated in yellow and blue. Deepah did not look at it. He was looking at the sky through the leaves of the tree, and seemed utterly content.

Eudora, no longer hungry, felt restless. 'It's half past two, we *must* get on to the Swami.'

Deepah rose and walked slowly to the jeep and consulted with the driver, then came back, shaking his glistening curls.

'Jeep is injured, madam.'

'What?' Eudora sprang up.

'The jeep cannot function,' said Deepah. He proceeded again to the jeep and sat in it while the driver raised the hood and inspected the interior with a disapproving air, meanwhile chewing upon a daisy held between his lips.

Eudora's good temper was gone. She stamped her foot. 'This is preposterous,' she cried. The children imitated her, stamping and dancing on one foot and laughing. Eudora walked to the jeep and looked under the hood. 'What's gone wrong? It was all right until we stopped here. Let me try, I can drive a car.'

Deepah said some words to the driver. He turned on the switch. Something sputtered, then died down.

'No sustenance of oil, madam,' said Deepah triumphantly.

'You mean no petrol? But why didn't you bring some more with you?'

'Tank leaks,' said Deepah.

'Oh dear, oh dear,' said Eudora. 'This is dreadful. How shall we get to the Swami, how shall I *ever* get back in time for the wedding?'

' "Let not impatience cloud your brow", Shakespeare, madam,' said Deepah. 'The driver will seek for petrol. Meantime, here on this pillowed bank we rest.' And he lay down again under the stone god, closed his eyes, and gracefully went to sleep.

'I think this is a put-up job,' said Eudora aloud. Her voice was trembling. The driver now walked away slowly, picking flowers from the hedges and putting them in his cap. The jeep stood with the fuel needle pointing to empty. She looked round her, felt desperately alone. Deepah was asleep. The children sat around, they had nothing to do but to look at her. It was a lovely afternoon, with sun drifts already slanting golden shafts from a sloping hill. There was a small breeze and somewhere bells ringing, a little drowsily. And Eudora was afraid and wanted to shriek. Instead she came back to Deepah and shook him and he opened his eyes. 'Take me back,' she screamed, 'take me back right away.'

'Of course,' he said amiably, and shut his eyes again.

'Right now, I said.'

Deepah looked at her in astonishment and sat up. Until now all this had been a play, a highly comical play, the discharge of his duty. He had no intention of dragging his father's jeep for twelve miles across this abominable road, using his father's precious, expensive petrol (five times the price it was in India, since it came by airplane), and getting a sore back. The General had said: 'Take her for a drive, don't bring her back before nightfall. But don't forget to feed her.' He had carried out paternal instructions. It chagrined and astonished him that Eudora seemed genuinely frightened.

'Madam,' he said, 'kindly becalm yourself.' Why could she not lie back, content, and daydream? Daydreaming was a familiar posture of the spirit in this Valley, especially in the spring, with the warm sun. He had seen Eudora's eyes cloud over in the jeep, she had been daydreaming then, something pleasant, he'd been sure by her expression. Why was she frightened now when really nothing had happened? The hours were there, unhurried and contented like beautiful women, wanting nothing yet pleasantly about, waiting one's leisure.

'I want to get back,' shrieked Eudora, more loudly. 'Take me back to the Royal Hotel, *right now*. How far is the Royal Hotel?'

'Three miles, madam.'

'Nepalese or English?' Eudora wouldn't be caught again.

Deepah drew himself up, insulted. 'The Kingdom of Nepal is a sovereign state, madam. All our miles are Nepal miles, there is no place for an English mile in Nepal.'

'I won't have it,' said Eudora. 'You're trying to kidnap me, I know. I've got no money, though. You'll get nothing out of me. I'll complain to the Resident, and you'll go to jail for life, young man. You won't get away with this.'

Deepah looked at her. He could not understand her threats or her fear. He did not know that any woman feels more exposed to outrage in a strange country than in her own. That is part of the myth that other peoples are not as we are. He suspected, however, that she was afraid of being raped, and the idea made him smile. She was not bad looking, not monumental like so many of these white women, but agreeably plump; but her hair was dyed, and from Deepah's poised teenage she looked vastly old, older than his mother, the Maharani, whose hair was ebony and whose fingers played on the sitar so beautifully. Of course there was always a submission, roundnesses of buttocks and breasts, a curiosity of handling which could be satisfied, but Deepah would never have dreamt of doing this to a woman committed to his charge. He had had women, willing maidservants in his father's house, and was now happily married and the father of two children. He began to feel insulted by Eudora's fear. His face became haughty and distant.

Eudora meanwhile was rapidly going to pieces. 'Take me back, take me back,' she cried. The hills, the friendly hills, darkened as the sun went above them. The peepul tree grew sombre, as a warning. The few grimy children left seemed hideous swarming little devils who would tear her to pieces with their hands like claws reaching for her. And then, shattering relief, she saw another jeep grinding towards them, emitting that peculiar noise of gear changes which Nepalese drivers achieve with such gusto.

'Help, help!' shouted Eudora, throwing herself forward and knocking down two small boys in the process. The little boys started laughing, picked themselves up, and ran after her shouting, 'Hellup, hellup!'

'Help, please help me.' The jeep had stopped. 'Help,' cried Eudora again, loudly in the silence.

'Yes, madam, what can I do for you?' said the occupant of the jeep. He was a small fat man with a very round face, long lobes to his ears which were under a round hat of yellow silk shaped like a pagoda roof with everted brim, and an amethyst embossed in gold on top. He had slant eyes and a smooth chin and straight stiff hair, very black and glossy. He wore a slit robe of orange silk, high boots, and carried a silver and gold prayer mill in a small, smooth hand.

'Why, you're a Chinaman,' cried Eudora, incredulously.

'A Chinese, madam,' corrected the man, twirling his prayer mill round. 'I am the Great Rampoche of Bongsor. My ancestors for countless generations were Chinese, but I have been here, and my father, and my father's fathers, for ten dynasties now. My estates are just between Tibet and Nepal, but I owe allegiance to His Majesty the King of Nepal. You know the saying, madam, render to Caesar.' He now leapt nimbly down from the jeep with a supple bending of the knees. Underneath his gown he wore a European shirt and black satin trousers tucked in his ornate black silk boots.

In the front of the jeep were three hillmen, Sherpas of the mountains, in fur caps, gowns of sheepskin, with kukris tucked in their belts and big boots to the knee. They had gold earrings, and two of them wore long droopy moustaches. They sprang out of the jeep, raced to the back, reappeared holding three efficient Bren guns, and stood behind the Rampoche, pointing their guns at Eudora.

'My body-guards and my driver. I am collecting my rentals,' explained the Rampoche. 'Ah,' he added, 'is not this young man with you Deepah, the son of my dear enemy General Kumar?'

Deepah now came to him, hands respectfully joined, and bowed very low to the Rampoche, who put his hand upon his forehead in blessing. Several men of Kirtipur and two old women appeared, who were similarly blessed.

'Please, Mr Rampoche,' said Eudora, 'this irresponsible young man dragged me here, then pretended the jeep was out of order. I was to be taken to see the Swami Bidahari, and discuss music with him.'

'Really, the Swami?' said the Rampoche. 'I didn't know he could speak again. Well, perhaps my driver can repair the jeep, madam, and you can proceed.'

'I don't want to go there now,' said Eudora. 'It's much too late, I'm afraid I'll have to cancel my appointment with him. Besides, I'm also expected at a wedding. At least, Father MacCullough – do you know him? – got me an invitation. But everything's so *strange* out here,' cried Eudora, 'I really feel I must get back to the Royal Hotel and rest. ...' She put a hand upon her forehead.

'And who may you be, madam?' said the Rampoche.

'I am Mrs Eudora Maltby, a well-known writer of inspirational music.'

'Ah,' said the Rampoche, gleaming all over his face, 'would you be a relative of my dear friend Dr Frederic Maltby, Chief Medical Officer of the Hospital at Khatmandu?'

'Why, yes,' said Eudora, bridging with intuition the last eighteen years. 'He must be my husband.'

'How absolutely ripping,' exclaimed the Rampoche, suddenly abandoning his Nepalese English and speaking like the Gurkha officers who came to recruit men in one of the districts he overlorded. 'I say ... by Jove ... I mean, I didn't know old Fred was married. He cured me of my piles, you know. O pray do not misunderstand me, madam,' he cried to Eudora, 'I pick up these ejaculations from my friends the British. I hope they are in keeping with the occasion.'

Eudora turned now to Deepah, but Deepah had retired by the stone god and was looking into space. Fate had willed the Rampoche of Bongsor to come along at this moment and inform the woman. He could do no more.

'I will take you and my dear enemy's son wherever you wish, madam,' said the Rampoche. 'I'm also going to the wedding, but first, collect some rentals. Our monastery,' he added unctuously, 'owns a considerable amount of houses and land in the Valley. At one time half the harvest was ours, but alas, now there is democracy' (like everyone in Nepal he pronounced it dam-ocracy, with the accent on the first syllable), 'and we only get a third of the harvests. Tax free.'

'Oh, I don't mind,' said Eudora, 'so long as we're back at the Royal Hotel before dark.'

'Then mount into my jeep,' said the Rampoche, shaking with laughter and whirling his prayer mill, 'and I shall take you back.'

'So what do we do now?' said General Kumar. 'She is at the wedding.'

'I told you it wouldn't work,' replied Unni peaceably. 'It would have been better to persuade Fred to see her.'

'But she is an ogre of the feminine gender,' said the General.

'You're behaving like children, you and Fred,' said Unni. 'Why so frightened of a woman?'

'You have always been lucky in *your* women, Unni,' the General answered, 'so you do not understand other men's woes. His women, madam,' he said, turning to Anne, 'throw themselves at his head and do not even demand fidelity in return.'

'I don't collect women, and you know it,' said Unni.

'That is because you are difficult to please,' replied the General.

'Please don't listen to him, Mrs Ford,' said Unni to Anne.

'Well, you who can do what you like with women, why don't you change Eudora?' said the General. 'Charm her, make her go away, seduce her ... anything, so she does not annoy my friend, I pray of you.'

'I will talk to her at the wedding,' said Unni. 'We don't eat before midnight, I'll have plenty of time to sort it out before then.'

Chapter 11

WHEN I came back from the wedding [wrote Anne] I realized that Unni and I had not spoken of the room with the parakeets.

A psychologist might impute some subtle, profound motivation to this lapse since all our lapses, even the stubbing of a toe, are symbols, distorted externalizations of inner states we conceal from ourselves. I think it was not a twist of the mind but the result of an awareness so profound that it remained unworded. Unni knew I had his room, and talk about it was superfluous. When we returned to the wedding I looked at Rukmini. This is the girl who painted the eyes and the parakeets. What love of loveliness, what unperplexed happiness, what longing guided her hand? It was humbling that I who came from elsewhere should now be here, looking at love made plain, admitted to that most secret and delicate torment, the feeling of a woman for a man. Rukmini in all her jewels sits, her wonderful childish eyes looking blindly at her strutting, silly, and yet sinister husband, and then looking at Unni. She sits in beauty and Unni does not look at her. It is a not-looking more heart-breaking than looking, acknowledging her better than smiles, words. Unni walked straight through the room to find Eudora; passing Rukmini without a glance or word. I could not weep for them, I could only accept that what I saw was best. I saw Rukmini accept it too, for she was radiant still, content that he should be there, not demanding anything else. ... He only had to say to her: Come, for her to follow him to the world's end.

There was the sputter of motor-cycles in the night, outriders of the King, bursting into the garden, and the sudden leap of music, the Nepalese national anthem. Under the brown lights walked into the room to the sofa draped in gold brocade, Their Majesties, a darkly clad, quiet couple, dark sun-glasses upon their eyes, moving softly, quietly, almost stealthy with unassumed grace. They sat, and the hours dragged round us. We talked to this or that one, moving about, waiting for the late banquet. I sat for a space with the Field Marshal, delightfully erudite, gentle, and witty, whose conversation was peppered with quotations ranging from Chaucer to Joyce. The Hindu poet also came to talk with us and discourse charmingly of books he had read and authors he had not met. We held plates heaped with rice and helpings from many different dishes spread out on long tables in a banqueting room arrayed with tiger skins.

'This is delicious,' I said. 'What is it?'

'Marrow of castrated goat,' replied the Field Marshal. 'Indeed a great delicacy.'

Thus I consumed, besides neutered goat, wild boar from the Terai, deer and pheasant, partridge and quail from the hills, and chicken and duck from the farms of the Valley.

'It's absolute poison for Paul, though I love it,' said Martha, when we met over a second helping, 'but he's had his snack, and we were back in time. Eudora was just ready to kick up a fuss. But she's under control now.'

I looked about me and there was Unni heaping Eudora's plate. He had not left her side since our return. Eudora's eyes were a little pink, but she was smiling bravely and appeared to enjoy his attentions, laughing up at him.

'Plucky little woman,' said a voice. It was the Field Marshal. And that is what she was. A plucky little woman, funny, but somehow sweet.

This morning I came to Unni's room by daylight. Through the windows I can reach with my eyes so far out, much further than I thought, across fields and fields, golden yellow, of rape seed; pink lines of trees, farmhouses, the top floor of a lighter brown than the ground floor, and further until the hills rise vigilant, and beyond them the sentinel snow peaks. The bungalow has a bathroom downstairs, efficient and modern, which would delight Isobel and many a hygienic minded tourist. There is a spare room with some derelict furniture in it. In front of the bungalow is a small lawn, with an arbour of roses enclosing a fountain, a row of walnut trees fringing it. The lawn slopes away from the bungalow to become fields following each other into a long, long view which apparently leads straight across the valley to the hills. I sat under the walnut trees, on a stone, for such a long time. The wind went through my hair with small cool hands.

I was late for breakfast. John was wiping his mouth, not in a good humour. For this I was responsible. Isobel was not there. History and Geography explained:

'She has a bad headache after the wedding last night.'

'It's terrible how they do go on at these functions. Absolutely killing.'

'And it's not over yet. The wedding goes on for two more days.'

'We *must* pray for her.'

'Since Isobel's not well, I'll take you to your classroom,' said History. 'I think you'd better start, hadn't you? Nuff loafing, don't you think?'

'Of course,' I said. 'I'm ready to start.'

'Oh, there won't be much to do today. Classes morning only. There's usually prep in the afternoon, but not today as the wedding's still on.'

I followed History. 'There's always a festival of some kind or other out here,' she said. 'I've never *known* such people for celebrating. Always playing music, blowing upon flutes, dancing, smearing those idols, day and night. We'd get nothing done if we carried on as they do. There are a hundred and sixty-five recognized feasts in the year, that's without counting all the private celebrating, like birthdays and weddings and building a new house or getting an extra wife.'

There were thirty-four pupils at the Institute, ranging in age from nine to nineteen. Twenty were married, and expected or had children. 'You're taking the Senior Class in English and prep. Miss Suragamy McIntyre takes the juniors and gym. She's Indian, but she's one of us. She's got a *beautiful* soul,' said History.

Miss Suragamy McIntyre was green; green skin, green sari, olive green coat on top of sari, spinster, Christian, with bad complexion and bad digestion. We shook hands with intense dislike.

'Miss Suragamy is a *most* valuable person,' said History. 'She Bridges the Gap for us. We wouldn't know what to do without her. She can tell us so many things about these people that we wouldn't know otherwise.'

We left Miss Suragamy McIntyre and walked down the corridor. The windows gave on to the courtyard, and suddenly History darted to one of them. In the courtyard, on the usual tennis court, a girl and two boys were playing, tossing balls haphazardly, waving rackets, and laughing as they ran about.

'Devi, Devi,' cried History, 'come here, this moment.'

They did not hear. They ran and leapt about and laughed with lovely graceful movements, a dancing grace, light on their feet, wrists twisting the rackets like ribbons. History's voice changed. Flat, acrid, it came from a mouth shuttered between two tight folds of flesh:

'Devi, I'm calling you. Up. Come up. Right now.'

The little girl looked up. She had on modern Indian garb, trousers, a long tunic slit on the sides, a thin scarf meant to cover her breasts for modesty and instead drawing attention to them with their horseshoe curve. The two boys playing with her also looked up.

'Come up here, all of you.'

The three appeared at the head of the stairs, holding their rackets, smiling disarmingly.

'Devi, go into my room right away and start knitting as I told you.'

'Yes, Miss Newell.'

'And you two, you know you're not allowed in here except by special permission from the Head. I don't want you to stay another minute. That girl's getting a bit above herself these days,' said History as we went on.

'What do you mean?'

'Always out playing with boys ... says they're cousins of hers. *I* know what she wants.' Her voice became vulgar, flat. 'That's what they *all* want. That's all they ever think of. Filthy I call it. Giving those boys ideas ... making them come here and play ... praise the Lord, I'll nip it out of her and keep her busy ... Satan won't have this one, I'll see to that ... make her take those flowers out of her hair ...'

I stopped.

'What's the matter?' said History. 'Aren't you feeling well?'

'It's nothing.'

'You look quite ill. It's the wedding, eating at these unearthly hours. ... Here, let's go and sit down somewhere. For goodness' sake, you aren't going to faint or be sick, are you?'

She looked at me shrewdly, and I could read her thoughts. Pregnancy.

'I'm quite all right,' I said.

The Senior English classroom (chandeliers and mirrors ripped out) contains eight girls, wearing saris, with flowers in their hair, glass bangles on their arms, gold in their nostrils, kohl round their eyes, lipstick on their mouths, sitting at small desks from which they rise as History and I walk in.

'Now girls,' says History briskly, 'this is Mrs Ford, your new teacher of English. Now Mrs Ford is a writer herself, and so you'd better look sharp and try to use whatever brains the Lord's seen fit to give you.'

They giggle politely. I try not to look foolish.

'Now don't forget to say prayers *before* and *after* each lesson,' she says to me.

I nearly answer: Why? They're not Christians.

'Well,' I say to my class, as History disappears, 'we'd better get acquainted. I'd like to know your names. Let's start with the back row.'

'If you please, Mrs Ford,' pipes up a voice, 'the others all started with the *front* row.'

The owner of the voice is round-faced, slant-eyed, dimpled, clad in an extraordinary garment like a lampshade with a light pink silk skirt with large hoops descending over a pair of yellow satin trousers to the floor. She has thick braids, like a ship's ropes, to the waist.

'All right,' I say, 'let's start with you.'

That is obviously what Roundface wants. She rises, her garments swishing round her. 'I am Dearest,' she says, 'the daughter of the Great Rampoche of Bongsor.'

I remember the portly man seen last night at the wedding, laughing all over his blunt and powerful face, who has foiled the General's plans for keeping Eudora away from the wedding.

'I will introduce the others to you,' says Dearest. 'I *always* introduce when a new missionary comes. Now here we have ...'

'One moment,' I say. 'I'm not a missionary, for a change, and maybe they'd like to do it themselves?'

'Oh *no*,' says the Great Rampoche's daughter complacently, 'they don't.'

There is a giggle of agreement, and several girls adjust the flowers in their hair and push their bangles up and down on their forearms.

'It's different for me,' says Dearest. 'I am very well educated. I speak English I learnt in the convent in Darjeeling. I also speak Tibetan as my mummy is the Dalai Lama's mummy's best girl friend. I can speak Sherpa, Newari, Hindi, and I am learning Chinese too. Last year when the Chinese Ambassador came from Peking he told me I must also learn Chinese as all our ancestors are Chinese. I'm going to be a doctor.'

'Thank you for telling me all this, Dearest,' I say. 'Now I would like *you* to tell me your name.' I address myself to the next girl. She giggles, smothers her face in her sari. 'What is your name?'

'You see,' says Dearest, 'they always laugh.'

I see that Dearest's Chinese mentality, practical, intelligent, gifted, is scornful of the less endowed. Dearest will run my class for me. She is a genius who must be sat upon, firmly.

'Then you will tell them,' I say, 'to tell me their names.'

Thus I obtain the names of four of my pupils, names of goddesses, Sita, Suchila, Amanda, Rada. Each one is pretty or beautiful; their glass bangles are gilded and picked with colour, bright blue, red, yellow. Some have a red spot painted upon their foreheads, some look more Indian; others have semi-Mongol features with delicate creamy skins and languid eyes. Dearest herself is not altogether Chinese, in spite of the enormous vitality she distils; her eyes are too round. I know what she thinks as she fixes those eyes upon me: Why do you waste time with this pack of girls who don't want to learn, never *will* learn anything except how to make babies, when there's me here, wanting to learn, hungry for knowledge, me? But she holds her owlish peace.

I come to the second row. A girl rises. She has no jewels, one rose in her hair. It is Rukmini. She smiles, gives me her name, slips back behind her desk. I pass on. Keshore, Amrita ... One girl, tall and thin, in a beautiful sari of pale green with golden flowers, has pushed her desk far from the others, so far that she is on the marble edge instead of the large carpet which covers the greater part of the floor and upon which stand all the other chairs and desks.

'What is your name?'

'Lakshmi.'

'She has five babies and also tuberculosis, if you please Mrs Ford,' says Dearest, unable to contain herself any longer.

'Oh. And how old are you, Lakshmi?'

'Nineteen.'

Something in the tallness and slimness reminds me of someone. 'Are you related to General Kumar?'

'I am his daughter.'

Lakshmi coughs delicately in her handkerchief. 'It is cold on the stone, Lakshmi. Why don't you move your desk on to the carpet?'

'It is forbidden,' she smiles.

'Of course not. If it is because of tuberculosis, you can sit at the back, there's plenty of room on the carpet at the back, and you'll still be away from the others.'

Lakshmi giggles and laughs. Everybody laughs.

I begin to understand the irritation of History and Geography and Isobel. I feel like a lady with a lamp striding into a sunlit room and everybody dissolving in mirth. Progress, I remind myself. Enlightenment. That's what you're doing here, you and Isobel and Fred Maltby and even Unni Menon. He also is the twentieth century walking into the eleventh, bravely holding a lamp up, and it looks quite ridiculous at times.

'Mrs Ford.' Dearest is helpful again. 'I wish to inform you ... Lakshmi is unclean now. Hence she cannot stand on the carpet, for the fibres, madam, would communicate this uncleanness to us.'

It takes me ten seconds to understand. Of course. Women here are unclean for some days each month, they cannot be in the sun, stand on the same mat as others, nor eat with them.

'So Mrs Ford, in these circumstances,' says Dearest, 'may we stay home when we are unclean, please, it will be *so much* convenient? Miss Maupratt says no, but it is devilish uncomfortable for us.'

The thin end of the wedge. 'I am afraid Miss Maupratt's decisions are final,' I say. 'Now let us begin.'

Where shall I begin, I wonder? History has been 'holding the fort'. She gave them an essay to write last week.

'Your essays,' I say.

Dearest gets up and places a bundle of papers in front of me. 'Mondays we usually do grammar.'

'I know. Can you do parsing? Good. I will write some sentences on the blackboard for you to parse.' Only comic rhymes go through my head, the Akond of Swat, the Pobble with no Toes, the Great Rampoche of Bongsor, the Cheshire Cat ...

I write: 'I've often see a cat without a grin. But a grin without a cat! It's the most curious thing I ever saw in all my life.'

'Parse that,' I say.

Even Dearest is quiet, reading the words, and then the whole class laughs, a gale of laughter. It subsides with little sighs, the bell-tinkling of bangles, adjusting of gold in nostrils and ears, and the girls start, their pens scratch, Rukmini's head is bent, she appears to write. All but Lakshmi's, for Lakshmi coughs, looks through the window at the sun-filled morning, and plays with her rings and her bangles and the flowers in her hair.

*

John watched his wife walk out of the dining-room with History, while Geography poured herself another cup of Nescafé. He remained in front of an empty coffee cup. He longed for Isobel to appear. Her vacant chair and unrolled napkin affected him physically. Poor girl. She'd been with them last night, at that wedding, with Ranchit and Pat, Ranchit's American lay. In a fraternal session in the men's lavatory Ranchit had dilated on Pat's physical satisfactoriness. 'I like European girls,' he kept repeating, 'they make a lot of noise and I like it. And some like being hit. I can make Pat do anything I like. She shuts her eyes tight and does it. She says I'm the best lover she's ever had.'

They had returned from this concupiscent interlude to find Isobel gone. By now there were a great many wedding guests about, John had had a few drinks, and all was a bit hazy, except Anne being there, and he had deliberately turned his back upon her, to show he didn't care. She'd returned from wherever she'd been with Hilde and spent the rest of the evening talking to women, or to the old Field Marshal, or to Paul Redworth. There had been no flocking of men round Anne such as there was round Pat and round another European woman, an Irish girl with a full bust who seemed to be very popular with the men, and whom John was able to get introduced to and to engage in conversation during dinner.

There had been the hot spicy food laid out in dishes on tables, rather like a country dance supper, and sweet pink champagne to drink. 'It's always pink champagne at these parties,' the Irish girl had told him, and went on to say how bad it was for her, she'd been brought up strict and still couldn't drink, and her mother had told her never to drink champagne, and even now, with this maternal injunction upon her through the years, she found champagne whatever its colour made her quite dizzy.

Perhaps it was the pink champagne which had produced another effect upon John: a smouldering strained half-sleep, a sudden waking and turning to Anne very early, Anne lying on the very edge of the hideous double bed. His hand had come to her, accompanied by his giggle.

Anne had taken his hand and flung it back at him with what seemed extraordinary violence, then got up, straight in her pyjamas, and gone off to the bathroom, taking her clothes with her; dressed and walked out of the bedroom, all without a word.

'Where are you going? Come back,' he had said hoarsely, not very loud, held back by a sense of finality, as if something dreaded in a dream had now come about, made real by waking up.

For a while he debated whether to stay in bed, to be ill, thus forcing Anne's return. If only he slept again, she might come back. But she might not. So he got dressed, slowly, ear strained for a sound in the corridor, other than the stamp stamp of the bearer bringing the hot water. A hillman, the bearer walked even on the flat corridor stones as if going up a slope, his heels down and slightly knee-bending. John had not noticed it until Anne had said it to Paul Redworth before the wedding, over the beer at the Royal Hotel, and now he was hallucinated by the walk of the bearer, he kept rediscovering it. He resented this seeing things in Anne's words, the only picture available to him drawn in the words she uttered. But he found himself mentally hobbled, unable to describe that stumping walk otherwise.

At breakfast Anne was not there, nor Isobel. The girls (History and Geography) informed him that Isobel had a bad headache. 'It's all those late hours.' Their nostrils were curiously pinched and the white efflorescence off their faces thicker. Reticent, they held long silences between bites of toast. Was it something he'd said or done? John wondered uneasily whether their preoccupation might be due to him, things he'd said to Ranchit last night which someone might have overheard. Then Anne had walked in, her face glowing, freshness about her, and History had taken her to the classrooms and he'd been left with Geography (she had a mole on her chin, History didn't), and Geography had edged her chair a little forward and sighed.

'What's the matter?' John had said, grateful for this sigh with its implied demand for him.

Geography didn't suppose she ought to ... but then he was a man, *reliable,* and it was a *great burden* to bear for a woman, but poor Isobel, dear Miss Maupratt ... was still in bed because, well, she couldn't take drink, poor sweet darling ... such a *wonderful* person, but last night Dr Maltby had taken her to the hospital and pumped her stomach out.

Geography repeated the last sentence twice, to make quite sure John had heard. Isobel was still in bed with a terrible headache. Sometimes she wasn't careful, she'd had heart trouble and a *little* brandy did her good, but she didn't know how much brandy these wretched Nepalese put in their drinks, and she wasn't really strong in spite of her size.

John listened, nodded, filled with a warm, tender, gentle melancholy. Poor Isobel. He quite understood. Of course not her fault. Not a word. Yes, he would help. Certainly. Anything he could do. Geography assured him again how glad, how *lucky* they were to have him in Khatmandu. This was a small place, and there really weren't many *reliable* men about, like John. Tourists came and went, poured in and poured out again. 'Three days in Khatmandu, that's the most any tourist agency books them for.' And then there were the artists. *So* Bohemian. Geography sighed again, nearly prettily. Well of course one ought to be charitable, but ... John understood. And he could see what the local people were like. And one had to stand by what one believed to be right, didn't one? And of course there was *so much* work to do here, not only teaching, progress, alleviating the wretched poverty, but most important, *showing* them (since one wasn't very much allowed to preach), showing what it meant to be Christian, to know the real TRUTH, true religion, so they could be really HAPPY in the Lord. One mustn't lose sight of that. And there was *such* competition ... Father MacCullough ... of course, Roman Catholicism was better than heathenism any day, but still, the Roman Catholics did not have the TRUTH. But they had money instead and were always so well organized. And John must come to the hymn meetings ... he would, oh goody goody goody. ...

Glowing with the grateful, fluttering look from under Geography's sandy eyelashes, John left the Institute and walked to the Royal Hotel. First he'd ask Hilde when their room would be ready. Then he'd see Ranchit there or Pat, or someone. He'd have a beer. The sunlit verandah with its tourists, always new, going or coming, drew him irresistibly. Seated there it was possible to know everything that would or could happen in Khatmandu. It was the centre of all contacts, the nexus of all rumours. And he was lucky, Hilde was there, shaking a sunlit mane, with lists in her hands and tourists about her; an expedition was camping in tents in the garden; the Indian Embassy was throwing a children's tea party and a lorry full of cakes made by the Swiss who made the butter had arrived, meringues, cream puffs, mocha soufflés, *babas au rhum*, the spread of a pastry shop in Zürich.

There was an amiable bustle about, and John felt happy as he settled at a table and hesitated between beer – too early – or more coffee. An American couple who had been on the same plane walked by and hailed him and sat with him. They spent their time doing safaris, they told John. They'd been on safari in South Africa, and they'd just come from tiger hunting with the Maharajah of Lagawore.

'And now we're going hunting in the Nepalese Terai,' said the woman.

'Where's that?' asked John.

'It's that strip of low jungle to the south of Nepal, just before getting to India. One of the best hunting grounds in the world.' They had been promised some good shooting by a Rana who was a retired Generalissimo. 'Just think of it, the Gissimo is *so* powerful, even the Princes of the Royal Household of Nepal come to do homage when he holds court in Khatmandu.'

'Yes, we thought the Ranas were finished, done for, like the aristocrats after the French Revolution,' said her husband, 'but they seem to be alive and kickin', they're still runnin' everything and formin' political parties too for the first elections, I'm told.'

'Well,' said his wife, 'I think it's a good thing to have aristocrats running a country. Otherwise the Reds might take over. I hope His Highness the Gissimo won't charge us too much for a safari in the Terai. These people seem to think that we damfool Americans pay *any* price.'

'Yeah, two thousand dollars we paid last year to shoot a tiger, and it wasn't even a good 'un, tiny small thing, had to be beaten right up by the beaters before it managed to crawl before our platform and be shot.'

'By the way, what was the length of the largest tiger you ever shot?' inquired the American of John.

'I'm afraid I've never shot any,' said John. 'Though I've got lots of friends who did, in India you know, before the war.'

'Yeah, I thought so,' said the American. 'We didn't meet many Britishers tiger-shootin' on our safaris. None at all, in fact.'

'Well, I guess we've taken that over from them, along with a lot of other world responsibilities, dear,' said his wife.

'We sure have,' said her husband.

And then Pat was down, looking worn out, sallow, and 'Hi, John,' she said, 'where's your wife?'

'She's teaching this morning,' said John, feeling Anne very far.

Pat now started talking about the 'real upper-class, aristocratic' wedding to the tiger hunters, who had not been invited, and who retaliated by saying once again that His Highness the Generalissimo, known as the Gissimo to his friends for short, was a much more prominent man, and from a much older and more aristocratic family than the Royal Household. The princes had come to pay court to him, in fact, and he'd told them himself that he was their uncle. The conversation took the familiar competitive flavour which such conversations have at gatherings of tourists, foreign correspondents, and would-be experts on the Far East; the tiger hunters produced a few names of rajahs, princes, and maharajahs, and Pat nonchalantly bowled them down. 'Those people? But they're not *a bit* in the swim now. When *I* was in Lagawore three months ago the only person to know was Shim Shikah Derr ... you mean to say you haven't met Shim? Why, he's the biggest guy out there, practically runs the whole place ... the Maharajah's just a puppet in his hands.'

And when the Gissimo was dragged in again with the exclusive, expensive, and hard to gate-crash Terai hunts, Pat said: 'But he's only a Class C Rana.'

'What d'you mean by that?' said John, who was feeling very much at a loss for something clever to say.

'Goodness, I thought everybody knew. The Class A Ranas are the ones whose mothers are also high-caste women, Rana or Brahman aristocrats ... they don't call them aristocrats but that's what they really are. The Class B Ranas are from not such high-born mothers, and the Class C are either from the local Newari girls, or hill-women, or what they call here maidservants. I guess they're actually slaves. We'd call them illegitimate back home, but out here a Rana can have as many wives and concubines as he wants, there's no such thing as a real bastard in Nepal.'

There was an uneasy silence, then John said: 'That's very interesting.' It fell flat because the tiger hunters were still morally shocked.

The madman walked in, stared at them, shrugged his shoulders, said: 'Spies,' and sat at his table.

'Now *my* friend Ranchit,' continued Pat, swinging her chair, 'he's a Class A Rana. He thinks we should organize a club out here, those of us who know this place thoroughly. A good club, I mean, select you know, keep out anybody who's undesirable. I know Enoch P. Bowers, a friend of mine, is sold on the idea. A real good cosmopolitan, democratic-minded club.'

'That's an excellent idea,' said John enthusiastically. 'Quite an asset to this place. I know when we organized our club at Mynah (I was club secretary, you know) it was very well received. The chaps all joined it, quite a link with the natives. But I'm afraid it's gone down a lot since we left, takes anybody now.'

'Let's make it a tiger hunter's club,' suggested the American. 'Y'know, only a chap who's shot his tiger could qualify.'

'Nothing doing,' said Pat, 'we want to encourage local participation. Our aim is building up democracy here and we need to recruit some talent, artists and writers as well as people in Government, and most of the local talents are Newaris, I'm afraid, and they've never shot a tiger, in fact the Newaris weren't allowed to hunt at all in the Rana days. It wouldn't be democratic to keep them out. Now maybe you'd like to help Ranchit and me and Mr Bowers organize it,' she said to John, 'with your experience of running clubs?'

'Certainly, I'd be glad to help,' said John.

They ordered beer. John looked round the verandah, feeling he belonged. They needed him here. Twice that morning he'd been asked to help. Once by Geography, and now. He had found his niche, and a club would be just the thing. He began to tell Pat about the club in the old days. He was very happy.

Chapter 12

Two days later the Fords moved to the Royal Hotel.

The room had twin beds, a coffered ceiling, deer skins on the floor, and a brand new bathroom.

It was a relief for both; not only from an enforced proximity now repellent, but in other ways as well. They both slept better the first night, and early the next morning managed without a word a tacit manoeuvring which reinforced their distance from each other with a minimum of occasions for contact. Anne rose first and went to breakfast; John appeared at the table only when she had already gone to the Institute. At night she returned late, arms loaded with exercise books. After dinner John sat on the verandah, formulating plans for a club with Ranchit and Pat and Enoch P. Bowers, a lanky man from Kansas who looked like Abraham Lincoln, but sadder. John formed the habit of talking to the tourists who flew in and out of Khatmandu. Anne would appear or disappear, going to the Institute, or on walks, or to see Martha Redworth, returning in time for bed. John would be in bed, immobile, pretending slumber. Or it was he who, after a party at Ranchit's palace, found Anne asleep, eyes closed in the semblance of repose. Thus they managed for some days to live at each other's side without having to speak to each other.

John had been genuinely frightened by Anne's new ways. His was a puzzled and somewhat cowed emotion. For the first time in his life, since that morning when she had thrown off his hand and gone from the room, he strove for a while to understand why she had done so. But thinking was unpleasant; it involved too much doing away with portentous attitudes and especially with facile words which fell so easily into sentences, formulae which in turn buttoned down his thinking, made it run along habitual seams of self-condoning. The words, once thought, replaced a dimly perceived reality of which he was frightened, sensing it different. *My* wife ... my rights as a husband ... it is a wife's duty to ... conjugal rights ... like bubbles from a drowning puppy these words swam up to the surface of his mind, to be mouthed, to spread out, suffocating, billowing over something he neither knew nor wished to know.

When Anne was away in the morning he still felt lonely, but not as much as before, because in Khatmandu there were so few people in the foreign colony that one was always meeting them, before lunch ambling at the U.S.I.S. library, or coming to the Royal Hotel for morning coffee, then having drinks or lunch with them, and often a party at night. Because the Royal Hotel changed its tourist population so rapidly he had the illusion of meeting many people, establishing a diversity of contacts. He found it pleasant of an afternoon to accompany each new batch round the centre of the city, pointing out the gleaming gold-shot Temple of the Kings, its bells ringing in the wind; or the upper storey window of a wooden shrine shaped like a house and painted ochre, Tibetan style, where two wooden figures glowed vivid: the goddess Parvati, painted in green, cinctured with gold, in the arms of the god Mahadeo, another incarnation of Vishnu; or exclaiming at the black enormity of Kala Durga, dancing upon her slain demons; or contemplating, with the required reprobation, behind bars with the whole of the King's palace behind her, the enormous copper-fanged head of Bhairab with gaping mouth, tongue dripping red, and Yama the Lord of Death as a seal upon her brow. Bhairab was the guardian angel of Khatmandu.

Very soon John, like Anne, like many another arrival in Khatmandu, suffered his own mountain change. Because the anthropocentric framework of the civilization which had moulded him was not tempered by a private originality in his own make-up, this change did not affect him in the same way. It became not, as in Anne, a dissolving, an understanding by osmosis, a relationship which accepted and found easy the acceptance of the fantastic and divine elements of the Valley. To John occurred an inflation of his own ego, phenomenon also recognizable in many others of the foreign colony of All-Khatmandu. Because these had no other living gods to worship except themselves (since religion, to them, was a thing apart, hebdomadal boring exercise to be kept decently away from weekday living), it followed that when the Valley changed them, insufflating them with its exuberance of life, this was transformed within their souls into a sense of their own importance. They became grandiose to themselves; and there was no way for them to mitigate this self-aggrandizement, to restore this equilibrium displaced towards the megalomaniac, by means which were at hand for the humble and the meek, who saw the Divine in all things, and who, at the same time as they became aware of their own godly attributes, also had to know that in the valley of the gods every tree, stone, pi-dog, cow, and ragged porter was also god, Divine, equal and One with themselves.

Such humility could not be John's or Isobel's, for their brand of Christianity had unconditioned them for it. And as for Father Mac-Cullough, to be the representative of the One Truth on earth is hard upon a human being.

John, who since his retirement had suffered from a sense of futility, now felt a person of great worth, an intellectual well on the way to becoming an expert on Nepal, to whom the tourists listened, to whom they said: 'Say, *you* seem to know a lot about this place. Are you going to write a book about it?' 'I'm thinking of doing so,' he would reply, seriously, with dignity, and quite believing it. The idea of the club grew in him in importance by the hour. It would provide the missing link, the magic bond that would cement the freedom-loving peoples of Nepal together with the other freedom-loving peoples of the world. It would become the fountain of western culture, where magazines gay and entertaining would be freely accessible, where education, through lectures, conducted tours, and Saturday night hops, would bring together the best of the Nepalese with the best from the West. It would combat communism. Sometimes John, thinking of the club, would feel near to awe at the tremendous conception which was his.

And now he had friends. A good many. Enoch P., that presidential, slow-spoken man, who would be president of the club. Professor Rimskov, who claimed to have spent five years in a mysterious valley in Tibet. Professor Rimskov had enormous buttocks, no hair on his head, and a high-pitched voice. He sat on the verandah every night, telling the tourists tales of the fabulous valley he had discovered. In the morning he sat too, with a stub of a pencil and foolscap paper and a few files in front of him, and a tall glass of blond beer. This was a familiar physical and spiritual posture on the verandah of the Royal Hotel, where there must have been more self-recognized authors and artists per square foot of verandah table than anywhere else in the world.

Father MacCullough John liked with reservations. Here was another man whose outward self was what he liked to think of as all of him. A religion, a dogma too exacting in conformity, produces a crust upon the living man, a cockroach-hard outer sheath, leaving the soft inside ungrown. A Church durable as the rock of ages is apt to petrify some of the vulnerable spiritual flesh of man, just as a life spent believing that one is administering, ruling, or guiding others not so able as oneself tends to make a man believe that the image he has created of himself is all of himself. But blessedly Father MacCullough escaped most of this outward hardening process, for the Church is very old, and has had many renewals. The phylogenetic memory of the Church's foibles within its infallibility procures for its believers a good measure of astute humbleness.

John also had long talks with Isobel Maupratt, talks which always made him feel virtuous, noble, and good. Her god was so sure the Head of the Girls' Institute was always right.

It was a god in her own image, monolith of perfection, with no nether side, no contradictions, no sin, and a complete knowledge of Good and Evil. Her god and John's god – who looked like a dignified colonial servant, efficient and still athletic, in white shorts and a carefully restrained expression, out to found a club of apostles in the Himalayas – got on very well together.

But none of these friends, not even Isobel, gave him the exaltation which Ranchit provided. And that too was a new departure, for never before had John, in his mind, been able to visualize a 'native' as a friend.

This need of Ranchit was quite unlike his need of Isobel Maupratt, and, in a small way, of Geography. Ranchit was wealthy, and did and said things which John would have liked to do and say. Ranchit had even offered him Pat. 'Any time, old boy.' A day without Ranchit was incomplete, lacked the stimulus of contrast. From Ranchit and the dubious parties at his palace John came back to enjoy deliciously puritanical teas with Isobel, and Geography's obvious, pointedly chaste admiration. From these meetings John went back to Ranchit, murmuring: 'These are good women.' Ranchit's depravity gave John not only a sexual stimulus but also a sense of his own goodness and superiority. 'That guy gets away with murder,' he would say to Enoch P. And it contributed to his self-gratulation that he should have a friend whose actions he could both envy and condemn.

Anne's metamorphosis was different. She felt exalted, but only as part of the general ecstasy of the Valley, an integration of herself with all around her. This she was trying to explain to the Field Marshal, to whom she paid frequent visits now. The Field Marshal was seated in an armchair at a large polished mahogany table and smoked a hookah; the long tube twined round his left arm and descended the side of his chair like a pet cobra to the tortuous container on the floor.

The Field Marshal nodded approvingly. 'You are blessed, Mrs Ford, with true humility. The humility indispensable for true seeing and hearing. Acceptance of being eye-witness. Acceptance of becoming a vessel of the gods. Lack of humility is a lack of the awareness of God, or the gods (whichever way the words appeal to you). And this lack of awareness is in man due to his ways of speech, to taking words too much for granted. How much of our emotions are only conventions created by the language we use! Words,' said the Field Marshal, 'are not communication, duologue, but a makeshift, signs like distress signals, and one never knows quite how much of them is to the other the sum of our meaning, the total essence of our anguished solitude. And when we begin to substitute the symbol for the reality, the word for what it represents, then is the beginning of spiritual pride, for we lose track of significance and therefore of reality, in pride of speech more than in any other way. How true it is that the worlds we inhabit are created by the languages we speak. Yes, truly, and also our heavens and our hells.'

'I think,' said Anne, 'that words, symbols, have a continuing life assuming different significances for different ages, and oh, it's hopeless, I am always stumped by the words I use. It is a perpetual restlessness with me, an obsessive malaise, to correlate the symbol to the thing, the word to its meaning. I just can't express myself and it makes me restless.'

'But it is this restlessness, this knowledge of the tame abyss you drag about with you on a leash, the abyss of language, which keeps *you* humble and therefore in touch with the Divine,' said the Field Marshal. 'Because you are an artist, seeking the meaning beyond the saying, you know at every moment how imperfectly you know; how limited by your own explanation you are; and you sometimes perhaps assume in others depths of meaning of which they are perfectly unaware – which is why, if I may venture to be so rude as to pass a personal remark, you are probably for ever *underestimating* yourself. Which is a good thing.'

The room around them was decorated with antlers and horns, but there were also books, books, and books, lining the walls behind glass; and these were not for show. 'I have somewhat dipped into them,' the Field Marshal said modestly. They walked through a long corridor lined with steel cabinets full of books, catalogued and separated according to subject. Anne mentioned a flower, an amaranth noticed near the pond of medieval justice. The Field Marshal opened one of the cabinets, produced a book on botany, the picture of the flower, its classified description. They discussed the hedges of golden dewdrop, and the Australian bottle-brush trees planted along the roads of the Valley. The Field Marshal knew their Latin names. Book Society choices occupied four special cases, and there were shelves of encyclopedias. On the large table in front of the Field Marshal reposed a thick leather-bound ledger, in which people wrote down their names and the names of the volumes they borrowed. Four works on political economy had been taken by the King, Paul Redworth's name followed with two complete poets. Anne put her name down as taking away a German–French volume on alpine flowers.

'I don't think I underestimate,' said Anne. 'I wanted to write once upon a time, but I'm not a genius, and I think the spark is gone.'

'Why qualify and delimit with a word which means exactly nothing, and thus diminish your powers, whatever they may be?' said the Field Marshal. 'Do not worry to give a name to what you do, my friend. Is it not sufficient that to you something is given, not to be buried in the ground, but to use? Use it well, with no thought of success or failure – but then I should not reiterate what you know better than I do.'

'I don't,' said Anne. 'I just don't always know what is right to do.'

'That is everyone's question. A problem, which only faith, belief in some creed, appears to solve. You can *believe* in all humility, seeking the depths of yourself,' said the Field Marshal, who sat like a small Buddha in his chair, his head wrapped in a cloth, his belly strapped in a large pink flannel waistband to protect it from the cold, 'you can *do*, but never be attached to success or failure in your actions. In other words, remain detached from the fruits of action. That is the secret of the Lord Krishna, the Lord of Life. That is living.'

'It is difficult to be detached and perhaps still to work with the same élan.'

'On the contrary, it is easier to work if you believe that you are but a vessel to do God's will, and divine to that extent, rather than to profess in all hypocrisy not to be a god (which leaves you a liberal margin of self-indulgence), and then act towards others as if you were God himself. Let God who made the world worry about it. Your duty is to *do*, and thus to revere life.'

The Field Marshal then abandoned his hookah and showed her old Nepalese manuscripts written in gold upon handmade paper. 'I lent one of these to a white man who told me he was a famous professor in a European university, and vowed he would return it. Yet he never turned up again, nor did my manuscript. But we must not generalize; this man may be shame to his country and his seat of learning; but my heart has not hankered after the manuscript, for he must have wanted it very much to keep it to his dishonour. It was the will of the gods, or God, and who knows? It may still turn up some day.'

They walked back through the corridors of books. Above the lockers hung pictures of the hunts, of the Field Marshal with rhinoceros, boar and tiger and bull. In his youth and despite his small stature he was a renowned huntsman. Between the lockers were rare bronzes of Newari design which he had collected. And then the Field Marshal had given Anne a book, the *Bhagavad-Gita*. On the first page, after the usual superscription, he had written: 'Let your prayer be: Oh Khrishna, Lord of Love and Life, give my roots rain.' 'You have doubtless read it in translation,' he said, knowing she had not. 'You will recognize this as also extant in your culture, my dear friend. You remember Herbert: For now in age I live again, I once more smell the dew and rain? This must happen to all of us, time and again, so that we never forget that life is all, and death only an insignificant tailpiece. Life is all, and Krishna, the God of Life, speaks here in these pages. And Krishna is the most beloved of all our gods, or manifestations of the One. Krishna is Life itself, life lived with delight in all its acts, play and work and love, sorrow and anger, pleasure and passion, error and wisdom. I think Krishna would be a happy companion for you, my friend, and he has so many shapes, so many loves, that even your lovely words could not encompass him. In this book you see him under one shape, but you will meet him in many other ways I think, and especially if you fall in love again, my friend,' he had added colourlessly, and then Anne had been outside, in the vast and well-kept garden where the black magnolia tree, the pride of the Field Marshal, was in full blossom.

She walked to the Ruby Palace, went to the bungalow, laid the *Gita* and the botany book upon her desk. There were a few more books lying about, she needed a small box where she could keep them. Perhaps downstairs, she thought. She walked into the abandoned lower room to rummage among the derelict furniture. There was nothing she could use. 'I'll have to ask Hilde for an old box or something.' She opened drawers in old chests. In one of them among old newspapers in Nepalese was a yellowed glossy proof of a photograph, discarded.

It showed a group of people seated on a lawn, under trees, with a mountain in the background. Anne brought it to the light, and saw Rukmini smiling, playing a sitar, and Lakshmi putting flowers in her hair, and three other girls laughing, and Deepah, the General's son, his hands tapping the small drums to accompany Rukmini, and Unni Menon with a cap and a flower above his ear, and a small, chubby baby girl laughing and clapping her hands, seated in his lap.

Anne wiped the photograph with her handkerchief, smoothing the corners, and put it in the *Gita* the Field Marshal had given her. She went to the window and looked out, a languid abstraction upon her. She sighed, opened an exercise book, and started to correct it. But the afternoon was too marvellous to relinquish to inattention. There was everywhere the cry of birds. She lay on the orange and blue raza, head flat, on her stomach, dreaming. And through the window came a small breeze, and the parakeets pecked in lively silence at the sunflowers, and she could feel every cell in her body throb with the passion of life.

And then there was a step, firm, unyielding, up the stairs, and a knock on the door.

'May I come in?'

I wonder what would happen if I said 'No, you can't,' thought Anne, as Isobel's face sidled her hungry eyes in the half opening, and on both sides of the door the painted eyes wide open looked ironically at Anne, as if to say: now, what are you going to say?

'Do come in, Isobel,' said Anne.

'I only came to fetch you for tea,' said Isobel. 'All of us girls have a cuppa and a get-together once a week. We thought you'd like to join us.' She said it without irony.

'I'll come,' said Anne, and followed Isobel, who turning darted her eyes about the room, sliding over the parakeets, the sun-flowers, not acknowledging them, cutting them dead as she had cut Dr Maltby after that disastrous walk together. Her eyes fell upon the book.

'Oh, a book,' she cried, swiftly taking a step towards it, 'may I see?'

'It's just a book,' said Anne, dreading Isobel's hand upon the cover. 'Someone gave it to me.'

'But what a nice cover,' cried Isobel, fingering it. 'It must be *quite* old. They don't do such good work now, everything's degenerated so much, one can *hardly* find a nice brooch or anything these days. Do take care of it, dear, you'd better keep it locked up in case someone steals it. The Nepalese are so unreliable, you know.'

They tramped down the stairs together, these yielding to the sound and the weight and echoing behind them, and were out on the lawn, with its walnut trees in a bent bow, and between the trunks there was a lovely, splayed-out mountain, and then Anne knew where the picture she had found had been taken. In front of this very bungalow, sitting in the shade of those walnut trees, with the mountain beyond.

*

Tea was a show-down [wrote Anne].

When I started this journal with the word Khatmandu, I thought it would be a saga of delight; on thumbing over the foolscap sheets I realize that to tell the truth I am also writing words which I dread re-reading. This hesitation to face the past is my weakness. I can be brave about the present, and the future. The past scares me. I receive suffering boldly, tranquil like a dumb animal, go on auguring it, even rushing upon it bare breasted. The sword goes in, I feel it not until growing, part of me, its livid passage unhealed after a long time, the day comes when I must turn to excise it, and it is a bigger wound than

I thought. One day, I tell myself, I will be very brave. I will face everything, even what is gone. Until then, I can only record and pass on to the future, the next hurt, tomorrow's pain.

History, Geography, Suragamy McIntyre, were in Isobel's living-room having tea and sandwiches and coffee cake, and I knew the moment I entered they had been talking about me. There was so much heartiness in their welcome, I was plied with victuals as if I had returned from an expedition to the snow peaks.

They did not cast about for a topic. Our move to the Royal Hotel was obvious, safe introduction. Did I like the room?

'It must be nice for Mr Ford,' said Geography, 'to be in the *heart of things.*'

'I hear your husband is writing a book.'

'Is he? I had not heard.'

'I think it would be a wonderful idea,' said History, 'for someone *really* competent to go round and collect material and write a *really* serious book about this place.'

'A lot of people come here and feel they want to write books,' added Suragamy McIntyre.

'But they're only *novelists,*' said Geography. 'I hear your husband is organizing a club. Such a wonderful idea.'

'Our drive for funds for flood relief could do so much better with a good club to organize our get-togethers.' That was Isobel.

I looked round mechanically for her knitting and found it, a flabby inchoate small monster lying navily in the shadow of a cushion.

'Some more cake? How do you like your class?' said History brightly.

'Very much,' I said.

Isobel cleared her throat. 'You've got a lot of married women in that class. I'm afraid they're a pretty hard lot to handle.'

'Oh, I don't find it so,' I said, imprudently.

'*Everyone,* so far, has found the last year difficult,' said Isobel stiffly. 'It's too early yet for you to be completely in the know, but one mustn't let standards go down.'

'Prayers, for instance,' said History, aggressive.

'I'm afraid I forget about prayers.' I shot myself down.

There was a silence, broken only by Suragamy McIntyre hitching up her sari and drawing the folds closer round her. She still wore her green coat on top. She was always cold, her circulation poor; the Valley was too high up for her.

The next bit got rather involved, as Isobel and History spoke nearly together.

'Well, of course –' Isobel began, and History said: 'There's always a tendency –', then they begged each other's pardon. Isobel was left to tackle me.

'I know that Father MacCullough had the same problem,' she began. 'In his boys' school. Prayers after class. Some parents objected. But Father MacCullough replied that those who did not believe did not *have* to recite prayers, simply to stand and listen, but not to join in. That's our policy too. The Board was explicit on that. Never offend, but uphold the Faith.'

'And besides,' said Geography, 'praying in front of them is good for them. They're in the grip of Satan.'

'That's how conversions are made. Quite suddenly, God will touch their hard hearts sunk in wickedness, and turn them from their evil heathen ways to the Light, and wash their souls clean.'

'All right,' I said, 'I won't forget prayers. I suppose the same as we had in Shanghai, Isobel?'

'That's right, dear,' said Isobel.

I passed to the offensive now. 'How did you like the wedding?' I asked History and Geography.

'Oh, not too bad,' they said, fixedly goggle-eyed, not looking at Isobel.

'I didn't like the way Rukmini, that Mrs Ranchit, behaved,' said Suragamy McIntyre, suddenly ominous.

'What did she do?' I asked.

'It's the way she looks at men,' said she, getting if possible pea-greener. 'It's not right. I'm having a lot of trouble with her sister, Devi, already.'

'I didn't know Devi was her sister,' I said, remembering the little girl playing tennis with the two boys, and then the three standing in front of us, fearless unshy gazelles, easily poised on their feet, knowing what to do with their hands and their eyes; and was the chubby girl in Unni's arms in the photograph Devi?

'Oh, she's a handful,' said History. 'They're both handfuls, actually.'

'And darn conceited.'

'Now if I were her husband, I'd lay her across my knee and give her a good spanking, that's what she needs,' said Geography with cold ferocity.

'I suppose you are talking about Rukmini?' I said, my anger rising. 'I think she's a beautiful girl.'

'But she hasn't got a beautiful soul,' said History angrily.

'I'd really like to know,' I said, 'what you have against her.'

'I'll tell you,' said Isobel, just as angrily. 'It happened very soon after I came. This palace was owned by Rukmini's father, who's sold it to the Government, who're letting us use it as a school. However, we already had our rooms and classes here, while negotiations were going on. And that man, Menon, he and a few others were staying here, as guests of Rukmini's father.' She took a noisy gulp of tea. 'Pretty soon I found out what was going on,' she said, her eyes dilating and her nostrils. 'It's really *so* awful, I can scarcely tell you. One morning I couldn't find *any* of the girls. They hadn't turned up for classes. I went round looking for them and then I found them. All of them. They were sitting on the lawn in front of that man's room, playing and singing, and crowned with flowers. And he was playing on the drums, to make them dance. Absolutely disgraceful.' She was quite pale. 'He should have known better, a grown man, in a high position, old enough to be their father, to tempt those girls ...'

'*And* in front of his room,' said History, shocked.

'I made him move right away,' said Isobel.

'But they still carry on,' said Suragamy McIntyre coarsely. 'I think so, anyway.'

I felt quite sick, nauseated. I must take a grip on myself. This way lies hysteria.

'If this is so, why then did you give *me* Unni Menon's room?'

'I ... why, I ...' she began.

'Why,' I said, suddenly acting like John acts, melodramatic, rising to my feet and extending an accusing index finger in her direction (oh, the compelling power of gestures, of words, to create emotions which are not), 'why then did you not have his room burnt down, or whitewashed, or something? Why did you bring *me* to it?' Disdaining an answer, I walked to the door. Then I over-played in the grand manner, throwing back at them finally their viciousness as if it had been an amateur show put on for my benefit which had not pleased me. 'By the way,' I said to Suragamy McIntyre, 'do you know anything about Krishna, the Lord of Life?'

'Oh,' said she, 'Krishna. Yes, of course I know it's one of the gods, there are lots of stories about him, but I'm a Christian,' she added defensively. 'It's a superstition. He doesn't exist.'

'I see.' Sounding almost like the Field Marshal, I walked out.

I went to my bungalow and locked the door of the room upstairs, and then went out and locked the outside door. They were Nepalese locks, very old, fixed at the bottom of each door to a ring in stone; and they were in the shape of animals, a hierogryph upstairs and a salamander below. I touched them with love, with ritual respect. I am learning reverence for all things, for all is alive; these locks are alive with beauty, the care and skill of awakened hands, the understanding hearts of the dead craftsmen who made them. To acquire them would be sacrilege; to handle them is richness enough. I had not used them before because I felt safe. But now after that tea party in Isobel's living-room I knew the parakeets in danger, the room threatened by those people with the faded tarnished hair and ropy necks, with breasts, large and pendant or small and arid, people who have forgotten or never known, never known the turn of the wrist, the gazelle look, the flowerlike gesture that plucks and that gives pleasure.

*

At the Royal Hotel, in the dusk at the foot of the steps leading to the rhinoceros heads and the crocodiles in the hall, was the golden fleece of Hilde, getting into a jeep with Unni.

'Hello,' she cried when she saw Anne. 'Come with us, Anne, we go to see Vassili at the jail.'

'Sure,' said Anne, and climbed into the jeep.

Unni smiled at her from the driving seat. 'Nice to see you again,' he said.

'I've just been at the Institute,' she replied. There was early twilight between them and she felt bold. Her heart beat wildly, her face glowed.

Hilde looked at her and said: 'Anne, you look fine these days. Khatmandu is good for you.'

'It is,' said Anne.

It was nearly a repetition of the evening of the wedding when they saw the gloomy jail walls topped with barbed wire and high watch towers, and the sentries' alacrity in opening the postern door. They walked the stone flagged courtyard, and towards them came a beautiful girl with blonde hair to the waist, free flowing, a twist of rubies round the neck and another round the wrist, the oval face, the swan neck, the green eyes of Botticelli's *Venus*. She was wrapped in a gold and white sari; her feet, with painted nails, were in golden sandals with a noose round the big toe. She saw Hilde and Unni and smiled and waved a hand, very white, upon which was only one, enormous jewel: two interlarded hearts in emeralds and diamonds upon a platinum ring. And behind her came Father MacCullough, who rushed up to Hilde.

'Why, hello there! Going to see Vassili? I've just been, he's fine. Yeah. He's very fit, Hilde. I've given him the catapult, the slingshot, he'll know what to do with it. Unni, I didn't know you were back in Khatmandu, I'd like to come and see you tomorrow, or will you be at the Royal Hotel after Mass Sunday! It's about that trip down the road.'

'Paul Redworth is coming with me day after tomorrow,' said Unni. 'I came back from Bongsor just a couple of hours ago. Yes, do come if you're free.'

'I'll get in touch with you tomorrow about it.'

'I won't be here tomorrow,' said Unni, 'I'm flying to Simra and back. Be at the Royal Hotel at eight the day after and I'll pick you up.'

'How long will the trip take?' inquired Father MacCullough.

'Two days.'

'Good, then I'll be waiting for you day after tomorrow at eight at the Royal Hotel,' shouted Father MacCullough, making everything sure and definite with words. And he ran to catch up with the girl, who had continued walking slowly towards the gate.

'That is the Prince's girl friend, such a beautiful girl, and very gentle,' said Hilde. 'The Prince likes Vassili a lot, he's certainly asked her to go to see him. Maybe there's some good news about release.' She walked more swiftly through the courtyards, one by one, surrounded by cells with heavy wooden doors and verandahs along which soldiers in khaki walked their guns, until she reached a courtyard which seemed to rock on its own with the sound of laughter; an open door, from which light escaped in a sprawl upon two guards squatting outside with their weapons across their thighs and grinning faces turned towards the open cell, and the recognized tones of a precise voice, saying: '... a do-no-good young chap, thumping good fellow at poker but otherwise full of God's mad wine.'

'The General!' said Hilde, and walked in the daub of light.

The cell was large, for Vassili was getting first-class jail treatment. It was vaguely reminiscent of the Royal Hotel bedrooms with its twin beds, but the windows were classically barred and small and high. The beds were planks with a thin straw mattress, there were sheets and bright razas on both. The room seemed full of people, sitting on the beds or on the floor, and at first they were like a crowd in a picture, immobile with strong brownish shadows and lights like a sombre modernistic painting, until they fell into recognition, assumed personalities and known names. There was the General, with a glass of whisky in one hand and a glass of milk by him. There was Deepah, standing behind his father. There were Rukmini and Devi, sari-wrapped and sitting with crossed legs on the floor. There was a tall and a very handsome young man talking to Rukmini, and there was Vassili, with the head of a wistful film Nero, kind blue eyes, a portly Roman body, capable strong hands gripping Anne's, a smile and a warm, enveloping sensation of kindness, humour, and Russian enthusiasm for life.

'So you are Mrs Ford? Hilde, why didn't you bring her before? It is nice to come and see me in the jail. Sit down on the bed, there, it is my bed, it is not that of that dirty fellow Sharma, full of bedbugs and lice. Sharma, meet Mrs Ford.' The handsome young man turned and bowed. 'This Sharma here is a poet,' said Vassili, 'so they put him with me for my sins and he keeps reciting poetry all night so I can't sleep.'

'I thought it was the dogs kept you awake,' said the General.

'The dogs and Sharma between them,' shouted Vassili. 'But now we have this.' He brandished the small brown catapult, shaped like a chicken's wishbone. 'A present from the Holy Church. When I was a kid I used to make little mud balls and shoot them, ping ping ping, my aim was always good. I could hit even a sparrow in flight. Have you brought the marbles, Hilde?'

'I have,' said Hilde, opening her bag. 'All those I could get on the market, Vassili.'

'Now we'll shoot those, putting some clay around first to make them stick a bit better,' said Vassili. 'Then I will also use it to stop my friend Sharma from writing poems at night, walking up and down spouting about pneumatic bliss. I'll keep him busy shooting the dogs.'

'Poor dogs,' said Sharma. 'I think Vassili is very cruel to interrupt their private ecstasies.'

'Any news about the Coronation, Unni?' said Vassili. 'Come, you great big expert, anything I don't know?'

'2 May, the Coronation,' said Unni. 'You'll be out before that, Vassili. Long before that, I'm afraid.'

'Too bad,' said Vassili. 'I was beginning to enjoy it here. No tourists to bother me. No accounts to keep. And my dear wife to visit me three times a week. And I was going to bring in a sofa for her. A wonderful life. So good for my liver too. No drinks and no temptation.' He sighed and looked at the General's whisky.

The General said: 'I know you will be out next week. That is what they say in all the government departments now, even those which are not on speaking terms with one another. So it must be true.'

'Oh,' said Vassili with interest, 'are the Public Works and the Interior still putting each other in jail by writing anonymous letters to the Vice-squad?'

'No, they've become friends again, but now a few other departments are not speaking,' said the General, shaking his head in mock sadness. 'I must tell you, madam,' he said to Anne, 'that one of the effects of democracy in my country is bureaucracy. In the old days, these terrible Rana days of horrendous despotism, when the Prime Minister, my father, wanted money, he just sent people to collect it. He said he wanted so many crores, he got it. What the collectors got was nobody's business. Then he just put it in a big room and when needed took a few handfuls and used it. But now we have government departments and files and offices, and we even have typewriters, in Nepalese. And it is all beautifully muddled and things get done because people who want to do things pay no attention to orders or counter orders but go ahead and do them.'

'That's true,' said Unni. 'One head of department last year issued an order to all those under him not to speak, write, telephone, or in any way communicate with those of another one. It made things difficult for us, as we had dealings with both. But very soon they were using me as a kind of unofficial messenger between them. It was a wonderful period, I got all I wanted merely by telling each in turn what the other was giving me. "What, that so-and-so is only giving you *two* trucks to cart the sand from the river?" one department chief would say. "*I'll* lend you all three of mine – collect them tomorrow." Then I went back to the first and got two more out of him. There were only ten trucks in the whole of Nepal, and only four in working order, but we fixed the remainder and used them all.'

'And what happened then?' said Vassili.

'Oh, they made up one day, grand reconciliation scene, and we had to hand back all the trucks, one by one. But the work was finished and everybody was very happy. They were very good sports about it, threw a huge party and made me blistering drunk.'

'That's democracy,' said the General.

'You should complain,' said Vassili. 'I'm in prison because of democracy. And so are you, Sharma. Though you deserve it, you lousy poet.'

'You'll be out soon,' said the General. 'And think how it will add interest to your life, when you write your autobiography. The Coronation is soon, and who will look after the many thousands of people then, my friend, feed them and drink them and bed them, and listen to their complaints about our country, if not you?'

'The lousy bastard who put me in will look after them,' cried Vassili, in an earnest violent fling of Russian temper. 'I will go to Calcutta with Hilde after this and open a club there and shake the lingamorous dust of this place off my feet. See if I don't.'

'Oh, you won't,' said Unni. 'The Valley's got you, Vassili.'

'If it wasn't for my liver,' said Vassili, 'I'd ... well, have a drink, Unni.'

Two bearers in livery with red sashes entered with drinks on a tray and curry puffs, anchovies, eggs, and caviar on small bits of toast, and olives stuffed with red peppers. They were sent by the Prince and his friend, who had also sent three extra bottles of whisky. 'What a sweet girl,' said Vassili. 'I must kiss her next time she comes to see me.'

'Then you'll stay in jail for good,' said Sharma. 'The Prince will see to that.'

At that moment there was prolonged howling from outside.

'The damn bitches,' cried Vassili, running to the window and climbing on a stool with great swiftness, catapult in hand. 'Hand me a marble, Hilde.' He took aim, let go. There was a series of yelps. 'That's one goner,' he shouted. 'My aim is still as good as when I was a boy. Pass me a drink, someone.' He stood on the chair, happy, looking down. 'Anne, have a drink. You don't mind me calling you Anne, do you, it suits you. And Rukmini, you're keeping so quiet, my beautiful. No, I think your little sister better stick to ginger ale. Whisky again for you General, Unni.'

Vassili's liveliness filled the small jail. Everyone was laughing, without quite knowing why. Sharma was talking to Rukmini, his eyes rapt upon her face, which she kept lowered, never looking at him, so that gradually he saddened. He was visibly in love with her. Unni went out to pour drinks for the sentries outside, who came in then to say thank you, and drain at a gulp and stand grinning, with empty glasses.

'No more for you,' said Unni, 'or you'll start wobbling and get caught.'

It was getting quickly cold and another sentry came in with a brazier piled with glowing coals. The hurricane lamp gave off a steady whizz. Anne felt quite drunk, half numb with a kind of saturated happiness like anguish, a feeling dolorous and pleasant, bruising somewhere, a drumming of her blood all over her body, an ache in whatever metaphysic bone her soul was made of.

Vassili was telling her the story of how he'd been arrested, and she couldn't stop laughing. He'd been arrested, and questioned, and though he had been questioned for days neither his questioners nor himself exactly knew what they wanted to find out nor did he know exactly what to reply, because all he knew was that he had been arrested, and he wanted to find out why, and they said to him very shrewdly and blandly: 'But that is just what we want to find out from *you*.'

And then there was a maudlin but happy discussion between Vassili and Sharma about democracy. 'We all think we talk about the same thing but we don't, because we use the same words, but we don't really,' said Sharma.

'That sounds wonderful, Sharma, but it doesn't help even you, because you're here and you don't know why you're here.'

'Oh yes I do,' said Sharma. 'It's political and anonymous. The favourite pastime of my countrymen is writing anonymous letters, or writing petitions claiming their wives have been raped or that they have been assaulted. And that's why I'm in prison – rape and assault – though I never saw the girl at all. But it is really a political move,' he added. 'Obviously political.'

'That's damn-ocracy,' repeated the General, who raised his milk glass, still full, squinted at it, shuddered, then poured himself another whisky.

'Peace, peace,' said Unni. 'Have another drink, Sharma.'

'Let's have a drink and a song,' said Vassili. 'You, my beautiful little one,' he turned to Rukmini, 'please sing us a song and fill our hearts with happiness.'

'Oh yes, do sing, Rukmini,' said Hilde. 'Rukmini has a beautiful voice.'

Rukmini shook her lowered head, then suddenly turned and looked straight at Unni, so that the red dot upon her forehead, catching the light, glowed like a drop of blood. Her eyes pleaded, resigned and yet with a fine radiant pride because he was there, and Anne, looking, understood her pride in her submission when he said, not looking at her at all, as the hubbub quietened, his voice low and grave, deep like the reverberation of a large bronze bell: 'Sing then, Rukmini,' and she began to sing:

> ' O the sun is now up and over the mountains,
> And the glad torrents come down from the slope,
> Why have you left me then, cradled in sorrow,
> And gone away, to the valley beyond?'

Devi chimed in, and the sisters sang together, feet folded, hands in their laps, their eyes far away, like those little girl oleographs the Ranas suspended on their walls. Their voices rose and fell like the sweet crested hills, Rukmini a soft contralto and Devi with a little warble, and the melody went heavy with sadness and love. And after a while Sharma and the General were also singing, Vassili and Hilde hummed it, and Unni whistled it softly; and the sentries outside clapped hands to the time, while with shining eyes and teeth and bayonets the guards crowded the doorway, listening and smiling.

It was cold night outside, the stars glittering packs chased by the wind. Anne had come without a sweater, and as she stepped into the icy courtyard Unni put his jacket, still warm from him, round her shoulders. Hilde, who had lingered with Vassili, caught up with them. Rukmini and Devi passed them, throwing their shawls about them, and joining their hands to say good-bye. Rukmini's bangles tinkled softly against each other.

'Come and have dinner in my house, madam,' said the General to Anne, 'and you, Hilde.'

'Can't,' said Hilde. 'I've got to be at the hotel in case the tourists want something or other, we've got a new batch in, and my three little padlocks have to be kissed good night by their Mummy, blast their sweet hearts. Usually they go to bed like angels, but when I go to see Daddy they don't sleep until I get back to tell them about him.'

'But you can come?' the General said to Anne. 'We will ask Dr Maltby also.' Anne was silent, struggling with herself. She should inform John, in all fairness. The General added: 'We will stop by the Royal Hotel certainly to ask your husband.'

But when they arrived John was not in, and the bearer reported he had left with Pat and Ranchit, and Anne felt suddenly quite gay. 'I won't be a minute,' she said. She hurried to her room, took her wool stole and came back to hand the leather jacket to Unni, who was in his shirt sleeves and did not appear to mind the cold. 'Thank you so much,' she said. He took the jacket and put it on again, without saying anything.

It was only a very short distance to the Serene Palace. They passed the nurses' private bungalow. It was lit, the sound of pianola music streamed out of it, people singing. They came to Fred's bungalow. He peered out. 'Oh, it's you, Unni,' he said, 'and Anne too. How very nice.'

It was a large room, with books and a heavy leather armchair and a desk. Beyond could be seen folding doors open upon the bedroom, with a big bed and a camp bed against the wall, for Unni was staying with Fred.

'We came to ask you to dinner with us,' said the General, 'but we shall sit down and have a drink with you first.' He spoke to the bearer, and in a few moments the Tibetan handmaid appeared with a tray and Vat 69 and glasses.

'Only one drink,' said Fred, who knew the General. 'Mrs Ford isn't used to eating so late, I'm sure.'

'I'll go up to the kitchen and tell them to get the food ready,' said Unni.

'Go up to the kitchen?' said Anne.

'Yes, the kitchen is on top of the house in a Brahman household,' said Unni, 'to avoid pollution.'

'Don't hurry,' said the General, 'we have plenty of time.' Like many of the Ranas of his generation he preferred to eat at midnight or later, drinking steadily through half the night.

From the next bungalow came another burst of music, and the words of a hymn:

> If you believe, your dreams will all come true,
> Embrace the Lord, and he will see you through,
> If you have faith, there's nothing you can't do.

'Ah,' said the General, cocking his head drunkenly and once again seizing a whisky and ignoring the milk glass he kept at his elbow but never touched, 'pretty.'

Anne was so tired she could not keep her eyes open. She dozed in the armchair. Unni was drinking steadily – he had had six or seven whiskies, but they seemed to have no effect on him at all.

'You're tired,' he said to her.

'Yes, I am.'

'Lie down inside there on the bed. Dinner will take an hour or more to prepare. I'll wake you when it's time to eat. Don't worry about us.'

'All right.'

He walked in with her, and she lay on the camp bed, too tired to realize that it was his, and he covered her with the raza. 'Just one thing before you fall asleep,' he said. 'Will you also come on the road with us day after tomorrow? With Father MacCullough and the Redworths?'

'I'd like to,' said Anne.

'Good,' he said, 'I'll arrange it.'

Then she was asleep, but in a turmoil. She rested in fitful restlessness, woke to eat a few mouthfuls, and Unni drove her back to the hotel. She fell into bed, noting that John had not returned, into a troubled sleep where there was danger and fear and hatred, and also a bell pealing, and then it was day. John had not returned.

Chapter 13

AFTERWARDS, when the time had come to say 'Do you remember?' Anne would remember that Friday and the Saturday that followed it in all its enchanted span; every moment of it compounded with happiness.

The dawn, when head still turned against the wall she perceived above the curtains of the french windows the glaucous slice of beginning Friday. Then spacious, all humbling, turquoise bold, the sky above the fake cupolas of the Royal Hotel, morning like a song flinging itself against the blue foothills, turtle doves circling about the roof alighting with a cardboard clatter of wings.

Anne got out of bed and showered herself with cold water and brushed her teeth, each action pleasure, ritual preparation for some wonderful event. All was ready, a change of clothing in the Shan bag, her tweed coat. She wore slacks, a shirt, a pullover. She picked up the bag and then came to a stop. John lay in the next bed, in a fixed immobility. She ought to say good-bye. She ought to say something.

'Are you sure you don't want to come?'

A quality of heaviness was already slowing down her gestures. Automatically she now lingered, went in front of the mirror to comb her hair again, and as she looked at her hair she saw at the crown the white hairs, two or three, standing up a little. She picked up her eyebrow tweezers and plucked them out.

John had not turned. He must be asleep. 'Well, good-bye,' she said, and walked out, to breakfast, hot coffee, the bearers squatting at the end of the corridor toasting bread on small charcoal burners; and Father MacCullough coming in with Unni as soon as she had sat down. Father MacCullough's face was white and nose was red in the morning, and he rubbed his hands with a rasping noise. He had two cameras slung crosswise round him, an overcoat, a hat with a feather in it, and the heartiness of a Boy Scout leader.

'Well, well, well, and where's that husband of yours?' he said.

John had reappeared, the morning before, slightly drawn, hangoverish, off-handed, watched Anne furtively at lunch. As she did not ask where he had spent the night he gave explanations, not to her, but to Hilde sitting at the next table, all about the curfew which was on at night, staying with Ranchit and how surprisingly comfortable the bed was. Anne did not comment until Hilde said, rather gauche: 'I think Anne is very broad-minded to let you go out with Ranchit.'

'Why?' asked Anne.

'Well, he's quite a Casanova.'

'By the way,' said Anne, addressing John directly for the first time that day, 'would you like to visit the new road tomorrow? Paul Redworth and Father MacCullough are going with Mr Menon, and we've been asked.'

'Oh, that is so fine,' said Hilde. 'We went once before Vassili got into the jail. We stayed in tents with the Madrassi Army Engineers who're building the road. They give you wonderful South Indian curries.'

'I don't think I want to go,' said John. 'I had enough curries when I was in Madras twenty years ago.'

'All right,' Anne had answered.

So now, the next morning, Anne said to Father MacCullough: 'John's sorry he can't come, he's got a previous engagement.'

And then John walked in, dressed in a woollen suit, shaved, carrying a suitcase. 'Good morning,' he said, 'glad to see you, Father. Would you care to join us for breakfast?' He ignored Unni.

'No thanks, I've had my breakfast,' said Father MacCullough, whose jaw had literally fallen with surprise at John's appearance. 'What about you, Unni?'

'I'll have some coffee,' said Unni, and sat down, Father MacCullough sat too. There was no awkward silence for Unni turned to give his order to the bearer, and then said: 'I think we shall have a clear day, hope you've got your camera, Mr Ford. There may be some good pictures.' He made small talk about the Hotel, while John ate eggs and bacon and toast, spoke of the poultry farm that the American Mission was starting, and the bee-keeping project which had fallen through 'because the bees didn't seem to like the hives, although they were scientifically designed to please any bee'; urbane, casual, he kept Father MacCullough busy anecdoting, embroidering the spun web of the genial, pointless conversation with extra information, thus forcing John to listen, mastering the occupants of the table, making them accept his presence through this subtle mastery. He did not look at Anne, but when she had finished her coffee gave her a cigarette and lit it for her with that dexterous long-fingered way of his, and then picked up her Shan bag and said they must go to the Residency to collect Paul Redworth, who was coming with them.

There were two jeeps waiting, a driver in the second, and pleasantly Unni flashed his teeth and said: 'The Resident will sit in my jeep with your wife. I hope you won't mind sharing the second jeep with Father MacCullough?' And 'Not at all,' replied John, hypnotized. He and Father MacCullough sat in front of the second jeep with the driver, their luggage was stowed behind. Unni put Anne's Shan bag in his jeep at the back, covering it with a tarpaulin.

At the Residency Martha Redworth, in a red flannel dressing-gown, was listening to General Kumar, dressed in his usual lounge suit but with a pink flannel band round his middle. The General was telling her and Paul that Sharma and Vassili would be released from jail the next day. 'According to my best information, madam.'

'How splendid,' Martha was saying. 'Oh, I do hope it is true. Wouldn't it be wonderful, Paul? Hilde must know. I'll go right over to see her.'

'We might go on a picnic to Mount Phulchoah on Sunday, if Sharma's fit,' said Paul. Paul wore a pair of real Tyrolean leather shorts, hand-knitted wool socks to his knees, a Tyrolean befeathered hat was on the settee. 'I only hope it is true. Where did you get the news from, General Kumar?'

'From my enemy, the Great Rampoche of Bongsor,' said the General. 'I despise His Preciousness, but he has nearly always the correct view of the scenery, the vile bandit.'

'Oh, come, come,' cried Father MacCullough, 'you mustn't be intolerant, General. He's not a bad chap. He gave me and a couple of friends from Minnesota a lot of hospitality up at Bongsor last year.'

'That miscreant would,' retorted the General. 'He has a toe in every custard ... ask Colonel Jaganathan of the Indian Engineers if you do not believe me. He tried to sell him one of his nieces in return for priority in a contract of stones for the road.'

'It is true that the Great Rampoche has a finger in every pie,' said Paul Redworth, replacing the General's version by the current idiom.

'Unni here probably knows more about him than anyone else. The Monastery of Bongsor is very near to where you're building the dam, isn't it Unni?'

'A few miles from us. I do have dealings with the Great Rampoche. A very powerful man.'

'Did he ever try to sell you one of his nieces?' said the General.

'Oh yes, three times,' said Unni. 'Two of them were quite attractive. The last one a blonde with blue eyes.'

'He owns houses of disrepute in Calcutta,' said the General. 'And with all the lamas going up and down the passes to and from Tibet, smuggling comes naturally. He is my enemy,' said the General, 'ever since our fathers duelled twenty years ago.'

'Over a niece, of course,' said John.

'Not at all,' said the General haughtily. 'My father had all the women he wanted. It was over the jawbone of a whale. My father and the Great Rampoche's father were in London at the same time; they heard of a whale brought into Liverpool by a whaling ship and went to see it. My father fell in a passion of affection for the splendid jawbone of the beast, and offered a large sum for it. He wished it taken back to Nepal, and as you know, at that time there was not even a steel cable over the mountains, but only porters, men carrying things for us, the Ranas, up the steep paths of the mountains. My father picked the best men to carry the jawbone, and he also had a great many other things besides. When they arrived in Khatmandu everything else was accounted for, but the jawbone had disappeared. My father immediately suspected the Great Rampoche, and though he had the porters whipped twice he could get no information from them. So my father went to Bongsor with a small army, but the Great Rampoche also had an army, and the end was carnage without a jawbone. Hence we are enemies.'

'What a pathetic story,' said Paul Redworth.

'My father was somewhere an artist,' continued the General, 'and his chief fear was that the Great Rampoche, not appreciating beauty but utility first, would chop the jawbone up into small pieces and sell it in China as rhinoceros horn, and you know the price of rhinoceros horn even today. It is the most spanking aphrodisiac on the market, when ground and taken in wine, banishing impotence like billy-ho. And that is why the present Great Rampoche, his son, and my father's son, are enemies,' finished the General, rising and shaking hands all round, ready for departure.

'What a wonderful chap the General is,' said Paul Redworth enthusiastically as he climbed into the first jeep with Anne and Unni. 'Wish I had the strength of mind to wear a pink flannel cummerbund outside my trousers. Wool inside gives me urticaria. Well, good-bye old thing,' he cried, waving to Martha. 'We'll be back tomorrow. Poor dear, she's so happy when I go off, and she can just potter about in the garden.'

They flashed over the pink roads lined with pink brick houses and fields. There were kingcrows upon the trees, and kingfishers upon shrines and sunbirds red upon the telephone wires; bricks still grey drying in mounds in the fields, hedges green and white and pink and yellow and mauve, all the colours of spring, delicate and vigorous at once. They passed Kirtipur, where Deepah had kept Eudora an afternoon, and after five miles encumbered with files of porters, women doing worship, goats, sheep, cows, pi-dogs, wedding processions, and holy men in a trance in the road middle, utterly unaware of jeeps or anything else, they arrived at Thankot, where the foothills and the new road from Khatmandu to India began.

In a few minutes, all about them were hills, a disarray of splayed out, soft and crumbly, micaceous ridges, swinging, rising and falling. The road curved and twisted, ascending all the time. At first all the slopes were fields, lentil shaped, descending like giant stairs to the narrow gully-like valleys below, still filled with morning mist. But as they rose the fields gave place to brush and then to trees, and these got thicker, and on turning a corner the slopes were covered with great masses of red flowers rolling up and down among a green sombreness of leaves. These were the rhododendron trees. There were little twisted paths strewn with loose stones between the slopes, nearly vertical, hanging above them as they roared past; and on these, here and there, woodcutters, chiefly women and little girls, with oval baskets with a strap across the forehead, and heaped upon the wood, a pile of red rhododendrons.

'They lighten their load with the flowers,' said Unni to Anne.

There were workers sitting breaking stones here and there in small pyramids. The road was in places just freshly laid stones. Among the Nepalese workers were the dark South Indian overseers of the Indian army, in khaki, and gang foremen, Gurungs of the hills, recognizable by gold earrings and embroidered black caps upon their heads. The road swung ever upwards, cut sheer in the cliff, and the raw face of the cut showed its layers, grey and flecked with mica, and somehow porous ... it looked as if there were cushions of air between the layers, and the layers themselves were frittered. At a corner there was what appeared a slip of grey stones like granite, but when the jeep wheels went over it they yielded like mud.

'Why, these hills are friable,' cried Anne.

Unni said 'Yes,' with a nod. He was driving fast, swinging round corners swiftly, and soon they looked down on many hills crowding like untidy flocks rolling sheepish backs around them, and the road could be seen twisting and turning in and out among them like a lasso. It was funny, looking at this thin strand, a decision of man, a decision hung in mid-hill between summit and base, surrounded by a world of ravaged rock. It was like a knifecut in butter, round which this rolling, indecisive, unsolid land wavered and crumbled, ready to let fall a cliffside upon them at any moment. The folds round which the road ran, in and out, had something fluid about their outlines, their thrust and fall was unpredictable like the toss of the wind shredding the mist below them. A stronger blast might dispose them otherwise, and then the puny road would veer, displace, and disappear. It was easy to see now that cutting a road through this land was not easy; for the rock was friable dust in the dry season, and pouring mud in the monsoon. It could begin to fall round them in fine ash, in grains, in pebbles, and then in larger rocks and in boulders, boulders heavy and hard yet still washable to mud. And later, after rain, a whole hill might pour itself down, sliding down upon the road, sliding upon the crescent fields, sliding into the valley, and losing itself, a red-brown ooze covering the fields, the ochre farmhouses, everything. And behind this fluid earth another hill would rear itself.

They stopped at a small pass, looking down into yet another valley spreading round them with fields and farmhouses, and a stony river bed right at the bottom which would be a torrent in the monsoon, and Anne picked up what looked like a piece of granite and crumbled it easily in her hand.

'Gigantic mudpies, aren't they?' said Father MacCullough.

They all got out of the jeeps, John took pictures, and Father Mac-Cullough had an acute urge to unburden himself of some geological knowledge. 'Weathered gneiss, that's what it is ... look at what the engineers had to do over there, to keep that hill from collapsing upon them.' He pointed to where two hundred feet of good stone stood against the hewn bare face of the rock, a wide, large wall, holding up the hill. 'That stone had to be quarried from forty miles away and brought here,' said Father MacCullough.

'Colonel Jaganathan will tell you that the secret of a good road is drainage,' said Unni. 'Drain, drain, and drain. Don't let water accumulate anywhere. He's put culverts everywhere he could, I believe. For after rain these hills swell and explode soddenly. Let's have some beer.'

The beer was ice cold, and they drank it, walking up and down.

'I'll pick some rhododendrons on our way back for Martha,' said Paul.

Swallows speckled the air, swinging in and out of the valleys, and crowds of little sunbirds came and went, and there were cuckoos calling each to each.

They drove again, the jeep clinging to the road as it wound, climbing still, roaring peacefully, powerfully, and trailing its little brown dust cloud behind it. They came upon bigger groups of workers, as the road bed here was being laid and the parapets built. And as they drove on, the road began to hypnotize Anne, the everlasting unwinding and looping and turning and twisting and Unni next to her, driving surely and swiftly, incorporate to the road and the jeep. She felt herself melted, fluid, also belonging, as he did. He knew the hills, gauging them, adjusted to the folds, giving in easily and reverently, fitted as to the body of a beloved woman, with inner consciousness which is vision and knowledge. And so she became conscious of him as a man. A man driving who sat easily the jeep, a rider sitting a horse, easy and light. Sometimes the jeep tilted and she was thrown against him, and felt his hard, lean thigh like a rider's, and she who for some years had found physical contact with men irritating, did not find it so. Every time was this impression of competent compact hardness, taut yet easy, and once as her side was thrown against the leather jacket of his arm she imagined his arm pressing a little against her; but then she was swiftly ashamed, and flushed, for he was holding the gear

173

in his hand, and it was she felt fortuitous contact and pure imagination on her part; and from then on she was careful, leaning towards Paul instead, not to touch Unni again. The jeep was going over the wide, squashy loop of a recent landslide, over which a bulldozer was working, planing and smoothing and pushing the mud and soft earth until it slithered in great lumps down the slope. The hillside showed the fresh, red scar where the earth had fallen away; a raw surface, like a granulating wound, and a little lower, like sponge cake. And she thought: if there was going to be another landslide now, he and I would know it right away. First a little fine mud-dust, dropping from above, and then, *wreplam*, the whole side of the mountain falling down, and she wanted to laugh, it seemed so funny to have a mountain fall upon one. But it happened, it would happen again, and the puny-looking men with picks and shovels clinging to the slopes, or in groups breaking stones, or the dark Madrassis standing and looking up, they knew the little roll of pebbles coming down, which meant a yell and *run for life*.

They stopped going up and came down again, into a small valley, the first camp of the Indian Army Engineers, an assembly of tents and small stone edifices on a kind of platform. There were lorries parked, and several jeeps. Their vehicle swooped into the camp.

'Ah, Jaganathan,' shouted Unni.

'Good morning,' said Colonel Jaganathan, 'have you brought the beer?'

'Three cases,' replied Unni.

If Anne had thought Unni dark, the Colonel was even darker; a pure, silken ebony. The sun upon his skin shimmered and split in little rainbows upon his bare arms. He emitted an almost blue gloss. Next to him was the tall blond young man, Mike Young, who had been talking to Rukmini at the wedding; he was the American engineer in charge of the American-built road which began further down in the Terai and climbed into other valleys.

'I thought I'd come over and see what you people are doing,' he said in his pleasant American voice. 'I'd hoped you'd be able to pick the rhododendrons on our road next year, sir,' he said to Paul, who had a rhododendron in his Tyrolean hat, 'but at the moment all our work's been washed away. Yes sir, the American road is at the bottom of the river right now. The whole cliff fell away with it, flat slap, into the river.'

'*Atcha*,' said Unni, 'I didn't know.'

'What a disaster,' said Father MacCullough.

'It would be one anywhere but in Nepal,' said Mike Young. 'Here that means we just start again, eh Colonel?'

Colonel Jaganathan grinned as he led the way to some chairs placed in a circle round a table, and offered beer or gin and a wash to everyone. 'It's happened to bits of our road too,' he said, 'and Unni here will tell you how he lost a large bite out of his waterworks the other day.'

'It was Mana Mani, the Wayward One again,' said Unni. 'But we'll tame her one day.'

The sun spread a loose, warm texture of happiness round them. Several other officers, young men, had joined them, and all the men were talking of the Road.

'My,' said Father MacCullough, slapping the table, 'I can always remember the day the Colonel brought in that steam roller in an airplane. That was a good story.'

'And do you remember the day the Minister of Transport was caught in a landslide and had to walk twenty miles up the road in full kit?'

'By the way, any trouble with your labour down here?' asked Father MacCullough wisely, putting his head on one side.

'Not now. But there was some trouble at the beginning, d'you remember, Mike?'

'You mean when the Nepalese stoned you at the airport?' said Mike Young to Unni Menon.

'Why not?' said Unni. 'They've got a perfect right to resent being helped.'

'There are always political agitators of one kind or another,' said Father MacCullough to Anne. 'They tried to rouse anti-Indian and anti-American feeling, in all sorts of ways. They said all these projects were for killing the Nepalese men, and taking the women away to India. They said they didn't want a road, or dams, or schools, or anything, as it meant that we wanted to occupy Nepal. They say all this Aid is really to annex the country and turn it into an American airbase or an Indian colony.'

'They've got the hang of the cold war psychology,' said Unni.

'At first the labourers were frightened of working for us,' said Colonel Jaganathan. 'They called us Kaffirs. They said we were black and ate human flesh, like the goddess Kala Durga.'

'Last year,' said Unni, 'when we started blasting, we had a good deal of trouble. They said we intended to cut all the water off, and starve them. And the Rampoche of Bongsor told them the gods of the river would revenge themselves and send a plague on top of a flood. We had quite a mutiny on our hands.'

'When we pushed the road over the Chandragiri Pass,' said the Colonel, 'I had to offer a sacrifice there before the labourers would start. They said the gods of the pass would be offended otherwise, and kill them. So I had to execute a chicken publicly.'

'I haven't had to do that yet,' said Mike Young.

'Your turn will come,' said the Colonel. 'They'll probably make you kill a water bullock. That's tough work, cutting off a bullock neck with one stroke of the kukri, you'd better start practising, Mike.'

'The Colonel's chicken, by the time the tidings had reached Khatmandu, had grown into twenty helpless virgins,' said Paul.

Thus the talk went, half serious, and then became more technical; of machines and men, landslides and bulldozers, and weathered rock and ways of mixing cement, and frost-bite in the cold of the mountain passes. And how no compensation was given by the Nepalese Government for the land taken in building the road, and how wretched the labourers were, though the Indian Government was paying three times the regular wages, and one thousand rupees compensation for any life lost, 'but what will happen when the road is finished, and thousands of labourers find themselves starving, no one knows'. And when the road was built, it would need maintenance crews otherwise it would disappear in three monsoons, and the Nepalese had no one to maintain it.

Anne listened, rocked by their words, happy that they had forgotten her, her eyes going from one speaker to the other, and Unni looked at her, and she smiled at him, sharing her pleasure, and he smiled back.

And then Paul Redworth said: 'Well, we must be getting on.'

They got back into the jeeps, climbing up and up. In one place there was a little shower from a cloud and the labourers went huddling in groups under umbrellas, five or six of them, like monkeys, with their backs outwards and the fronts close against each other, and one in the middle holding the umbrella above them all. As they climbed the vegetation changed. There were now pine trees and oaks, and the wind singing a strong tune among them, and lichens and mosses, and it became colder, until they had crossed a pass at nine thousand feet and come down again amid the long shafts of the afternoon sun like golden prongs, and in sight of their camp for the night at a place called Lamidanda. And as they roared among the tents it was suddenly very cold. A booming wind, with the noise of trombone, suddenly pelting sand, was upon them in a moment.

'Just in time,' said Unni happily, 'we're going to have a thunderstorm.'

Paul, John, and Father MacCullough hurried from the jeeps. The wind threw large handfuls of sand and gravel in their faces.

'This way,' shouted a young Indian officer, and they found themselves in a small concrete structure, with a fireplace, some easy chairs, some magazines on a shelf. It was the common-room for the officers of the Engineer Corps living in this camp. Now the shutters were being closed. A fire of logs was lit in the room. Through the window Anne could see the sky suddenly change from turquoise blue to bronze, and then it was as if a huge black carpet was rolling up, blotting out everything, and soon it was pitch dark, with thunder and livid strips of lightning blazing and crackling all round them.

The young officer who seemed in charge of arrangements now asked them if they would not like to go to their tents and have a wash and change. Unni had disappeared already; going outside Anne could hear his voice; he seemed to be telephoning. In a file they went, each one had a small tent, but the wind had blown sand inside each, and it was bitterly cold. An orderly brought Anne a pail of hot water and she washed her face and hands, shivering; she had brought a coat with her, and a change of clothing, but it was too cold to undress and she kept on her clothes and hurried back to the common-room. Nobody else was there and she crouched by the fire, warming herself. There was a hurricane lamp swinging from the ceiling. Then the door opened and in came Unni, and the rain, sudden, shouting, in sheets, sweeping in through the door.

'Lovely storm,' said Unni, and walked to the recently closed shutters and flung them wide open. Through the door came umbrellas with Father MacCullough and John.

'My God, couldn't we shut those bloody windows?' said John.

'I just opened them,' said Unni. He stood in front of them with an air of intense happiness. It was as if suddenly that slight distance and formality which until now had muted him, at the wedding, and on the way down, had dropped away as the rain fell. Anne crouched nearer the fire, trying not to show she was cold, and then just as suddenly as the rain had come it went, rolling down.

'The storm is now going towards Khatmandu,' said Unni. 'They say a rainstorm thus, just before the Feast of Siva, is a good omen.'

'Oh, indeed,' said Father MacCullough politely. He too was cold and stood toasting his back at the fire. 'Tomorrow's the Festival, isn't it?'

'Yes. We'll be back in time to see it.'

Anne involuntarily rubbed her hands.

'You must be cold,' said Unni, surprised. 'I'm sorry, I forgot.' He shut the windows. 'I love storms so much, I forgot you are not used to the cold.'

'It's all right,' said Anne. Her facing was burning now. I must have been sunburnt on the way, she thought.

Several other officers came in, and Paul Redworth, who, now revived with a whisky and the fire, discussed lengthily with Unni the customs of elephants. And then Colonel Jaganathan and Mike Young arrived; they had been in the storm and seen it pass.

'It was as if the heavens were being rolled up,' said the Colonel. The rain had been very heavy though brief, and they'd been lucky, no landslide on the way to the camp, 'though no one knows what has happened behind us'.

Anne was tired now and so was Father MacCullough. As to John, he looked grey and worn and kept very silent. But in true Indian fashion Unni and the Colonel were now completely relaxed and ready to go on talking all night. But dinner arrived early, chicken curry, very hot, South Indian fashion.

'Oh, my poor stomach,' said Paul Redworth *sotto voce*, and was relieved to find there was an alternative dish of mutton chops and omelette, as well as a sweet afterwards. Anne was very hungry and loved chillies burning her inside, and as she ate her tiredness ebbed, and she found herself laughing and talking with the young Indian officers. Soon after Paul Redworth made a signal to retire.

In each tent was a soldier's narrow iron bed, with its mattress and sheets, and one thin Army blanket on top. The tent flaps were closed but it was colder than ever. Anne shivered, and debated for a moment whether to ask for another blanket. She went out. After the storm it was icy dark, in spite of small, far, glittering stars and a hard, brilliant crescent moon. In the tent just beyond hers she heard Unni and the Colonel and Mike Young talking. No one was in sight. A sudden shyness overpowered her. She had only to cough outside the tent, say: 'Excuse me, may I have another blanket?' ... or grope outside in the dark, up the slope to the common-room ... but she felt she could not do it, and in the end she did neither of these things, though she could never understand afterwards why she had been so shy. She put her coat on the bed, and the Shan bag, and under the coat spread all the clothes she had, and shivering got into bed in her pyjamas and a pullover on top. At the last minute she remembered she had a pair of woollen socks in her Shan bag, and she put them on. It took her some time to get a little warm, and all night she woke up, off and on, feeling the cold. But at last she fell sound asleep, sleeping till the bearer came in with the tea at six-thirty in the morning, crashing the tent flaps open on to a world of terrible splendid brightness.

Sand-strewn, in the morning, the narrow iron bedstead, the sheets, the Shan bag; all visible, and all covered with damp sand.

Sand in the hot water pail brought to Anne. Now she could strip, wash, change, the water running sandily on the sand-strewn tarpaulin floor of the tent. Her face was hot and burning and painful. Sunburn. Her hair was stiff with sand, the brush was brown after brushing.

Outside the sun was a bright heap of sand, the white tents, and forget-me-not blue sky, and ridges and crests with green pine trees all standing a-tiptoe, robustly; and under her feet a large green valley with a stony, sandy river going on and on, and twisting behind a hill; and a blue-green haze, flat, on the horizon, and beyond it an ochre haze: the Terai, the Nepalese jungle strip and hunting ground, and beyond that India.

The Colonel was up already, on the terrace of the common-room, sun-drenched, with Paul Redworth, Father MacCullough with binoculars, and John, who smiled at her wistfully, tenderly, and said: 'I nearly came in to see how you'd slept.' His face was drawn and pale as if he had not slept at all.

Anne thought: goodness, I've forgotten him completely until now, ever since the storm. She had these lapses, now, writing in the parakeets' room, or teaching the girls, or walking in the sensuousness of the sun-filled Valley. But it had not happened at night before, for with nightfall she returned to the common, conjugal bedroom. Soon I'll forget that I'm married to John, she thought, and the thought amused her pitilessly. She felt less about him at that moment than about Paul or Father MacCullough, as if John was some stranger about whom none of her emotions had ever wrapped themselves. She looked at him, detached, wondering whether he would ever again precipitate in her those turmoils of helpless, useless emotion which manacled her to her marriage; and then Unni came up the steps, in a bush shirt and with bare arms and looked at her face and said, with deep surprise: 'You're peeling.'

And suddenly everybody round her began to laugh and laugh and laugh. And in the swift exultation of laughter everything joined, the mountains and the toppling sky and the camp round her and the faint peter of the work lorries, and somewhere, boom boom, the echo of blasting was also deep laughter of the hills. In exultation's shell, her skull, container of this mirth, she repeated: 'Now I understand ... now I know,' felt hovering on the threshold of a vast glad knowledge, a beholding of happiness, of which this laughter was the bell-peal of warning echoing round.

They had Indian *dhosis*, baked flat cakes, for breakfast, made with flour and onion, light and savoury, though Paul Redworth stuck to a standard English breakfast. John had rallied, was now talking and laughing frequently, his face bright red, asking questions about the road and the camp from the Colonel, and every now and then turning to Anne.

'We might do a bit of walking,' he said, 'go straight down by those mountain paths and rejoin the jeeps lower down.'

'In winter,' said Colonel Jaganathan, 'our workers get on their spades and ski down the slopes.'

Then it was time to get back on the jeeps, and Unni turned to Anne and said: 'Would you like to drive?'

'I don't think I could, I've never driven a jeep. And not on a mountain road.'

'Then it's time you tried.' He went round to the front of the jeep and said: 'Jump in. It's yours.'

'Is Anne going to drive?' said John, and began to laugh.

'Yes, Mrs Ford is going to drive,' replied Unni, smiling.

'Well, well,' said Paul Redworth, climbing in with a fraction of hesitation. 'Have you ever driven a jeep before?'

'Never,' said Anne, very loud and clear. 'But I'm going to.'

Unni sat in the middle between Paul Redworth and Anne. 'The road's clear,' he said. 'Blow your horn round the corners, as you never know when a lorry may be driving up and those Nepalese drivers never blow *their* horns. That's all. The rest you'll do easily.'

'But it's a left-hand drive, and she's never driven anything but a right-hand drive, and she's not good with a car,' said John, still laughing, but with irritation.

Unni looked at him speculatively from his seat in the jeep. 'Go on,' he said to Anne, 'start.'

Coming with Unni the road had looked difficult, but they had winged over unmade portions rough with boulders and stones, pot-holes and narrow places where small slips had dented the road-bed; but now, driving herself, Anne felt every pebble. The jeep tilted and she had an uncontrollable urge to throw herself inwards and away from what she had not noticed until now, the precipice, a few thousand feet down, which bordered the road all the way.

'It didn't look that far below us yesterday,' she managed to say between clenched teeth at one moment, and Unni replied:

'I rolled two hundred feet down one day and I'm still here.'

She swerved too quickly and Paul Redworth on the other side uttered an exclamation of fear as his shoulder grazed an overhanging rock.

'That's all right, there was an inch to spare,' said Unni. He himself appeared completely happy, he had no hat on, his dark hair was ruffled, his leather jacket open, both his arms enveloped the two seat backs on either side of him. 'I like this,' he declared. 'It's relaxing.' He closed his eyes.

'For heaven's sake keep your eyes open,' implored Anne tensely, 'I'm frightened.'

'I thought you enjoyed this,' said Unni.

'I do, but I'm scared.'

'Can you sing?'

'Not very well.'

'It's awfully nice to hear singing up a mountain road. I'll sing to you then.' And suddenly, effortlessly, he began to sing a Nepalese song, and it was the song that Rukmini had sung in jail; then he sang another, then whistled it, looked at Anne, and said, 'You're doing fine.'

They were climbing up to the pass, and at a turn Paul said: 'Ah, there they are, the snow peaks.'

'Where?' said Anne.

'Don't look now,' said Paul. 'Stick to the road, lass.'

'We get down just below here and have a rest and some food and look at the snow lords,' said Unni.

Further down they stopped, got out, and climbed a hillet upon which was an upright concrete slab on which had been engraved:

TO THE MEMORY OF
THE OFFICERS AND MEN OF THE CORPS OF
INDIAN ENGINEERS WHO LOST THEIR LIVES
BUILDING THE ROAD

Round them in an immense arc, bounding the rim of the world, were all the snow peaks in their rifts and folds, watchful magnificence in being and in name.

'Breath-taking, breath-taking,' said Father MacCullough, and with binoculars he and Paul started identifying them, reciting their names: Dhaulaghiri, Manaslu, Nanda Devi, Himalchuli, Annapurna, Gosainthan, and suddenly Paul said: 'Look, look, there's Everest, I'm sure.'

Small and grey between two nearer and seemingly larger peaks, with a grey spume which was the snow blown off its top by the eternal wind, was Chomolungma, Everest.

They had sandwiches and there was more curry, in containers, and coffee in Thermos flasks.

'There's no doubt about it, Indian Army hospitality is magnificent,' said Father MacCullough. 'I'm so glad I came to see the Road. It's going to make all the difference to Nepal having some means of communication other than a daily Dakota. Bring the price of food right down I expect. Incredible, isn't it, to think there's a perpetual food shortage in the rich valley of Khatmandu? By the way, I celebrated Mass and gave Holy Communion to the officers this morning. Quite a few of them are Catholics. Did you know that, Unni?'

'No,' said Unni. 'But I know you're always hoping that I'll become one.'

'Of course,' said Father MacCullough. 'I'm sure Our Lord will find a back door to Heaven for you Unni, Catholic or not.'

Unni lay the whole length of his body on the ground, in the sun. 'Just shift a bit,' he said to Anne, who was sitting bolt upright next to him, 'there, so that I may have your shadow over my eyes. Ah, wonderful.'

There was a cold, cutting wind up above, but on the slope where they lay it was windless, the sun beat down and soaked into their bones. Paul put his Tyrolean hat over his face. John, who had gone a little further among the Indian oaks and the holly scrub, now came back, looking ill, his face mottled.

'What time shall we be back in Khatmandu?' he asked.

'Round about evening,' said Father MacCullough, seeing Unni did not answer. 'What's the matter?'

'I think it's a touch of indigestion, or the sun,' said John. 'I'd like to get back early. I think you'd better let Menon drive from now on,' he said, addressing Anne. 'We've wasted quite a lot of time getting here.'

'But I do not wish to drive,' said Unni agreeably. 'I love being driven. If you want to get back earlier, why don't you let the driver take you back first and we'll follow?'

'Yes,' said Paul Redworth quickly, 'I think that would be a good idea, if you're really feeling the sun.'

'Oh please,' said Anne to Unni, 'I don't want to drive any more, really. I'm too scared.'

'Nonsense, m'dear,' said Paul gallantly. 'I enjoy scraping the cliffs with my right shoulder.'

'Mrs Ford always leaves at least four inches between the wheel and the precipice,' said Unni gravely. 'We're quite safe in your hands, Mrs Ford, and beside you may never have the opportunity to drive on an unmade mountain road again.'

'Well, I'm not going to stand here and listen to all this claptrap,' said John loudly. 'Are you coming with me, Anne? I want to get home quickly. I don't feel well.'

Anne looked at him stonily. 'All right,' she said.

But Unni was up already. 'If you're feeling as ill as all that of course I'll drive you home, my dear chap,' he said, and managed to fit a world of insult in the sympathetic phrasing. 'You'd better lie down at the back of my jeep.'

'I don't want to lie down,' said John. 'I'll be quite all right sitting up.'

'Then Mrs Ford, do you mind going with Father MacCullough?' said Unni. 'Your husband will sit in front with Mr Redworth and myself.'

'All right,' said Anne.

Unni now went whizzing round curves, reflexes incredibly swift, avoiding potholes and stones and oncoming lorries as if by miracle, and soon leaving the second jeep far behind, whose Indian driver smiled at Anne with great pride, saying: 'Sahib, top class driver, top class body.'

The cliffs exuded a deep pink glow slowly turning to mauve, and the valleys were filling with blue shadows as they approached Thankot, and fell among pilgrims, a sea of pilgrims, suddenly filling the road, issuing from everywhere, flowing towards Khatmandu.

'SIVARATHI,' yelled the driver.

'The Siva Festival,' interpreted Father MacCullough unnecessarily. Over the past two hours he had made observations on the geology, the history of Nepal, on personalities he knew in Khatmandu and who were of tremendous and first-class importance in stemming the tide of communism and likely subjects for Anne's pen. Like many Americans abroad, Father MacCullough had the mild and understandable defect of judging, of seeing people of a certain mental or social status not as human beings but as personalities to be manipulated as bulwarks against Red Aggression, or shunned as vanguards of communism in Asia.

But there appeared to be something on his mind, a corrugation of perplexity upon his sunburnt forehead. Anne had lapsed into that daze, that mute and nearly hostile silence which so often enveloped her, made her self invisible, her words reluctant monosyllables. But inwardly she was a turmoil of incommunicable, smouldering pleasure and pain and total awareness, which made her remember all the colours, the birds, the curves, and the sounds of the hills, and now another pure delight of the senses, the jeep honking slowly as it plunged into the flood of pilgrims. Pilgrims in grey and saffron and green and gold and amber and magenta, with earrings and nose ornaments and sticks in their hands and their faces transfigured, their eyes upon Khatmandu; and the veils and the robes falling lovely as the folds of the hills, and here and there the last flash of sun on a copper pan, and all beginning evening blue around them. They walked, an army on naked graceful feet in the bronze dust, and among them small crowds of goats with anxious eyes and hooves, stammering across the way, shepherded by no one; and to be in a jeep among the living walking was sacrilege.

One day, thought Anne, I will take off my shoes and walk with the pilgrims.

Transported by the same ecstasy, a believer? something sang in her, mockingly.

I don't know, she replied.

'Now I expect you're worried about John,' said Father MacCullough, unaware of Anne's silent disputation with herself. 'I'm sure he'll be all right. Prayer always helps.'

'I'm not worried,' said Anne truthfully.

Father MacCullough did not believe her. It was conventional to be worried about one's husband or wife, even if husband and wife could not stand each other. Even Eudora worried about old Fred. Eudora had come to the priest, tearful, two days ago. She'd had a long talk with 'Oh, such a nice man, Mr Menon. A dear.' He understood her so well. Arranged for her to meet some famous Indian singers, and would also extend her visa. But he'd asked her *not* to try to see her husband for a few days. 'I'd so like to explain to Fred ...' she'd said, she was worried Fred would not understand, and 'he ran away, ran away when he saw me,' and the tears had gushed down her face. But she'd promised Mr Menon she'd be patient, wait until Fred came to her. ...

'Marriage is a wonderful thing,' said Father MacCullough. 'The holy union of man and wife, *nothing* comes between, whatever people may say or do. That's the mistake a lot of people make, Mrs Ford. They think that when everything's over, as they say, they can divorce ... but there are things no amount of legal jostling can sever, only death. I hope you'll give Mrs Maltby your sympathy and help if you have the time.'

'Of course,' said Anne, absent-minded, and meaning to do nothing at all. And then they spoke no more, for the jeep was wading among pilgrims, and it was at a crawling pace that they arrived at the Royal Hotel.

As Anne went up through the hall, between the rhinoceros heads, Fred Maltby was coming down the steps.

'Hello, Anne,' he said. 'My, you're sunburnt.'

'Yes.'

'I've just seen your husband,' he said, lightly. 'There's no need to worry, none at all. A temporary gastric upset. He'll be right as rain in a few days. By the way, Unni left me a message to deliver to you. If you wish to see the Siva Festival at Pashupatinath tonight he'll take you.'

'I don't know if I can,' said Anne uncertainly, 'if John is ill.'

'Oh come, come,' said Fred Maltby with medical testiness, 'you mustn't pamper him, you know.'

'I don't,' said Anne, surprised.

'Well, I suppose not, but I don't see *how* he can object to your going for an hour or so to the temple to watch the pilgrims go in and out. Quite a throng. It will be very interesting for you, as a writer I mean. Pity you won't be allowed in the temple though. They don't allow Christians inside.'

'I doubt if I am one. I have no baptism certificate.'

'Well anyway, do try and make it. It's worth the effort. And Anne?'

'Yes, Fred?'

He put a hand on her arm. 'Remember,' he said, 'we all need help, we are none of us invulnerable. We need other people, sometimes. I'd think it a privilege if I could help you.'

She looked at him, half smiling. 'I'm one of those dumb animals, you know,' she said lightly.

'I know. Not a word. But sometimes we need to break out. What are you trying to do, punish yourself for what?'

'I've just had two wonderful days,' said Anne unsteadily. 'Yesterday and today. Let me hold on to that.'

'Right. Who am I to talk, anyway, with Unni having to take care of my wife for me?' said Maltby bitterly. 'I must go now.' And abruptly he left.

In the room John was sitting up in bed; he had had a bath and looked cheerful, rested, and not at all ill. He greeted Anne with a full, blue-eyed look and an uncertain smile, and she immediately suspected some treachery.

'Dr Maltby told me you had a gastric upset.'

'Yes. Very slight. I'm really quite tough. I'll be as right as rain in a few days, right as rain.'

'That's what Fred said.'

'I must say Dr Maltby was very prompt. I've had a bath and my bowels have worked. All these curries, oily stuff. Absolute poison. I've had some light food and now I'm going to take my sleeping tablets, and go off to sleep. I couldn't sleep last night in those wretched tents. Everything was full of sand.'

Anne stood up. Oh God, she thought, it's worse than ever. I can't even look straight at him any more. I loathe him. Yes, I loathe him, she thought fiercely, delightedly, and the thought admitted gave her composure, a narrow, obstinate watchfulness.

'Have a bath, you look filthy, you've got sand in your hair,' said John, jocose. 'We both need an early night in bed, I think. You look fagged out.'

'I thought I'd go out and watch the Siva Festival for an hour or so,' she replied.

'Out again? My dear Anne, you're insatiable. We've just come back from two hundred miles of bloody road, and back you want to jump in among a lot of vermin-ridden pilgrims.' He laughed, so artificially that Anne wondered what was the matter. 'Why not relax, just once, have a good night's rest in bed?'

He patted his pillows playfully, lay down with a blissful sigh, shut his eyes, mimicking beatific sleep.

Oh God, thought Anne, at the same time realizing she'd never invoked the Deity so often, please, please don't let me give in now. Not to this kind of thing. How many times do I have to learn that I cannot go on all my life tied to this, feeling this constant repulsion, of every moment, every gesture, every mood, good or bad?

'I'm going to the Festival,' she repeated, a little too defiant.

John's eyes opened slowly. He looked at the ceiling. 'Don't shout,' he said, 'I can hear you. You're going to the Festival. You've only just come back, I'm ill, in bed, I've had an injection, at any moment complications may set in, I could die, and all you want to do is to run out again, after Dr Maltby no doubt. You saw him in the corridor and you fixed it up with him.'

'Oh, don't be silly,' was all Anne found to say. Why is it that in the middle of these stupid, pointless, off the mark scenes which kept recurring between John and her she could only give stupid answers back? It was nearly automatic. Like those children squabbling. You did, no I didn't, yes you did.

'Well, let me tell you,' suddenly John erupted into the customary violence which was his way out of these scenes, 'if you go out you can stay out, I won't have you back. I don't want a tart for a wife.'

Anne walked out of the room. She had scarcely closed the door when something heavy slammed it. John had thrown his shoe against it.

She walked down the corridor in darkness, to the Ladies' Room, favourite refuge of her boarding school days, and shut the door. It took her a little time to collect herself physically, but when she had done so she found herself glad, breathing evenly. She was going to the Festival. And she need not hurry now. She would take her time. And tomorrow ...

I'll ask Hilde for another room, she thought. I don't care what people think. I won't stay with John any longer.

The light was bad and as she came out of the Ladies' Room and into the dining-room to look for Hilde she bumped into someone, who said: 'I beg your pardon?'

It was Ranchit, alone.

'Ah, Mrs Ford, so nice to see you. I heard feminine footsteps and I came out to see who it was. You know Vassili is out of jail tonight? We don't quite know the exact time but Hilde has gone to the jail to fetch him. I think it will be quite late. My government likes to release prisoners round about midnight, it makes less commotion with relatives and the family welcoming them back.'

'I'm so glad,' said Anne. 'Yes, I heard.'

'Won't you have a drink with me? I guess where you come from. From our dear invalid upstairs. May I say that you look charming? A trifle perturbed, but charming. Kiss, oh kiss those tears away ...'

'I'm sorry,' said Anne, edging away, 'I'm in a hurry.'

'Oh, not now,' said Ranchit in surprise. 'John surely can't think of it now, for a few days. Doubtless it came as a shock to you. But you're a lady of the world. I think I will have the woman severely punished,' he said gravely. 'Severely. I am a very powerful man, you know, Mrs Ford. I can still command the services of many devoted followers. She shall be whipped for it.'

Anne stared at him. He now grabbed her arm and led her to a table in the deserted dining-room at which he had been sitting. There was a bottle of whisky and several small bottles of soda water on a tray upon it.

'You must not blame him, Anne ... may I call you Anne? You have been Anne in my heart many days now. You are enchanting, you know, Anne. I am, myself, a poet at heart, I care not for these foolish young girls. A woman like yourself, with wisdom, maturity ...' his hands went up her arm in a standard gesture, then his fingers raised behind her ear, searching for the sensitive, nerve-ridden exquisite spot to rouse.

Anne stood, rigid, unflinching, seemingly unaware of the hand upon her neck. 'You mean John has had a woman and now he's ill?'

'Of course. Five days ago, and again three nights before yesterday. But it's only a minor ailment, I assure you. One injection usually clears it up. Please do not blame me. I told him not to trust Suriyah, she is quite low-class, but ... why talk of such things? Here, in front of me, is a most lovely blossom ...'

He withdrew his hand, which obviously had had no melting effect upon her, and put it back round his glass, and took a gulp, lustfully eyeing her, a manner which he thought would achieve what the hand had not.

'Good night,' said Anne, and walked out, so swiftly that by the time he had got to his feet she was down the stairs and running across the garden and out into the road. For a moment he thought of pursuit, getting into his car, ordering the driver to follow while he would

shine the lights upon her, keeping the lights playing on her body ...
But there was plenty of time. With so many pilgrims about the
streets, it might be difficult to find her ... he poured himself another
glass of whisky.

Anne walked through the gates of the Girls' Institute. The building
looked deserted, but a few lights were about. She went round the side
and was in the smaller garden, past the rose arbour. She crossed the
lawn and saw a dark figure standing on the steps of the bungalow.

'Unni,' she said.

'Yes, Anne.' He looked even taller in the darkness, and from where
she stood she could feel the warmth of his body radiating from him.
And suddenly all pain was gone, and time stretched, timeless, beautiful.

'How did you know I would come here?'

'As my friend General Kumar would say: one guesses,' said Unni,
moving his head from side to side. Anne burst out laughing.

'Aren't you going to invite me in?' said Unni. 'I assure you I have
no sinful intentions. Just so that the bearer and the maidservant I have
engaged for you may begin their duties?'

'How do you know ...' began Anne, then shook her head. 'What
duties?'

'Cleaning the place, up and downstairs. Looking after you. Cooking, preparing tea or coffee, washing your clothes, running errands. I
know you live at the Royal Hotel, but you come here often, by day,
in the evenings, to work I think. The General likes you enough to
insist that you should be looked after properly. Don't ask again how
does he know ... there are the invisible, the anonymous human
gadgets that one forgets ... bearers, servants, room boys ... like the
proverbial monkeys, they know and see and hear all.'

'I didn't realize that,' said Anne.

'It happens everywhere,' said Unni, 'only here it is more evident.
The Valley is small, and everything is brought together, gods and
men. From now on you will be protected, I think. These two' – he
indicated two figures in grey, crouched beyond the bungalow, waiting – 'are trusted servants of the General. He wants you to have them.
You must pay them, of course, ten rupees a month each.'

'Ten rupees,' said Anne, 'why, it's ridiculously cheap.'

'Human labour is cheap here. In Nepal a labourer is only paid four annas a day. When the Indians on the road paid twelve and sixteen annas a day, there was quite a commotion. They were accused of pampering the workers. And tomorrow there will be a driver with a jeep for you. Whenever you want him just say *jeep* (a very long ee), and the servants will fetch it.'

'I can't take this from you or the General,' said Anne.

'Why not? This was my bungalow,' said Unni. 'And it still belongs to me. I'm the rightful owner, not Miss Maupratt. Right up to those trees, under which I'm told you often sit. I wish the place to be looked after. You may want hot water for a shower, you may want to have a friend to tea here, on this lawn, where it is so pleasant in spring and autumn, under the walnut trees, looking at the mountains. You may even consider one day asking *me* to have tea with you here.'

Anne sat on the doorstep. Unni leaned against the door. He took something out of his pocket and started to throw it up and catch it in his hand.

'Is that a coin?'

'An old coin, a charm. I've had it since I was a little boy at school. I keep it always on me. I play with it when I think hard. At the moment I am thinking very hard.'

Anne laughed again. 'You say such silly, simple things,' she said, 'and I think it's funny, and I laugh. Only ...'

'Only what?'

'Only nothing. I'm all mixed up at the moment.'

'I can't detect any confusion,' said Unni, 'except sand in your hair. Guessed rather than seen. It will be very cold soon and you've come out without a coat, as usual. Shall we go to the Festival now, since you're not opening the bungalow?'

'I haven't got the keys. I left them in the hotel bedroom.'

'Then you will allow me to give the bearer a duplicate set, which I have on me.' He extracted them from his pocket and called the bearer, who proceeded to unlock. 'What a shock for Isobel if she knew that all this time I've had the keys to her bungalow. How her fecund imagination would seize upon this to conjecture the worst. And now the bungalow is all yours. Shall we go now to the Holy Temple of Pashupatinath?'

He helped her to rise, took off his leather jacket, and put it round her shoulders. Underneath he had a soft woollen sweater.

'You think of everything,' said Anne.

'Almost,' said Unni. They stood looking at each other, then he took her hand gently in his.

'Come, let me guide you to my jeep.'

In the flickering burnt gold shadows of torch flare the pilgrims were beautiful and frightening. They filled the roads and the lanes between the houses. The jeep went slowly, at a man's pace; and round it the milling pilgrims at first jostled, then seeing a man inside it a few of the younger boys began to put their hands upon it.

'Climb in,' said Unni, and in a moment the jeep was a mass of pilgrims, laughing as they settled at the back, or stood on the running board. There were many torches about, and many other jeeps, lights on, nuzzling and honking their way through the dense crowd. They went down the cobbled uneven lane and parked a little way from the Temple, for it was now impossible to drive. They walked, or rather were pushed by the pilgrims around them, till they reached the golden main gate of Pashupatinath, the same gate from whose threshold Fred Maltby had fled at sight of Eudora.

The gate seemed impassable, for the press going in and out; two soldiers guarded it to prevent desecration by Christians or tourists trying to get into the holy precincts of Pashupatinath. The courtyard inside was lit with torches and fires, and the huge golden bull, the steed of the Lord Siva, upon his seven-foot marble pedestal, glistened and shone in the various lights, as did the hundreds of gods carved and gilded upon the beams, the copper finials, the carved ornate walls, and doors of gilded copper. Up the pyramidal tiers upon which rose the main Temple steps was a pullulation of pilgrims; and everywhere the double pulse of drums, the wail of flutes, and the fresh and deep singing voices; and with the music and the fires a windfall light upon everything, it was like being in an ocean, an ocean of golden light and music, a world of its own.

'We are going in,' said Unni. 'But first, are you a Christian?'

'I don't know.'

He hesitated.

'Oh,' said Anne, 'I do not wish to commit sacrilege.'

At that moment, in that soft, ethereal way which he had, General Kumar materialized near them. He also had come to worship, and spoke to them without preamble.

'All the Valley is here, and nearly a hundred thousand pilgrims from India have come in and gone out of the Temple in the last three days. Would you like to come in, madam? It would be a blessing upon you for ever.'

Anne looked at Unni.

'Are you a Christian, madam?'

'I don't know,' said Anne. She saw her mother, in pink, climbing from the rickshaw. She saw Isobel Maupratt's mother, heard the voice of History ... 'I don't really know whether I am or not.'

'She has the reverent spirit,' said the General to Unni. 'Let her take off her shoes and go in with you.'

The soldier barred the gate to Anne. 'She is a white woman,' he cried to Unni and to the General.

'She is my woman,' said Unni. The soldier hesitated, looking at Anne's face quickly, then at Unni.

'All right then,' he said, 'if she is yours.'

Anne took off her shoes. She wore no socks, having forgotten the only pair she had, worn because of the cold in the night before, in her Shan bag in the hotel room. The ground was wet with water, strewn with flowers and petals crushed in the mud. They went in, stepping over the high lintel of the gate, and immediately Anne was lost, lost in the way she and those of her kind have, in that awareness which makes people round them call them absent-minded and forgetful and children still. She was plunged in this new consciousness where vision and hearing was all, in which there was total forgetting of self, the body moving without knowing itself in movement, wholly transported in this same ecstasy, the tranced concentration which here made her one with all the thousands gathered. She forgot Unni and the General, her naked feet, and where she trod. This was the instant of Siva the Lord of Death and also of Birth, poised between an unmoving dream and the sole moving moment, time timeless, the unending point in space and time which is eternity, beginning and end, when knowledge becomes self-knowing, when one learns, at last, to eye-witness what is seen, to stare with utter sober passion at the most ordinary things as well as the most uncommon, to become rather than acquire, to know impermanence permanent, and deceitful immortality only the selfish echo of man's memory.

And so she went, not knowing the stones underfoot, across a small maze of lingams, each one strewn with flowers and grain, and with pilgrims queueing for devotion from one to the other. Along covered area-ways, cloisters of stone, sat groups of women, singing and dancing, their bracelets and heavy anklets tinkling and their heads crowned with flowers. Like a bronze statue in the light of a fire of burning pine branches stood a naked man, with a thick mane of hair, stained yellow like a lion's mane and streaming down his back, and the body of an adolescent Mercury, holding a trident, staring in adoration towards the main Temple. And in a carved stone alcove sat a man with his body dyed all blue playing on a flute, for he thought of himself as an incarnation of the Lord Krishna, the blue God of Love and Laughter, and a cluster of pilgrims round him. Next to the golden bull with its head raised towards the Temple were men in white loin cloths, round another bonfire, singing and playing small drums and wooden instruments and steel rings and clappers, and blowing on clarinets like shawms, and the fire flickered fantastically upon their bearded apostles' faces as they chanted: 'Ram, Ram, Sitaram,' the shadows of their moving arms were thrown about them, and the logs of the wood spurted and sizzled, still full of the live juice of the tree.

And though there were thousands there in the courtyard, yet each was alone in his own worship, bent, drawn inward in the sweetness of his own preoccupation with his God, his personal adoration; and out of each individual, like a small lamp at a festival, came his own intent faith, until all together the Temple blazed with light and rang with the clamour, like the internal tide of the sea, of the unharnessed multitudes which would never merge, because they were, in their multiplicity, the universe and the essence of the One. Pilgrims eddied, swirled, shifted in the vast courtyard, and Anne became a particle in the movement like a tidal wave which bore her, first round, and then irresistibly to the Temple itself, and slowly pushed, up the steps, inescapably now, towards the yawning open copper door.

Above her bent the gilded gods, in all their multiplicity of faces and arms and hands, a numbering now essentially simple, for all that was single and divided was not a part of a whole, but the whole itself. It seemed to Anne so clear that as each man, human, is a crowd, each with various aspects and powers, traits evil to some and good to others, so it must be in all that lives. For we only knew others through our relationship with them, and that relationship is a fragmentary affair, mutable, various, not revealing all but the part we call all, because it is all that is possible in that one particular relationship and we remain ignorant of the rest. No man is a monolith, and not to admit his many faces, complexities, uses, contradictions, is to reject the reality of the man. As she went up the steps she saw them all, those she had known, in an instant flash, her mother, Jimmy, John, Isobel, all, like the gods above her, infinitely diverse in their humanity. It was this complication, this intricacy, many-layered, faceted like the single eye of a fly, which was the essential hallmark of Oneness. Life never reproduced twice the same leaf, the same ant, stone, the same face, and permanence was only achieved through change, just as eternity was only the birth of new things out of old and dying ones. Perhaps Christianity was confused deeming immortality a static, imperishable continuation of a single identity, thought Anne, resigned and absorbed and carried up the steps, and suddenly finding herself, squeezed against others throwing flowers and shouting with gladness through the open door, coming into the Temple itself. In sudden compunction she stepped aside, pushing herself out, in a seizure of reverence for the faithful round her, those who really believed, while she did not know. She had no right to go in. She had only time to see, like a vast mirror face, the huge gaunt stone, four sides carved, upraised, glistening with water poured upon it, strewn with flowers, and down she was again among the dancers and the singers and the ecstasy round the steps singing, that life and the power of life was wonderful, and death but the gateway to life. Or so Anne felt, until it was suddenly much quieter, and the General and Unni were with her, walking out of the Temple.

They found their shoes where they had left them, and put them on, Unni taking a handkerchief from his pocket for Anne to wipe her feet. She meant to say: You think of everything, but he said 'Almost' before she could say it, and she smiled as he answered her unspoken thought, and squeezed her feet back into her shoes.

The General went a little way with them in the jeep, then abandoned them. 'I am going to discuss the betrothal of my friend's daughter to her tree,' he said, and melted into the darkness in the silent way he had.

'Another wedding?' said Anne.

'A betrothal. Perhaps more important than a wedding. Among the Newaris little girls round eight years old are betrothed to a tree, the Bel-tree, so that they can never become widows. Hence they've never had suttee or such cruel customs because, technically, a girl or woman's first husband being a tree, the others are supernumeraries. And the tree is not allowed to die, that is prevented by cutting it off and throwing it into the river.'

'What an agreeable arrangement.'

'Yes. Unfortunately the Ranas, their rulers, follow Hindu custom, and their women are not so happy. But the Newaris of the Valley seem to have solved all the riddles of contradictory creeds and their petty cruelties very well. That's why all the temples and gods here are so mixed up. There are Hindu gods in Buddhist temples, Buddhist saints in Hindu temples, and many shrines and gods have several identities and names. It makes life easy, tolerant, and sane. Words, names, and their symbolic limitations, no longer fetter, they become interchangeable, and you can call reality what you will. I hope that people of such tolerance will be able to acquire the mechanics of progress very quickly, without losing a sense of humour about its absurdities.'

They rode on. Unni whistled the tune he had sung that day, Rukmini's song; a faint melody underlining the silence of the streets, near deserted now that all the pilgrims were at Pashupatinath.

'It is so strange,' said Anne.

'What is strange?'

'That so much happiness here, in a day ... when I have known whole weeks, whole months in my life and nothing's happened ... and now, every minute is crammed full of meaning. Look at today for instance.'

He said nothing for a little, as if waiting for her to go on; then as she stopped, he said diffidently: 'Human contact is full of the power of giving life. It is the only way.'

They were nearing the Royal Hotel. It blazed with lights, laughter, the music of a party going on. Vassili was out of prison and celebrating, and All-Khatmandu was there.

'Vassili loves a party. He gives magnificent ones.'

'I don't think I want to go to a party now,' said Anne, 'much as I like Vassili.'

'You are tired?'

'Yes ... no.' How could she tell him? The exaltation, the marvellous moment at the Temple, were subsiding gently, but they had changed her. Or rather, the change begun with the word Khatmandu had now proceeded irrevocably, until even Anne herself knew she could never turn back. My identity, she thought. Like the gods, like the many-armed, many-faced goddesses, she was someone else of herself. And to that she would be faithful now. She remembered John. She did not feel she wanted to lie in the bed next to him and pretend to sleep again, but she would do it tonight, there was no other way. It was something to be done tonight, but it meant nothing, no annoyance any more. There was tomorrow.

'Shall we drive round,' said Unni, 'if you do not wish to go into the hotel now?'

'No, you must be tired too.'

'I am never tired.'

That was true. He was never tired.

'Well, I'd better go,' said Anne. Tomorrow, she thought, I will move to the parakeets' room. Tomorrow.

She turned round to say good night. Unni was looking straight in front of him.

'Thank you.'

'There is no need. I am going back to the dam tomorrow.'

'Yes.'

'I'll be back in about three weeks. I fly there, it's about fifty minutes by air, though it takes two weeks by mountain path. May I come to see you when I return?'

'Yes.'

He climbed down from the jeep and helped her out.

'Good-bye,' she said. He nodded and stood for a moment as she went up the stairs. She did not look back.

At the top of the stairs she fell headlong into noise, laughter, clamour, voices, music from Radio Nepal, and the gramophone. Isobel with History and Geography, Major Pemberton, all the Americans, the Irish girl, Pat and Ranchit, Martha Redworth and

Paul, Hilde gorgeous in a blue sari, and Vassili superb, who ran and embraced her, and put a glass in her hand. Everyone seemed to her to be screaming words at the top of their voices, words completely incomprehensible to her.

Isobel came up to her at once. 'Where have you been?' she asked; she was full of authority, powerful, wrathful even.

'To the Siva Festival at Pashupatinath.'

'But John's not well upstairs. I went to your room to fetch you. I found him ill in bed.'

'Yes.' What was the use of explaining, defending, justifying? Isobel's eyes looked full at her, then she turned on her heel scornfully.

'I say,' said Major Pemberton, 'quite a crowd down there at the Temple.'

'Yes.'

'Oh, did you go into the Temple?' said History.

'Yes. I took off my shoes.'

'Indeed? Fancy doing that! And they weren't stolen?' she added incredulously. 'I should have thought they'd disappear in no time, unless you hung on to them.'

'I think I'll go now,' said Anne, moving from them.

Vassili shouted: 'Anne, Anne, come back!' But she shook her head and walked away. They would destroy, kill the beautiful moment with their questions exuding meanness. Not Vassili or Hilde, so happy now, but the others. And she wondered that the world of the blind, the narrow-grooved, should have such power to shatter the bauble of the beautiful and the alive. But it was so, and Anne, dragging her feet up the steps, back to the room with John in bed, knew then that it had always been so; that she herself had compromised with the never-enchanted, the ruthlessly dull, who were frightened of beautiful things and wanted the whole world cut to their small, niggardly measure. She must stop coming to terms with them, or she would become like them. Tomorrow, she thought fiercely, tomorrow. There was a refuge all made, and this time she must truly go to it, believing in herself, and not in others. She must go where there were parakeets among sunflowers laughing, and the exquisite agony of all-seeing eyes, seeing what people tried to hide even from themselves. What did it matter that in subtle irony it was another woman who had painted them, that it was the product of love disenchanted, perhaps of a curious despair? The gods in their careless wisdom had given this to her now, and she must use it.

'Tomorrow I will move.'

She got into bed. John did not turn. It was only towards the grey morning, waking up, that she remembered she had not even washed her feet, and they were caked with the dry mud and crushed flower petals, and God knows what else besides thought Anne, feeling that Isobel would disapprove, and History and Geography talk of germs and dirt and spit, and this made her so happy that she fell asleep again, until the winged sun was full upon the courtyard and upon the circling, cooing, clattering doves.

PART THREE Way Up

> Before my highest mountain stand I, and
> before my longest journey, therefore must I
> first descend deeper than ever I descended.
> NIETZSCHE: Thus Spake Zarathustra

Chapter 1

APRIL was come to the Valley, with risen sap and oratories of leaves; with roses, hyacinths, irises and bee orchids, gentians and yellow double jasmine; with shadows lying subtle and moving upon the hills, and love strong as a man of war among the birds; and matching these machinations of spring was the hurry and bustle, among the humans and the gods, in preparation for the King of Nepal's Coronation on the second of May.

Perhaps the birds should come first, setting the tone of exuberance, the rapturous energy which animated other beings in their different motivations. The birds filled the Valley with effervescent laments of love, paeons of straightforward passion, and their minstrelsy made the words of men seem futile, as the complicated lifelessness of mirrors is futile, screening but not being the vivid world of substance, mountain-rimmed, sun-blossomed, bird-enchanted.

The crows went about, scolds of the air, filled with strident alarms, voracious and quarrelsome. Their tearing voices in no way ruffled the harmony of the Valley. All day long the lorikeets screamed chee chee chee, the orioles poured warbles of defiance. The paradise flycatcher, in silver with long silver tail, frolicked a loud singsong near the airfield. Sunbirds, colourful like gems round the necks and wrists of the Maharanis, rioted in rebellious mobs. Kingcrows attitudinized and kingfishers glowed at the fields below them. Among the rhododendrons went jaunty tits, and bulbuls meditated everywhere. In the peepul trees of the market place, at the gate of the Taleju Temple, fifty young egrets swayed delicately on long thin legs, and the small breeze that sent the bells chiming ruffled the white-gold feathers on their heads and breasts. Kestrels and barred eagles poised like small black suns in the sky. Parakeets, in spurting trails like windblown leaves, went calling in great excitement across the gardens. And nowhere was there fear among the birds, but boldness in song and presence.

It was April and the time of expeditions up to the peaks. Vassili, restored to freedom and to the Royal Hotel, was immensely busy.

'As soon as I've got rid of the mountaineers and the spring army of tourists there will be the newspaper correspondents and the photographers and the Coronation official guests. ... I don't think I shall live through all this. Perhaps I had better go back to jail. But next time I take a good sofa with me. For Hilde.'

The language, apparel, and behaviour of the climbers was as various as the song and appearance of the birds. There were Japanese, climbing Manaslu; Argentinians, Swiss, Frenchmen, Englishmen, come to reconnoitre future attempts; a Texan expedition, led by a bona fide Texan in oil, to look for the Abominable Snowman, complete with an entourage which included a publicity agent who wore a mink coat and high-heeled shoes. There were free-lances, self-styled climbers, fed and housed by Vassili, and who afterwards classically forgot to pay.

'Never mind,' said Vassili, 'these chaps really were broke.'

'Vassili, we'll never be rich,' said Hilde.

'Never mind, my little one,' said Vassili, 'it will be given back to us in the Valley of Paradise, I don't think.'

And round the tables on the verandah of the Royal in the warm springtide of Vassili's happiness and the postprandial content of sumptuous food (for the Royal Hotel's two Madrassi cooks turned out better *caneton à l'orange*, meringues, soufflés, *bombe Alaska*, than could be found anywhere else east of Suez, including Saigon), there would be loud talk of arêtes and glaciers, of crampons and cwms; and humorous gossip, of how the Swiss, prosaic ever, stolid even in triumph, had come down from the summit in a blaze of reporters and photographers, and the immortal words they found to say were: 'Oh, it was quite high.'

The Japanese had more cameras than men, and more spectacles than eyes; were charming, polite, and paid, 'which,' said Vassili, 'I am no longer accustomed to.'

The Irish girl and a few of the other unattached lady-artists at that moment in Khatmandu attached themselves to the Argentinians and the French, and red-hot passions sprang and died, in the fashion of the ephemerae, and nothing as constant as among the birds, in a matter of hours.

And then there were the usual spring hitchhikers, artists of course broke, young men and women in love with sunburnt faces and no money, experts, savants who called themselves professors. Vassili fed them, boarded them, forgot to charge them, loaned them money, and sometimes in part-payment received gifts of paintings, unpublished manuscripts, or other works of art, bric-à-brac, which accumulated, along with Rana portraits, tiger pelts, hunting photographs, unclaimed letters, and unpaid bills, at the Royal Hotel.

But overshadowing all were the preparations for the Coronation of the King.

The diplomatic circles of Khatmandu became each and every one involved in tragedies of protocol, precedence, and diplomacy. Who would attend the Coronation as representative of each country; in which order of precedence they would walk; upon which elephant and in whose company on the elephant's back they would be in the solemn pageant of the Durbar after the crowning; where they would sit at which banquet or function; what orders, medals, decorations, honours, would be presented to whom, when and where; and which would be returned upon the breasts of who and how; who would be lodged where and for how many days and would there be enough food for the lot?

Every diplomat of Khatmandu, and all the first, second, third secretaries, and trade and cultural attachés went round with the harassed and intent look of birds in search of a mate. ... There would have to be a great deal of deft timings.

A Chinese Vice-Premier and a Chinese Ambassador from what was called in Khatmandu 'the real China' would come as official guests, for Nepal had now recognized Peking and there would be presentation of letters of credentials from the Chinese Ambassador to His Majesty the King at the Durbar Hall; the fifty-strong United States Point Four Mission must not be seen anywhere near the Chinese Delegation at any function, cocktails, dinners, garden parties. The State Banquet would be a nightmare in protocol and etiquette and seating. It was reported in quarters hostile to the Americans that the Nepalese were aggrieved because they felt that only a Vice-President of the U.S.A. could be the equal of a Vice-Premier of China, and they did not know the name and had never heard of the intended U.S. Representative, who was said to be merely a university professor, and professors abounded on the verandah of the Royal Hotel. On the other hand, rumour in the vicinity of the U.S.I.S. Library affirmed that the Nepalese were aggrieved at the Chinese because they, the Nepalese, had issued invitations to the Dalai Lama and the Panchen Lama of Tibet to attend the Coronation, and the Chinese would not let them come; replying that both the Lamas were in too delicate health to venture through the Tibetan passes at this inclement time of the year.

The Embassy of another Western country was now reported in high disfavour because of a religious *faux pas*. His Majesty the King of Nepal was at first reported due to receive a very high Order from that certain Western country; but then, most untactfully, this was cancelled because the Order in question was only given to Christians, and could definitely not be given to heathens, and the King of Nepal was a Hindu King. This was enough to rouse the dormant passions of racial and religious bitterness: was not one religion as good as another, just as one man was as good as another man, whatever the amount of pigment his skin contained? 'We are not blinkard heathens,' said one of the Secretaries of the Foreign Ministry coldly at the Royal Hotel, unconsciously quoting Swinburne. The unhappy Representative of the said country took to his bed with a severe diplomatic illness until a formula could be reached.

Paul Redworth looked harassed and had bags round his eyes. 'My dear,' he said to Anne, 'how I wish I were the French Ambassador, our lucky, charming, erudite Count Ostrorog, whose Gallic civilization enables him to be at home anywhere, and especially in this Valley. For here prurience and prudery, Kinsey and Freud, and all those other unhappy and lugubrious products of the Teutonic strain in us Anglo-Saxons do hamper one a lot, don't you know. We are never at home anywhere because we are not at home with ourselves anyway ... old D. H. Lawrence, God rest his soul, was only too right about us, "with our moral itches and our virtuous hypocrisies".'

But Count Ostrorog had no such handicap. 'How I pray to the gods to be a Nepalese in my next incarnation,' he had exclaimed fervently and with such unfeigned delight that the Nepalese had immediately known him a brother in spirit and flesh, and gone on liking him for his zest for the food, his appreciation of the carvings, his respect, courtesy, and erudition.

'He is civilized,' they said.

And Count Ostrorog would not be embarrassed by Christian or

non-Christian medals. He would give the *Légion d'Honneur*, and everyone would be happy.

Three weeks before the Coronation diplomatic frenzy had reached a peak of confusion. Despite the efforts of all the local embassies and diplomats, the Nepalese Government, whose Ministries functioned in a huge edifice called the Singha Durbar (a palace to out-palace all others, with such a complexity of rooms and corridors, wafting a strong ammoniacal odour, that it was impossible not to get lost in it), had not produced one date, one hour, or anything vaguely resembling a programme for the Coronation. Nothing seemed planned at all.

'They never send an invitation for any official function until the very day of the function, and even then the invitation card sometimes comes after it's over,' said Enoch P. Bowers, quoting Isobel. Enoch had nominated himself President of the Valley Club (John was the Secretary, Ranchit Treasurer, and Pat Vice-President), and in this capacity was hoisting himself into invitations at all official functions and to the State Banquet as well.

The only diplomats to remain unruffled were the Indians. Seasoned in haphazardness, they knew the best of plans altered by rain or natural calamity, and the astrologers busy interrogating the stars for an auspicious minute for the crowning. There was no reason to worry unduly; everything would happen in due course. And the hair-trigger suspense in which the coming Coronation was wrapped, as the Ultimate Reality is hidden from us by the Mist of Appearances, did not disturb them. But this happy fatalism was not shared by the Western colleagues of the Indian Ambassador, who found it very trying not to be able to produce schedules for their governments, and therefore the small Indian post and telegraph office was kept uncommonly and wastefully busy with frantic cables and counter-cables, with coded orders timing and mistiming functions, and yet other cables cancelling all previous cables, until even the Indian patience of the operators became exhausted by the sound and fury of the Westerners.

'Wait till the newspaper correspondents come, it will be a hundred times worse,' said Vassili to them consolingly.

No one knew what the Chinese were up to. Although the Chinese are maniacally tidy, and this fanatical orderliness was now worsened by a political theory which thought it could sweep minds as tidy and clean as it regimented bodies, yet they seemed strangely unruffled. It was known that the Chinese Representatives would arrive a few days before the Coronation. They would stay at the Royal Hotel. It was said that the Point Four Mission would avoid meeting them at all, an injunction difficult if not impossible to carry out. Vassili wondered whether he could find a Chinese cook in Calcutta.

'But suppose the cook is a Nationalist and something happens?' said Hilde. Vassili's enthusiasm ebbed.

'Don't take life too hard, my dear fellows,' said the Indian Ambassador to his colleagues. 'Everything will be *perfectly* all right. I know our Nepalese friends. You will see, at the last minute everything will fall into place.' And suavely his sensitive hands made a silken gesture of appeasement. To no effect. The Westerners rampaged, the burden of their lament inefficiency, carelessness, lack of organization, muddle of the Valley, their prophecy disaster.

'May is the driest month of the year. There won't be any water. Not even to drink.'

'Why, there isn't a stick of furniture in the Government Hostel. Not a bed.'

'There's no petrol.'

'Where will the transport come from? There are only ten taxi-jeeps in Khatmandu.'

'They've just had another landslide on the road ... the supplies will be held up for days.'

'No, they've cleared it now, but they're only allowing ten lorries a day up the road.'

'There are only ten lorries in the whole of Nepal, anyway.'

'There won't be any water to drink,' said Isobel firmly.

Isobel scrounged a bathroom from Vassili's last consignment. History and Geography roamed the market place and wrote to friends in Calcutta and went to Gaucher Airfield every day to receive parcels of tins of food. 'Prices are going to soar, my dear, there'll be a dreadful shortage of everything.' Miss Suragamy McIntyre produced a fiancé who was a Christian (he attended hymn singing), who had very curly dank hair, and who told Isobel he could purchase some petrol for her in the name of the Institute because there would be an acute shortage.

'I'll want about fifty gallons, I think that'll be enough for all of us,' said Isobel, and gave him a letter so that he might apply to the Ministry for the gallons required.

The fiancé thoughtfully added a nought and purchased five hundred gallons, Isobel received her fifty and Suragamy McIntyre stored four hundred and fifty, hoping to sell them at inflationary prices during the Coronation.

Chapter 2

Anne wrote:

THE Nepalese clean their temples and shrines, splash pails of water upon the golden gates and the bronze lions and the stone statues, and repaint the gods, for the Coronation of the King. In Khatmandu, as also in Patan, Bhadgaon, and Kirtipur, the other three cities of the Valley, there are more temples and shrines than houses, more gods than humans, and every corner of every street is studded with symbolic lingams or phallic divinities. And among the fields the shrines of the black Tantric goddesses lie, an older creed, demanding blood sacrifice.

This is the land of the gods, and here their service is the most common single activity; whereas in other regions work and human pleasure, the pursuit and achievement of human satisfactions and greeds, gear the pace of all activity, here worship takes precedence. Here more food is given to the gods than to humans, and though there is always a food shortage in the Valley, the cows and bulls are fat and the children go hungry. Here religion is not only an integral part of life, it is the first, the foremost energy-consumer. All human doing is subordinate to a divine interpretation, implicit in all actions. Birth, copulation, and death are not the cycle of the anthropocentric, sapient animal, but the material, inadvertently human manifestations of a divine eternal cycle of which all happenings in the Universe are but a reflection, straws blowing in the wind of Being. And therefore all has meaning beyond human meaning. It is precisely this notion that everything is sacrament: eating – a communion; sexual intercourse – a marriage; and death the final, exalted adoration; that has become alien to us. Perhaps we need to remember it sometimes. Michael Toast, the young Englishman whose sexual advances are so unsuccessful, puts it in the language of our non-divinity conscious world: 'The place drips with sex and religion and the two really hang together.'

This Coronation spring cleaning, then, is first a cleaning of the gods. It seems to involve the whole population, the population which is not engaged in portering. For about half the people one meets in the

Valley seem to be porters, men and women with oval baskets held by a thong across the forehead, going in long files somewhere else than where they come from, like ants which move, yet always in the moving file are others going in a contrary direction. Some of these baskets are loaded with two tins of petrol of forty pounds each, or paper, cloth, salt, wool. The porters come up the steep paths from India, as their forefathers did when they carried for the Ranas. But others are what I should call refugees, displaced peasantry whose fields have disappeared under the floods of last year and who have joined the international battalions of the dispossessed, and now, with their goods slung on their backs by the leash across their brow, go here and there, hungry and asking for work.

The rest of the population are busy sluicing the gods, on perilous scaffolding cleaning the temples and daubing the beams with what looks like a mixture of straw and mud and cow dung and which, the General's son tells me, has marvellous cleaning properties, 'even being used by the Newari women for their hair', and painting everything that can hold colour. The painting is the most gratifying part of this renewal. In beautiful colours, vermilion and saffron, gentian blue, limpid green, ochre, magenta, and in Chinese white, effulgent and happy, the roof beam gods and goddesses look down upon us in glowing animation. And what a burnishing of bells and prayer wheels, of lions and naga snakes, of old Mallal kings of Nepal whose gilded statues, wearing hats exactly similar to that of the bridegroom at the wedding, kneel upon high pillars of carved marble. The bulls, steeds of Siva, the bird-gods or Garudas, steeds of Vishnu, the elephants, the rams, all, all are being scrubbed and painted. And the magnificent and famous golden gates with which the Newaris adorned their cities shine like the entrances of apocalyptic heavens.

'As you know,' says the Field Marshal (who knows I do not know and thus instructs me at the cost of appearing obtuse), 'His Majesty the King of Nepal is, to us, a God – as we all are in some measure. His Majesty is the incarnation of the Lord Vishnu, the second person of our Holy Trinity of Brahma, Vishnu, Siva, and the Preserver, the Continuer of Life.'

Upon the carved houses along the streets leading to the market place the new paint reveals intricate loveliness. Not one window, not one door, not one pillar is exactly like another one, never have I seen one carving repeated twice. All these lintels, pillars, cornice friezes, door jambs, window frames, are first daubed in ochre or in black, and then the carvings picked out in white, until the whole looks like starched tiers of lace standing stiffly out on a Renaissance portrait. And from the centre hollow, square or round, of these openings, the smiling and beautiful Newari women and children look out.

Yet all this carving was done by Newari craftsmen with simple rough chisels. 'The Newaris always were great artists,' the Field Marshal tells me. 'In the twelfth century our famous Newari architects, with crews of sculptors and artists, were called to China by the great Mongol Khan to build pagodas and temples and gates. There is still a gate of Nepalese design in North China, and most of the temples which adorn Lhasa in Tibet are Nepalese work.'

I must not forget to mention what our foreign colony attempts to suppress by never mentioning them. The erotic motifs. These also are being repainted with meticulous care. Perched on scaffolding tied with ropes of straw, the artist (there is no other word for the love with which he works), with a few small pots of paint next to him on a flat plank, his palette, spare brushes in his mouth, paints eyelashes, smiles on languorous lips, strawberry nipples, and does not forget the white tips of finger and toe-nails. I have remained to watch him, and he, a not too clean little Newari, small-boned and jaunty, pleased with my attention, smiles tenderly at me around his brushes, then goes on with his joyful labour, brow gleaming with concentration. At the feet of the shining gods, the humans engaged in their amatory preoccupations emerge. Some of these poses I have read of, described in those pseudo-scientific terms acceptable to us because they are written in our ponderous, apologetic jargon of science, those perennially popular books which our Western civilization produces as an index to our ignorance about ourselves: *Happy Marriage; Science and Sex; The Technique of Marriage.* Recipes, recipes for human success, achievement; in sex; in business; in making money. Do this, do that, think this, think that; eat this, eat that, copulate in this or that manner, and you cannot fail to be rich, to be happy, to achieve an orgasm, to wangle a pension at the end of your career, to get into heaven. All emphases on performances, ritual gestures, devoid of divine meaning, consecrated to the greeds of man and not to service of the gods. They teach us bigger and better, possibly more efficient magical passes and formulae, and I see now no difference save that our type of ritual is devoted to the religion of man, and the other, the Nepalese one, we call inefficient and medieval because it is still devoted to the gods who don't care about man at all. I can see no difference now between the woman who rubs herself on a lingam stone and waters it with milk and water and crowns it with flowers, and the woman who rubs a brand new kind of lipstick upon her mouth, both believing that it will help them in their heart's desire; no difference between the magic worded in pompous scientificalese which passes for knowledge, and the choir of splendid and fantastic fables about the deities; no difference between the 'modern attitude to sex' which smuggles the titillation of our senses under a heavy protective odour of antiseptic and presents it in the only guise we find justifiable for an experience – functional, purposeful, priced with a moral and a financial value – and these carvings, save that they are so much happier. We can no longer accept pleasure and beauty for God's sake, or pleasure's sake. It must be morally useful or it makes us feel guilty. The Nepalese have converted sex into a function of worship of the Deity, and perhaps that also is a way of escaping a concealed sense of guilt?

Meanwhile these smiling, elastic, pink bodies appal Isobel and nearly everyone else. Tourists go the round of the temples, wriggling uncomfortably, surreptitiously adjusting their sunglasses (why do sunglasses make one feel that one can look without the evident glance being caught by fellow tourists?). They are nervous, restless, deprecatory, above-it-all, indignant.

'Rather ... outspoken.' (Giggle.) 'I'm afraid I don't care for that sort of thing ... do you?'

'Of course not.'

The tourists pass on, like Queens of Spain, existing only from the neck up, no entrails, no belly, certainly none of *these* things. But under the artist's fingers they emerge, pose after pose, and some are undoubtedly perversions; in Patan, along a side temple, are several lesbian scenes; in Khatmandu on the façade of the old Royal Palace, now badly crumbling, polygamous ones. There is a beautiful miniature of a man making love to two women at once. But there are no reproductions of male homosexuality.

I am neither shocked nor stirred; perhaps being a woman the visual presentation of erotic scenes does not affect me; according to scientific pundits it is men who get visually excited. With women perhaps what comes first is an intuitive, an emotional upheaval, something mysterious, unexplainable, a state of mind rather than an arousal of body. I do not know what makes a woman, any woman, love a man, and without love it seems to me, as it probably seems to most women, sex is either unthinkable or a painful, mortifying experience, to be endured rather than enjoyed.

Besides the scouring and cleaning of temples and gods, other things are being done, but they are not so obvious. Now that I have a jeep, and even a driver (but I prefer to drive myself), I go about in the evenings and at night, much further than walking would achieve. I went to Gaucher Airfield last night. It was a firelit fresco of Nepalese labourers pounding stones, lorries bringing up barrels of bitumen, wood logs glowing under cylindrical tar mixers, steam-rollers gawking and purring with that familiar noise of crushing stones into a smooth surface; there was the smell and glisten of hot liquid tar poured upon them. In place of the two wind-flapped tents of our arrival there was now a small, white, concrete building. And in the middle of it all stood Colonel Jaganathan, our host of the road from Khatmandu to India. He was picking up stones and trying them in his hand and gesturing disapprovingly. I hailed him.

He turned round and I received the flash of his smile.

'Oh, hello,' he said. 'What are you doing here at this time of night?'

'Having a drive. And you?'

'Working, as you see. We're enlarging the airfield. We've got to hurry up a bit to get everything done before the Coronation. I've just discovered they've quarried the wrong stones. These are so soft and friable there'll be potholes in the metalled surface in no time.'

I got down from the jeep and walked round with him. I found him a companionable man, easy to talk to.

'We've got to finish this airport building for the V.I.P.s when they begin landing for the Coronation. And tarmac a five-mile road to Patan. And a few other things besides. Have you seen the new electric power plant?'

'No.'

'I've got to go that way. Let's drop in. All the machines have come now, and been screwed into place. In a few days we'll have much better electric light. I think it's silly, of course, to have an electric plant in the Valley.'

'Why?'

'Because we've got to import so much oil to keep the diesel engines running to *produce* the electricity, and all this oil has to come in barrels, either by road or by air, and it is awfully expensive to transport it ... whereas we could have tapped electric power off a cable from a large power station just across the hills in India ... but Nepalese national pride wouldn't have it. The politicians, as usual, had their say. They didn't want a cable line from India. Nepal was an independent kingdom. Their electric power must be independent too. Well, that's the way it is. Honour is safe, at a ruinous cost. Though I think when Menon's dam is up in a few years' time we shall probably have some hydro-electric power inside this country.'

Round us crowded the short, sturdy Nepalese, grinning; and they were all round the power station, too, staring at the grey machines, at the dynamos like couchant beasts behind their grids, at the blond German technicians bolting them in place; for these were the new temples, the new shrines, the new gods; not places to pray, but places to work; dams and roads, bridges and factories, and airfields. Perhaps the new way of worshipping the gods of life was work. If only we could think of it that way!

Chapter 3

In a tragedy my leaving John would be the climax, the spire-like summit of an ascending drama. But this is real life; and in real life something terrible occurs and no one knows. People stop, stare, and go on chewing, or weeding their garden, or reading the newspaper. Perhaps it is me; I lack a tragic sense, just as I lack a self-defensive attitude, an armour, and find myself wounded, with astonishment, later. A comic handicap. Because I cannot throw the operatic high note at the conventional climax I find myself imbued with a sense of guilt, as if mistiming reaction was also an index of felony, of hard-heartedness. It was so when there was the baby. I felt nothing, except a vague guilt about the baby, until now. How strange, John's and my baby, when John is now a total stranger to me. And I've had to wait nearly a week before being able to write about leaving John.

Let me try to describe that Sunday morning six days ago, when I left my husband. It was the Sunday morning after the Siva Festival at Pashupatinath ... oh, how entranced I am again, pierced with arrows of delight, at the memory of that hour away from myself in the lights among the fires and the pilgrims! That morning I rose; washed myself in the bathroom, cold water, then warm water, and then cold again; I went on and on, lapping the water, the lovely running water swimming like a silver fish upon the skin of my arms and my belly, and thus I became acquainted with each particle of my body in a way I had never been before. This was my body, particular, intimate, unique, given to me, impermanent and the only habitation I would ever have. I had forgotten it for so long. This was my body, and rubbing it dry, I knew it awake and clamorous. There could be no more traitorous half-sleep, no persuasion of appeasement. This is my body. I stood drying myself, looking at it in the mirror. I saw it young still, elbows and clavicles and hips pointing in a deceptive adolescent angularity ... but however flat the stomach, clean the thighs, there was a lack-lustre about it, an incipient aridity. The thin white scar in the belly's middle was hardly visible now. Well kept, no sag anywhere, no fat, and with walking in the sun an Amazon flavour. But looking I said, 'I'm dried up.' Dryness within. This was my body, house of me. Perhaps I had a soul, somewhere, but it was not separate from this my body, it could not function apart from this mirrored flesh, and further than the mirror I would not look any more. I dressed, went back into the bedroom, and started to pack.

John was lying still, too deep a stillness for sleep. I packed two suitcases and my Shan bag. I opened the door, put the suitcases in the corridor. I closed the door. The room bearer was standing in the corridor. He took the suitcases without a word. We walked downstairs, perfectly timed conspirators who had not even consulted each other. It was very early, no tourists were about, only the bearers, hands and feet, eyes and ears, and they all knew I was going away. Sitting against the walls near their toasting charcoal braziers reading their English primary readers (for they all want to know English now), they smiled at me. Some in the dining-room were listening to Radio Nepal. They asked if I wanted coffee. They spoke softly.

'No coffee, but I would like a taxi,' I said to one of them, a very beautiful boy.

'But your jeep is waiting to take you to your house, Memsahib,' he replied, surprised.

Of course. My jeep, my house. I should have known that as in a fairy tale 'my' coach would be there to bear me away in time, but instead of wheeling me to a harsh cinder reality, this was where I would step out into fantasy, the dream that is, choosing deliberately, choosing my body, choosing myself.

We drove in the fresh morning, already the snow peaks were lovely living flames leaping into the sky, ice and fire, fire and ice. We passed the gates of the Serene Palace and I glimpsed Fred disappearing inside the Hospital, his walk accomplished. I remembered Eudora, vague, receding like everything else. Father MacCullough wanted me to help her, but how? I had just committed what Fred had committed many years ago; left the marriage partner, the conjugal bed.

'My' servants were there; they had not turned to mice in the daylight. There was hot water in the bathroom, and even toilet paper, stamped 'Government Issue', undoubtedly a black market scrounge, for the rolls thus stamped belong exclusively to the British Residency bathrooms.

In the downstairs room the derelict furniture had gone. There was a table, covered with a table-cloth stamped Royal Hotel, three chairs, a small brazier. Regmi, my bearer, grinned at me and rushed to the brazier to make toast.

Upstairs the room was aired, windows open, the couch made up as a bed. They had known I would come.

I took off my clothes again and went straight to bed. This was my room, my bed, my body in it. I looked at the parakeets. The sun shone upon them. I went into a dream, and Mita, my maidservant, called from the door, a soft, fresh voice, and brought toast, eggs, and coffee. I ate, I slept, I woke with voices from below.

Isobel and John were there, on the lawn. Regmi stood in front of the door, not letting them in. John was angry, shouting 'Let me pass, you bastard,' but the door was shut, barred from inside, and John started pounding on it and calling my name, 'Anne, Anne!' Isobel looked up to the window where I stood, with that agony of hunger in her eyes. I stepped back, I don't know whether she saw me. She also began to call 'Anne!', then she said something to John. They stood awhile there, then went away together.

Round me the room glowed, sparkled. I lay on the bed, body beating like a drum with fear and elation and hatred. I lay there, staring, staring at my life, at what had gone, what was to come. This was my body, alive. Relentless, irresistible, at last, the past came pouring over me, like the tide of the wind in that storm at Lamidanda on the road over the hills only two days before. And now, seeing all my own mischance, I cried a little with the pain of the lost past, yet I was sure with the knowledge that I had done what had to be. I had not wanted to look at this pain, wishing to remain unmelodramatic, sensible, to stay put. But there is no safe anchorage, no harbour for me. I must go out, alone, and live. Meanwhile, in the passage from the old Anne to the new, there will be pain, and doubt, guilt, and fear. And of course sorrow. Never mind, I would surmount them all. Looking at the parakeets, the sunflowers, watched by the deathless eyes at the door, I wept a little, but not very long.

*

Dr Maltby's out-patient clinic was on Monday, an auspicious day. Tuesday was not a good day in Nepal for starting enterprises of any kind, and few women would have come to have their complaints seen to.

Geography, distant, palely powdered with long-suffering patience (just enough to make Fred feel that she disapproved of him, but that she would continue to help him), stood in the doorway.

'No more patients, Miss Potter?' said Dr Maltby, stacking the patients' cards, engrossed and frowning concentratedly so as to avoid looking at her.

'Only a visitor, Doctor,' said Geography. 'Mrs Ford.'

'Oh –' Frederic Maltby looked up, his face lit with a smile. 'Anne. Why, do let her in.' And without waiting for Geography to do so he was at the door calling, 'Come in, Anne, how nice of you to drop in.' He was so pleased that he did not notice Geography shut the door with the suggestion of a slam.

'Thank you.' Anne looked round. 'You're very busy –' she began.

'Very. What a goose you are, Anne. I've just finished and I'm free until tomorrow morning. Do stay and talk to me. I don't seem to have had any relaxation for ages.'

'I didn't know Geography was your nurse,' said Anne.

'Geography? Oh, I see, Miss Potter. On Monday afternoons. We're very short-staffed. And she's had some nursing experience. She's a good sort really, worries a lot about the patients. Just had a note from Unni,' said Fred Maltby, to make conversation. 'He's coming back in a fortnight, he tells me, round about the 20 April. For the Coronation. I hope you enjoyed the trip on the road with him?'

'Yes,' said Anne. 'It was wonderful.'

'I hear Paul, Tiddlywinks we call him, was paralysed with fear when you drove the jeep,' said the doctor, laughing. 'I say, it *is* nice of you to come. All patients safely tucked away and Miss Potter – Geography – will see to them, and no emergency operations, so let's have tea.'

And after the tea had come, with some rather damp biscuits, he said, in his dried, physician's way: 'I also hear you're no longer at the Royal Hotel, Anne.'

Anne smiled. 'It makes it easy to start, that way. I left a week ago. You remember saying to me: we all need help, someone to talk to? This time it's me, *I* want to talk.'

'About John?'

'Yes, of course.'

'Everybody knows, in Khatmandu. Sometimes people know things before one knows it oneself. I'm sorry, Anne, but John'll be perfectly all right soon. But I suppose you're very hurt. It *was* wrong of him.'

'No.' She shook her head. 'No. If you mean his getting gonorrhoea, that has nothing to do with my leaving John. Absolutely nothing. I really couldn't care less. I'd have gone even if he'd remained what people call faithful. But of course John thinks it's because of that, and so does everyone else. It's much more complicated. It all begins really years and years ago, with me. It may sound tragic in parts, but it isn't. I suppose each one's life story can be either a comedy or a drama, depends how one tells the story – just like the gods in Nepal with their wayward biographies and their many incarnations, both good and evil. In a nutshell then: I'm cold, I'm frigid, I tighten up, I don't want to make love with my husband. I hate it, hate it, hate it with him. And now I've left him. I'll never go back to him. Not as a wife. Not if he were the last man on earth. I don't want him to touch me, it makes me sick. I'd rather kill myself.'

Fred Maltby said: 'Was there someone else before John, someone you loved?'

'Yes, there was. Otherwise I don't suppose I would have married John. I was twenty-two. It was 1944. We fell in love. Only a few months, and then Jimmy was killed, in a plane crash, during the war. I haven't actually missed Jimmy for years, I'd accepted his death, I think, long ago. For a while there is the clutching at memory, a pain cherished, more precious than the joy that was, and then the gradual self-effacement of the dead, and then, nothing. Or what we call nothing, an equanimity, acceptance.

'I was born in Asia, in Shanghai. That too has conditioned me, made it easier for me here, harder for me to understand John perhaps. I didn't know my parents well, my father died when I was very small, my mother was supposed to be a dancer. She worked hard to keep us both, and me at school in Shanghai. The Maupratt Boarding School for Children of European Parentage. Isobel was the daughter of the Principals, Mr and Mrs Maupratt. They were missionaries. Then war broke out in China, and I was sent to school in England, and there later, earning my living as a secretary in an office, and then doing war work, I met Jimmy, and it was bliss and youth. We planned to get married. Suddenly I found that I could write. I wrote short stories.

Then Jimmy died, I grieved, and wrote a book, which was published, and I've gone on writing since, the ability to pour out words which came with love for Jimmy stayed with me when he died. But I myself seem to have changed, dried up slowly, like a mummy in a sarcophagus, features recognizable, inside hollow.

'But when I married John I was still alive, still hurt and eager and wanting to do and to be. I wasn't in love with John. He said our marriage would be based on reason and friendship, more lasting than love, and I believed him. Love had been brief, with a cruel and bitter ending, like punishment. I'd been hurt, and I was too young to understand that it wasn't *love* which hurt, but the lack of it. John was older than I by about ten years. He spoke as if he knew. He used phrases which I now recognize to be mere clichés, out of books. But at that time I felt he was a good, steady person, safe and solid. He would take care of me. "You'll learn to love me. We'll be quite happy. I'm a very reasonable man," he said.

'You said you shouldn't have married Eudora. I shouldn't have married John. *Because* everyone said he was safe, stable, kind, good. Clever too, not brilliant or anything like that, but good at his work, reliable. Marrying him was an act of cowardice on my part. A retreat to security. I shouldn't have done it.'

'Everyone is a coward at least once in their life,' said Maltby. 'It is so complicated really always to know what is right. Sometimes to do right by our inmost selves seems to be cruelly wrong to others. Where women are concerned there is so much emphasis on safety, security. Women have such ages of subservience behind them. Even the best of them still get married for security's sake, or because they're lonely, and for nothing more.'

'One person didn't,' said Anne. 'My mother. I scarcely knew her. I could only remember being at the Maupratt School in Shanghai, and later being sent to England, and money coming to pay for my education, and then Jimmy, and the war. Sometimes I worried about her, she stayed in Hongkong all through the war, caught there, but it was like worrying about a distant relation. Then the war was over and suddenly I wanted to go and find out what she was like, and I said to myself: as soon as I've finished writing my book, I'll go. Then the lawyer's letter came to say that my mother was dead.

'I knew my mother was a dancer. It was something I'd been

ashamed of, at the Maupratt School, spending agonized nights there thinking myself illegitimate. Even now I remember Isobel and a few others, at night in the dormitory, sticking out their tongues at me and dancing round my bed chanting: "You're a bastard, you're an ugly little yellow bastard." To find out I was not, to find among my mother's papers her marriage certificate and my birth certificate – I remember it well because under Religion was the word "None" – was nearly a let-down, because by that time I'd got used to the idea and accepted it. And there were my father's photographs, a dreamy man, and my mother's, a dark small woman, looking straight at people under straight brows. I found their letters to each other, yellowed and faded, read how they loved each other as I thought only Jimmy and I could love. But their love was better: my mother's diary, terse, to the point, proclaimed it. She worked hard, a widow, alone, to keep me. She did not marry again. She wasn't frightened of being alone. She thought to spare me hardship by putting me away from her and her hard-working life in a "good" school, the Maupratt School, an expensive school where I was always made to feel ashamed of my mother and bunched with the very few charity cases the Maupratts took in to show visitors – "these poor girls, you know". And the visitors would say, "I'm sure they must be very happy here", and Mrs Maupratt (she didn't look at all like Isobel, but much more like Geography) would purse her pale lips and say in that flat, complaining voice of hers (she had a voice that trailed its goloshes at all hours), "I try to be the mother they don't have", or "This is a home from the homes they haven't got", and then the visitors would look at us with pity, their children grasped their hands and stared at us with incredulous horror, and we felt like murdering them all.

'In my mother's diary was an entry which hurt when I read it, as it must have hurt her to write it. It said: "Today three o'clock went to see Anne." She was out of a job at the time. "Borrowed a dress and shoes. Bought some chocolates. Arrived in a rickshaw. Anne ran away from me. She is shy, growing girl. Waited for her in the parlour. She did not come. Left the chocolates and went away." This is what I had done to her, and it must have hurt her terribly.'

Anne was now crying softly, and Fred Maltby, very embarrassed, gave her his handkerchief and a cigarette. She recovered and went on. 'There were so many other things she wrote, and each one hurt me, across the years. Of my holidays by the sea, while my mother danced in the night clubs of Shanghai, Hongkong, and Singapore. School fees, sending me to England, paying for books and a winter coat ... then no diary, not a word, throughout the war. She had not been interned, the Japanese did not seem to bother about her. But there were many letters written after the war, from people she'd helped in internment camps, passing food and letters. So it was only after she was dead that I found my mother.'

'She must have been fine, a magnificent and courageous woman,' said Frederic Maltby. 'She only erred, perhaps, trying to spare you. Perhaps one should never spare one's children. She kept you away with the best intention, to give you a better life, a better education than she'd had.'

'I know,' said Anne. 'I got over it. I wrote it all down. A collection of short stories. And I put Isobel's mother in too. I wrote them all out of me, and then I was emptied I thought, emptied of the past, the Maupratts, my mother, Jimmy, everything. I married John.

'Words, self-expression, like Christian confession, like communist self-criticism, lighten, they don't eliminate guilt. And I was guilty. I'd run away from my wonderful mother. Obscurely Jimmy's death now became partly my fault too, a queer expiation, a fated atonement. Then I met John in Hongkong. I had some money from royalties. There was nothing much to do, after I'd finished writing. I wanted to be respectable, longed to be good, to start a new, clean life. So I told myself, not knowing that I wanted security, safety, relief from emptiness inveterate as old remorse. John proposed and after a while, warning him I didn't love him, I married him. I told him about Jimmy, there had been no one else, and he was very man-of-the-world about it. Afterwards it was one of the things he used to bring up against me, time and again, saying that Jimmy must have been a weak, effeminate chap because he wrote poetry, that he had no guts. "All these Air Force people are quite unstable. That is my considered opinion," he used to say. "It's a good thing he died. You'd have been thoroughly miserable, married to him."

'I was full of good resolutions. I would be respectable, devoted, a worthy wife and helpmate, leading a beautiful life with John, as my mother had with my father. My mother would be pleased to see me happy, well married.'

'As if marriage must of necessity be a conspiracy of happiness,' said Fred. 'That's the great lie we're brought up to believe. And in yours the essential ingredient, love, body, and soul together, love was lacking. It wasn't even a marriage, then.'

'I felt lack of love was a guarantee of stability,' said Anne. 'I never wanted to be hurt again as I had been by Jimmy's death. And John had said, "Oh, you'll learn to love me, just give me a chance," squaring his shoulders and looking me full in the face with that lowering look not unpleasant then, and intolerable now.'

'You did him great wrong, and he should have known better, but neither of you were honest with yourselves.'

'There was our wedding night. There was something, something I could not put a name to, would not even take notice of, some indefinite non-reachableness between us. I told myself I was very happy, acted the willing and happy bride. For years I would go on thus lying to myself, less and less efficiently – until I came to Khatmandu. And lying made me die inside. But at the beginning there was nothing that I would not overcome with my desire, my anxiety to please, to be Wife, Friend, Helpmate ... not to begrudge body or spirit. A week after marriage I found, curiously enough, that the curtain between us was not getting less but more dense.

'I felt that it was my fault. I had never thought myself particularly attractive. The Maupratt School did not teach one to be aware of one's body except as a kind of gawky impediment in an ill-fitting uniform. Women only feel beautiful and are beautiful if they are loved, if a climate of love is entertained round them, and it was not in John to make me feel beautiful. From the beginning I got on best with him by mothering him. Mothering can be pleasant, but it left me curiously tired and irritable. Even the prelude to love-making had to be a kind of mother-act in that I had to fondle him, I had to talk to him as to a baby, and I did not like it. I wanted him to take the initiative, to be my lover, I did not want this sniggering, furtive baby-act.

'Two months after our marriage I became pregnant. I waited three weeks to make sure, then told him. "John, I'm going to have a baby. Isn't it wonderful?"

' "What?" he said. "What? What's that?"

' "A baby, John. I'm so glad, aren't you?"

'He threw his newspaper on the floor. "Blast you," he said, advancing on me. "You go and muck up everything. I don't want this baby. You'll just have to get rid of it."

'I couldn't believe it at first, so I laughed. "Oh, wipe that smirk off your face," he cried. "Can't you even use a rubber cap or something so you wouldn't get yourself pregnant? It's going to muck up our whole life. I tell you, I don't want this baby."

' "It's our baby, John," I said, stupidly.

' "I'll kick it out of you, then," he said savagely, clenching his fists just above my head. John has never hit me. He just likes to strike threatening attitudes, then he lets them drop. But I was not to know that. I am always easily frightened of human violence, loud voices, slammed doors. Terrified, aphonic, I sat, unable to move. He picked up his newspaper and it was all over. In the evening he brought me some flowers. The next day I lost the baby.

'Losing the baby had nothing to do with John. The baby had got stuck in one of the Fallopian tubes; it was an ectopic pregnancy. I got a funny, sudden pain, nausea, vomited, became dizzy, and blacked out. I was taken to hospital and operated on right away. John was wonderful then, sitting by my bed, offering his blood to the doctors, no one could have had a more devoted husband.

'He told his colleagues that he lived for me alone, that he would devote his whole life to making me happy. Everybody said to me afterwards that I was very lucky to have a husband so much in love with me.

'On the fifth day he came and sat by my bed. He looked sombre, I was filled with post-operative euphoria, tenderness, a kind of happiness too. I had suffered. Perhaps because we are brought up that way, we feel there is something ennobling and purifying in pain itself, without asking ourselves why.'

'That's only human beings,' said Maltby conversationally, as Anne stopped speaking, preparing herself for the next painful paragraph. 'Only humans get so confused, attributing an absolute rather than a relative value to renunciation, patience, endurance. Actually those virtues have no moral value in themselves at all, but they are essential to the attainment of satisfaction, and often we confuse the means with the end.'

'Go on,' said Anne.

'I'm being scientific,' replied Fred. 'Using words devoid of emotion dupes us into thinking we've discarded emotion. We humans have acquired a conditioned reflex to suffering: climbing a mountain on foot instead of by funicular, doing things the hard way, so that finally the satisfaction of desire, if straightforward or direct, without obstacles and complications, appears to us shocking, pointless, and immoral. And because our friends and betters the Nepalese enjoy their enjoyment, we call them immoral. I often think our way of life is essentially masochistic. Man has become a pain-seeking animal, experiencing pleasure only in pain first with pleasure deferred. And this pain-seeking applies to sex perhaps more than to any other domain of activity. The greater the pleasure, the happier we are if pain comes mixed with it.'

Anne went on: 'John sat by my bed and I said: "Oh darling, please don't worry. I'm fine now. And later on, when you like, we'll have another baby. It was a bit early to start one now. ..."

'I said this, thinking it would make everything well. "Or we won't have any, it will be just as you like."

' "This," he said, "is going to make a lot of difference to us."

'I said "Yes," happily, thinking we had at last shared something together, a common pain, since our common pleasure was so curiously remote and unspeakable. I was unprepared for the snares of his outward self, those attitudes and postures, the formulations of his state of mind. "This is going to make a lot of difference to us" ... I still hear him say it, and I can feel my own elation rising like a plumed bird rustling its feathers and shimmering in the sun, and then suddenly, like the crash of the hunter's shot, his words. "It's all been so messy. It's mucked up all my feelings for you. And that operation. The scar will be horrible. I don't feel you're a woman any more. I don't think I can make love to you again."

'I said, "What?" stupidly. It is my ears, the wind roaring, the morphinic post-operative nightmare, it is a great big joke.

' "Oh," he said, "why do these things have to happen to me? *Me?*"

'A few days after that I left hospital to go home. I was a bit stiff and had backache. But I was determined that nothing would interfere. John did make love to me, but not before I had cried and begged him not to let the operation make any difference. I had thus again manoeuvred myself into a feeling that it was my fault. The scar became a fine white line, the surgeon was very pleased with it. "Practically nothing to show," he said. And it was true. I wrote it up in a short story, the last short story I ever wrote, five years ago. I put it on someone's face, and got rid of that too.'

'What luck,' said Maltby smiling, 'write it down and get rid of it. I wish I could.'

'I can't always,' said Anne. 'I could take little things, like the scar, and weave them into a story, but the heart of the matter, the wound inside myself, the truth, I did not dare to look at. I could not face it. Until now. I was lying to myself, and so of course I died. In all ways.'

'You became frigid,' said Dr Maltby. 'So many women do in marriage. So many many women ... It is the usual story.'

It was getting dark in the doctor's office, and Maltby rose to press the light switch. Passing the window he noticed someone in the garden below and thought it looked vaguely like Geography. Then the office was bright (the new electric plant was in action) and blotted the evening outside.

'Is that all?'

'Nearly all. We made love less and less. You can guess the medical side. The unreality which I'd felt about sex now grew and swallowed all feeling. It became just a painful thing to endure. John said I was cold, and unnatural. Of course I accepted the verdict, nearly with gratitude. But I felt intellectually responsible for my marriage, and I went to see a doctor. A woman gynaecologist, brusque, masculinely handsome, intelligent, and didactic. She told me she'd "fixed up" any number of marriages that were going on the rocks. She examined me. I was suffering from tightness, she said. Sometimes a little operation helped. In my case it was psychological. "Of course, you writers are all *very* highly strung." She made me feel that writers, like dancers for the Maupratts, must of necessity be queer, unbalanced, and taken firmly in hand and allowed no nonsense. "You've got a perfectly good husband. Englishmen are always a bit slow and reserved, got to get them going. I tell Edward: Come on now, hop it, get on with it. (It sounded like a steeplechase, the way she described it.) She gave me pills. I left feeling guilty, inadequate, deficient (why couldn't *I* just lie down and say: come on, get on with it?). I didn't know how to handle a man, I didn't have the proper feelings. That night I tried. I put perfume on. John did make love to me. I pretended, as usual, what

I could not feel. I wanted to be sick and had nausea. Now I have nausea even at the sight of him.

'I saw the gynaecologist again a few days later. "Well," she said, "how are the pills working?" "Oh wonderful, wonderful," I said, hearty as she, "everything's fine." "I'm so glad," she said. Her lined features lit up with simple happiness. Another marriage saved, and I had lied as usual.

'Now I know I have lied, lied to myself, which is much worse than lying to others. Now I know I want a man, but not John, never John. I had to leave him. I had to be alone, by myself. I couldn't go on.'

Fred said, very carefully: 'Is there anyone around, Anne, in whom you've begun to get ... interested?'

'No,' said Anne, 'not that I know of, consciously. Actually I really started coming alive when I heard the word Khatmandu. I wanted to come here, and I did. And everything else has followed since. So you see it's nothing to do with John's illness, or another man. It's just me.'

'John's illness is the most satisfactory explanation for All-Khatmandu.'

'It's as if I'd wakened, coming here to the Valley. It's the mountain air.'

'Possibly,' said Fred. 'It's quite true that one becomes different here. More oneself. I too ...' He did not go on.

'I've taken a long time,' said Anne, rising. 'Doctors never get a rest, do they?'

'Doctors,' said Maltby, 'procure themselves strength and power from other people's diseases and failings. Themselves, however, they neither help nor cure. I can't even do what you do so well, get rid of problems by writing them out of you. I don't quite know what to say to you, except that you must not lie to yourself again. And I think you will cure yourself. You've begun already. You're really very strong, Anne. Terribly strong. I'm not worried about you. I feel you've done the right thing at the moment. Given yourself time and space to work things out.'

Anne turned at the door. 'Something puzzles me. Why did Isobel give me Unni's bungalow? Without it leaving John would not have been possible, you know.'

'Perhaps she too is pricked by Christian guilt,' said Fred. 'She's a repressed woman, with a strong sex drive and nowhere to use it. You

did not feel anything when you heard that Isobel was here in Khatmandu? No panic, no fear? Then you'd outgrown her and the Maupratt School all right. But she is still frightened of you, possibly
because she called you a bastard and danced round your bed, and
therefore she has to make gestures of love at you. A ritual placation.
I wouldn't be surprised if suddenly it turned to hatred. It must have
cost her a good deal to give you that room. Because of Unni, of
course.'

'Why?'

'The effect he had on her. He has some magnetism, call it animal,
or sexual if you will, which people either succumb to or resent at
sight. But he is not always conscious of his attractiveness as a desirable
male. He reminds me of Shakespeare's lines: "They that have power
to hurt and will do none, that do not do the thing they most do
show." Unni likes women, and women adore him. But Isobel couldn't
confess this attraction to herself. Unni was living in the bungalow
where you are, Isobel negotiating for the larger palace for her school.
It was the talk of Khatmandu that Isobel was going to get Unni to
leap into bed with her. She's not bad looking, with that reddish hair,
handsome in a large, magnificent way. They were out two or three
times at parties together. Isobel made great play of having him fetch
and carry for her and Unni is very good natured. There were bets
laid whether he would or not. In Khatmandu, as you know, there is
very little else to do except talk and think and make love. No theatres,
no plays, nothing to take us away from ourselves, to make us forget
the fundamentals. And so our sexual selves, which we repress elsewhere, emerge and we're made conscious of what we try to forget.
And then, of course, there's that famous mountain air.

'After a few weeks Isobel began to say openly things about Unni:
that he had women in his room, that he had made improper suggestions to her. Then we all knew he had turned her down. Anyway, he
wasn't much here, only appearing for a day or two, and then off again
to the hydro-electric project at Bongsor, but when he came his friends
crowded the bungalow. They came to talk, to eat, to sit on the lawn,
to play music, to sing, to dance. It was like a perpetual party, in the
sun, under the moon. And they came in families, with the children,
the girls were all a little in love with him, Rukmini among them.
Krishna, Rukmini called him, the Lord Krishna. And Rukmini, then

229

a child of thirteen, painted the parakeets in his room, working with a crowd of friends and lookers-on one day, for fun, painting the walls of his room. Before her marriage to Ranchit everyone said she had talent and should go to Europe or to India to study painting.

'One day there was a picnic on the lawn. The General was there, and his wife the Maharani, brothers and cousins, Rukmini and other girls, and Unni. They thought of playing the music of the dance of Lord Krishna with the milkmaids. Krishna, most beloved of all the gods, faithful and faithless lover of all women. Krishna when a boy stole milk from the milkmaids' pails, and then danced with each of them in turn to console them when they wept. So they played and sang and Devi danced, she was about ten years old. The older girls did not dance, for that would have been considered immoral. Rukmini played the sitar and Unni the drum. I was there, flat on my back in the sun, clapping my hands in time. Isobel came marching upon us, her face mottled, shouting ugly things. The floodgates were open, and what came out was so unmissionary that Rukmini put her hands over her ears and burst into tears. I tried to intervene, but Isobel turned on me too. Unni stood there, listening, and when she had finished she spat in his face and turned on her heel and marched off. So Unni moved to stay with me at the Serene Palace, and the whole incident was hushed up. For Isobel's sake.'

'Why didn't she have the bungalow whitewashed, or burnt, or something?'

'Well, it's not her property. In fact, she had no right to give it to you. It belongs to Unni, he is still the owner, and to no one else. I feel that in some way you and her feelings about Unni must seem to her related.'

Anne turned her face away. 'I must go,' she said. Her voice sounded constrained, polite. 'Good-bye, Fred. And thank you.'

'Good-bye,' said Fred. 'Let me see you to the door at least, Anne.' He wondered: what have I said to make her suddenly so abrupt? He peered at her face and could not understand.

Anne climbed into her jeep, and Fred, feeling suddenly bereft, walked back to his office. I'm certainly not sorry for her, he thought. She'll work her way out. It was John and Isobel who were the inadequate ones. Hard, like cockroaches outside, but soft within. Anne was not like that. Under that deceptive softness and quietness was something very strong, ruthless even, relentless certainly, working its way out. Anne was not to be pitied at all. On the contrary. I pity whoever crosses her path, thought Fred. Like the gods, so were the humans. And just as Parvati, gentle goddess, smiling tender lady of plenty, was also Kala Durga, the black, the terrifying killer, so a woman like Anne might well destroy emotionally a weak man like John, yet to someone else be the very breath of love and life. 'One man's poison, another man's meat,' said Fred, reassuring himself with a cliché. He lit his pipe, turned off the light, and sat in darkness, plunged in thought.

Chapter 4

FATHER MACCULLOUGH was busy and anxious and beset with pre-occupations. Like everyone else, he half convinced himself something would go wrong at the Coronation; and the tenor of his life was heightened by the expectancy of disaster. He would anxiously ask news of the road: 'Had there been a bad landslide? Was it being cleared? How would it affect transport?' And he dropped in at the Royal Hotel to see 'what progress was made'. 'None,' said Vassili. 'I'm still waiting for the money to buy the liquor. Without liquor there is no Coronation in Khatmandu.'

Father MacCullough's concern for his fellow men was genuine. Despite his small foible – a liking for helping them overmuch – he was unselfish in his present anxieties. He shared Isobel's apprehensions about water, food, and petrol, but not for himself; his was a wide-spread concern for all in the Valley; and he badgered the elusive, evasive, and charming Nepalese Government officials to 'do' something about the black market in petrol, food, beer, and photographic films, which had already begun.

But because we all tend to pinpoint our worries, so Father Mac-Cullough, worrying about all souls created by the One God, was particularly worried about the soul of Anne Ford.

Eudora had worried him too, but not to the same pitch. Unni Menon (for whom Father MacCullough had a particular affection) had taken her in hand. And Eudora had decided to wait in the Valley, and extended her visit to four weeks, and now she would stay for the Coronation. How she and Dr Maltby had not met in these weeks in the small valley was prodigious jugglery.

Fred Maltby did his morning walks (shorter than usual); operated, saw his patients. But he did not come to the Royal Hotel; instead, Vassili and Hilde, and Father MacCullough, dropped in on him acci-dentally once or twice a week, to keep him company and to inform him of current rumours. Hilde and the ladies of the Point Four Palace, the Irish girl (also one of Father MacCullough's pets, in spite of the disrupting effect of her generous propensities upon husbands), and

Martha Redworth, all had done their best by Eudora, asking her to teas and informal dinners; and the Hindu poet and Sharma had produced music and musicians. Eudora remained, and Father MacCullough approved.

Father MacCullough organized a sight-seeing tour of the Museum for ladies only. There were a lot of things worth seeing in the Museum, but some of them were of a type which could not be shown to anyone. Some of the statues were serene in contemplation, others a fury of dancing arms and legs and feet stamping the pulse of the world's magnificence. The worst were the bull gods, advancing phallos erect upon ecstatic women awaiting their embrace; and those Tibetan paintings, designed to fortify the lamas against temptation, representing temptation at its most rosy and lustful. When the day came, Father MacCullough shepherded his flock into the right rooms and showed them all that could be shown. The little museum curator, a charming and tiny Newari, imprisoned many long years by the Ranas for 'dabbling in education' (four of his comrades had been hanged and quartered, but he, having Rana blood and being a Brahman, could not be killed and was thus merely jailed for eight years), had afterwards taken tea with Father MacCullough and congratulated him on his great knowledge of Nepal. The meeting had been a success. Even Eudora had come (clad, of all things, in something resembling a sari, probably to show a spiritual affinity), but Anne had not appeared. And Father MacCullough had felt dejected.

Should he go to see Anne? He waylaid her at the Royal Hotel where she had lunch daily with John. Father MacCullough approved of this concession to the public *mores*; it showed that all was not over between them. They could still be invited together at parties and cocktails. He thought Anne had a different look about her, restless, glowing, so that sitting with her felt uncomfortable, as if near to something pent and waiting to be released. Somehow the small talk, the endless repetitive things about Nepal, Professor Rimskov's tall tales about Tibet, the conjectures about the Abominable Snowman, the tourist question and answer, the high intemperate voices of women, the rumours, the gossip, it all frittered away, went to pieces before the solemn inattention of her polite, immobile presence. All of them felt that she was not listening to anyone at all, but turned inwards, waiting.

Anne became endowed with a peculiar importance: haunting, unexplainable, and therefore much discussed. And many talked to her, and talking, suddenly embarrassed, casting about for a topic, they would start talking about themselves, discovering a great urge for self-exploration, taking themselves to bits and handing the pieces to Anne. There were drawbacks to this elevation into one of the Valley's chief topics. Geography and History hinted that Anne was man mad. 'She's probably having affairs with *countless* men,' said Geography.

'She's probably a communist, too,' said History.

As for Isobel, she pursed her mouth, and twice in a week invited John publicly to tea.

Father MacCullough thought he knew the reason why Anne had left. That John had had an 'accident' and Anne, in a fit of temper should have gone away for a few days, was only human and would fit Father MacCullough's theory of human nature and the marriage relationship well; yet somehow he felt this was not the entire truth.

He had thought of Anne as convertible material right from the beginning, for though all souls are equal, for some a priest felt more enthusiasm than for others. Eudora might be convertible material too, but Father MacCullough did not feel particularly interested whether she became a Catholic or not. Not that he would not be pleased if she did; but quite honestly he felt like doing much more for Anne, or Unni Menon ... those were souls worth catching, he felt, and if he had been asked to say why he could not have said why. It had nothing to do with importance. He wanted to approach Anne and talk to her, and yet when they met and he talked it was as if she had taken a pair of scissors in her hand and nipped, neatly, all the words from him. She did that to a lot of people. It was the way she simply did not care what they thought about her. Her attention was elsewhere. He lent her books, gauche, not quite knowing what else to do, how else to establish a contact with her; unfortunately there were not many books about, except the Field Marshal's. Finally he picked a few he thought might become, not an indication of his own erudition, but a symbol of his concern for her: *Catholic Writers*, *Writing for God*, *Saints are not Sad*, Chesterton's works.

'I'm sorry it's all such muscular Christianity,' he said, with a wry attempt at humour, to Anne. 'Now promise you'll read them.'

'I will,' she said gravely.

A day later, as an afterthought, he gave her another book: *The Holy Sacrament of Marriage*. Anne took the book and did not comment. Father MacCullough felt he had been rude, and was more worried and uneasy about Anne than ever.

'How am I doing?' asked John.

'Fine,' said Dr Maltby. 'Everything seems to have cleared up. I'd like to repeat the blood test, though, say in about a couple of months, and again after that. We've got to be sure we haven't masked anything, mustn't risk trouble later.'

'Of course,' said John. 'I quite understand.' He laughed easily. 'First time anything like that has happened to me. And in this God-forsaken hole of all places. Most annoying.'

'Yes, isn't it?' said Fred Maltby. Something in his tone made John stare at him with that deep, profound attentiveness which Isobel and Geography found so engaging. Only yesterday at tea Geography had managed to convey (while Isobel was away for a moment) what a wonderful masculine person he was. She'd sighed, looked out of the window towards Anne's bungalow, now screened from sight by the full spring foliage of the walnut trees, and then smiled at John. Isobel had come back, and Geography had lapsed into submissiveness, demure sandy lashes down, while Isobel and John talked of the Coronation and the chaos it would be.

'Just one more thing, if you can spare me a little time, Dr Maltby,' said John, not letting go with his eyes of the doctor, who was playing with a silver paper cutter on his table.

'Of course,' said Fred Maltby.

'I'd like to say a few words about my wife,' said John. 'I'm worried about Anne, quite frankly. Her mental state. I don't want to complain or to make excuses for myself, but what did happen was partly her fault. She doesn't seem to be quite normal as a woman.'

'You mean to imply that you were driven to sleeping with another woman and catching gonorrhoea because your wife wouldn't sleep with you,' stated Fred.

'Well, I wouldn't put it *quite* that way. I suppose it does boil down to that. I'm a normal human being. I'm not a saint.'

He paused. Fred was looking intensely at the paper cutter in his hands.

'But when one's got a wife who's just like an iceberg, well ... Anne pushes me off, deliberately, and in such a violent manner, most unwomanly. I love my wife very much, but I do feel that she has to take part of the blame for what's happened. I may be wrong, but that's the way I look at it.'

'Did you stop to think,' said Fred Maltby carefully, 'that this coldness you complain of in your wife might be due to your own attitude?'

John flushed. 'Certainly *not*,' he said. 'There's nothing wrong with me. Of course we've been married years now. Anne's very romantic, you know. She can't expect me to spout poetry or that sort of thing. I'm just a simple, normal man. I don't know what my wife has said to you. Afraid she's got a habit of saying things about me behind my back. She's very high-strung. It's her background, having no children. I believe she is unable to have any now. I'm not a doctor, so don't ask me to tell you what went wrong with the first one, but I believe she had some internal trouble.'

Dr Maltby remained silent.

'Well,' said John, 'I don't like talking about Anne. It's disloyal. Whenever anyone has attacked her – she's artistic, never got on with other wives, too nervy, and people always gossip about anyone like her – I've done my best to quash it. This has involved a good deal of sacrifice on my part in the past. Anne doesn't seem to realize what it's meant to me. Five thousand pounds, that's what it cost. Because if I'd only stuck it for another two years, the colony was given self-government, and I would have received another five thousand pounds instead of just the pension I was entitled to. But I left early, and I must say it was due to Anne.'

'I suppose you've told Anne all this?'

'I've never *blamed* her,' said John. 'Never. But as her husband I think I am entitled to some consideration. I've made sacrifices for her. But she doesn't seem to realize it. I wonder sometimes whether she's suffering from a kind of early menopause.' He paused, awaiting a sign from Maltby, but the latter said nothing. 'It is not very pleasant for me, as a husband. And now I suppose you know she's taken to living in that bungalow next to the Institute. Well, I don't mind. I couldn't care less what people say, but it's not very good for my wife's reputation.'

'She probably needs to be alone for a while, to think things out.'

'But she's always thinking,' cried John impatiently, 'and certainly *I* never interfere with her thinking and her actions. She's perfectly free to write *what* she likes and she's always gone off on her own, daydreaming and leaving me all alone. I'm not trying to force her to do anything she doesn't want, but I've got some rights too, as her husband. I can't go on like this indefinitely. I thought as a doctor, and a friend of hers, you might get her to recover her balance, to see things more normally, as a *wife* should.'

'I don't think this is the time to discuss all this,' replied Dr Maltby. 'If I were you I wouldn't hurry matters. Anne has been unhappy for quite a while. She needs –' he stopped abruptly.

'But what about me?' cried John. 'Don't you think I need some attention too? I may be old-fashioned, but I feel that I haven't had from my wife the love and care to which a husband is entitled. Not once. D'you think it's nice for me to feel her go away from me, to see her stare right through me without seeing me? I've been very good and patient; I only want what's mine by right. I'm asking you to help Anne to return to her wifely duties. I can't be happy without her, and I'm sure that once she gets rid of this nonsense about wanting to be alone, she'll be quite happy with me.'

'I'm sorry,' said Dr Maltby, rising, 'I can't do anything at the moment, I'm afraid.'

'Well,' said John, heavily sarcastic, 'I should have known. I suppose you've got enough of your own worries on your hands at the moment. Good day to you, Dr Maltby.'

Fred sighed, ran his hands through his hair, glanced at his watch. 'The poor clot,' he said, 'the poor clot. Not at all a bad chap. Quite likeable, really, and really terrified of Anne.'

And then he stopped thinking of Anne and John. He was thinking of Eudora.

Eudora came walking across the lawn, lifting her feet in Mexican slippers above the grass. She wore a wide coolie hat of that Chinese style much seen upon tourist heads from Italy to Tokyo. Eudora had become perceptibly thinner in four weeks in the Valley. Her hair, so blonde on arrival, now showed mousy streaked with white at the roots.

'I do hope you won't mind my coming to call,' she said to Anne, who sat under the walnut trees. 'I've wanted to say hello for a long time. My, what a pretty place you've got here. And that cute little farmhouse there. And that mountain, across the fields. What's its name?'

'Mount Phulchoah,' said Anne. 'It's a hill, really.'

'It's beautiful,' breathed Eudora. 'How lucky you are, having a bungalow all your own.' She gazed with inquisitive wistfulness at the small white building, the lawn, the arbour of roses, and the little fountain under it, and then her gaze went back to Mount Phulchoah.

'Paul Redworth will tell you that it's not a mountain, but a goddess, lackadaisical Nepalese fashion,' said Anne. She was not annoyed by Eudora, but she had liked being alone. *Je ne parlerai pas, je ne penserai rien ...* it was wonderful to sit here, not thinking, not talking. Rimbaud's clarities came naturally in such a civilized, harmonious landscape ... *mais l'amour infini me montera dans l'âme.* Love, this swelling, silent tumult. Love or longing?

'Oh, do tell me about it,' said Eudora, clapping her hands.

'The goddess is supposed to be one of the two wives of a god, I forget which, and patron saint of handicrafts; Newari women take their daughters up the hill, with flowers and spinning shuttles, pray and make offering of these to the goddess that she may turn them into clever housekeepers and weavers of cloth.'

'How too too sweet,' said Eudora, a trifle distraitly. 'You know, this place does funny things to one, don't you think? I mean, it's quite another world, isn't it? One gets all at sea, you know that feeling that everything you've thought or done appears ... different? As if the unimportant mattered and what one thought important isn't, really.'

'Maybe it's a way of finding oneself,' said Anne.

'Yes, well that's what Unni Menon said. We've had such long talks, he and I. I was so unhappy, so angry ... about Fred. Fancy everyone knowing about Fred and not telling *me* ... but Unni is a real nice person. He spent the whole evening with me that first day at the wedding ... and he's been to see me often. Only the other night at the Royal Hotel, when Vassili was out of jail, and everyone was at the party but I felt I just couldn't face it ... I went back to my room and I had a good cry, and then Unni was there. He's a really human person,' said Eudora with a sudden glow, 'such a man. And yet, you know, I'm never frightened with him. Not one bit. I mean ... once or twice after parties here people have wandered up and down, and there's a chap, I needn't mention names …'

'I know, Michael Toast,' said Anne. 'Comes up and says: "How about bed, old girl?" And if you say no …'

'He says: "You must be a lesbian."' Eudora giggled. 'Yes. A few others too, who think that because this place is far away and different they can just let go. That's what makes Asians look *down* upon us so much,' said Eudora vehemently. 'But I wasn't scared with Unni, though he's so dark, really. Know what I did? Threw myself in his arms,' said Eudora, blushing and giggling again. 'Such a relief, just seeing him. He's coming back soon, isn't he? He promised to come and see me again.'

Anne did not answer. Her hand was in the grass, and she pulled, gently, the tough grass, and felt it domesticated, tame, pulling back at her, a friendly tug. It was curious, this effect of reciprocity, between all things. She'd never had it before coming to the Valley, and feeling her body fall into the curves of the hills round her; as if the meandering dogs and cattle, sharing space and air with humans on equal terms, and the grass underfoot and the trees above her, all collaborated in an inextricable pattern of existence. And now Eudora, and the words she brought, conjuring more figures to add to the pattern, Eudora coming and plumping herself down next to her, like one of those insolent and fearless crows, sure of their right to share with her, to eat, to live, unafraid.

'And now I'm being good. I promised Unni I would be,' said Eudora, with a return to her girlish manner. 'It is difficult, but in another way I'm beginning to understand what patience means … don't you think one *needs* that sort of thing nowadays?' She bent her eyes upon Anne, who nodded, embarrassed. 'I've met such *nice* people here, it really does make one feel life is beautiful in spite of, oh well, one's private troubles. There's the Hindu poet, and that perfect darling boy, Sharma, don't you think he's so handsome? I wish I were twenty years younger,' said Eudora in a burst of candour.

'Would you like some tea?' said Anne. The maidservant was bringing tea and cakes bought from the Swiss baker, and which now appeared for Anne three times a week, alternating with biscuits which Anne recognized from their particular mouldiness as coming from the General's palace across the road.

'By the way,' said Eudora, 'I'd like to ask you and your husband, if he'd like to come, to a little party I'm organizing in a few days. I find the foreign colony here does not get round to knowing the real Nepalese, the true values of Nepalese life. Like everywhere else, they're cutting themselves off from the life of the people.' Eudora enlarged on this theme; she felt that she alone had penetrated to the hearts of Asians; to begin with, she had always had the right political approach. 'Even in London my flat used to be crowded with those darling Asian students. We had meetings every Thursday. I made friends with so many people who later went back to help their countries become independent. I feel in a very small way I've helped them to find themselves. D'you know what some of them used to call me? Mother Asia. Fancy giving me that name,' said Eudora, emitting again that particularly nervous, high giggle which Anne now felt must have been one of the things Fred Maltby had run away from. She pulled some more at the grass. The afternoon, the bland, unthinking, lovely surging afternoon was gone, shattered by that voice, that giggle, that terrible goodwill, little girl willingness to do the right thing ... and then compassion came to Anne. Poor Eudora. With the clarity of those whose instincts have taken over, she knew that Eudora had not forgotten Fred. She was still, queerly, in that state which could have been described as 'in love with Fred'. The many years had gone, and here she was, in the same valley as Fred, waiting, waiting for a sign, a word ... it was terrible and comical and tragic and funny. And all she did, Anne, was to raise barriers of glass between herself and this other woman. ...

'I've just left my husband,' she said, too casually. 'I live here alone. People must have told you.'

'Of course they did,' said Eudora, leaping into humanity, all pretence abolished. 'Father MacCullough told me. That's what made me feel I wanted to talk to you. I was trying to talk, but I didn't know how ... somehow one's talk doesn't come out the way one plans it out here, don't you find?'

'It doesn't. Father MacCullough asked me to come to see you, but that was before I left John, and I'm afraid I'm growing very selfish. I just sit here and let the wind blow round me, and I wasn't going to do anything about you at all.'

'Neither was I. I don't think you need help. What you're doing is all wrong, and yet, somehow, I feel it's right. Just as what I'm doing I feel is right, just waiting, I don't even know why.'

'Would you like to come for a drive?' said Anne, after a silence. They had said all there was to say. Anything more would be otiose, sentimental, losing in the insular grammar of each woman's island, the eloquent silence, understanding all.

'I was just going to suggest it,' said Eudora, bounding up. 'Let's drive to the airfield. The plane from India must have come ages ago and it's about time for the plane from Bongsor. That's where Unni Menon works at the dam, you know.'

'I didn't know there was a plane every afternoon from Bongsor.'

'Not every day. Once a week or ten days, and not at all if there's too much cloud. It's only a tiny little plane, an old DC.3 thing, but there might be a note from Unni for me. I asked him to write to me, otherwise I'd sure go mad with loneliness here, just waiting, I'm not quite sure for that ...'

'All right, let's go to the airfield,' said Anne.

*

Anne wrote:

Eudora and I drove to the airfield. There was for her a blue air-mail envelope. A sloping even writing, nondescript, the capitals are scarcely larger than the other letters. From Unni Menon.

The next morning Dearest came walking across the lawn, with her father, His Preciousness the Rampoche of Bongsor.

His Preciousness, an Asian Churchill, wore a zoot suit. Dearest was muffled in an organdie sari, pale pink. Both had thick black sunglasses upon their eyes. Sunglasses are the fashion in the Valley. Their Majesties wear them nearly all the time. It is reported that some people go to bed at night with their sunglasses on.

'Hello, Mrs Ford,' called Dearest in her gushing, fervent manner. 'This is my Daddy, I've told my Daddy about you, my Daddy has been wanting to come to see you for a long time, he want to invite you to lunch today.'

I make an effort to shake the uneasy, yearning inertia, semi-coma, which possesses me. I tell myself I must go. I must move about *with* people. Yet all I want to do is to lie under these walnut trees, looking at the mountain opposite. *Je ne sentirai pas, je ne penserai rien, je laisserai le vent baigner ma tête nue.* Here the wind comes stiffly through my hair, an invincible caress. Here is the passion of a peace with myself which I cannot tire of. At night I drive for hours alone, I need to be alone. ...

Dearest has seen the *Bhagavad-Gita* lying on the grass. She stoops to look at it but does not touch it, being a polite Asian, keeping her hands to herself.

'Oh, that is very beautiful, Mrs Ford. We have some at home like that too. My Daddy collects old books.'

'This is the Field Marshal's.'

The Rampoche nods. Dearest does all the talking, while the Rampoche's black button eyes (gleaming as with an extra gloss of polish upon them) look around, pecking at things, swift, sharp, and accurately as a bird.

The Khatmandu house of His Preciousness is in Tibetan style, a graceful façade with moulded cornices and not too much carving. The family live on the first floor, in spotless rooms (we take off our shoes to go in). On the floor boards is a thick layer of linoleum, and on top of that Tibetan handwoven carpets and mats. On the walls is the usual jumble of photographs, oleographs, the sublime and the ridiculous comfortably together. Reproductions of living Buddhas, Dalai Lamas, and other important Tibetans to which Dearest has added dashes of colour ('My Daddy says I am artistic'), angels holding palms, golden statues of Buddha, the Shwe Dagon, a Sacred Heart, the Potala of Lhasa; some of the more covered pin-ups; 'Daddy' photographed in full regalia with various notables, the King, Ambassadors, mountain climbers, signed faces of people who have stayed with His Preciousness expressing appreciation, gratitude, appropriate sentiments in French, English, German, Spanish, Dutch. A gallery of Asia's great men with Nehru, Mahendra the King of Nepal, Mao Tse-tung, the President of the Philippines. No tusks, no tigers – the Rampoche does not hunt.

In glass cases, on tables, *objets d'art*: the usual hideous clocks from Paris, coupled with beautiful carved jades from Peking, a good Swiss chronometer; Dresden statuettes, little ornaments from Selfridges, the priceless and the shoddy, unabashed in proximity. There are kukris with scabbards embossed in silver or gold and encrusted with turquoises and agate. There are silver bowls and cheap pink glasses of Hongkong manufacture.

A head peers from the door and I recognize the Tibetan woman who was in the same airplane when first I came to Khatmandu. 'Auntie' to Dearest, she smiles at me, displaying fine square teeth. Her several children troop in to fold their hands in salutation and say 'hello'. Dearest shoos them off, settles by my side, and continues talking. She never stops. On and on, an unquenchable babbling stream, her unpunctuated talk flows. There is nothing to do but settle down and let this ponderous host of words pour over me; the Rampoche sits and nods. Perhaps he too is submerged under his daughter's volubility.

'And you see when I said to my cousin the Serene Lama's third stepsister who is in Lhasa and is also related to my Auntie but you shouldn't cut your hair because even in Goldsmith's *Essays* it is written that it is woman's crowning glory and she said but I am independent and equal now she did not listen to me and her husbands objected very much because they said all of them they liked long hair but my cousin is clever and she got her second husband to say that he also liked short hair and he was modern and they went to the films together and so when it came to a vote in the family it was fifty-fifty and now she is marrying a fourth who likes short hair but they all have to move to a bigger house as the house is too small for the five of them but I said to my cousin you will lose your husbands one day because your hair is short but she is not listening now she is sure that she is quite right but I don't think so as I think long hair is crowning glory and even if I am a doctor later I will keep hair long as it is now although it is more trouble my Daddy says and sometimes it is too heavy and gives me headache Mrs Ford don't you think I might be a doctor I don't know where to study medicine Peking or Calcutta I can speak Hindi also but it is not necessary for medicine as it is in English in Calcutta my Daddy says perhaps if I like I can study in America and now he is trying to get a scholarship for me to America Mr Bowers do you know Mr Enoch P. Bowers he is tall and wrinkled but I don't like the colour of his skin too pink I am crazy about William Holden he is much more handsome than Mr Bowers I saw him in a film he is quite tan we do not like a man too white but I think a woman should be pale in the skin don't you that is what we all think and my Daddy says in Lhasa now everybody is using face powder and also lipsticks as well as Parker pens because everybody likes Parker pens and what is your opinion but as I was saying about Mr Bowers he promised to help with a scholarship and so my Daddy promised to join the Club you know Mr Bowers is President and of course we want also your help as your husband Mr Ford is Secretary so Mrs Ford can you help me to get a scholarship to America?'

Dearest has come full stop so suddenly that I'm taken by surprise and I say 'Uh?' The Rampoche smiles benignly and says something to his daughter in either Nepalese, Tibetan, Sherpa, Hindi, or any other of the dialects she speaks. Obviously today he knows no English, although fluent at the wedding. Dearest replies. They argue animately, then Dearest turns to me:

'My Daddy says never mind about the scholarship but if you write books again perhaps you write about me and say how very very much we all appreciate U.S. scholarship here in the Himalayas and ardently love dem-ocracy and Mrs Ford there is a little something else that my Daddy wanted me to bring to your attention for him he says please excuse him he did not wish to speak about the scholarship now he knows that being your pupil *of course* you will help me if you think that I am hopeful and we know the Americans are looking everywhere for talented young people good stuff they can send to the United States for getting their brains very dem-ocratic so perhaps later we can arrange the scholarship but at the moment my Daddy says can wait but there is something else my Daddy says would like to talk to you about because he is sure you magnanimous and great and noble lady likes to help everybody to understand each other and it is about Unni Menon.'

Pause. Again the pause is so abrupt that I am caught still floating in the backwash. This time it takes me two seconds to react. I react with with a reflex defensiveness. 'What about Mr Menon?' I say. And inexorably, slowly, unthinkingly, despite myself, I blush, blush from head to foot, solemn, inarticulate, helpless, and furious. I don't know the man, certainly I have no feelings for him. Certainly not. I interrogate myself, poised, cool now, in front of this white sheet which is meant to record in words the new self I catch glimpses of. What do I feel for Unni Menon? I have to answer: I don't know. Do I wish to see him again? I don't know. I am angry, angry because Eudora is waiting for Unni Menon, and now the Rampoche too.

'I have absolutely nothing to do with Mr Menon,' I say stiffly. 'I don't know him well at all.'

'Oh you are friend of his *great* friend he trust you very much Mrs Ford he never treat any other woman like you,' says Dearest, goggle-eyed. 'We are all admiring so much beautiful friendship no other woman Mr Menon very handsome tall very lady-killer but a little too dark otherwise just like William Holden only slimmer hips because not American but Indian and all Americans a little too fat because very wealthy but Indians poor cannot afford to eat so much but usually Mr Menon like all men so many women around just take to bed if you will pardon me and then forget anyway not interested but good worker and my Daddy tries to help him but Mr Menon sometimes does not understand how my Daddy very anxious help him and so perhaps when Unni comes back you can come here with him and my Daddy explain to him how he tries to help him yes?'

'I'm sorry I can't promise to bring Mr Menon anywhere,' I reply. (I now remember the nieces.) 'I have absolutely nothing to do with his work at all.'

'Lunch,' says the Rampoche briskly, rising and clapping hands and laughing Jolly Miller fashion, ha ha ha. We rise, are led to another room, sit upon a settee lined with cushions, and each one of us is supplied with a small table, upon which, in the shape of lotus leaves of beaten silver, are large plates. Upon these plates Auntie heaps food. Like Dearest's talk, it is too copious: rice, curry, two kinds of chicken, three kinds of meat, four kinds of vegetables and a special mushroom from Tibet, *dahl*, curds. The Rampoche, a follower of the Tibetan type of Buddhism, is not a vegetarian. Auntie informs me that the title Rampoche is the equivalent of bishop, while the word lama means ordinary priest.

Dearest talks of her school, her plans for the future, Auntie talks of her three husbands and children; she has taken two husbands and all the children to the Valley for the Coronation, and left her third husband home 'to mind the house and the furniture'. The Rampoche eats and grins at me. After lunch I go home, feeling fit to burst, plied with a parcel of the famous Tibetan mushrooms, and Dearest waves from the door.

'Bye bye Mrs Ford so kind of you to come please don't forget we are all friends of yours real friends never talk not like some people yes we never talk gossip about people see you soon when Mr Menon comes back.'

Strange that I should teach Rukmini. With the same heart-wringing docility with which she sat at the wedding she sits in class. She does what she is told to do. 'Read, Rukmini.' She rises with effortless grace, as she rose when her husband Ranchit came up with Pat, the American 'artist', to introduce his mistress to his wife. Dutifully she reads, eyes lowered. I see her again, sitting on the floor in Vassili's cell, and hear Unni's dark, deep voice saying: 'Sing, Rukmini,' and she sings. She has no consciousness of the wealth of her beauty, her charm, her grace. She only knows how to give, to give of herself, her smile, her loveliness, accepting that others should rule her. Dearest, the Rampoche's daughter, bullies her. Rukmini adorns Dearest, coiling her thick, straight hair (so unlike her own soft, curling hair) into a graceful, heavy bun. Her hands are skilful with flowers and silks and jewellery, and that she cannot produce an English sentence without a spelling mistake does not matter at all.

'That girl still can't draw a plain contour map,' cries Geography in despair.

I set an English composition yesterday: 'Describe a Wedding in your own Country.' According to the rules I should have added: 'Use not more than three hundred words.' Dearest reminded me.

'Please, Mrs Ford, how many hundred words for this composition?'

'As many as you like.'

Dearest's satins stir and vibrate to and fro. Her round gleaming face and glasses display considerable agitation. 'But Mrs Ford, the other missionaries always –'

'I want you to feel free to write it down your own way.'

The experiment has not been a success. Three hundred words was a limit, the end of a tiresome span of writing. The freedom I imposed they could not use, except Dearest and Rukmini. Dearest, owlish as ever, puts on my desk a bulky tome entitled: 'A comparative study of wedding ceremonies among the different peoples of Nepal.' It is a fascinating work, and Dearest deserves praise. She must have sat up all night writing it, and it is well done. I congratulated her in front of the whole class, and she became very red, hopped from one foot to the other, and threw me, across the barrier of her spectacles, such a look of utter, intense devotion that I felt humbled and ashamed of having tried to put her down. She cannot help being brilliant, bossy, vigorous of mind and body, and the thing to do is to direct her over-abundant intellectual energies into worthy channels.

Lakshmi is away. 'She is just pregnant again, please Mrs Ford, and desires to be excused as she is vomiting mightily.'

Rukmini rises, predestined victim, and places in front of me a little piece of paper, on which is written: 'Mrs Ford, I did not write my composation. Sorry, Signed Rukmini.' After class I call her back. 'If you do not like to write words, Rukmini, is there anything else you like to do?'

She looks at me, doubtful, uneasy, a little frightened.

'Draw or paint, for instance?' I say, and blush to the roots of my hair as I say it, having exposed her and myself. We stare at each other, two women in a turmoil of emotion, all the things felt and unsaid between us. 'You know I am staying in the room you painted once, Rukmini? They are very beautiful, the parakeets ... are you drawing or painting now?'

'Yes,' says Rukmini, 'sometimes.'

'Rukmini,' I say, 'if I can help, I would like to help.'

She does not seem to understand, smiles, and softly draws her sari over her head, across her face below her eyes, and thus, veiled and wordless, walks away.

Isobel is sure there will be a water shortage at the Coronation, and is having the cement tanks in the garden filled in advance.

'That's because she's got enough brandy on hand, otherwise she'd be worried about that,' says Hilde, tranquil, but as a fact.

Vassili is not disturbed about water, but about liquor. 'Over a hundred and fifty foreign correspondents, photographers, reporters, and a Megalorama team, and possibly only Coca-Cola to drink, and the pink grenadine they give you in Calcutta on teetotal days and call fruit juice! I need a half-dozen Dakotas full of whisky and beer.'

And when the Hindu poet – who is to write an ode in honour of the Coronation, and who, being a strict Brahman, fasts on Saturday and drinks nothing but water or tea – hints mellifluously that it is better for the soul to drink only fruit juice:

'Comrade,' says Vassili impressively, 'one can see you're an idealist. You don't understand the gullets of the Press. It doesn't matter what you do; if you haven't got the means of alcoholic lubrication the wrong man gets crowned.'

And then Vassili is called to the Palace, and tells me confidentially that he may soon be getting thirty thousand rupees to go to Calcutta to buy liquor 'as soon as they've collected the money in taxes from the people. But keep it quiet, or I shall have to be giving bottles of whisky away to all the Ranas before the Press have even got their visas stamped.'

Today I receive some letters; one from Leo Bielfeld, to tell me that he and François Luneville, our French photographer friend, are coming to Khatmandu for the Coronation.

'*Anne, ma sœur Anne, ne vois-tu rien venir?*' writes Leo. 'I have always been fond of that French story of Bluebeard, but one thing only stuck in my mind: the picture of Anne, the sister of Bluebeard's wife, high on her tower looking out at the road for help. And her forlorn, hopeless reply, "*Je vois le soleil qui poudroie et la poussière qui tournoie …*" It is your distant look, Anne, which makes me think of this. Will you greet me, I wonder, with that cold yet watchful, Anne-on-her-high-tower glance when I reach Khatmandu?'

Dear Leo. In Calcutta it was with real astonishment that I observed his sexual antics. They were to me no more than an external, inexplicable agitation, meaningless, out of focus, nothing to do with me. And now? Anne, Anne, do you see nothing coming? How can I talk of this, how can I describe this murmurous rising sap in me which is nameless, which has not coalesced yet into one shape, one name? But I know it now, I know the endless bounty of desire again, the torment which renews the world … but I must not think of this. High on my tower I remain, watching and waiting, a little while more.

A Swiss agriculturist drops in at the Royal Hotel to speak about last year's desolating floods. Whole valleys have disappeared. Hundreds of thousands of people are starving and refugees will pour into Khatmandu. It's nearly impossible to keep them out. Although the road to India is not yet finished, already every day twenty to thirty lorries are coming up, laden with food from India for the people of the Valley. 'Otherwise there will be famine and riots, not very nice for the Coronation.'

I have been to tea at the American palace, where the Point Four Mission stays. Geography enthuses about it. 'So cosy. And *clean*. Quite a dream. Little America really.'

Father MacCullough bounds in and out; he is so weighed with responsibility one would think the success or failure of the impending Coronation depends entirely on his efforts. Yet at the same time he is lovable, helpful, and kind. He is off to the other school he runs, six thousand feet up in the hills. 'Don't forget Mass at 8 a.m. on Sunday, right here, come if you can,' he says to me. Father MacCullough celebrates Mass in the grand salon of the Royal Hotel, among the chandeliers and the mirrors.

A very tall American in long white trousers and white shirt (his laundry bill must be something) complains to Hilde about the Nepalese Government. He has been here nearly five weeks, trying to get a permit to take films from the air of the Himalayan ranges. He has called on all the important people; the King, the Field Marshal, the Prime Minister ... everybody. Five weeks. Vassili laughs heartily as the American relates his experiences with Nepalese Government officials.

'Tomorrow,' they say, 'tomorrow, maybe we shall know whether we can let you have a permit.'

And when he insists, they hold up their hands with great surprise: 'But why today,' they say, very politely, 'when it can be done tomorrow?'

'That's the motto of the Government,' says Vassili. 'Why today when it can be done tomorrow?'

When the American is gone, he tells me: 'He will never get this permit. It is madness to ask for it. What? He wants to take a plane and shoot photographs of the Himalayan ranges. That means the Chinese frontier. Do you think any Nepalese government in its right senses would allow an American in a plane to go and shoot the Chinese frontier?'

'The man must be mad,' says Hilde consoling. 'Or innocent.'

'Neither,' says Vassili. 'All the Americans in Nepal seem to have a formidable attraction for the northern passes. They're for ever asking for permits to go "trekking" up there, or for building hospitals or schools along the frontier. That's what makes the Nepalese so suspicious about all American Aid. Americans can't think of Aid without automatically thinking of it in terms of anti-communist money, anti-Chinese money, and so everybody suspects that they don't really aid, they have military motives in mind.'

The madman walks in, talking and smiling to himself, and bows to Vassili, who bows back at him. 'I'll miss him if he stops coming,' says Vassili, looking at him affectionately. 'I hope they never go modern and put him in a mental home.'

I ask Vassili to make sure there will be room for François and Leo at the Royal Hotel. Vassili tells me that the rooms are booked twice over, a hundred and fifty correspondents have applied, and there is not a stick of furniture in the Government hostel, which is to house a few score of official guests. Vassili is going to put extra beds in an annex to the Royal Hotel, and pitch tents in the garden. He is hiring eighty bearers from Calcutta. He does not think they can come up by road, there are not enough trucks. They will have to be flown in. 'I'll have to borrow a plane from Unni, if I can get at him.'

Hilde says some prawns have arrived from Calcutta as well as *bekti*, a fish, and some river trout. Fish is a great delicacy in Nepal. Sharma, the young man who was in jail with Vassili, wanders on the verandah, disconsolate. We have a beer together, waiting for lunch.

Sharma is very good looking, with large luminous eyes and a beautiful mouth. When he talks the words tumble out of him, quickly, in a pleasant torrent. He tells me he has a wealthy father, refugeed in Zürich from Nepalese income-tax, which is only just beginning to be imposed. Quite a few of the Ranas live abroad, and invest their money in Switzerland and America. Then he talks about Rukmini. 'I have been loving her for ages, but her father is an old reactionary. He married her to Ranchit. It was a political marriage. She should have married me. Or Unni. But preferably me. I don't think she would have been happy with Unni. He only loves work and mountains, and has a spiritual indifference to women. Spiritual only; he is not a poet, like me.'

Sharma is a poet, which means that he believes in love of mankind, equality, freedom, is in love with Love, and sounds far more revolutionary than he is.

Vassili tells him: 'You're a lousy poet, Sharma, and you don't understand politics.'

But Sharma vehemently denies this: 'How can I be a poet, write POETRY, when round me my countrymen are trampled underfoot to starve? No, I am a socialist, I am politically progressive. No Asian writer can remain in an ivory tower. All of us must lead the people in our struggle for the future.'

In Asia, young, didactic, idealistic, the social novel must also be the political novel, the writer the fighter; talent used merely in the service of art, art for art's sake, is considered outrageous, selfish, and wrong. Sharma sees himself leading revolutionary masses, though he is truly a poet, and shrinks from the courage (or the cowardice) necessary to give shape in selfish solitude, away from the vile realities of economics and demography, to the graceful fantasies which visit his heart.

'You better keep your mouth shut, Sharma, or back you'll go to prison,' says Vassili.

Sharma's eyes flash. 'Ha,' he says, 'they would like to put us down; but wait, wait and see. Wait till the elections. The King will have to promise elections at his Coronation. But the Government is corrupt to the core. Nepotism, bribery, corruption – twenty miles from here, there is no Government. A friend of mine has just come back from a tour of the western valleys. The people are starving there. They do not even have enough seed to sow the spring harvest. And the landlords go on treating them like slaves. They have to do a hundred and fifty days' work a year free for the headman and the priests. It is absolute tyranny, just as in the Rana days.'

'You'll get into trouble,' repeats Vassili, drinking his Vichy water. Vassili, since his liberation, drinks *eau de Vichy*, less pernicious than ordinary water since partly medicinal and *bon pour le foie*. It used to come by air, but now a consignment of bottles has come by road, and Vassili hopes that some of the beer can also come by road. 'If Colonel Jaganathan doesn't confiscate it, and drink it up himself.'

John now appears with Enoch P. Bowers. Enoch P. is definitely President of the Valley Club, and John its Secretary. The Club is 'scheduled to open at the Coronation', as Enoch puts it. 'The Club would then have its official delegates attending all official functions,' he says. Sharma whispers that Enoch, as President, hopes to attend the State Banquet.

We have lunch with Vassili and Sharma and Hilde. We eat

bouchées au roi Boris, stuffed with chicken, mushrooms, chillies, and cream. The pastry is soft, flaky, melts in the mouth. And after that we have the fish, the precious *bekti* from Calcutta, fried with slices of ginger and a dash of white wine, extra-sec. And pineapple ice cream to follow. I've seldom eaten better in my life than at the Royal Hotel. Vassili and I spend the lunch hour inventing new dishes.

'But what is the use of the art of cooking to me?' says Vassili. 'You, Anne, understand something of food. But you are one in ten thousand. The tourists ... give them something different and they will look suspicious, poke at it with their forks, and wonder about cholera germs. In bed as at the table the average Anglo-Saxon is still a Stone Age man. The superstitious Americans, they only eat things which they believe have magical properties, like promoting health, giving them vitamins, or keeping them slim.'

Sharma says: 'How strange it is that there should be no fish in the Valley, for you know, once upon a time, it was an inland lake. There are many such in the Himalayas, five of them in and around Pokhra valley and a beautiful one at Bongsor, where Unni is trying to build a dam. At the dawn of history the Nepalese chronicles say this Valley of Khatmandu was a great lake, full of snakes. And there was a self-grown lotus in its middle, which flowering, later became the small hill upon which our holy Buddhist temple of Swayambudnath was built. It was because of this lotus, a very God appearing on earth in flower shape, that the Buddhas and the gods were attracted to the Valley at first, and came here and desired to make it habitable. At that time the hills formed a great circle round the Valley, rimming the waters in so they escaped not, then came the giant god Manjusri from China, and in his compassion drew his sword and struck a cleft in the hills to let the waters out. You can see the place just about ten miles from here, it is called Choba, or sword cut, and there the River Baghmati runs in a stony gorge scarce forty feet wide between two elevations. That's the Buddhist story, but our Hindu chronicles add that the Lord Vishnu, the Preserver of Life, seeing the many snakes left after the waters receded, took pity and came here upon Garuda his steed, the bird-god, and Garuda destroyed the snakes. Hence he is always seen in stone with a collar of snakes round his neck. The Valley became habitable and fair and beautiful, and the haunt of gods, both Hindu and Buddhist, and of sages and saints.'

'Wasn't Buddha born in Nepal?' asks Hilde.

'Indeed He was,' answers Sharma. 'At Lumbini, two thousand five hundred years ago, the Light of the World, the Lord Gautama was born. And that is why here, where all gods are friends, walking in company together, you will find no segregation in temples or shrines, and there are no untouchables, as in India.'

'But you've got Tantrism,' says Enoch. 'That's really primitive, isn't it?'

'It's an older, more primitive type of religion. The Tantric deities are female, goddesses, and as everybody knows it is the female who is bloodthirsty and vindictive, and demands blood sacrifices. Always the blood of young male animals.'

'It's a most frustrating situation for serious study,' John says, pompous. 'People here tell stories which flatly contradict each other. I was asking about a shrine I saw this morning. "What is the name of the god?" I asked some of the worshippers. I got three different names and five different stories. Most off-putting.'

'Not at all,' says Sharma. 'What's in a story? It is only an interpretation, an assembly of words to express our feelings about an event. Some of the worshippers adored the god under one of his incarnations or names, and the others under a different one. Even in our religious festivals there's always improvisation and change. That's because so many different blends of ritual come in that one is never quite sure what is due next. It is most creative and stimulating.'

'I find it completely inefficient,' says John. 'It's hopeless trying to make a scientific, serious study of religion in Nepal. It's a mess. And the more one goes into it, the more degenerate and obscene it all is. Worse than India.'

John seems very purposeful. At the end of the lunch, as the others leave, he asks me again, as yesterday: 'Well, Anne, when are you going to come back to me and stop this childishness? It's very awkward for all our friends. ... I've had to *beg* Isobel to be patient or she'd have turned you out right away.'

And again I reply: 'I don't think I'll come back.'

He bursts out laughing, in high good humour. 'Oh dear,' he says, 'don't sound so dramatic. You'll get over this tantrum in a few days and then you'll come back to me.'

Chapter 5

MARTHA REDWORTH walked across the lawn with Vassili lumbering good humouredly in the rear. They stopped by the rose arbour and Vassili plucked a rose and put it behind his ear. Martha threw an expert glance at the rose bush, muttered something about pruning, then tripped on, the wet grass rustling under her shoes.

'My dear, dear Anne, do forgive me butting in while you're still at breakfast. Yes, thanks, I'll have more coffee. I was on my way to the airfield and we thought we'd drop in on you. Why is it that meals outside taste so much better than in one's home? This coffee is *delicious*. And you look *so* well. Tiddlywinks is off for two days with Major Pemberton ... the Gurkhas, you know. ... I thought I'd start getting myself organized, there's *so* much to do for the Coronation. We shall be having eight guests, people staying with us ... all those menus to plan for each day ... can't give them the same thing twice. I mean Tiddlywinks and I can have some cold meat and salad but it won't do for the V.I.P.s at all. Vassili's helping me compose the menus.'

On she rattled, making a cheerful noise, covering the small emotions of the meeting with a tinge of official sanction. Vassili looked at the table-cloth. Perhaps he recognized it as coming from his hotel.

'And now we've got the garden party. I simply don't know how I'm going to get proper lighting installed. Last year at the Queen's Birthday Unni helped so much. Put up some wonderful lamps and bulbs and things. I'm just going to give the pilot at the airfield a note to take up to Bongsor to tell Unni that Tiddlywinks and I are in a fix about the garden party. I hope he comes soon.'

'So do I,' said Vassili. 'I've got a French woman at the hotel who's got a letter of introduction to him. An unattached female. "*Où est Monsieur Menon?*" she shouts. "I 'ave a letter from a friend of 'is in Bombay. 'e must take me around." It appears she has written or is writing a book, *Men of Five Continents*. It's supposed to be a classic encyclopaedia on the different ways men have of making love all over the world. I think she wants to add Unni to her collection. He's not exactly inhibited, and she's not bad looking. It'll be a nice change from his dam.'

'Oh dear,' said Martha Redworth, 'how wicked you men are, and so early in the morning too. I think Unni is a dear. Positively the only man I would trust with my own daughter, anywhere.'

'It's not what he does, it's what the women want him to do,' grinned Vassili.

'Well, I must be going,' said Martha, consulting her watch. 'Goodness, it's stopped again. I must pop into the Hospital, and then the airfield – there's a woman journalist coming to interview me for an article on Khatmandu. She wants to go and see some clay pots. The trouble we've already had with those clay pots! I've asked Sharma to come with us and stand right behind her ... it wouldn't do at all if someone pinched her bottom.'

'Why not?' said Vassili. 'Isobel survived.'

'But this woman's from the *Manchester Guardian*,' said Martha.

*

Anne wrote:
Another tea session with History, Geography, and Isobel. These weekly meetings are held on Wednesdays in Isobel's drawing-room.

I enter and the slight buzz of voices which I could hear from the corridor stops. History and Suragamy McIntyre are sitting on the sofa. Isobel is standing, arms folded across a Boadicea bust. Three faces look at me. This time disapproval is plain, and Suragamy sniggers openly, olively. Although it is warm she wears a sweater, dark brown.

Geography comes in, bustling, a little dusty. 'Oh, sorry,' she says, 'I'm late. I walked to Father MacCullough's. I thought I'd make it in time. Ta,' she says, as Isobel hands her a cup of tea.

There follows a horrible three minutes of arch talk.

'You walked? You don't mean to say you walked all that way and back?'

'Indeed I did. I like walking.'

'All that dust and everything?'

'It isn't the dust I mind, that's natural,' says Geography generously. 'Jolly good exercise in this weather, walking. It's all those pagodas and things on the way. There weren't any pilgrims about though, they've all gone back now the Siva thing is over.'

'Thank God it's over,' says History fervently. 'It's the worship of the Golden Calf, that's what it is.'

'Pure wickedness,' says Isobel, her voice more shocked than usual.

'You went to Pashupatinath I hear,' says Suragamy McIntyre. 'How did they let you in?' She holds her teacup with a crooked little finger.

'I don't know,' I say, trying to sound offhand.

'Praise the Lord,' says Geography, '*some* of us are saved.'

'I wonder they let you in,' persists Suragamy McIntyre. 'They never allow Christians or white people into the temple, never.'

I'm not going to fight, so I just smile and help myself to a cake.

'Well, I hope it was quite an experience for you,' says Isobel. 'I suppose you'll write it up for a magazine article, or something.'

'Yes, I suppose so,' I reply. Meek and docile. I imitate Rukmini's voice in my retreat into gentleness.

We go on drinking tea. They are all angry at me, but they do not dare to say what they want to say. We talk of classes instead. We are supposed to give a weekly report to Isobel.

'Lakshmi has dropped too many attendances,' says Isobel sharply. 'Do you know the reason?'

'Yes, I believe she's pregnant.'

Isobel's hands are flung on the table with consternation.

'What, again? It's hopeless.'

'By the way, you haven't been to one of our hymn meetings yet,' says History. 'How about tomorrow? You're free, aren't you?'

In a moment of weakness I say yes.

The thunderstorm has not discharged itself when I leave.

*

'Well!' said Geography to History.

'I'm disappointed with the Head,' said History, 'very disappointed. I think she ought to have said something right here, don't you?'

'I think it's a dreadful, perfectly dreadful situation,' said Geography with relish, 'and such a *bad* example for the girls.'

'And then she walks in here, brazen as brass, quite cool. And only left her husband a week ago!'

'Ten days ago, dear. She left him on Sunday before last, and today is Wednesday the week after. And then she was with Fred Maltby, night before last, shut up in his office, and the lights didn't go on for *at least* an hour.'

'Oh,' said Suragamy McIntyre, at the window, excitedly. 'Look, Miss Maupratt is going towards the bungalow.'

'Oh, is she? Let me see,' said History and Geography.

All three crowded the window, looking out. Isobel was seen walking towards the bungalow, then disappeared as the trees, thick with leaf, hid her from sight.

'Oh, goody, goody,' said Geography. 'That woman's got it coming to her, I hope.'

'Well, I think we'll be having another lecturer in English soon,' said History.

'Praise the Lord,' said Suragamy McIntyre.

'Come in, Isobel,' said Anne.

Isobel walked in. She did not sit down. She looked round. There was no change, except a bronze lamp neatly hung from the ceiling throwing bars of light and shadow across the room, increasing the sensation of being in another world, a planet on its own whose tone was gold, while outside the blue soft mists of evening gathered round, as the sea gathers round a lonely ship.

'Well, you've made yourself quite comfortable, I see.' In a recess in the wall behind a curtain, half-drawn, of handwoven Nepalese cloth, grey with a small blue and yellow pattern, hung Anne's dresses. Isobel fixed her glance upon them, accusingly. 'I do hope you won't mind my saying so, Anne, but there's been an awful lot of talk lately. About your leaving John. I do hope it's not true.'

'It is true,' said Anne. 'I've left him. Ten days ago, to be precise.'

'May I sit down?' said Isobel. 'This is quite shattering, I must say. I do hope you know what you're doing. I don't want to judge ... I don't know what is the matter between you and John ... but I feel you're not giving yourself a chance.'

Anne squatted on the orange raza, folding her legs under her as did the Indian girls. Her hand fingered the book which lay upon it. The *Bhagavad-Gita* given her by the Field Marshal, The Song of God, of the Lord Krishna. Inside it, the edge protruding, was the photograph taken on the lawn. Unni with a flower above the ear under a Nepalese cap, smiling Rukmini, little Devi, Lakshmi, Deepah ... the beautiful, the careless, the heathen. ... Perhaps Fred Maltby had taken that forgotten snap.

'You must confide in your friends, Anne, who're trying to help you, and especially in God. There's nothing that God can't do in his Infinite Mercy.'

'Yes,' said Anne. 'Believe in God, and he will pull you through.' Those were the words of the hymn she'd heard, floating on the air that evening, after visiting Vassili in prison, when she'd been so tired. Only which God was one to believe in? Christ or Krishna? And which God was it that Isobel invoked? And anyway, what did God have to do with all these petty affairs of man? She felt like saying petulantly, flippantly: What I need is a man, not a God. A real, tall dark 'n' handsome honey of a man. Honey ... a voice like dark, dark honey ... suddenly there it was, the voice, the hands, Unni Menon, so vivid, so entire, that Anne put both her hands on her face, abruptly wanting to cry out.

'My dear,' said Isobel rising, rushing to the couch, putting an arm round Anne. 'You must be quite upset with all this, most upset. One *must* pull oneself together, though, it does *no good* to lose one's control. This way lies wickedness and Hell, believe me.'

But the shoulders under her hand were not heaving with sobs as she had hoped. Anne's hands dropped from her face. She looked young, thin, and had black shadows under her eyes.

'Here,' said Isobel, 'you look quite worn out. I'm sure you're going through a lot, though I think we often make ourselves suffer unnecessarily because we have no faith in our true friends, and especially in the One True Friend. I'm sure if you think it over and pray tonight, you'll feel better and you'll go back to the Royal Hotel tomorrow.'

'No,' said Anne. 'I don't think I'll go back.'

'Why?' said Isobel. 'What's happened? What *can* have happened to make you do a thing like that? It's a very serious thing, my dear. I can't believe it's anything that John's done. He's got a very fine character. I came here with John on that Sunday, but you were asleep, that bearer of yours wouldn't open the door. John was *quite* desperate, he'd rushed up to *me*, poor man, begging for help, as soon as he'd found you'd gone.' Isobel's nostrils quivered with compassion, her frame squared with responsibility, bearing John's distress upon herself. 'He was *utterly* prostrate. You know he wasn't well. Taken ill after that dreadful, hair-raising drive on the road. I couldn't blame him if he lost his temper with you when you wanted to go out again that very night. But he certainly didn't expect you to run away like that, to leave him, especially when he was so ill, just because he told you not to go to that obscene Siva Festival ... surely Anne, you were behaving like a spoilt child, don't you think?'

'Perhaps,' said Anne. She hadn't really listened to Isobel's version. Her heart was painful, knocking against her ribs. Unni Menon. Unni. Of course. Unni. His voice, his hands ... her arms and legs were now covered with gooseflesh and the waters of desire in her mouth; the yearning, the fire, the sweetness in the marrow of the bone. Call it what you will, there it was. If only this woman would go away, leaving her alone with this, this cruel and wonderful sweet lust, desire come like a lightning flash streaking the sky, showing her a whole new world.

'Well, now,' said Isobel, 'forgive and forget, that's my motto. I guess you were hurt, and that's why you came here. But it's giving rise to a lot of talk, and it's not good for your reputation, nor for the Girls' Institute, so may I just send a note round to John to come and fetch you, say tomorrow morning?'

'I lunch with John,' said Anne. 'I go to lunch at the Royal Hotel every day. He sees me then. We talk.'

'Oh,' said Isobel, taken aback. 'I didn't know that. Well then, don't you think it's absurd, going on as you're doing?'

'I'm not going back. I must be alone, think things out for myself.'

'I'm sorry,' said Isobel, rising. 'I'm sorry to hear that. I should have thought this was *quite* simple, really. John was not well, lost his temper a bit, and off you go. ... I was able to reassure him,' she continued, 'I asked him to be patient, to give you a week or so to recover your balance.' Anne smiled, remembering that John had said that it was he who'd asked Isobel to be patient. 'You make me feel sorry I ever gave you this bungalow, Anne. It's being misused at the moment. As a writer I thought you might need a place of your own. I didn't mean you to stay here though. I was *very* surprised to find you'd changed the room downstairs and got two servants to come in without asking my consent. Very surprised indeed.'

'I'm sorry, Isobel, but the bungalow does not belong to you,' said Anne. 'It belongs to someone else. You had no right to give it to me in the first place.'

'Why,' said Isobel furiously, 'of all the ... I can guess who told you that. That sex fiend Unni Menon. If he dares to show his face here I'll have him arrested. Runs after every woman he can get hold of. Can't keep his hands off them. Let me tell you that the whole place is rented by our Board, and I've a perfect right to this bungalow. I'll take it up with the Government. We shall see.'

She stood, ravaged, angry, powerless, defeated, and bluffing. 'I don't think there's anything more to be said. You're heading for disaster, Anne, I warn you. I'm afraid if you persist in your strange conduct we shan't be able to keep you, it would be most detrimental to the reputation of the Institute.'

Anne did not answer, and Isobel went firmly past the ironical, unwinking eyes, and downstairs.

As a river begins, trickle, seep, spurt, and then strong tide, flood deep and wide knocking at its banks, so did the anguish in Anne grow through the days.

The journal started, intimate, her own self self-explained, now receded, detached, and she was reticent towards it as towards another person, noting down events but not what happened to herself. And therefore the paper yellowed in the typewriter, while she lay on the orange quilt, sluggish yet tense, torpid and sensitive at once, no longer in that fine exaltation which had lifted her from the stagnant laguna of the plains, but in this extinguishment which made her inarticulate. Yet there was a change in the fabric of her silence. Lying flat or sitting for hours clasping her chin, staring between the trunks of the walnut trees at the soft mountain beyond, non-doing was not an empty, hopeless staring at nothingness. It had become the immobility of one helplessly carried, carried stupefied by a current too strong to resist.

Around her shone the temples and the shrines, new scrubbed, painted, daily more revealing; above the hills, the snow lords were incandescent at dawn and sunset, gleaming blue and white till noon, then muffled by cloud mushrooming round them like some bulky sky vegetation.

In Anne's room the parakeets hurt to look at, like something that cannot scream its distress, cut flowers, a dumb animal wordless under blows. The painted eyes, unblinking, challenged her to look at herself. Who could escape their gaze? In dreams she saw them, felt watched. They would not let her escape herself. They were the All-seeing Consciousness, the eye within the grave looking at murderer Cain. The superfetatory lines of Hugo floated back out of time, out of French learnt at the Maupratt School: *L'œil était dans la tombe, et regardait Caïn.*

Ever since the day when, with Suragamy and Isobel, History and Geography, Anne had climbed the hill of the lotus, and painfully the lesson of inward sight had begun for her, the eyes had not let her go.

Four days after her last encounter with Anne, Isobel announced to the staff that they must have a picnic on Sunday. Everybody *must* go. They'd pack sandwiches in a basket, visit Swayambudnath, the Buddhist temple built on a hill – 'It's the least indecent of the lot' – then go on into the valley, find a nice spot to eat lunch, and return home again.

'Swayambudnath is the hill which is supposed to have been a lotus and turned into a mountain. Don't you think all these heathen superstitions are funny? Like children's fairy stories,' said Suragamy to Anne. For the past four days the staff, including Isobel, had suddenly begun to treat Anne with an overwhelming friendliness. Christian charity, or feminine reversal?

Anne remembered Sharma's story of the living lotus, floating upon the waters when the Valley was an inland sea, and transformed into a hill when the Valley became the abode of gods. It was about three miles from the city, and from the air the golden spire of Swayambudnath protruded amid green trees.

Jovial, dank greasy hair dripping brilliantine, Suragamy's fiancé came with them. He informed them that he always got up very early, and had already done a lot of 'business' that morning. He and Geography talked of the last hymn meeting.

'By the way, you missed it, though you said you'd come,' said History reproachfully to Anne. She must come next time.

'It's in the bungalow *next* to Dr Maltby's at the Serene Palace. Two of our nurses live there,' said Geography.

The fiancé volunteered to drive the Institute jeep. It was a squeeze with Isobel and History and Geography in the back, Suragamy, her fiancé, and Anne in front, with squeaks and giggles and History calling, 'Shove off over there!' and inching of buttocks on unprovided space.

'Girls, girls, behave yourselves,' cried Isobel, indulgent.

The jeep stumbled from crest to ridge to pit in the humpy dirt road across the fields, while round them the April morning produced thrushes treading among fat green leaves, and diminutive people in homespun the colour of the earth hoeing long rows by hand, cauliflowers and cabbages in baskets sunning at door sills, and onions hanging in thick braids from roof eaves, a world patient and tranquil within the cup of the near hills. The sun was upon them all, and History and Geography were excited by it and kept wriggling and uttering exclamations and remarking on all they saw.

'Coo, look at that child carrying a jar – it's as big as he is, poor thing.'

'What do they wash their hair with that mud for, Suragamy?'

'Oh, another procession. I wonder what it is. ...'

And so on.

The sun upon Suragamy made Anne think of moss and slime clinging to rock, there was an inherent biliousness about her and her clothes.

Isobel sat erect, like some benign statuary. 'I daresay I shall be able to climb those awful steps,' she said. 'I feel quite well these days.'

'You didn't last year, dear,' reminded History, 'you were out of breath in no time.'

'I'll take them easily,' said Isobel. 'I'll beat you girls to it, see if I don't.'

The hill was soon reached, sparse of grass, stony and shaded with old tall trees. At the foot were two large Buddhas with rapt faces of inward equipoise. There was about the tranquil slopes a holding in beatitude, stillness debarring triviality. On either side of the steps climbing up the hill elephant-headed and bird-headed deities of the Hindu persuasion, daubed and flowered, and meditative Buddhist saints, were placed in the usual confusion of dogmas; the elephant gods, trunks fondled to nothingness by patting, reminiscent of Rome and St Peter's fast disappearing foot destroyed by devout kisses. And everywhere, upon the gods, among the trees, on the steps, scratching, picking fleas, clambering, swinging from boughs, eating, copulating, staring at the visitors, were monkeys.

'Oh,' cried Suragamy, terrified. 'Monkeys! They bite, and then you *always* die. I had a friend who was bitten, and she died seventeen days later.'

'Don't be a silly-billy,' said Isobel. 'I'm not scared of monkeys.'

But Suragamy clung to the fiancé, who clutched her, blanched, as frightened as she.

They began walking up the steps, Isobel first, valiantly, Anne behind, lagging, their backs disturbing her constant painful–pleasurable dream, but better than their faces with mouths flapping. Then she felt watched, and raising her eyes above her companions and the monkeys, saw the egg-like, enormous white dome, the large golden cube set upon it like a face brooding above a cloud, a face crowned with a high golden cone, and two large painted eyes with winged brows arched in concentration looking down; the One Consciousness, All-seeing, All-embracing, spreading the protection of its gaze upon men, beasts, and gods, in the Valley of Khatmandu.

Above the cube, from the spire, the wind wafted long white streamers inscribed with Buddhist prayers. The stairs went up, up, narrowing and becoming steeper and encumbered with small shrines and stupas on both sides, and the formal symbols of Siva, the phallic lingams, thrust of life, disguised with Buddhist carvings. Among them the monkeys with little pinks hands and faces went nibbling and spilling the flowers and the offerings and uttering guttural small cries.

Up they went, step by step. Anne looked, turned, paused to stare at the Valley that was being encompassed by the eyes, a pink daze of roofs in milky sunlight, the white tower of Bhim Seng's Folly, a profile of tiered pagodas, a horizon of hills.

'Oh my,' cried Isobel, panting, 'these steps *are* something.'

The last forty were divided in two by a hand-rail and mounted very steeply. The eyes were now near, looming above them, unwinking, never letting go. Between them was a dot upon the golden forehead, and below it the nose was drawn like a question mark. With laughter and loud voices a crowd of Tibetans came hopping and skipping down. A baby monkey ran in front of them and Suragamy cried with fear. The mother monkey appeared, baring her teeth. The Tibetans called at her, snapping their fingers, saying 'Hey, hey', as if to a dog. The mother collected her baby, who clung between her hind legs, and went off into the trees.

'Come on,' shouted Geography, 'come on, you slow-coaches.' Arms akimbo, legs apart, with the eyes just behind her, she watched Isobel and History race up the last steps.

They were now on the circular marble platform surrounding the central egg-like edifice. The platform was untidy with a prolificacy of shrines, stupas, bells, statues of all sizes and shapes. Round the waist of the egg went hundreds of Tibetan prayer mills in two rows, bronze cylinders each incised with the words *Om Mani Padme Hum*. There were the usual pi-dogs nuzzling among the offerings of rice upon leaves and flower petals and milk, there were pigeons and doves and crows in foraging squads, and everywhere among the gods, eating, scratching, copulating, were monkeys. Walking round the prayer wheels, turning them with one hand as they walked in the act of prayer, making offerings at the smaller shrines with sprinkling of marigolds and hibiscus and food and water, were men and women, many from the Buddhist northern valleys, Sherpas and Bottyas and Tibetans.

Slowly the staff walked round the terrace, exclaiming at all they saw, and Anne felt them coarse and lacking reverence, and was ashamed to be with them.

Behind the central stupa they came upon a larger shrine with a black and silver image inside it and cascades of bells, big and small, in front of it. There knelt a man and a woman, Gurungs from the hills. Gold encrusted with turquoises hung in the woman's hair and in the lobes of her ears, so distended that the round hollow hole seemed to Anne like another empty eye staring. On the woman's lap lay a parcel, a bundled baby, face covered with a small dirty grey cloth. Next to the man and woman was the usual muffled and ragged little Newari priest; in front of them pewter jars and flowers and offerings wrapped with leaves on a tray.

'Oh, what is it?' cried Geography, bending over the group. 'Ask them what it is,' she said to the fiancé.

The fiancé spoke to the priest, who seemed to conduct the ceremony with the usual indecisive casualness, and grinned at them, pleased with an extra audience.

'The baby has had smallpox and is blind, so the parents have come to pray to the Goddess of Smallpox,' said the fiancé, indicating the dark image.

The mother turned her face upwards, smiling at Geography. Her gaze caught the eyes on the golden cube, and she pointed at them and then at the baby.

Geography took charge. She squatted by the mother, uncovered the baby's face, lifting the cloth. From a mess of crusts and pus two white stones stared at the sky.

'Oh, how horrible, how perfectly monstrous,' screamed Isobel, covering her face with her hands. History also made indignant noises. Suragamy wrapped her coat tight round her and took three steps back. But Geography bent over the baby, her face worried, concerned. She took the stinking bundle in her arms from its unwilling mother. Anxiously she egged the fiancé to translate. The parents MUST take the child to the Hospital, down in the Valley, not far. She gave directions. They could go, right now. Half-heartedly, with that infuriatingly resigned shrug of the half-Westernized Indian contemptuous of his own people, the fiancé translated. Geography looked pleadingly at the mother. The mother smiled, saying neither yes nor no. The priest went on chanting. The father rose, went to the black image, fondled and kissed its hands and poured milk upon its head.

Geography, defeated, stood up. Her lips were trembling, she seemed on the verge of tears. Her feet were in sandals, there was a large bunion on the joint of each big toe. It must hurt her to walk. And now Anne was ashamed of herself. She'd mocked, scorned Geography, felt she was vulgar and narrow-minded, yet it was she, with her aching feet, who had tried to do something for the baby. It was she, and people like her, who would one day convince other mothers not to let their children go blind. ... Anne could only stop, look, and pass on, 'and maybe write it down to make myself feel better'.

Isobel now said they wouldn't be able to eat anywhere on this hill with all the monkeys about. They left by the back of the hill where a filthy lane ran between decrepit priests' houses and then went diving down the slope, and in the blue sky they could see a black ridge, snow encrusted, and further behind that a snow peak unsmothered by cloud above the ridge, inviolate revelation. There was a twist in the path, and Khatmandu was below them, soft and silvery below their feet.

Another pair of eyes of the All-seeing Consciousness, from yet another face of the golden cube, went following them as they walked down. Anne came home to find the stare again, in her own room, a contemplation now associated with the pale stones that were the baby's eyes. And it was added desolation that the Ever-watchful, All-seeing Consciousness should be stone-blind.

The General came across the lawn, looking like a tall flag-pole on an amble.

'I hope the servants look after you well, madam?'

'I am very happy here,' said Anne.

'Happiness is difficult, for it is non-desire, madam, non-attachment as the Lord Krishna teaches us in the *Bhagavad-Gita*, and that is very difficult.'

'It is difficult,' admitted Anne, 'to control one's desires.'

'Who said control? The man who represses himself without knowledge is as evil as the man who abandons himself to evil. Is it not written in The Song of God:

> The abstinent run away from what they desire,
> But carry their desires with them;
> And desires unfulfilled corrupt inwardly.

But the way to detachment is arduous, more so than climbing the highest mountain. For that one must, it seems to me, have wandered in the valleys and the foothills, tasted many of the joys of life, and have a full heart, before letting go.'

'My heart seems to have shrunk in the past few years.'

'That it does,' said the General. 'For we are frail, we humans. The heart shrinks, it shrinks under blows, it shrivels and dies. O Miracle, it blooms again, but with great timidity, and that is the perilous moment, the moment of choosing.'

When Anne looked up again, the General had gone.

> Time of renewal, when I come back from where I go
> I shall know
> What to do next, lizard shedding skin,
> Renewing same old lizard.

Now where on earth, thought Anne, did I get that quotation? And then she saw Rukmini coming across the lawn in the sunny afternoon with a cardboard file under her arm.

Rukmini sat down upon the grass, her legs folded under her, in the supple way which Anne had practised and now could also do. She drew some large sheets of paper from the file.

'I painted this.'

It was the wedding.

'You were there,' said Rukmini.

'Oh Rukmini, it is so good!' Anne held them up. Gay, splendid, the wedding: the musicians, swaying and playing their flutes, agile brown hands tapping a ta-la upon the drums; the groom in a shimmer of silk; the Maharanis in satin liquefaction of clothes and jewels with long lovely eyes and flowered hair. And there was Anne, standing by the piano, with her face raised, looking up, a hand extending, towards nothing at all.

'It is excellent, Rukmini. You'll be a great artist one day.'

They sat together on the grass. Rukmini did not speak. She looked round her, a floating gaze, resting with equanimity upon the fields, the trees, the bungalow, the mountain. She took out some pencils from a bag and began sketching Anne. Anne read the *Bhagavad-Gita*. They had nothing to say that would not be trivial. They understood each other well. They were both waiting for the same man's return.

And then was a wan, pale night when Anne woke, hearing his voice say 'Anne!' outside; went to the windows, half-closed because of the sudden cold when the sun went down; bent out to peer, all her skin gooseflesh at memory of his voice; walked downstairs, past Regmi and Mita asleep bundled in the corridor; lifted the heavy bar of the door, and was in the bleak outside, in a landscape of grey sifted silver, and nothing there but all alone the sleepless moon.

Until the evening darker than night when returning from a drink with the Redworths she saw, beyond the shadows of the fountain and the rose arbour, in the dense fall of the walnut trees, a denser shadow standing, and knew it as if her eyes could pierce the night. She walked slowly across the small lawn, trailing her feet in the grass, filled suddenly, full as a fruit with sweetness and darkness, with this new thing so new, and stood in front of him unmoving, and they stared with their night-blind eyes at their unseen unsmiling faces, enemies before a battle measuring each other. And then Anne spoke, not words from the conscious self known as Anne, but from the depths of a being beyond words of mouth, primitive, female, and hungry.

'Will you help me,' she said, 'Unni, will you help me, please?'

Perhaps he was looking at her, but she could not see it and could only guess the pain in him as he said: 'Then I shall be enmeshed, I shall be caught ... you are asking me for myself.'

'I want to be alive. Alive, not half dead, not like this.'

'Ah,' he said, but not bitterly, 'and now love must turn to passion first, and through our bodies play the compulsory game.'

'Don't you want to be enmeshed?'

He was silent, deciding.

'Yes, I think I do.'

He took her hand, as at the temple. She listened to her own steps up the stairs, but did not hear his, until they were in the golden light, and she was frightened suddenly of him, for he was a stranger.

'Put out the light,' she implored. 'Put out the light.'

He lifted his arm in that grave, masculine elegance with which he moved. She walked to the bed in the darkness and he lay along her, and there was nothing else, no other world but this new world of being, of darkness and delight.

She woke, thinking herself at sea, dreaming still. The wind howled an oceanic sound outside the windows. The lamp swung as from a cabin ceiling, swinging its light across the parakeets. Even the bed under her seemed to move gently.

O wind, deliverer, you've blown me clean with rain, away, away.

'It is passing,' said the voice of Unni. 'It will be over soon.'

The baying waters bounded and clattered and finally stopped, and the heaving of the grass and the leaves came to her, and the smell of rain, softly, softly.

She saw him then, sitting in the chair, lean and long in his shirt-sleeves and trousers, smoking, looking at her in bed. Already the room was different: it seemed to leap at one, singing, it wore a mild, cheerful untidiness. His leather jacket was thrown upon the floor. A bottle and glasses were on the desk, there was the smell of his cigarette, and his bigness, the warmth and size of the man as he rose seeing her awake, walking to the desk, pouring whisky and soda in a glass.

Gradually the feel of her own body was coming back to her, a slow, relished tiredness. She stretched and said 'Aaaaah.' Unni came to the bed and stood, handing her the glass.

'Where on earth did you get whisky and soda and ice cubes at this hour, Unni?'

'Sent Regmi over to the Royal Hotel for these.'

'In the middle of the night?'

He nodded, and Anne laughed, and then couldn't stop laughing, spluttering in her glass, putting her glass down on the floor the better to smother her face in the pillow with laughter. Unni ran his hand through her hair and she stopped laughing, shivers running on her skin, arching her muscles, her body already ready again, desirous again.

'Oh don't,' she begged. 'It's terrible what you do to me, Unni. I just don't understand it. I'm supposed to be frigid. And here I am.'

'You're liquid fire, I shiver too when I look at you. And I want it this way. I want you to desire me. And I shall please you ... at least, I hope I shall.'

'I suppose it's quite wrong,' said Anne, 'but I don't care.'

'Of course it's wrong, but we are a man and a woman ... and the gods are merciful. They will understand.'

'How familiar you are with your gods.'

'The skin on your face,' he replied, 'is very soft, like silk.'

'I peeled right off, after those two days on the road. This is my new skin. Do you remember the road?'

'Do I remember. I've thought of nothing else, these three weeks away from you. And the Siva Festival. That's when I decided to do something about you.'

'You gave me your jeep to drive. What a mad and dangerous thing it was, Unni. Tiddlywinks was terrified. I don't think he's quite forgiven me yet. Why did you do it?'

'Didn't you guess? I was putting my life in your hands, giving myself to you.'

'Don't make fun of me, Unni,' she said, a little sadly.

He did not reply. He tugged thoughtfully at her hair.

'I wonder what will happen,' said Anne, trying to sound detached, composed, and objective. 'I wonder if this is going to last, I wonder ...'

'Hush,' he said. 'We haven't started yet. Time enough for our other selves to take over, ideas, fears, principles, moralities, to torment us. Virtues grow out of our passions and I suppose we too shall turn our passionate angels into righteous devils. But tonight is for you, for your body, and the heart in your body which needs tenderness. Look, the rain is over, soon it will be day, and until day don't let us think too much, shall we?'

'Oh Unni, if I could only tell you ...'

'One day you will. But now to deny what is, is to lie. To fear to love is to run away. To fear to give too much is to be a miser of life. I am whole-hearted in this, and if you are only using me as a male I shall know it one day, for I do not wish to be used, least of all by you. But I don't think you are, Anne. However, we shall see.'

'Hold me,' said Anne, 'hold me again.' She must not say too much, not try to mouth words over what was real. He was there, with her, and she remembered the glad surprise, the cry of happiness when he had taken her, skilful, gentle, and strong, and she had found no obstacle, only her own body, fervent, leaping to his in that frantic passionate attention, which is the act of love. This physical excellence, felicity achieved, was rare and precious enough, and now it was hers. *I shall not ask more, not demand eternity when beauty and time is mine, now.*

And so it was, until the pickaxe voice of the cock broke the night, and from its grave Lazarus day came forth reborn.

Chapter 6

LIKE birds in spring, first one, then a cohort, came the correspondents, the reporters, the photographers, and the guests for the Coronation of King Mahendra in Khatmandu.

Among the earliest, Leo Bielfeld.

'Leo's arriving,' Anne told John at lunch at the Royal. 'D'you wish to come with me to the airport to fetch him?'

'Can't, I'm afraid,' replied John importantly. 'E. P., Pat, and I are going this afternoon to see the Megalorama people.'

'Yes, Mrs Ford,' said Enoch P., 'that's right. Megalorama's arrived with their equipment. John and I are going to see what we can do to help them organize their social contacts.'

Megalorama was, said E.P., a fabulous affair. Megalorama had flown in its own men, technicians, machines. That had meant chartering a special airliner (a fabulous machine) from the States. Since the airfield at Khatmandu was much too small for this giant Skyliner, it had landed at Delhi and Megalorama had transferred to a number of smaller craft to fly into the Valley. The entire team would live in its own tents, away from the population and every possible other contamination.

'They've got everything thought out. It's fabulous organization. Special clothing made of insulated fabric treated with antibiotics against leeches and mosquitoes and bugs and fleas, which will cover their feet and their bodies while they work so the chances of catching anything will be absolutely nil. And they've had special inoculations against smallpox, cholera, yellow fever, sandfly fever, polio, typhoid, paratyphoid, and they're getting extra vitamin shots. They've also made their own catering arrangements. All their food cooked and flown in sterile containers in special convoys of airplanes from Delhi every day. The scheduled cost is two hundred Indian rupees per head per twenty-four hours. That's only about forty dollars U.S.'

'Two hundred rupees per head per day!' exclaimed Anne, aghast.

'Yes, ma'am,' said Enoch with great pride. 'They're fabulously efficient. They won't see anybody except those main personalities that we'll be arranging for them to meet. But we've got to work fast. There's only six days to go before the Coronation now.'

The talk, as usual, veered to Nepalese inefficiency. Both John and Enoch P. had called upon and tried to 'fix up appointments' with various 'prominent personalities'. They'd got the list of Who's Who in Nepal from the State Department 'back home'.

'But these people just don't seem to realize how important it all is,' complained Enoch. 'Why, we've called three times on the Prime Minister and he's not been at home. Not once. Though we left our visiting cards and all.'

And though less than a week remained before the Coronation, there was still no schedule issued, no official programme, no furniture in the hostel, no bearers, nothing.

'Never mind all that. What's worse, there's no liquor,' said Vassili. 'Where's that Unni? I've been waiting for him all morning. He promised to drop in to help over the liquor and the bearers.'

'Probably busy with some woman or other,' said John. 'Indians just can't keep their hands off a skirt.'

'He was here this morning, quite early,' said Vassili, 'to fetch Miss Valport for a drive. She's the French girl. She's got a letter of introduction to him given by a friend in Bombay. But they can't be in bed together because at the moment Miss Valport is lunching with the Indian Ambassador.'

'That's probably an excuse, you know what I mean,' said John, winking heavily at Anne. The word 'French' still had for him in Khatmandu a sniggering connotation.

'If we do see him, we'll tell him you're waiting for him, Vassili,' said Enoch P. 'Say John, it's getting late. We'd better get going.'

'I'll collect Leo at the airfield,' said Anne, rising to leave.

'One moment, Anne,' said John. 'I want to speak to you.'

Enoch left to fetch Pat, and husband and wife faced each other across the hotel table.

'I wanted to say just one thing,' said John. 'It's about the Coronation. The place will be absolutely crawling with people, correspondents, journalists, what have you. Not only Leo and François, but a lot of other people who know us both. I happen at the moment, as Secretary of the Valley Club, to occupy an important, a responsible position in Khatmandu. And in no time at all there'll be talk about us. There is already, I expect. Though I've done my best to quash it.'

'What about it?'

'Don't try to be more obtuse than usual,' said John stiffly. 'I'm not going into the rights and wrongs of the case now. I've got work to do, I need *all* my energy to concentrate on the very important liaison work we're doing, trying to make the Coronation a big success. You can see what these people are like here. Worse than the Indians, when it comes to organization. I simply can't afford the time to try to make you see reason. If the truth were told I'm sure most people would be on my side. You're angry with me because you think I've gone off with another woman. Let me tell you that the way you've treated me, no man could have stood it. I think in all fairness you must realize that it's damn well your fault what's happened, and in fact if I got ill it was your fault too.'

'I know,' said Anne. 'All these years, everything's been my fault. Always.'

'Don't say it that way,' cried John. 'I won't have it. Making a martyr of yourself. You just distort and twist everything I say. What I say in simple, plain English is: are you going to come back to me as a wife now so we can have a happy Coronation together, and give up this nonsense about living alone at the Institute?'

And as Anne stared with profound composure upon some vision in front of her in space: 'That doctor chap says I'm perfectly all right. There's nothing wrong with me at all, whatever you may think.'

Anne rose and made to turn. John put a hand upon her arm.

'No, you're not going to get away from answering. I want an answer, right now. I'm not going to be ignored any longer.' He was shaking with something which Anne mistook for anger, and which was fear; his eyes were fixed upon her, under their glaze she could not guess how much he wanted just one word of affection, one small tenderness. Her gaze went up and down him, deadly, measuring, comparing, and she smiled.

John clenched his fists. 'You're a filthy bitch,' he said, in a low voice. 'A real tart, that's what you are. And I know who it is who's putting you up to this. It's that bloody doctor. Just let me get my hands on him and I'll break him, and you too.'

'Oh, John,' sang the voice of Pat, Vice-President of the Valley Club, 'yoohoo, are you ready, Jo-ohn?'

'Yoohoo, yes, ready!' John called brightly, slapping a smile on to his face.

Anne drove to Gaucher Airport to fetch Leo Bielfeld.

'Why, Anne,' cried Leo, 'I nearly didn't recognize you.'

'Have I changed that much?' said Anne, knowing she had changed.

'I can't describe it. There's something ... something ... I know,' said Leo, hugging Anne, 'you're having an affair.'

There was that flame in her face, an inner translucency, a lightness, something in her figure that touched him immediately. If he had automatically desired her before, he now felt puzzled, apprehensive, and upset. She's beautiful, he thought, astonished. How beautiful I'd not quite realized.

'Anne,' he said, moved by his own emotion towards her. 'You're beautiful, d'you know that?'

'I'm glad,' said Anne. 'I want to be.'

'Who is the lucky man?'

'I can't tell you. I don't even know if I'm in love.'

'Love,' said Leo, 'is glandular. And mountain air is wonderful for one's glands. A woman always *vibrates* more in the mountains. I remember a superb skiing holiday in Austria ... I resolved always to take my best girl friends four thousand feet up at least ... it made them vibrate so much more.' His eyes shone. He squeezed her arm. Anne had come off her pedestal. She was having an affair, and sensible, not romantic over it. He brightened with avidity. 'Whatever it is, it's fantastic the change it's made to you,' he said gaily. 'How long has it been going on?'

'I'm not in love,' said Anne, talking to herself. 'I don't think so. I feel too free, too unimpeded –'

'You look all that. Don't worry about love, Anne. Just have some fun. Sex is jolly good fun, isn't it?'

'I don't know, Leo.'

They went through the Customs in a flash. The officials smiled at them approvingly. Anne drove to the Royal Hotel.

'Ah,' said Leo, 'what a marvellous place. Fantastically beautiful. This soft air, so refreshing after the plains. It's already frightful in Calcutta. I suppose you've rented out your flat?' Anne nodded. 'And how's John? I came a few days before I needed to very much because of you. I wanted to see you again.'

He launched into the recital of his latest.

It was in Delhi he'd met Kisha, a receptionist in a hotel. She was crazy over him, crazy in that fulsome, sensuous, dramatic Indian way, had thrown herself in his arms. And the perfection of her body was such that he had had to look at her face, not so perfect, the skin a little too greasy, not to be surfeited.

'But you know what Delhi is like; only the Ridge, with jackals howling and shuffling all round the car, and now they even have snoopers with torch-lights. It's getting quite impossibly puritan, like every other capital in Asia.'

Kisha had started ringing at all hours of the day, and coming to his hotel room at night, and she got hungry in the small hours and leapt out of bed and ate bananas.

'She's a lascivious little thing,' said Leo complacently. 'Quite sex-mad, and so whole-hearted about it.'

And the manager had made remarks, so it had to be the Ridge and the jackals and the snoopers again.

Kisha's over-abundant physical perfection become cloying, Leo was glad to visit Nepal; escaping Kisha by sending himself an urgent cable, inviting himself to the Coronation. She had accompanied him to the airfield, trampling in her sari and pale with tragic sorrow; he had felt embarrassed. It was so conspicuous. 'Indian men still like their women shut up ... they don't really understand sex equality.' They'd been rude to Leo and her at the airport. He hoped that she would not descend upon him here in Khatmandu.

Leo professed himself enchanted with his room, which was small; and Hilde, whom he found strikingly beautiful. He was going to call upon one or two people in the Government, and upon the British Resident, Paul Redworth. 'I always try to get those necessary calls over in the first twenty-four hours. But let's have dinner together tonight.'

'I'm busy this evening,' said Anne, 'but I'll stay and have tea with you, if you like.'

They sat on the verandah and soon upon them swooped a group of people: robust, splendid, with smooth shoulders and flaming hair,

Mariette Valport the French girl, followed by Ranchit and Professor Rimskov.

'Vassili,' Mariette was saying, '*mais où est-il, ce* Vassili? Look what I 'ave.' She held up a bronze statue of a goddess, hieratic features and bronze hands. '*N'est-ce pas que c'est beau?*'

Professor Rimskov advanced upon Leo with exclamations of pleasure. It appeared they had met before.

'In Geneva,' insisted Professor Rimskov, 'I am sure it was Geneva. Two years ago. Before I went to Tibet.'

'Oh yes, of course,' said Leo, laughing with all his face, 'of course I remember now.'

Anne and Mariette found themselves seated at the same table. Mariette's skin was firm upon rosy flesh, her eyes sparkled, her voice was gay and loud. She exuded a kind of happy sexiness, with roving round black eye and sumptuous mouth, bust well shaped, hips not as stocky as most French women.

'*Et puis, moi, je dégringole, je monte, je descends* ... I agitate myself to take zese photographs ... but what a reward, when I arrive in Paris, all ze professors of the Sorbonne, zey are wild with joy. Zey come to my flat ... I arrange a small party, and I show my pictures and ah ... *ils en sont tout paf. Ils restent là à regarder* ...' she turned to Anne, '*et vous, madame,* you take photographs, yes?'

'No,' said Anne, 'I don't.'

'But what a sacrilege, *quel sacrilège,*' trumpeted Mariette Valport. 'Not to take pictures of all zese beautiful sings. But you cannot appreciate zeir beauty, madame, if you do not take photographs. For me, I cannot leeve wizout my camera, and I will sell all my photographs to ze best magazines. I will also write a book on my travels, I am sure it will be a fantastic success. I cannot understand people who are not for taking ze pictures. You know, I travel alone, and in Siam and in Indo-China I was always for finding small little *patelins, des tout petits patelins de rien du tout* and I used to say: zis will be a magnificent photograph, unique. And I am always right. *Et comme ça, j'en ai eu, moi, des bonnes prises* ...'

The men were getting restive; Professor Rimskov wanted to talk of Tibet; Leo wanted to talk about himself and wore an amiable listener expression upon his face; and Ranchit, at first fatuous, scenting new conquest, was now looking round, regretting Pat's more laconic presence. But Pat these days was taken up with Valley Club activities and Enoch P. With exclamations Mariette charged, riding the spirited charger of her own conversation, caracoling from subject to subject.

'... and I wanted to come to Nepal. Zen I 'ad a letter of introduction to Mr Menon from a friend. 'e told me all about 'im, zat 'e would 'elp me. And now zis morning I see 'im. I want to go and see ze mountains and ze dam 'e is building too. 'e is so 'andsome, like a bronze Apollo, zose shoulders, zose 'ips, and especially zose long long *cuisses*, like steel. *Magnifique. Et tellement froid, brrr ... c'est tellement excitant, un homme froid.*'

That hint was enough to bring back the men's attention to her, an attention spilling like sand under the spattering fountain of her verbiage. Ranchit pulled his little moustache. 'Don't waste your time on Menon, madam,' he said. 'He is a complete barbarian. He is quite incapable of appreciating a beautiful woman.'

'Oh, *vous croyez*?' said Mariette, laughing throatily. 'Well, Monsieur Ranchit, *I can* assure you zat Mr Menon is very appreciative.'

'In Tibet,' began Professor Rimskov in his high-pitched voice, 'the women –'

Murmuring something about being late, Anne slipped away. Leo followed her downstairs.

'What a charming gay girl, that Mariette Valport,' said Leo enthusiastically. 'Such a change from Kisha.'

Already Anne could see Leo returning to the table, settling by Mariette, listening and laughing, with motive in his smile. The compulsory game, the compulsory game. And suddenly she was swamped by the desire to see Unni, to hear him, to be with him in the darkness alive. She drove the jeep fast. She passed the main building of the Institute. A figure bent over the verandah railing, watching her return. Isobel or someone else? There was no one under the walnut trees, or on the lawn.

She entered the bungalow and there he was, sitting on the stairs, waiting for her. And it was as if a great burden she had been carrying had slipped off her shoulders.

'You're back,' he said, standing up smiling.

'Yes, I'm home, Unni,' she replied, putting a hand in his to walk up the stairs.

They had made love, then washed, sluicing water over their bodies, then eaten; Regmi serving them chicken curry with tender alacrity, while Mita sang in the darkness of her unpolluted kitchen where Anne was not admitted; and whatever was left of Anne's food Mita would throw to the birds, for Mita was a Brahman, though not a thorough-going one.

'In the first meeting, all at once, love caught me in the net of his eyes,' sang Mita.

'How they love love,' said Anne.

They lay together, companionably smoking, already the small habits of lovers established: the way a head moves to find a shoulder, nestles into it one way and no other; the way fingers light a match, hands cup to prolong the flame's existence; and the long touch of two bodies, desire appeased, lying next to each other, suspended in a tranquillity prelude to desire renewed. Now Anne could talk, not listening to herself, and Unni heard as if he were not there, thrusting no attentiveness upon her.

'I just cannot understand it ... I've made more love with you in the last few days than I have in the past three years. I didn't know I could ... it was all gone ... but I know you won't believe me.'

'I do believe you,' said Unni.

He got up to pour her a drink; a white linen dhoti was tied round his waist, and Anne's eyes followed him with an artist's which is a lover's delight in physical beauty of shoulders and flanks and burnished skin. Part of his physical attractiveness was a suave precision, an effortlessness in movement and in the handling of things, whether machines or bodies or, more subtly, relationships with other people. And he dressed and undressed with the dexterity of his people, who bathe in public rivers, change their clothes without exposing their bodies. A grave reticence was now incorporate in the pattern of their togetherness, their own climate of love and being, weather of their souls, landscape of their new liberty, and perhaps appointed imprisonment of each other. Now they could with difficulty imagine a time when it had not been thus; and Anne's astonishment at the ardours of her body, contrasted with its total abeyance for so many years, was already transmuted to an intellectual preoccupation round which the other selves which dwelt in her as a human being would hang their moral condemnations, their spiritual scruples, and their philosophical rationalizations. The physical revelation was endured, assimilated, the astonishment that it should be so remained.

'And I'm not even ashamed. At least, not when I'm with you. Although I know it's wrong, I'm being unfaithful to John.' She said it with a certain unfeeling smugness, due to the word 'unfaithful'.

'You'd been unfaithful to yourself long enough,' replied Unni, handing her a glass with a little whisky and a lot of soda in it. She had disliked whisky, but he drank it and remained unaffected, and now she liked to nurse a glass, twisting it round, watching the bubbles consume themselves into nothingness, sipping, slowly and always leaving more than half. Meanwhile a fecund timelessness surrounded their mental exploration of each other, consummating the physical harmony achieved.

'That's not an excuse for unfaithfulness,' said Anne. 'John's my husband; there is such a thing as for better, for worse, in marriage.'

'I'm not making excuses. When were the platitudes of adultery valid excuse for the platitudes of marriage?' He looked at her ironically above the glass he was drinking from, then put it down, ground out his cigarette in the Cupid-ringed ashtray (from the General's Victoriana), and lay down by her side again.

She was stung by his words. 'I earned that,' she said. 'I threw myself at you, like all the others.'

'What others?' He was genuinely surprised. He had not meant to hurt her by a general statement.

'The other women, Unni. Everywhere I go I hear your name coupled with women's names, this one or that one.'

'Who, for instance?' His fingers followed the insipid pattern on the quilt.

'Oh, well, just as a late instance, this French girl, Mariette Valport.'

'Anyone else?'

Rukmini, thought Anne. He is waiting for me to say Rukmini. And if I say it, it will be all over. She shivered, seeing the thin perilous margin upon which she had trod. He's like me, she thought in a flash, deceptively mild, and then one day it's over and he's gone.

'That's not the point at all. I didn't say I *minded* about other women, did I?'

'You're not worried by my polygamous tendencies? How very broad-minded of you!'

'Not a bit,' said Anne, laughing now, teased back into the languorous good humour of after-love.

'I love your laughter. Laughter cleans the teeth, and all extremes are reconciled in the orbit of a smile.'

'What an enchanting thing to say. Did you make it up?'

'It's a proverb from my native dialect.'

'Oh, do stop teasing, and don't stroke my hair. It makes me lose what little sense I'm trying to make. In our civilization a woman is conditioned to resent polygamy intensely. But I don't seem worried about it where you're concerned. I don't know why it is so. I am, however, worried about John. About the fact of adultery. People all assume that I left John because of his going off with another woman. It'll appear a more valid excuse than any other for my doing this. And John's excuse, of course, is that he was driven to it by my coldness. But all those explanations don't alter the fact that I am committing adultery, and it is an ugly word.'

'It is,' said Unni, 'an ugly word. Let's leave it at that.'

'I'll have to tell John one day,' persisted Anne. 'Otherwise it isn't fair.'

'Yes,' said Unni, '*we* will. In good time, when *I* decide it's right to do so. You will leave it to me.'

And that was exactly the way Anne had really wanted it, though she had not known it until he had spoken. 'I'll leave it to you, Unni,' she replied, and shivered with pleasure.

'And by the way, I too was at Ranchit's party, the same night as John.'

'Oh,' said Anne, sitting up straight.

'Don't get excited,' said Unni. 'I want you in my arms. Come, lie down again. I was there, and John, and others too. Ranchit is extraordinarily depraved. Organizes these parties, with women brought in, and isn't happy unless his guests avail themselves of the pleasures he provides.'

'Is that why John was so rude to you at breakfast that morning when we were going on the road?'

'I suppose so. John is easily frightened. He is a good fellow, lets not his upper nature register what his lower performs. Ranchit was not interested in making John misbehave. He wanted to debauch me. "Come on, Menon, another drink." Then he started. "Come on,

Menon, you great big lady-killer, show your stuff." Interspersed with long anecdotes about his own prowesses. "I don't eat meat out of a spittoon," I told him. This made him furious. "It's because you can't – you're impotent," he shouted. "I know it's just bluff with you. I've had every woman that you've tried to make," he said, "and I *know*. They've told me. You're no good. You're impotent. You've got nothing between your legs."

'Ranchit has always wanted to beat me at things, tennis, flying, importance, and now sexual potency. We went to school together, we're distantly related, he's a Class A Rana and I'm a commoner with only the vaguest claims to a fairly low caste. But in the world of today I am more important than he is and the only thing left at which he can beat me is women.

'And then, there was Rukmini.' Unni lit another cigarette, poured himself another drink, walked to the window to peer through the curtains at the night. (A pair of curtains had appeared, to Anne's surprise. 'I bought them,' Unni had said when she expressed surprise, 'you'll need them with me here.')

'I never touched Rukmini. She was always a child to me, a beautiful and distant cousin (yes, we're related too, all the Ranas are inbred). The day she reached puberty she was shut up for two weeks in a dark room, as is the custom; after that I never saw her alone again. She was not allowed to go out freely, to mix with males even of her own family. Three months later she was married to Ranchit. Her father needed money. That is why he sold his palace, which is now the Girls' Institute, and it's considered shameful for a Rana to rent his property. And Ranchit had money as well as caste. That was three years ago.'

'Poor Rukmini,' said Anne, 'poor, poor Rukmini.'

'I don't like to talk about it,' said Unni, 'so we shall not discuss it again. Shall we?' It was an order, and Anne accepted it. 'As for other women ...' he mused, smiling, his eyes going back over the women, all the women in his arms before Anne, and Anne saw them, saw him remembering each of them, 'I find it difficult to make love just glandularly, as Leo puts it. The preoccupation with amorous conquests which permeates so many men bores me now. But of course I've made love to women. Of course, though not so many as Leo.

'Sex measured in quantitative terms – that's what Ranchit and Leo

281

(though intelligent otherwise) think they want. A hunting record. I think they are afraid to love, that's why. They prefer to become emotional castrates, separating the act of their bodies from their feelings. They are afraid of suffering, of getting involved, so they cut themselves off from their actions emotionally, and sex becomes "good fun". But we believe that no one can perform without getting involved. We think that each man is imprisoned by his own deeds, and their kind of promiscuousness is dreary and just as desiccating as the abstinence *you* went through.'

'How do you know,' asked Anne, 'that I'm not like that too, wanting you to make love to me and no more?'

'I don't think you are. I never thought so. And I am not, Anne. I am in love with you.'

'Love,' said Anne. 'I always associate love with a great deal of pain and suffering. This is too gay and light-hearted, too fearless and easy.'

'How do you know you won't suffer terribly one day because of this?' said Unni.

Time and again, in those first days and nights, Anne was to argue her scruples, in the release by passion from the cloud of passion; elaborate them at more or less length, treading round and round like some feline which goes shoulder glancing off the iron rods of its encircling cage; as she knocked against the word-made barriers of oughts and shoulds, she knew that she was only giving herself more reasons, in words, for continuing to make love with Unni Menon.

In lucid intervals (or thinking herself so) her intellect prodded and probed, trying to discover flaws in their relationship, to find in their motives and intentions the imperfect and the impure, interrogating the future with rational, cold logic.

'It's only because I was starved,' she threw at him (after losing herself in a paroxysm of sensuality of which she had not known herself capable), 'it's just that I needed a man, I'd been starved too long.'

'Certainly,' said Unni. 'But why then did you wait until me? Whatever your friend Leo may think, you and I make love not because of glands alone. Otherwise, it might be Leo here, now. Or Ranchit.'

Against this simple faith she exhausted argument and as her body changed, flowering, blossoming, shaped to lovely flesh and moulded to beauty in his arms, so the habit of earnestness dropped from her, and one night she had no more to say and burst out laughing.

'I'm so tired of fighting, trying to put all this in words. Right or wrong, Unni, please look after me.'

'I will.'

'Would you marry me,' said Anne, 'supposing John divorces me – would you?'

'No.'

'Why not?'

'Is it the paint that makes the timber stiff? You need a rest from marriage. I'll live with you and cling to you and be yours. Maybe a couple of five-year plans from now I'll marry you, but not before.'

Anne, though laughing and knowing he was right, was not altogether convinced. She doubted herself being able bravely, proudly to say: I love this man, without first clamping him and herself down into an accepted, legalistic formula. And yet the idea of marriage *was* now distastefully allied to her physical repulsion of John. The reality was Unni, and chiefly the discovery of her body and its sensual power, the pleasure she gave and received, unknown and now fascinating revelation. These were solid, real, vivid, the world of substance which is, upon which the world of words imposes its interpretations and distortions and its conditioned emotions.

'Methinks I twist myself into too many knots. Or verbalisms, as the Americans would say.'

'Methinks you do. Don't let's ask, like the gods, to be always right, Anne.'

And so, in Unni's arms, Anne began slowly, gropingly, to seek all of herself, even though she remained unbelieving.

Chapter 7

EUDORA now decided to give her little party, planned some days ago, and to have it on Anne's lawn.

'I do so want a little musical soirée now that Unni's back,' she said, coming trippingly to Anne in her too young way and emitting that high giggle which now, to Anne, sounded what it was, an unsure frightened sound, evoking protection.

'Of course, Eudora,' Anne replied, in new-born kindness and gentleness which so often follows gratified desire in woman. 'I'll ask Isobel's permission.' It was a mere formality, but Anne felt punctilious in these small matters, such as lunch with John.

Anne knocked at Isobel's door, heard the chink of glass before the door was opened with moderate violence and Isobel stood sternly there.

'Oh, it's you,' said Isobel. Her breath smelt loudly of brandy. But she was more statuesque and imperious than ever.

'May I have a word with you, Isobel?' said Anne.

'What is it?' said Isobel, not asking her in.

'Eudora, Mrs Maltby, wants to have a small party at the bungalow. There won't be more than a dozen people, and some musicians. To-morrow evening.'

'Oh,' said Isobel, looking curiously at Anne. 'What a funny idea. Why doesn't she give it at the Royal Hotel?'

'It's getting very crowded there.'

'Fancy asking to borrow *your* place,' said Isobel, and produced what could only be described as a sneer. 'I mean, in her position.'

'In which position?' said Anne.

'Well, I suppose some people will do anything,' said Isobel. 'I have no objection ... the bungalow is far enough and I hope I shan't be disturbed.'

'Thank you,' said Anne. 'It's very kind of you.'

'Why was Isobel so astonished at Eudora giving a small party here?' said Anne later in the night to Unni. He had come, as usual, hoisting himself easily over the crumbling pink brick wall surround-

284

ing the Institute; Regmi, an admirable conspirator, keeping watch without being told, with as much sureness of instinct and zeal as if it concerned his own dalliance.

'She thinks you're having an affair with Fred.'

'Fred? Why Fred?'

'Because on your first day here you went for a walk with him (so they say) and were gone hours and hours, and *everybody* knows he's a depraved character because he had a Nepalese girl, once upon a time, who died. On the next occasion you left your husband right after meeting Fred on the stairs, after John's little accident, which Isobel makes herself believe was sunstroke. A week later you remain closeted with Fred until dark, and no lights for a long time. ... You see how well informed I am about you.'

'Some day they'll know it's you.'

'Of course. I want everyone to know ... but not before the Coronation. Paul Redworth, as the Resident, wouldn't like a scandal like that at this moment. Later, we'll see. Later you may lose your job at the Institute. Would that worry you?'

'Would I have to leave Khatmandu?' said Anne.

'You'd come to Bongsor,' said Unni. 'I'd take you to my young mountain. I must show her to you. She is so beautiful.'

And Anne wanted to say: More beautiful than I? but only smiled, and went into his arms.

The next day, Friday, four days before the Coronation, it still looked as if only the gods in Khatmandu were ready to receive the worldlings from outside the Valley. The Government Hostel was still bare of furniture, the Royal Hotel in turmoil. The liquor had not arrived, nor the bearers. Vassili changed shirts three times a day and had abandoned Vichy water because, he said, 'My brain can no longer cope on just this stuff.'

The eighty bearers who should have been airlifted from Calcutta in order to look after the official guests had disappeared; reported somewhere in the Himalayan foothills, there was no news of them. Seventeen cases of whisky had been impounded by Customs; much beer was on the road from India to the Valley, and Vassili loudly feared it would never arrive: 'Colonel Jaganathan will drink it.' Five hundred chickens in cages had been waiting two days at Patna to be airlifted into the Valley, and it was said half of them had already died of sunstroke and thirst.

Along the streets of Khatmandu ambled the Royal elephants, happy beasts, being fed or feeding themselves as their massive feet trod down the pink shards and all traffic went on the side. They seized the baskets of cauliflowers and radishes at the doors of huts. They tore up young branches from the wayside trees, or dragged boughs protruding over the walls of the Rana palaces. Every morning several could be seen sluicing water over themselves from the public pond of justice. With golden toe-nails and painted faces and ears, caparisoned in gold and silver and velvet, they would carry the guests of the King in the Coronation pageant.

Leo sat on the verandah, sipped a Martini, and brooded in so far as his gay, volatile nature allowed him to brood. In spite of the eroticae of Khatmandu and the stimulus of Mariette Valport, he was uneasy and unhappy. His disquiet was Anne. He had seen Anne twice – at the airfield, and the next day at lunch with John. John spoke incessantly of the Club, and lectured Leo on the religions of the Valley. He appeared healthy, robust, purposeful, and no whit worried that Anne had left him. It was all very strange. Comical, also, this lunching together and sleeping separately, thought Leo.

'You are not listening to me, *chéri*,' said Mariette.

'Of course I am, you were speaking of going to Patan to see the naked dancers. I can assure you that there are no naked dancers in Nepal.'

'But zis *monsieur* says there are.' Zis *monsieur* was Suragamy's fiancé, now a self-promoted guide and eagerly sought by the tourists, since the local inhabitants did not seem to get the hang of guidesmanship. Besides providing jeep-taxis (Isobel's petrol would come in handy at the Coronation, at a price even the Americans called fabulous), the fiancé was organizing 'dances' with prostitutes (whom he called temple virgins) doing a kind of Egyptian belly wiggle, which was new to Khatmandu.

Anne suddenly appeared, looking absent-minded and young. Leo stood up and called: 'Anne! Please come and talk to me for a bit. I haven't seen you at all.'

'I know, I haven't been kind to you.' Anne sat down, looking radiantly, unseeingly at them. The fiancé cringed and bridled, uncomfortable, insisting loudly that the dances he would show were ritual, sacred dances, and Mariette talked of taking photographs. *Les rites sacrés* she called them.

Anne stared at Mariette as if just awakened, a long, knowing, appraising look, a look Leo had never seen her use before. Sensual, lifesure, almost insolent. It made him angry. She's become quite a bitch, looks at us like vermin ... it can't be just an affair to have made her so sure of herself, so physically arrogant. But this new-minted shining boldness, this knowledge of the power of herself, now compelled his pursuit not only with the usual instinct of the collector with a hunting record, but with an obsessed, fearful, and angry bafflement, an intellectual effort which infuriated and exhausted him. Never would he be able to put his hands on her casually again. Her desirability to him had increased with her own increased estimation of herself. Leo felt as if Anne were something so rare and so precious that the rest of his life depended on her, all his conquests ash-weary false starts, the possession of Anne all he had ever wanted. He could not remember desiring anyone else.

'Well,' said Anne to Mariette. 'I'm sure you'll enjoy the dancers.'

'I must talk to you, Anne,' Leo said. 'You've quite neglected me. And I came to Khatmandu centuries earlier than I needed to, for you.'

'I've been busy.'

'I know, my pet. But how about dinner tonight? Just one night?'

'We're having a music party.' She looked at him speculatively. 'It's Eudora's party, Mrs Maltby, she's giving it where I live. In fact, if you'd like to come, I'm sure she won't mind.'

'Good,' said Leo, disregarding Mariette and the off-handedness of the invitation, 'I'll be there.'

'John isn't coming,' said Anne casually, and left.

When she had gone Mariette turned to Leo: 'You abandon me tonight, *mon ami*?'

'Anne is a very old and dear friend.'

'An ancient mistress?'

'No.'

'Oh *alors*, I understand ... *l'attrait de l'inconnue*,' said Mariette good-naturedly. 'They say she is having an affair with the doctor, Dr

Maltby. But truly, what do you men see in her? She never says anything, no brilliance, no wit, *elle a l'air de dormir debout.*'

'*Méfie-toi de l'eau qui dort,*' said Leo.

Leo's enthusiasm over the lawn, the bungalow, and the view sounded flat amid a din of evening crows cawing their flights home. Anne gave him a drink, and they waited for Eudora and the guests. Anne wore a soft grey dress of handwoven silk. Suddenly she had wanted new clothes. It was Unni, fingering her dresses (she liked the way his fingers evaluated surfaces, learning them; he loved textures, told her, eyes shut, which was the better material by feel alone), who had started it.

'You don't like my dresses, Unni?'

'I do, but –' he hesitated, then suddenly: 'I want your beauty in silk and gold. I'll buy you some, and jewels, too.'

'Oh Unni, you mustn't.'

But she had accepted, knowing his pleasure in adorning her, and discovering his passion for beautiful things upon her. And the grey-silver silk, extravagantly expensive, so fine as to be weightless, had been brought by a pilot friend from Benares. Martha Redworth knew a little Indian tailor clever at making dresses in two days, and Unni had spent an hour with the tailor, arguing about how to cut the dress, both men looking critically at Anne, folding the material on her, Anne immobile as a mannequin, something she had never done before.

Leo watched her as she walked or sat, with a passionate bitterness. He knew all the signs, he told himself, of desire gratified, the extraordinary bloom upon the skin, the serenity, the calm, and a kind of innocence, fragile, vainglorious perhaps, in the straight supple body moving now with so much grace; her hips were slimmer and her waist, more rounded her shoulders and her breasts, and her arms flowed from her. Leo could not stop looking, and she, unconstrained, let herself be looked at, smiling and happy to be admired, conscious yet unthinking, but it seemed to him wilfully, openly taunting him with her beauty, and insolently sure he would not dare to touch her, having vowed that she would always refuse him. Well, thought Leo, we shall see.

'You quite bowl one over,' he said to her.

'I'm glad,' she replied, thinking of Unni, but he hated her for saying it.

Gaily chatting by her side, he felt acutely forlorn, yearning, and for the first time afraid that he would fail. Anne, *ma sœur* Anne, this cruel and sensual goddess moving in silver? What is happening to me? cried Leo in his heart.

'Lucky blighter,' he said aloud. 'I'm sorry it wasn't me, Prince Charming to bring you out of your sleep, to wake you up, sensually I mean. Well, here's to your happiness, now and for ever.'

'For ever doesn't matter,' she replied. 'Now is good enough.'

She sipped her drink slowly, sweeping her eyes briefly over him and then dropping him, in that new way of hers. She was drinking, he noticed with surprise, whisky with a lot of soda, but drinking nevertheless. And he remembered clearly how she had always said she loathed the smell of whisky ... the man surely must be a whisky drinker.

The Redworths with Eudora now came through the darkness, and Sharma and the Hindu poet and Unni. Eudora professed herself charmed to meet Leo, and Leo, knowing she was the doctor's wife (was Anne's affair with the doctor?) was charming to Eudora. He had called upon the Redworths at the Residency, and he recalled enthusiastically their meeting and plunged into a discussion of Gurkha recruitment. Sharma joined them, maintaining that Nepal should not let these men enter the British Army to fight in the Gurkha regiments abroad, but use them for herself instead.

'But without the money they bring in, their districts would be even poorer,' objected Paul.

Eudora meanwhile demanded to go upstairs to Anne's room with Anne, in order to freshen up though the Royal Hotel where she stayed was only five minutes by jeep away. 'Oh, I do hope it will be a success. I did so want to give this little party. No, of course I don't mind your bringing Leo. I did ask you to bring some of your friends too. I meant it. I hear the Indian singer is quite marvellous. Just too perfect. How do I look?'

'You're looking wonderful,' said Anne.

Eudora was wearing a sari again, with a broad golden hem. It suited her, gave grace and a longer line to her body.

'Unni had a few saris sent over from Calcutta. He asked me to choose one. So thoughtful ...' She turned round, so taken with her own appearance that she missed the parakeets though she was in the room for the first time. She now sat at the desk, after looking in vain for a mirror in the room ('It's in the bathroom,' explained Anne, who did not go on to say that a mirror would have been out of place here, with the eyes and the birds), and proceeded to do her mouth again.

'Anything about Fred?' asked Anne. Since their talk on the lawn there was no false reticence between them.

'Not yet,' said Eudora to her compact mirror, trying her lips, arching and pouting and then snapping the lipstick back into its case. 'Unni and I had a long talk about Fred. It's inevitable that we should meet at some of the Coronation functions. It's really very silly of Fred, just like an ostrich. But he was always like that, you know, running away from things in one way or another.'

'Don't we all?' said Anne.

'Perhaps. In a way,' answered Eudora, 'I mean, it's hard always to face up to ourselves. If it weren't for Unni I'd have ... oh, I don't know what I'd have done. I'm leaving right after the Coronation now. I've got work to do and I can't wait for ever.'

'You're still in love with Fred,' said Anne.

'I don't know,' said Eudora, looking at the parakeets with unseeing eyes. 'It may be just curiosity, a sense of untidiness. I want to know what went wrong with us ... oh, I've had lovers since, of course, but I've never bothered to divorce Fred. I won't know until we meet. By the way, Unni's very much in love with you,' she said suddenly. 'Please don't hurt him, Anne.'

'Hurt him?' said Anne. 'How could I hurt him?'

'Oh, I'm just talking,' said Eudora. 'Only, he *is* in love with you. What a beautiful room,' she exclaimed, 'so pretty, so cute. You're very lucky, Anne.'

On the lawn Father MacCullough had arrived, and was talking to Leo about the floods and 'the situation' in the other valleys of Nepal. 'Something will have to be done, otherwise communism will find a footing,' then proceeding to outline his strategy for out-witting communism. The General and the Maharani, his wife, completed the guests. The Maharani kept an imperishable smile upon her round and flawless face. She could not talk to anyone, she knew no English, but it did not discountenance her. Happily she smiled, and smoked, as the General did, through her hand folded to function as a cigarette-holder.

All at once there was light in a soft fluid cone from a Tilley lamp, revealing Martha and a dark stooping shadow, Unni, tinkering with the square reflector. 'Too bright,' he said, and spread out some crêpe paper over the glass.

'Yes, that will do perfectly,' said Martha. 'I was just telling Unni I want at least a couple of these lights for my garden party,' she explained. 'Quite essential, otherwise the American Mission might get near to the Chinese Delegation, and that would be terrible, wouldn't it?'

Unni rose now, saying: 'I want a drink,' moving towards the table where Regmi presided over glasses and bottles and a pail of ice cubes, and Anne said: 'I've just poured it,' handing him a glass. They looked at each other, and then Leo knew, and at first did not feel even surprised. So, it was Unni. So. And then, slowly, slowly, slowly, it began to hurt.

'Here,' said Father MacCullough, 'I don't believe you've really met.' He walked Leo up to Unni, repeated the introductions. Leo assumed the bubbling, voluble approach always successful in Asia, his desire to shine enhanced by the piercing curiosity, the ravenous pain he felt, regarding this man who had managed to capture Anne. Capture was the right word. She was caught, body and spirit too, for women, even the more perspicacious ones, were fused together more tightly than men; and the best guarantee of a woman's soul was her body, as cynical Boswell knew. How much insight did Anne have about what had happened to her? A gifted stud horse, was Leo's verdict, looking at Unni and pleased with his apt phrase.

'Mr Menon? Yes ... I've heard about you. And the dam, of course. I would so much like to see it ... nothing to see? But of course there should be, ha ha ha, perhaps after the Coronation? ... what interests me particularly is your relationships with labour, the goodwill of labour and other neighbouring vested interests, landlords and so on ... in some cases these modern projects bring much resented dislocation to the traditional ways of life. ...'

Father MacCullough said: 'Sure do.' He proceeded to tell Leo how, in the new road to India, the farmers were not being compensated by the Nepalese Government for the land taken up in building the road. 'The Indians are paying their labour three times the rate which the Nepalese pay theirs in Khatmandu, and even that is less than a rupee a day.'

'Same at the dam. High rates for our labour. Yes, landlords are a problem. The Rampoche of Bongsor is the biggest landlord there. Spreads rumours that we offend the deities who'll bring plague to the valleys.'

'What about using old Gurkha material, ex-pensioners, and so on?'

'We do, the more intelligent ones as gang foremen. But on the whole the Gurkhas are slow and stupid, lacking in initiative and know-how. They make good soldiers, but not good technicians.'

'But they're such happy people,' said Paul, who occasionally fell into the British way of prizing the stupid above the clever, calling them children of nature.

The musicians now arrived in a jeep, the singer with three accompanists. Rugs appeared, laid out on the grass, they were the General's, brought by a file of servants.

Eudora was pleased. 'Oh, General, how you do spoil me.'

'Madam, it is delighting to my heart to do so,' replied the General gallantly.

Sharma and the Hindu poet suggested more rugs. 'For us to sit on. It is not right to listen to music sitting in chairs.' These were now brought, and the singer and the musicians took their position, cross legged, facing their audience, establishing a preparatory silence while they prayed, collecting their vital essence to pour it forth into the divine harmony of music.

Father MacCullough unsuccessfully tried to sit upon his crossed legs. 'How do you do it?' he asked Anne.

'Practice.'

Leo settled near her, his knees up to his chin. 'It must have been painful practice. The hip bone rotates outwards completely, and then you sit upon your crossed legs.'

'Hurts at the beginning, but I'm getting better at it.' Provocation, uxorious insolence had gone. Her face was candid, pure. She smiled at Leo vacantly, seemingly more accessible, but he, moving himself nearer to her, could feel her absent, unaware of him. His eyes went seeking Unni, and with a shock found him seated right behind Anne. The stud horse moves softly, he thought, cynical.

Sharma announced: 'The song will now be of the Lord Siva dancing the dance of the world.'

'Oh, yes,' breathed Eudora, rapturous, joining her hands and indicating by a facial straightening a profound spiritual attention.

The singer was a portly man of forty, face flashing like copper in the light, black moustache and eyes. At both sides and behind were the musicians: a man with a sitar, an over-sized guitar with six steel strings, a very long handle, the body made of two gourds to give resonance; another man with a long, fluted drum, tapped at both ends with the fingers; and a man with a lute. The singer closed his eyes, joined his hands in the Indian salutation, bowed deeply to the company, and then, with his right hand making the gesture of plucking a flower, started the first note, his voice plucking it out of air. Quick, industrious, the melody followed upon it, like a spider with a thread waving and swaying it in emptiness and ready to spin, spilling note after note, building a structure of sound, the web's marvel. The voice, agile, running, pausing, ringing, holding and letting go, pulling and twisting and turning and throwing the thread of melody round and about them. The sitar's great and beautiful tones went on, a majestic pulse, and the drum beat like a heart beating time, while the music coursed and zigzagged and always sprang back again at the singer, recalled to him in tranced obedience, as the thread is never detached from the spider's body. Soon the listeners were part of the music, became the notes, bodies strung on the invisible scale the singer compelled, woven into the invisible architecture created out of silence; and then imagination bent them to many visions. They were driving through a mist, seeing fantastic shapes float past and dissolve, and the spun thread of sound was a road to follow; and upon this road everything they would ever know; pain, young as the mountains, and pleasure, vast and old; wonderment and knowledge, acceptance, and a hint of that which is Beyond encompassing even with blind obedience. For Siva was dancing, and under his feet the Universe was coming to birth. A tremendous bringing forth, of which this music was but an echo: somewhere a hammer thundered, and from its sparks the suns burst forth and the stars flashed, the worlds created went whirling on, more and more of them, and none could stop the blossoming, as the unfolding of the curled petals of a flower, the gentlest thing in the world, cannot be stopped. There was nothing they could do, caught in inexorable recurrence, and even Father MacCullough sat tranced, unmoving until it was over, and then he blew his nose violently, and clapped.

'Oh, it was beautiful, beautiful,' said Eudora. She was genuinely moved.

There was a pause, some whispers, they felt subdued, a little stunned, hastily regaining their consciousness, isolated once again into particled selves. The General now spoke to the singer, and one of the musicians came over with the sitar and handed it to the Maharani, who established herself upon a separate rug (modesty forbidding her to sit with other males than her own husband).

'My wife will play the sitar now,' said the General. He was thus doing a great favour to Eudora, for the Maharani had never played in public. 'She has been praying and reading the *Gita* that her spirit might be worthy of the music. She thinks she has improved a little now.'

The singer began again, the hymn of Rada and her love for the Lord Krishna.

'Rada was the first wife of Krishna,' explained the General, 'Rukmini was the second one.'

The wistful evocation ended; the Maharani's sitar sent its last long low vibration across the garden. The singer's hands came together. It was over.

Unni bent forward, Anne turned her head, he gave her a cigarette, lit it for her, his hands cupping the match in the same gesture as the singer, curving up, holding the luminous fragment with his palms longer than needed, so that he could look at her face in the light, and thus looking at her betraying himself altogether. But Anne was not looking at him, because she was satisfied with his looking at her and because she feared the sudden assault of desire which leapt at a glance, a touch, between them.

'How beautiful you are,' he said lightly, and then: 'I'm being stupid.'

She did not reply, turned her head slowly away, giving him her face, her neck, in the turning, and as she got up it was as if her whole body was one long caress under his hand, the skirt of her dress brushing his sleeve. And Leo understood it all perfectly, saw them move, among the others, apparently free, yet really revolving round each other, walking and turning, until they met and passed each other again and stood together for a moment, and then again appeared to leave each other, only to swing back as in a dance, each one the other's fulcrum, centre and nexus of desire, all revealed in their apparent indifference. Leo was spared nothing, wondered the others did not see, or appeared not to. He too was revolving, turning round them, trying to engage them in talk, forcing their attention to him; he found himself next to Unni, who was seated next to Eudora having an argument about polygamy with the General.

'Oh no, madam, two wives for the Lord Krishna is nothing. Polygamy for gods and for men, monogamy for women, that is the Natural Law. For women it is the child that is important; and the man who gives her a child takes her soul as well as her body. Hence monogamy for her, if possible,' the General said.

'Well now, how typically conceited and masculine,' cried Eudora. 'That's what I don't like about you Asian men, you might be very modern in other ways, but you all feel that woman's place is just bed and board and that you're superior to women, and therefore you can have a lot of wives and treat them as you like.'

'Not as we like, madam,' corrected the General, 'but as they like to be treated.'

'You've got no real idea of equality at all. Polygamy is the curse of Asia,' said Eudora.

'There's no such thing as sex equality,' replied Sharma, who under the influence of music and a drink was being impossibly 'Asian', with a passion of historical memories and feelings against the whites, trying as many Asians do in emotional moments to find virtues and a code of living in Asian traditions superior to the West, and now ardently defending polygamy, not because he really believed in it, but because it seemed to him a way of life opposed to the doctrinally monogamous West. 'Look at what monogamy has done to the Americans. I went to the States last year, and I can tell you there was not a woman there that I could not have slept with, if I had wanted to. Whereas our women are chaste still, and it is because we keep ourselves superior to them, and are male.'

'To obey the male, in sheer love, that is the happiness of woman, perfection in the world. Women do not like it if their men are meek,' said the General. 'They want to be mastered in any country. And if men do not master them, women become tyrants.'

'I do agree,' said Paul. 'I think we in the West have given far too much equality to our women. England suffers from a surfeit of masculine-minded women, and they're unhappy in their independence.'

'How perfectly wrong-headed you are, Tiddlywinks,' said Martha placidly. 'You know jolly well that it's you who wanted me to become more independent and take up war work and do all that sort of thing, when I'd have been happier just pottering in the garden and looking after you.'

Leo now took over, possessive, explanatory, very much the European who has his emotions strung to the framework of scientific logic. 'Love is really a much exaggerated phenomenon,' said Leo. 'It is purely an outpouring of glandular hormones, but we like to illusion ourselves that it is a communion of souls. Women especially tend to attach far too much importance to love, and that is why, where monogamy is enforced, women suffer from a pampered romantic complex which makes them feel that to give their bodies is a mystic and sacred thing.' This he said in his lightest way, hoping Anne was listening.

But Sharma had not finished with his attack on the unnatural vice of monogamy which, he and the General maintained, destroyed the very foundations of the moral order of society. 'The white man's neurosis.' Sharma went on. 'Americans have got some of the best-looking women in the world, and they simply don't know what to do about them. They can't satisfy them emotionally; because, no matter how many times one repeats the sex act, it isn't the body's orgasm alone that matters, it's the spiritual climax. A woman is *not* happy unless she feels she is embraced by a god and not a subservient sex organ which she can despise and revile and use. It is the psychological and emotional overtones which give sex its value and its importance, not technique or the relief experienced.

'And in revenge you white men exploit female physical sexuality as no so-called barbarian ever dares to do. There is no country in the world where the acme of degradation of woman as a human being is carried as far as in the United States. No Asian country would greet its artistes with demands as to the precise dimensions of their mammary glands. Only in the West is woman's sexuality constantly cheapened, her thighs and the shape of her crotch being used to sell anything from toothpaste to presidential elections.'

'These practices,' murmured the Hindu poet dreamily, 'evoke an interesting comparison with some of our Tantric rites here in Nepal. In order to become admitted to the priesthood the men go through a door which is in the shape of a woman's vulva. And in the city of Bhadgaon there is a temple where the window through which the offerings are made to the temple is also thus shaped, and painted red. It offends a great many tourists, yet they buy their cigarettes under practically the same auspices.'

'And so Western men have become de-sexed sex salesmen and are horribly frightened of their women,' said Sharma rudely. 'They become impotent, emotionally if not physically. Then the woman revenges herself because she is unhappy and frustrated, she becomes vindictive and spiteful, tyrannical and destructive.'

'That is what I said,' the General put in stubbornly. 'Our women remain women because we are male, givers of love and pleasure, not to one, but to many. Imprison a man to one woman's pleasure, he loses the spirit of enthusiasm in love, it becomes drudgery and monotony. Hence polygamy is essential to keep a husband a good lover.'

'Nonsense,' said Eudora. 'Do you honestly believe that your Asian women like polygamy? Do you ever stop to think of the terrible amount of hidden suffering which women in Asia still put up with? You, General, can you truly say that your wives rejoice when you bring another concubine to your palace?'

'No, madam, they do not rejoice, but they are used to it and they don't say anything.'

'They are used to it, they don't say anything, they put up with it, because they've no right to protest, they are your property. They are like caged animals, suffering dumbly,' cried Eudora dramatically.

'The soul of man craves many women,' said the General. 'Man's soul finds itself in love, first of the many, then of the One. A man must pass through the passions to reach non-desire. To man, woman is a temptation and a hindrance to his soul, yet he must go through these desires to reach understanding.'

'And have not women souls then?' said Unni. 'And cannot they too find the growth of their individual selves in man, not one, but more than one? And can they not too aspire to the divine?'

'Women's souls,' replied the General, 'are different from ours.

They are more earthy than we are, and even when they aspire to God, it is not a God as we men see it, but as a Lover, who fills them with bliss and pierces them with arrows of desire. In other words, my friend, and as you know so well,' added the General slyly, 'women find their God through a man they idealize. All the gods of women are ideal lovers, and their prayers are addressed to these in the name of Love. That is why women love Krishna, Lord of Love. And even among Christians,' continued the General wickedly, 'nuns vow chastity because they have married themselves to their God and no mere man can have them.'

'General, Milton and Blake thought like you,' said Sharma enthusiastically.

And the Hindu poet, who had been waiting for this opportunity, began quoting from his favourite Blake:

'The virgin
That pines for man shall awaken her womb to enormous joys
In the secret shadows of her chamber: the youth shut up from
The lustful joy shall forget to generate and create an amorous image
In the shadows of his curtains and in the folds of his silent pillow.
Are not these the places of religion, the rewards of continence,
The self-enjoyings of self-denial?'

'Oh, Blake,' said Eudora, 'Blake was a mystic.'

'Mr Blake was polygamous, madam,' said the General, 'and so was Mr Milton and even that scamp Shelley, so much like my first cousin. Polygamy for man, monogamy for woman ... for with woman there is the child, and woman's whole being is concentrated upon producing children.'

'Not since family planning,' said Martha Redworth. 'With family planning a woman just isn't a child-producing machine any more.'

'But we don't like family planning in Asia,' answered the General.

Father MacCullough, who had been coughing violently for some time, succeeded in making his throat discomfort heard, and Paul Redworth tactfully changed the subject and spoke of the Coronation, which was due to begin with a Purification Ceremony on the first of May, a Tuesday. A detachment of Gurkhas under Major Pemberton would take part in a Durbar, which would be held on May the second in the afternoon; there would be thirty-five elephants and he and his diplomatic colleagues would ride upon them in great discomfort and in solemn procession to the Durbar on Coronation Day.

Leo looked at his watch and said in a tone of polite surprise: '*Déjà minuit?*' He thought, I could have sworn it was later.

Mariette's facile laughter gushed. She leapt out of bed with a prancing pretty swivel of the hips, her buttocks had shadowed even dimples. She went to the mirror to put on lipstick, sitting on the stool, her legs a little apart, then came walking back to bed, humming to herself. Her breasts swung well from her shoulders, her round belly had a navel placed exactly right, the dark V of the hair, curly, thick, hung down in a point. Leo began comparing her with the Kisha he had left in Delhi. Kisha also used to leap out of bed, not to put on lipstick but to have a snack.

'She was like a highly spiced Indian dish, a little too rich. Though she was so young, there was already too much of her everywhere. I was a bit overwhelmed by so much wealth, and had to peer at her face, less perfect, to send myself off. *Mais toi, tu es tout à fait charmante. Tout à fait,*' said Leo, planting a kiss upon Mariette's new red lips to confirm it.

'*Bien, mon chéri.*' Mariette wriggled back into bed, smooth as soap and ready for gossip. 'Oh, it has not been easy for me, with all zis travelling. Lots of men, most of them... *complètement impossible.* But one can speak with you. One is not alone.'

'*Mais tu les as tous, les hommes,* they all turn round you ... *et maintenant, avec tous ces journalistes ...*'

'*Je sais bien. Mais ce n'est pas ça que je veux. Il y a un type ... celui-là, si je ne l'ai pas, je me sentirai flancher.*'

'*Qui donc?*' said Leo, and knew before she said it the recrudescence of pain, forgotten for such a short while in Mariette's bed.

'*Celui qu'on appelle Menon, le grand brun. Ce qui est le plus rigolo, j'ai une lettre d'un de ces amis, me recommandant à ses soins ...* Figure yourself. I arrive, with zis letter. Of course I demand to see zis personage. I hear much about him, his work, and how good looking he is. At first he is away. Then he arrives, one morning, very polite. I 'ad written to him. I was having my *petit déjeuner.* I see him come in. You have seen him too. *Six pieds, et ce teint, ces épaules, ces jambes.*'

'Of course, you did your best,' said Leo, ironic and bitter.

'Of course,' replied Mariette, laughing again her rich, fruity, easy laugh. '*Donc* he says: "I am at your disposal madame." I look at him, and I say: "And I at yours, monsieur." He says: "Do you wish to go for a drive?" I say: "Wiz pleasure." We go for a drive. He shows me ze temples, I had seen before, *je m'extasie. On revient.* I say: "Come into my room for some photographs I took in Siam I wish to show you."'

'*Et alors,*' said Leo, '*rien du tout?*'

'*Pas encore,*' said Mariette. '*Mais je ne me décourage pas pour si peu.* I try again, next day. Very early, after breakfast. I breakfast in my dressing gown, of course. *Je me penche sur lui,* to make him admire the photographs. He says: "Would you like a cigarette?" I invite him to sit near me, on the sofa. He sits. Zen he says he is busy, will come again when I need. He goes.'

Leo laughed. 'Next time,' he said, 'try after lunch. Perhaps breakfast is too early.' The reason why they had gone to bed together, reflected Leo, was precisely that he and Mariette found it so easy to relate to each other their amorous exploits; both considering themselves of more than usual calibre. And if they had not spoken like craftsmen of their bedmanship, there was nothing else to talk about except Mariette's photographic talent, and that bored Leo.

'*Moi,*' said Mariette meditatively, her head upon her chest, and the fine double chin showing like a collar round her face, '*je crois que c'est un pur ... c'est très excitant, un homme pur et sensuel quand-même.*'

'*Il est probablement impuissant,*' said Leo.

'*Je n'en crois rien. Ranchit dit ça. Mais moi, je crois qu'il a toutes les femmes qu'il veut, et je m'y connais, mais il joue froid. Il y a du feu dans ce glaçon-là.*'

Fire in ice, thought Leo, feeling himself hit again. Anne, Anne, fire in ice. And how irritating of Mariette to say it about Unni. She's really stupid, thought Leo, looking at her. And too fat. Most women were too fat. What he longed for was a thin, agile, supple body with no showy curves, an intensity of passion which this exuberant flesh would render grotesque, elephantine.

'*Je le trouve lourd et vaniteux ... un poseur. Je le crois bête.*'

'*C'est possible qu'il soit bête, mais c'est une bien belle bête.*'

'*Et bien,*' said Leo, '*si tu le veux, je t'aiderai.*' Yes, he thought, it would be wonderfully amusing if Unni were brought to bed by Mariette. What would Anne say or do? The thought excited Leo, and so in a rage of passion for Anne he kissed Mariette again, declared himself *tout à fait remis,* and effaced his hunger for Anne in Mariette's willing embrace, so boring in such a short time.

'Jolly good party, that was. Anne's looking very well these days,' said Paul to Martha as they settled in the huge double bed at the Residency.

'Grey's a very good colour for her,' said Martha carefully.

'Yes, I think so too. I'm glad for her, dear, aren't you?'

'Yes, Tiddlywinks. I hope it lasts.'

'I never did care for that husband of hers,' said Paul. 'Though, mind you, one does hope nothing bursts out before the Coronation. Simply terrible mess. Spoil the garden party and everything. Shocking and all that. I mean, we couldn't have them all here together then, could we?'

'No, we couldn't. It's hard enough with Eudora and Fred.'

'Oh, we'll have to invite both, separately, of course. Unni's promised that everything will be all right before that.'

'I doubt it,' said Martha. 'Fred's still hiding in the Hospital.'

'Unni'll have to hurry if he wants them to meet,' said Paul. 'Only four days left, and lots of work to do.'

'And Anne,' said Martha.

'And Anne,' agreed Paul, settling back in his usual stance, prepared for sleep.

The General and the Maharani on their way back from Eudora's party visited Fred Maltby in his bungalow.

Fred was not yet in bed. He had had an emergency operation to perform. The General's thin face and the Maharani's round one came out of the blackness of the open door to smile at him.

'Do we disturb you?' said the General.

'No, not at all. Do come in,' said the doctor.

'We shall only stay a few moments,' said the General. And sent for his whisky. 'I wish to speak with you, my friend, about your wife. We have just been to her party.'

'Oh,' said Fred, looking at his watch. 'I wish you wouldn't. Speak about her, I mean.'

'It is impossible,' said the General, 'for you to go on avoiding her.'

'At one time,' reminded Fred, 'you did your best to make me avoid her.'

'That was weeks ago. But now,' said the General, 'you cannot do so honourably. Nobleness obliges.'

'I'm very busy.'

'You are frightened,' said the General, swaying on his legs.

'I'm not frightened,' replied Fred, truculent. 'It's unpleasant, that's all.'

'I like her,' said the General. 'She is stupid, but she understands music. And she loves you. If Unni were here he would tell you to see her. But he is himself mad with love these days.'

'Here he is now,' said Fred, surprised. ''Evening, Unni.'

'Good evening,' said Unni. He sat down, reached for the whisky, and poured himself a peg. The General looked at him and then looked at the Maharani, stupefied. He opened his mouth, but the Maharani pulled his sleeve vigorously.

'We were just talking about the doctor's wife,' said the Maharani. 'Don't you think a meeting should be arranged?'

'Certainly,' said Unni. He drained his whisky.

The General looked at the Maharani again, and the Maharani, with great tact, rose and said it was time to go to bed, and they went, effacing themselves gently.

Left alone, the two men did not speak to each other. Unni went to the bathroom, had a shower, returned twisting his dhoti round him, threw himself on his camp bed, and was still.

Fred did not look at him. Something was wrong, since this was the first night Unni was in his own bed, but they had never spoken of women to each other, and words now would not help. Anne and Unni, Unni and Anne. Two proper nouns, two words, two people. An event. An event which had not surprised him when he had known, and he had known soon enough, the first afternoon that Unni had been back from the dam. He had come in, had a cup of tea with the doctor, walked about restlessly, then disappeared. Fred was by now well attuned to understanding without words. 'It's a woman.'

He knew. And the next morning the General had told him: 'It is Anne, my friend. Our Unni was there all night.'

'I'm glad,' the doctor had said.

'Do you think Mrs Ford will ever go back to her husband, later, when you have cured him?' the General had asked, in simple-seeming innocence.

'I wouldn't know,' Fred had replied. Of course the General knew that Anne would not go back. 'At least, I don't think so,' diagnosed Fred.

Tonight, going to bed in his turn, he also knew it was not so simple as saying: Unni and Anne. Unni was consistent, clear, intelligent, and happy-natured, deep in his emotions and nature, quick in his reflexes but thoughtful, not given to self-torturings, to mental agony, and fecund doubt, to shallow sudden obsessions. And he was in love with Anne. He had fallen in love, as he did everything, wholehearted, unafraid, giving all he was. Fred had never discussed it with him. I just know, thought Fred. So does the General. But what about Anne?

'She will love him too,' the General had said confidently. 'What woman would not be happy to love such a beautiful man? And she is very lucky. Many others have tried to love him, and he has told them he did not love them. This woman is not talkative, she will be good for him, and he will make her happy and she will fulfil him too.'

'I wouldn't know,' Fred had replied. 'She is a writer, you know, a modern woman. It's not so simple as all that. Writers serve no one but their own demons, in the long run.'

The General had replied that a woman is always a woman first, Unni was man enough to keep Anne and give her children, and make her forget all about writing. 'What will she need to write for, when she has such a man to look after her?'

Fred had not explained. He himself wasn't sure, only saw vaguely what might or might not be the truth about Anne. And now, aware of Unni in the next bed, feeling him unhappy, he wondered uneasily. For woman is a selfish beast: war, and all the genius and invention of man, the rise and fall of empires and revolutions, are nothing to her but a background, a tapestry, a robe to garb her and to discard, adornment to her own self and foil against which she could play the tragic comedies of her emotions. Would Anne use Unni for her needs, whatever they were, and then throw him away, discard him in a hoard of words, a story, a novel, a book? This living love, passion of life, beauty and tenderness, that this man could give her; would she abandon it for shadows upon a page?

I'm getting fanciful, he thought, and turned on his side and fell asleep.

*

For ten days I haven't written a word. Shall I begin again? How shall I begin to write again? For ten days I have had a lover. I have not had time to think. The discovery of myself overwhelmed me, blotting out words. But the urge to face myself rose again, and so I turned to Unni tonight after Eudora's party – he was waiting after the others had gone, waiting for me to decide whether he could stay or not. Always he does this, never presuming, never forcing, and it pleases me very much. But this time I said – quickly because it hurt me to take back my solitude and yet it had to be taken back – I said to him: 'Unni, I'd like to be alone tonight.'

There was darkness and Regmi taking up the chairs quietly, no moon and us. I waited to hear what Unni would say, do. If he had begun to argue why, something would have snapped, would have been finished between us, so fastidious have I become, so finicky that I must needs have my lover guess at my slightest mood. Teetering over a knife-edge, ready to note the least syllable which sounds false, the smallest gesture forced, implacable towards Unni where I have put up with so much, so many small foulings, so many maudlin enactments with John. … Unfair, because Unni is as he is, strong, invulnerable; because I came to him for help he now has to repay me in intangible ways for the dreary clumsy laxities, miscalculations, bunglings that have gone before. Can anyone call this love?

Unni did not ask: Why? He did not surmise, build an edifice of suppositions, ask for explanations, express doubt. He stood calmly, finishing his cigarette, his drink. He was not even in silence asking me to explain, he had accepted already. But silence bullies. Because he did not say Why? I was compelled to explain. (And now at last I understand John, poor John, so little in control of his emotions – whereas Unni and I are to each other like instruments of precision in this field –

compelled to ask me questions because I keep silent, compelled to flatten himself in ridiculous repetitions, miserable because I do not look at him.)

'Unni, please don't misunderstand.' (He wasn't misunderstanding.) 'I want to be alone because … I just want to be alone.'

He could have risen and said: Certainly, or: Of course I understand, masking whatever blow to his vanity this rejection would inflict in a phrase which would have been 'appropriate'; or swaggered out, saying: See you tomorrow; played the gentleman, or the lout, anything. But he did none of these. Instead, he took out of his pocket the charm which I had seen him play with before, and started throwing it up and down, up and down in the darkness, and since there was not a word we just sat on and I wanted to take back what I had said, but I could not. I was now totally fascinated. I waited for what would happen. Trial by fire, or by water, Holding the flaming bar, would he burn himself? Submerged, would he come up spluttering, unable to hold his breath?

He said: 'You are my dearest love,' and his voice was happy. He walked away.

And now I wanted him to stay, to return, now I loved him, oh how I loved him, and his voice, his hands, how could I forgo them? Once again, as so many times in the last ten days, he had said, done, the right thing, not the obvious, the conventional, the false. 'Push me in the fire, says Gold, I shine the brighter. But please don't measure me against the dross of lesser things.' That is a Nepalese proverb he taught me. I thought it naïve then. But his happy voice released me from guilt, and now I am alone.

I am alone: to recollect myself in tranquillity, sacrificing but really not sacrificing his presence for something, more important at the moment than his mere physical presence, a sum total of awareness of Unni. I must stop to look at him. I cannot do so when he is with me. If he had stayed with me tonight, persuading me, if he had asked: Why? this moment would not be the moment when I want to write the word 'Us' for Unni and myself, acknowledging him in my life; writing *us* and thinking *us* and later being *us*, without turning back.

And to begin with it is not all true, the things I wrote when I arrived in Khatmandu, and in the first burst of ecstasy became intellectually excited, discovering a new world. That was only the

outward gleam, the poetic lustrous garb of what is now. This fundamental urge which (laughing at me and at all my words) has pushed
me steadily, inexorably, towards today, Unni. A pattern clear as the
road through the foothills, a constant direction, twist and loop and
bend, and still for all its turns a constant direction.

Now, after ten days, with an expert eye I look round me at other
people and measure them from no other standard but this true instinct which tells me exactly what people are like: not the intellectual,
the bright chattering masks which they put on their faces for show,
but the small naked candid features, the bodies that they are in bed, the
embryo within the armour with its obscenities and fears, delights and
greeds, all the lies to themselves. I see Leo now with his thousand
women, a thousand blind alleys, a mere number, a repetitive tediousness, intense, excessive, unceasing functioning of his sex in order to
prove himself to himself. I see him, as Unni says, desiccated by
promiscuity as others are by abstinence, for he has merely functioned,
he has not loved.

But this true instinct also tells me something more disquieting. It
tells me that within this complicated self of mine also resides a small
demanding demon, a vanity, a demiurge, which turns everything
into words, which takes the bright, beautiful life lived and mercilessly
reduces it to those perpetuating symbols, mummies of our thoughts
and emotions. And it is this demon which tonight has made me tell
Unni I wanted to be alone. I wanted to write. I could have told him
so. I could have said: Tonight I want to write. But I did not wish to
tell him. I wanted him to know, without words. 'If he knows without words, then I will believe.' Of us two, he is the one who is sure.
Well then, let him understand, without being told. He uses the word
love as if he knew all about it. He seems quite certain every moment
of what he does and says, whereas I am still frightened of emotion,
frightened of prediction, frightened to say love, frightened of making
another word-made world. Well then, since he believes, let him perform the miracle: let him make *me* believe.

I said to him yesterday: 'You will get tired of me. Of the way I
doubt our feelings, or what we presume to be our feelings, analyse
and tear to pieces and argue and discuss.'

He replied: 'Carry on, I like it very much. You're just like Mana
Mani, the young mountain I'm going to lick one day.'

It was so folklorish and grandiloquent that I felt quite irritated and I said: 'How conceited you are!'

And he replied, with the dangerous softness he wears upon his voice when he is strongest: 'The men in my country are conceited because they are men.'

Chapter 8

THIS Saturday morning Isobel assembles us, and with an air of exhausted triumph produces sheets of paper, the programme for the Coronation Ceremonies. She reads it aloud.

'Sunday, 29 April, that's tomorrow. Investiture at the Durbar Hall.'

'We haven't got cards for that,' says Geography.

'Never mind,' says Isobel, 'nobody's had cards yet. I've asked the Resident and I'll ask him again. You know what these Nepalese are. The cards will arrive when the ceremony's over. We might as well just go.'

'*You'll* be quite all right I expect,' says Geography to me. 'Your husband's got cards, hasn't he?'

'I don't know.'

'Of course he has,' says Geography, telling me. 'He's Secretary of the Valley Club. The Nepalese wouldn't *dare* to leave him out of the official functions ... *of course* you'll have cards for Mr and Mrs Ford.'

Conversation at the Girls' Institute is still that of the garrison of a beleaguered fortress faced with imminent deprivation of all the amenities of life; even though now Vassili, catering for over a thousand official guests, V.I.P.s, and correspondents, has managed to airlift three hundred chickens from Patna (only a couple of hundred perished on the way), twenty wild boars cured and laid out in the deep freeze, rows of partridge and quail and pheasant, caviar and prawns and bekti for the State Banquet and various other diplomatic dinners.

'There's still not a stick of furniture in the Government Hostel,' says Isobel dramatically.

'It says on the Schedule,' continues Isobel, '1 May, Purification Ceremony, time 9 a.m. I doubt if that's the right time, we'd better inquire. Coronation: 2 May at 9 a.m. Consecration, 10.33 a.m. That's what the astrologers gave as the exact minute for the crowning, isn't it? The Ceremony's at the Hanuman Dhoka, that's the old Royal

Palace, the one with that dreadful blob of stone in front, supposed to be a heathen monkey god or something.'

'I bet they'll change all the times at the last minute,' says Geography. 'They always do, those astrologer wallahs; look at the stars and change the time, or ask their birds. They keep parakeets in cages. Supposed to tell them things.'

The talk goes on, and my blood boils. I perceive why we, the Christians, are so disliked. We exhibit an extraordinary grossness and vulgarity about other people's religion. We have no respect for beliefs not ours. In the coarsest, the rudest way, we speak of other gods with contempt, derision, utter lack of courtesy. Here Father MacCullough scores; whatever he may think, the old and deep wisdom of the Catholic Church, approximating Asian courtesy, leads him not to pass judgement openly upon the creeds of his hosts. But here at the Girls' Institute we have intolerance and narrowness, among the faded flowers of the sofa, among these women with faded skins and corded necks, and the vague, antiseptic smell. (Except that Isobel isn't faded or antiseptic; her hair is strong, her body firm and massive; held in by that vast hunger of hers for something her creed does not allow her. Isobel was made for a farmer's robust love-making, for love and healthy children. Thank her God she drinks. Otherwise it might be even worse.)

'The King's supposed to be Vishnu, isn't he?'

'Yes. They've got a Trinity kind of thing: Brahma, let me see, that's it, Vishnu, and Siva. Siva's the worst.'

'That's Siva, all these stones and things' (the word lingam has never been uttered by those pale lips), says Geography. 'That's why they don't allow you into temples if you look like a Christian. Beastly things they do there.'

'Thank the Lord for that. I'm glad I *look* a Christian.'

After these affirmations of faith Geography also produces some typed sheets of paper. It is coyly entitled *Mountain Peeks* and it is written in that extraordinary, breezy, slangy, oh-so-jolly style favoured by modern muscular ex-China missionary Christianity.

'I wonder if you'd like a look at this,' says Geography, handing it to me. 'It's *ever* so good. Gives one the real dope on all that goes on.' (Is it its influence, Geography is now always at the Royal Hotel before lunch, even has an occasional lemon squash with the correspondents?)

I read:

Eileen Potter is one of our younger nurses. Eileen says she became interested in nursing while still in the doll stage. She stuck out for the wide open spaces and is now slipping up those hills at the weekly rural dispensary in Patan ...

The Hymn Auxiliary met at the Nurses' Home last week. Nine ladies were present, dessert and coffee was served by the hostess, Miss Spockenweiler.

Miss Spockenweiler was presented with many lovely gifts for her birthday ...

Everybody square dance: Yep. Shore hope to see you there. Put on yore jeans and loudest shirt and bring yore best party spirits.

SWING YORE PARDNER!!!

(This item is flowerized. I mean, little flowers have been drawn round framing it. Ugh.)

'Thanks a lot,' I say, and hand the paper back.

'It's got a wonderful article, *everything* about the Coronation, on three pages in the middle,' insists Geography. From the way History looks modestly at her hands I guess it's History's own contribution to *Mountain Peeks.*

'I'm allergic to clichés,' I say in my politest tones.

I know, how well I know the laudability, the true heroism of their efforts. The devotion, the missionary spirit, the Doing of Good, the Fight Against Disease ... the latter seems an overwhelming reason to compel belief in our own superiority, for we have now a materialist faith, and the ethics of our age have a different goal. If it was the aim of medieval ethical speculation to find the way of Heaven by fulfilling the Commandments of Moses and caring not a bit about our vile bodies, in our century this goal is reached by furthering the health of one's fellow men, and all our Christian Churches have harnessed themselves to this task. And this anthropocentric aim of our religion seems to entitle us to look down upon people who care only about their souls still, as we did nine centuries ago. The work we do appears noble, unselfish; or is it only a greater selfishness, the satisfaction of our spiritual pride in doing something for lesser mortals? But it is a social ideal which we now call Christian, because our modern Christianity has grafted on to itself the dogmas of progress without which the poverty, the misery of this country would never change. Alas, why is it that the vessels of this doctrine should themselves be so uncouth, so unpleasant, so little capable of beauty, and so arrogant?

The correspondents are here.

Five shifts of airplanes a day have brought, yesterday and today, the hordes of the Press. Along with them are the photographers; most of them will be camped at the Royal Hotel.

The earliest to arrive, Vassili tells me, is the sole Chinese correspondent, inconspicuously installed in a room by himself. In the next plane the *New York Times*, closely followed by *Time, Life,* and *Newsweek,* make their Khatmandu début. In the same morning arrive the British Press, the Indian Press. By noon the air is full of competition and rivalry, the tables crowded with men and women with their backs firmly turned to the sun and the Valley, and their faces magnetized to each other. The Coronation, suddenly, has become something to be written up, adjectivally, in all its verbal aspects. Enoch P. circulates, and the word fabulous circulates with him.

Twenty taxis have arrived from India, I don't know how. The Chinese Delegation is lodged at the Royal Hotel in a suite. The electric light has failed. So have the pumps. There is no hot water. But, worst of all, *there is no liquor.*

The correspondents drink orange juice, Coca-Cola, and grenadine. Then Coca-Cola gives out. There's only grenadine left, sweet, sticky grenadine.

'I cannot stand it any more – I think I go back to prison,' says Vassili. He sits in his room with his head in his hands, dictating to Hilde a letter to the Field Marshal. The Field Marshal is in charge of the Coronation Programme.

'Your Excellency,' he writes, 'My patience is exhausted. The correspondents are drinking water' – ('Water!' cries Vassili desperately, knocking his forehead with his fists) – 'and I am afraid that the Coronation will be a complete disaster. Twenty-five guests of the Government are arriving tomorrow, and they will have to eat with their fingers and sleep on the floor.'

The correspondents are full of demands and inquiries. They want guides; they want to know the way to this, that, or the other. Hilde does what she can. The Irish girl is most willing. The lady artists have reappeared. Pat is laughing with the British Press.

The correspondents keep track of each other. They move in a body, for fear that someone might get on to something that the others would miss.

'Where's Blumenfeld? Haven't seen him for the last hour.'

'He's writing,' says *Newsweek*, a young man whose face appears perpetually blenched with anger.

'Writing?' (Look at the watch.) 'But we've only been here one hour.'

'Always writes three thousand words within first hour he gets any place. Calls it a preliminary survey.'

At that moment Blumenfeld, tall, bald, camera round neck, sheaf of cables in hand, appears: 'Can anyone of you fellars here tell me,' he demands plaintively, 'who the hell is Vishnu?'

Lunch is in relays. Since the electric power is off the ice cream is liquid.

The Press organizes itself. *Newsweek* goes round distributing hand-bills. There will be a twice daily Press bulletin, circulated round the correspondents by a committee of three. It will tell them exactly what to do, where to go, and when. 'Can't rely on the Nepalese to tell you anything. We'll do it ourselves.'

'Honest, this is going to be fabulous,' says Enoch P. John, he tells me, is at the Residency trying to fix a date for the formal opening of the Valley Club. 'We want to do it during Coronation Week.'

Leo is nowhere to be seen. Hilde tells me that Mariette Valport has gone off to Pokhra this morning by airplane to take photographs. 'She's a good sort really,' says Hilde.

There is a noise of engines downstairs. We all go to the verandah to see. Some lorries have arrived. Vassili is happy. It is the beer, the beer has arrived. And also some whisky. It had been impounded by Customs, and the cases have now been released. Vassili is happy, and shouts:

'Gentlemen of the Press, the drinks are here!'

And we all feel that now the Coronation will be a success.

After the tea at the Royal Hotel I go to see Fred Maltby at the Hospital.

(Oh Anne, you liar. You did not go to see Fred Maltby. You were looking for Unni. Everywhere. All the time. At the Royal Hotel, before and after lunch, waiting and talking to the correspondents, laughing, pretending you liked the company, lingering, lingering, hoping he would come ... and because he did not come, you went to see Fred Maltby, knowing that Unni lives in his bungalow when he is in Khatmandu. You were hungry and thirsty for him, and afraid, because last night, so surely, so insolently you said: 'I want to be alone.' And now you are frightened that he will not come back ...

But if he does not come back, then I know he is shallow, stupid, that he does not understand.

But you've been doing this for days, arguing aloud with yourself, in front of him, taking what he has given you to pieces, shaking the fragments, making them ring on stone, to see if it's true. You are so afraid of being hurt, Anne.

I never want to be hurt again. I keep on trying to find out ... how valuable this is.

Did he not say to you: 'Go ahead, you're like my young mountain'? And all you found to say was: 'How conceited you are.'

But he *is* conceited. He is so sure of himself. He says: I love you, as if he knew what love is.

Why should he not know? 'How can you tell me what I should or should not feel?' Don't you remember he said that?

I don't believe.

You don't believe ... does that give you the right to say he lies? You are a miser, Anne, a miser of the heart.

That's what Unni said. And now I am afraid that he won't come back.

You are afraid to give, and afraid to take. What if he should tire of these complications? What if he is tired already, and gone?

Oh no, please God no. Please.

It will be your fault.

My fault, as always. We are the owners of our deeds and the heirs of our actions, enwombed in our gestures and refugeed in our words.

How you live words, Anne, instead of living.

And so, very near to breaking down, in these colloquies with myself which I cannot stop once they've begun, feeling upon my face a

look akin to Isobel's – perhaps, after all, drink does help – I go to Fred
Maltby in the Serene Palace across the street.

The garden, is large, and I have no sense of direction. I nearly lose
my way, finally reach the bungalow. The door is open, Fred is at a
desk, typing. He does not see me at first, and my eyes go across the
study to the bedroom whose folding doors are open, to Unni's bed,
the narrow camp bed pushed against the wall in the wide bedroom
he shares with Fred Maltby. Why hasn't he got a room of his own?
Perhaps he does not need one. Perhaps he is always in one or another
woman's bedroom when he is in Khatmandu. I am hallucinated by his
bed. I keep staring at it, as if suddenly Unni's shape, the whole length
of him, with those narrow flanks and long hard legs guaranteed to
make any woman go limp, could materialize out of the quilted raza.
But there is nothing, not even his linen dhoti, not even a pair of
slippers. He is not here.)

'Oh, come in, Anne, come in.'

Fred looked cornered. It is Eudora. Last night, *en aparté*, the
General said to me: 'It is time that my friend stopped hiding
in his Hospital, behind nurses and patients and operations. I
thought Unni would put sense in his brain, madam, but Unni does
nothing.'

'What can he do?'

'Every wise man has a foolish fragment. It must be forcibly removed out of him, like a tooth.'

'Dr Maltby wouldn't like it, General. It's his private life. We can't
really interfere.'

'Private?' the General replied, astonished. 'That is *why* I must interfere. My friend's private life I must aid to my hindmost.'

I remembered that Asian conception of privacy is not ours. It
is an old misunderstanding of ours to think that what is private does
not belong to the community. I apologized to the General, who for-
gave me and turned back to his whisky.

Fred is very glad to see me, and soon in easy companionship we
speak of Eudora.

'I know I ought to see Eudora. I intend to, of course. It's simply
that there's not much point to it, is there? I mean, she hasn't asked to
see me. Don't think she wants to.'

How like a man. The procrastination, the shelving, passing the buck. Soon it will be Eudora's fault if they don't meet. Sardonically I say: 'You're bound to meet her soon, with the Coronation.'

'That's what I think,' replies Fred, relieved yet worried. 'There's no point in doing anything now, is there? She really would not like it. In fact, I feel sure that she probably does not want to be bothered at all.'

And having explained Eudora away to his satisfaction, Fred changes; becomes austere, full of quiet authority and wisdom. Physician, healing me.

We do not speak of me. We gradually come round to talk of female frigidity. 'D'you know that I've never had a case yet in a Nepalese woman? Yet I've seen plenty, in practice ... I think the country where I saw most of it was Australia. I saw a lot of it in England too of course, only I was there eighteen years ago when we called it nerves or muscular spasms, we didn't go in so much for psycho-analysis then, we still thought that women were of two kinds, the hot and the cold. The subject was altogether indelicate. But six years ago when I was in Australia it was mentionable. Women came to complain of it. They knew that sex should be something more than lack of lubrication, pain, passive putting up with. Though there were still plenty of the other kind among the women who were my patients: "My Bill is ever so good that way, he doesn't bother me much," and "After all, it's the man's enjoyment," sort of thing. I found this attitude popular among a lot of the wives of Service officers in the colonies. A conservative lot hemmed in by regulations.

'Among Asian women there's another problem. Neglect. Many Asian countries are polygamous. And with polygamy lots of married women simply have no sex life at all. They've been discarded sexually, though officially they're still wives. But at least they all seemed to know what sex was about and to know they should enjoy it, and they made no bones about it. It's because Asian men on the whole have always been taught that they must please the woman – whereas a lot of our men don't know that, or don't appear to worry about "coldness" in their wives.'

Fred inhaled deeply, his mind busy on the medical aspects of sex.

'We don't seem to bother enough about what Asians think and feel. And they know so much more about us than we do about them. We really need an Asian Kinsey, for comparison's sake.

'I was saying to Unni only this morning' (I sat up, this was enough reward already for me to go on listening, hoping for another mention of his name ... Unni had spent the night with Fred, he had been there that very morning ... o balm, o bliss, o foolish Anne who goes leaping at the sound of a name, like any moonstruck teenager), 'there's a changing pattern of *mores* all over Asia. But ideas and feelings don't catch up with material progress. There is Unni, building a dam which will revolutionize this country far more implacably than any political theory. It will alter the whole pattern of living for hundreds of thousands of people, but ideas, emotional make up will lag behind for another decade at least. It's a kind of inverse revolution that countries of Asia are going through ... not from within out, not from ideas to implements, but from out to within, from machines to ideas, and that's why sometimes they appear to mishandle the things which are being brought to them. It's because, psychologically, they're not yet in possession of the implements we put in their hands.

'Unni and I, we're the greatest revolutionaries in Khatmandu today. He with his dam and me with my Hospital. I wish sometimes we could delimit the extent of the changes we're bringing about ... but we can't.'

'Unni,' I said, practising the word in public, though my heart beat so loud I did not hear myself, 'isn't at all a social theorist. He's a technician.'

'Same as me,' said Fred. 'Doers, not thinkers. We're so busy doing, we don't think at all ... just as those scientists who were busy manufacturing the atom bomb, they didn't think of the implications, and how it would change the whole texture of war and the future. That's what I mean. We keep on saying ideas are dangerous, and talking utter rot about containing communism and all that stuff, when communism is just one of the logical by-products of this technico-medical material revolution we're having even in such places as Nepal and Tibet. If it were ideas alone, they could be kept out, die of themselves, like plants without soil and water; but it's the bulldozers, the steam-rollers, the jeeps, the airplanes, the dams, the factories, the roads, the material building up we call progress, that's what changes the country. And that isn't kept out.'

And then Fred wandered on to medicine again, to frigidity, and his London student days. 'Even ten years ago it was quite the thing to operate for a condition we called vaginismus. That means a tight spasm in the woman, barring entry. Now we give hormone pills and psychiatry.' He'd never seen a woman naked before, and on his first day there were twenty in a row, laid on tables like so many pigs; or rather, he did not see them, but only their exposed vulvas, knees draped like two white columns, and the portals of sex between, like a row of doors. 'It was an awful shock, but we all sniggered, and pretended we knew all about it.

'And that is why, perhaps, things went so wrong with Eudora. She was impatient and I was so inept ...' His voice trailed off. 'She too became cold, Eudora I mean ... and for me, too, it was a relief to think she was cold. I wondered how many husbands at this very moment bluff themselves, as John and I did, that their wives are naturally cold? Now I know that it is woman's way of passive resistance, the road she always chooses, turning herself into a non-sexual being. Perhaps because of the centuries of female subservience behind her. Anyway, there it is. She's nice and cold, until one day ... You're very lucky, Anne, you know, with Unni ... you don't mind my saying so, do you?'

'No,' I said . 'I want you to say it. Where is Unni? I am looking for him.'

'Unni? I don't know. He went off this morning, early. We had some coffee together and chatted a bit. The General ought to know.'

But the General was out, and so I came home, it was already darkling; half-expecting a shadow on the lawn, but there was none; half-expecting him on the stairs, but they were empty.

Slate grey dawn, I know it by heart from peering out of the window. He will not come.

That I would have to endure this, this utterly humiliating cliché-ridden state is comical. I observe myself going through the incomprehensible antics of anxiety, the agony of waiting, the imagined steps, the non-existent jeep heard, and the peering. ... I catch myself doing it and I am angry and then I do it all over again.

How pitiful, how ridiculous, how contemptible ... yet even great poets have suffered this, for none escape the pettiness with the ecstasy, the grandiloquence with the suffering, the idle twist which deflates a tremendous emotion like a pricked balloon, the glory and the singing stars and the terminal burp, the smut with the sacrament. Some tediousness and some voluptuousness, that was ever the burden of the poet's song.

As children and psychologists look at ink spots and deduce fantastic theories or crazy images, let me look at myself. Stocktaking on this my journey. As a mountain climber, having assembled his expedition, counts the porters, watches the loads, checks the gear, then turns his face towards the summit ... only it is Unni who talks of mountains and summits, and not me. I have not yet plumbed my own depths.

Like the Queen, facing her mirror, asking for truth, I have been to the mirror downstairs. I see a woman still young, a grace I look at with pleasure. I have changed: gloss of skin, lustre of hair, brilliance of eye; from every pore comes happy knowledge that I am beautiful. But the years are going, the running grave of time tracks behind me, my own shadow, and what have I done? Tried to be good, respectable, and dead. Wound myself to near death in my own cocoon of respectability. No more.

I look for the white hairs, at the crown. There were two yesterday I plucked out. I find another one.

I look at my belly, with the fine scar down the middle. Nearly invisible. I know Unni has seen it. Of course he has. I can feel him learning me, inch by inch. The memory of his hands, two days ago, holding my waist between thumb and finger, bringing me to him. ... Then I hear the sound of a jeep.

There is one jeep which is like no other. One can always tell a jeep from another jeep. ... I listen, listen. But it drags its small roar away. And this is the final twist, the prick in the balloon. Suddenly all the content of my emotion drains, like a pail overturned, at once emptied, nothing left, no charm, no subtlety, no pain.

Unni, a word, hollow with non-meaning. The ridiculous, didactic manner in which he speaks, unblushing, confident, of love! Going up the stairs back to my room, I feel myself all over, bewildered by this reversal, this disappearance of all emotion. Thank God, it is all gone. I am free, free, myself, and happy again. On the walls the parakeets mock. Bright, shining passion? Nothing but the slate greyness, paling slowly, the bed slate grey.

Chapter 9

SUNDAY, 29 April 1956. Lunch at the Royal Hotel had the flavour of snatched meals at a busy station restaurant. The languorous, sun-drowsy mood of the verandah had vanished, replaced by a steamy, hectic agitation like a gigantic halo which emanated from the teams of correspondents and photographers seated at the tables.

That morning the first official function of Coronation Week had taken place at the Durbar Hall. This was an edifice of white stucco and indeterminate 'Western' architecture adhering, with an air of trying to tear itself away, to the Hanuman Dhoka, the old rambling Royal Palace, where the King no longer lived, preferring his pillared and stucco replica of Buckingham Palace. The old Palace had towers with multiple roofs which through age and decay sagged and crumbled, tiers of carved beams quietly rotting above the courtyards. It would now be open to a select assembly for the ceremonies 'for the first time in the history of Nepal'. History's article in *Mountain Peeks* asserted it and proceeded to give dates and various data on its archi-tecture. Unmentioned in *Mountain Peeks*, the Palace also contained the most worthy and original erotic carvings to be found in the Valley.

The Durbar Hall, in its whitewashed, Calvinistic ugliness, boasted nothing better than a few score of chandeliers, and along one wall of the marble-floored audience room, with its golden throne rearing a nine-headed snake above the monarch's head, were the usual oil portraits of Ranas, tempered with a few recent Prime Ministers of the democratic age, Edward the Seventh and Queen Alexandra, and even one or two Kings of Nepal.

That morning Megalorama hád made its first public appearance. A machine on wheels, many bent attendants at its service, a prosaic rope tied to one of its gadgets enabled it to be wheeled back and forth at a slant to the Durbar entrance, and thus to snap the dignitaries alighting from their cars from the moment they stepped out till they dis-appeared into the Hall. Ambassadors, Rana generals, diplomats, marched into view of the Cyclopean, bleak round eye of the machine until their faces alone filled its lens. Conscious of this mechanical vision (an all-consciousness more dangerous and precise than the Eyes of Buddha upon their golden stupas, since Buddha's vision only extended to their immortal, eternally recurrent spirits, whereas this one would engrave upon the eyes of millions their infinitely more cherished delible mortal traits), one and all straightened their shoulders, moulded their visages into tallow solemnity as they passed in front of the all-encompassing Megalorama.

Anne too had attended the ceremony, with John who had entrance to the Diplomats' Gallery, a fact which he and Enoch P. extolled. 'Our role is liaison, the promotion of social contact between the Nepalese and ourselves,' the latter reiterated to the many correspondents who spasmodically assembled round him and round Father MacCullough, as experts invested with oracular status in Nepalese custom and history.

Enoch P. now called: 'Hi, T. S.!' to a portly Nepalese in full General's regalia. 'General Torula Sham Sher, very nice chap, fixin' to join our Club,' he explained, in loud *aparté*, to the impressed correspondents. 'Actually introduced me to his Maharani (that's his wife), a great honour. Means they trust you when they take you to see their wives.'

All-Khatmandu was there. All-Khatmandu could scarcely avoid meeting itself there. Anne, brought to face people she had seen, saw, and would see at least several times a day for the next few days (encounters unalleviated by the maximum conventional expressions of pleased surprise, effusive delight, with which these repetitions were enriched), felt nearly suffocated in the Diplomats' Gallery. Michael Toast, languid and lanky, attached himself to her.

'You've got something the others haven't got,' he preambled.

'Now what can it be?' she asked, half weary, half pleased.

'You're normal. I don't think I can put it better in any other way. Most of the other women,' his glance swept the gallery, brooming aside behatted and gloved Americans, the Girls' Institute in full blossom, Suragamy in red speckled silver, Isobel high in colour in a floral design and with John attached to her like clam to rock, a natural gravitation; 'most of these other women just don't have any artistic impulse at all.'

The conversation was taking its usual twist, and Anne replied: 'Normal, but not available,' left him standing under the portrait of

King Edward the Seventh, and was soon cut off from him by the wives and interpreters of the Chinese Delegation who now swarmed up into the gallery, all smiles and stiffly curled hair.

In spite of the chandeliers and the Press and Megalorama, a Nepalese atmosphere of cheerful feckless good temper, suave certainty that all would go well by supernatural agency if not human effort, had invaded Khatmandu.

'You see,' said the Indian Ambassador to his British colleague, 'everything is going fine.'

The Chinese Ambassador presented his credentials to the popping of many cameras, and the Indian Mission presented a sword, and both received from the King the tokens of welcome (the Chinese Ambassador for the occasion deploying a very clean, very new handkerchief to receive the gift of scented water and pan from a golden casket by the King's own hand).

At the Royal Hotel, released from the restful charm of Nepalese officialdom with its evasive answers, serene and diffuse smiles, soothing promises, and masterly inactivities, the correspondents maintained their own ulcer prone atmosphere of strain and tension. Lapped in the warm gusts of nervous strain, indispensable to them as the temperature of a hothouse to orchids, these men of the tired saliva and the keen skidding eye – so apt to chisel what was alive into sensational headlines, so clever at avoiding becoming affected by what they wrote about, rounding their backs and looking at each other to avoid seeing what could not fit into the patterned words of their column – chewed and threw at each other little pellets of false dope, true dope, and withheld dope, dispensed only to get back equivalent secret dope.

Anne sat, in the discomfort which the agitation of others produces upon one who does not partake of its stimulant effects, at a table with Leo, Michael Toast, and some correspondents whose talk of the moment was all of Blumenfeld, the incorrigible Blumenfeld, who had once again monopolized the sending apparatus and was doing five thousand words on the morning's ceremony. His colleagues had retreated to beer and malignancy about Blumenfeld.

'That guy's going nuts.'

'Crazy, I tell you. D'you know what he said yesterday? Collared me and said: "D'you realize that Krishna is only another incarnation of Vishnu?" "So what?" I said.'

'He'd better be careful, he'll go batty with all those gods in his bonnet.'

'Yeah, they kind of haunt you after a time. All those multiple personalities.'

'He's swotting up the Hindu cosmogony now. Bet he'll take up Yogi next.'

'That'd be fine. Get him looking at his navel and out of the cable office.'

Newsweek's elegant young man was loudly complaining of inefficiency. His jeep had not arrived, for three consecutive days he had called on a famous politician and found him at prayers, at a wedding, and finally engaged in love-making with his wife. 'At 3 p.m.,' raged *Newsweek*. 'Can you beat it?'

Vassili was happy. He swore profusely at Colonel Jaganathan. Out of a hundred cases of beer, seventy-nine had turned up. Vassili was convinced that the missing twenty-one had been requisitioned by the Indian Army engineer while in transit on the road. 'You don't know that fellow. I bet he's downing the beer at this moment in his tent and laughing his head off. Wait until he gets here for the Coronation. I'll show him his drinks bill for the year and he'll pass out.' Meanwhile sixty of the eighty bearers had turned up, and the Field Marshal, as if by magic, had produced furniture, linen, plates. 'It'll be a success,' said Vassili.

Hilde, walking back and forth, busy finding extra beds, checking the plates and the laundry, was also fending off the amorosities of two stalwart pressmen and three photographers, who insisted that a pagoda's finer points could only be appreciated with blonde Hilde in the foreground.

Leo was intensely depressed, due to a cable just received: ARIVVING ON FRIST MAG THUNKING SMUCH OF GOU CANNOT EAT LOVE KISHA, which was comprehensible even if garbled, and enough to make him dread the prospect. Kisha was coming on the first of May, eve of the Coronation, the day after tomorrow in fact. Where *could* one go away, hide, disappear, in this handkerchief-size valley, where? For a moment he contemplated going to Pokhra. Mariette had gone to Pokhra by plane the day before, planning to return on Monday. She had taken with her a tiny, rotund little Swiss, a self-dubbed explorer, who for some days had been contemplating Mariette with gluttonous adoration, exactly the same expression in fact (thought Leo) as the bulls of Siva in front of the lingams. Laden with forty pounds of photographic equipment, he had smiled heroically while Leo kissed Mariette at the airfield. And then Leo had noticed Unni and a group of men at the airfield, getting into another plane. Where was Unni going? He asked the Customs officials, who all knew Unni. Pokhra, they said. Leo smiled, pleased. Then Mariette would inevitably meet Unni at Pokhra. Had she arranged it with him? No, he felt, otherwise she would have told him. 'We'll see, we'll see,' he had said to himself, elated by the coincidence. But the cable from Kisha had put Mariette and Unni out of his mind.

Anne, sitting opposite Leo, was preoccupied and off-colour, kept looking around, answering briefly, impatiently; whenever a jeep came to a stop outside the Hotel she half raised her head, looked over the verandah railing. There was something hard about the way she answered Michael Toast while he drawled small talk about the Newaris:

'Curious customs they have … Newaris much more free than the Ranas, who've no originality in art or in amour, copy everything from India … a Newari woman can divorce her husband simply by putting a betel nut under his pillow at night. Would like to see his face waking up one morning to find a nut instead of a woman in his bed. …'

'All the Newari girls are married to trees,' said Anne. 'Marriages to men are merely second-hand makeshifts, only the original tree counts as a real husband.'

'I say, most awfully convenient for the woman, isn't it?'

She nodded. At that moment there was a sound of feet and voices on the stairs, and she turned her head, her eyes and face lit up, but abruptly the light went out again. Two Indian pilots, tall and dark, swinging in for a drink. The pilots were all working overtime. Shift after shift of planes were coming into the Valley. They complained of overwork, gulped a drink, chaffed Hilde, slapped Vassili on the back, and went out again, jeeping back to the airport to take yet another plane to Patna and back again to Khatmandu.

'Unlax, unlax, they need unlaxing,' said Leo, tense and wound up himself, and yet unable to tear himself away from the atmosphere, unable to go. I know what's the matter with Anne, he thought, she's waiting, waiting for that man to turn up. He wondered if he ought to say something about Pokhra, and Mariette and Unni being there together. He watched her anxiety, it was alleviation of his own about Kisha.

A couple of correspondents came in with cameras, they had been taking pictures of the temples. With them was Suragamy's fiancé, voluble, sweating oozily, who now went from table to table, as if soliciting. Anne caught snatches of his talk: '... temple dancers ... ritual performances ...' His eyes swivelled in promise of curvaceous delight.

The madman walked in, carrying his briefcase, and looking round for his own table which was occupied. Vassili shouted an order, and the bearers brought in an extra table and a chair and wedged it somehow into an exiguous vacant space. The madman sat in solitary grandeur, drumming with his fingers and looking benignly round him. Among the correspondents small waves of interest began: a Nepalese, obviously important, since he had a briefcase and a table to himself; a native, must be full of local dope. Slowly an enveloping movement began, with *Time* and *Life* in the lead, the *New York Times* and *Newsweek* neck and neck behind, converging upon this mysterious V.I.P.

The Chinese Delegation, not addicted to drink, walked by, soberly dressed, stiff and precise in demeanour, and disappeared in the direction of their suites, followed by the free stares of the Press. They were objects of speculation, as if they were not quite human, as if they could not possibly eat, drink, and talk like other people, and anything they were reported to have done or said was scrutinized for hidden falsities. The lone Chinese correspondent, an amiable and handsome young man who spoke excellent English, sat with some Indian newspapermen at a separate table and toasted co-existence in fruit juice. Blumenfeld had tackled him the day before. 'Does the Peiping Communist Government intend to render any monetary or other so-called Aid to Nepal?' he had bawled.

The Chinese had gazed at him thoughtfully, and parried: 'If we do, will it double your so-called Aid?'

'If *you* do, we'll cut off every cent,' shouted Blumenfeld.

John now came in with Ranchit. Ranchit for the past twenty-four hours had been taking out a woman journalist with an enormous amount of yellow hair piled on top of her head. He caught sight of Anne and immediately made his way to her table, and from the sneer upon his pale, amber face, outlined by his thin little moustache, Anne knew he was going to hurt her.

'Well, Leo, what've you been doing with yourself?' said John genially. He was in the swim. He had a new suit on, as Anne had a new dress. She had noticed the suit at the Durbar Hall, and wondered whether he saw the dress. It was a beautiful yellow silk, with sleeves and high neck, moulded to her with a little flare at the back. Somehow the tailor seemed to work twice as well now with Unni talking and arguing with him about texture and seams and gathers. She was beginning to learn Unni's taste in clothes ... oh, if only he would come, if only he would be here. Desperately she turned round again. The crowd was thick about her. Even if he were there, among them, she might not see him immediately. ...

Ranchit was watching her, smiling covertly, talking to Leo about the United Nations, 'I don't see they're much good, they can't stop anything ...', meanwhile his eyes kept glancing insolently at Anne, then back at John. That man knows everything, thought Leo, and John doesn't. Poor chap. John was very self-assured, his voice loud, laughing frequently, stopping the conversation to hail people, to promise to 'see to it', explaining all about the admission passes the Club had received. 'Very satisfactory seating too. First few rows, the F.M.' – John referred to the Field Marshal in charge of the Coronation programme as the F.M. – 'will see to it we get the best seats.'

Ranchit suddenly stopped Hilde by holding familiarly to her arm as she went by. He liked people to think that all the women about had been his.

'Hilde, my beautiful, have you seen that fellow Unni about?'

'Unni?' said Hilde, disengaging herself. 'No, I haven't. Ask Vassili.'

Ranchit laughed heartily. 'He must be still in Pokhra, enjoying French leave,' he said, winking at John, who laughed back. 'Of course,' added Ranchit, 'who wouldn't? Miss Valport is charming, a beautiful woman, and an eminent writer too.' His eyes slid over Anne, up and down, disparagingly. 'She's really *most* attractive. I think Unni will have a jolly good time, eh?'

'Ha ha,' laughed John.

Ranchit also roared with laughter and clapped him on the shoulder. 'Nothing like a French girl, eh? She'll come back purring like a cat that's had a full saucer of milk.'

In the silence that followed they heard the madman speaking loudly now to correspondents who had worked their way to his table. At last, their expressions said, here's a native knowledgeable and willing to talk. Apart from his theories on Lenin and Stalin, the madman was fully aware of what went on round him.

'Yes, gentlemen, the Throne of the King, the great golden Lion Throne, rests upon seven skins, bear and lion, wild boar and tiger, elephant, rhinoceros, and human.'

'Human?' said the correspondents.

'His Majesty is monarch of all he surveys, of all creation. Human skin cannot be omitted,' said the madman gravely. 'It was left out by the last King, and His Majesty's reign was short and unhappy. If King Mahendra omits a human skin,' said the madman threateningly, 'he will have a tough time.'

'François,' shouted Leo, rising.

François Luneville was advancing towards them. He had just arrived by the seventh airlift of the morning.

How terrible, thought Leo, everybody, but just everybody I know, will be in Khatmandu for the Coronation.

François bent to kiss Anne's hand, shook hands solemnly with John, was introduced to Michael and Ranchit. He was a small man, thin, with a long sad nose and a long face, and extremely intelligent eyes. '*Vous avez tellement changé, Anne,*' he said in his measured tones. From Lyons, spare of speech, he disliked meeting new people. The populousness of the verandah inhibited him. 'I am going to make myself clean. I come back and have lunch with you, yes?'

Anne said: 'Yes, do.' Sitting, sitting and waiting. And Unni was in Pokhra. And Mariette. Now she felt she must go home, right away ... he might be back at home, he might not be in Pokhra, Ranchit was lying, Unni was in the bungalow, waiting for her. ... Here she had been, wasting her time at the Royal Hotel, when he was at home waiting for her. ...

'I must go back for a minute,' she murmured, half rising. 'I forgot something.'

Ranchit now seized her arm, moulding the flesh hard under his fingers, hoping she would show pain. 'Without lunch? Oh, come Anne, you *must* stay and eat ... you're getting so thin. John, you shouldn't let your wife *work* so hard ... is it really something very important you forgot? If not, why don't you let me fetch it for you? Or go later? We're all having such a good time together, why not have another drink first?'

'You don't know my wife,' said John. 'Anne's never happy the way other people are. You're sure it isn't something you forgot at the Hospital?' he added brutally.

'At the Hospital?' replied Anne, puzzled. 'Why?'

'You seem to go there very frequently.'

'I do occasionally pop in and have tea with Fred. I like him. He's nice.'

'No man,' said John, suddenly quarrelsome, 'no man who refuses to meet his own wife is nice.'

'The King will be anointed,' the madman declared in a loud voice, 'with water from the seven seas, collected and poured over him; and his skin will be touched with mud from the five sacred mountains.'

'That's Fred's business surely, whether he and Eudora meet,' said Anne.

'I don't see why you have to defend Dr Maltby,' replied John. 'Everybody thinks he's a coward.'

The General came floating softly up the stairs.

'General,' exclaimed Leo, in the joyous, exuberant tone he adopted to parry unpleasantness. Really, I might be a butler announcing entrances, he thought; and the next one will probably be Kisha. Or Unni and Mariette.

'And there will be seven sisters,' chanted the madman, 'seven ladies of ill-fame, whores to you, gents, to remind the King that he is Lord of the meanest as well as the highest.'

'Good day, madam,' said the General to Anne. 'I went to the bungalow but you were unpresent. I meditated you might have deposited yourself here. I have a letter for you.'

'Oh,' said Anne, blushing furiously. A big Nepalese envelope, corn coloured. She looked at it, half in fear.

'It's from the Field Marshal,' said the General. 'He regrets that he has not seen you in the past few days, or he would have handed them to you personally.'

'Can I see?' said John, bending forward.

Anne opened the envelope. In it were passes, such as John had. The momentary elation dropped, leaving her numb.

'Your wife,' said the General gravely, 'in her quality as an intellectual, is receiving her own passes, as well as the double passes that have been issued to you.'

'What an extraordinary idea,' said John angrily. He fingered the passes, mentally noting the number, in case Anne as an intellectual received better seating than he did.

Meanwhile the General casually extracted a blue envelope from his pocket and handed it to Anne; only a line of the familiar, so familiar (though only once perceived bending over Eudora's shoulder at the airfield) unemphasized writing: 'After lunch Monday Royal Hotel.'

And the whole of Anne had changed, happiness skylarking, making her suddenly vivid, glowing. Leo and Ranchit saw and knew the message Unni's. John, having missed it by a few seconds' inattention, handed back the passes with a 'Very interesting,' which meant nothing at all but was his way of filling a gap in talk when he could think of nothing to say. Anne turned upon them with a sudden, extraordinary radiance: 'Shall we be going in to lunch? I'm hungry.' She was transfigured.

'But François will want a drink,' protested John. 'And you, General, what about a drink?'

'Certainly. Whisky,' said the General.

At lunch Ranchit immediately started again on the subject of Mariette Valport. 'A most interesting woman, most fascinating,' he repeated, stroking his little moustache. 'Writing a book entitled *Men of Five Continents*. It is a study, a really serious report, on the love-making habits of men in every country she visits.'

'Menon will help her write a chapter,' said John, heavily witty.

But it all fell flat, and the General carelessly said to the air round him: 'Such ladies have come in great numbers to Khatmandu in times past, and always retired hence muddlefied and impregnated.'

'I beg your pardon,' said Leo, 'I didn't quite catch what you said?'

But the General did not elaborate, he turned to Anne, spoke of his daughter Lakshmi, and the baby she was expecting, and how she would soon go to Switzerland for her cough, and soon after took his leave.

The next day Anne was there, waiting in the hall between the rhinoceros heads. Above her head the verandah's noise: John, Ranchit, François, Leo, a rueful Leo haunted by visions of Kisha. 'Yes, Anne, she's coming tomorrow. It's terrible, I tell you. Once I've been to bed with a woman I simply can't stand the sight of her, sometimes I get so disgusted I never want to see her again.'

Anne had left them, walked downstairs, prudent, fearing that Unni would miss her. She wondered he had chosen such a public place, then remembered that the Institute was full of visiting missionaries. She stood in the hall waiting, wondering whether the day might ever come when she and Unni would look at each other with hatred and disgust, would never want sight of each other again? But I'll know, she thought, I'll know. His body and mine, they will tell us before our minds do.

And then she felt hot all over, going molten and weak, liquid fire rising under her skin, the pure, exquisite, excruciating goose-flesh, for he was there, come walking, she had not heard any jeep, he was walking towards her, familiar and incredibly unknown. He stood in front of her and she caught the warmth of his body and the faint smell of leather and sandalwood. Ambrosial dusk, she thought, the ambrosial dusk of you. ...

He said, smiling: 'It's wonderful to see you. Have you had lunch?'

'No. I'm not hungry.'

'You will be. I've got sandwiches in my jeep.'

'You think of everything.'

He looked at her, and it seemed to her that they both swayed. 'I think of you,' he said.

'Where are we going?' She was parched with happiness.

'To the airfield. I've just come back from a trip to Pokhra. They've got a project there and I had to go to see it. I left a message for you. Did you get it?'

'Yesterday, Sunday. The General gave it to me at lunch time.'

'Only yesterday? You should have had it Saturday.'

'It doesn't matter. I wasn't worried. I knew you'd come.' And at that moment it was true. She was sure she had always known, never doubted.

They walked, keeping prudently to the wall, unperceived from the verandah. They both shared a natural, almost crafty quietness of movement.

'I'm taking you for a plane ride to Simra. I've left my jeep outside the hotel. Get into yours and drive to the airfield and I'll follow you.' And as if ashamed of prudence, he added: 'I'm sorry. I hate this.'

They arrived together at the airfield, parking their jeeps not near each other. Anne pleased even by the fact that their vehicles stood in the same line.

The pilot was a thin, sallow faced young Indian with a small moustache, and the co-pilot a fresh faced Eurasian with green eyes and brown hair, a little more stocky than Unni but nearly as tall, with more girth round the waist and buttocks and thighs.

They climbed in the airplane, an old DC3. Raja, the pilot, complained that there would be cloud.

'I'm having five days off starting tomorrow. Been flying up and down from Patna six shifts a day, and two shifts to Pokhra, and now Simra. After this job, I'm going to resign. Every time I fly into Khatmandu a few more of my hairs turn white.'

'It's quite dangerous, especially in the monsoon,' said the co-pilot.

They stood in the cockpit, and there seemed to be clouds, great romping roundnesses, rising on every side. 'There's the road,' shouted Raja, pointing down below.

'That's the road,' said Unni in Anne's ear.

Between the drifts of cloud were the hills in their medley, and the irregular zigzag among them, pale like a scar, of the road, insignificant from here. And then they were flying over the green swampy belt of jungle known as the Terai, and going down, following the cord of a river, down into the plain, Simra.

The heat of the plain struck them bodily as they came out of the plane, and the heaviness. The sky above them was like poor quality china, and Raja looked at its vacancy, and spat.

'I don't think we'll be able to go back today. Cloud coming up.' He was very tired.

The runway was rough and bumpy and only big enough for two or three small airplanes to manoeuvre. There was a hut with thatched roof, a few mat sheds strewn about. At one end of the small airfield, lashed with ropes, were barrels of tar in mounds, laid out, waiting to be flown into Khatmandu.

'I take one load, no more,' said Raja. 'You can fly the others if you like, Smithson, and kill yourself for a few damned rupees.'

He went into the shadow of the sheds and flopped on the hard earth floor, and drew another cigarette.

A little man with a large crease of a smile came up to Unni. 'Good morning, sar. We've also got twenty bearers here for airlifting.'

'Twenty bearers? They'll have to come by road,' said Unni, 'we can't do it.'

'But sar, I had a message from Mr Vassili ... you were coming to fetch them.'

'Mr Vassili was told they'd come up by road,' said Unni. 'I've come to talk over some things with your supervisor while the tar is being loaded, and go back with it.'

Smithson came back, shaking his head. 'Captain Raja doesn't think we can get back today. The sky doesn't look very nice, sir. Captain Raja says too many clouds.'

'I think we'll let Captain Raja rest for a while and give him some drink and cigarettes,' said Unni. 'He's been up since early morning, flying from Patna and back several times. This airlift is enough to kill any pilot.'

'Yes sar, shall we load the tar, sar?'

'You might begin putting in a few barrels. I'm sorry,' he said to Anne, 'Raja's been living on his nerves for a long time. All the pilots have been overworked. Let's give Raja time to calm down.'

'Maybe he resents my coming,' said Anne, a little anxiously.

'He wouldn't, in ordinary circumstances, he'd be delighted. But he's just not feeling well, and I didn't know it. However, he'll feel better soon.' Unni sat on a tar barrel and stretched his legs, and began talking to the supervisor who had now come up. Anne wandered on.

The plain was long, it went on and on, sometimes breaking into clumps of trees. There was a ruined wall, which must once have been a farmhouse, several hundred yards away, and Anne walked towards it. It was very hot in the sun, and she was unused to the heat after the cool, high Valley. The grass was dry, already coarse, brown and rustling beneath her feet, end of April dryness. There was an occasional small, stiff breeze coming in and out of the plain, nobody knew from where.

She heard the call, coming near, of a bird she could not identify. The sound grew stronger as she approached the derelict farm. A large tamarind stood a hundred yards from it, and she sat in its shade, mopping her face. It was a bird calling, but what bird? A voice brassy, resonant, raucous, ringing. The bird must be very near, and it seemed to be shouting at the top of its voice. Then she saw the bird, or rather the dazzling blue flash of its wings. Such a blue she had never seen. Such a bird voice she had never heard.

The bird was now calling unceasingly, louder and louder, until it seemed the plain echoed with its ringing voice. It flashed its astonishing, incredibly blue wings, a never-imagined sapphire blue. The bird was about as big as a jay, and it behaved extraordinarily. It somersaulted, catapulted above the stones, glided down to grass level, hopped back into air to whirr in a great circle and came back, meanwhile calling, calling in ear-splitting fashion. And then Anne noticed the other bird round which this one wheeled and rolled and called, which then took flight, also flashing blue wings from a bluish-brown body, and settling, as a woman chooses a more comfortable seat, upon another crumbling heap of bricks.

'How wonderful. They're *nilkants*,' said the voice of Unni behind her. He had come up and now stood with her, looking. 'I think you call them blue jays in English. They're courting. I've never seen *nilkants* courting before, have you? That's the male, of course, throwing himself about like that. ...'

The bird was now hopping up and down in a series of leaps in mid-air, then turned round on itself and nose dived again in a paroxysm of screams.

It was so marvellous, such an unstinted passion squandered on the dry plain, that the humans watching felt moved and taken up, wrapped in this bird delight in the bird-echoing plain, brown, dusty, and sun-powdered, the bird indefatigable in his labour of love, filling the air with the excesses of his voice and his beautiful lustful body.

Anne looked at Unni, but he was looking at the birds, unconscious of her; and then feeling her looking at him, he turned his head, and their eyes met, and they smiled at each other with pleasure. And then, with pleasure shared, communication delicate and sensitive of minds knowing, acknowledging each other's delight in this mutual contemplation, swift and overwhelming, coursing up in them, gushing into their eyes and their mouths, came desire, ardent, and their eyes now locked, they were caught again in this lovely illumined mesh, bright, insatiable, all-absorbing, and Unni's hands came up to Anne's shoulders, and she said, 'No, no,' moaning already in her throat, already twisting her head sideways in the refusal to look which is consent to be taken, her limbs melting, fire sweet and strong in her loins. 'Your body says yes,' he said, and pushed her down, and she found herself helping him, at the neck of her shirt, the belt of her jeans, with swift hands, abetting her own stripping, and then his body pressed to hers and his swift entry, pleasure so intense that she heard herself cry out and hid her face, biting the back of her hand, and the jagged golden lightning of the storm was loosed, and the kettle drums of thunder beat, and the flame blew whiter and whiter, until 'I am going to die, I am dying, I am,' and then felt the lovely shock of his coming, more pleasurable than hers, the final stunning dumb blow within her which sent all her nerves tingling in an exquisite cacophony and slid her into the blankness which was fulfilment.

She came back to find the abyss of the round sky above her, its spacious bell and eternal security, and a deliberate slack silence. To find herself washed clean, pure, pure and golden and sighing with innocent peace, knowing the soft dove's feet of love which rule the world, and all her armour gone, stripped from her like an old skin too small, entirely shed at last, and the innocent tender young she within blinking at the sun, infinitely vulnerable, naïvely tender, all given, tremulous with new candour, fulfilment, nothing short.

'I thought I was dying,' she said. She heard her voice very far away, faint and white, colourless as the sky.

'So did I.' His voice, laconic, held a leash in it, secretive over a consummation he would not blister with words, but it brought him back, near to her, where she had been one in her transfiguration. He was lying, eyes closed, his head upon his arm. Her arm began to hurt her. She moved it, and he also moved, rolling away from her and half rising, drawing her clothes around her protectively with that modesty which she liked so much, and then he put on his own, and sat up. His shirt was still open and his skin glistened with sweat, and she put out her hand, gliding it on his naked chest, on his arms. She was feeling the smooth, even skin, so wonderful now to her, so alive, touching him with love and gentleness and sensuality, the comprehension of knowing that this brutal tender impalement was really the gateway to all the rest, the beginning and the source, dark frontier of creation, a flame within to keep alive and to be kept, to give life in darkness throughout the whole scintillating, many-faceted self. And this was body, the humble, patient servant who was also the lord, the much despised, much insulted body, which however took its own revenges if hated too much. And now body was one great reason, a plurality with one sense, a war and a peace, a flock and a herdsman, a pentagonal sense-bound prison for the universe, end and yet never end in itself. Behind the body man had created a spirit, an arrogant fluttering self, and sought to separate the two, calling the spirit noble and the body base. And that was the great crime, the sin against the Holy Ghost, committed again and again. For body and spirit must be together, indivisible, responsible to and for each other, each one the other's owner and servant, and whoever divided them did perish and murder others.

He was dressed, and looked at her troubled, moved as she was. Their silence declared their new knowledge, the space between them a stronger bond than their touching. Silently, softly, they kissed, as if freeing themselves by contact, measuring their bodies along each other in acknowledgment and giving. And then they walked back to the plane.

The afternoon was rapidly becoming the afternoon it had begun, as if time which had slackened and stopped, held back by their love-making, had now resumed its normal speed. Time was different stuff here now, a bustle about the plane's hard insect lines; the tar barrels loaded, and the twenty bearers, docile, stowed in two rows in the plane's body, the tar barrels roped securely down in the middle.

'I hope they don't roll,' said Raja, who seemed recovered and was smoking.

The supervisor now came up with a sheaf of papers, waving them at Unni. 'Here are the forms, sir.'

'We take off now,' said Raja impatiently.

They got into the cockpit once more. It was hot, and Anne squeezed in a corner. They stood while Raja and the co-pilot angled into their seats and adjusted their earphones.

'I'll take a look around,' said Raja amiably. 'Maybe you'd like to have a view of the Himalayas before we land?'

'Yes, very much,' said Anne.

'Okay,' said Raja, as if proffering a spin down a nice country lane. And then the airplane lifted, and they were off, in the mid-afternoon, with the plain falling away in industrious patterns, brown and green, like delicate veins under skin the small canals, here and there a pond with toy water buffaloes on the banks.

There were about them the clouds again, the airplane shadowed and rainbowed upon them; Raja's elation gone, he shook his head and spoke to the co-pilot, re-entering gloom and irritability as they went into cloud. The airplane picked its way in and out, suddenly they went flashing back into blue sky and straight before them, barring the way, were the peaks, one by one, the Himalayas, so near it seemed they could be touched if one but stretched out of the plane window to finger their dazzling flanks. The colour of the sky was peculiar, an azure that looked as if it would break, there were blue shadows upon the monstrous summits jutting frighteningly about them; and down below cloud, all cloud.

Raja made signs that he wished to turn, and even Anne knew that they had to turn or they would hit something, there were so many ridges now, suddenly, out of the clouds, sharp and traitorous humped ridges like teeth, like black icebergs wind-swept clean of snow except in crevices, appearing here and there like dolphins leaping out of the sea of clouds; and it was getting very cold and hard to breathe.

Unni was behind her, not touching her, and she knew he too was afraid, as Raja was, and the co-pilot, for they could no longer find the valleys, only cloud and snow peaks.

'Look at the mountains,' he said to her, 'and I'll look at you. I see them more beautiful through you than by myself.' He wanted her staring at the summits, beautiful and serene, divorced from the fear of men. And she obeyed.

The airplane caught in a gulf of air and lurched violently, the engines seemed to stop, and then went droning on.

'If anything happened now, it would really be the right minute for it to happen.' For a moment she knew that death was quite possible, entirely within reach, but the word death was but a sound, a name of air, not to be uttered, though it was all about them now.

And then Raja made a gesture. They were flying parallel to the black ridges and turned again, then again, caught some elusive tear in cloud. Down below were green hill slopes. Raja was sweating profusely and the small muscles of his jaw tight like cords, painful jutting. They plunged through, and they were droning at peace. There was the

Valley, with Khatmandu, like a sword laid down. Raja brought the plane down without a bump, sat in his seat, unmoving.

'Come with us and have a drink,' said Unni, when the engines had stopped.

But Raja shook his head. He was still dripping with sweat, green as if he would vomit at any moment. He did not wish to speak and impatiently waved them away with his hand.

They came out. The co-pilot was also pale. 'That was close,' he said, his voice shaky. 'Raja just took a chance. He won't fly for some days now.'

They left the plane together, followed by Raja, staggering a little, walking away from them, hostile, nursing his relief like a grievance.

The airfield was ringed with people, correspondents, tourists, cameramen. Anne saw several familiar faces, but vaguely, not impinging on her at all. She did not care, she could not care any more.

'Leave your jeep here,' said Unni, terse and taking charge. He was suddenly withdrawn from her, not looking, not tender, nearly angry, and climbed in his jeep after her, wordless, hard, shot away, driving too quickly, and she knew he wanted her again, and was as helpless as she was.

The scent of wood smoke, the houses, the familiar things rushed by. He drove through it all, caught her hand and squeezed it hard, hurting her. But it was such pleasure to be hurt, she wanted to be hurt, wanted him to do what he would do, and knew he would do it till it pained everywhere. They drove straight to the bungalow. Unni threw the keys of his jeep to Regmi, who came running, and Regmi climbed in and drove it off. Even now Unni did not forget a measure of caution. No tell-tale jeep parked outside.

'Let's go to your room,' he said, tightly, and climbed the stairs after her.

Upstairs, closing the door behind them, she turned to face him. He stood with his hands in his pockets, and jerked his head towards the waiting bed, as if she were a slave, and watched her walk to it, and slip off her shoes. There had always been something a little off-putting for her about taking off her clothes, a diminution of desire; but not with him, for he held her down with one hand and took them off for her, and she had to submit, lie naked, to be looked at, palpated, her flesh explored, his fingers thoughtful as his eyes, until she cried out with unbearable hunger, and clung to him, avid, voracious, clamorous with small moans and sighs. And time was not, nor space, the hours could not be, nothing existing but this tremulous fusion, fathomless falling, plumbing the depths of self, half-conscious unconsciousness and the ferocity of passion released; and now she no longer could examine it, for her word-fledged world had fallen to pieces about her.

And then Anne knew and believed; for in fulfilment of pain and pleasure, her body sewn to his, she was all of herself, at one, the other dabbling conscious selves fusing within her, coalescing, submitting to his voice, his hands, the imperious will that gave her no mercy; and now his simplicity, which said: 'I love you,' was a shining and wonderful token, she utterly believed it exactly the way he meant it.

For as he had made her whole, so had she made him entire and complete; as she had need of him, so had he needed her, body and soul; this she knew though he did not tell her so. And all unnecessary and crowing words twisting the pure meaning of life were useless and would not be used.

Mita and Regmi did not disturb them with food or footstep. The bungalow slept. They slept, woke, slept again, locked in each other's arms against all evils and all betrayals.

Anne heard voices, still dazed went to the window, saw John and Fred Maltby grasping each other's throats and swaying backwards and forwards on the lawn. It appeared to her highly comical and she began to laugh. What on earth are they doing, she thought, so early in the morning on my lawn? And then she woke completely, and there was Unni sitting up in her bed, looking at her and listening to the voices, coming to stand behind her to look, turning back and picking up his clothes, scattered on the floor, beginning to dress.

'What is it, do you think?' said Anne, getting back into bed because she felt cold.

He smiled at her, detached as she was, immune from reality by a night of love-making. 'I believe I see your husband downstairs with the doctor.'

She laughed more. 'Why are they here?'

'I'd like to know.'

'What on earth are you going to do, Unni?'

He was thoughtful, buttoning his shirt, then replied: 'I'm going to put on my shoes,' with intense seriousness, and did so. Anne laughed again, rocking and smothering her head in the pillow, and Unni grinned. 'Stop laughing,' he said, 'or I'll want you again, you look so nice in the morning.'

'Oh dear,' said Anne, and then, 'but I'm really very worried,' and went on laughing, and the more she laughed, the more she thought how funny it all was. Unni drew a comb from his pocket and combed his hair, and she thought that was more funny than anything else. She laughed until she ached. 'This isn't at all the way to behave when one is caught in adultery,' she managed to stammer between gusts of mirth.

They could hear John's voice downstairs shouting 'I'll bash your face in!', something indistinct from Fred, the shrieks of Mita in the kitchen; Regmi came pattering up the stairs, Unni walked to the door and opened it slightly, Regmi spoke urgently to him, Unni answered, Regmi went down the steps again.

Unni sat on the bed, took Anne in his arms, and kissed her very deliberately. 'Now,' he said, 'we've got to act. Put on a dressing gown and go down. Stand inside the door and ask what is the matter. Regmi has barred it from inside. Take off the bar very deliberately, stand on the threshold. Regmi will shut the door behind you again, and stay talking with them for about five minutes before letting them in. That'll give me time to get away, and Mita to do your room without John rushing in. But don't let him walk away. Keep him here. And Fred.'

'Then what?' said Anne.

'And then,' said Unni, 'I'll be back.'

'You think of everything, don't you?'

'Not this time,' he replied.

She went down, stood as he had told her, moved on to the front door step, heard the door shut and the bar click into place behind her, while she faced John, with froth on his lips and clenched fists and bulging eyes, and recognized immediately that he had worked himself up into 'one of his states'.

'What on earth is the matter?' she said, and felt again like laughing.

'What is the matter?' screamed John. 'How dare you ask me what is the matter. Here he is, here' – he pointed dramatically at Fred

Maltby – 'your paramour. I meet him here, outside *your* bungalow at this time of the morning.'

'Well, what time is it?' said Anne.

Fred looked at his watch and said: 'About seven.'

'Don't talk to each other,' screamed John. 'I forbid you to talk to him. I'm your husband and you must obey me.'

'If you mean Fred,' said Anne, 'he is not my lover.'

'Don't you lie to me, you bloody whore. I've been patient enough. For the last five weeks I've put up with being treated like a dog, an unwanted dog. But I've known this all along. I was just waiting for this opportunity to catch you. I saw you come out from this man's room the other night, and now I've caught him here, and I shall destroy you both.'

Anne looked at Fred, and said: 'Why did you come here this morning, Fred?'

Fred readjusted his shirt and Tibetan sweater, and said: 'I just came up, back from my walk. I … I felt worried. You know, there's an official function today at nine. I was foolish I guess, I just wanted to ask you to come with me … then Regmi told me you were still asleep, and then this lunatic came rushing up the path to tear my shirt.'

'Go and tell that to someone else, not to me,' said John. 'I saw you, I tell you. I saw you come *out* of the bungalow. I'll have justice. I'm not going to be made a fool of. You'll both pay for this, I'll see to that. You won't be able to hold your heads up and go to the Coronation or to anything. I'll have your cards cancelled. I'm going right now to the Resident to tell him the whole thing, and I'll start legal proceedings against you. Yes, you, Dr Frederic Maltby. I'll have you run out of Khatmandu.'

'Honestly, I've never heard anything so silly in all my life,' said Fred. 'Now, if you could only keep your temper, I'll explain …'

'I won't keep my temper,' John screamed, like a child. 'I find you coming out of my wife's … my wife's … room at this hour of the morning, and you ask me to keep my temper. I'll smash your face in, I tell you,' and he advanced again on Fred with clenched fists, his mouth working.

He was more thick-set and slightly taller than Fred, and the latter withdrew a step.

'Honestly,' said Anne, 'what a fool you are. Fred is worried about meeting Eudora, and that's why he came here. He didn't come *out* of the bungalow. You met him on the lawn.'

'Don't tell me I'm lying,' screamed John. 'You've got the damned cheek to stand there and tell me I'm lying? I've never told a lie, I always speak the truth. You tart,' he screamed, foul-mouthed.

'What is all this commotion?' said Isobel, coming suddenly from behind the rose arbour.

John now made an obvious effort to control himself. He passed a hand across his sweat-beaded forehead. 'Good morning, Isobel,' he said, in nearly normal tones, 'I am very sorry indeed that this should happen, today.'

'But what has happened?' said Isobel. 'What has Anne done?'

'What has Anne done?' repeated Anne, suddenly angry.

'Isobel,' said Fred Maltby, 'let me explain.'

'You've got nothing to explain! The only one who has got the right to open his mouth here is me. I catch you coming out of my wife's room at this hour of the morning, and you think you can still explain anything?'

'Oh, Dr Maltby,' said Isobel, in her most shocked tones.

'But it's nonsense,' said Anne. 'Fred wasn't here. He just came here to talk about something and he found I was asleep so he was walking off.'

'To talk, at this hour of the morning?' said Isobel, icily.

'And then I caught him,' said John, 'caught him walking out as cool as you please from this ... this ... bungalow,' and he pointed theatrically at it.

'This is completely ridiculous,' said Anne. 'Isobel, you're not going to believe him? I tell you, Fred was not here until now.'

Isobel did not reply. She put her face in her hands, and then she said: 'This is absolutely terrible. I knew something like this would happen. It will *ruin* the Girls' Institute, and just the day before the Coronation too. Dr Maltby, how *could* you do such a thing, and with your own wife in Khatmandu?'

At that moment came the sound of a jeep chugging up the gravel alley. It roared to a stop behind the trees. Someone called gaily: 'Thanks for the lift,' and the gravel went spitting under shoes. Passing the rose arbour and fountain, coming to the lawn where they stood, in jeans and her tourist hat, was Eudora.

'Good morning,' said Eudora. 'Nice morning, isn't it?'

Nobody answered. They stared at her, stupefied.

'Well,' said Eudora, 'here I am, Anne, ready for breakfast. Remember, you did ask me to breakfast this morning.'

'Asked ...? Yes ... of course, of course,' said Anne, then she burst out laughing.

'Good morning, Fred. Good morning, Miss Maupratt. Good morning, John,' repeated Eudora.

'Good morning,' they said, docile.

'Well,' said Eudora, 'how *nice* to see you all here. Are *you* having breakfast here too? Miss Maupratt? John? What about you, Fred?'

'Yes, Fred,' said Anne, 'won't you join us for breakfast?'

'Erh ...' said Fred. It had been impossible to run away, he stood face to face to Eudora, and found to his surprise that there was no fear left.

'Did you enjoy your walk, Fred?' said Eudora conversationally to her husband.

'Yes, oh yes,' he answered.

'Just a minute,' said John. 'Mrs Maltby, there is something I think you should know.'

'Something I should know?'

'I found your husband,' said John, 'coming out of this bungalow this very morning, just half an hour ago.'

'You did? That's funny. Half an hour ago I saw Fred walking along the main road. I was in a jeep. Mr Menon's jeep, in fact. We immediately turned back, of course,' she added, too lightly, 'Fred doesn't like to be disturbed on walks.'

'Well,' said Isobel, 'I don't know what to say.'

'Then you shouldn't say anything,' replied Eudora, as viciously as her nature permitted. 'Anne has asked me to breakfast this morning. I hope you don't object?'

Isobel drew herself up. 'Your private concerns, Mrs Maltby, are none of my business. I do hope, however, that such disgraceful incidents will not recur, or I shall have to take action.' And her glance above Eudora's head went to the door of the bungalow, as if she expected to see inside it.

'Disgraceful?' said Eudora. 'Come, come, Miss Maupratt. There is nothing disgraceful in Fred and me having breakfast with Anne, is there?'

'Mrs Ford shouldn't be here,' said Isobel violently. 'She should be with her husband. She is infringing the laws of hospitality by staying here.'

There was a commotion as the door was suddenly flung open and Regmi dragged a table and some chairs on the lawn. Mita stood, arms folded, as if to say: You can look now, you won't find anything. There was the smell of toast and coffee from the kitchen.

'How about asking me for breakfast too?' said John.

Anne looked at him. 'I'm sorry,' she said, 'I'll see you later, at the ceremonies.'

'Oh, come, come,' said John, jocularly. 'I am sorry, Dr Maltby. I can see now there was nothing in it, but I must say I have been very upset lately, very upset. You must forgive me if I'm sometimes not myself.'

'Yes, I know,' said Dr Maltby.

'I may be old-fashioned,' said John, 'but I don't think a wife should run away and leave her husband. There's such a thing as the sanctity of marriage vows. I think I may say that a woman who behaves badly lays herself open to suspicion.'

'I think,' said Eudora, 'that the less we say now the better.'

'Mrs Maltby,' retorted John, 'I've got my rights as a husband.'

'For heaven's sake,' said Eudora, 'don't let's have any of this conjugal rights business now. I want my breakfast.'

'Will you stay and have some breakfast, Fred?' said Anne.

'Yes,' said Fred.

The three sat down. John and Isobel stood, hesitated. Anne did not look at them. They went away, uneasily, not talking to each other. Anne poured coffee.

Eudora chatted about the Purification Ceremony due at nine. 'I'm really interested in the music they will play. Some very special old Hindu music.' She was knowledgeable about music. It was tacitly agreed they would go together.

'I'll go and change and we'll meet, say at the Royal Hotel,' said Fred, addressing Anne, but he was including Eudora, already.

Eudora did not jump up and ask for a lift to the Royal. She waited until he had gone, then turned to Anne. 'I must go and change too.'

'Thank you, Eudora,' said Anne.

'My dear ...' Eudora suddenly hugged her. 'You deserve to be happy. You ...' she ran away swiftly.

Alone, Anne thought of Unni. She was suffering now this peculiar sense of aloneness and despair which follows love; for the more desire is accomplished, the more it fails to accomplish its end, extinguishment. She longed for his presence, the sight of him, as never before. But at the same time she was repulsed. He was too clever. It was too clever, bringing Eudora, flinging her in the middle of the scene, and thus, at one stroke, accomplishing two aims: forcing Fred to meet his wife in a situation where he could not run away, and completely disarming John by making him look ridiculous.

They must tell John. Otherwise her relationship with Unni would be corrupted with safety and guilt. Safe but guilty. It was unendurable. They must face whatever there was to face, together, she and Unni. Looking at John and Isobel, departing together, she had been torn with compassion and pity for John, for his stupidity, the inane way in which he handled his emotions, the methods he used to express them. But it was the means he used she disliked; she had no doubt that in his own way he thought he loved her. In his own way. He did and said everything in a way which worked against himself. Where she was concerned he was his own worst enemy. She pitied him, although she knew this pity destroyed her.

Unni was too clever, and for a moment Anne felt as trapped by this cleverness as she had felt suffocated by John's stupidity. Then she remembered the baby, and her mind hardened, the mood passed. She would never go back to John. His weakness had preyed upon her long enough.

Chapter 10

FOR the next two days Eudora and Fred clung to Anne, their new-found communication, fearful of losing her and thereby each other. Together they went that morning to the Old Palace for the Purification Ceremony. At the gate John waiting, eager, repentant, helpful, voluble.

'A husband is always the last to know.' A husband. John, trying hard to please. Anne went stiff as wood when she saw him, shoulders raised, coming towards them smiling. He had waited, he said, to show them their places. They would sit together, through the Ceremony. Lunch afterwards, together.

Under the eye of Megalorama John ushered them into the court-yard of the Old Palace. They were instantly swept by gazes: rows of eyes, from the All-Khatmandu; ranks of the Press with its barrage of cameras and goggles, lenses big and small. How many knew, thought Anne, as she and John walked together to the seats. John's devotion was thick-heaped upon his features, there was a swagger in his arms and legs which conveyed his modest triumph. It was as if the recon-ciliation of the Maltbys was due to his efforts and a double of his own marital harmony.

'I think this is yours, yes, you'll see all right from here. I was par-ticularly careful that you shouldn't be in the sun ... the Ceremony may be quite long and it might be a bit tiring.'

People who had no seats were standing; Isobel, a few Americans; the General, in a uniform folded round his thin waist, a borrowed garment, for his own had been lent to a nephew, who had pawned it in Calcutta. The King had forbidden the Ranas to wear their jewelled headgear at the Coronation, and they appeared in service caps or in modest casques with dyed red and yellow feathers. The officials of the Nepalese Government were in black coats, white jodhpurs, and black silk caps; the Indian Military Mission wore British-type uni-forms; the Press wore lounge suits.

Anne looked round, espied François, behind his camera placed in a corner of the courtyard, who raised his hand sedately to her; Leo, his face nervously twitching, was next to François. Leo felt safer here, safe from Kisha. Kisha had arrived as threatened. The previous evening Leo was just saying to François: 'Well, the last plane-load of tourists is in, and she hasn't come,' when 'Ah, darling, darrling, here you are!' It was Kisha, behind him, heaving, pearly beads of sweat upon her upper lip, surrounded by six turbaned and bearded men whom she introduced as her Sikh cousins. They stood, towering battlements of headgear and hairiness looking down upon him, as 'My fiancé,' Kisha announced proudly. Six enormous hands were thrust at him.

Leo had not dared to contradict. Sikhs, he knew, placed great value upon the chastity of their women, were quick with the knife. The cousins fingered their beards, smiled, showing immense white teeth, François had offered drinks.

Later Leo had gathered enough courage to tell Kisha and her cousins how very difficult it might be for Kisha, a Sikh, to marry an unworthy outsider to the faith. All the Sikhs laughed and shook their turbans in denial, one of them waved these scruples aside.

'Yeah, I know how you kinda feel,' he'd said, in a pure Bronx twang, 'but so long as Baby loves you and you love Baby, that's fine for us. We're modern, see?'

Fortunately propriety had directed that Kisha should stay the night with an aunt, and the cousins had gone with her. She had whispered passionately that she would find a way out 'when Auntie's asleep'. Leo had spent a dreadful wide-awake night, but Kisha had not turned up.

At the Purification Ceremony Kisha was not in the courtyard. Leo felt safer.

'*Ne vous en faites pas. Elle ne vous mangera pas*,' said François.

Mariette was also there, with the little Swiss in tow, the latter still carrying her equipment as Leo had last seen them, emplaning for Pokhra. Leo felt comforted. He could always refugee himself with Mariette. Then he saw the Fords and the Maltbys, heard the comments.

'I thought they weren't speaking.'

'Who? The Fords?'

'No. The Maltbys.'

'Oh, *they* weren't meeting.'

345

'Well, well, well.'

'I thought *she* was with the doctor.'

'Wonders will never cease.'

He kept his eyes on Anne, hoping she would look back at him.

'*Elle est très belle,*' said the taciturn voice of François. 'I am very 'appy.'

Anne turned, saw them, smiled, then her glance wavered, slid over the eye-carrying faces round her. John looked when Anne had turned, saw Leo and François, and waved amiably, turned to Anne to say something. She did not look at him, and he seemed to slump back in himself. Whatever happens, I'll feel sorry for that chap, thought Leo. One couldn't help feeling sorry for John. He did depend on Anne so much.

There was a stir, distant fanfare, sharpness in Mariette's voice ordering the Swiss about: '*Mais mettez ça donc par terre, mon cher: vrai, vous êtes un empêtré.*' Unni came in. Jealousy-sharpened, Leo felt, as Anne did, the powerful drag-net of the man's sexuality; knew Anne, looking at Unni, would be getting that small shock in the chest; heard two women talking, nudging each other, their lips curling to form his name. Damn you, thought Leo bitterly, venomously.

Unni sat down and began to look round him, exactly as Anne had done, till he had seen her, and then he stopped looking and spoke to Mike Young by his side, while Anne spoke to Eudora.

'My dear fellar, watch how some people cover their tracks.' Ranchit, behind Leo, addressing him. Leo pretended he hadn't heard.

At one end of the long courtyard, in a recess, chairs had been placed for the diplomatic envoys. At the other end of the courtyard was a four-sided hut, twenty feet square, made of green tree boughs; it had a thatched roof and no walls. Inside this enclosure the King and Queen now stood, now sat, Asian fashion on carpets, while the Buddhist priests chanted prayers and made offerings, anointing the King. Just outside the enclosure was a small brown cow and her calf, as witnesses of the Purification Ceremony.

The Press and the photographers, breaking decorum, surrounded the hut, shoved aside each other to within inches of the King's nose. Gradually the chairs became deserted as, except for the diplomats, most of the guests now mingled with the Press and crowded round the hut. John was among them, camera levelled, manoeuvring a place for himself at the enclosure. Soon all etiquette had been abandoned, the hut was ringed by cameras and bodies. Through his dark glasses, while the priests in saffron silk poured flower petals and water upon him, the King stared at the crowd outside, said something to the Queen. Two officials attempted to restore order; but flash bulbs were popping, cameras clicking, and some of the more enthusiastic photographers climbed on chairs to get a better view.

Eudora had also moved nearer, and stood happily wrapt, listening to the singing which went on to the music of a small Nepalese orchestra. Anne stood near Fred, seeing the backs of priests, and between their legs catching glimpses of the King, in pure white, the Queen in a red sari with silver stars. Anne moved away. The keeper was patting his cow; smiled at her as she also touched the cow and the small calf nuzzling its mother. From here she could look towards Unni, who had not moved from his chair, and was looking at her. He got up. He was going to walk to her in front of everyone. She was afraid and swiftly went back to her chair, for her composure disappeared when she saw him move.

'May I sit down near you?' he asked.

She indicated the vacant seat.

'Oh darling,' he said fiercely, not looking at her (remembering the malicious eyes), 'I can't bear it. To see you ... with so many others around. To hover, not touch you when the very marrow of my bones cries for you. I can't bear it.'

'It's the same for me.'

'It was horrible this morning, wasn't it?'

'Not horrible, vile.'

'Yes. You did not like my bringing Eudora, did you?'

'I thought it was too clever.'

'I couldn't let John bully Fred, though I doubt he would have done anything, really. John knows there is nothing between you and Fred. John doesn't *want* to know about me.'

'Why did you bring Eudora?'

'It seemed the right move. I didn't know I was going to do it. Then I did it. And it's turned out all right.'

'Was it to save us?'

'Not to save us from discovery. We are guilty, and we'll be caught when the time comes.'

'When?'

'It will come. I promise you, my darling, I won't be clever always.'

'We must tell John. Right after the Coronation.'

'What exactly do you wish us to tell John?' asked Unni slowly.

'That you and I ... are together.'

'Do you think he will understand?'

'What do you mean?'

'If I were to go up to him now and say: I love your wife, John would laugh in my face. And I cannot say to him: I make love to your wife, can I? Not unless I can take you away when I go.'

She had forgotten. 'Go?'

'Back to the dam, Anne. And then the monsoon will be here. I'll be able to come back to see you sometimes, but not every day. And I cry for you. I have never wanted a woman so much, with everything in me. And I cannot take you with me now. Not to the dam. We're not allowed to have women up there. Later, quite possibly, on my own. Not when I'm working. I must leave you to face John. What can I say to him before I go, and leave you to him, and to Isobel?'

'When are you going? No, don't tell me,' she said quickly, 'it hurts too much.'

'As late as I can. And I will be back. Whenever I can. Whenever it clears and I can come. Promise you believe me. Anne. Please have faith in me.'

He rose, John was returning. He bowed, said: 'You are my dearest love,' she nodded coldly, and he went.

'What's that fellow got to say to you?' asked John, sitting by her side.

'Nothing much,' said Anne.

The King and Queen now came out of the hut. Outside, in flat woven baskets, in coconut shells, on trays, were grains and fruit and leaves: the produce of the earth, to be blessed by the King.

The reporters and photographers followed, trooping behind the King as he left the courtyard, and Enoch P. now came to shake hands with John and Anne. He looked hot but happy. He had actually secured a seat in the Diplomats' Gallery. It was at the furthest end of the courtyard, and between it and the hut was a platform upon which stood the State Throne, so that it was nearly impossible to see anything. But it was the V.I.P.s' stand, and he'd been only two chairs away from the Chinese Delegation. 'I could have heard everything they said.'

'What did they say?' asked John.

'They didn't say anything. Those Reds are jolly careful. Never say anything in public.'

At lunch at the Royal Hotel Unni was in one party, Anne with John, Fred, and Eudora at another table. Then came the unending afternoon. Anne said she would go back to rest, hoping to be alone, but she had scarcely reached her bungalow when Leo was there, flee-from Kisha and her cousins, arriving with François, throwing himself on the grass comically, not forgetting to be comical for Anne's sake. François took pictures of Leo, '*le lion prostré*', went down into the fields and pulled two ears of wheat on their stalks, put them in Anne's hand. '*Virgo, vous êtes Virgo, n'est-ce pas?* I'm an Aquarius myself, I really belong in a pond, with the fish. That is how I see you, Anne, *déesse des moissons*, Virgo with two stalks of the harvest, only your harvests are words, not corn, are they not?'

'Impossible.' François shook his head. 'You are writing, Anne, already in your head. I see it in you. *Il faut en profiter* . . take the wind that comes, like this.'

About them the nourishing wind, lord of the sky, blowing their hair softly in one direction only. Leo listened, wondering; he had not known François in such a mood.

'You're nearly a mystic, François.'

'*Un mystique sans y réfléchir*,' replied François. He tapped his camera affectionately. 'My *témoin*, the eye-witness of my days, like that gentle cow there in the courtyard, the only true witness and the only dumb one. Did you notice above the cow's head the superb erotic carvings? Such art, such sensuality. What a wonderfully alive people these Newaris must be, deep in themselves. That is why they are so beautiful, in spite of horrible poverty.' He raised the lens, snapping Anne unprepared. 'With this, my own dumb witness, I perceive not only people, but their auras. Your aura, Anne, is golden. Virgo of the harvests, in golden sunlight. It was different, in Calcutta.'

'I'm a different person.'

'Not altogether. Let us say that you are a bigger person. *Mais ne soyez pas trop sage*. Do not be afraid to jump over the moon.'

And then John arrived, with Isobel, Geography, Enoch P., Pat, Fred, and Eudora self-conscious.

'Hi!' said Pat. 'We thought we'd look you up. Nothing to do till this evening, the Royal Garden Party, thought we'd pay you a visit. Everybody seems to be visiting everyone else today. What a cute little place,' she exclaimed, sitting on the grass.

'Yes, just the right kind of environment for a writer,' said John. One felt he had ordered the landscape specially for Anne's benefit.

So this is John's game, Anne thought; John would infiltrate here. He would come, flanked by Isobel, Geography, or other people; soon he would be here any time he wished. Day or night.

The hot afternoon made them a little sour. Isobel argued with François. She had exclaimed over the 'nonsense' of the Ceremonies that morning. 'As nonsensical as some of the horrors we perpetrate in the name of Christ,' he replied.

'But how can you say that?' Isobel was arguing. 'I know we have our failings, human failings. But we do bring these people through our religion an infinitely superior way of life. I don't see how we could accomplish it without Christian ideals. Think of the improvements, the progress ...'

'That is where you make a mistake. The progress, the improvements, the medicines you give and the education, are the products of humanism, not of religion. And in order to survive in the modern world religion had to take up a full-scale programme of sociological progress. Without that it would have flickered out long ago, for it was only preoccupied with the soul, as is still the case here in Khatmandu. It is schools, and public health, roads and progress, which will destroy the temples here, and not your Christian preachings.'

'We're *not* allowed to preach Christianity here,' replied Isobel. 'We merely show, by example, what a higher and nobler ideal it is than those revolting idols and all that preposterous throwing about of flowers.'

'Just what I like about them,' cried Eudora. 'So utterly unsophisticated, so pure and spontaneous, without all this abominable guilt-complex about sex. They just don't think about it ...'

'They think about it all the time, all the time,' shouted Isobel, so angry that her voice shook, the deep red flush which came more often now suffusing her face and neck and arms. 'They're immoral. Sunk in Godless impurity.'

'Religion and morality are not the same thing,' replied François with a Frenchman's logic.

'I say,' John interrupted, jocose, 'that's a controversial statement of yours. Religion and morality must go hand in hand. I mean, one must have an integrated personality, don't you think?'

'Why?' said François. 'What is an integrated personality?'

'Oh, I mean a person, an individual, must always stick to what he believes, act consistently.'

'But what do you mean by an individual?' asked François. 'What is a person? What is an individual? I for my part never know quite what is going to come out of me. All artists have this same puzzle to solve: the search for their real self, or selves. Even normal personages, like yourself, Monsieur, become different when faced with different situations. We may have *un fond*, a definite fundamental self, but the modalities we exhibit are infinitely varied. I prefer to think of a human soul as just a mass of relationships, not as anything solid. A complex linkage of energetic electrons, dancing in mutable and for ever changing orbits.'

'I think I'm quite solid,' said John huffily. 'Thank God, I'm always myself.'

'How very boring,' said François. 'You must bore yourself, I mean. And I don't believe you.' He raised his lens, snapped John. 'With this' – he tapped it – 'I have already seen you become three different people: one with your wife, one with me, and one with that lady.' He indicated Isobel. 'And I am sure, madame,' he bowed towards Geography, 'will be able to produce yet another John Ford out of you.'

'Why, I ...' simpered Geography, blushing under her floury skin, 'I think you're a great big tease.'

'Well, we haven't got time to listen to all that, however interesting,' said John. He looked at his watch. 'Nearly time to get dressed for the Garden Party. Coming, Anne?'

'I'm not sure.'

'Shall I wait for you?'

'No, you'd better go ahead. I'll go by myself. I've got a pass.'

'It would look better if you went with me, your husband,' said John loudly.

'I haven't made up my mind.'

John turned to the others. 'Did anyone ever have such a capricious wife?' A heavy silence followed.

And then, as in a pantomime, from behind the rose arbour came Kisha and her six bearded and turbaned Sikhs.

'The moth and the flame,' murmured the Field Marshal, 'they can't stop seeking each other.'

The Field Marshal had a talent for picking out, even in the dense crowd at the Royal Garden Party, the faces of people he was interested in. He stood unmoving and saw exactly. Father MacCullough laughed fortissimo; Enoch P. was being interviewed for the third time that day, only once had the newsmen approached Father MacCullough for the low-down on the situation in Nepal. Isobel talked with the Minister for Education; the latter's enigmatic lotus smile taught the Field Marshal the denunciatory content of her conversation; History, interviewed by *Life*, was overcome with emotion; Geography raised abashed eyes at John expounding to a group of Nepalese officials; Mike Young stared at Rukmini in the midst of some Nepalese women adhesively banded together in tittering propriety; François, unprehensile, elastic, camera round his neck, went recording the moment of instantaneous meaning, split second when all facial plications, eye glitter, complications of movement, come together in significance; there stood a wilted Leo, looking as if he had sweated a great deal, and a Kisha, buxom, uxorious, exudative of everything too much, hitching her sari over her promontorial shoulder, knocking down with her plastic bag a tray of drinks; Mariette, in off-the-shoulder dress, long gloves, and roses in a bustle low at the back (a prodigious bustle, hypnotizing the Hindu poet), arched her body towards Unni; and Unni's eyes went to one side and the other, looking for Anne.

Groups merged and broke. Unni moved, bringing Mariette to Leo, manoeuvring the Hindu poet from his contemplation of the roses at the back to Mariette's front, edging sideways to speak to Father MacCullough, and from him to Anne, with Eudora and Vassili on the other side of the priest. Side by side again, they both laughed, looking straight in front of them, at what Vassili was saying. They drank, glass to mouth, behind the partial mask their eyes met.

Ranchit appeared, talked to Anne, taking no notice of Unni. Anne drifted back to Father MacCullough, and Unni turned to speak to Colonel Jaganathan, then to François; he circled a narrow orbit, till he was with Anne again.

Fred, looking a little lost, was with the Curator, and Father Mac-Cullough, now abandoned by Anne, brought Eudora to him.

Well played, the Field Marshal thought, well played, Eudora.

Ranchit was again with Anne, fingering his little moustache, looking impudently at the outline of her breasts under her dress; and Mike Young laughed with Rukmini a few steps away.

Another swirl, and Fred was with the Field Marshal, Eudora awash in a group of Americans.

'What a crush,' said Fred.

'A fascinating *mélange*,' murmured the Field Marshal.

'I don't know,' replied Fred. 'Feels unreal to me.'

Said the Field Marshal gravely: 'Permit me to express my admiration for the way you are handling the situation. With utmost diplomacy. Utmost.'

Fred wanted to protest, but he was pleased, though he knew the compliment undeserved. Weakly he said: 'Oh, now, well ...' but his eyes sought Eudora. Not bad looking. Small bones. Agreeable to talk to. Sharma and the Hindu poet liked her; the General thought highly of her; Unni was her friend; she certainly knew a lot about music. And she didn't appear to hang on to him, which would have been unpleasant. She did not bother him, not once had she delved into the past. Or asked for explanations. Or wept. Or anything.

This astonishing Eudora, so unlike the picture he had tenaciously maintained of her, contributed to the unreality which possessed him since the morning's scene with John. A cloudy out-of-touchness, a pleasant disembodiment, like those Tibetan lamas who step out of their bodies and look at them two feet away, like the physical tiredness after some gruelling operation when one was ethereal with fatigue, dreaming standing up.

This sensation Fred often had with other people. His extra-sensory, clinical perceptions assessed them physically and emotionally, as any good doctor will do. Their speech, gestures, the lines on their faces, the lies or convictions colouring their voices, revealed to him after twenty years of practice a diagnosis of the being as a whole, not as an assemblage of organs. Thus with John – John dominating the morning, first with his rage, then with his good humour at the Purification, a happy, forceful John contradictory to the frothing, filthy-mouthed John of the morning. Only a doctor, aware of the conjugation of opposites which is the human being, knew they must be the one John. Fred mused on John's behaviour, his quick-change appearances, the range of his emotions, so conventional, so expected, and therefore so palpably false. Some people were most themselves when they were acting, as if they had to act what they were expected to feel before they could feel it. One common factor in pseudo-feelings emitted by people who had no genuine emotion was violence. Exaggeration was the symptom of factitiousness, as artefacts, cardboard castles, theatre backdrops, are more highly coloured, more sharp-angled than the reality they imitate. Perhaps over emphasis was necessary to convince themselves of the reality they did not possess.

Fred's reflex to the false was this sense of unreality. That morning, while tugged at by John, the predominant concern in his mind was that his sweater should not be damaged. Bemused, he studied the puppet, Dr Maltby, whose strings were pulled by Fred, who did not mind being with Eudora, who gave conventional answers, smoked a cigarette, moved about where he was pushed by a tide of faces, voices, gestures, eyes, cameras, lost in the crowd at the Garden Party until deposited by the side of the Field Marshal.

From there Fred also watched the Garden Party and its by-plays. Saw Anne and Unni and the distance between them more vibrant than touch, laden with their longing for each other; saw Rukmini, a little smile at the corner of her mouth, listening to Mike Young, saw Sharma come up to them. 'Both are in love with her,' he said to the Field Marshal.

'Young is the better man,' replied the Field Marshal. 'I think Rukmini should divorce Ranchit and marry this American.'

'I didn't know you were so liberal-minded,' said Fred, astonished.

'I do not like a beautiful thing in the grip of nastiness,' said the Field Marshal, 'nor talent overthrown by stupidity, emotional stupidity.' His eyes magically picked out a hilarious John, making his way to Anne, dragging some people behind him. It was obvious he was going to introduce them to his wife. 'I have drawn Mrs Ford's horoscope,' the Field Marshal said. 'A goodly destiny, though people will not think so. Men are apt to believe that a man must be all to a woman.

But sometimes comes a woman with more than usual passion for life. For her the state of happy wife, housekeeper, and mother is unhappy: there is not enough triteness in her for that.'

'I hope everything turns out all right,' said Fred. 'Unni is my friend, and I am very fond of Anne.'

'As you perceive,' replied the suave Field Marshal, 'everything has inevitably begun.'

'I'm going mad, Anne. Like this,' It was Unni.

Crowd, prying on them with all its eyes and ears.

'It's torture. I want you. To hold your hand, be with you. Every minute without you is a century of hell. And tonight there's an official banquet, a theatre – I won't be able to come away till late, but I'll come.'

Miss Spockenweiler walked up to him. 'Mr Menon, how about a lecture from you for our Point Four Ladies' Get-Together? You did promise last year.'

They met, crossed, lost each other; like swimmers in a separating sea.

And never had they felt time running out on them with such desperate speed.

It was four-thirty in the morning before he came, breathing as if he had run. Anne, wide awake, holding out her arms to him, caught him to her, eager. And so soon day, Coronation Day.

Rocking her pain and his in his arms, he said: 'Believe me, believe me, one day we shall be together. I'll take you to the mountains, one day.'

'I believe you,' Anne replied, not adding that it was fate, her own destiny, that she doubted.

It was clear morning when he left under whatever eyes watched. Neither he nor Anne cared. They longed for discovery as for a release.

Coronation Day started with the usual din of crows and the crowds, the men in homespun and caps, grey lines along the streets; the women a confused, sparkling, dazzling army, in squadrons, in battalions, seated or standing on the pagoda tiers; the pagodas vanished, replaced by solid pyramids of women to the roof tops, women smothered in beads, nostrils and ears flashing brass coins, shining dark hair bedding turquoises and gold, in heavy dark skirts, holding umbrellas, women everywhere, between the gods, upon the roofs. In the streets a lane was kept free by soldiers and policemen, but children ran between their legs and nearly under the jeeps and cars which went, slowly honking at each revolution of their wheels, pushing their way into the main square.

Like the Purification Ceremony, the Coronation was in the large central courtyard of the Old Palace. The crowd was thicker than the day before, the diplomats in their stifling gallery, the generals and officials in their chairs, the reporters and their batteries of cameras everywhere, the cow and calf, the priests, a handful of peasant women chanting, and Megalorama.

Again Anne with Eudora and Fred sat with John, today surly and inattentive, coated with a new hardness towards her. Ranchit sat next to her, unasked, looked insolently at Unni, as if defying him; John walked away with a group of exasperated Pressmen unable to obtain a plausible explanation of what the cow was there for: 'Say, John, come and help us, will you? We just can't figure out what this guy's saying.'

'Beautiful Anne,' said Ranchit. 'How can anyone leave your side?'

Anne looked away.

A fat woman with a round, happy face, very dark hair, now sang, leading a group of peasant women in a Greek chorus by the side of the hut. 'That is Suriyah,' said Ranchit. 'A courtesan, and a good singer. All castes and crafts represented. Even the oldest profession. Charming, isn't it?'

'Very humane,' said Anne. Perhaps that was why John seemed uncomfortable. As if it mattered to her.

John was back. He cast a furtive glance at Suriyah. Blumenfeld came with him, talked of the significance of what they saw.

'Who are these women?' asked Blumenfeld, pointing to the group with Suriyah.

'Singers,' said John.

Blumenfeld snapped the group.

'It's a fabulous show,' said Enoch P., passing them to go to the Diplomats' Gallery. 'We've even got a correspondent from Radio Iceland.'

There was a blare of trumpets, a military march, a squad of red-coated soldiers, followed by standard bearers with glittering peacock fans encrusted with small mirrors, priests in yellow silk robes. The King and Queen arrived on an elephant, which knelt at the gate to allow them to dismount; and from there, under the gleaming red and gold umbrellas, with heralds waving the peacock-tailed fans about them, the Royal pair entered the courtyard, to disappear into an inner apartment, where the priests and a few high dignitaries followed them. Meanwhile the courtyard waited in the sun and the music of two orchestras, the military red-coat band, and one with horns, drums, and clarinets like shawms playing Vedic religious chants from South India.

After an hour the King and Queen came out and sat in the thatched enclosure, the same used for the Purification the day before, and the Ceremony then proceeded, incomprehensible to most of the on-lookers. Brahman priests and Buddhist priests anointed and chanted, round the hut pressed the correspondents and photographers, Megalo-rama clicked and whirred. And then, at 10.33, at the minute fixed by the astrologers when the sun, the moon, and all the planets propitiated by the priests were in the right conjunction, the Royal High Priest placed upon the King's head the Crown of Nepal, a casque of pre-cious gems, pearls and emeralds, surmounted by a Bird of Paradise.

The King and Queen then sat on the nine-headed Snake Throne, erected on a canopied platform next to the thatched enclosure. Under it lay the hides of water buffalo, deer, elephant, lion, and tiger. The Royal Family and Princes came down from the first floor gallery, where they had sat, to kneel and pay homage and to throw coins on the floor in front of the King. One by one the special envoys and the diplomats also came to pay homage, and then the Rana officials and all the representatives of each caste and trade and guild. And in the flux round the throne Anne and Unni were together again; thrown against each other's side, enough for them to be once more beside themselves, fevered, hallucinated by this endless thirst.

Lunch at the Royal Hotel, with the usual drift in and out, and Blumenfeld talking of Vishnu; Leo, a querulous shadow of his all-spring-and-angles self, with Kisha and her cousins and Michael Toast, all at one table; the utter weariness of eating, Unni not there. Mike Young coming in with Colonel Jaganathan (Day and Night, Vassili named them, one so blond, the other so dark); Mike seeing Ranchit and immediately looking for Rukmini – but Rukmini was not there; then Dearest, the Rampoche's daughter, in bright orange and green satin, swishing in through the vociferous gathering, going straight to Anne.

'Mrs Ford, I am so glad to see you. My father wants to invite you, and Mr Ford, and oh so many other people to some simple Tibetan repast.'

'What's that?' said John.

Anne introduced.

Dearest looked worried. 'You must come, all of you. My father has already invited a congregation of gents and ladies. He is asking the Indian Ambassador and Mr Bowers and some Generals and Mr Menon and –'

'So sorry,' said John, 'we're eating here now. Perhaps some other time.'

'Then there is this letter for you from my father,' said Dearest, and thrust an envelope in Anne's hand.

'Who is she?' asked John suspiciously.

'One of my students,' Anne replied, keeping the letter in her bag.

After lunch, going to the refuge of the Ladies', she read the letter:

My dear Niece,

I am writing this note to request you that yesterday I had asked our Mr Unni Menon regarding sand and lime stone powder contracts to which Mr Menon did not take enough interest.

Previously several people had received various contracts from our Mr Menon. My dear niece, we must help each other. I consider you as my own daughter, thus I am not hesitating a bit to give you trouble. If you don't mind please try your utmost to procure the sand and lime stone contracts. The man who needs those contracts is my intimate friend. He has been worrying me since a long time. I have promised him to obtain contracts because I knew you would help by requesting our Mr Menon to give those contracts. Please believe me, I shall be ever grateful to you and to Mr Menon for the kindness.

More when we meet again.

> I remain,
> Yours affectionately,
> RAMPOCHE OF BONGSOR

Anne read, smiled incredulously, tore the letter up, and threw it in the waste-paper basket.

In the afternoon a Durbar was held on the large open meadow of Khatmandu; but although scheduled for two o'clock, it was four when, from the tents under which the guests sat away from the hot sun, could be seen coming along the road in swirls of dust and clamour, like walking pagodas, the painted and caparisoned elephants, their toe-nails gilded, their ears like screens with arabesques of flowers, and palanquins upon their backs. Masked dancers went dancing in front of them, until the elephants stopped and knelt at an arch which led to the meadow. The diplomats on their backs dismounted (the French Ambassador, superb in a tricorne, leaping agilely down the flanks of his beast), walked up the red carpeted lane to the central pavilion where the King, from a throne, would deliver the Coronation Speech. Lining the way to the pavilion were two hundred gods and goddesses, eight feet tall, with golden faces and sumptuous clothes and headgear of jewels, sheltered from the glare by red umbrellas of state and fanned by their own retinue of human attendants. They had come from the temples of Bhadgaon, Patan, Kirtipur, carried here to attend the Durbar. Around them milled the thousand odd guests and the Press, complaining of the heat and making frequent raids upon two small stalls where orange juice could be purchased.

Another commotion, a great stir of trumpets, and on the largest elephant of all, robed in scarlet and gold and with beautiful tusks, the King and Queen arrived, accompanied by the Megalorama machine moving in front of them, strapped on a lorry. As the Royal pair, in their robes of state and crown and tiara, walked up the red carpeted lane, in front of them went the machine with its attendant men, another, a mobile god.

'Here, King! Here, King – not so fast,' called one of the cameramen as the King strode forward. The pale, stern young face of the sober King of Nepal showed no emotion, perhaps because of the dark sunglasses. Preceded by Megalorama and followed by everyone else, the King and Queen mounted the steps of the pavilion and sat on the Throne.

'I wonder if the Nepalese will get angry at what we are doing?' said Eudora.

But the Nepalese were not angry. They considered the machine a happy joke, or a new, amusingly inquisitive deity, and its curiosity did not ruffle their inward peace. And so with touches of comic opera, the Coronation was still a dignified ceremony.

The microphones broke down and nobody could hear the King's Speech, and the Durbar was suddenly over.

Sweating, the diplomats reascended their elephants. Paul Redworth, throwing an agonized look at Anne, shared one with the Earl of Scarborough, scarlet face sweating above his velvet cloak and blue ribbon, the Chinese envoy in a workman's cap and a thin black silk uniform. A detachment of Gurkhas played a military air, and the crowd began to go home, gathering in families, walking away in groups.

Later, when memory, unclouded by the torpor of being with John (he takes my eyes and my ears from me, Anne thought, looking malevolently at John, having no other way to describe the palpable abeyance of her perceptions when he was near), had become more precise, she was to remember also the police beating the crowds back with sticks, the clay jars along the road in which the King would throw coins, a whole pyramid of women with black umbrellas, like a single gigantic jackdaw with a new, upstanding kind of feather. She had come, as in the morning, with Eudora and Fred, but now, walking back to the far dusty place where the cars were parked, Unni was by her side.

'I am taking you back.'

The time of caution was past, she would go with him whenever he asked her, wherever he went. They drove off in a slow queue of vehicles through the streets of Khatmandu.

'We have another forty-eight hours together. I will have them all.'

Suddenly she was angry with him and with the whole apparatus of circumstances which made it possible for her to be angry, because he moved her so much and she was no longer her own, he but had to look at her and she was his. All through the day their bodies hungered for each other, and now she was tired, tired and ready to weep.

The sun was going down behind the mountains, and under the young trees the wind was pushing the grass the usual way, and Anne sank on to the grass and said, 'I am tired, tired.'

'Rest your head on my shoulder,' said Unni. He lay back against a trunk, she put herself in the crook of his arm, her shivering body, paining as after a mauling, was quiet. Any moment she would sleep. Was it minutes or hours later she felt the shoulder pillowing her head stiffen, and opening her eyes saw first the shoes, and up from the shoes the trouser legs, and then the faces of Enoch P. and John?

There was a stillness, a moment's petrifaction, Anne's head resting on Unni's shoulder, and in that moment everything was cut-glass clear: the shoulder behind her head, the face of Enoch Bowers, the look of John. She had not noticed before that Enoch's upper teeth were false; now, looking up, it was the first thing she knew.

'Hello there,' said the voice of Unni, a vibration through the cloth of his shoulder. The shoulder moved slightly. If the shoulder is taken away, then it is all a lie, he has lied, he is a coward. Even as she thought the words his shoulder had receded, not more than half an inch, certainly not more, for she still perceived its warmth behind her. And he had not risen, he was behind her, so that never in her life later would she be able to know whether in that fraction of movement he had been afraid, or merely adjusting his position.

'Oh, er –' replied Enoch P.

John's mouth worked. Oh please, please, Anne prayed, as she saw his lips slacken, the blue eyes cloud with pain, yet not any pain that she could do anything about, please don't let Unni be too clever. For in this instant also with the shoulder's retreat she knew the guile of his simplicity; knew him wary and for ever cool-headed; he had thought of this encounter, rehearsed its enactment; forearmed with anticipation, gauged John's reactions, and would handle this with the unsurprise of competence, as he would a punctured tyre. And this speed and precision of his adjustments which made it appear as if he manipulated events at all times, was exactly unbearable. He'll play with John like a cat with a mouse. Even if he says and does nothing, it will be choice, not compulsion. All she could do was to stare, at Enoch's false teeth, at John's horribly stupid, genuine suffering, and hope and pray that Unni would not out-clever himself.

'Well,' said Enoch P. 'I ... we came ... Miss Maupratt told us, I mean, there's a party, the Valley Club party in two days, we wondered ...' He looked at John.

Unni got up. He did not brush his clothes, which would have been a gesture to fill in a pause. He stood facing John. He did not look at Enoch P.

John stood, his face going stony, yet still astonished, refusing belief.

'Good evening,' said Unni, quiet.

'Good evening,' John replied. It started him functioning, again. The pain died down, a stunned incredulity remained. 'We came to speak to Anne, my wife.' The last words seemed to anger him. He scowled, looked Unni up and down.

'Well,' said Enoch quickly, 'we really wanted to tell you, Anne, that we're organizing a small party for the Valley Club at the Royal Hotel day after tomorrow. Practically everybody's coming. We thought it would be a good idea to launch the Club now, with the Coronation and all that. John suggested dropping in here and telling you about it. We've seen Isobel.'

'Thanks,' said Anne. 'I'll see if I can come.'

'Well,' exclaimed Enoch, 'that's fine! I guess we must be going, John. Got a few more calls to make, and it's been an awful long day. Hope you enjoyed the Coronation as much as we did, Anne.'

'I liked the elephants.'

'Oh yes, the elephants, yes. A fabulous pageant. Well, be seeing you tonight maybe, at the State Theatre.'

John turned on his heel violently, not saying a word.

They lay back in silence. At last Unni said: 'John does not wish to know it's me. As long as he does not know, he feels he won't have lost you. When I'm gone, he'll make a row. But not before.'

Chapter 11

CORONATION WEEK eroded itself away. There was a hot afternoon of National Sports, the most applauded item a game of musical chairs with Paul Redworth and the Commander in Chief, the Foreign Secretary, and one or two Rana Generals running in the sun; there was the Redworths' garden party, at which the Tilley lights suddenly failed, and for fifteen minutes – during which Unni could not be found – utter darkness prevailed; an exhibition of Nepalese handicrafts, some banquets.

All partings but the most abrupt are prolonged in time and space. The expected bereavement of physical presence remains, a hovering unease about these final minutes, hours, or days. In both Unni and Anne a certain downrightness prevented future pain from exalting present joy. They were aware of the taint, apprehension of suffering, which tilted the balance of every moment towards reminiscence even in its enjoyment. Anne felt these hours a burden, over-ripe fruit just withheld from decay. With Unni it had become elemental to her to make a pattern of words, and discover that it would always be possible to say anything she felt, and that he would understand, for the clairvoyance of love goes through the physical barriers of sight to insight. And this also was fulfilment.

'It is one of the best things we have together, Unni, that I can talk to you.'

'You don't talk *to* me. You talk aloud to yourself, and I listen.'

The last hours were the seal of a new closeness in understanding; they were accepting their gift of each to the other, making no demand upon the future. Finiteness in time, marking with a limit their life together, was a frame round this fragment of living till it became a whole in itself.

'Sometimes I can't bear waiting for you to go. I wish it were all over already. I wish you were gone, that I needn't wait for departure to take place when it is already a fact.'

'My darling,' he replied, 'you'll remember every word so much better when I'm really gone.'

And thus it was in retrospect, departure accomplished, that their spring together was as a fruitful autumn, to bear fulfilment. Tracking each episode, weaving into pattern the strands of experience, Anne would find this portion an explicit whole before the next lap of her journey towards herself.

Micaceous dawn, seeping light gathering strength, a morning's small eternity, the breakfast coffee and toast with its rich scents and taste. Then the General, frail, swaying as if the breeze was too much buffet, the Maharani rolling her hips, her head majestic on her shoulders, as a Coronation elephant, Lakshmi swathed in pregnancy, Deepah faun-like and golden, and Unni in shirt sleeves and bare feet, come down from the bedroom, playing with two smaller children, a baby girl of three and a little boy of five, the General's offspring.

'It is such wonderful sun, let us drive to Bhadgaon,' said the General. 'A little jolting will do great goodness inside.'

As the jeeps passed the main building Anne saw the flitting, milk-pale figures in their summer dresses, watching from the verandah.

Bhadgaon, the old city, with trees bearing many pink and wavy roofs between their leaves, all upon a hill; along the cobbled streets clay jars, and women washing themselves at the fountains. In a large depression, as if the ground had sagged beneath its weight, the market square, centre of Bhadgaon, with an enormous five-roofed pagoda straining towards a very blue sky, a piling of roofs upwards, an avalanche of stairs downwards flanked by stone gods and beasts in order of puissance, the last pair, the lowest, human jugglers. Filling the square, a crowd in homespun, listening to a loudspeaker on the lowest tier of the pagoda surrounded by fierce young men with chiselled faces. Above them moved a bright red crackling flag with the hammer and sickle.

'Let us not disturb their politics,' said the General. He stood in the shadow of the pagoda, achieving a kinship between the building and himself by his elongate elegance, an air of old, uninsisting nobility. The General pointed to the pagoda and smiled. 'It is like a Christmas tree after Christmas, much beautiful, a little ridiculous, and still standing.'

The crowd's easy attention now centred upon the jeeps, children and women began to mill round, and Unni drove away, circling the market square.

'We should not disturb,' repeated the General, 'even though they make empty promises to fill hungry stomachs.'

Up another street they went, past projecting balconies offering trellises of carved birds, friezes of snakes, front doors painted with parakeets and eyes, to the small temple of the goddess Kala Durga, the black demon-slayer. They passed a murky courtyard encumbered with bric-à-brac, rickety stairs with a rope for the hand, came upstairs to a dirty room with a dark image surrounded by lights in pewter and silver cups. On the walls hung rows of beautifully painted masks used by the dancers of Bhadgaon in their autumn dances. Driving back, Unni swerved to avoid, in the middle of the road among the cobbles, one larger stone chalked and smudged in red. 'The guardian of Kala Durga. There are ten of them, four for the four points of the compass and four in between, one in heaven and one in the centre of the earth.' To run the jeep wheels upon them would be sacrilege. Anne remembered placing a foot against a stone at the corner of a street. An exclamation behind her had made her withdraw it. This unshapen pebble was a god, and two women and a man were looking at her, as angrily as their faces would permit.

A last look as they left, to see the pillar surmounted by the golden statue of a Mallal king, handsome and supercilious, a Ranchit face, kneeling with hands folded in front of the famous golden gate he had given to his city of Bhadgaon some centuries ago.

And then on the way back there was the General's sudden horror: 'Look, look!'

They looked. A bull, heavy, ill-looking, with a bleeding raw stump of a tail.

'Someone has cut his tail,' screamed the General, pale with anger. 'A criminal.'

And Deepah, just as moved: 'An odious criminal.'

Father and son went to the animal, spoke to three peasant women standing there.

Lakshmi was as indignant. 'They will catch the criminal and beat him to death. In Nepal it is a crime to kill or maim a bull or a cow.'

Unni kept silent, his hands on the wheel. Then in a matter of fact voice he said to Anne: 'It will take time to change this. To kill a man only costs a thousand rupees, that's what we pay up at the dam when there's an accident. But to kill a cow is murder.'

'They will catch the monster who did this,' repeated the General, climbing back into the jeep. 'They will hack him to pieces with their kukris.'

Then they spoke of it no more, leaving the bull, with its tail hanging, a sodden mass, between its legs.

Regmi had locked the bungalow, and now came from the back, explaining that 'too many people had been roaming about'. The Rampoche and his daughter had come, he said, and also 'the white man whose face is all lines like a dry mud field'.

'Leo,' said Anne, smiling at the description. She must remember to tell Unni about the Rampoche's letter. Then she forgot.

François arrived with Eudora, without awkwardness falling into the mood under the walnuts heavy with leaf.

'C'est un Manet,' said François of the landscape, and he was in ecstasy over the General: 'Quel homme épatant, qu'il est beau,' staring at the white shock of hair, the dainty rakish cap, the clothes on the scarecrow body.

Eudora spoke to Unni: 'I'll be leaving soon, what about Fred?'

'Let Fred be. He will think it over, it will grow in absence if it is worth anything. And try again, in the autumn perhaps.'

And the General: 'Patience, madam, the dew falls on the grass when the night is most silent.'

Eudora laughed (funny, thought Anne, her giggle has disappeared). 'Patience, oh patience ... General, here, where time is timeless with mountains to look at, patience has meaning and the world seems always young, but where I go back to people measure time by their watches, and they are very impatient, and old age is a terrible evil, and I am afraid to become afraid of it again.'

'True, madam, there are places where time is an evil thief,' said the General, 'but you are proof against time now, and you will conquer.'

'Oh,' said Eudora, 'I'm not young, you know.'

'You're as young as our mountains,' replied the General gallantly. 'Ask Unni. He will tell you the Himalayas are only a million years old.'

Lunch came, Nepalese food, hot, spicy; *pilau* rice, so good only eating with the fingers would do, the metal of spoon or fork spoilt the flavour. The General nodded, sniffing in the aroma of the dishes, but ate nothing. 'My stomach is so delicate, madam Anne, it withholds from itself all too solid victuals.' He drank whisky and asked for a glass of milk.

After lunch François, a postprandial Frenchman, became eloquent. 'Here I return to the heart of myself, as you have done. I wish I could stay for ever, but I must not. In the world outside often I do not know what I want; pulled to shreds between so many things, the faces of hatred and love, yearning and disgust, until the texture of my attention to life is lacerated. But here all is true and becomes whole and part of myself, and I desire to become utterly myself, to encompass my own universe of awareness. It is something to be sure of a desire. Sure as a child is sure of living.'

The General, overhearing, said: 'God is here, Himself, in the pleasant wind and walking on the joyful grass.'

Sun-drenched drowsiness after lunch, sudden awareness of Unni's body; the Maharani picking herself up, gathering her husband, daughter, Eudora, François, Deepah, disappearing without lingering good-byes; as if she had guessed, thought Anne, neither ashamed nor awkward; and Unni taking her hand, naturally, as if they had been together all their lives; and still the feeble business of being scrupulous and foolishly upright. 'Supposing people come. What will they think?'

'What can they think,' replied Unni gravely, 'except that we are a man and a woman doing what is expected of us?' And seeing her dubious face, he laughed: 'Come, Anne. Do not worry. Regmi will say you're out.'

And then their bodies taking over, his arms and the feel of him obliterating all else, annihilating all doubts and questions, creating its own non-being.

Loveliness; the discovery confirmed, of the promised land, the flesh in beauty, swinging with it in unison the spirit; a great hurt in the breast, and all the words that this pain has created through the ages come true; the lovely words, more rousing, more important than caress of hands or contact of flesh in the sumptuous creation and maintaining of desire; and wonder that this man should know that to make love it is to speak love, that he should say: With my body I thee

adore, in so many ways, and mean it, and do it in speech and in gesture; that she should know how true the words, empty, vague, before.

She clung to him, saying fiercely: 'Keep me, take me, I am yours.'

He replied: 'And I am yours.'

And she felt this was true marriage.

Anne now was the earthy one, rubbing herself against his side,
putting her head in his armpit, smelling him, enamoured again: 'Tell
me again,' she said, 'tell me I am yours.'

'You are my woman,' he said. 'The first time, at the Temple, at
the Siva Festival, I knew it. You are my woman.'

Was not this enough? Adoration of her flesh, holy with beauty
created in his eyes, adorned by his words, made precious to her by the
love poured upon it by hand and eye, lip and body. The acceptance of
her spirit, accepting her own growth, accepting to be all his and yet
for ever separate in her absorption in things not him. And even as
they said: 'I am yours,' and meant it wholly, in unlimited giving
and receiving, they were also accepting all the things they could not
share together and a future they could not shape.

Now she knew herself free and whole, for the first time. I must not
ask too much, not ask that this love of man be the law of a god, nor
the statute of a law, nor a landmark for me to beyond the earth, to
paradise. I shall love with little prudence and less reason: for this
bird has now built its nest with me, now with me it sits. And so
knowing this sacrament and creation, wholly mortal and not to
recur, she said:

'Make me a child, Unni, please make me a child of you.'

The Coronation guests were leaving. The crowds about Khatmandu thinned as Sherpas and Bhottyas, Tibetans and Gurungs,
drifted back to their own valleys and villages. Like a long-tailed salamander, Coronation Week went on indecisively trailing a sparse programme.

'At least they give you plenty of time to fade away if you like,'
said Vassili.

A tattoo, organized at the sports stadium (where part of the new-
built wall had fallen in under the weight of its own empty seats) had
bugled and detonated its *feu de joie* and other martial items till late at
night.

The next morning saw Leo, his own cheerful self again, coming across the lawn when Anne was having breakfast.

'Anne, how gorgeous you look!' She wore a soft shirt and jeans and looked young and happy. 'Coffee? Certainly. Isn't this heavenly? This is the most marvellous spot, the best in Khatmandu I should say. And your job is fascinating, lucky you, teaching English to a lot of little married teenagers.'

'I guess I may have to give it up.'

Leo looked up quickly. 'I did hear there was some debate about your being here. Isobel's making a fuss.'

'Isobel would like me to resign. She hasn't said it but I feel it. And I'm expecting John to turn up now, any time, for a showdown.' She poured herself another cup of coffee.

'Why?' said Leo, 'I should think by now he's accepted the *fait accompli*.'

'What is the *fait accompli*? John knows, but he'll have to make gestures, strike attitudes in keeping with his status. But he had to wait until Unni was gone to do it. "He'll make a row when I'm gone," that's what Unni said.'

'I hate rows,' said Leo. 'They make me shiver.'

'Me too. They paralyse me. I never know what to say, I'm strangled with fear. But now, waiting for one (a John one, possibly later an Isobel one), I feel rather curious, I'd like to know how I'll react now, if I've changed at all.'

'You'll have to tell him, of course,' said Leo, 'unless Unni has spared you that trouble.'

'He hasn't. That's not like Unni. I mean, going up to John and saying: "I love your wife and your wife loves me."'

'I should have thought,' Leo was sarcastic, 'that it was the only decent thing for a man to do. Especially when he's – I beg your pardon – compromised you so hopelessly.'

Anne laughed. 'Dear Leo, you sound comical saying conventional things. Unni won't pronounce the word love in front of someone who, he says, is not capable of understanding the word. He has not said anything.'

'And left you to face the music,' said Leo.

'And left me to do what is right. I didn't leave John for Unni. I left John for my own sake, for myself. Unni is a development, if you

369

like; even if he had not happened, I would have left, sooner or later. Unni will speak for us both, when the time comes.'

'It's all very intricate, possibly very idealistic,' said Leo, rather irritably. 'And it seems to me that Master Unni is an opportunist getting away with a lot.' Damn the woman, fresh as a rose, explaining Unni to him. Leo's sexual aggressiveness, Kisha-smothered with surfeit and boredom, was freshly aroused. He strove to maintain a light run of talk to keep the contact achieved with this new Anne, who spoke, giving pointers to herself, instead of remaining sequestered in silence. How well he remembered that day in Calcutta, the grinding rumour of buses, Anne's voice: 'I'm nicely dead.' Look at her now, nicely alive, clad in the hues of the Valley, her willing soul transpiring at every pore with sensuous knowledge.

'It's not that, it's being wise as serpents and simple as doves,' said Anne. 'How Isobel would sound and fury if she heard me quoting the Bible.' She threw herself back in the chair with mirth. Leo had never seen her so childishly vindictive. She can't be much in love, he went off yesterday, there she sits, roaring her head off.

'Anne,' he said, trying to interject a note of adulthood, 'but seriously, what is going to happen? What are your plans?'

'Haven't any.'

'Now that is too childish,' said Leo, sounding very German. 'You cannot *not* have a plan. Surely you must have decided, since you've left John, to ask for a divorce.'

'Why?'

'Why? Because this is an impossible situation, impossible,' cried Leo. 'You can't go on like this. Poor John might come upon you and Unni at any moment. He might get very ugly.'

'You think he would get ugly, don't you?'

'I really don't know John at all well. On the other hand, if you asked him, frankly, he might consider giving you a divorce. Or you might try to catch him out. That would be simpler.'

'Oh, you mean Suriyah the pro,' said Anne. 'That doesn't count. Not really.'

'My dear girl!' Leo became practical. 'I know, I respect your attitude. But just consider. Sooner or later something *must* be done. You *must* get a divorce.'

'What for?'

Leo was so irritated he nearly said 'My dear girl!' again.

'What for? Well, you sweet dear, because everybody gets divorced if they're in love with someone else and no longer with their marriage partner. So that they can be free to marry again.'

'Does divorce really make one free?' said Anne. 'I don't know.'

'Perhaps you don't need to worry about divorce in Khatmandu,' said Leo, 'but you're not staying here all your life. It's a hole, really. You'll want to go elsewhere and it isn't convenient, legally I mean.' But even as he spoke he felt his practicality, the logic of his assurance, the implacability of the arrangements one made with society ebb from him, and a sense of happy folly come seeping in from the grass on which he had planted his thin buttocks, at Anne's feet. There was dew on the grass and he was damp; somehow it was quite immaterial, it didn't worry him to have a damp backside, the sun and the wind would take care of that in their casual and irremediable manner. So he said: 'Oh, let's leave it. It's too beautiful a morning to talk of such things. I hope you're happy. You're very lucky, I know.'

'Why is it that everybody says I'm lucky and nearly everybody says, Poor John?'

'Why?' Leo was perplexed. 'Perhaps because you ... well, you're obviously so much stronger, more able, sure of yourself ... in fact, you could be hard as nails about some things. And yet you do get hurt very easily.'

'It's a different kind of hurt now, not a self-pitying retreat as before, scanning its own lacerations and bawling its head off. It's joyful pain. That's even harder for other people to forgive. Do you know that thing in the Bible about if a man force thee to go one mile, go with him another two? If you're alive you feel like that. Everything turns into good fortune, even one's worries. Just as absence makes love clearer, it's the other side of presence, and just as necessary. Solitude is necessary, don't you think?'

'Shall I leave you then?' said Leo. 'Would you like to be alone?'

'Oh dear Leo,' cried Anne quickly, 'please. I'm so full of myself, I forget other people. Do stay, I love your company ... and by the way, you seem relieved and more relaxed than I've seen you for days. Is Kisha gone?'

'Not gone, but off my hands,' said Leo triumphantly. 'I wanted to tell you. Toast's finest hour. She's probably breakfasting off him now. If I remember correctly, she's quite insatiable. Quite.'

'And the six Sikh cousins?'

'I don't know,' said Leo, 'but if they appear I intend to be properly indignant about her tremendous treachery to me.'

He had spent the night with Mariette, and had learnt, incidentally, that she had not met Unni at Pokhra, but a distant member of the Royal Family, whose concern for her comfort had made her decide to stay another week or so in Khatmandu.

'And you, Leo?'

'Me, my darling?' He looked round him. He was happy, just now, sitting with a wet backside in the damp grass. He did not even desire Anne at the moment; and with him physical desire being always the exact equivalent of love, he was sure he had 'got over' his exacerbations about her. For his perceptions were uni-dimensional, and he proceeded to understand himself and others rationally as he would have written a report. Wordless sensations could not exist simply because there were no words for them. If one didn't want or desire, one couldn't love. 'Me! Nearly in a Buddhist Nirvana. I'm really ideally happy at the moment. And I shall leave tomorrow, carrying this wonderful picture of a small, enclosed Eden: this bungalow, these trees, and you Anne, sitting here, looking lovely, having breakfast and talking to me.'

'And like all paradises, here comes the angel with the flaming sword,' said Anne, rising. 'Good morning, John, I was waiting for you.'

Chapter 12

'PERHAPS I'd better go,' said Leo hastily.

'Yes, do.' Anne was watching John, alone and striding purposefully across the lawn, squaring his shoulders, thrusting his chest out in that so familiar gesture of filling himself up with air. And she was annoyed to find herself slowly going frightened as he drew near, step by step, afraid not of John but of his violence, human violence, producing in her now all too quickly a dry mouth, a fast-beating heart, a mind unable to declare itself clearly.

'I've come to have it out with you once and for all. Yes or no – are you coming back to me?'

I can't say yes, thought Anne, and I'm too frightened to say no. She lit a cigarette to give herself time, concentrating on steadying her fingers.

'That's one more thing I don't want you to do,' said John. '*I'm* going to be master here from now on. I don't want you to smoke. I hate people who smoke, it's a filthy habit. I'll take these cigarettes away from you. From now on we'll see who's giving the orders.' He snatched the cigarette from her hand, ground it into the grass under his shoes. Then he stamped up and down, shouting: 'I've put up with this long enough. I won't have it any more. It's six weeks now that you've been living in this place, behaving like an absolute tart, having men coming round, like a real whore. I've had enough.'

Suddenly, in a flourish of rage, having got himself over the first lap, he planted himself in front of her, thrust his face to hers, and said: 'And what's this about that black ape, Menon? Lying on the grass here, in front of everybody, pawing you with his disgusting filthy, black hands?'

'What about it?' said Anne, despising herself for only parrying, yet in her physical fear unable to do anything else.

'You whore,' screamed John, stamping away, 'I'll smash your insolent face in, you ...'

There were people, thought Anne, who made it impossible to tell them the truth. They invited prevarication. If it had been anybody but John she would have replied without fanfare or hedging, only telling the truth, Unni is my lover; but it was John. Unni had known. 'John does not wish to know it's me. He wants to have his tantrum, but he also wants to be deceived.'

'Don't tell me any more lies,' John was shouting. 'I know what you're after. A phallus, that's what you're after. You've lost all sense of dignity. First it's Fred Maltby, and now that I've scared him away, you throw yourself at this black syphilitic Indian. Don't smile. I forbid you to smile. *All* Indians are syphilitic. I know them. I've been years in India. Not content with one paramour, you want that black bastard to — you. But you'll soon find out who's important here. I won't have men snooping around, sitting on the lawn with you like that bastard Bielfeld I caught just now, having you rub yourself against black bastards like that Menon. He's filthy, black, black, dirty. If I were a woman I'd be sick just to look at his face. I won't have it, do you hear? I'll smash his face in, next time I see him. You'll see him come snivelling and going down on his knees, the coward, while I smash him, like that.' And he whizzed his fists in the air about her.

'Well,' said Anne, 'why didn't you smash him when you saw us?'

John lunged towards her, and she moved quickly backwards. He hit her with clenched fist on one side of the head. She fell on the lawn while he stood above her, screaming 'You dare say that to me? To me! You whore, you dirty ...'

She picked herself up, facing him, retreating slowly while he advanced on her as if to strike again. Now she had the breakfast table between them. John's eyes fell upon the toast rack, the coffee pot, and the cups; he picked up the coffee pot and hurled it at her, and then the cups and the toast rack. The hot coffee streamed down her neck and blouse, and she said 'You brute!' and started wiping herself, mechanically, and then suddenly John fell into a chair with his head in his hands, and began to sob.

'Anne,' he moaned, 'Anne – you don't love me. You've never loved me.'

Anne went on wiping. He had spent himself and she was shaking. Both had avoided the issue. Never, perhaps, would they discuss it. They would circle round it, draining their energies, complaining of this or that, not daring to tell the truth. How could Anne say to John that it was the words he used, the way in which he reacted to situations which made it impossible for her to talk to him? John was his own worst enemy, for he had never any control over the way in which he expressed himself. And Anne felt again the compassion she'd always felt about John. John was frightened of her, had always been frightened of her, yet this knowledge did not help her to speak to him, to break the conditioned reflexes of his reaction to her and hers to him. They were caught in the vicious whirlpool of their own gestures, they reacted to their outward shells, not their inner selves; they went on, as in an eternal ball game, throwing back hostility to each other. The difference between them was that she had insight enough to know this, to pity him because of it, but not enough sublimity to disregard it, not enough to love him. And because he knew that she could not love him, because he could not acknowledge in his small vanity that he acted like a fool, because he loved the ways of his short-sighted violences more than he loved Anne, he went on raging, as a blind bat will go, hitting the ceiling of a room until it breaks a wing. Futile, shattering, wholly destructive, their semi-contrived scenes would go on, in themselves a catharsis for him, for her an accumulation of hatred, scenes which as the first frenzy wore off always showed themselves an act not entirely real.

Now his tears, head sunk between heaving shoulders, were nauseous, irritating, false as his rages. It's just hopeless, completely hopeless. I suppose that's what's called incompatibility. I can't reach him, and he can't reach me. We don't talk the same language.

'Anne,' said John. 'Come here, Anne, please.'

If he'd left it at that perhaps she would have come, in silence, but taking a step. But he had to go and spoil it by lifting his wet red face from his hands.

'I'm your husband, you know. You *must* come if I ask you.'

And that kept her where she was.

He looked at her now, mouth open, openly crying.

'How can you be so hard,' he said, 'so cold to me? I've never been happy. Not once have you been kind to me.'

'I'm not kind, wasn't made that way.'

'You bitch,' said John. 'You're unnatural. I never knew you were so vindictive. Any other woman would take pity on me. Anybody with a trace of human feelings – but you haven't got any. I think you're not normal. You're quite inhuman. You're ruthless, and you're trying to destroy me. You've destroyed me mentally and physically already. You've tried to make me impotent too, you cold unnatural woman. But I'm not impotent, d'you hear? I'm not!'

'I don't want to destroy you,' said Anne.

'Yes, you do,' said John, standing up, walking about in an ecstasy of anger, squaring his shoulders and throwing his arms about. 'You do. First you try to make me impotent and then you run away from me. You won't talk to me and you muck around with any man that comes, anything in trousers. Well, I'm going to fight back. I won't have it, and to begin with you're coming back to the Royal Hotel. I'm not going to have you stay here any longer.'

'I'm staying here.'

'That's what we'll see. I'll do what *I* like round here. Here you!' He shouted to Regmi, whose frightened head appeared cautiously round the corner of the bungalow. 'Take Memsahib's things down right away – she's coming back to the Hotel with me.'

Regmi disappeared, and John bounded up into the bungalow and up the stairs.

'What are you doing?' shouted Anne, and ran behind him. 'Stop, John. Don't you dare go upstairs.' She didn't want John to go into her room. But he was already on the landing, and she, looking at his back as he crossed the threshold into the room with the parakeets, said: 'Now it's really over. Now you've done it. I'll never come back to you again. Never! Not if you were the last man on earth.'

She heard John opening and shutting drawers, flinging coat-hangers about, turning round the room, coming out again; in his hand the *Gita*, picked up from the desk where she had left it, near the typewriter. Her diary, on foolscap in the bottom drawer under her clothes, he had not seen.

'What's this?' he shouted, holding up the *Gita*. He opened the book. The snap fell out. He picked it up, tore it, hurled the book down the stairs at Anne. 'Take that,' he said, 'you can stick it up your — if you like.'

'You're mad,' said Anne. 'You're mad.' The words he used made her want to vomit.

'You call Isobel,' said John satirically, 'she'll throw you out.'

'Here! What's going on here?' It was Leo, pale and anxious but resolute. He had not gone far. Behind the rose arbour, ashamed of his cowardice, he had turned, heard, and seen everything. He was quivering, and Anne knew him frightened, but he now faced John. 'I'm appalled,' he began, 'absolutely appalled at your behaviour.'

'You keep out of this or I'll smash *your* face in,' said John. 'You ...'

'John,' said Leo, 'will you please stop behaving like a madman? Remember you're Secretary of the Valley Club.'

Anne was picking up the *Gita*. Several sheets had come loose. The back was damaged and the cover bent. It hurt her as nothing else had done. She held it to her as John came bumping down the stairs and passed her. She followed him with a look of hatred as he and Leo, expostulating in a low voice, went away together.

The Valley Club party at the Royal Hotel turned out more lugubrious farewell than happy inauguration.

'We should have had it a day earlier,' said Pat to Eudora. Pat was in the receiving line, with John and Enoch P. Tonight in an off-the-shoulder dress of black satin, her mouth painted scarlet, and her hair piled on top of her head, only the chunky fake jewellery round her neck and from her ears was reminiscent of her more slipshod past. All-Khatmandu was there, and Pat was striving hard to please, but it was not Ranchit she was trying to please.

Eudora, in a sari, looked dignifiedly back at Pat. Dignity was all the women present strove to achieve in various ways, for Enoch P. boomed this occasion was 'unique'. Shaking hands with the guests he imparted the feeling of a senatorial pre-election venue.

Fred came with Eudora, their presence together now unsurprising. Fred did not want to come; but the urge to see Eudora again had made him come, although he was resentful towards himself for giving in to it. 'Good thing it's in the garden,' he muttered, 'stifling inside.'

'Yes, isn't it?' said Eudora. 'We can walk out as soon as you wish,' Fred.'

'Oh, we'll stay as long as you like, I don't mind,' replied Fred magnanimously.

There was nothing more they could say, and they turned with relief to their drinks.

Vassili had mixed the drinks, and they were strong and perfect, Manhattans and Martinis, Bronx and Sidecars. The General stood near him, he had brought his own whisky as usual. Many of the correspondents had already left the Valley, the remainder would go the next day; the Coronation was past, and they talked of other assignments away from Khatmandu. All but Blumenfeld, the non-pareil Blumenfeld, who appeared dragging a Buddhist priest with him, spurned all the drinks and called for Coca-Cola.

'Which plane are you on, Blumie, the 8.30 or the 8.45?'

'I'm on the ten o'clock.'

'Phew, won't we feel the heat in Calcutta after the Valley?'

Blumenfeld had adopted the Nepalese style of dress, jodphurs and a tunic, tied with ribbons slantwise across his chest. He informed Vassili and his colleagues that the tunic was derived from the Chinese style of dress in the tenth century.

'On the other hand,' said Vassili, 'the Nepalese will tell you that the Chinese copied it from them. Just like the pagodas. We always think they're Chinese. But they were built in China by Nepalese architects. Have a drink.'

'I'm going to come back here,' Blumenfeld said, refusing heroic-ally. 'I feel there's something here that we haven't got in the West. Yes, Vassili, maybe it's wrong of me to get emotionally involved with places and people, but I'd kind of like to come back and do a real study of this place. And put some order in the religion, maybe. I'm all at sea with those names.'

'We like it that way,' said the General. 'What's in a name?'

Leo was waltzing on the stone pathways with Hilde. At times he stopped completely, and his mirth dropped from him as he scanned the gradually thickening crowd.

'Are you waiting for someone, Leo?'

'I wondered whether Anne would come,' replied Leo, because it was Hilde asking.

'Is she coming?' Vassili stirred the champagne and looked at Hilde, in a brown silk dress with a pattern of golden flowers, her long fair hair pulled to one side to fall in a turbulent wave.

'I hope so.'

'Madam Anne will not come,' said the General. 'She is fast asleep.'

'Everyone here is waiting for her to turn up,' said François. 'They are ferociously ready to tear her to pieces.'

'She will not come,' said the General. 'She is more happy alone.'

'Then,' said François, 'I will go to write to her a letter.'

'Hey, you can't leave the party,' cried Vassili.

But François did not return.

The garden was getting full. Enoch nodded with satisfaction. So many of the Ranas, a prince or two. 'A very select crowd,' he murmured. But, alas, the Field Marshal was not there. 'I fear me many a friendship will founder at your Club,' he had told Enoch P. suavely, when the latter had solicited his membership.

'Oh, now, Your Excellency, that's not our aim. Our aim is to cement the traditional friendship between the free world and Nepal.'

'Let me not mar your merriment,' replied the Field Marshal. ''Tis high iniquity to meet again at the Club people I meet – and occasionally become inebriated with – almost any day of the week. Seeing too much of one's friends is nefarious to the emotions.'

Kisha, who now cut Leo dead, hung on the arm of Michael Toast, and her six towering turbaned escorts surrounded him. No one could tell them apart save by the colours of their turbans: pink, canary yellow, a tender lime, a vivid white, a turquoise blue, and a cinnamon.

'Poor Michael. He just said "How about bed?" once too often,' Leo whispered jubilantly to Eudora.

Michael was telling everyone that he'd nearly finished his book, and would soon have to leave for England 'where they're sure to lap it up'.

'Wiz me!' Kisha cried. Already she saw herself, the star in Michael's film.

Michael looked at the Sikhs, who all looked at him. 'I want a drink,' he said, and Vassili, moved with pity, gave him a strong Paradise.

Mike Young was dancing a staid waltz with Rukmini. Holding her, precious and delicate, decorously far, betrayed by his rapt, happy face. Rukmini sat down and Mike fetched her an orange juice. Ranchit, very drunk already, was mauling the blonde journalist behind the margosa tree.

Vassili, uncorking a bottle of champagne with a tremendous pop (which made History and Geography start and exclaim), heard the talk floating by him, driftwood on the sea, marking the high tide of public knowledge in All-Khatmandu.

'Yes, that's the Maltbys. Separated years and years ... just made it up.'

'She'll be staying here, I expect.'

'I wonder whether I should send her a card for our next Get-Together?'

'Might get a job at the Institute.'

'Especially now.'

'Yes ... did you hear what I heard?'

'What did you hear?'

Whisper. '– her face is so bashed in she won't appear.'

'Who told you?'

'Miss Newell. She was there. Hiding, of course.'

'It was absolutely terrible. Apparently he was there all the time too. Ran away when he saw you know who.'

'The doctor?'

'No, no. Not the doctor. That man over there. Leo Bielfeld. He came specially to Khatmandu for her.'

John and Leo approached each other, and both conversed earnestly. All-Khatmandu held its breath. Nothing happened. Leo walked away, and John went to confer with Geography, and then asked the Irish girl for a dance. He seemed very happy.

Isobel also was missing. 'She has a terrible headache,' Geography explained brightly to everybody.

God, thought Vassili, pouring some more drinks, what a party. No go at all. It's a great big flop, all right. He wondered how to make it go. Everybody was getting quickly, coldly, mutely drunk. In spite of the music, the soft night, the lights well placed, there was tension, nervousness, a palpable air of waiting. Groups stood immovable, glued to each other, talking without smiles or looking round vacantly. When there was laughter, it was Ranchit's, raucous and outrageous. An ugly party. A dull, dead-alive party. Something was wrong. Everybody was saying nasty things.

'Goodness, listen to them,' said Eudora, outraged. 'The nonsense they do talk about Anne and poor John.'

The General was arguing with a bright, tall girl with an incredible Mayfair accent, who had been staying with a Maharajah's son (called Pooch), and would now be staying with a Prince (called Pet). 'Absolutely too darling of them to ask me,' the well-bred, carrying voice said. '*Couldn't* be sweeter, really. I'm absolutely broke. Couldn't have come if Pooch hadn't bought my plane ticket.'

'Our hospitality, madam, will be even greater,' said the General belligerently. 'Many a lady like you has come here and retired impregnated.'

'I beg your pardon?' said the Mayfair accent.

'The General means impressed,' said Vassili quickly. 'He means overwhelmed, impressed.'

'That is enough,' said the General, suddenly angry. 'My English is not ungood, my friend. This female does understand me, even if I do create new words by copulation of syllables hitherto separate. You are welcome to Nepal, madam; and may our masculine hospitality be equal to that which I found among the female natives of your glorious country.' And then the General walked away, a little sideways as if tilting at the night.

By eleven p.m. the party was a desperate, woeful affair. Ranchit and the journalist had disappeared, Mariette had gone, the Hindu poet was reciting loudly and disconsolately. Rukmini sat in a pretty pose, the only gay thing, twining her rubies round her fingers, while Mike Young gazed at her raptly. From time to time she raised her eyes and opened her mouth and said a few words. Then they both smiled.

At eleven-thirty p.m. Enoch P. made an announcement: 'Ladies and gentlemen and guests of the Valley Club,' he began, 'it is with great pleasure that I and my colleagues greet you tonight, in this fabulous city of the Himalayas, Khatmandu.'

Enoch P. had prepared his speech and held a little paper in his hand, while Vassili sympathetically swayed a torch over his shoulder to enable him to read it. But the atmosphere of the gathering discountenanced him, he stuttered and became muddled. The Valley Club, he said, had been formed with the idea of promoting friendship 'among all democratic elements in this far-off, remote valley'. He spoke about the free world and the 'good work done by those people who are hand-picked to come to this fabulous, far-off kingdom'. He put in a sentence about Club fees, which would be thirty rupees a month 'which we feel sure you'll be glad to hand over'. There was a slight stir at this point, since the nominal salaries of most of the lower officials of the Nepalese Government were round sixty rupees a month, this precluded them from belonging to the Club, and thus Enoch's announcement that 'we feel the Valley Club is truly representative of the best democratic elements of the country' only applied to the wealthy Ranas and the foreign element of Khatmandu.

Finally, Enoch P. wound up with 'two announcements, which I am sure you'll greet with a mighty glad hand. The first, the engagement of Miss Kisha Kaur to Mr Michael Toast. ...' At this Vassili clapped loud and long, and everybody else clapped as long as he did. 'And the second ...' Here Enoch P. tried to look coy. 'Folks I want to tell you I'm the happiest man here tonight. Miss Pat Arbuckle, whom you all know as Pat, has said the word.' Overcome with emotion, he let the handclaps rock over him, while Pat came forward, and they both held hands together over the microphone.

John surged with History and Geography to shake hands and to kiss Pat with the usual expressions of pleasure. Enoch P. solemnly gripped John's shoulder. 'Thanks, John. And thanks for your co-operation in making the Valley Club such a success.'

'Not at all, old boy,' said John enthusiastically. He sounded gay, he looked happy, but he was miserable. Pat and Enoch, standing there, reminded him of his own engagement, his wedding, with Anne. He wanted to groan aloud with pain. Instead, he began to laugh, nearly hysterical. Well, Anne wasn't there. He wouldn't let that worry him. Shutting his eyes, because he felt them smart, he raised the champagne cup with which the bearers were providing everyone, to drink to the health of Michael Toast and Kisha, Enoch P. and Pat.

Fred and Eudora had long since retired to the verandah, where sitting in comfort they gazed upon the guests.

'I wonder how John stands it. He looks quite normal.'

'I wonder. He can't acknowledge that he knows, because then it's all over for him. Maybe he's rationalized the position – he sticks to the people who tell him how wicked Anne is. But he's really afraid of losing Anne. He's like an animal in a catatonic trance, afraid to move, yet growling and baring his teeth.'

'That's awfully involved,' said Eudora, feminine.

'It isn't really. So long as Anne stayed with him, even hostile, he had something. Now he is afraid that she is truly gone, body and spirit. He can't face that, there'd be no point in his living then.'

'That's why we all say poor John,' said Eudora. 'What will Anne do?'

'Probably nothing,' said Fred. 'The kindest thing she could do would be to force him to see the truth, but you can't really force people to see what they don't want to see.'

'Why not, if it's the right thing?'

'I said the kindest, not the right thing. I don't know what she will do. I feel she'll just sit there, mulishly, and let things happen. She has a great capacity for sitting things out.'

Like someone else I know, thought Eudora, but held her peace.

'For Anne the problem isn't to have a clear-cut situation, but to weave a pattern with what has happened,' said Fred. 'In other words, she's more preoccupied with the significance to her of what is happening than in controlling events. She may feel she mustn't make a gesture on her own which might put the whole thing away. Do I make myself clear?'

'Artistically, yes,' said Eudora. 'It's like having a melody in one's head, and being afraid to move, lest you break the thread.'

'That's a good simile,' agreed Fred.

Anne again had been their link, their way to each other. The subject of Anne made them appear perspicuous to each other. But it could not be discussed for ever.

'Well,' said Eudora brightly, 'I must toddle off to bed. Got to catch a plane tomorrow.'

'I'll come and see you off,' said Fred, 'if I may.'

'That's very sweet of you, Fred.'

They stood, uncomfortable, perched on the brink of dismalness. Eudora then said, her voice very small: 'Would you like me to write to you occasionally ... I mean, just to keep in touch?'

'Yes,' said Fred, 'I'd like that ... it's very nice of you to think of it.' He added: 'I'm due for some leave at the end of the year. I was thinking, I haven't moved from this place for ages. I might take a trip.'

'Yes,' said Eudora brightly, fearful of saying too much, 'I'd love to hear your plans.'

It was silly to say good-bye. She said: 'See you tomorrow.'

'Tomorrow,' he mumbled.

She left him, going to her room, head held high, running a little, afraid she might start weeping before she got there.

'Anne!'

Anne peered down in the darkness, already in her heart a drumming of hope that it was Unni. 'Who is it?'

'*C'est moi, François,*' said the shadow modestly.

'Oh, François.' There was a slight disappointment in her voice, and it hurt François. He was looking at her. Behind her the light was diffuse gold, heavy as oil upon her shoulders and hair.

'*Anne au balcon,*' he said. '*C'est très romantique, comme ça.*'

'What brings you here, François?'

'My good-byes to you Anne. I am leaving tomorrow.'

'Oh,' she said, 'everybody is leaving Khatmandu. Season of farewells.'

She went down to open the door and he walked in. She wore a dressing-gown of some golden material with embroidered peacocks. François looked at her.

'Unni gave it to me,' she said, caressing the material.

She now sat at the typewriter, a neat pile of foolscap on the desk. François looked at everything slowly, a look like an inhalation.

'*Que c'est beau. Comme j'aime ça.* It is nearly frightening, Anne, your beautiful tower of gold.' He stretched on the carpet on the floor. It was a Tibetan rug, blue and scarlet with a dull gold background. '*C'est fou comme tout paraît beau ici,*' said François. 'I must come back and understand and capture, capture this moment of vision, for which the price of a life is not enough.'

They were caught in enthralment of the beautiful moment, the light, the carpet, the golden gown, the lovely life upon the walls, the pleasure of being able to see, to hear, to feel the delight of this paradise in their hands; and yet at the same time knowing the constant self-discipline which this awareness demanded, the delicacy of restraint to be for ever practised, a skill like that of the pianist who has to exercise his fingers every day.

'I will lose this,' said François, 'I will lose it, for sometimes I am not myself, I am dead, as everybody dies many times before their death, and is born again. Then I come back to life. Perhaps it is good to come to life only occasionally, like this. Otherwise one would be suffering too much.'

'It's people,' said Anne. 'Some people take away my eyes and my ears, and others give them back to me. I suppose real freedom is just that, to be aware without needing too much of other people.'

'One always needs other people,' said François.

'That's what Unni says,' said Anne. 'To eye-witness what we see, that is how he put it.'

'Unni is a very remarkable person,' said François.

'Oh no,' said Anne, 'Unni is very simple – but he is wholly himself, so he can say these things, without thinking about them. Like a child giving you a pebble because it is pretty.'

'And he forgets, and you, Anne, take the pebble and start building a monument with it, because you are in love.'

'Am I in love? I don't know.'

'You are, I think,' said François. 'Of course, it depends what you call love.'

'It depends, rather, the kind of love one chooses,' said Anne.

'Most people cannot choose,' said François. 'They have to go away. Or do something. Or they cannot get involved. Or they give themselves no time to find out.'

'What Unni calls emotional castrates,' said Anne, 'afraid of pain, so they cut themselves off.'

'I have written something, Anne,' said François shyly, 'and please do not laugh. It is for you.

'J'aime la pierre qui fleurit
Sarabande érotique et sacrée, beauté dansant dans le bois, le bronze,
Les lions, les gryphons, les éléphants, les oiseaux,
Dorés sereins les rajas sur leurs hautes stèles
Priant devant leurs dons, leurs dieux,
Le délicieux arc-en-ciel des déesses en délire
Parmi les serpents phalliques.

'J'en ai mal un peu partout, de ce bel amour.
Poser le pied sur l'herbe joyeuse, c'est beaucoup trop bouger.
Les enfants sont comme les moineaux, bien moins loquaces, même si gais,
Ils se bousculent pour voir ceux qui regardent.
Sur une joue des trous de la vérole, dans un visage des yeux de pierre
Lèvent quand même leurs paupières au soleil,
Divinement heureux.

'Tout tourne autour de ce nombril merveilleux, centre du monde,
Poutre qui perce le ciel;
Tout danse autour de cet axe invisible, soleil en soi-même.
Les gens sont comme leurs peintures dans le cadre de leurs fenêtres
    ajourées,
Leurs yeux de lotus vivent sans se mouvoir,
Yeux des Newars artistes et rêveurs
Créateurs fantasques et indigents des dieux.

'Ils vivent émerveillés
Sans connaître autre chose que la misère de l'homme.
À travers les trous de leurs haillons, les étoiles de leur rêves sont à l'aise,
Ils n'ont pas besoin de sens pour voir,
Entendre, sentir, toucher.
Ils aiment, et cela explique tous les miracles:
Ils aiment, et sont Dieu Lui-même.

'Car sans amour toute pureté est sale, tout zèle et dévotion vérole,
Toute création néant.

'*Voilà*,' he said, getting up suddenly. 'I only wanted to see you and say good-bye, for I am going tomorrow.'

'We'll meet again, François,' said Anne, 'nobody ever leaves anyone. No human being.'

'Perhaps not,' said François, suddenly taciturn, tongue-tied. He nodded briefly, said: '*Au revoir*,' and walked away swiftly.

And although Anne knew his pain and his need, yet her own fulfilment, like the silk gown on her body, interposed a veil between its realization and herself. François must go and she must stay, and that was that.

*

In driblets the correspondents and the tourists have gone. The Coronation is over. The spring is over. Already, scanning the white porcelain sky, the General speaks of the monsoon to come.

One trip to the airport and I have disposed of my farewells. François and Leo go together. The laconic François has said all last night, now wanders in the white heat, waiting for the plane; is already withdrawn, departed.

Not so Leo, voluble, unperspicacious Leo of the wandering fancy and the ever-recurrent small zests. Leo goes once again over our last meeting, and John's tantrum. Tantrum is the only word which applies. Leo has still not left, he is still verbalizing the scenery (I feel like saying décor, it becomes a décor when surrounding Leo), the climate, the alarums of the Valley.

'My dear Anne, to think of *you* having to put up with this kind of thing. It really made me feel like climbing the wall. You know I spent the better part of the day afterwards with your husband, trying to make him *see* that he must release you?'

'Thank you, Leo.'

'He seemed quite normal at the Valley Club party that night. It was a funereal party, Anne, and *so* much gossip. I think a lot of people were waiting for you to appear, in a way I am sorry you didn't.'

'I was writing.' I tell Leo casually the most important thing about me, but Leo is distrait, and the news glances by, the winged moment goes unperceived. Unni would have known what a gift I made to Leo by telling him. But Leo has not heard. Unni knew without being told.

'I think John will be more sensible now, after our talk,' says Leo. 'I don't think he will behave like this again. Paul Redworth also had a talk with him. I think he'll behave now.'

'Thank you, Leo.' I find it easier to thank people.

The airfield is crowded. Blumenfeld, clad as a Buddhist monk but with three cameras round his neck, a few other correspondents, consult their watches, make sure of the plane, talk about the heat in the plain. Kisha and Michael Toast are seeing off the six Sikh cousins, Vassili and Hilde wave to a gaggle of tourists and a mountain of luggage.

Colonel Jaganathan is here also, in full dress uniform, strangely despondent.

'Waiting for two brigadiers from Delhi,' he says, 'coming to investigate a mild case of rape.'

'Of rape?'

'Yes, my own. My dear Nepalese friends at their favourite pastime. Someone or other is supposed to have been raped by me; anonymous letter to Headquarters.'

'Too bad,' sympathizes Leo.

'Damn it,' says the Colonel feelingly, 'and I haven't had a woman for months!'

Leo proffers immediate solutions. 'But why not,' he exclaims, 'with all these unattached tourists ...?'

'All the money wasted,' continued Colonel Jaganathan, 'sending two brigadiers from HQ all the way from Delhi. They'll stay here a few days, drink my beer, and go off again. Next time I'll demand a couple of generals.'

'Take care your brigadiers don't get involved in some mild rape while they're here,' says Leo.

The plane is ready, and with sudden haste the people file towards it across the apron, Leo shakes both my hands and has tears in his eyes.

'Anne, darling, how I hate to leave ... you will look after yourself, won't you?'

'Of course, Leo.'

'Don't be discouraged, Anne, everything will turn out all right.'

'Everything is all right,' I reply, surprised that he should think me discouraged.

I watch the plane, remain looking at the sky. There is cloud behind the hills, and the mountains are hidden.

Chapter 13

THE Valley became grey-hot. The mountains disappeared. The clouds, jungle of the sky, feared by air pilots, had the snow peaks, abode of the gods. At first it thundered drily, lightning zigzagging across the rents in a steel heaven, then it rained; thick, ropy rain, falling with the sound of hurtling bodies upon the gardens, the streets, the palaces, the temples; rain in pails, in sheets, elephantine rain, solid and grey, with trumpeting blasts of wind suddenly from nowhere. The filth swelled out of the courtyards into the streets, the mud in the streets ran ankle-deep. The hills became waterlogged and sodden. Their water-riven flanks ran sheets of red mud over the new road, and finally cut through the road-bed. Sometimes a small hill would heave without warning and slither down, together with its boulders and trees.

In the cities of the Valley the Newaris huddled in their steaming, fetid, dungeon-like rooms below the overhanging carved balconies. There was little food and the grain to eat went mouldy in its sacks.

In the hills the Indian Engineers' unit sweated in their tents, and drew up the balance sheet of what the monsoon was doing to the road. Many people said the road would be entirely washed away in one monsoon. It was a point of honour with the Engineers to keep the road open. Whenever it cleared for a few hours they would go out with the bulldozers. Coming to the landslides the bulldozers would set to work, pushing and heaving the muddy soil in front of them until it had evened out, tumbling the extra mud into the ravines.

In the high mountains the winds held the sky in thrall, the air was a sea of cloud raging and breaking among the crests. There were gulfs and gorges, swirling vortices between the tremendous hosts of clouds rolling across the slopes. A great west wind blew and broke itself on Everest, throwing her snow plume that could be seen two hundred miles away. Sometimes the storms broke on one side of the mountains and left the other side dry, the clouds could not pass the high crest-lines.

In the Terai, the jungle of the low plains of Nepal, leeches flourished in the hot steam of the downpours.

'It rains leeches there,' said Father MacCullough.

The modern bulldozers which the Americans had brought lay half buried in mud washed up from the flooding streams. The river, the nefarious river, never content within its shallow bed, went swinging into a new channel overnight, leaving behind it twenty miles of boulders and slime and desolation along a length of a hundred and forty miles.

'My God, do we need that dam,' exclaimed Father MacCullough to Anne. 'Got to stop that river. It's absolute ruin. Famine in its wake every year.'

Every year it was the same. Like a pendulum the river went swinging its ominous, beautiful arc between two ranges of hills eighty miles from each other. Seven times in the last ten years it had changed its course, going west, then going east. In Khatmandu the peasants from the flooded valleys lay in the filth of the rain soaked streets and begged for food, and the ribs of the babies showed very clearly above their huge copper bellies.

This was the landscape of the monsoon; greyness of invisible sky, blotting of earth, the Valley floating waterlogged cities surrounded by sodden hills.

'Even my brain will be growing mushrooms pretty soon,' Father MacCullough pointed with sour delight to the green mould which grew on his shoes, on the books in the bookcase, on the statues and furniture of his school (also a converted Rana palace). 'The worst time of the year, until in September they chase the Rain God away, after that it's fine and sunny till the next monsoon.' He peered through the window, like a prisoner, at the sky. 'No planes today. Feel quite cut off when there's no letters for a few days.'

He walked with Anne downstairs, pointing cheerfully to the maps pinned on the walls which showed the swing of the flooded river charted by years, and watched her walk away to the jeep.

'You should buy an umbrella,' he called after her.

'Don't like them.'

'Those artists,' muttered Father MacCullough to himself. He wouldn't go out without his umbrella, but some people actually *liked* to be drenched with sky water. Unni for instance, went for long walks in the rain, came back soaking wet, sat in wet clothes, happy. 'If someone had told me, I wouldn't have believed it.' But Father MacCullough had seen him do it. He'd told Anne about it. He sighed and went back to his study. There was her cup, the stub of cigarette with lipstick on it which he threw in the wastepaper basket. I must remember to pray for them. Sad, very sad. Sternly he told himself again: fornication, a mortal sin. It wasn't adultery to Father MacCullough, since his Church did not recognize Protestant marriage. Just fornication. He should be shocked, more than he was, but in truth he was not shocked. If Father MacCullough had been shocked he could not have lasted very long in Khatmandu, and besides, charity did not consist in being shocked – but he must remember to pray for them. The ways of God were mysterious. The priest was shrewd in knowledge of the human heart, as are the truly great sons of the Holy Church, percipient enough to wonder whether through this love, illicit, immortal, but also beautiful in passion, in these souls satiated by sin, God might not through the very sin they committed open a way to His Grace. It had happened. The wondrous ways of God. Anne had become so much more approachable, for instance, dropping in to have tea with him, never done that before. ...

Father MacCullough went into a daydream in which both Anne and Unni were converted to the Faith and married each other, but he knew it was a dream the moment he started it.

Isobel was also dreaming, in her living-room, alone. The monsoon did funny things to her. There was little work. It was a very trying time. Put into a word, she always described it as 'trying'. Trying, to have fungus in your shoes, the cornflakes in the kitchen soaking, the jam mouldy, the butter dripping with water, the mattress damp, and all the mosquitoes in a cloud in the evening when the rain lightened. The Institute was closed, the girls stayed at home, the married majority started new babies, and when the Institute began classes again it was as if they had never been there. All the good work undone, they'd even forgotten the words of their prayers.

There were few tourists in Khatmandu during the monsoon. No explorers, no mountain climbers, no trekkers. Everyone was irritable and tired, even Vassili complained more of his liver. Isobel complained of her heart. She had attacks of panting, fits of weeping, the heavy damp was bad for her. In a corner of a monumental wardrobe, in a helter-skelter of shoes mouldering in an odour of wet dog, stood the bottles that she kept in reserve for these crises. One nip, just a small nip, then another. That was how it had begun some years ago. A doctor had told her to have a nip of brandy when she felt breathless, and she'd had attacks of breathlessness in her youth, rheumatic fever leaving a weak heart for which brandy was the sovereign remedy. In the monsoon there was little else, and the brandy made her dream.

That afternoon, sitting in her room, looking at the wardrobe furtively, wondering whether it was time to have another little nip, she heard the jeep. *That woman's jeep.* She went to the verandah, saw Anne driving to the back garden, to her bungalow. Under the wheels of the jeep the water splashed, insolently.

'Damned bitch,' said Isobel, shaking with fury, a passion which tore her to shreds. 'How I loathe her, wicked, dreadful woman, and *so* arrogant! And to think it was me, I, who brought her here. I who gave her the job, and the bungalow.' Now Anne wouldn't even stop; wouldn't even come in in the afternoon – the rainy on-for-ever-afternoon when she must *know* that Isobel was all alone, all alone, looking at the wardrobe. She wouldn't even come up the stairs and knock at the door and say hello. Drove straight on as if the place belonged to her.

Isobel opened the wardrobe.

'The whore of Babylon, the adulteress,' now in her bungalow laughing at Isobel, and she wouldn't even move away, though she knew she wasn't welcome. She stayed there, and in the silent night when it didn't rain hard Isobel could hear her typewriter tapping, tapping. Isobel sometimes prowled around the rose arbour at night, clad in a mackintosh, listening to the typewriter.

Isobel was feeling warmer now, with the brandy. Strongly the daydream took over. She saw herself rising, going to the Minister of Education. He would receive her – of course. Had not Isobel at the Royal Garden Party told him a few plain truths about his country, and had he not agreed with great politeness that all that she had said was correct? Now she would go and talk to him about Anne.

The Minister, tall, thin, opening the door for her, delighted to see her. 'Miss Maupratt! Do come in, of course I love to see you. We wouldn't know what to do without you here. The Girls' Institute, such a valuable contribution to the progress of our country.'

'I am afraid,' she would reply, 'that I've come to speak to you of something very painful. It concerns one of our lecturers – Mrs Ford.'

The Minister's brows would come together. 'Mrs Ford,' he would say, 'what about her?'

And Isobel would tell him. 'Most unsuitable. She's left her husband and she's behaving in a scandalous manner.'

And the Minister, indignant: 'I agree with you. Do you know who else is implicated in this disgraceful business?'

'Yes. I'm afraid it's that man Unni Menon.'

'He shall be deported out of Nepal in the next forty-eight hours,' the Minister of Education would say, crisply, perhaps ringing the little silver bell he kept on his desk.

And then Anne would come to her crying, no longer driving straight past in her jeep, but stopping, climbing the stairs (those long brown legs of hers running away, so many years ago, from her own mother), knocking at her door, saying: 'Isobel,' sobbing.

Flushed, feeling hot, sweating with triumph, Isobel was carried on, the dream no longer about Anne, but about herself, Isobel. A substitution preceded by the official deportation of Unni, but now Isobel was peering out of the window of Unni's room, and Unni was behind her, his arms closing on her. ....

Relentlessly as the rain, tapping like a gigantic typewriter, her mind was back at starting point: three years ago, a hot sultry three o'clock, heat dropping from the leaves, the sky blank, and silence but for the click click of her shoes on the gravel, going to the bungalow.

(But like a camera in reverse, spooling into the past instead of the future, there had been the morning scene, not included in the dream, a fugitive, lurking around the fringes of it, obstinately refusing to be shut out.)

'They're having a little music in front of Unni Menon's bungalow.' Dearest, industrious, sat in the morning classroom and reported on the flight of her companions. All the others out, like birds in the honeysuckle sun. Isobel walked towards the bungalow, felt the terrible devastation of this spring morning sweetness, but what she had seen on the lawn turned the sweetness into blind rage.

Evil, pure wickedness, lewdness ...

Laughter, music, dancing, people with flowers in their hair, Unni tapping a drum, those long dark hands holding the oval body of the drum, caressing the skin tight at both ends, tapping lightly, enticingly.

Something had snapped in Isobel's brain then.

She had returned and paced, paced, paced up and down, for hours in her room ... as she was pacing now, three years later, only now the heavens outside were pouring with grey rain, closely the dun curtains of rain encompassed the past, not letting go, never letting go, never letting her go free, except with brandy in the dream.

The pacing had stopped. She was sweating and yet shivering, and had walked out in the spring heat, in the afternoon. Three o'clock. Going towards the bungalow, hearing the click of her shoes, to 'have done with it, once and for all'.

'And I was right, I was right, I was right ... such sinfulness, leaving the classroom without permission, dancing right there in the sun ...'

The bungalow lay tree-lapped in drowsiness and heat. There was no one about. Even the grass was straight, one could not make out the imprint of those evil sinful bodies who had sat on it in the morning. The door was open. Isobel went up the stairs, cunning, agile, and stealthy. The door was to, unlocked. Craftily her fingers prised it open.

Unni was stretched in bed, naked, sweat glistening over his long body. And underneath his lay another, a woman's, with ash blonde hair. Piercing Isobel's sight, like nothing else had ever done, and now back again like an arrow in her pupil so that she said 'Ah!' with pain, she saw the white breast of the woman, enfolded in Unni's hand, only the nipple showing, like a bud plucked, his hand round it.

Suddenly his eyes were open, looking at her. Before she could move he was up, had drawn the sheet over the woman, saying: 'Someone's here, don't move,' seized a garment on the floor, holding it in front of him, walked to her, taken her wrist, and pulled her with him downstairs.

She had gone with him, only half unwilling. His hand round her wrist did not hurt her. He was taking her somewhere, and she followed. They came into the downstairs room. (Just as Anne now did he had used it as a sitting- and dining-room.)

'My dear Miss Maupratt, it is wrong to enter without first knocking.'

'It's filthy,' she had whispered, 'wallowing there, with that woman, it's a sin, it's horrible. Who is she?'

'That is irrelevant. You had no right to peep. Most un-missionary. Now you'll stay here until the lady upstairs is gone. I don't want talk about her.'

'Filth, filth, filth.' Isobel's head, body, was throbbing. 'How can you, how can you? And in the afternoon.'

'I like making love in the afternoon,' he had replied. 'Wait here until I let you out.' He had turned, she had seen the naked buttocks. He closed the door, she had stayed there, waiting, eager for his return, hearing the hasty steps of the other woman going away. Then the door had opened, but it was the servant, Regmi (the servant he had now given to Anne). Isobel had walked out, back to the Ruby Palace, in the hot, panting, dripping afternoon. She'd had a heart attack that night.

And the next day Unni was gone, moved out.

But the General had come to see her, and in his mild way, as if talking to air, had said that any stranger who defaced Nepalese property was liable to instant deportation. 'But drowning is also possible,' he had added.

And so the bungalow had remained untenanted and intact, except for some broken furniture Isobel had had thrown in the downstairs room.

Filth, filth, filth ...

Relentless, the long rapiers of the rain, piercing the earth, splashing watery stars.

But now Isobel, lolling on the sofa, bottle emptied, changed it all, changed the afternoon of three years ago and made it come right, added the true, necessary end, as it was meant to be, as it had to be. Here it was Anne, that body (the blonde hair changed to dark in the same glorious now-is-everything-made-right last judgement), and Unni pushing the body, slim, slack, out of his bed, until it fell thuddingly on the floor, the face grimacing with pain. 'I don't want you.' Unni held out his arms to Isobel, Isobel flying to him across the floor, treading on Anne, the body prostrate on the floor.

'Come, my beloved, my beloved.'

And then another scene. She was looking through the window of Unni's room, and there was Anne running away (she'd know those

395

brown legs anywhere), and behind Isobel Unni's hands, closing upon her breasts. 'Doves, twin doves,' and the plucked buds of the nipples issuing from the dark hands were hers, her own, and the agony and the delight hers, burning like burning water.

Relentless the downward blows of rain, hammering the earth. Hammer, hammer, something was hammering, somewhere.

'Come, oh come,' she shouted. She was panting. A mouth was opening, opening, inside her, twisting her body on the sofa. If only he would come, as she had seen him, come in from the rain, all wet and raise his hands.

The door opened, the face of the one who had been knocking came in, the olive, surprised face of Suragamy McIntyre's fiancé.

*

I go to tea with Father MacCullough [wrote Anne] and I think he is pleased. With coy excitement he shows me his books, his maps. Upon the deal table (the furniture has the usual monastic flavour) is a copy of *Mountain Peeks*.

'I suppose you get *Mountain Peeks*?' says the good Father to me.

'No,' I say, mesmerized by his obvious desire that I should read it into picking it up:

'FATHER MACCULLOUGH SPEAKS ON NEPAL. On Wednesday the Combination Tea Party organized by the Point Four Ladies' Get-Together and the Valley Club Cultural Group Meet-Up, after having won Father MacCullough's reluctant assent, presented him in person to our assembled members. What a thorough display of our free world co-operation! What a victory! What a turnout!

'Father MacCullough rose, but not until he had been further plied with tea and sandwiches delightfully served by Miss Spockenweiler, Miss Potter, and other members of the PFLG and the VCCG.

'The subject of Father's speech was the history of Nepal, and the gist of it was that Nepal is a pretty grand country and has been for a long time.'

'Oh, you mustn't believe all they say.' Father MacCullough is modest.

I try hard but find nothing, except 'Wish I'd been there.'

'I had to leave out the more ... hmm ... unmentionable parts of the history of Nepal,' he adds, again with that modesty which takes my breath away. Since the history of Nepal is one long record of palace intrigue, assassination, adultery, and atrocity sprinkling every main event, I wonder how much of it, expurgated by Father MacCullough, remained to excite the Ladies.

'The listeners left,' I read on, 'with an already healthy interest stimulated to the determination to read and learn further about Nepal.'

'What a pity I didn't know about this.'

'Well, now, I do think you ought to come out and mix more,' says Father MacCullough, 'keep in touch. I'm sure our Point Four ladies would be delighted, absolutely delighted. They're really very cultured, on the whole. I think they're conscious of their responsibility. Every American is a Point Four ambassador, that's my motto. I passed it on to them some time ago.'

Round us the rain, a dense curtain. Father MacCullough speaks of the floods. I close my eyes, and half my ears. Yesterday, because it brought me nearer to Unni, I went for a drive in the hills and was caught in a storm. Rain-ploughs rending the interstices of the hills, warping their contours, the cliff spilling squashily, sudden deep gashes in the firm slopes, running torrents of soil and friable boulder. It was very frightening to find the earth so unsolid, the water so irresistible. And then it stopped, and the hump-backed sun glowed in the puddles, a thousand sundrownings. And the rainbows came out, spanning hill to hill.

Father MacCullough talks of Unni naturally. 'He goes walking in the rain. Last year, would you believe it, I saw him coming all dripping, walking through the worst storm I'd ever seen. Came in here, sat in his dripping clothes on that chair. How he didn't die of pneumonia beats me.'

This is my reward, handed to me as to a candid child, for having come to tea with Father MacCullough, for having sat here, listening patiently. And I know the man kind, to have said this purposely. That is why I come here, go to the Royal Hotel, go to the General's insane grand salon and sit on the mammoth furniture. To hear them talk of Unni. And they always do. They know it makes me feel better.

Fracturing the stolid hours of the night, a loud banging, at first confused with the rain's rampage, Regmi's voice, someone screaming: 'Mrs Ford, Mrs Ford!'

'Who is it?' I call.

'It is me, me, Suragamy!'

Suragamy McIntyre. Regmi unbars the door. A settee and two arm-chairs have turned the downstairs room into a diminutive replica of the General's salon. But why should I insist on 'tasteful' surroundings and thus cut myself off from the wisdom and the wit, the urbanity and the easy goingness of the people who come to see me and who feel more at home on hideous plum plush?

Suragamy, dishevelled, twists her hands towards me. 'Mrs Ford, Mrs Ford, you must, must help me, I tell you. You are the only person who can help.'

'What is it?'

'It's Mutti,' she says. 'He is in trouble, terrible trouble.' She rolls her r's and her eyes and wrings her hands. Her neck snakes upon her shoulders and her hair swings down her back.

'Mutti?'

'Mutti Aruvayachelivaramgapathy, my fiancé. And Miss Mau-pratt. She is a wicked woman, a wicked, crafty, wily woman. The doctor is there, and the police. She says Mutti ...' Sobs break out of her.

'She says Mutti tried to assault her?'

'It is a lie, it's a great big damned lie, she's had her eye on Mutti for a long time,' says Suragamy McIntyre, entirely out of character. 'I tell you, she's man-mad.'

'Oh, come, come,' I say.

'You say that because you're a white woman too,' shrieks Sura-gamy. 'You always stick together, you whites. And they will put my Mutti Aruvayachelivaramgapathy into jail, yes, and shoot him or hang him, because he is not white.'

'Oh, for heaven's sake, you're years behind the times, you know. This is Asia. It's much more likely that tomorrow Isobel will be accused of trying to rape him.'

'But that's just what she has tried, man!' cries Suragamy McIntyre.

The scene at the Institute is in keeping with Suragamy's émoi.

There is a small knot of policemen in the corridor outside Isobel's room; they apply eye and ear to the keyhole, one after the other. Suragamy and I arrive and say 'Excuse me,' and knock at the door.

Another minion of the law opens, hesitates to let us in. I catch a glimpse of Fred and wave. We are admitted.

Isobel lies on the sofa, covered with blankets, breathing stertorously. Geography has a finger on her pulse. History pours tea. Fred stands with a stethoscope round his neck. The General and the Maharani sit in armchairs, as at a play. Two plain-clothes men in jodhpurs and Western jackets hover; one corpulent man in uniform and boots sits at a table writing. A beautiful young boy with a jaunty cap and a brand new camera slithers behind the sofa and takes flash bulb pictures of all of us. He slips each of us a calling card: 'Reporter-in-Chief, *The Khatmandu Times.*'

'Isobel,' I say. There is no reply.

History says: 'She's in a state of shock.'

'Don't touch,' warns one plain-clothes man.

'Finger-prints,' hisses the other.

The camera pops.

The Chief of Police (the man in boots) gives an order in Nepalese. Gingerly, a handkerchief wrapped round his hand, one of the two plain-clothes men picks up the empty bottle of brandy on the table. The Chief looks at it intently, then nods and starts writing once more. Another bottle is presented. He sniffs it, nods again.

'Dr Maltby,' says Geography, 'her pulse is getting faster.'

'You have been long acquainted with this lady, madam?' says the Chief to me.

'Miss Maupratt? Yes, I've ... we were at school together.'

'Ah ...' More writing. 'Is she a lady of good morals?'

'Oh, yes,' I say, 'excellent.'

'Ah. Rape,' he says impressively, 'a most revolting crime, if committed.'

'How many times?' asks the General.

'We don't know as yet,' replies the Chief of Police. 'Our investigations have only begun, General. They will have to be pursued to the very end.'

'Ah,' says the General admiringly, 'how fortunate our democracy in having you, sir.'

'My unworthy self is abashed, Your Excellency,' replies the Chief of Police, rising and bowing.

'The question is, I assume,' says the General, 'who raped who?'

'Of course,' says the Chief of Police.

Suragamy McIntyre bursts into violent tears again.

'That, indeed, is the question,' continues the Chief, his head going sideways on his shoulders.

'In these entanglements between a man and a woman, who can be wise?'

'Who indeed?'

The General and the Chief, born Lifemen, look at each other gravely. Fred, all doctor at the moment, is completely off track.

'Ayaaaaaaaah, my Mutti Aruvayachelivaramgapathy, I shall never see you again,' wails Suragamy McIntyre.

'Of course you will,' says the Chief of Police. 'In prison. Visiting hours every three days five to midnight for close relatives.'

Suragamy has hysterics on the spot, and History gives her a cup of tea.

'Doctor,' says the Chief of Police, 'can the lady now be moved?'

'I don't think so. She's ... in shock,' says Fred, looking apprehensively at the small mountain of Isobel snoring on the sofa under her blankets.

'In that case,' says the Chief gravely, 'we can wait. There are few crimes in Khatmandu during the monsoon.'

'Raping,' the General informs me, 'is usually accomplished in the spring and autumn. This case is out of season.'

'There may have been other elements,' says the Chief of Police, glancing frowningly at the bottles. 'We shall have to analyse the contents. For aphrodisiacs. Or poison.'

The camera pops again. The plain-clothes men also glare at the bottles. The General nods approvingly, and reminds us he was at one time Chief Judge in Nepal, 'when our methods were not so scientific. Then, madam, we would have submerged both sides in the Pond of Justice. An infallible method.'

Two bearers appear suddenly with cups of tea for the Maharani, the Chief of Police, the plain-clothes men, and the reporter. The General mutters: 'Whisky!'

The door bursts open and Vassili, Hilde, Enoch P., and John come in.

'Isobel ...' says Vassili, then stops short. 'Is she badly hurt?' he asks Fred.

'No, no,' says Fred. 'It's just shock. Er ...'

Vassili's eyes light on the bottles and look away again.

The Chief of Police has risen and is talking and laughing with Hilde. 'What a pleasure it was for me when Vassili was in my jail, madam.'

John is by the sofa's side. 'Isobel,' he cries, 'Isobel!' in agonized tones. Then to Geography: 'Is she all right?'

'Of course she is,' Geography replies acidly. 'Just shock, you know.'

'Oh, I'm so glad,' says John. The emotion he has brought with him into the room wilts on its own.

Enoch P. says: 'This is terrible, terrible.'

'Oh, please, please, Mr Bowers,' says Suragamy, joining her hands, 'he didn't do it. I swear he didn't. By all the gods I swear.'

'Suragamy, remember you're a Christian,' says History, indignantly.

'*She* raped him,' cries Suragamy. 'She tempted him. He is an innocent, a pure boy. Never would he think of such a thing by himself, never, never.'

'What's going to happen, Chief?' says Vassili.

'I have already apprehended one of the parties,' says the Chief of Police gravely. 'I am waiting for Miss Maupratt to recover sufficiently to remove her also. *Corpus delicti*, I think that is how you would express it.'

'Take her away?' say Fred, John, and Enoch together. 'Where?'

'To prison,' says the General. 'We always put both sides in prison.'

'But you can't do that,' says Enoch, John, History, and Geography together.

'She will have first-class jail, like you, Vassili,' says the Chief. 'I will attend personally to it.'

'But this is terrible,' cry History and Geography.

'This is monstrous,' says John. 'The Resident must be informed.'

'Mr Chief of Police,' says Enoch, 'sir, I'd have you consider that Miss Maupratt is holder of a British passport. She is a *European* woman.'

This is obviously the worst thing to say. The Chief of Police looks like a statue of stone. He is very angry. Hilde makes signs with her hands at Enoch and John to stop talking.

Suragamy twists her hands and shrieks: 'I told you so, I told you so, they will use their white influence, and my Mutti will die.'

'Nonsense,' says Vassili, 'nobody dies for rape. Only for killing cows.'

'But he will lose his scholarship, his U.S.I.S. scholarship,' says Suragamy. 'That is terrible.' She turns to Bowers: 'Oh, Mr Bowers, promise me you will help him. He is a pure innocent boy.'

Enoch P. looks very cold.

Isobel moans, turns round, and starts snoring again.

Fred, Hilde, and Vassili approach the frozen Chief. There are low expostulations. Hilde smiles. He unbends slowly.

Meanwhile John walks up and down, hands behind his back, an expectant father.

'I'm afraid this is serious, quite serious,' says Enoch P. 'I'll be involved.' Enoch is one of the two sponsors of Suragamy's fiancé for a scholarship to America. 'He appeared entirely suitable to me, very democratic.' But he must have had a bad streak in him 'to attack a defenceless woman'. Mutti's scholarship is done for.

The Chief of Police turns and gives an order. He has decided that Isobel, in view of her health, would stay at the Hospital, under police guard. Vassili and Hilde thank him profusely.

'How about a drink for you, Chief?' says Vassili.

The General's whisky bottle appears. The gathering round Isobel on her sofa shows signs of becoming a Royal Hotel party. Already the bearers hover with glasses in their hands. But Hilde pulls Vassili away firmly, and regretfully we all leave.

Outside the rain is like a deluge. Enoch catches up with Fred and myself and tells us that John will stay at the Institute tonight.

'The girls are very frightened,' he says, 'they'll feel better with a man around. I feel perhaps I ought to keep him company,' says Enoch, hesitatingly, 'except that Pat might get worried. Vassili will send over John's blankets and bedding in a jeep.'

The General laughs to himself and rubs his hands. 'Rape out of season, madam, is fruitful of much thought,' he says, as he and the Maharani under huge black umbrellas disappear in the rain.

*

'Bad show,' said Paul Redworth. 'Damn nuisance.'

Anne, Fred, the General, were at the Residency, summoned by Paul to a confidential meeting. It was a week after what was known in the foreign colony of Khatmandu as the Maupratt Affair, *The Times of Khatmandu* headlined it differently: THE AFFAIRS AT THE GIRLS' INSTITUTE. On the settee and the floor were strewn newspaper clippings, with translations, of the Nepalese press; three or four small newspapers which appeared spasmodically, but were now booming on what the General called 'this unseasonal copulation'.

'I've been re-reading *A Passage to India*,' said Paul. 'Quite incredible, you know. Here we are, thirty years later, and it's exactly the other way round.'

'And in Khatmandu, of all places,' said Fred. 'As if no Nepalese had ever heard of sex before.'

The General said: 'Someone is behind all this. I suspect much.'

With disgust and a growing feeling of dread, Anne read a translation: 'WHITE WOMEN WHAT ARE YOU DOING HERE? Unable to satisfy their lusts with their own eunuchs in the West, these demonesses come here where our men are virile ...'

'Ugh.' She put the paper back carefully on the rug, as if it were dynamite.

'It reminds me of the Tenzing business,' said Paul carefully, 'only much worse, of course.'

Fred was gazing at another clipping. It showed a picture of two bottles (Isobel's brandy bottles) with the caption: 'Containers of Love Philtres Forced upon Mutti Aruvayachelivaramgapathy.'

'Oh my God,' said Fred, 'I can't believe it. The Nepalese don't act that way. This is a put up job, obviously.'

'Perhaps that makes it more serious,' said Paul. The Resident was deeply worried. 'There have been such campaigns before, as you know. Political intrigues. Against the Indians, for instance, the Engineers building the road. Against the Americans and Point Four Aid.' He turned to Anne. 'You remember when we were on the road, Anne, how we laughed about it?'

'Yes, I remember.' How comical she had found Colonel Jaganathan and his 'mild case of rape' just after the Coronation! Only it wasn't funny now. It was ugly, dirty, sinister.

'It isn't the people,' repeated the General, 'it's the politicians. Agitators. People who want Nepal to be shut in again. Very few of our people can read, and so if it is political there will soon be trouble-makers around, making speeches. Fortunately it is rainy weather, so public demonstrations and riots are not so easy to arrange.'

'Oh, lord,' said Paul Redworth. 'What will the F.O. say?'

Anne picked up another clipping: 'What are all these self-styled friends of Nepal doing in Our Country? Under pretences of Aid they spy, they take photographs, they blast our mountains, kill our people, they treat Nepal as a conquered land. Officials in high position rape our women, and now their women are shamelessly depraving our men. Yet they come to be teachers of our own virtuous maidens! We hope to publish details of further true cases of orgies among these foreigners before long.'

'I know the Government is doing its best to stop this filth campaign,' said Paul. 'I've been assured that they'll take steps. It'll all blow over, but it's damn unpleasant. We've got to be most careful. Most. And anyway,' he added irritably, 'who fetched the police before coming to me about it?'

'I don't know,' said Fred. 'I was called by History and Geography, in terrible excitement. I found Isobel lying on the sofa, she had passed out. She was, quite frankly, inebriated, and her clothing disarranged, but not so that ... not enough to suspect violent rape,' he added.

'I can tell you how it began,' said the General, 'although I was un-present. The servants told me. Miss Maupratt was comforting herself with her usual invigorant when she heard knocking at the door. It was this young man – as you know, a great rascal whom in olden days I would have whipped – with two friends. Their intention was to ask Miss Maupratt to let them have permission to buy food for the Institute. Of course, they are trying to corner the little food there is, in the name of the Institute. There is a big shortage and many hungry people. The friends remained outside while the rascal penetrated in-side the room. Suddenly the friends heard lamentations and screams, and then the other two English maidens and the Indian one came hurrying to the door. The screams became worse, they opened the door and the young man rushed out. "Call the police, call the police!" shouted Miss Maupratt. The maidens also began screaming for the police, and the bearers were so frightened they ran to the police with-out thinking. The young man and his friends were afraid, they too went to the police, for in our democracy the one who complains first wins the case. The Chief of Police was by great misfortune inspecting the new Police Station for the first time. When he saw all these people in their jeeps he was forced to do something, instead of ignoring the matter as he would have done in other circumstances. He had to arrest the young man and his two friends, *and* also Miss Maupratt.'

'They should have called me first,' said Paul. 'I was kept out of this until much later, when Vassili came and told me.'

'I think, madam,' said the General suddenly, 'that it is good that your name does not appear. All the other ladies are named, but not you. That is fortunate.'

'It is,' said Paul. 'Let's hope it keeps that way.' He spoke abruptly, but redeemed himself with a kind smile. 'I'm sorry if I sound huffy, m'dear, it's nothing to do with you, but it's just that with the er ... rather inexperienced type of judges we've got here, the less people involved the better, don't you agree?'

'Of course, Paul.' She knew what was in his mind. It was in hers too. The dim fear, the dread, slow mounting. Her own case. She could already see it in the newspapers: orgies at night; white woman, coloured man. The squalor. And this time in reverse. Not John, a white man, screaming at her and calling Unni black, but the other way round, the Asians, people like Unni, getting exactly the same sadistic thrill out of the strong, heady mixture of Colour and Sex combined. But not in Khatmandu, not in the blessed, smiling Valley, so wise in the ways of humans and gods. It wasn't possible here.

But of course it could be whipped up. Like anywhere else. The inverted lechery of Colour-cum-Sex was a man-made perversion. Man would make himself believe the most fantastic lies, whether it was in Johannesburg, Tennessee, or Khatmandu. Everywhere a difference could always be phantasied into a monstrosity and a crime. And difference of pigmentation was the easiest to make a crime of, its obviousness most accessible to condemnation. There would be no thrill in the colour bar if it wasn't the sadistic thrill of the sex bar. The two *had* to go hand in hand. Love-making between two humans *must* be made into unnatural vice for the madness of racialism to be successful, anywhere.

'I'm sure it'll straighten itself out,' said Paul. 'But I'm afraid we'll have to go through an Inquiry, or some such thing. Though it will be in private. At least, I hope so. Nobody is sure. You see, there are no laws yet on this thing ... the new constitution isn't quite clear yet ... it's going to be quite a mess.'

'The weather is bettering itself,' said the General, as they came out of the Residency.

Anne looked round. The sun, shining faintly, dewily, the grass steaming a little.

'It's a break in the monsoon. We'll have a couple of clear days,' said Fred.

'The planes will be coming in then,' said Paul. 'They've been held up by bad weather.'

They were warning Anne. A break in the weather might mean Unni. He might be dragged into this. They'd rake up the past, Isobel's accusations, John.

As she drove back through the streets already she felt the Newaris' smiles derisive. At the Institute gate the porter sprang to attention, his wife, nursing her latest baby, laughed as the jeep went by. They knew about Unni. All did. And then her heart stopped beating. A jeep was there, unfamiliar; perhaps a messenger with a letter. There was at least one letter from Unni whenever the small airplane from Bongsor came to Khatmandu.

The bungalow door was ajar. No Regmi, no Mita. She climbed the stairs. Someone was there.

'Unni?' She was doubtful, yet full of hope.

'You've got the wrong name, but I'm still glad to see you,' said a voice, and looking at her was the fatuous handsome face of Ranchit.

*

I had not seen Ranchit for a month. The monsoon season is sociable, with teas and cocktail parties; but my 'situation' gives me a reprieve from many 'functions' where we're not invited together, John and I, and this is pleasant because time is short when I hoist myself from the typewriter to sleep and then find myself back at the typewriter again the next day.

'What are you doing here?'

'Need you ask, goddess. I come to see you. You must feel lonely without ... John.'

John has left three days ago. He has gone to Delhi to see a lawyer. His bachelor brother had died, leaving him money, the Calcutta flat, a mass of papers to sign. John has now become quite a hero, not only as protector of Isobel's virtue – he spent two nights at the Institute on guard – but also because it is now rumoured that he is fabulously wealthy with his baronet brother's demise, and an 'estate' in Sussex.

'I usually see people in the downstairs room,' I say, moving towards the door. 'Not here.'

'But I like it here. Here,' he waves his hands, 'where the walls are covered with the efforts of my beloved wife, and where, on this bed, the lovely woman I dream of reposes at night. It is sad to think of a beauty like yours neglected, goddess.'

'You're being offensive, Ranchit.'

'Offensive? Me? When I come to offer myself to you? I mean to be your lover,' he adds gravely.

I want to laugh, but laughter is dangerous. Ranchit is creating about us a heavy sexual atmosphere. And I am half fascinated. Since Unni, I have become susceptible to men, aware and curious about them. In the subterranean universe of sex I am now versed in the speculative look, the stimulating indifference, the expert tentacles of foreknow-ledge which envelop, appraise, discard; skill of the jungle tracker who can tell the passage of an animal and its direction by a bent twig, the twist of leaf. This awareness, older and deeper than any ethical or intellectual knowledge, flows through me; with it I know Ranchit disturbing, though vaguely loathsome; fascinating yet repulsive. He knows I know. He comes forward, near, not too near, making of the right distance between us another hold, like the exact separation of magnets.

'Tell me,' he says softly, dreamily, 'what does Unni do to you? How lucky he is, goddess ... to have plucked you frozen from the grave of the senses in which John had you fast and dead, to have brought you to life ... and look now, how beautiful you are. Lucky Unni. But I can do better. I can please you as you have never been pleased before. I can teach you things which your simple Unni would not dream of doing. And you are tempted, I know you are. For you are inquisitive, and you have imagination. I have seen you absorbed, reaching out deep into the nature of things, heedless of yourself. I want to see this trance on your face, in my arms. Will you not try, goddess, will you not let me show you the great mysteries of love?'

'You speak like a salesman, Ranchit. It does not become you.'

He is cut short in his canticle of eroticism. 'Oh fie,' he says, mincing a little, 'you are brutal like all foreign women, Anne. And I thought you different. Most of them are so ... coarse in love-making. It is amusing sometimes, but I felt you could be a real artist. You have the hidden charm of great courtesans. It is a pity to deny your gifts because of a stupid attachment to one man alone.'

I cannot reply. Because his words are reminiscent of Unni, in that short delirium five weeks ago when he returned from Bongsor and came straight to me. He was again in that perfect fury of passion for which there is no reasoning, no brake. Lust has its own innocence; and with Unni I can always be totally myself. I told him of my curiosity towards other men (a thing I could never have told John). As always he gave me a total and detached attention. 'How odd,' I said, 'now that I have you, it is easier to imagine my having a casual affair with someone else, where it would never occur to me before.' 'I don't think you'd do it, though you could, you are so wonderful to make love with. But women on the whole like to be faithful to one man.'

Now here is Ranchit. Half attractive, half repellent. I know I should be indignant, appalled, instead of being merely fascinated and curious. I cannot reply, and Ranchit presses on.

'How about offering me a drink?' he says gaily. (I have all the time in the world, his face proclaims.) 'Have you got any whisky?'

'No, I haven't,' I lie. 'Mita and Regmi ... by the way, where are Mita and Regmi?'

'My dear, I incarcerated them in the kitchen. Not to interrupt our conversation. I'm a Rana, you know, and they're still very respectful to us, very. I'll send my own chap to the Royal Hotel for some whisky, shall I? With ice, of course.'

That is too much. 'Get out,' I say, 'get out. This moment. Or I'll scream the place down.'

'Goddess, what is the matter?' says Ranchit. He is really surprised.

'Get out, I tell you, or I shall scream.'

He laughs, his falsetto ugly sound. '*You* call for help, goddess? Who will come, who will hear you? Run out, to the Police perhaps? Do you wish more talk about the Institute? About you and the men who come to visit you? Did you not wonder, Anne, why your name alone was kept out of the newspapers? It was due to me, my influence. I am a Rana, remember.'

'So you're behind this,' I say. 'Why? Why do this to Isobel?'

'I didn't do anything,' says Ranchit. 'I didn't rape her, did I? But the monsoon season is so boring, goddess. And now,' he stretches luxuriously, 'the newspapers may start on you, for a change. And everybody knows about Unni ... I need only drop a hint ... So, my dear, you must be reasonable and pleasant. Let us enjoy each other's bliss, and I promise you nothing will happen. Deny me, and read the newspapers tomorrow. About you, and what you teach the girls, and Unni. He'll lose his job, I promise you, when I've done with you and him.'

'You hate him. How you hate Unni,' I say.

'Of course,' says Ranchit. His complexion has gone leaden with hatred. 'He stole Rukmini from me. He steals all women, with his false air of chivalry and nobility. He is a liar, and a thief. I can do what I want with her body; but I cannot have her worship. He cast a spell on her, and she cannot forget him.'

'He did not touch her,' I say.

'That only makes it worse,' says Ranchit. 'To catch a soul is worse than to take a body. You don't know what it is to hold a shell of a woman, the heart gone, taken out of her by someone else. I've already had some revenge.' His eyes went round to the walls. 'She did that for him ... She won't touch a pencil again, I've seen to that. And I'll destroy Unni. I'll kill him in front of her one day, I'll ...'

Madness peers out of his eyes.

'You're all tangled up, Ranchit. I wish you could understand. Unni doesn't try to attract women.'

But that is too much for him. He screams with anger, a curious feminine noise, clenches his fists, bites his lips. It is like a fit.

And we might stay there, for ever, imprisoned by each other's presence, but that through the window I see two figures approach, and we go down together to meet them. It is Dearest and her father, the Rampoche of Bongsor.

'Ah ah,' says the Rampoche on a rising note, 'and with *Sri* Ranchit! What a pleasure!' It is obvious he merely thinks what comes naturally to mind, in Khatmandu or anywhere else.

'Mrs Ford it is such a long time no see and now my Daddy says must come to see you on our visit to Khatmandu and I hear you give private tuition during monsoon holidays I must have and my Daddy always thinking of you as one of our family.'

'A niece,' beams the Rampoche. 'I could not care more for your health and happiness, dear Mrs Ford, if you were my elder brother's youngest daughter.'

'My Daddy wants you to come to Bongsor for a week or ten days it would be excellent for your health truly Mrs Ford quite a few friends are coming every year we make big party and this year Mr Bowers and Mrs Bowers and the French lady Miss Valport and maybe others like Major Pemberton and Father MacCullough and Professor Rimskov who knows five words of Tibetan all bad and we are hoping you can join it will be very fine soon when monsoon is over.'

'We came from Bongsor by plane last week,' adds her father. 'Oh, the rain has been bad! A calamity everywhere. The goddesses are angry. I am afraid much of the work on the dam is washed away. The mountains are angry at all this interference. And there is a lot of fear and malady among the workmen too. I think a plague will come.'

'That's not surprising,' says Ranchit, 'all these filthy workers dirtying the valleys.'

(It is Unni they are talking about.)

'Well,' says Dearest brightly, 'these low classes are very lazy scamps really and we must sometimes beat them to make them work.'

'Join our tourist party to Bongsor, Mrs Ford,' says the Rampoche. 'You will not regret. It will give you a great stimulation to your writing. Although much trouble at the dam, yet all is peace and holiness in our Monastery.'

The three leave together.

I go to the kitchen to release Regmi and Mita, who come out contrite and weeping as if it was their fault they were shut up, and then walk as fast as I can go without actually running, to the Serene Palace to see the General and Fred.

There is a conference in the grand salon. On the three-seated contraption the General, the Maharani, Lakshmi; Fred and the Field Marshal in deep armchairs.

'Off with his head,' says the General loudly as I enter, ushered by the Tibetan handmaid.

'We were talking of the editor of a newspaper, madam, and his latest rascality. He has now demanded that the Hospital should be closed as it is debauching the nurses.'

Fred is very quiet.

'There is nothing to worry about, Doctor,' says the Field Marshal. 'It is a cabal, an intrigue, merely. Do not let printed words affect you so much; you know their value doubtful. In another week or so the whole plot will have foundered. It won't affect your patients,' he adds with a twinkle, 'since, fortunately, they do not read the papers.'

'The people don't read,' says the General, 'but I am tinged with alarm. After all has been stopped in the papers, rumours in the bazaar and elsewhere will take it up; word of mouth is more potent in our country than in others; and suddenly one day, after the monsoon, there may be trouble ... especially if the people are too hungry.'

The article on Fred, fresh from an afternoon paper (hence we did not see it at the Residency this morning), is being read by the Maharani and Lakshmi, who seem to find it extremely amusing, and burst into laughter, alternately veiling and unveiling their faces.

I tell briefly, omitting details, of Ranchit's visit. It is difficult to make it sound coherent, and the Field Marshal's steady look away from me, contemplating the carpet, makes me feel that he knows all I leave unsaid. I have been to see him during these last weeks, to borrow books, to talk of poetry, of philosophy, of the ways of Nepal and the rest of the world. But we have avoided the personal because our very friendship made it difficult for me to speak to him of Unni.

The General accompanies the Field Marshal home. The salon's largeness, pushing the walls away, isolates Fred and me from the rest of the world.

'An awful mess, Anne.'

'Don't worry too much, Fred. I don't think much harm will be done.'

'Hope not. Isobel, by the way, is quite crackers. You'd better go to see her. Might pull her together.'

'More likely to pull her apart.'

'Such a mess,' says Fred. 'It isn't really Isobel they're trying to hit. It's deeper than that. It'll spread. If this is political, then the next thing they'll go for is people like Unni and Mike Young, and the engineers on the road ... anybody who *does* anything new. There's an awful lot of feudalism and ignorance about, and it's easy to try to prove that natural calamities like floods and bad harvests are due to our meddling. ... Paul is worried about it all.'

He sucks meditatively at his pipe. He is longing to talk about Eudora. He misses her.

'I'll have to write and tell Eudora not to worry about all this,' he says, 'in case something leaks out. You know how difficult it is to keep anything bottled up once it's in the newspapers. It gets all distorted.'

'I hear things are not going too well at the dam,' I say.

'Did Unni tell you that?'

'No. The Rampoche of Bongsor.'

'I wouldn't put too much faith in what he says. He's just the kind of chap that would love stirring up trouble. He's afraid of losing his hold on the people of Bongsor. You can't build a dam and start paying people decently and building a small hospital and latrines and a school and some decent housing without creating a minor revolution. The dam might mean the end of His Preciousness, as far as influence goes, anyway.'

'Is that what Unni is doing?' I say, bursting with pride. 'He never told me. I want to see the place, don't you, Fred?'

'Oh yes, after the rains, when Unni's back, he might take you I suppose,' says Fred.

The next morning I went to see Isobel, now warded in the Hospital.

Isobel was in a dressing gown on the balcony, her arms folded, a favourite attitude.

Isobel looks older. She seems to have crossed the edge defining a still verdant middle age into the raddled, indefinite realm of those for whom there is no return of youth. It is not so much a physical change as a radiation. The look she turns on me is frayed and full of resentment. I would wish it less futile.

'Fred told me you were better, Isobel.'

'I've never been ill,' says Isobel with asperity. 'It was just shock. But I feel that I cannot carry on. I've tried my best, but I'm afraid this country is entirely given up to Satan and his works. ...'

'Oh, well,' I say, 'things like that do happen, they're awfully unpleasant, but I think they'll blow over. ...'

'If you mean what that monster tried to do,' replies Isobel, flushing as expansively as ever (even the backs of her hands now change colour), 'that's *not* what I mean. I mean the whole thing,' she brushes the landscape with her hand, 'the treachery, the baseness ...' she shudders, 'my own staff,' she says, tragic. 'My own staff.'

'Suragamy,' I begin ...

'And others,' says Isobel. 'Not only Suragamy.'

She obviously means me. Am I in combative mood? Not at all. I don't want to manufacture an artificial thunderstorm, to release her pent up hatred upon my head, I flatten myself like water, hands in the pockets of my jeans, eyes vague like mist upon the garden and the fields.

'All this would not have happened,' says Isobel, her voice shaking, 'if only ... if only people behaved like decent human beings, instead of ...'

She wants a fight. And now I don't mind fighting, inquisitiveness makes me pursue. After all, Isobel fascinates me. She is one of the characters growing within me, in this double pregnancy of mine. For with the human seed which now has taken root within my body is also the urge to create, in words, to fashion something as much a living part of oneself as my baby, wrung out of me by this sweaty urge to pour forth life in other forms than the biological cell. And this, which is perhaps our only claim to exist as human beings, a rung above other creation, came first, before Unni's child.

'Instead of what, Isobel?'

'Oh, you know.' She tosses her head equinely. 'Nothing of this would have happened, if I hadn't been betrayed ... if *you* hadn't taken advantage ...'

'Me?'

'You heard me.' Isobel tosses again, as if tossing off unpleasant memories. 'I don't suppose you'll listen, but I do feel that you've been responsible for *shattering* my work here. I hope you'll realize one day the harm you've done ... it's not for me, I don't matter ... but it's God's work we were doing here to try and help these people, and now it's all gone, all gone. Complete fiasco.'

'Then why did you give me the job? Why did you give me Unni's room?'

We're back at starting point. Back to the afternoon when she opened the golden orange world, forbidden fruit, to me.

'There you go again,' says Isobel, 'trying to head off your own responsibility. You've always run away from facing up to things, I know. I'm sorry, yes, terribly sorry that I ever did recommend you for the job. I suppose it was only human of me. ... I felt you might need the job, you wrote and asked for it.'

'No, Isobel. All this goes back further than that, to our school days.'

'Well, of course,' says Isobel, 'we were at school together. Of course that's why I recommended you ... how wrong I was!'

'Do you remember, Isobel, you and some others one night dancing round my bed and calling me a bastard?'

'Me?' says Isobel. 'Dance round your bed? But I never did that. Are you sure you're not making it up?'

'Quite sure. I remember it very well.'

'*I* don't,' says Isobel, 'and I would, if I'd done it. It's your imagination, I'm afraid. You *do* imagine things, you know. Things that aren't. That's why all these awful things have happened. Because you've let your fancy run away with you. You don't really know people, however clever you may think you are. You're not. You make mistakes ... whether you are deceived or you merely deceive yourself I wouldn't like to say. I don't want to get personal and anyway the whole subject is dreadfully repugnant to me – it would be to any right thinking person – but I was right when I said you were heading for disaster. It's already happened, and I'm afraid we're all suffering for it.'

'It depends what you call disaster,' I say. 'I consider my marriage to John was a disaster. And I don't see how anything that happened to me could possibly have brought this about.'

'But it did,' says Isobel, 'we're suffering now, because of you.'

'That's not true.'

'Not true?' says Isobel. 'If you weren't so blinded, Anne, so carried away by an insane, a ... a ... sinful way of life, you'd see more clearly what you've done. I hope the Lord will forgive you, Anne.'

'The truth is that you want to go to bed with Unni. You hate me because it's me, and not you, in the room, in his bed. And that's why all this has happened.'

Isobel does not flush. She breathes deeply, once. While I remain bewildered by my cruelty, she nearly smiles.

'Me, not you ... you, not me ... *you* think he cares, you think it's you he loves. Let me tell you, that man doesn't care about any woman. Except Rukmini. He loves Rukmini, not you. He's Indian. He takes things as they come, women as they come. I've seen it with my own eyes ... I tell you, I saw him there, lying on that bed, your bed, with a woman under him ... and he was covered with sweat. You think you're the only one ... why, at the dam, right now, he's probably in bed with a Tibetan girl.'

'I don't care if he has twenty women, so long as I'm one of them.'

We've come right down to earth, right down to the primitive, amoral, ferocious female, more ruthless than any man could be.

Returning, the sun is hot. There is no breath of wind on the lawn, where Regmi (still much subdued) is pulling a table and two chairs for lunch in the shade of the trees.

'The Master is back,' he says.

Unni has come back. The scene is nearly domestic. Thus I used to wait for John to come back, for lunch.

I shower and change, do my hair, and watch Unni through the window coming towards the bungalow.

I hear his voice asking Regmi, Regmi telling him I am upstairs. His step, and he is there, at the door, waiting a little, then coming in, smiling, happy, saying, 'Oh, how nice you smell,' and instantly amorous again.

'Oh no Unni, not before lunch.'

'I'm more hungry for you than for lunch.'

I give in. But something has happened to me. We kiss, he is eager, I respond; but only part of me; another me, clear, all too clear, cold, and untouched, observes; I make the necessary adjustments to his body's movements, his changes of mood. I have closed my eyes, but open them from time to time, rapidly, to gauge the stage at which he has arrived. I find his expression, at first gentle, ardent, changing slowly as he multiplies his efforts to please me without attaining his aim. I feel absolutely nothing. It is not unpleasant; not the nausea-making, painful forcing of John. It's just that I feel nothing at all. For a while I think that I might act again, pretend the orgasm I know now I will not attain ... but if I did he would know, and not forgive me.

'Darling,' he says, stopping, 'what is it, do I not please you?'

'I don't know ... I'm tired.'

Swiftly, neatly, without a sound, he ends and leaves me, drawing the sheet upon me as he does. As he turns to put on his clothes I see his back, glistening with sweat.

He gives me a cigarette, lights it, says: 'Shall I see you downstairs for lunch, later?' He walks out of the room. I find him, waiting for me on the lawn, throwing up and down his little charm, and staring at the mountain opposite us.

Lunch is pleasant, I eat heartily. I discover a new Unni, or rather, rediscover the old one, the one of the first days: distant, with small talk and courtesy, unreachable. What a charming man he would be, anywhere in the world. I tell him so. 'You know, Unni, you're really terribly attractive.'

He smiles, and I feel again how physically attractive he is.

After lunch, I don't know what to do. For the first time we have nothing to say to each other. Unni smokes. I can practically hear him think. But I can do nothing to help him. At last he says:

'Can't you tell me what it is?'

'I don't know what it is.'

'Have I annoyed you in any way?'

'No. Unni, I ... I think it was Isobel. But I can't talk about it.'

He looks at the mountain. There are dark clouds coming up. We'll have some more rain, before evening, to relieve the heat.

'What did she say?'

'You know she herself wants you, I suppose?'

'I know. It's in the newspapers too.'

'In the newspapers?'

'Yes. Ranchit has made good his threat to you. Half a page devoted to my misdeeds among the staff of the Institute. Think of it, Isobel, Geography, History, and Suragamy ... and you.'

'So you know about Ranchit coming here?'

'The General told me this morning, while you were with Isobel. I don't know, however, what she's said to you.'

'It's all horrible, I don't want to think of it.'

'Let's leave the subject. You have to go to the Inquiry tomorrow morning.'

'I didn't know.'

'I do. I saw the Chief of Police also while you were Isobelling. And I shall have a talk with Ranchit tomorrow morning.'

'As usual, you've thought of everything.'

'Not everything, since I appear to have lost something in the process.'

'Don't sound so melodramatic,' I say sharply.

I don't know what is the matter. I only know that it is because of Isobel.

We go out driving, and later to the Royal Hotel, where Hilde and Vassili greet Unni with exclamations of joy.

'Unni,' cries Vassili, 'what's this I hear about you? The whole staff of the Girl's Institute, that's good going.'

'History and Geography will never live up to it,' says Hilde.

The bearers grin admiringly. Mariette Valport drapes herself round Unni.

'Unni. I am so 'appy to see you. You 'ave been away so long ... why don't you come to see me sometimes now, you naughty boy?'

Then Mariette embraces me. 'And Anne, 'ow well you look ... may I call you Anne? *Comme elle est jolie* ... no wonder I never could get anywhere with you, Unni.'

Unni disengages himself gently, gives her a tap on the bottom. 'Go away, Mariette.'

'She's got good hips,' he muses, in answer to the look I throw. I am mortified, jealous, and hurt, all at once.

Enoch Bowers nods to us coldly. Pat appears, cuts us dead, and goes to sit by Enoch, who greets her effusively, pulls out a chair, appears to hang on her every word.

'They're always like a couple of love birds,' says Hilde.

There are two sharp lines between Pat's brows, a perpetual puzzlement.

We dine, we dance. Unni dances with Mariette also, and with Hilde, I with Vassili. When Unni holds other women in his arms, I want him dreadfully; but when he sits near me something hard, resentful, is between us. What is it? We go home together; to bed; I lie in his arms but he does not make love to me, and I hate him because he does not, and if he did I would repulse him. In the palpable darkness he breathes evenly, holding me in the crook of his arm. I am safe with him, yet I don't know what he thinks, I do not know what he is going to say. I too have lost something. And all because of Isobel.

Chapter 14

THE Inquiry took place the next day, in the General's grand salon.

'Don't be worried, my dear,' said Paul Redworth to Anne, who called at the Residency first. 'Our friends the Nepalese are really doing this very well, very well indeed. They wish to clear up everything very quietly. It's strictly a private chat, don't you know, the less one talks the better. I've had a few minutes with Isobel and I've told her everything is just a misunderstanding. I do hope she'll take my advice.'

There were two clerks with one pen between them sitting at the monumental marble-topped table; three policemen, weaponed with dripping umbrellas, at the door; History and Geography on a settee, affecting not to see Suragamy McIntyre accompanied by a tall thin young man ('my lawyer') and a crowd of female relatives, all talking all the time, armed with smelling salts, plastic handbags, extra shawls, coats, cigarettes, bouquets of flowers, and several of those wreaths wrapped in cellophane paper that in India and Nepal are put round the necks of heroes, visitors, bridegrooms, Prime Minister Nehru when he climbs in and out of airplanes, and visiting diplomats from any part of the world. They formed a solid, seated phalanx, openly confronting History and Geography. They did not appear hostile to Anne, who was informed by the most voluble of the lot that the wreaths and bouquets were destined for the fiancé 'when he has triumphantly won his case against that wicked woman'.

The General and the Field Marshal now came in, with a rotund short man, whom the General introduced as a Magistrate and 'my nephew, madam, they magistrated him because he is afflicted with much offspring'. Finally, swaggering, oily hair streaming with perfumed brilliantine, accompanied by two young men ('Lawyers, by their smell,' said the Field Marshal), and his two friends, the fiancé. Regmi, who had come out of curiosity, and other servants, began moving chairs and sofas and armchairs until there was a row of seats spaced along each wall. At the large table two Gothic armchairs were occupied by the Magistrate and the Chief of Police. Now, in close succession, Fred, Isobel, and Dr Korla, the small Nepalese doctor, friend of Fred, who operated and treated his patients in the courtyard of a local temple, filed in. Enoch Bowers and Vassili also walked in and closed the door behind them.

'Where is Unni, is he not coming?' asked the General.

'He drove me here, but he has something else to do,' replied Anne.

The policemen began pushing out a few of Suragamy's friends, who protested volubly. One of them ran back to pass a wreath round the fiancé's neck, and all the others clapped.

'They can wait downstairs,' said the Magistrate. He invited the Field Marshal and the General to sit at each end of the table as impartial umpires, and the hearing began.

'This is really the strangest procedure I've ever seen,' said Anne to Fred. 'Why is the Magistrate starting with Vassili?'

'Just to get warmed up,' replied Fred. 'It may look odd, but believe me, these people are clever and wise in their own way. They're doing their best, they haven't really got their judicial procedure worked out yet, so we mustn't compare with our own systems. They'll sort things out.'

'You sound just like Unni,' said Anne, 'when you say that.'

'We are usually so intolerant of people who do things differently. They get results just as quickly and efficiently their own way as we do in ours.'

Vassili's evidence was very brief. He had been called, he said, by a bearer, and had come 'with my wife, who is busy at the moment', and found everything, he said, already in the able hands of 'His Excellency, the Chief of Police'.

Well satisfied, the Chief of Police nodded, and passed on to the next witness, the General.

'My worthy friend has said all,' said the General. 'I was also called, to find that His Excellency the Chief of Police was already there.'

'Most praiseworthy speed,' said the Magistrate, and the Chief of Police got up and bowed.

At that moment a commotion at the door ushered in Paul Redworth, who mopped his brow, excused himself for being late. The Chief of Police beamed at him.

'You're the next witness,' the Magistrate informed him amiably. 'Just say what you saw.'

'I saw nothing,' replied Paul, 'as I was called late, and everything was already in the hands of our excellent Chief of Police.'

Things were going swimmingly. The Magistrate and the Chief of Police wagged their heads and smiled at each other. The Magistrate then called on Anne, who said she had been called by Suragamy.

'And what did you see?'

'I ...' began Anne.

A discreet cough from Paul Redworth gave her warning.

'His Excellency was there,' she said, 'everything looked quiet and orderly.'

The Chief of Police positively rubbed his hands with glee.

'Medical evidence, next item,' called the Magistrate.

Fred and Dr Korla got up.

Dr Korla was asked what his analysis of the contents of the two bottles (produced by one of the clerks) were.

'After due analyses and much prayer and thought,' he replied, he had come to the conclusion that it was an 'invigorant for the heart'. 'I have examined the lady in conjunction with my eminent colleague, Dr Maltby, and I found she was suffering from heart disease and general weakness,' he concluded.

Fred confirmed that Isobel was 'in a state of shock' when he had seen her. 'I have nothing to add to what my able colleague has just said.'

Dr Korla and he bowed to each other, and they sat down.

'Oh, Fred,' whispered Anne, 'this is wonderful.'

'Hush,' said Fred. 'The art of lying without lying, Father MacCullough will tell you, is one of religion's chief accomplishments. The Jesuits are magnificent at it.'

'Why did they ask Dr Korla?'

'Unbiased testimony from a Nepalese. We're all whites, aren't we? Only natural we should stick together, lie to save one of ours ... it's been done before, in British India. The Nepalese remember. That's why. It's to save us from ourselves.'

'How nice they are,' said Anne.

'Madam Maupratt,' said the Chief of Police. 'She can give evidence sitting down, I understand she is too weak to get up.'

The three lawyers, the fiancé, his two friends, and Suragamy snorted heavily and nearly together.

Anne found herself, like everyone else, craning slightly forward to listen to Isobel.

'Miss Maupratt,' said the Magistrate, taking over from the Chief of Police, 'did you give this man permission to buy food for the Institute?'

'Not a bit,' said Isobel.

Suragamy McIntyre broke out in indignant chatter. 'That is a lie, my Mutti helped her to buy many things. During the Coronation my Mutti ...'

'Ah-ha,' said the Chief of Police, 'that is just the point. We have here a receipt signed by Mutti Aruvayachelivaramgapathy for five hundred gallons of petrol during April and May, purchased under our controlled price. Did you purchase five hundred gallons through this young man, madam?'

'Certainly not,' said Isobel indignantly. 'I merely asked him to get fifty.'

'Ah-ha,' said the Magistrate and the Chief of Police together, and they smiled to each other more than ever, as if to say: see how clever we are.

'But sar, but your worship –' said one lawyer, springing up.

'We protest,' said the other two lawyers.

'Case closed,' said the Magistrate briskly. 'Mutti Aruvayachelivaramgapathy, we detain you for forging and obtaining, under false pretences, five hundred gallons of petrol, controlled price, for your own private uses, and for assault upon the person of this noble lady when she refused to allow you to purchase food in the name of the Institute for private use; and for maligning the good name of this noble lady, and for making false charges against her honour. I think that's all,' he added, turning to the General and the Field Marshal.

'It is,' said the Field Marshal and the General together, happily.

'Well,' said History to Geography, 'they didn't even call for *our* evidence.'

'I thought ...' said Geography, depressed, 'I thought it was going to be ... quite different.'

'How different, madam?' inquired the General.

'Oh ... you know.'

'Surely, madam,' said the General severely, looking at History and

Geography in turn, 'you *could* not expect the soul of honour that is the Chief of our noble Policemen to mention such ignoble things as sexual encounters in front of virgins like yourselves and Madam Maupratt? And besides,' he added, seeing them thoroughly crushed, 'rape is out of season during the monsoon.'

Outside the clouds were thick and darkling. The break in the monsoon was over.

Anne hurried back to the bungalow. Relief flooded her. Now she wanted to see Unni, she wanted to run to him, tell him everything. What a fool she had been ...

'Unni,' she called, 'Unni.'

But there was only Mita, dusting her room. 'The Master has gone out.'

'I'll wait.'

He would come later, like yesterday, and how different this time. She would say: Oh, darling, and tell him all that had been bottled up. ... She felt slightly dizzy, tremulous, and strangely tired. She would show him the foolscap, piling up slowly, her new book. 'You see, darling, because of you, because of the happiness you gave me, I can write again.' She could write again, live again, body and spirit, both. Flower of the body and flower of the imagination, blossoming. She would tell him, slowly, the wonderful, sweet secret, the life beginning in her ... as if (smiling at her own feeling of wonder) this was the first time in the world that anyone was having a baby. My soul doth magnify the Lord. How well now she understood the words! Every mother should feel like that. Behold, she thought, a woman fulfilled.

She did feel a little giddy. This morning, rising, she had had a slight blackout. Suddenly everything had gone dark, but only for a second, she had recovered immediately. It's happened twice in the last two days. It's the baby. I'll lie down. Lying down, she felt better, felt herself uncommonly lucid and clear, thinking clearly, seeing everything so clearly.

My dearest, she thought, how blind, how wicked and egotistical I have been! I came to you, to ask you to help me; and you gave me love, tenderness, your human warmth, and sympathy. And then, because of a few words from Isobel, because of a past full of childish fears and hatreds, I had to hurt you, try to hurt you. What it is now that started this I do not know ... was it Isobel saying she saw you with another woman, here? And what of that, I did not even exist then, why should this come between us? And even if now there were someone else, *also*, that you care for beside me, I think I would understand, I would have to learn to accept it, somehow ... though it would be hard because I am a woman and I love you. But I would hate to restrict you, to cut you down to my own measure, to make you fit me like a garment, for you are yourself, and I must love you as you are. I must learn to love, she thought, I do not know how to love, not really, not as Unni knows. That is really the whole trouble with us, with Isobel, John, Leo, myself. But Unni, and Rukmini, *they know*. They know how to love, love with generosity and gentleness and abnegation, asking not for tomorrow, asking nothing. ... I must learn from them.

His step and he was there, before she could rise.

'Oh, darling,' she said, half crying, holding out her arms to him to be held close. 'Look after me. Please forgive me and take care of me, I am such a fool.'

'You're a woman with wonderful gifts and always yourself, and I am so grateful that you have chosen me,' he said, stroking her hair.

'You don't know, Unni. You don't know.'

'Of course I don't know everything,' he replied, 'but I have faith in you, and that is enough.'

'I've hurt you.'

'No,' he said, 'truly, you have not. How could you hurt me, when I accept you as you are? How can you hurt me if I love you? Even if you were to send me away now, to say: I've done with you, I would go smiling and happy because this has happened and cannot be taken away. I think I must have done something wonderful in a previous life to deserve the happiness of you.'

'How can you love me?' she said. 'So many other women are more beautiful and attractive than I am.'

'I don't know. But I did not love deeply until now, and that is true, you must believe it.'

'I believe you,' she said.

'And don't think you owe me any reciprocity,' he added, holding her from him, 'because you don't. You aren't going to be guilty, or responsible, for anything I feel or do.'

She laughed, raised her head, raised herself from the bed, and felt giddy again, so dizzy she wanted to fall.

'What is it?' said Unni. 'Are you not well?'

'It's nothing. I'm a bit dizzy. I'm probably hungry. Let's go downstairs to lunch.'

But at lunch she could not eat a mouthful, she felt nauseated.

'I think I'll lie down,' she said, holding off the delicious moment of letting him know about the child.

He came round to draw her chair, and then she noticed his left hand, swollen, daubed with red.

'Oh, what is it, Unni?'

'It's an argument I had with Ranchit this morning.'

'I had forgotten ... what an absent-minded person I am,' she cried. 'Did he hurt you?'

'No. We just hit each other a bit, though I tried to be polite as long as I could.'

Everything he said or did appeared to her funny. Laughing, she began climbing the stairs, and suddenly, lifting her foot, was rent by pain, doubling her up, making her scream. He was behind her instantly, supporting her, or she would have fallen. The pain was unbearable, she could not speak.

'What is it,' he said, 'what is it?'

'Lie ... down,' she whispered, racked with pain.

He carried her upstairs, laid her on the bed. She kept her hands on her belly, where the pain was subsiding slowly and instead she could feel the slow beating pulse of her own blood, filling her belly from within, and she knew what it was. Putting up her hand to Unni's face, touching it gently, tracing the contour of the forehead, cheekbones, mouth, she said: 'Darling, I'm so sorry. You'll have to call Fred. I've just ruptured inside. It was your baby, I'm afraid.'

Pain, lapping up like a surging tide, Geography with the hypodermic saying 'There, there,' soothingly, and feeling, after a while, the pain recede, and drugged sleep.

Nightmares, vision of the red bottle dangling above her, and then suddenly consciousness, discomfort and pain, and the shape of Fred in white gown, fluid to look at, saying: 'Now you'll be up in no time.'

'Fred, it was the other tube that the baby was in, wasn't it?'

'Yes, Anne. Quite an early one. Ruptured ectopic.'

'That means I can't have any more babies now ... a woman's only got two tubes.'

'Don't worry about that now, Anne.'

'Where is Unni?'

'He had to go back to the dam, after he knew you were all right, right after the operation ... he'll be back as soon as he can.'

Sweat. Tired already after a few words. She closed her eyes. She heard Geography's whisper and caught its drift.

'What about John?'

'John's back. He's sent you some flowers.'

'Does he know?'

'No. We said it was appendicitis.'

Geography nurse, and Geography school teacher, two different beings. Watching her deftly propping her pillows, Anne thought: the Field Marshal says the gods are projections of ourselves, and that each of us is a crowd. Geography the nurse is wonderful and good, showering happiness in this hospital. Her pale freckled hands are deft and kind and filled with soothing, healing power.

'I hope your feet don't hurt today?' said Anne.

'No, dear' (to Geography every patient was 'dear'), 'how did you know my feet hurt me?'

'That day, when we went on a picnic, the blind child, remember?'

'They never turned up with that baby,' said Geography. 'It's certainly dead by now, poor wee mite.'

She laid Anne back gently on the raised pillows; took a com' and began to comb Anne's hair, adjusted her nightgown. The room was full of flowers.

'See how popular you are,' said Geography archly. 'My, what lovely blossoms. So hard to get too, in Khatmandu.' There was a bunch of mountain irises and little white daisies. 'My my,' said Geography, 'someone must have gone quite high up to get these. No name, no card. I wonder who it is, don't you? You might have some visitors today, I guess. Doctor said you could if you wanted to.'

'How is Isobel?' asked Anne.

'She's fine,' said Geography heartily. Mention of Isobel altered her, snapped her back into her other self. 'The newspapers were fined, you know; the whole thing blew over; that dreadful man was deported out of Nepal. We're reorganizing the Institute, and re-opening next month. Isobel is very busy trying to get someone in place of Suragamy. By the way, your husband's asked if he could come to see you. I hope that's all right?'

'Certainly,' said Anne. 'I'd like to see John.'

Geography suddenly looked angry and walked out.

Anne looked at the irises, the white small daisies in clusters. Whoever had sent them, they meant so many things, visions of the summits, the snow peaks, blue sky, and icy summits ... she must have fallen asleep and when she woke it was abruptly, startled to find Unni standing watching her and John just walking into the room.

Only in real life, thought Anne, do things happen like that. Meeting between husband and lover in front of wife's sick-bed. No novelist would dare to write this down for fear of cheating.

'How do,' said John.

'Hello, John.'

'I'm back from Delhi,' said John, turning his back upon Unni. 'Sorry to hear you've had appendicitis. You look quite fit to me. Fred Maltby says you'll soon be up and about. That's good news.'

Now or never.

'I haven't had an appendix,' said Anne. 'I've had ... another ectopic pregnancy.'

'Oh, don't make up things, Anne. You're dreaming, you know.'

'I'm not.' She was already exhausted by the effort of talking to John, of finding, once again, this wall that was John, blocking her view, blocking all avenues towards the adventurous, the free highroads of imagination, by his own being. He's always done that, just by being himself, by talking and thinking the way he does. He's always given me that feeling of helpless rage. ... She turned to Unni. Her eyes said: You must do what you think is right. For both of us.

'John,' said Unni, 'it was my child that we lost, Anne and I.'

'Oh, balls,' said John. 'What is this big ape doing here anyway?' he asked Anne. 'Tell him to get out of here. I'm your husband. Not him.'

'Let us both get out,' said Unni. 'Anne is not well. We can talk outside.'

427

'I won't go out, I'll stay right here. I'm her husband. I've got my rights and I want them.'

'Oh, balls, as you say,' whispered Anne, laughing with rage and exhaustion.

'You may think me old-fashioned,' said John, 'but I believe a wife should keep her marriage vows. Laugh at me if you will, but I believe in the sanctity of marriage.'

'How many prostitutes,' said Unni, 'did you have in Delhi, John?'

'That's a filthy lie,' shouted John. 'How dare you talk to me like that? I'll bloody well knock your face in.'

'Here, here.' Geography appeared, brisk, bustling. 'Who's making all this noise? Oh, John … I'm sorry, but you mustn't talk too loud as Anne is still quite weak, you know. I think you'd better go out, and you too,' she added, giving Unni a hostile look. 'You poor thing,' she rushed to Anne, 'look at her, covered with sweat. Shall I put some cologne on your forehead, would you like that?'

'I wish John wouldn't talk as he does,' said Anne, 'it really makes me want to throw up.'

'Oh, he wouldn't be so bad, in the right hands,' replied Geography.

'I want to talk to you,' said Unni, keeping pace with John swiftly walking downstairs.

'And I don't want to talk to you,' said John, hurtling himself down the steps. 'I've got nothing to say to you. I'm going to take proper action with the authorities. I'll write to the Aid people and get you fired.'

Unni reached out a hand and pulled him by the tie. 'We talk, now,' he said. 'Or I'll punch you until you won't leave the Hospital.'

John lunged at him, Unni stepped back. John came another step forward, and Unni dealt him a blow which glanced off the side of his head. John kicked Unni in the stomach, and when he was doubled up hit a fist into his left eye, but Unni had caught John's legs and pulled and brought him crashing down, then put a knee on his chest and seizing his ears knocked his head hard, twice, against the stone floor.

'Now will you talk,' he said, 'now will you talk?'

'You brute,' cried John, stunned, 'you brute.' His fists came forward, he punched Unni in the stomach again.

Unni got up and kicked him in the ribs twice.

'God,' cried John, and rolled on his side, groaning.

'Now will you talk? Or do you want some more?'

'You brute,' said John, gasping, 'striking a man when he's down.'

'We talk, or I kick your teeth in.'

Round them, at respectful distance, a circle of hospital attendants and patients, who clapped hands at the spectacle, shouting: 'More, more, more!'

John got up, doubled with pain. 'I've got a broken rib,' he announced, groaning.

'Never mind that,' said Unni. 'We talk.'

'Kicking a man when he's down.'

'In here. This room is empty.' He pushed John into a room similar to Anne's, a private ward on the ground floor. A nurse ran up, protesting. 'I'll borrow this room for a few minutes' talk,' said Unni.

'But it's a room for private patients.'

'There may be one patient in it by the time we've finished our talk.'

The Nepalese nurse burst out laughing, while the more able patients surged out of the building to surround the balcony upon which the ward opened, hoping for another fight.

John dropped in the armchair. Unni sat on a chair, astride, his hands on the back, which he had turned, facing John.

'I love Anne, and I am her lover. This was my baby. Will you give her a divorce?'

'Not on your life,' said John. 'I mean to destroy her, and you too. The wicked must be destroyed. She's an immoral, a vicious woman. She must be punished.'

'If I hit you again,' said Unni, 'I'll probably kill you. Is this final? Will you divorce her, and cite me?'

'You'd like that, wouldn't you? You dirty nigger, you'd like to go round with all your filthy friends saying you've — a white man and taken his wife from him?'

Unni got up. 'Get out,' he said, opening the door, 'before I murder you.'

John gave a sneering laugh, now he knew he was safe. 'Menon,' he said, 'this isn't the end. I'll make you pay for this. Just you wait and see.'

Fred was in Anne's room when Unni walked in again.

'Oh,' said Anne, looking at Unni's swollen face. She laughed weakly.

'John and I had an argument.'

'You seem to have a good many these days,' said Fred. 'I had to treat Ranchit after your argument a few days ago. He's flown to Calcutta to have some teeth replaced, I'm told. What have you done to John?'

'Kicked him when he was down. Most unsporting. He told me so.'

'D'you think he'll need me? I've got out-patients this afternoon.'

'He says he has a broken rib.'

'Well,' said Fred, 'the patients and the staff had a good time. Don't get too tired, Anne dear. All this emotion is bad for your insides.'

'What did John say?' she asked, when Fred was gone.

'Marriage is of supreme sanctity. The marriage bond indissoluble and holy. He will hang on to you.'

'Poor chap,' said Anne. 'It doesn't really matter, does it? I'm yours, not his.'

'It would matter if you had lots of children and were financially dependent on John, and I could be fired as he's threatened to do. As it is, it will merely be inconvenient. Some people will cut us dead. Which won't hurt us too much.'

'I suppose I'll have to resign,' said Anne.

'Are you worried,' asked Unni suddenly, 'are you worried because we won't be married?'

'No,' said Anne. 'You weren't going to, anyway.'

'Only because I thought it wasn't right to fetter you again in wedlock. But now I'll marry you any time. I want to. And I promise never to hold you down. Never. I love you too much for that.'

Anne said dreamily: 'I would have liked your baby. Married or not. And now I'll never have any children. Never. I don't feel bad about it, not yet. But what about you? All Asian men want sons, don't they?'

'There,' said Unni, 'I've again been too clever. I already have two sons.'

Anne sat up so suddenly that she fell back again with a groan, having forgotten her stomach. 'You never told me.'

'I have so little to conceal, that I must sometimes not speak otherwise you'll get tired of me too quickly. I was married at sixteen and a widower at eighteen, having killed the girl-child I was married to by my family with too much love-making and two children in two years. She had heart disease and no one knew it, least of all the young and impatient male I was.'

'You mustn't feel bad about it,' said Anne, 'it wasn't your fault.'

'I don't feel bad or guilty. Our society puts a lot of the burden of our individual guilts upon fate, the wheel of rebirth, and so we are less demanding of our destinies and more trained to accept what happens. We don't feel responsible for anything except the responsibility of being true to ourselves. But this marriage and its death stopped me from falling in love, until I met you. It is a simple brief story,' said Unni. 'Please accept it.'

'I do accept it.'

'I love you, Anne. It is something which keeps on growing in me. May the gods keep me unselfish in love. That is all I pray.'

'Just before this happened,' said Anne, 'I was thinking about you, and about love. I wanted to say: teach me to love, I am only beginning to understand ... or rather, I am learning yet another aspect of this enormous, endless thing. I say to myself, this is it. This is real love. This is true marriage. Then I find something else, and now it seems that I am only beginning to see, as in a glass darkly, and I want you to teach me.'

'But it is the same with me,' said Unni. 'Every day reveals new things. I had that feeling from the first day I met you, that we were setting out on a journey together. I didn't ask whether it would be long or short, and certainly I did not know how far together we would go. But dreary it would never be, and no one else did I want for a companion. And that it would last till death is far too much to ask. It was enough that I had found you, to walk with, a little moment or a long time. And all my life I would love you for this being together a while.

'The night we went to the Temple I said to the guard at the gate: this is my woman. I did not know it, but it was true, as much as human things are true, within the limits of their own reality. You were my woman, my lover and excellent companion, and even if you had never slept in my arms or loved me, my life was changed by the fact that you existed. It was in the Temple that night that you were revealed to me; the absorption in your face, self-forgetful in the awareness which our poets sing of. It was then I loved your spirit, solitary, in solitude listening and waiting and searching. I am not as delicate-hearted as you. I have no gift of expression. And I longed to give myself to you, that you could find us both in your words, that you might be revealed to yourself, that we should fulfil each other, and that I should hear your voice declare it. I did not know how to do this. And then you came to me, and asked me to help you.'

'Why then did you say,' said Anne, 'then I shall be enmeshed, we shall play the compulsory game? Why were you afraid?'

'Who is not afraid in front of love?' said Unni. 'I was afraid of my own possessiveness. For with the body comes passion, and though it is beautiful yet it is also possessive, scheming, mean; it is attachment, greed, fear, and suffering. We are taught non-attachment as a supreme virtue, and that the pain which is illusion comes from clinging too strongly, wanting to own what we have merely received. I was afraid to defile, to hold too hard, to mangle the flower in my hand with too tight a grip. Constant is my prayer that I should not possess, but we should grow and fulfil ourselves, together or apart.'

'And are you still afraid now, are you still frightened?'

'I don't think so,' said Unni. 'To make love body and soul to you, my beloved, is like a prayer now to me. And that love which begins with the body's communication can go on, permeating all our awareness and our actions, till it becomes something greater than the self. At least,' he added diffidently, 'so I like to believe.'

'Go on,' said Anne. 'I want you to say this, and more.'

'I think it is one of your Christian saints, Saint Teresa, a woman (you see how, because of knowing you, I have had to enlarge my own horizons ... I've taken to reading the saints as well as the poets), who said there were four sorts of prayer: the first a weary effort with small returns; the second internal prayer, like a tree putting forth leaves and buds; the third, love of God, enabling us to converse with Him face to face; natural, like a tree blossoming in the sun. And the fourth cannot be described in words. Then is no more toil, the seasons no longer change; flowers always blow, and the soul enjoys undoubting certitude, the heart loves and does not even know that it loves.

'And as I read it I thought of you, and the ascending journey which is that of all poets and seekers, good or bad, whether they fall early by the wayside or reach the summits. I thought there might be many stages of love. Lust, straight and wearisome desire, which makes one take a woman and be done. Possessiveness, most often mistaken for affection, vampire clinging to victim, sanctified by all legalities, gravestone over the corpse of love. That which nourishes the spirit as well as the body, a psycho-physical wholeness, the most successful human love between man and woman. Then another step upwards, a deep tenderness, a will to understand, to be involved in other people's lives, demanding nothing, perceiving without effort, the love of saints for humanity. And perhaps, beyond all these, the complete beatitude. The unattainable summit, always desired by man, the only thing which seems to give sense and point to his living and the source of all his myths, creeds, and religions, the goal of all his searches in and out of himself. What it is I do not know, and we're certainly not ready for that. Not yet.'

Anne said: 'In my country and in quite a few others in the West, we are near making a cult of boredom and cynicism. We have love-ennui, obsession with obscenity, love-titillation, love-clever, love-sex. The more we go on describing and detailing and gorging ourselves with the physical processes and the mental failings of the activities we pursue under the name of love, the less fun we have, the more bored we become, until we become ashamed of being in love, of "taking ourselves seriously". It still happens, of course, that people do love each other, but then we immediately want to keep it, embalm it, own it Frigidaire-fresh. We're so afraid of its decay that we mummify our loving. We take our love into barred houses and close doors and windows upon it, shutting out the housebreaker life, till it dies of suffocation. And now I am frightened, I am afraid that much more may be required of us than I want to give. I am so happy now that I too want to keep this fixed.'

And Unni, replying and yet not answering, said: 'I love you as a man does a woman, and it is hard not to be possessive, for I am only a man.'

They looked at each other smiling, and Anne understood what a great gift she had been given in this man. She knew his presence, saw his face, transient, yet for her immortal. They did not pledge permanency, their impact on each other already eternal. It had happened, that was enough for ever. Now Anne knew that by taking their child away the gods had not been cruel, only exacting, putting her among the blessed, those that life made unattached and fleet by suffering and vision, crippling of body and enlarging of horizon, so that they might not be chained down by common happiness. She could say: At the foot of my height I dwell; how high my mountain peak, no one has yet told me. But now I know my valleys and my depths.

'I am so glad, Unni, that you have sons.'

'They are healthy and clever, the future theirs. They do not belong to me, and therefore we love each other. You will see them one day, Anne. Perhaps during the winter holidays, when they come to Nepal.'

Anne smiled again. The desire to go to the dam was strong in her. She might not be able to stay with Unni there, but she could go, when she was well, for a few days, coming with a party of tourists on one of the Rampoche's organized tours. As soon as I'm well, she thought, waving to Unni leaving (he was going back the very same day, but would return if he could within a fortnight), I'll surprise him; I'll go to Bongsor.

Convalescence is an exhilarating phenomenon: Anne's visitors suddenly became profoundly interesting, lovable, and at the same time excruciatingly amusing. Everything was enhanced, a Wordsworthian childhood.

It began with Father MacCullough and his book *How to Help Your Husband be a Success*. Anne managed to gasp 'Thank you' between moans of laughter. Every time she laughed she was in agony with pain.

Father MacCullough had given a pint of blood to Anne, and this endeared her even more to him. 'How's my blood relation?' he called from the door. Then: 'How's John?' he asked, a little apprehensive.

'Broken rib,' replied Anne coughing with mirth.

'Too bad,' said Father MacCullough, who knew everything. 'Talking things out is worth trying, though.'

Isobel came, doing her duty, to tell her that the Institute would be starting again pretty soon.

'I intend to resign,' said Anne.

'I don't suppose you'll wish to stay in Khatmandu,' replied Isobel.

'I don't know,' said Anne.

Fred took out the stitches. He had managed to cut along the old scar, the new incision was clean and neat. 'You healed up beautifully. It really won't show much.'

'I don't mind if Unni doesn't mind.'

At this disconcerting frankness Fred replied: 'Oh, I don't think he'll mind at all,' and blushed.

Hilde and Vassili, with a basket of mountain irises and camellias.

'John got a broken rib rolling down the Hospital stairs while visiting you, I hear,' said Vassili.

'No,' said Anne, 'you know Unni kicked him.'

'Good,' said Vassili. 'I'm sorry, Anne.'

'I'm sorry about the baby,' said Hilde.

'Oh, I don't seem to mind,' said Anne, 'it's rather funny, how I don't mind.'

They talked about Isobel.

'I wish I could do something about her. Find her a great big bull of a man. She'd be such a nice woman then.'

'No doubt about it,' said Hilde, 'mountain air does things to one's inside. Khatmandu is the worst place in the world for Isobel. Now the monsoon is over people's thoughts are turning back to sex.'

'They never left it,' replied Vassili. 'Can't go wrong in Khatmandu if you keep your mind firmly on sex.'

Unexpectedly Michael Toast came for a farewell visit, with the announcement of Kisha's elopement with an American. 'A Texan. Told her he'd make a star of her. She started dieting.' He did not seem unduly upset, and added that he'd lost a lot of weight and was now putting it on again. He was going back to write another book on Nepal. Kisha would figure largely in it.

Pat walked in saying: 'Hi!'

'Hi!' said Anne. 'How nice of you to come and see me.'

'Went to get a check-up with Fred, thought I'd pop in to see you. How's the tummy?'

'It's fine.'

'Funny things, appendixes. Mine went when I was nine. There wasn't any sulfa or anything then. Had to have a tube in me for ages. That's why I never could have kids, I guess. Oh well, I couldn't have had such an interesting life if I had. Say, mind if I ask you a question?'

'Go ahead.'

'Well, maybe it's indiscreet, but ... did you and John have some kind of incompatibility or something? I know it's awful of me to ask ...'

'Yes,' said Anne. 'I don't like to go to bed with him. I tried but I couldn't. And now I won't try again. Never.'

'It's funny, isn't it, how that kind of thing happens? D'you ... was he impotent, or something?'

'No, it was me. I couldn't stand it. I dreaded it. I became all tight and it hurt. And then of course I pretended it was natural, I was getting older, not interested in such things ... you know how women always give themselves excuses, and men, husbands I mean, are only too happy to say it's the woman who's abnormal, cold, and so on. As if it were a virtue, a guarantee of chastity. Of course it isn't at all.'

'But you like to make love, don't you?'

'I do, with Unni. I love it, with him,' said Anne, and felt that sweet burning inside again, locking into her body.

'And I did, with Ranchit. It was lovely. But I can't stand it with Enoch. I can't stand it. It's awful.' She suddenly burst out weeping. 'I feel like a mattress,' she said, 'nothing more.'

'Then why did you marry him? Pat, I'm sorry, but why did you?'

'What can a woman do? I'm not getting younger, you know, and one's got to have someone around. ... You know what Ranchit's like. There was no future in it with him. I *liked* Enoch. He was rather sweet. He looked the kind of steady fellow who'd look after me, not stray too much. He's got a good job. Sure, I knew he wouldn't be great shakes in bed, but I didn't think I'd turn into an ice cube like that.'

'Is that what you went to see Fred about?'

She blushed, as if only now was there something shameful about it. 'Yeah, well, I thought perhaps Fred could fix things up ... I'd heard of an operation they used to do ... but Fred said no, it's not done any more. Nothing's of any use, he said, except Victorian resignation, taking to religion, or change of consort. "Try a heart-to-heart talk with Enoch," he told me. But that's the most difficult thing of all. I simply can't *speak* to him about it. How could I tell Enoch I can't stand his smell? Because that's what's worse than anything else, his smell. I never noticed it before.'

A day later John, pale, walking heavily with a cane, letting himself down in the armchair of her room and wincing lengthily.

'Ouch!' He grimaced with pain.

'Does it still hurt?'

'That blackguard kicked me in the ribs when I was down. I've got a fracture. Fortunately not compound.' John's head was thrown back, eyes closed, breathing heavily. 'I came,' he said between breaths, 'to apologize for having lost my temper when you weren't quite fit. If that fellow hadn't been there, there are lots of things I wanted to say to you. He annoyed me. I really will have to teach him a lesson.'

'Oh, come off it, John. What's the good of playing this comedy with me?'

'I'm not playing a comedy. I'm being sincere, as I always am. You're always accusing me of acting. It's you who're acting, to yourself. You're high-strung and you're now pretending that you're in love with this fellow and he with you. Well, let me tell you, you're not. Now you're in this bloody mess he'll be quick to get away and leave you flat.'

'This bloody mess,' said Anne, angry and also desperate at finding herself involved again in the hopeless treadmill of mutual invective, 'this bloody mess, as you say, is paradise, is heaven compared to the bloody mess of my life with you. At least Unni *wanted* a child; we *both* wanted one; he didn't threaten to kick it out of me, as you did, all of six years ago.'

'I ...?' said John increduously, 'me? My poor dear Anne, you're making all this up, you know. I never threatened you at all.'

His voice rang with sincerity, and Anne perceived that with him, as with Isobel, the mechanism of moral self-defence had functioned, obliterating unpleasant remembrance. He had truly forgotten, just as Isobel had, and Anne was left alone with a useless sheaf of accurate memories. I alone am left remembering. They have forgotten. It doesn't exist for them.

'What have you come here for? To annoy me, to try to shatter me with another scene? To show me your broken rib? I don't want to see you again, John. I will never live with you again. What is the point of all this?'

'It's just like you,' said John, 'running away when things don't suit you. Isobel's right, I'm afraid, when she says you've got a weak streak.'

'Oh, blast Isobel. Why don't you marry her? You'd make a perfect match.'

'Don't be insulting,' said John. 'Just because Isobel is a good and sensible woman you can't stand her. But I'm afraid she's right. Just as I was when I said there was something wrong with your insides. It's proved now.'

'You're not a man, John, you're a bitch.'

With tears of exhaustion and weariness she sank back on her pillows. There is no end to this, no end to this. I have no way of making John go. All these people who tell a woman: why don't you tell him to get out? All the women who put up with this kind of oppression. Only brute physical strength can toss John off from where he sits, in my room, a husband come to visit his sick wife. It is no use consoling myself with visions of all the women, everywhere in the world, worse off than I am; afflicted worse than I am, enduring in this unspeakable relationship which marriage can become the suffocation of the other being, sitting there. So long as in this one relationship, that between man and woman, husband and wife, brute physical strength is unequal, I can never push him away if he wants to come and bother me. This is a fact that in our civilizations, full of the rights of women, sex equality, and so on, still persists. How many women, I wonder, are still held by fear as well as sheer physical impossibility of chucking a man out, bodily? How many women would like to do it? Soldered by hate, John and I sit and quarrel, growing bitter and ugly, wasting life. And I have no way to push him off.

Chapter 15

THE Field Marshal seldom left his palace, where, with his books and his Maharani, the most beautiful woman on earth, he felt sufficiently in touch with the affairs and emotions of the world. Yet when Anne returned to her bungalow, ten days after her operation, the Field Marshal came to see her, accompanied by Sharma. They sat under the walnut trees gazing at Mount Phulchoah, abode of the Goddess of Good Spinning, a Chinese landscape wrapped in fine blue mist.

'I do believe,' said Sharma, 'that an artist would never tire of looking at this. It is perfection, the fields, the little farmhouses, and the mountain.'

'God is a great artist,' said the Field Marshal, 'if we but see the wondrous patterns he draws with all that is and lives. Every life can be a work of art. A platitude, as are all things we know so well that we always forget them.'

'It is not difficult to see beauty,' said Sharma, 'if one accepts without fear everything that is.'

'It is difficult to accept,' said the Field Marshal, 'for it is the eternal problem of being which each one of us must solve for himself. What to do, when to do it, and how, in order to *become* ourselves. It has concerned our philosophers everywhere since man invented language to perpetuate himself in time and space. Confucius, two millenniums ago, prescribed the rules of correct and harmonious existence in all their minutiae. To the Chinese mind the issue has always been the problem of relationship to other human beings. Perhaps that is why the group spirit, the welfare of the collective, becomes so readily their social pattern. The theme of existence for medieval Europeans was as for us, the Nepalese today, our relationship with the Divine, a spiritual exploration. The Renaissance, however, diminished and withered this intent upon God, replacing it by an immense preoccupation with the phenomena of the external world. For centuries this new aim of existence was a glorious success. Nature, the world, human beings, all became solid, condensed matter, which could be understood if analysed into their components. The mechanistic movements of life thus taken apart could be reproduced by machines, an extension of man. It made the white man sure of himself, a spiritual arrogance which alone could have assured him he was always right in subjugating others. And then suddenly the world for him became unsubstantial and precarious too, for always there was something, beyond the split atom, which clouded understanding, always shifting quicksands below the all too solid machinery. Now I think Europe, and America too, will be driven back to God, to the search for the meaning of self in living.'

'But,' said Sharma, 'so long as there is poverty and hunger in Asia, we Asians have no right to become selfishly immersed in the quest for self in God. *We* must now go through the Machine Age, and the Industrial Revolution, as Europe has done. We can't practise detachment for art's sake when it is selfish and inhuman to do so, when round us people – humans like ourselves – have no dram of life to spare for anything but the quest for food. In short, we have no right to speak of the Kingdom of God before we've made the earth a kingdom for man. We've got to become materialists in our turn.'

'That view, my friend,' said the Field Marshal, 'honours you. You are a poet, and therefore man's inhumanity to man will always move you. Are you not glad that in this day and age people all over the world are conscious of this need for social justice? I am an old man, and known as a conservative, yet I do not fear communism nor socialism, because it seems to me they are, in Asia, necessary if harsh steps towards abolition of the poverty round us. But all political creeds such as these are indexes of our failures to be human. If we were really conscious of our brothers' needs, and acted accordingly, their necessity would not arise. But since we are selfish and ignoble, amassing for ourselves and murdering our own kind for gain, real or imagined, we must pass through the crucible of such dogmas in order to learn again that humanity to the body is the first step to divinity of the soul.'

But Sharma did not agree with the last sentence. 'What holds us back in Nepal,' he said, with flashing eye, 'is precisely this belief in divinity, religion and all its paraphernalia of waste and cruelty, superstition and ignorance. If we want to progress, we'll have to do away with it, all of it.'

'I think some of its more wasteful aspects will wither away,' acquiesced the Field Marshal, 'because there will be factories built, and schools, and roads, and such things as the dam of Bongsor, which will change our country as nothing else has done before. The Industrial Revolution will inevitably bring spiritual changes in its wake.'

'They're having trouble at the dam,' interjected Sharma gloomily. 'Nothing to worry about, though.'

'I didn't know,' said Anne. 'Unni did not tell me.'

'Oh, nothing much,' said Sharma, now sorry he had spoken. 'Just local prejudice. Religion and superstition, that's all. And it's only a rumour. Much exaggerated, I'm sure.'

'Tell me, please,' said Anne, feeling wan, 'or I shall begin to worry.'

'Unrest is due to hunger,' said the Field Marshal. 'The valleys are flooded, there is famine, as usual, as always. And starving men have little reason.'

'No harm done,' said Sharma. 'Just a few demonstrations. People always need a scapegoat. Agitators have told the people of Bongsor that the goddesses are angry because of the dam. Of course it is not so. But humans are unreasonable, they prefer to believe their prejudices and their passions rather than to think clearly.'

'The dam will succeed,' said the Field Marshal. 'This is not the first time demonstrations happen, and Unni has won the rioters over without bloodshed. He is very able with people as well as with machines.'

'I'm not worried, really. I'm grateful you told me,' replied Anne, but disquiet made her voice waver.

Sharma spoke of the difficulties of sending a letter in Nepal. 'Mail from outside Nepal is handled by the Indian Postal Service to Khatmandu and out. But it's different inside the country. Our local Post Office doesn't sell stamps, and Dr Korla is away pounding pearls and mountain honey for the Swami of Bidahari, who is awaiting death in one of the courtyards of Pashupatinath. There are no postmen because no one paid them for two years. I'll send my letter by runner.'

'What's Dr Korla got to do with stamps?' asked Anne, surprised.

'He holds the monopoly. The Post Office found it too difficult to keep selling stamps, so many of them disappeared, got stolen. They sold the monopoly to Dr Korla. An up and coming man in our democracy,' said Sharma, half humorous, half bitter.

'There is high iniquity in our country, bribery, corruption, all the evils of democracy without public spirit,' murmured the Field Marshal. 'When this goes on too long, we too shall have a revolution.'

'We are in a revolution now,' replied Sharma. 'The valleys are seething with discontent. We are importing food from India, even into this Valley, one of the most fertile in the world. I put my faith in the dam, in the factories, not in the gods or the virtues of man. Spiritual mountaineering is out of date anyway. What we need are picks and shovels, bulldozers and syringes, to remove the high cliffs of poverty and injustice and pestilence.'

After Sharma had gone, the Field Marshal remained, gazing at the mountain.

'I feel out of date,' he said, 'with this nice young man.'

'I am worried,' replied Anne, 'about Unni.'

'Do not worry about him,' said the Field Marshal. 'Unni will be all right. I feel sure of that.'

'I'd like to go there,' said Anne, 'to see it. To see the dam, and the mountain that's so troublesome, Mana Mani … do you remember?'

'All mountains are troublesome things,' said the Field Marshal, 'especially the Himalayas, because they are young, active, and mischievous. But at the moment it's not Mana Mani which is troublesome. However, Unni has a way with him, and will conquer.'

'I'd like to go,' Anne said again.

'I can no longer give you advice,' said the Field Marshal. 'To go may be unwise, but to stay may be cowardly. I do not know.'

'Unni said that women were not allowed at the dam.'

'It's a precaution. The work is dangerous, and there is also the element of emotion. Women are a source of distraction and trouble everywhere,' said the Field Marshal, smiling, 'and particularly up in the mountains, where people get *very* emotional. Of course, the workmen and the local people have their families with them, but not the directing staff. But I feel you will go. The Rampoche organizes tours at Bongsor, in the autumn after the monsoon. Why not go then, as a tourist, for a few days? That is allowed.'

And Anne, thinking back to the letter from the Rampoche about stones and contracts: 'I would like to go … but I wouldn't like to hurt Unni by going. The Rampoche is very mercenary, isn't he?'

'Of course, all Tibetan lamas and priests are excellent business men,' said the Field Marshal. 'And the dam is sapping the Rampoche's sources of revenue, it is changing the minds of the people, who previously gave a hundred and fifty days a year free labour for the

Rampoche, but now are working at the dam for wages. The Rampoche does not *like* Unni, but I don't think he would hurt you. It would do him no good at all.'

Anne felt reassured. Should she write to tell Unni? Perhaps better wait a few days. Unni had said he would be back soon. The next airplane might bring him. 'Perhaps I could go back to Bongsor with him. I must get well quickly, so that I can go.'

Two days later in the morning there was a sudden rumour in the streets, crowds of women with flowers in their hair, nostrils and ears flashing gold, each carrying a bundle of fresh clothes under her arm.

Mita was not there. It was Regmi, with eyes respectfully downcast, who discreetly brought morning tea to Anne in bed. He wore a hibiscus in his cap, dangling over his forehead.

'Where is Mita?' said Anne. 'Is she not well?'

'She is well, memsahib, but today is Woman's Day,' said Regmi. Nepal, he informed Anne, had many such festivals. There was Animal's Day, in the spring, when cows and goats and pi-dogs were garlanded with flowers and fed; Pictures' Day, when families brought out and revered the snapshots, paintings, and oleographs on their walls; Father's Day, Children's Day. Today was Woman's Day, twenty-four hours when women did no work. They bathed in the sacred river to purify themselves, put on new clothes and flowers in their hair, sang and danced in the temples. To honour the women men wore a hibiscus in their caps, the flower of love. 'For it is good to rejoice, memsahib,' said Regmi, 'when life is so beautiful to live.'

Anne spent as much time as possible on her feet, for her desire was to be well by the time Unni came. I want him to make love to me, she thought, a little fiercely, and felt herself torn to liquid fire at the thought. Then all would be well, he would tell her whether she could come to Bongsor for a few days. She suddenly loathed the Institute; dreaded to see John or Isobel. It's all over, I'll never compromise again. I'll never put up with such people again. The very thought flooded her with hate.

She decided to go out in the jeep, and took the driver with her. 'Go to the General first,' she ordered, 'I may pick up a friend there.'

At the gate of the Serene Palace was the General himself, talking to his porter, bent in respect, his hands cupped to his mouth. The General saw Anne, and she thought that instead of the pleasure usual and instant upon him, he recoiled, but already he was smiling though a little constrainedly.

'Ah, madam Anne, how rejoicing to see you. Do you wish to visit my wife?'

'Yes, General,' said Anne, surprised at this unusually domestic overture. 'I'm told it's Woman's Day. Could I go with the Maharani wherever she may be going?'

'Certainly,' said the General. 'My ladies are all in the grand salon, some still combing their hair. Today,' said the General, 'we men count for nothing and must withdraw modestly.'

At that moment Anne saw Fred walking along the gravel driveway with Mike Young and Colonel Jaganathan.

'Good morning,' she said, pleased to see them. Fred waved at her. They came forward. Was it fancy, or were they glum? Mike looked ill. His blue eyes were red-rimmed. His skin had a sanded look, as if it grated. Fred's brow was furrowed. Only Colonel Jaganathan looked as usual (but that, thought Anne, is possibly because he is so dark, and I am not clever at perceiving emotion on faces darker than mine).

'Good morning, Anne, what fair wind brings you here?' said Fred.

But how artificial, how terrible ... thought Anne. Panic seized her. Something was terribly wrong. Fred didn't talk that way. Only one thing could be wrong, in the whole world, only one thing, supremely important above everything else. ...

'What's the matter?' she said, her voice strangled. 'Has something happened to Unni?'

Fred stared at her, and then he said: 'Now, now.'

'Something's happened to him,' she cried, 'something's happened, and you're not telling me. ...' Her voice rose nearly to a shriek. She got out of the jeep, as if getting down would bring her closer to the truth. 'Tell me,' she said, 'tell me.'

'Now, now,' said Colonel Jaganathan, 'steady, steady.' His big hands shot out, holding her shoulders. 'You're not very strong. There's nothing the matter with Unni, I swear to you.'

'Is that true, Fred?'

'Of course it is. Anne, you're not well yet. There's absolutely nothing the matter at all with Unni.'

She was shaking all over. 'I'm sorry,' she said. 'I'm all right now. It's the way you looked.'

'Madam,' said the General, 'I will call my Maharani to come to you here. Our stairs are hard to climb.'

'Oh, no,' she said, 'please don't bother.'

But he was off, leaving Anne standing with the three men. There was an embarrassed silence.

'I'm sorry,' said Anne, 'I'm a nuisance.'

'Now, please stop talking like that,' Fred replied warmly. 'Anne, you shouldn't overtire yourself. Better go and lie down. You're not quite recovered yet.'

But she shook her head stubbornly. 'I'm all right, just a little emotional. I'd heard, you see, that things were not going well at the dam, I thought ...'

'Nonsense,' said Mike Young. 'Of course, there's always a bit of trouble with the workers, but it's absolutely nothing. Unni is quite capable of coping. He's gone through far worse.'

He spoke with such conviction that Anne felt remorseful.

'I'm awful,' she said. 'I really am ashamed of myself. So spineless, and then to break down like that ...'

'I think you're a hundred per cent woman,' said the Colonel enthusiastically. 'We like that type, we Asians.'

'Here comes the most serene woman in the world,' said Mike, with a vast effort at gaiety. 'Good morning, Maharani.'

The Maharani, with a bundle of clothes under her arm, came majestically towards them, rolling like a galliass. She smiled at Anne, taking her hand in her two gentle ones, her full dark eyes beaming with affection.

'She will bring you with her to the temple, madam Anne,' said the General, 'there to see the maidens bathing, a most becoming view.'

'It's a lovely day, Woman's Day,' said Fred. 'Eudora would have enjoyed it. I've just had a letter from her,' he went on diffidently.

'I'm glad,' Anne replied.

Meanwhile the Maharani had been saying something lively and mischievous to Colonel Jaganathan, who burst out laughing and appeared to defend himself energetically.

'*Nai, nai,*' he was saying, the Indian word for no, shaking his head.

The General smiled lugubriously. 'It is ever so,' he announced in English. 'The good are discomfited by the ungood.'

'Is Jag discomfited?' said Mike Young. 'He doesn't look it.'

'The Colonel is a child of the happy gods,' said the General, 'and doesn't feel woe when he should. Rape is a word not untedious I feel, of calamitous intent.'

'What, rape again?' asked Anne.

'Not again, merely once, madam,' replied the General. 'That rascal who encumbers the earth with his iniquitous deeds – a distant nephew of mine, to my shame – accused as you know our Colonel of forcible carnation with his Maharani, a dastardly lie, of course. My Maharani and I have since undone him, she by sitting on his chest until he had produced an apology. Meanwhile,' he added dreamily, 'I mangled him somewhat by means of ten thoughtful kicks.'

'That was well done,' said Fred. 'Hope you hang on to the apology, Colonel.'

'Ah,' cried the General, carried away by his exploits, 'kicking is *so* artistic! As you know, madam, undoubtedly the Siamese boxers practise it with great delight. Democracy must sometimes be strengthened with such terrific, poisonous, and confident stimulus. I remember,' he continued, hitching himself upon the jeep as if all the morning in the world were his, 'a boxing championship in my young days, when I had acquired some ingredients of the Siamese cultural arts. It was a revel, though I lost and was carried out to the hospital, yet my opponent could not be a man for many weeks, which made his life hell with complaints from his wives. Yes, indeed,' said the General in happy reminiscence, 'nothing was worse.'

'In my country,' said Mike tactlessly (he had obviously not heard of Unni's feats), 'you don't kick a man when he's down.'

'Not kick a man when he's down?' said the General, astonished. 'Then when, pray, is it convenient to kick the fellow?'

'I'll give you ten bottles of whisky, General, one for each thought,' the Colonel promised, still laughing.

'Thank you,' said the General. 'But I think you should accept the maiden whom my Maharani is suggesting. She is swooning with love for you, and all the diplomats, even some of the Americans and Indians unfortunate enough to live in our Valley, finally acquire such raptures to keep their tempers even.'

But the Colonel laughed and went on shaking his head, and Anne knew him shy, because he blushed, or rather turned a more glossy ebony; and the General, exclaiming that chastity was an unrequited virtue, 'you will get the slander, and others the nectar', now floated away.

Anne climbed back into the jeep, this time with the Maharani, and they drove off, with the men waving at them. What a fool I am, everything is all right. I'm too emotional ... aftermath of my operation. I imagine things. The Maharani, sitting by her, oozed comfort and motherliness. They were soon at the Temple of Pashupatinath.

On the stone ghats where the river ran narrow between the main edifice and the sacred hill of lingams, hundreds of women were sitting, standing, walking into the stream and slapping water over their faces, hair, and bodies.

'Three hundred and sixty times,' said the Maharani, 'one for each day of the year, do we wash ourselves.'

Nimbly she stepped down, in all her clothes, and stood in the river between a very old woman with dark skin and a young girl plaiting her long hair, her strong breasts outlined by the clinging damp sari round her.

Three hundred and sixty times the Maharani slapped water all over herself, so that all the sins of the year should be cleansed. Then stepping out dripping, she managed to dry and dress herself in her new clothes without exposing an inch more skin than that on her face, arms, and neck. All around her more women were arriving, stepping into the river, throwing water over themselves, dipping in and out again, to change their clothes in the same unrevealing way.

Anne and the Maharani went back in the jeep, passing groups and processions of women walking, singing in chorus, dancing, all with glistening hair, and hibiscus and camellia, red and pink and yellow flowers, and much gilded brass, about them.

Along the narrow streets and in the market place, on the stone stairs of the temples, Newari women, their heavy pleated skirts bundled at the waist into a pouch-like waistband from which chickens and sometimes a small lamb protruded, were selling bangles. And such bangles! Reds and greens, golds and blues and dazzling pinks, rows and rows of bangles in great splashes of colour. In front of their spreads squatted the customers, with arms extended; the seller of bangles would knead their fists into smallness, pushing and squeezing the bones of the folded hands until she could slip the bangles one by one, a dozen or more, upon the forearm. Hanging from frameworks of bamboo were braids and tassels of red thread, to be wound into the hair. There were stalls and stalls of flowers, camellias, hibiscus, wild roses, and mountain irises. All was glitter and dazzle and laughter warbling as an amused river, as the women flowed about the streets, and men, homespun shadows, walked effacedly.

As it was a holy day and there could be no killing of fowls of any kind in her house, the Maharani could not ask Anne to lunch, and suddenly desirous of company Anne went to the Royal Hotel. Her body ached, she was easily tired still, but more than physical pain she felt parched, hungry and thirsty for a word from Unni, in default of his presence. It was odd, this silence. There ought to be a plane. Perhaps this afternoon. Perhaps Unni himself would come. He had promised. Meanwhile she took human comfort from sitting with Hilde on the verandah, and the sight of the madman, solemnly staring and courteously bowing to the tourists, was also soothing. John did not appear. If he had been there, Anne knew she now had the strength not to notice him at all. Never again would she sit facing him, pretending to eat.

But even here, in Vassili's and Hilde's uproarious company, later eating soufflé merveille and drinking Balkan brandy, she could not shake off the sense of unease.

'When's the Institute starting again?' asked Vassili.

'Soon, I think, but I've resigned,' said Anne.

'I'm sorry,' said Hilde.

'I am too,' said Anne. 'I liked the girls.'

'If you stay in Khatmandu,' said Vassili, 'they'll take private lessons from you.'

'That would be nice, but I'd hate to hurt Isobel. She's so hurt already.'

'She won't find another English teacher that soon,' said Vassili.

'What about finances?' Hilde was always practical. 'I don't suppose John gives you any money?'

'Oh, I'll manage,' said Anne. 'I've got a little bit saved.'

'Life isn't cheap in Khatmandu,' warned Vassili.

'I know,' said Anne. She did not want to say: But I'm living through all this, I'm living and I'm writing, and I've got to live this through, store up life, enormous life, to be spilt out in words. 'As soon as I'm better I'll think about making some money.'

She felt exhausted after lunch, and returned to the bungalow to lie down, hearing the singing of women and the small drums and flutes as they passed the palace walls.

Maybe I'm spineless, she thought. Looking back, she could not remember doing anything positive ... except one thing, she corrected herself, coming to Khatmandu. Certainly all this time, all these years, were blurred like a half-awake state. She seemed to be a mere passive object, floating on the stream of events, and yet, somehow, perhaps this was as it should be.

Illogically, deep down in herself, she knew this passivity essential, its awareness a preparation, like a pregnancy, when one is both observer and participator in something which happens within oneself but which is uncontrollable, once it starts. Pregnancy ... she had tried it, her body inhabited with the beloved's seed, and now it was gone for ever, never would it happen, and suddenly the full, the wrenching and hideous tragedy occurred to her. I am sterile, I am sterile now, for ever. She was too weak to cry, and closed her eyes, letting the paroxysm pass. And as it ebbed away, she did not feel as unhappy as she should have done. Perhaps I'm learning acceptance. Meanwhile she must remain like this, feeling spineless, insecure, but accepting insecurity against all logic, all reason. Accepting. She took the *Gita* lying on the table. In spite of a small Nepalese workman who had cunningly hammered it back into shape, there was still a dent in the beautiful jewelled cover, a small dent which she had strongly to will herself not to notice or hate would flood over her again, a helpless and shattering exhaustion. She read:

Thus said the Lord Krishna, Behold my divine forms, hundreds upon thousands, various in kind, colour and shape. O conqueror of sloth, you shall behold the whole universe made one.

For I am the beginning, the life-span and the end, the radiant sun and the wind-god; among the stars I am the moon. Among the mountains I am the highest, and the ocean among waters. I am the Love-god, begetter of children, and I am Death, who distributes the fruit of all action. Among those who measure, I am Time; I am the knowledge of the knower, the logic of those who debate, the strength of the strong.

There is no limit to my manifestations, for I am Life.

In the evening, restored by sleep and hugging loneliness about her (no Unni, no letter from Unni, the hunger for sight and feel of him almost unbearable), Anne went back in the jeep to the Temple of Pashupatinath.

There was the golden flare of torches, as at the Siva Festival in the spring; the cobbled, singing streets, shoving, laughing crowds.

On a grassy open space a group of men sat on one side facing a concourse of women at the duet game of love-singing. Each group had its protagonist. The man and the woman chosen sat in front of their backers and sang to each other, upon the theme of love, extempore poems of their own making in a contest of wit.

'Aiii, I waited for you in the shadow of the peepul tree by the fountain;
I waited for you in the heat of noon and was burnt by the sun;
I waited for you and was blenched by the moon;
But all in vain, all in vain,
For you did not appear, and my honey,
The lovely golden honey, which I had climbed the hills to fetch for you,
The stolen honey for you to taste,
Was left with me
To be eaten by the ants ...'

'Aiii,' sang the woman back,
'Why should I burn myself in the heat of the sun
To go to the fountain to see you?
Why should I blench my bones in the light of the moon
To peer for you under the peepul tree?
Do I not have enough water from the fountain
In the jars of my house?
And what need have I of your honey,
For I have honey of my own,
And yours might give me
A belly-ache ...'

There were peals of laughter at this retort. Several of the men hastily surrounded their champion, whispering suggestions, while the women did the same to theirs, who, Anne saw, was fat Suriyah, the prostitute, sitting like a golden goddess, dappled with light and darkness from the flickering torches, with rings and bangles and jewels in her nostril and hair and ears. On Woman's Day was no class nor caste; prostitute and Maharani together bathed, prayed together in the temple. Today all were clean of sin.

Suriyah's opponent had no ready wit. Time went by while he anxiously listened to his friends' whispering and pondered, and finally the women shouted: 'Enough, enough,' railing at the men, clapping their hands with glee at Suriyah's victory, and the groups rose, to go towards the Temple of Pashupatinath.

In the inner courtyard, around the main edifice housing the enormous lingam of Siva (but now the gleaming doors were closed upon it), went the women, walking always clockwise. Bodies covered the steps, the stairs, filled the galleries, lay sleeping or awake singing or talking to each other. Groups danced round the bull and the shrines. The ground was thick and moist with petals.

Anne felt her arm tugged at. 'Mrs Ford,' said a voice, 'Mrs Ford.'

At first she did not recognize the young girl who now clung to her.

'Devi,' said the girl. 'Devi, Rukmini's sister.'

'Oh, Devi,' said Anne, 'how you've grown. How are you, and Rukmini?'

'I would like speech with you,' said Devi. 'Let us go to your house.'

Anne, whose strength was ebbing, nodded. She pushed herself physically to the limit of her endurance, testing herself, yet there came a moment when she could no more until she had rested. Trying not to bend her body (the scar hurt again, felt as if it would burst as the weak muscles cramped), she walked out slowly with Devi, clambered into the jeep, signalled to the driver to go home.

'My family might be looking for me later, they are at the Temple,' said Devi. 'Can you drive me back?'

'Certainly,' said Anne.

Devi was afraid to return alone with the driver, a man. Her reputation would suffer. She kept looking round her fearfully. 'My sisters are praying,' she said.

'Is Rukmini also there?'

'No, not Rukmini ... I must speak of Rukmini ... you must help her.'

'Of course, Devi. If I can.'

Devi began to weep.

It was a terrible effort to climb the stairs to the room and Anne threw herself on the bed, exhausted. 'Sorry,' she said to Devi, 'I'm not too strong yet.'

Devi sat on the chair. How pretty she is, thought Anne. Not as delicate of feature as Rukmini; there was something more sturdy and less ecstatic in Devi. Under the lamp she glowed softly. Her hair was down in plaits. She was still a maiden, but she would soon be ripe for marriage, all of thirteen years old.

'Would you like something to drink, tea or coffee?' asked Anne.

'No,' said Devi. She twisted her hands. 'My father does not wish me to speak,' she began, 'neither do the others, they do not wish to tell you, but I am afraid ... I am afraid that Ranchit will be very angry. Ranchit will be cruel to her.'

'Why, what has Rukmini done?' asked Anne.

'Rukmini has gone away. She is gone to Bongsor, to find Unni Menon.'

Isobel, at the Institute, had embarked on what she called a thorough spring-cleaning. The road to India was now open to traffic, and more things entered Nepal at less cost. Salt, bales of cotton, food, grain, furniture, machines, came up in dangerously loaded Nepalese lorries from the frontier. Isobel ordered some of the unused rooms to be opened; only to shut them again as the cost of cleaning and furnishing them proved discouragingly high. Two more bathrooms were installed. An army of bearers scrubbed, mopped, and swept under the watchfulness of a new gym teacher, an Anglo-Indian girl, doe-eyed, yet intensely ugly. Isobel said the Institute must prepare itself for an increased enrolment of pupils for the autumn and winter, and sallied forth daily in the jeep to visit notables in order to acquaint them with the attractiveness of the education she provided.

But although outwardly busy, strenuous, and single-minded, Isobel's internal fragmentation proceeded. There was no hint of it in her customary peremptoriness. At breakfast she presided over History, Geography, and the terrorized gym teacher with her usual self-assertion, reinforced hypnotically by the glass vases now filled with paper orange blossoms, a gift from the Eurasian. 'How very chi-chi,' History had sighed to Geography. The two had been planning an excursion to Delhi during the winter holidays, with the Bowers and possibly John.

'I do think he's got to pull himself together and make a decision soon,' said History tentatively.

'I am sure he's making up his mind right now.'

'A trip to Delhi in the winter would do him good.'

'Certainly, otherwise I wouldn't have dared suggest it to him.'

They looked at Isobel covertly, testing her humour with little snippets of talk. A dull roughening had come over her in the past few weeks. From hair to hands, a brittle, under-skin coarseness infected her.

Geography experienced a vague disquiet. A thought crossed her mind that there was something terribly wrong with Isobel ... but the breakfast table was too usual, the clatter of cups and tea-pot too familiar, the drizzle outside, tail-end of the monsoon season, dulled cosily. 'It's less muggy today, isn't it?' she said brightly, re-entering the self of herself she liked best, the sure one, useful, good, kind, who didn't miss anything in life. Surely not a man. Dreadful nuisance they were, men.

Isobel nodded. 'Yes,' she said. 'We must start on a new footing, this time.'

And the others drank their coffee soundlessly, overwhelmed by her earnestness, the inapposite reply to Geography's weather remark.

After breakfast Isobel went back to her sitting-room and opened one or two ledger books. But there was nothing much to do except to write to the Board informing them of Anne's resignation, and asking them to provide a new lecturer in English. Anne's letter of resignation lay in her drawer, and she enclosed it in her letter to the Board, relieved. 'Good riddance,' she said aloud. After a few orders to the Eurasian, and inspecting the bowed backs of the workmen scrubbing the dirt and the mould off the corridors' stone flags, Isobel drove off in her jeep to call upon some more potential supporters of the Institute.

There was in everything she did a curious lack of depth, a bottomless, falling-out-of-space sensation. Purposeful action, enthusiasm, all went off like popping balloons, suddenly shrinking into nothing. What did I do yesterday? What am I doing this for? It had no meaning, it all disappeared into a yawning, horrifying emptiness. The Institute ... what was it about the Institute which suffocated Isobel now? It was abhorrent to her to sit at breakfast, looking at History's and Geography's bleak, mild faces, hearing their girlish laughter and their to-each-other talk. She had to steel herself to face them, to give orders, to appear to know what she was doing, and why, when everything was wrested from her in appalling meaninglessness. And this present chaos began to spread backwards into the past. There was nothing in her life she could point to, only a sifting and heaving as of ashes, devoid of shape, smell, sense. She felt gritty with ashes inside and out. All the years, all the years, burnt-out.

Recently she had had many headaches, when she would walk, up and down, up and down, dizzy with this ashy rage and the pain of her head. What was worse, when the headaches came they made her want to scream words, words she could feel rolling in her mouth, hungry-tongued, filthy words (and the very notion they were filthy was relish, made saliva pour forth, made her want to lick her mouth all over), flurrying words like froth at the edge of the sea, worrying and snarling and growling inside her. Even at the Education Ministry where she had gone to tell the official in charge of Anne's resignation – 'And we're not sorry, Your Excellency, the woman's been quite a disaster to us' – she'd suddenly had an attack, suddenly felt like letting loose a stream of abuse. Against this she had struggled to suffocation, red in the face, vehement, talking louder and louder of how she'd had no help from the Education Department, 'nor the consideration we're entitled to'. The official had been as mellifluously exasperating as ever, all smiles and transverse nodding, so that his evasive compliments turned into wafts of breeze, gentle, unseizable, and utterly confusing. He had agreed to everything, then absentmindedly annihilating, with a caressing gesture of his hand waved in a dancer's pose, his approval of Isobel's denunciations of Anne, he added: 'My wife is very fond of Mrs Ford. We may ask her to give private tuition in English to our daughters,' and bowed Isobel out.

After the Inquiry, and during Anne's operation and stay at the Hospital, Isobel had begun going about, visiting everyone she knew, at the Royal Hotel, the Residency, the Point Four Palace, explaining, accusing, amplifying, pouring an avalanche of words over what had happened. 'It couldn't have happened anywhere else but here.' Everywhere she had stayed on and on for hours, deriving assuagement from the fact that her restive but polite hosts listened to her. 'I want them all to know the truth,' she said. But it was an effort constantly to be renewed, and gradually she became aware that many listened out of curiosity, derision or because they had to, but that they already had their own convictions about 'this shocking affair'. Human instinct here had worked swiftly and surely, even though for once there had been a singular lack of gossip.

In spite of Geography's natural love for the dispersal of information, there was one magnificent staunchness in her. As a nurse she was incorruptible. Her story was that Anne had had an acute appendix, and even History could not get another word out of her. But in spite of Geography's heroic reticence, her mouth drawn down in exiguous firmness, All-Khatmandu knew without needing to be told that Anne had had a baby, that the baby was Unni's, that Isobel was furious because she herself had wanted Unni to go to bed with her, that John, the complaisant husband, was so madly in love with Anne that he'd do nothing about it, even though he had been assaulted by Unni and kicked in the most unsporting way while lying prone on the floor of the Hospital, and that Isobel was going man-mad and would explode 'any moment now'.

Isobel pitted herself against an edifice of fact, bolstered with downright instinct, which no amount of prolixity could shake. Hence, driven further afield, she on this morning mounted her jeep to pay a visit to the Museum, ostensibly to inform the Curator that the Institute would open soon, and to solicit his help.

The Curator proved the most satisfactory listener she'd had so far. His study was a small room encumbered with old Nepalese books, hand-written on fine slabs of parchment, Tibetan prayer books with sheets of beaten gold. Isobel's voice rattled and was thrown back at her by the walls, it exploded and lapped round, while the Curator, his charmingly square Mongoloid face set in an unalterable smile, sat in the Buddha lotus pose of unalterable patience. Isobel became quite heady with the sound of her own self. She experienced the deep satisfaction of being listened to, while she burrowed into the spiritual degeneracy of Anne and of Unni. Her indignation grew as she told the Curator how she'd found Unni with women, in the afternoon, lying on his bed, in full daylight, and how there were men coming out of Anne's room at all hours of the morning, and how the Institute had suffered, but now, thank God, that woman was going, and the

Curator must help; he must deny all rumours spread by evil tongues, this was the truth. ...

As she paused, nearly exhausted, the Curator nodded his head from side to side, and rose. 'A fascinating cautionary tale, dear lady. I regret that the Museum's finances do not yet run to a tape recorder. We hope to get one next year. Would you fancy some tea?'

Isobel declined tea. 'I must be going,' she said, pretending to consult her watch, her excitement ebbing a little, but still full of energetic satisfaction.

'Not before a look at our Museum,' said the Curator amiably. 'We have acquired some new sculptures and paintings. From Tibet. You know what excellent smugglers these lamas are. The Chinese don't let them take valuable works of art out of Tibet, but they still do, when they need cash. It is indeed highly sinful.'

He guided her footsteps towards the show-case, waved vaguely, and excusing himself 'just for a moment', disappeared.

Isobel had not been in this part of the Museum before. She was still palpitating, tremulous inside and out from her talk, taut yet elated, with a throbbing pulse. She stepped towards the room indicated by the Curator's hand, and found herself in the regions which Father MacCullough had eschewed from his conducted tours.

The recent acquisitions were there, a row of Tibetan paintings, all presenting the same scene: among paradisal flowers, demons and gods and flames, the black figure of a god and his female counterpart, in the act of copulation, the goddess raising herself on one leg, the other round the god's body, a halo of multiple arms thrashing the air about them.

'Oh,' said Isobel. 'Oh! Oh!'

Something tremendous in her rose at the sight, a deafening vast scream. She looked quickly round her, surprised that no one had heard the shouting, but she was alone. Avidly she came nearer, scanning. Then moved slowly to confront one of the bull gods she had never seen before. It was about two feet high, with three heads and many arms, twisting in power and glory; from him protruded the phallus, four inches long, with the tip realistically daubed red; and crawling towards it, legs ready to twine, arms open to embrace, a woman figure, clad as a goddess, ecstasy upon her face.

How long Isobel stood there only the Curator ever knew. When he thought she had had enough, she heard his discreet cough, and with a start turned and gazed intently at the serene figure of a Buddha on a lotus, in pure prayer, next to the bull-god.

'Ah yes, madam, highly interesting. See the workmanship, a triumph, veritably. And so true. The sacred and the profane side by side. For without the act of fusion which is the essence of being, we are as without knowledge of ourselves, atoms separated, fragments without synthesis. Do you not find it so?'

'I ... it's perfectly dreadful,' cried Isobel, 'perfectly dreadful!' And the Curator saw her run out as if the bull-gods and the demons, so pre-occupied with the act of love, were pursuing her. Her face and arms had turned brick red.

'Poor lady,' sighed the Curator, watching her escape, 'poor dear lady.' Isobel had come to him, savage and angry, in her eyes the de-vouring look of fiendesses in torment. I have tried to help, thought the Curator. Perhaps I have done wrong. What did the *Song of God* say? 'Action is mine, but the fruits of action are not, they belong to God.' Comforted, he went back to his study to pray. It was time for prayers, the absorption of his mind in the Mind of the One. Unlike Father MacCullough, the Curator would not intercede with God for Isobel or anyone else. Humility precluded it. But he knew that no one life could, with impunity, interfere in someone else's life, cross another being's destiny. However, Isobel had come to him; he had prayed while she spoke, then he had done what he had felt was right. Given her the choice of looking or not looking. God would take care of the rest.

But it was John who brought about Isobel's final fragmentation, and at the same time, in the way untoward events and calamities have, a re-sult which in the end was accepted as inevitable and even pre-destined.

John came to tea at the Institute. Geography, Isobel, History, were waiting for him, looking rehearsed. He sat down, wincing only slightly. It didn't hurt any more, and he had to remind himself to wince. 'Fred's just changed the plaster, getting on all right. Three broken ribs. But I'm quite tough, I heal up quickly.'

'But ...' said Geography, and then subsided. The X-ray had shown only one doubtful fracture.

'I'm afraid I'm not a doctor. I believe Fred told me it was three,' John added a little warmly. And she did not contradict him.

'What's all the commotion in the street for?' Isobel asked. Her headache was very bad, but she passed the tea-cups precisely.

'Oh, don't you know? Of course, you weren't up till late this morning,' answered Geography, brightly daring. 'It's Woman's Day. All the women parading in the streets. Dancing and singing and all that.'

'They dip themselves in the river to wash their sins for the year,' said History. 'Fancy believing that.'

'A bit like baptism to them, I suppose,' said John, benevolent.

'Baptism is *quite* different,' said History sharply. 'I mean ... they're only heathens, so it won't wash away *their* sins, I'm afraid.'

'I'm afraid not,' Isobel concurred. 'However, it's better than some other things they do. It's a bath, anyway.' (All laughed at this.) More sandwiches, John?'

'Thank you,' said John. 'When does the Institute reopen?' He let his gaze float, in superior and tender affection, upon the three women. How fond they were of him. What good women they were. He felt masculine, sure of himself, with them. They admired him so much.

'After the Rain God ceremonies in about ten days,' said Isobel. 'It's just one festival after another out here. Woman's Day today, then Father's Day, then another feast (I've forgotten what *that* is), and then a whole week for the Rain God. We're short-staffed as it is,' she bit her lip, having purposely said it, but pretending it had escaped her. 'Anne's resigned, as you've probably been told.'

'No, I didn't know,' replied John. 'I'm never told anything.' He said it sadly and softly. 'I wish sometimes Anne would be more ... trustful.'

'I wonder what she'll do now?' said Isobel.

'I don't know,' said John, still with the same soft sad deliberation. 'I'm very much afraid that, without any restraining influence, she'll ... destroy herself.'

Geography and History listened with bated breath, and sighed in approbatory unison.

'It's tragic,' said Isobel, 'but certainly there's nothing *you* can do about it, John. You've done your best, your very best.' For a moment she was again the semi-regal, vibrating Isobel. 'She was probably born with a lack in her character.'

'She's been terribly punished,' said History, shaking her head solemnly. 'Terribly.'

Geography looked bashfully at John, and sighed again.

'Well, now,' continued Isobel briskly, putting down her cup, 'the point is, what are *you* going to do, John? Surely you can't spend your life looking after her. You *must* have a thought for yourself. You're entitled to some happiness, I think.'

A Christian chorus of approval rose.

John looked mournfully at the three. 'That's very kind of you. Very. Few people seem to ... worry about *me*. It's true I haven't been happy. I've had my ... feelings, my hopes, well, what the average chap expects in his marriage, everything, dashed to pieces ... it's been ... years ...' He gazed at the past, in the mid-distance above their heads, with unflinching eye.

Geography coughed briskly.

Isobel put out a hand. 'Steady there, John. You mustn't think back, you must look forward. Make plans for the future. You can't let this hang round your neck for ever. You must make a clean break, I think.'

'Start life again,' murmured Geography.

'Yes,' said John dreamily. 'I'd thought of that. If you knew how much I'd thought about it. And I know what an *ordinary* chap would do. Divorce Anne. I've got sufficient grounds. In fact, I know that's what that blackguard is hoping for, so he can drag her down to his level. ... But my mind is made up.' His voice firmed, he sat more erect. He had been sitting in a pose he adopted nowadays, legs stretched and parted, slumping, a pose which ill-suited him as it pushed forward his heavy belly, spread his buttocks apart, so that he looked boneless and soft. He was putting on weight now, rapidly, and his head seemed larger than normal as he thrust it forward, through habit rather than pugnacity. 'Whatever she's done to me, she's still my wife. I won't fail her, even if she's failed me. I may be old-fashioned in thinking a wife should be faithful to her marriage vows, but I also think that a husband should protect his wife, through thick and thin. I'm not going to divorce Anne. I know she's making a mess of her life, and mine. She's heading for disaster. All I can do is wait until she comes back to her senses, that's all.'

In his mind he saw it, Anne, poor, ragged, white streaks in her hair, coming to him, pleading, begging to be taken back, loving him at last, him alone, and nothing else in the world for her, none of this damn absorption into things around her, staring at trees and people, sitting at the typewriter, quite gone away, having forgotten him. ...

He looked round to see the effect of his words. Isobel was staring at him with strange fixity, biting her nether lip over and over again. He heard Geography's voice, falsely bright: 'Well, Martha Redworth asked me to go and help with the chrysanthemums. I must go now, or I'll be terribly late.'

Walking out later John wondered, with mortified incredulity, what had gone wrong. It was strange. They hadn't quite appreciated his nobility ... perhaps they were stunned. Certainly Isobel's hand shook. Fine woman, getting a bit long in the tooth now. Didn't like her colour. Brandy didn't help ... though she'd never misbehaved, really. She just couldn't take it, that was all. If he were more interested, he'd make her lay off it. He squared his shoulders, walking through the feminine crowds back to the Royal Hotel. Woman's Day. Flowers and bangles and colour everywhere. Laughter round him, someone threw a flower teasingly. He smiled, pleased. Pity Ranchit wasn't back yet. Still in the flesh-pots of Delhi or Calcutta, having his teeth fixed. Must be pretty hot down there. Up here, it was turning fine. Oh well, he'd had himself quite a time in Delhi, while the lawyer was doing the papers and things ... and those Indian girls always had such fine big breasts, even if their bones were small.

Paul was saying good-bye to Mike Young, on the doorstep of the Residency, when Geography appeared, striding hurriedly up the drive.

''Afternoon,' said Paul, waving his pipe. 'Looking for Martha? Shall I call her? She's down in the garden, near the chrysanthemum patch. How about some tea first?'

'No thanks,' said Geography, very agitated. 'I've just had tea.'

An hour later, in the twilight, Martha came to Paul, reading in the study. He looked at her from over his glasses. 'Have a good time with Geography?'

'Terrible,' said Martha wearily. 'The monsoon's over and everybody is getting emotional again. The poor girl was weeping and snuffling all over the place. Over John Ford, of all things. She's worked herself up into believing herself in love with him.'

'Wonders will never cease,' said Paul. 'I thought Geography was a sensible gal.'

'Of course, she wouldn't say it right out. Started on how wonderful he was, perfectly noble, how much she admired him ... went on and on all about his sacrificing himself. Seems he's refusing to divorce Anne. Still loves her and will wait for her to return to him.'

An expletive unusual at the Residency came from behind the pipe. 'Nobility be blowed. Play-acting all the time. Hasn't got a spark of any real feeling about him. Not divorce Anne ... damn selfish of the brute. Wants to hang on, that's all. The man's a leech. Never liked the fellow.'

'Maybe he does love her,' said Martha.

'That's not love, that's blood-sucking,' retorted Paul. 'Hanging on to her, trying to make her pay in this way. It's mean. And I guess he fancies he's being noble, just like that chap in that book, you know, that husband refusing to give a divorce ... what's the name of that book?'

'*Anna Karenina,*' said Martha. 'You gave it to me to read, right after we were married, remember? Mum was shocked.'

'So I did,' said Paul, smiling. 'What a thing to do to one's bride.' He became gloomy again. 'I've got news too, dear. Mike Young's just been to see me. The poor boy is very upset. You know he's in love with Rukmini, Ranchit's wife.'

'Everybody knows that, Tiddlywinks. And so's Sharma.'

'Yes, but it's serious with Mike. Well now ... Rukmini's left Ranchit. She went last week, ostensibly to visit a relative in the next valley. But she never got there. Instead she's now in Bongsor. Where Unni is. You know how she feels about him. If Ranchit gets to know, the whole Valley will blow up. I've advised Mike Young to go to Bongsor on the quiet, try to bring her back. And not to tell Anne. Anne mustn't know. That would be the last blow for her.'

'Can't believe it,' said Martha. 'Unni isn't like that.'

'Of course not, but will Ranchit believe it? And the others? They'll be only too keen to fasten something on Unni. Women,' said Paul, 'women. They never know how to leave well enough alone. For God's sake, let's keep Anne out of this. She's had enough to go through.'

'She was resting in her bungalow this afternoon, Geography told me. I'll go and see her tomorrow,' said Martha.

But when, the next morning, Martha reached the bungalow, she was told by Regmi that at dawn the Rampoche and his daughter had come in their jeep and taken Anne with them to catch the airplane to Bongsor.

It was Anne's jeep, going away in the evening, then later returning, chugging into the deep evening, biting the honey sweet darkness.

'Ooooooh,' moaned Isobel, 'oooooooooooh ...'

Right after John's departure, the wardrobe.

She could still hear the gurgle of the brandy as she drank, wondering why she did it; she had felt no pain. Like a mouldy house suddenly falling, a confusion of soft splintering sounds and smothered bricks and dust, she had felt something give within her, and now contemplated the ruin and its waste, herself.

'Isobel Maupratt, Miss Maupratt. The chosen of the Lord.' She giggled. Profanity came easily after the giggle. Words she did not know that she knew. 'Oh Lord, how Thou smitest me,' she cried, then screamed abuse.

The bearer who came to announce dinner fled. Remembering the previous uproar and its sequel, he did not say a word to History, Geography, and the Anglo-Indian drinking their tomato soup before the hymn meeting.

'Where's Big Memsahib?' asked History, between two spoonfuls of soup.

'Big Memsahib no hungry,' replied the bearer.

The staff went on eating.

And now Isobel too went out, out along the verandah, through the back door; towards the bungalow, always towards the bungalow. The bungalow was lit and alive with a sound of voices, but no words heard.

Isobel stood in the darkness by the rose bush outside, lifting her face towards the windows, the golden glow.

Always it was like this. Damn unfair. Damn. God is unfair. He is unfair.

'Oh God, oh God, why have You forsaken me?'

She was always waiting, staring; waiting for something and some-

They twisted and turned their bodies like the goddesses on the wall. The priests turned and sprinkled Isobel with blood from the lamb.

Isobel was shouting too with the others. Someone thrust a clay cup in her hand, and she drank. Again and again and again.

They were out now, dancing in the light of a very small moon, upon a hillside. And screaming.

'The blood of the lamb,' screamed Isobel, 'the blood of the lamb. I am clean, clean.'

She clutched at her blouse. It tore easily. The women with her laughed, clapped hands, shouting. She heard the cloth tear. With a thrill of pure pleasure she heard the searing sound of cloth tearing. The women crowded round her. The drums beat.

PART FOUR Mountain

> *Thus said Krishna the Enlightener: 'The world is imprisoned in its own activity, except when actions are performed as worship of God. Therefore you must perform every action sacramentally, and be free from all attachment to results.'*
>
> BHAGAVAD-GITA (The Song of God)

Chapter 1

By the sea, in the plain, in the valley, people talk of mountains, raise their heads to stare at mountains, not knowing this sense of vast fate which is mountains seizing upon the horizon. Here in the mountains at last is no refuge from the overwhelming, the magnificence, the thrall they engender. One becomes lost in smallness under the wavering sky.

The true Himalayas, miles above the sea, are still in the throes of creation. The mountains are young, very young, adolescently dinosaurian, terrible with ruthless youth.

Here is laid out for man to see the turmoil of earth's change since its crust folded and twisted and thrust this corner of the world, the Central Asian plateau with Tibet and Nepal, up into heaven. We become all pettiness in the scale of the enormous upflung rock hurled skywards. Strong wind and water, ice and snow and baking sun have carved their gradual breakdowns into the shapes we see, which like evolutionary mammoths last their aeons of slow travail before vanishing into new forms.

In the plane I acquire this knowledge of mountains, not beauty, splendour, vision, but primeval, awful insentience. The wings of a Himalayan storm have caught us, and our plane is tossed about until we no longer hope for anything but quick, merciful crash. Such is my last moment inquisitiveness (convinced of death, death held no fear), that while the Rampoche huddles telling his beads, his mouth opening in silence (no one could hear his shrieked prayer in the cyclone of sound hurtling us about), I cling to the frosted window-pane, curious whether we would perish in snow, bare rock, or boiling river. Dearest becomes so sick that she faints. Mike Young is lividly unhappy, and Professor Rimskov has given up. As for myself, I have one more look, and that is too much. I join Dearest on the floor.

But then, suddenly, we arrive. There is a great outburst of calm, as if we have already died. We descend, too swiftly for comfort, the wind dying about us as we plunge through misty drizzle. The Rampoche is the first to stagger out of the airplane. We follow, a dismal company: Dearest, myself, Professor Rimskov, Mike Young. The Rampoche watches us down the plane ladder, and though still a funny verdigris himself and swaying a little on his short legs, shakes hands with us gravely as we set foot on ground, and says: 'Welcome to Bongsor. All that I have is yours.'

I am now accustomed to these quick personality changes, from the Rampoche and everyone else. Man makes the gods in his own image, and it is only logical that the Rampoche should own multiple identities, as happily disconnected from each other as possible. Schizophrenia I know as man's normal state. How otherwise could man express his many-layered complexities than by a diversity of wildly inconsistent agents?

The airfield of Bongsor is tiny, a floating fichu square of flat brown, mist encircled now, but the tilting backs of the lower ridges are not far to guess. Professor Rimskov says: 'We're nine thousand feet up here. This level plain is an old, dried-up glacier that brought down too much silt with it and trapped itself, and then churned another escape further away. You'll see the mountains as soon as the mist lifts,' he says, 'it is fantastic, fantaastic.' He pronounces the word lengthily, which makes it more effective. 'Now Bongsor is four miles from here as the crow flies, over the ridges into the next valley.'

Out of the fine spraying mist looms a fearful galaxy of men, half goatskin robes to the knee, kukris in the waistband, guns in their hands, earrings with a turquoise or an agate round as a small egg in earlobe.

The Rampoche claps his hands. 'My servants.'

They surround us with threatening friendliness, pointing their guns, but merely relieve us of our bags. Others clamber into the plane. Two jeeps also appear, each flying a dark orange silk banner, the flag of the Rampoche of Bongsor.

'I had these jeeps brought in by plane last spring,' says the Rampoche. 'It cost me too much money, by Jove.'

From the plane's bowels are produced objects vaguely familiar, wrapped in straw and paper with strings, protruding smooth, china-white rims and curvatures. It is easy to guess what they are: the insignia of progress, sanitary fixtures, bought by the Rampoche, not for his Monastery (he assures us) but for the hotel he plans at Bongsor. 'It will be a limited company hotel,' he says. 'I'm calling it the Dam View Hotel. Perhaps a little too early, don't you think?'

Another jeep passes us, khaki grey, in it two men. Mike Young's eyes light up.

'That's the jeep from the Aid project at the dam, Anne,' he says excitedly. 'I'll give them a message for Unni, shall I? They can take it back with them. I'll ask him to get in touch with us.'

At that moment the Rampoche strikes his head-gear (he is wearing a tweed cap with his zoot suit) and groans in anguish. 'Alas,' he says, 'alas, the atrocity of it! The letter!' he cries, writhing. 'I could disembowel myself, my dear niece' – this is to me – 'the letter from our beloved engineer, Mr Menon, the pilot gave it to me and I forgot to give it to you when we were in Khatmandu. Here it is, I think' (going swiftly through his pockets), 'no, it is not here. It must be in the luggage. By Jove, I'll forget me own name next.'

There is nothing I can do. Not even become verbally indignant at the trick. The jeeps shiver into motion, cough uphill. A trick has been played upon me. By the Rampoche. Why, I do not know. Perhaps, if I had read the letter last night, I might not have come. But Rukmini is here. Devi, her sister, asked me to see her. And Mike Young, grim and young but reassuring, sits by me, so that I feel protected. As long as nothing happens to Unni, what else can go wrong?

On the four-mile long abominable jeep track (an enlarged bridle-path) from the airfield to the town (or is it village?) of Bongsor, over the ridge of two mountains, with zigzagging curls and spins, and with the long melodious thunder of the river below us, I fall into fevered dreaming. In the unreality of disquiet and physical discomfort last night reiterates itself.

Devi is sitting in my room. I am flat on my back, hear myself saying: 'Rukmini is at Bongsor?' and my voice is pale and lifeless.

'Yes. She left twelve days ago by airplane. You were in hospital then.'

That could be the same plane as the one Unni had taken back to Bongsor, when he left me, in my hospital bed, twelve days ago.

'Please,' says Devi, 'can you not go to Bongsor and bring her back?'

'Me, Devi?'

'Yes, you,' says Devi. 'Nobody else can do it.'

Of course I must do it. It is the only thing I can do. 'When is the next plane?'

'I do not know,' says Devi. 'Only one person would know, the Rampoche. He came back two days ago, he flies up and down very often on business.'

So there was a plane, two days ago, and no Unni and apparently no letter from Unni was on it. He had not come, and he had not written to me. Suddenly a disfiguring despair seized upon me, a swoop of utter helplessness, growing swiftly, enormous, frightening like the dark storms they have here, obliterating sky and land. 'I'll go to the Rampoche now and ask about the plane.'

Devi rises, looks at me steadily. 'You will see Unni. Please ask him to be good to my sister Rukmini.'

'I don't think Unni would hurt Rukmini in any way.' I don't believe anything I say, but the sky does not fall to pieces. It never does, after all. Humans are not so important as they think.

'For Rukmini Unni is god, the Lord Krishna. Yet Unni thinks she is a child, that we are both children. Tell him ... Rukmini and Devi, they are not children, they are women.'

I brought Devi back to the Temple, then my driver took me to the house of the Rampòche. It was dark, quiet after the singing streets. Perhaps no one was there, the plane had already gone with the Rampoche (as everyone in these miscalled primitive countries, he hopped on a plane as blithely as a Londoner takes his bus), I would have to wait days before the next.

But the servant, opening the heavy hobnailed doors, said the family was in, and stiffly climbing the narrow stair I nearly fell upon Dearest, her face covered in white clay (a beauty mask for the complexion).

'Mrs Ford what a delight my what a pleasure my Daddy will be enchanted truly will you step into the parlour my Daddy is just finishing prayers.'

The Rampoche sat in the contemplative pose, legs crossed with feet turned soles upward resting upon his thighs, on a bed with yellow silk curtains; his hand upon his knee slipped smooth beads between thumb and index finger. His face was serene and golden. Behind him on the clean bed his quilts were piled, the topmost one artistically folded in pyramidal waves, like a range of Chinese mountains in perfect equilibrium. On a small table was a Buddha of gold, about a foot high, in front of which burnt four butter lamps.

I made to withdraw, muttering about disturbance, but 'Nothing disturbs my Daddy when he is holy,' cried Dearest with loud delight, and so I sat on a low chair, sipping tea out of a silver cup, while the Rampoche finished his prayers, then rang a bell to change himself out of his holy self, bowed with forehead touching the table in front of the Buddha, poured some more melted butter into the lamps, and turned to me. His face, until then as smooth as that of the statue, became full of vivacity, eyes creased in smiling wrinkles, and a great deal of laughter issued from his mouth.

'My dear niece,' he cried, 'how jolly to see you are now so well.' He clapped his hands and shouted an order for food. 'I hope you will join us in a simple and frugal meal,' he said.

It was in vain I protested that I had already eaten; the little tables were set, the silver dishes of chicken, quail, meat, breadfruit, radishes, and what Dearest called 'Himalayan herbs to promote vigorous health and radiant intelligence' were laid out. But I conveniently had a giddy spell, and was stretched on the low couch which ran along one side of the wall.

'I am not yet entirely well,' I said, as I came to in a few moments. 'I am not allowed to eat more than twice a day.'

'My dear, dear niece,' cried the Rampoche, and extracting from his sleeve a strong mint-smelling green paste in a tiny silver box, rubbed some on my temples. 'This is the famous Tiger Balm of China,' he said gravely. 'I never travel without it now.'

Dearest meanwhile had produced some red powder, a Tibetan medicine, which I was made to swallow with some tea.

I could now refuse dinner, and asked the Rampoche about the plane to Bongsor.

His eyes suddenly became like small oysters in their shells, the white rimming the dark pupil all round. There was feigned surprise, some triumph, but also a kind of cunning calculation in that look. He knew why I wanted to go to Bongsor, and was quickly assessing the effect of my arrival.

'Why,' he exclaimed, 'that is indeed a good idea, yes indeed. Yes, in the pure air of Bongsor you will become strong and young in half the time. I always feel quite ill myself when I come to the Valley. I am a man of the mountains, breathing the pure air above. There communion with the Divine, my dear niece, is within grasp, while here, in the filth of the city ...' and his gesture was deprecatory, as that of an evangelist tossing the dust of his sandals against the lascivious cities.

'When is the next plane?' I asked again, pertinacious.

'Why, tomorrow morning,' said the Rampoche, laughing widely. 'Tomorrow, early in the morning, my dear niece. And you will be in time for our Rain God ceremonies next week. That is *really* when some wise people come to Bongsor. Because our ceremonies are much better than here, in Khatmandu. You will be a little early if you come now, but I suppose you must come tomorrow,' he said, accepting the inevitable.

'Yes, I'd like to book a plane seat for tomorrow.'

'Certainly,' said the Rampoche. 'The modest price is but eighty rupees, and it is a mere forty minutes to an hour (depending on the weather) from the Valley. Ah, my dear niece, how we shall look after your health.' He beamed. 'My humble property will be honoured by your visit. And many hearts will rejoice.'

On this ambiguous double-decked statement I left the Rampoche, to go home to pack with the help of Mita and Regmi. My warmest clothes, typewriter, paper. That was last night. At dawn Dearest and the Rampoche came to take me with them to the airfield. There I saw Mike Young, waiting for the same plane, going on the same errand. We did not need to speak one word. He gripped my hand and helped me up the ladder. I did not leave a note for anyone. Everybody would know soon enough.

'The Himalayan Drugs and Potions Company Limited', 'The Mountain Fur and Wood (Yaks, Goats, and other Useful Animals) Company Limited', 'The Ever Restcure and Happy Drinks Corporation Unlimited'. Along the tilted main street (a wobbly assemblage of praying stones, pot-holes, *chortens*, stupas, stone hovels, yak dung, climbing steeply up a dark brown slope) these signs of progress greet us. Each one of these embryo companies, with their enormous signboards in English and I suppose Nepalese and Tibetan, belong to the Rampoche of Bongsor.

'My Daddy is so progressive sometimes though at other times quite prehistoric as you can see Mrs Ford and what a pity there is a fog still otherwise you could see how much more but soon all will clear and the mountains will be with us.'

The mountains are hidden, but Bongsor lies about us with brown slopes. Tibetan houses, black and white with narrow windows, piled atop each other on the steepnesses. There is a wind-whipped, boulder-strewn, coarse and uncompromising violence about. We have passed meagre fields of barley and corn, tawny like the moth-eaten leopard skins on the walls of the Rana palaces in Khatmandu. The road twists about half way up above the fields, and down in the gorge rages a boiling torrent, its noise after a time dazing our ears so that we no longer hear it. A procession of yaks pass us, going their slow yak-pace, loaded with tea and borax, their black matted hair exudes a strong smell; long-haired goats are tied to stony bare walled-in patches of ground at the side of the houses. The women have flat square burnished faces, striped aprons, shawls about their hair in thick plaits. There are many weapons in the men's waistbands, but people come out to join hands and bow to the Rampoche, who blesses them from the jeep.

Atop the climbing street and the houses of Bongsor is the Monastery, a massive fortress with toppling battlemented walls, heavy wood and iron gates, four corner watch-towers, and a piling of stone going up and up, a miniature Potala. For we are now near Tibet, though in Nepal, and Lhasa is spiritually nearer than Khatmandu.

The Monastery gates are open, they clang to behind us, there are armed men around it, guards of the Rampoche. We have driven into a large inner paved quadrangle, bounded on both sides by galleries with rooms opening on to it. There are ponies saddled, a small fire burning in a corner, some monks about squatting, drinking tea, more armed men, boys with shaven heads and dirty robes, young apprentice lamas. These are the stables and the outhouses for servants and unexalted guests of the Rampoche. We drive into a second courtyard, and stop. Here is a parking shed for three jeeps, more rooms strung along the rampart of walls, and a newly white-washed Tibetan house with its back to the ramparts and its framed windows facing the courtyard.

'This is our new hotel for welcome tourists,' says Dearest proudly.

Beyond this courtyard is still another, smaller, from which rises upon steps, like St Paul's Cathedral, pyramid-shaped edifices of stone. This is the Monastery proper, the residence of the Rampoche and of his deities, his lamas, disciples, henchmen, and soldiers; here also are his granaries, cache for arms, and treasures. A medieval fortress, back to the hill upon which it stands, dominating the town of Bongsor at its foot.

I manage to say, before getting down from the jeep, to Dearest: 'I want to see Rukmini, as soon as possible, please.'

'Of course,' says Dearest, no whit surprised, 'I am sure my Daddy will arrange it she has been our guest as you know though my Daddy tried to tell her this was too rough but Rukmini is living behind a veil in ecstasy enchanted with much prayer for Unni Menon's sake and here is my Daddy now with the letter he *thinks* he forgot to give you last night.'

The Rampoche comes down from his jeep, and after blessing a good many lamas in very dirty stained robes, who have appeared from orifices (door is too wide a word) in the stone walls of the fortress, approaches me, and hands me, at last, Unni's letter.

Mike and Professor Rimskov and I enter the hotel, where our rooms await us. Each room seems hewn out of stone, narrow windows wood-shuttered give on to the courtyard and the rest of the Monastery. The view is non-existent (that is why the Rampoche, with Tibetan sardonic humour, calls it the Dam View). The floor of stone is covered with tough wool carpets of yaks' or goats' hair. Dearest has come with us to show us with great pride the bathrooms, always a first with tourists, across the corridor, stone tubs with tin pails standing by. The lavatories are labelled Gentlemen and Madams, they are the squatting type, easy to keep clean, if somewhat strenuous for limbs unused to the effort. There is a pail of water with a tin can ladle for sluicing. It is all nearly modern, and extremely clean.

'Now you must all rest and wash,' says Dearest brightly, 'and then the gong will ring for lunch but tonight you have a welcome dinner with my Daddy.'

We are left alone, and gradually become invaded by a curious sense of imprisonment, of paralysis, of semi-cataleptic stupor. The thick walls, the obscurity, the ensconcing of the building between ramparts, within the fortress of the Monastery, its only view the courtyard, the large clanging gates, the groups of armed men hinting at sudden onslaughts by night, raids, and medieval wars, the near-sinister pyramidal piles climbing the slopes beyond us, with those slit windows behind which we imagine vicious bows and arrows, gun muzzles, pails of boiling oil … Mike Young and I stand in the corridor, not daring to look at each other for fear of revealing our fear; we both feel the same oppression (and because it is higher than the Valley, we both pant slightly after walking upstairs and about), a mental airlessness as well as a physical one. Professor Rimskov, bald, broad-beamed, and beaming, whose high pitched voice relieves our unease, comes out after inspecting his room, rubbing his hands. Here he is the Expert.

'Ah, Mrs Ford, Mr Young. Do you like your lodgings? Not bad, is it?' He looks purposeful, happy, and at home. 'I will just permit myself to call some servants, you call them by shouting at them in the courtyard … I thought each one of you would like a servant … one has to hire them, there are none in the hotel.'

Professor Rimskov does speak a mixture of Tibetan – more than the five words all bad which Dearest imputed to him – and the local Bongsor dialect, and in no time three grim, weaponed dwarfs are bringing in a pail of hot water for each of us.

'First a good hot bath, then we shall have lunch, and then if you like I will take you around, yes?'

'I want to find a friend of mine who is here.'

'I am at your service, Mrs Ford. I know my way all about this Monastery, we shall find her if she is here.'

The hot water is soothing, washing away tiredness, depression. The small room seems safe. I dress again, lie down to rest, exertion at ten thousand feet makes me light-headed as well as breathless. After half an hour in the horizontal position I am much better. Then the sense of imprisonment returns, and restlessly I get up. There is a knock at the door. It is Professor Rimskov again. Instead of being irritated, I am happy. How indispensable he is. He comes in holding at arm's length a large jar of cold cream.

'For you, sunburn cream. You forgot – tourists always forget. I never travel without it. In Tibet I used butter. You will need it here or, forgive me, your skin' – he drools round the word – 'will be ruined. And now,' after watching me with ample satisfaction put on some cream (he directs it to be rubbed well into nose and mouth and round the eyes), 'the sun is dispelling the mist. Let us go up to the roof and watch the mountains.'

There is a flat roof to the structure; to it we accede by a wooden ladder, pushing open a trap-door, emerging into bright, blinding sunlight. For a moment I blink, unable to see, then look round.

I am looking at a huge horseshoe of snow peaks, some far and some near, fenced from us by a circus of animal brown and green slopes going sheer down to the boiling, green-milk torrent below. All the snow peaks seem so near, the blue sheen of ice upon the crevasses, the shadow-filled hollows, the spume of snow like smoke blown about them against the background of the dark sapphire sky, their immensity increasing our personal insignificance, and yet at the same time exalting us as nothing else could do.

Professor Rimskov's high falsetto is now honeyed with emotion. 'Are they not incredible? That is why I cannot leave. That is why they say I am crazy. I am. About the Himalayas, because there is nothing else in the world like them ... except perhaps the Antarctic, or the moon. I think it the superlative degree of every impact to which these mountains subject one ... an extreme of shock from which one does not recover, perhaps. More than woman, more than love, more than anything else. I can never return to anywhere else. Can you understand that?'

'Which one of these is Mana Mani?' I ask.

Professor Rimskov sounds nearly hysterical as he replies: '*La Belle Dame sans Merci*. Right behind you.'

Because of looking northwards towards the enormous half-circle of mountains, I had not turned my head, thinking only the Monastery behind me. Now I looked. Beyond the Monastery riding the hill, beyond the brown, untidy, wolf-pelt shaggy hill crest behind it, suddenly straight up in the sky, there she was, Mana Mani, a tall white spire, an impossible mountain, so lovely, so unexpected, so slim and chiselled so dangerously that it seemed, if one looked long enough, she would suddenly overbalance and fall upon us.

'Mana Mani, the abode of the Goddess protecting Bongsor,' says Professor Rimskov. 'But if you ask the people here, it's really five goddesses. They belong to an old religion, far older than Buddhism and Hinduism. You also find their cult in Mongolia, in Tibet, and in Khatmandu in the countryside shrines, where they are worshipped at night with sacrifices. Five goddesses, each with two names, two identities, one good and one evil. But their names are so terrifying it

478

is forbidden to pronounce them, and so gradually Mana Mani has come to mean the goddesses instead of merely the mountain.'

I went on gazing at Mana Mani. She took one's breath away. No wonder Unni was haunted by her. 'Mana Mani did this ... did that ... she threw half the road down.' It was easy to give a more than human malevolence to this dazzling, uncompromising perfection for whom all the sky was background, for whom the Monastery crouched at foot level in shadowy worship.

'She doesn't look benign, does she?'

'No goddess is. They're so bloodthirsty. The blood of male animals, lusty and strong, that's what they want.'

At that moment a brass gong rings somewhere, and the Professor interrupts himself.

'Lunch,' he says with alacrity. 'I am afraid it is a very bad lunch here, but the evening meal is better because the Rampoche eats with us at night.'

He is suddenly hungry, uninterested in the mountain, responding like a Pavlovian canine to the sound of the gong.

'I'll come in a moment,' I say, and he goes down the trap-door first. I stay gazing at Mana Mani, and the more I look the more I feel troubled, afraid, desolate. Looking at her I know her merciless. A stifling cruelty. *Le Belle Dame sans Merci*, Unni's *Belle Dame*. Unni ... Rukmini. I look again at Unni's letter in my pocket. I have read it already at least four times, merely because it says so little:

Anne, I cannot come to you by this airplane. Please wait for me. I shall come to you as soon as I can.

That is all. Not one word more, though I stare and stare. If I had received this letter in Khatmandu, would I have come to Bongsor? Would I have come, even if Devi had asked? And I knew I would, I fold the paper up, soon I scan it again, hoping for a miracle, a word of love. But there is none, no word of love for me; not a word about Rukmini. Yet Rukmini must have been there when this letter was written. Unni must have known it. She must have been in the same airplane. He does not mention it. Of course there was the dam; there had been trouble at the dam, that was what had kept Unni from coming back to me; that, and not Rukmini. That is why only this heartless, pitiless line on the blue paper, for me to twist between my fingers.

I look up at Mana Mani again. The mountain is watching me. Under her icy hostility I feel my thoughts fall apart, another self of mine disclosed, a self merciless as she. The gong rings again, and I go to lunch knowing I will not eat.

Professor Rimskov has buff-coloured soup, a curiously scented hash (buffalo, goat, or yak), and a glutinous sweet flyblown at conception. The Professor eats with audible relish, more to show he is immune to mountain sickness and at home in Tibetan surroundings than out of real appetite. He finishes both our sweets with gusto, then demands buttered tea, Tibetan fashion.

'This is really Tibetan country, though it belongs to Nepal,' he says. 'Takes a few days to get acclimatized. This gorge is nearly ten thousand feet, at least four thousand higher than Khatmandu. It's one of the lower passes to Tibet.'

He chatters on, while I wonder where Mike has disappeared. Mike's lunch is laid, but there is no Mike. And once again comes dread, this certainty of isolation and impending danger. I want to look over my shoulder and see if Mana Mani is there, watching me, my disquiet irremediably linked to the existence of that haughty, inimical spire climbing so whitely above us.

We are having tea (mine ordinary) when the hotel reverberates with noise, a frightening clangour as it roars on and on and on, pouring into and among the echoing slopes.

'Oh my,' cries Rimskov, 'the big drums of the Monastery. Now why?'

This is followed by the weirdest noises, like sirens howling, high and wild and sweetly dreadful, on and on, shrieking each to each.

'They're blowing the rams' horns,' says the Professor, disturbed. 'That's a call for prayer against great calamity.'

Whatever the cause, the ensuing tumult is evident. Shouts are heard, the shouts swelling into a pandemonium of sound. The courtyard is filled with people running and galloping goats and whinnying ponies. A confusion seemingly endless, but out of which someone is speaking now, aloud, screaming, a lama in amber waving his arms above his shaven head.

'What does he say?' I ask Rimskov.

'Can't hear from this far,' he replies. He is listening, it is obvious he cannot understand. The mob is shouting again, beginning a new

480

frenzy, rippling up and down. The lama turns towards the Monastery, his arms go up, and everyone turns too, putting their arms up and shouting. On the battlemented walls the armed body-guards are carrying long trumpets, which they blow, turned towards Mana Mani.

'I think they are praying to the goddesses,' says Professor Rimskov in my ear, 'but I don't know why.'

Then I see Mike Young push himself through the crowd, leaving a ripple of jeers behind him, but no one tries to stop him. He stands with us outside the Dam View Hotel, looking at the courtyard of people, looking at the trumpeters on the medieval walls.

'Isn't it fantastic?' he says. 'This beats anything.'

'Mike, where have you been?'

'Went to have a good look round. Wasn't very hungry. Everybody seems to have vanished. No Rampoche, no Dearest, nobody. I went right round, into the village too. Thought I'd get some information. But nope. Nothing. This is the craziest place. What are they making all this noise for? I hope Unni turns up soon. Tried to organize myself some transport to the dam, but didn't get anywhere. Seems all the jeeps are busy today bringing in things from the plane.'

I look at Mana Mani. The lower portion of the spire is in cloud, cloud like enveloping hands. I feel stifled with apprehension, yet at the same time strangely detached. As a Tibetan lama, I too am floating about my own body instead of being inside it. A terrifying detachment, being on the edge of a precipice and tempted to throw one's vile body over.

The courtyard is emptying now, the men drifting inconsequently away, the women pulling children back to their aprons, all going through the gates, and soon nothing is happening. Only the mountains, clouding up around us, with a hint of end of day and a curious desolation.

'We can't stand here all day,' says Mike. 'What are we going to *do*?'

'Oh,' cries Professor Rimskov, 'you Americans, always wanting something to *do*. Here it is best to *be*, to meditate on *being*. Come, I will take you round the Monastery, there are *most* interesting things to see.'

'I've been already,' says Mike, 'I've been walking all round the place.' But he comes with us.

We cross the courtyard and enter the bulky main edifice. The doors here are narrow, of heavy wood, reinforced with metal strips, bolts, bars. There is a triple girdle of rampart, wall, and gates round the inner Monastery. Somewhere in there lives the Rampoche. Somewhere in there must be Rukmini.

Mike strikes his fist, suddenly raging, a pitiful young fury. 'I wish I could blow up the whole thing. I'm sure they're hiding somewhere. I wish I could lay my hands on His Preciousness. I'd twist his neck.' He is incoherent and angry, and of course it is Rukmini, but he is not going to say it.

'Mike,' I say, 'Rukmini came here of her own accord. She is a friend of Dearest. There is no sense in the Rampoche keeping her a prisoner. *She* may not want to see us.'

'That's possible, of course,' says Mike. He looks so unhappy that I slip my hand under his arm. He throws me a quick grateful look and squeezes my arm. 'Oh Anne,' he says, 'I do love her so much, and I thought one day, last spring, I began to think – she might in time love me a little too.'

'I know, Mike.'

'You think Rukmini is in love with Unni, don't you?' he asks.

'I don't know. It's not as simple as that.'

'I know,' says Mike. 'She thinks he's a god. It's really hero-worship. I think she's very young still,' says Mike, and my heart is wrung with pity. 'And her husband – less said the better. I thought there might be some hope for me. I would try to make her happy, give her all she wants. ... Unni's a great guy. But seeing he doesn't care for her, seeing it's *you* he cares for, Anne, I thought I had a chance.'

I do not reply. What can I say? Does Unni's loving me make any difference to Rukmini's feelings for him, or to his feelings for her, if he has any? I hurry forward, Professor Rimskov is waiting for us impatiently on the steps which lead up, cathedral-wise, to the massive pyramids whose composite aspect is so forbidding. Most of these piles of masonry and stone are four-storeyed, each storey smaller as it rises upon a lower, and round each runs a narrow battlemented terrace. The windows are slits, and the rear of the fortress protected by the body of the hill itself. No wonder that the General's father, leading troops to Bongsor to attack this medieval stronghold, produced only fearful carnage and not the whale's jawbone. I wonder vaguely about the jawbone's present whereabouts as we penetrate into the butter-rancid musky interior, where many small fumous lamps pattern grotesque dancing shapes about.

We go from room to room, confused in a haze of incense and shifting light and soft-footed lamas praying. The inner architecture seems extraordinarily haphazard, with corridors of stone leading into pillared recesses where on altar tables dwell the gods of Tantric lamaism; many of them representative of the terrible couple, the Father and Mother of All, in the symbolic embrace, Origin of All. They are crowned with skulls, rear their bronze passion amid an aureole of arms. Others are the serene, contemplative reflexes of the Buddha, hands in the teaching or the praying position, negation and affirmation of Being, just as the embrace is the summit of sensation and at the same time its end, consummation to emptiness.

'As you can see,' says Professor Rimskov, lecturing us with the fervour of the uninterrupted, 'here is practised a perverted type of Buddhism, mixed with Tantrism which itself is a medley of magic, Siva worship, and a primitive animism. In Khatmandu are many Tantric shrines, especially in the countryside, with rites similar to the European black masses, the witches' sabbath, and the Bacchanals of ancient Greece. The chief feature of Tantrism is the introduction of female goddesses, the *female* principle, instead of the male. The whole of this region is dedicated to goddesses, and they are all incarnations of each other, manifestations materializing in two forms, one benign, the other malignant. When I was in Tibet,' he adds, mechanically turning a huge copper prayer mill, taller than a man, standing in a corner of the room, 'I tried time and again to get the names of the malignant forms, but no one would tell me. Only the benign names are spoken or written, because to utter the evil ones would make wickedness put on *being*, take shape and form and life. Everywhere in the world you find this,' says Professor Rimskov, as he leads the way further into the maze, past hundreds of prayer mills inscribed with the formula which is supposed to keep the world safe from obliteration by Total Evil, *Om Mani Padme Hum*, 'this fear that words *are* the thing they represent. In the beginning was the Word, and the Word was God, and the word was made flesh. That's St John. He was near to Buddhism when he said that. The Word made flesh … that's what everyone is afraid of. The creative power of the Word to *become* reality in our minds. ... That's why the repetition of prayer, of words, accumulates merit in the other world, in every religion.'

'And calling on the name of God dispels demons,' I say.

'Exactly.' Professor Rimskov beams. 'I believe it's fundamental to the human being, isn't it, this almost magic feeling of respect and awe in front of words and their power? That's why authors are often felt to be endowed with something a bit monstrous.' He giggles waggishly at me. 'It's a very old feeling, that feeling about language. What is once uttered exists, what isn't spoken or written doesn't exist ... don't we all really believe that?'

Fascinated, compelled, Mike and I follow the Professor. I note the flitting shapes of the acolytes and lamas in their dirty maroon robes and their high felt boots, the walls with painted frescoes dim with smoke, the steps up and down, the carved writhing friezes over the doors, and here and there, in prayer upon cushions made of some kind of plaited yaks' hair, or pouring melted butter into the small cups of offered lamps, the men and women, some well dressed, others in rags. And everywhere, all the time, like a great beehive hums the endless reiteration: *Om Mani Padme Hum, Om Mani Padme Hum.*

'What I don't understand,' says Mike, abruptly shaking off his own trance, 'is the Rampoche being such a crook, and at the same time spouting so much about non-attachment and beatitude and Buddhist Nirvana. I've heard him talk about merging with Beatitude, then I've seen him ten seconds later, without batting an eyelash, offer a bribe or a girl to some guy with whom he wanted to clinch a deal.'

Professor Rimskov laughs his hen-cackling laughter, as he agilely leaps over a threshold and down a few steps, passing a small courtyard with a strong smell of urine, leading the way into a staircase plunging below ground. 'All is illusion. For the Rampoche neither money, nor women, nor any material thing, exist. They belong to the substantial self of his doomed to annihilation, that self which deals with illusions of the flesh, and it can be abolished by an effort of will, a concentration of thought upon the One, or the repetition of *Om Mani Padme Hum*, words which *create* the substance of good. That's lamaistic casuistry, and that's how they get the best of both worlds.'

We now stand in front of a dark red curtain with a pattern of crosses. Professor Rimskov lifts the curtain. Contrary to the other rooms, dark with but few lights to relieve the gloom, here is abundance of lamps; hundreds of small glass and pewter vessels, in rows on the altar table, in niches in the walls, blazing upon two enormous drums mounted on stands, long Tibetan trumpets, longer than a man, with the opening resting on the ground, and huge rams' horns twisted and convoluted and shiny with handling, with silver mouth-pieces. Upon the altar stands a fantastic figure, the Female Multiple One, fiendess and goddess, with a pyramid of heads and a nightmare whirling of arms, feet upon a world of humans and animals.

'That's Mana Mani, or rather the goddess of Mana Mani, the Five-in-One, or rather Ten-in-One,' says Professor Rimskov. 'Notice the ten heads piled on top of each other. Her name is sacred, hence only the mountain's name is used to designate her. Curiously a Hindi name for a Tantric goddess.'

There is malevolence in the bright room, perhaps because the horns, the drums, now silent, remind us of the sudden tumult, the heart-leaping fear which had infected the fortress so short a time ago. In the fantastic light the complicated figure moves and dances, the heads shake and sway. There is a festoon of skulls round the neck.

'Rukmini,' cries Mike suddenly, 'Rukmini.'

With the eyes of love Mike has seen her first, and the sound of his voice splitting the hostile silence about us makes us come out of our fantastic semi-torpor, this frightened and frightening lethargy which binds us as people whose feet are entangled in a nightmare, unable to escape.

Rukmini, a pewter jug in hand, is pouring melted butter into the lamps round the goddess. She has come from the back of the altar; at least, it *looks* like Rukmini, turning to a small boy-lama (is it a boy? — under the grime on the face, the bulky robe, the felt boots, I suspect a girl's body) with a tray of lamps, lighting each lamp from a flame on a spill, holding each up to Mana Mani in supplication, and setting it down on the altar. It is Rukmini, but she gives no heed to the sound of her name.

Mike is by her side in a second, looking at her, saying 'Rukmini,' overpowered by her far-away trance, this sinking into another universe, a god-surrounded atrophy of self. Even his strong, American individualism here is powerless to touch her. He keeps on repeating: 'Rukmini, you're here. Please listen to me. Please, darling, look at me, only *look* at me.'

I don't think he has ever suffered so much as when she turns to look at him, her lovely face dreamy, enchanted. She wears a long striped skirt, flat in front, with a buttoned sleeveless tunic in the Tibetan style, the pale sleeves of an under-robe protruding. She has no ornaments in her hair. When she moves her bangles tinkle softly, that charming golden sound intimately associated with the presence of a woman, subtle and enduring as perfume.

'Is my lord come,' she asks, 'is my lord come to fetch me at last?'

'Oh,' says Professor Rimskov, and starts to laugh. His laughter is nervous, it has no mirth, only pity and horror.

Mike is a young man, not preoccupied with mysticism, thoroughly Western in his reactions. I anticipate his next move. From my own cataleptic state, I see him in my mind's eye turn on his heel, fling himself out, taking the words at face value, not searching within.

But Mike is in love with Rukmini, and because of that, because love gives insight and understanding above and beyond selfishness, because he too has known the hell of lovers harpooned by love helpless and hopeless, concealing under his gay, grinning face and cheerful laughter a treasure of unused devotion, he understands at once. I see him grow in the space of a few seconds into a state of pure unselfishness, made so by love alone.

'Not yet, my darling, not yet, but he will come. Very soon.'

'You will bring him to me, Mike,' she says, dreamily putting another lamp in front of the goddess. 'Because you love me, don't you?' she adds, cruel and careless.

'Yes, Rukmini,' says Mike, 'I love you.'

She smiles through him, her eyes ecstatic. 'I'll see you tonight,' she says, 'at dinner, when my lord comes, perhaps.' And moves away, is gone.

Mike comes out of love then, out of the transporting moment, the moment of ecstasy unshared with Rukmini, transcending mortal greed and desire, a moment to redeem the corruption of a whole world. He is what he would have called 'himself' again. 'God,' he says, 'do I need a drink. It's stifling in here, let's get out.'

Even Professor Rimskov had no heart left for guiding, so strong had been Mike's suffering he had felt it and wanted to be out of it, as did Mike himself. We walked out, in the courtyard flooded in sun,

our discomfort remained to haunt us, an inner darkness. I was tired,
lethargic, half giddy all the time, but I did all I did as if lifted out of
myself, so that later it was always to remain a dream, poised upon a
mountain-top, yet a dream to drag round with me, always. ... We
came out of the Monastery into the humping downward street of
Bongsor, a sparrow battery of ragged children found us and followed
as we made our way to the Ever Restcure and Happy Drinks Unlimited, which turned out to be a dim cave scooped out of rock, with
ramshackle chairs and tables at which nobody sat, and the following
elucidation below the vast new title-board I had seen from the jeep:

> FOR THE FAMOUS
> ROSE LIQUOR
> NEPALESE BRANDY AND WHISKY
> AND OTHER RAVISHMENTS
> VISIT OUR CAFÉ

One of the walls of the cave was decorated with the posters of an
Indian film, a crowd of buxom dancers, with a lengthy caption:

> GRAND GALA RELEASE – IN GORGEOUS TECHNICOLOR
> A sensational picture for all masses and classes
> A heart troubling love story supported by
> Grand Musical smash told amidst
> TEARS AND LAUGHTER

'I wonder how this poster got here?'

'Oh, ha,' said Professor Rimskov, heavily winking. 'I'll tell you
later.'

Later he told me: this was a brothel at night, hence the Unlimited,
and hence the poster, as near an approach to pictorial pornography as
was allowed outside the Monastery (inside, of course, it was not
pornography, but mysticism).

Our entrance produced the proprietor from behind a curtain. He
was a charming ball of a man, so round and oily one suspected him of
rolling himself in a blanket of melted butter at night. He and Professor
Rimskov had met the year before, and renewed acquaintance with
exclamations of happiness.

'My friend, Tenzin Lama,' Professor Rimskov introduced.

'*Kushog* Rimskov' – (*kushog* means lord in Tibetan) – 'it is indeed a famous day when you come to visit my poor house,' exclaimed Tenzin Lama. He clapped his hands, and three surly looking girls, very pale, with heavy necks of goitre and their hair in little plaits tight and stiff with dirt, appeared from behind the curtain, were plied with orders for whisky and Tibetan beer.

'These are from the next valley,' the Lama explained. 'Refugees. There have been such terrible floods we have many such. I give them food and treat them as my own nieces.' He laughed, as if with glee, to denote the exact status of the girls in his establishment, and shook his head to indicate sorrow at the floods. 'Such calamities we have never had before, Kushog. You felt the earthquake this afternoon?'

'Earthquake? There was no earthquake.'

'Oh, there was, there was,' said Tenzin Lama solemnly. 'Many people felt it.'

'Did you feel it?' asked Mike.

'I was sleeping,' replied Tenzin Lama. 'And I am not holy enough to feel with my body all that the goddesses mean when they shake the earth in anger. But others, they have felt it. Why otherwise would the great drums beat, and the horns be blown? Oh, it is bad, it is bad, the goddesses are very wrathful. We shall have plague as well as floods and hunger, and it is all because of the dam.'

'Ah,' said Mike, crashing his fist down on the heavy table, 'that's it. That's what they're after, all of them. The dam.'

'Look here, Tenzin Lama,' said Professor Rimskov, 'you are an educated man. You have seen dams and roads in other places. You have had floods before the dam was even thought of. Then how can you say it is because of the dam?'

Tenzin looked uneasy. '*I* don't say it, Kushog,' he said. 'Of course I have travelled ... I was a soldier once, myself, in the Gurkhas. I went down to Singapore, also, selling turquoises and agates. I have seen the world. But here in the mountains it is different. You know, this is the land of gods and goddesses, and their wishes come first. And Mana Mani is angry. Some say,' he added with casual carelessness, 'some even say that the goddesses are restless because they want a man, Kushog, a new husband.'

'You mean a human sacrifice?' said Professor Rimskov, shocked.

'I only say what I hear,' Tenzin persisted. 'Everyone knows that all goddesses have their hungry moments, like women. And, of course, being female, what can they like but the blood and the seed of males, Kushog? A young, handsome man. That is what some say. In our valley, before, there were such offerings, and the goddesses were pleased.'

'I should have thought,' said Mike, 'that being female they'd like a woman chopped up for a change.'

'Oh, sahib,' Tenzin was profoundly frightened, 'please do not say this, it is terrible.' And his hand went tremblingly inside his robe, open to form a large breast pouch confined by his belt, extracted from it a rosary of amber beads, which he began to finger, muttering prayers to counteract the evil of Mike's words. 'Not a woman,' he said, 'nobody *can* harm a woman or a girl in this valley, or any female animal. The goddesses look after their own, Kushog. But it is well known that females like blood, the blood of young males. The gods are not as cruel,' he laughed, 'they only want flowers and fruit and grain. But Mana Mani, she is very cruel,' he cried, and under his oily coat of butter and cheerfulness he was uneasy with terror.

The slope left us breathless as we went up again, passing the armed men in the outer quadrangle, conscious of the peering faces from the rooms on both sides, the high ramparts enclosing the sky above us, re-imprisoned, stifled in suspicion and hostility and this eerie uncertainty, a dread which evaporated all other feelings and desires and rendered us unreal to ourselves, until we scarcely knew why we had come to Bongsor and what we were doing there.

'I think I'm beginning to see the pattern,' panted Mike. 'They're trying a frame-up. They're scared of the dam, so the Rampoche is working up people with fake earthquakes and things.'

'Mike,' I said, 'what are we going to do?'

'I don't think we can do anything until Unni gets here.'

'Do you think Unni will come?'

'Sure,' said Mike, 'bound to. As soon as he can. My guess is to-night. If I could only get a jeep, I'd go to the dam. It's only about eight miles from here, but it's eight climbing miles. If he doesn't turn up, think I'd better try to get there tomorrow morning. I can walk it, once my breathing gets easier.'

'Maybe the Rampoche will lend us a jeep?'

'I tried. It was no go today.'

'Maybe tomorrow,' I said, 'if Unni doesn't come.'

'He must come,' said Mike simply. 'If he got my message, he knows you're here.'

And then Professor Rimskov called us to see Mana Mani once again. We went up on the flat roof. The Monastery was already in shadow, but Mana Mani behind it was radiant with the poured gold of sunset, the circus of mountains was a splendour of pink and golden ice against a magenta sky streaked with long shafts of shadow, reflections of the peaks into the air above them. In loveliness the mountains stood about us, and looking down in the courtyard we saw small fires, intent people crouching in the cold over a smell of boiling meat and the smoky sting of burning dung; we heard the hubbub of chants far off, a tinkle of bells, muffled drums, miscellaneous, unarranged noises which indicated preoccupations with living and with prayer. In the Valley we had left such noises were immensely comforting, we became part of them; but here on the Mountain all was strange and desperate and evil and hallucinating, a phenomenon of horror and a spell upon us, living observed from the flat roof, and yet also an estrangement from all we were and knew.

'It'll be all right when Unni comes,' repeated Mike.

And then Dearest was calling in her cheerful voice, making the world ordinary again: 'Mrs Ford Mrs Ford,' poking her head through the trap, a Dearest in a thick wadded robe. 'Oh it is so cold at night Mrs Ford and *of course* you do not have warm clothes so I have brought some for you they are mine but our size is the same and my Daddy has now finished praying and so shall we go and dine I am so glad you have come really Mrs Ford.' She hugged my arm, sincerely happy, intensely affectionate. 'I hope you stay many days Mrs Ford so I can practise my English and also Rukmini though she is behind a veil now her mind in ecstasy but when Unni Menon comes here she will be more twentieth century again.'

I was so weary I could have wept, standing there, bawled like a baby. Rukmini, Unni, me. Me, Unni, Rukmini. Something wrong, something gone awry. Something I alone, perhaps, could put into words, but did not want to. In words what had not existed would become real, my words giving it shape and life.

Going down the trap-door with Dearest I was weary to tears with more than physical tiredness, but what it was I would not say, not even to myself.

The Rampoche was holding forth. Clad in a fur-lined robe, seated on a long spreading settee from China covered with carpets, he pressed fragrant Chinese green tea upon us, saying it helped to dissolve the fat in the food, and discoursed freely, vaingloriously, in that sudden expansiveness which comes upon men of much cunning and great contrivance when they no longer hold themselves in, and feel an irrepressible urge to boast before underlings or people who cannot hurt them, even if they reveal their plotting meannesses and their rapacities.

Although proud of a Chinese ancestry, the Rampoche had a strong admixture of Tibetan blood, and was therefore more violent and more boastful than a true son of that meticulous and modest race. He also liked Tibetan beer, or *chang*, which he drank instead of the Chinese tea he gave his guests. Its smell nearly killed the delicate fragrance of the latter in the hermetic, thickly carpeted room, but its absorption made the Rampoche exuberate.

'For many years, hundreds of years, we have owned much land, all the land here, and also across the passes to the north. I have much property in Tibet as well as Nepal. Always the Monastery has looked after the people of our hills and mountains. An obedient people, religious, until now.' He took another quaff of beer. 'Alas, now times are changed. Religion leaves their hearts, and there will be much trouble, much trouble. They care no longer for those who protect them, and the Spirits are angry.'

'I thought I had noticed, indeed,' said Professor Rimskov with a foxy look upon his rubicund countenance (he had dressed for dinner and looked very Prussian and correct), 'there were far fewer butter lamps than last year on the altars.'

'Ha ha!' exclaimed the Rampoche, raucous and Tibetan, his voice guttural with anger (and suddenly I knew the dangerous violence encased in the genial little man). 'You have noticed, honoured sir ... I am glad you have noticed.' He took another gulp of *chang*, his face had become very red. Dull hatred suffused it. Dearest giggled. She was sitting next to Professor Rimskov, Mike, Rukmini, and I faced them, while the Rampoche occupied the top of the room. Each of us

491

had in front of him a small table on which the food had been laid. The middle of the room where, in the West, a table would have been, was empty, covered by a beautiful rug.

'Fewer butter lamps, much less butter for the lamps. Oh, it is bad, bad,' exclaimed the Rampoche. 'Instead of bringing the butter from their flocks the people keep it for themselves. I cannot get anyone to cut my wood; no one to care for the goats of the Monastery; our fields lie neglected. People have this new terrible greed for money; they would rather work for money than for the goddesses and me.' He shook his head and groaned aloud. 'Punishment will come,' he prophesied. 'Alas, alas.'

'Serve you jolly well right, Rampoche,' said Mike. 'A man shouldn't be a slave and made to work a hundred and fifty days a year for anybody, not even for a goddess.' And he raised his cup of tea.

'Oh Mr Mike,' said Dearest. 'don't upset my Daddy he is so sore already everybody asking for money now and soon I suppose even trade unions here,' and she tut-tutted most charmingly.

'It is the dam,' said the Rampoche, at first quietly, but as he spoke his voice rose until it roared and thundered. 'I have been patient, very patient about this dam. At first I thought: it is as they say, it is good for the people. I even tried to help with contracts.' (I remembered the letter written to me at the Coronation, trying to obtain a contract from Unni through me.) 'It was I who told the people here: go, go and work for the honoured engineer at the dam. I told them. I tried to help with supplies too. I told the dacoits and the thieves: don't attack the food convoys up to the dam. I told the people: now be good, don't turn into dacoits and bandits and take the supplies. I never refused to carry anything in *my* airplane for them, anything they needed. And now they have complained to the Government that I was charging too much, and organizing thieves to stop convoys. But the dam is not a good thing. It is badly planned. It is upsetting the balance of the mountains. It is a dangerous thing, not scientific. See, never have there been so many earthquakes. There was one this afternoon.'

'Oh, blah,' said Mike rudely. Rukmini sat, a few yards away from him, beautiful and absent, he stared at her, and his knuckles were white. 'There was no earthquake, Rampoche,' said Mike. 'Only a lot of drum beating, but no earthquake. I guess somebody was trying to hypnotize people into believing there was one, that's all.'

'Gee,' said Dearest happily, 'are you trying to psychoanalyse my Daddy Mr Mike?'

The Rampoche looked at Mike, a look of anger, animosity, and also calculation. He allowed a silence, full of the tick of a clock, and then he went on slowly, deliberately. 'The goddess is angry at the dam. You who laugh now, you will be sorry and you will weep blood. The goddess will not allow her mountains and rivers to be polluted by the dam. Already twice there have been landslides, and all the work washed away. Now the men will refuse to work, unless ...'

He stopped, looked round us all, a malevolent glare.

'Unless there is a human sacrifice. A man must die. I have tried to prevent it. I have warned Unni Menon. He does not listen. Now it is too late. Today the wonder-worker drew the horoscope. Someone will die in this valley. Soon. And then we shall *all* weep.'

It was disagreeable and melodramatic, and in the close room, with the dipping lamps, horribly convincing. Nobody spoke. And then, slowly, deliberately, we heard the drums, booming slowly, gently, like the enormous steps of some quiet giant walking. The Rampoche looked up. Boom boom boom went the drums, not loud. We heard the long soft melodious roar of the gates being opened, one after the other.

'A visitor,' said Dearest.

Then the flurry of voices downstairs at the foot of the long staircase up to the room where we sat.

Mike and I stared at the door, hearing the steps come up, and I knew them, I knew his steps, and for the first time I was afraid, afraid of Unni, afraid that I had done wrong to come to Bongsor, afraid that something terrible would happen because I had come.

'Ha ha!' cried the Rampoche, 'Kushog, you have come at last.' He turned derisively to Rukmini and to me. 'Your lord has come,' he said tauntingly, addressing us both. 'This is indeed an honour for me.'

It was Unni, and my heart leapt to see him at the door, standing so tall, so quiet. And suddenly all unease had gone, all fear. Unni was there. I was safe. Perhaps a few weeks ago I would have moved towards him, gladly, saying his name. But I had learnt so much now.

493

I had learnt that Asians like Unni did not like these demonstrations centred upon one's own emotions. They liked public reticence in a woman, however frenziedly passionate she might be in private. They became embarrassed otherwise, and Unni would be embarrassed by outward display of what should remain delicate, muted, secret. Especially in front of enemies, such as the Rampoche. I remained exactly where I was (though we had all risen, as is courtesy), and thus we stood, Rukmini and I, while the Rampoche taunted us by calling Unni our lord, and I knew Rukmini's face now radiant, I could hear the soft breathing of her happiness. I knew Rukmini looked just as she did at the wedding, when over my shoulder she had caught sight of Unni when Hilde had walked in to us alone, before I ever saw Unni, before he had even meant anything. ... I had only seen Hilde walking in, but she had seen Unni. ...

And if Unni had been an American like Mike, convention would have made him come to me first, to demonstrate publicly his affection. But here this would have been an insult to me, for only public women are publicly acknowledged. Unni did not look at us, neither at me, nor at Rukmini. He looked at the Rampoche, placing his hands together in respectful Indian salutation. The Rampoche waddled up to him, a Rampoche suddenly effusive, diminished, bustling, for all the world like the Little King, and placed both hands upon Unni's head in blessing, murmuring a prayer.

Then Unni turned (and when he moved my heart moved too, all of me tied to his least gesture), saluted the wife of the Rampoche who had come in with him and stared at him with an unaffected delight in his handsomeness, her hands under her striped Tibetan apron. He saluted Dearest, shook hands with Professor Rimskov, said: 'Hello, Mike, so good to see you.' He turned to us and bowed, his hands folded, and we did the same.

'Bring a seat, a seat,' shouted the Rampoche.

Unni sat, stretching his long legs, opposite the Rampoche, so that the oblong we formed was now closed, a geometrical balance. His Preciousness, no longer the ferocious, powerful tyrant, was now a little man jabbering and full of smiles. For Unni had brought with his long body and easy gestures a new power, flexed, easy, and yet to be respected. Before it the bombinations of the Rampoche seemed trivial. And Mike was relaxed, laughing, having a companion now, another man like himself, nothing that he could not understand and be sure of.

'It's good to see you again, Unni. I thought you'd never come.'

'I came as soon as I could, Mike.'

'I knew you would.'

The Rampoche laughed with great and totally false joyousness. 'Our noble engineer is for ever busy,' he proclaimed. 'Truly, a great and tremendous responsibility is upon him. The care of many souls at the dam.'

'Wouldn't be so tremendous if you stopped trying to make trouble for us, Your Preciousness,' said Unni conversationally, picking up the tea bowl and drinking, Chinese fashion, from under the saucer covering it.

'I,' said the Rampoche, 'make trouble? Honoured sir, that is indeed unfair. How often have I not prayed you to honour me with a visit, so that we could discuss matters and smooth little mistakes? Trust is a beautiful virtue,' said the Rampoche. 'Look at me. People trust me, because they know I am good and kind and I will help them.'

Unni drank again. And suddenly I knew that over the rim of the tea bowl he was looking at me. But when he put it down his eyes were upon the Rampoche.

'I hope that one day I too shall be able to trust you.'

'Ho ho ho!' said the Rampoche. 'Ha ha ha! You are insulting me, my friend.'

Unni smiled, good-naturedly. 'You know very well, Your Preciousness, that you've given me enough trouble today to keep me busy a week. That was a very nice riot you tried to organize this afternoon, Rampoche.'

The Rampoche sighed, yet I could detect satisfaction and smugness in his sigh. 'You are indeed labouring under illusions,' he said, shaking his head sadly. 'I did my best to pacify them, this afternoon, after the earthquake.'

'Indeed a most formidable earthquake,' replied Unni gravely. 'Take care, Rampoche, that you do not overreach yourself. If the people suddenly run amok and really demand a human sacrifice to Mana Mani, you will not be very happy.'

'How misunderstood I am,' cried the Rampoche. 'But it is ever so, that good intentions are mistrusted. I complain, my friend, that you take all my labour away. Did I not myself supply you with labourers? But they have now become proud, and refuse to work for me, as tradition demands. And so the goddesses and their fields and flocks are neglected, there is no one to do any little building for me, free, as is the law and the tradition, or give me the churned butter for lamps for the altars. I have to pay, PAY,' shouted the Rampoche with great indignation, 'to get my water, the wood for my fires, anything done.'

'Never mind, Your Preciousness. Think, when the dam is built, how wealthy you will be,' said Unni. 'You can put your money into so many other things when we get hydro-electric power and Bongsor becomes a town. It is very foolish of you to start these riots in the name of the goddess. It won't give you more butter for your lamps.'

'You are not treating the workers well,' sighed the Rampoche. 'You closed the canteen.'

'Only because you were cheating them. When you sell good food, we shall give you back the canteen.'

The Rampoche turned smilingly to Mike Young. 'I think,' he said, 'that Mr Menon is a communist. So many changes, so quickly. It is not natural, it is not good. Change should come slowly, or the people will become arrogant and irreligious. Communists, like across the border.'

'I guess if there were more people like Unni around, there'd be fewer communists,' replied Mike.

'Ah,' said the Rampoche. 'Illusions again. One day, my friend, you will realize how much I have tried to help, how I have laboured to remove obstacles and keep the traditions – ach!'

'Ooh,' said Dearest, giggling, 'Daddy sounds terribly feudal tonight.'

They rose, the Rampoche indicating that they were free to go. 'Why not stay here tonight,' he said affably to Unni, 'there is place at my hotel. I call it the Dam View, you see, in omen of the future.'

'You are very kind,' replied Unni. 'When the dam is finished, Your Preciousness, I will stay with you.'

'Ha ha ha,' laughed the Rampoche, again with helpless jollity, 'that won't be for ten years. Yet I thought you might stay just for once, if not for my sake, for the sake of your friends.' His eyes did not move, but his meaning was clear.

'I would like to talk to the Lady Rukmini for a while,' said Unni.

'By all means,' said the Rampoche hastily, suddenly serious. 'By all means. In this room, if you wish.'

'Mike,' said Unni, 'will you stay here too?'

'Sure you want me to stay?' said Mike, whose face had gone very white.

'Yes.'

The Rampoche and his family left, descending the staircase, and Professor Rimskov and I followed them. But this was what Unni wanted, and I obeyed, because now I was sure, I knew, and there was nothing but a great clearness, as if I sat under a great tree, at peace, having suddenly received illumination. Now he would talk to Rukmini. And I knew how it would be.

The cold outside was like a whip-lash in our faces. Professor Rimskov and I hurried back to the Dam View, panting with the exertion and the icy air blurring our breaths about us. The rooms were warm, the Tibetan servants having brought in small braziers with wood. I put on more cold cream, then wiped it off. I did my hair again. He would come to me, when he had spoken to Rukmini. I lay on the bed, to wait for Unni, all my bones hurt, and I was very tired.

He was in the room before I knew it, I woke up to find him bending over me.

'Oh, Unni,' I said, 'I fell asleep.'

He did not answer. Just stood above me, looking down.

'Please sit down, Unni.'

He sat down on the edge of the bed. He gave me a cigarette, and I found his hands again, so loved, their sight alone stirring me already, cupping the light, near my face; then lighting his. I looked at him, gazing my fill, fulfilled by sight alone.

There was nothing to say between us now. What could we say? I had come. I was here. Rukmini was here. And now that I knew that Rukmini would always be here, always with us, always part of us, what could I say?

'What does Mike feel about it?' I asked at last.

'Nothing,' said Unni. 'Happily he does not understand fully.'

Then I noticed how thin Unni had become. Thinner than two

weeks ago, when I had seen him last, in the Valley. A care-worn look. It moved me so much I longed to throw myself in his arms, instead of lying there too tired to sit up.

'Oh Unni,' I said miserably, 'I understand only too well.'

He was on the bed then, on me, his arms round me, his face pressed against me until it hurt. And I put my arms around him, knowing him unhappy, needing consolation; for the first time in our knowledge of each other, it was he who needed tenderness and comfort and soothing, not me.

'I did not come to see her. Until tonight, I did not see her. You know that, Anne.'

'I know it makes it only more valid, Unni. Your love, I mean. For Rukmini.'

He had forced me, forced me to put in words what lay between us, what had always been with us, in our knowledge of each other, forcing me to elucidate, for himself and for me, what he had not known about himself. And thus making me also search within me to find in myself what this would mean to me, what I would do with this new knowledge, whether it would *do* anything to Us, the Us that was neither Unni, nor me, but this emotion together. Love, it was called. It had brought me to life. Would I now have to relinquish it? Because of Rukmini? Or rather, because now I knew and Unni knew what had always existed, but latent, hidden, unknown, until called to birth by my words?

Oh foolish I am, Unni, I cried bitterly to myself, always to put things in words, and thus to give them existence. The Word made flesh – that was it. Rukmini. Unni loved her and had always loved her, and now not only I knew it, he also knew it, through me. Without me, my presence, he might not have known. And now my words had stamped a perfect seal upon it. *This love is*. Knowledge, not only for tonight, not only with Rukmini there, but always, for the rest of our lives.

And so, with his hands in my hair now, his weight upon me, he mute and strong and yet so hurt, so vulnerable now, sensitive as no woman could be, I had to ask myself at last what kind of love I was going to choose. Until then I had been content to take what Unni had given, to accept the emotional security, the physical fulfilment, to embody my love in his relationship to me. I had taken and taken from him, from his quietness and his talent for understanding, his passion and detachment and forbearance, and now I had to give.

In this Tibetan room, where I could feel ourselves enclosed, closer in spirit than we had ever been – while outside the icy mountain night cocooned us, and the hostility of the Rampoche, and next to us, beyond walls opaque to touch but transparent to our feelings, Mike's tangible pain assaulted us until we clung to each other tight for protection – I had to learn how to give love to Unni because he needed it.

'You have not asked me,' I said, beginning carefully, 'why I came here.'

'Mike told me.'

'Are you angry because I came?'

'No. You had to come.'

'Do you think,' I said, 'that I came because I was ... jealous of Rukmini?'

'No, I never thought that.'

'Have I no cause to be jealous?'

'Anne, you know you have every cause.'

'Yes. You betrayed yourself, Unni, when you said: I did not come to see her. I did not see her until tonight. You know that, don't you?'

'Yes,' he said simply, 'but I did not know it myself. I mean, I did not know that I loved Rukmini too, until I saw you, and her, together. You told me, just now, and I believe you. You see,' he added, reflectively, straightening himself, and suddenly I was reduced again in size, no longer *mater consolatrix*, but a woman, his woman, with whom he would sleep if he wished when he had finished speaking, 'Rukmini is so young, I could not believe it.'

'She is half my age,' I said, merciless. 'But she is not a child. Devi wanted me to tell you this: tell Unni, she said, we are not children, Rukmini and I, we are women.'

He sighed then, got up, put another log on the brazier. Already he was accepting the facts of emotion, weighing them in his mind, as he threw the little charm up and down. He came back to me, taking off his leather jacket, underneath he had a woollen knitted sweater.

'This is nicely done,' I said, about the sweater.

He nodded.

'Where did you get it?'

'A woman knitted it for me.'

There was a silence. What could I say: it was true, and he was as merciless as I am. We would always be thus, unable to escape our own cleverness and our own turpitude. Once I could have lied to myself, but now, after Unni, there was to be no more lying.

'Was Rukmini in the same airplane as you to come here?'

'She was.'

'What will you do now?'

'I do not know, Anne. It depends upon you. Truly I love you.'

'I do believe it.'

'You are the need of my heart and my flesh,' he said. 'I cannot speak to Rukmini as I do to you. But she haunts me, she is part of me; she is helpless and all that is male in me wants to protect her and look after her. I cannot stop myself.'

And then he was kissing me, and the sweet, torrid overwhelming that we could not prevent ours; as always he knew my body better than I did; knew me tired and aching but eager and a little apprehensive. And was fierce yet gentle, imperious yet patient, until there was no barrier between us and I had gone beyond ecstasy to find him still with me, holding me tightly in his arms. Never had love been so good or so complete, and I could not help but know, later, between sleep and waking, that it was perhaps because of Rukmini. I had accepted her in him, and so had exorcized whatever withholding there could have been. In the darkness, while he breathed gently, passion spent (and soon would rise, to go back to the dam, for he would not stay, he said, till daybreak and the Rampoche found him), I deemed it strange that what is one's perfection must be another's woe. And because Rukmini for impossible reasons loved, so in her pain for me the bright birds sang. 'It is you, Anne, you the need of my heart and my flesh.' I must not ask more. I could not take away from Unni anything that was him, diminishing him would also diminish Us. There was no way out but total acceptance. What was this nagging rhyme in my head? *For the error bred in the bone, is to ask to be loved alone.* Well, certainly not in polygamous Asia. Many loves, I thought sleepily, in his arms, many kinds of love; perhaps it was difficult to ask anyone to love one alone, at any time.

And was it not the same for me? Did I not take of Unni's spirit and emotion, had I not demanded of him that he should know and should accept that other love of mine, love of words, a demanding demon which took me away from him, which even in the first glow of discovery had made me turn and say: Go away, I wish to be alone tonight; which condemned me to secret, unshared emotions, away from him?

This then was really to love, not to immure and entomb in selfishness, but to fulfil the loved one, to free him and give him not a cage, but the vast liberty of the world. Unni was given to me completely, because I had accepted to give him up. He would love Rukmini, unguiltily, tenderly, because she was gentle, beautiful, a natural victim, needing protection. Then what would happen? Somehow I could not worry overmuch, for tonight Unni was mine, he was near me.

I fell asleep and during sleep came the transformation. I woke, no longer benign, but a fiendess, tortured by resentment, and Unni was gone.

Shall not a woman weep as the night wears on? As the night wore on my nobility had worn off; the scarcely human detachment, the serene composure, had vanished as I woke to find Unni gone. In those small hours before dawn when people most often die, when people wake up feeling desolate and life merely a long wait for death, I woke to find myself lost in jealousy and rage and pain, racked by the demons of hate, a malignant creature, hating the self that had played at being generous, feeling it unreal because it was there no more. Time, and sleep, had effaced it, replacing its outworn (and now ridiculous) sentimentalism with a strong and cunning beast, formidable in hatred and greed. But of course at that moment I did not call it greed. I had entered my own hell, but found it natural and right, at this dead time of darkness, the soul's stagnant ebb. There was only me, and I had been mortally wronged. Even now, as I write this, now that the Mountain is no longer with me, now that, fallible and knowing, I await the return of love, I still remember how right it felt, how true it felt, how justified I was in the great wrong done to me by Unni and Rukmini.

I crouched in the empty bed, my body on the sheet where he had lain, still lapped in his warmth, hearing his voice, that voice of loin-stroking sensuality whose recall was enough to drive me into obsessive desire. A spectre of love lay wan by my side, to which my body responded and stirred, with all my skin standing gooseflesh, and yet I was drowning in hate and jealousy. He is mine. It is too much to ask me to give him up, to share. I want him. All of him. You've already taken my child, our child. You've taken everything. You won't have Unni.

And gradually the rending dialogue with myself.

To take is to lack, to give is to receive.

I won't, I won't. This is all nonsense. It is not real. This is real, this, that Unni loves me and I love him. Rukmini ... she is a dream in his mind. Tomorrow, in the day, he must forget. He will.

He will remember, at night, by your side.

No, because I have already sterilized the memory of Rukmini, embalmed Rukmini, with the beauty of my clever generosity of last night, which is not me, which was never me, which was a me possessed by something I do not want. By a foolish abnegation which now terrifies me. It was hypocrisy. Not me. I've had enough of being hungry in mind and body. I am lucid now. I am clear now. I want my share of happiness, I want my pleasure and my love. I've got a right to it. I've suffered. I want happiness; I want to be beautiful and young, not to become dry again, I want to live. I have a right to all those great commonplaces of feeling, mainspring which each of us has to rediscover every time. This is true. Rukmini is not true. She's a little girl playing at gods and goddesses. Playing at ecstasy. Mary at the feet of the Lord. But I do not want to surpass myself. I am Martha, perhaps, but Martha wasn't a hypocrite. I stay with my feet on the ground. I won't give him up.

Love devises not the imprisonment of the loved one but his greater release.

Nonsense. He said it himself. I am the need of his heart and his flesh. I can give him what no one else can. What can Rukmini give him? I won't let a chit of a girl, an illusion, a brief dream of a child in ecstasy, dreaming of a god, come between us. Unni is taking this much too seriously. He is a man, she is beautiful and gentle, she appeals to his protective instincts. He cannot love her and me at the same time. It is impossible. No man can love two women at once.

It happens all the time, everywhere.

I was silent, terrified that it might be true.

You are doing to Unni what John did to you. Putting up the shutters on the house of life, keeping the housebreaker life out of your neat, ordered house, keeping him locked. He is *yours*. A possession. Take care.

All right, I said. I'll play at being generous. Anyway, it works better. But you know it is false. You know I cannot do this, I cannot give him up. You know I'm going to suffer torment, perhaps a self-made hell, but hell all the same, from now on, and for how long?

I felt myself become cunning, ruthless, a plotter, insidious as the Rampoche, but far more clever. There was no peace for me and I went up to the roof, to breathe, for I suffocated in the room. I wanted to see Mana Mani again, Unni's malevolent mountain. How well I understood her now, the female, goddess, jealous and black-hearted, cunning and scheming to keep the mountains and the river to herself, demanding a human sacrifice, the blood of a man, lusty and strong. Of course. That's how she remained young.

It was true. Here incredulity was out of place. Trances, visions. The air alive with demons and fiends was not only possible, I believed it completely. Had I suffered an illusion last night? I was myself now.

Mana Mani took the dawn with a pink splendour mantled upon her. She was more lofty and arrogant than ever. Very soon the sun was rolling down her steep flanks in a golden tide, when all the Monastery was still in pansy coloured darkness. Where Bongsor hurtled steeply down to the valley, thick mist lay masking the river whose perpetual soft roar was a silence itself. Now was a kinship between us, the mountain and I, for we had established a secret pact.

Mana Mani ... Unni's voice, talking affectionately, amusedly, of the mountain. Living years in view of her; acknowledging her power. What a small, laughable thing the dam must look, with Mana Mani looming on the back of it, the dam, taking the river from her, blandly, under her haughty stare. Ants' work. Man's work. Ants, grovelling about, yet conquering in the end. 'I'll tame her one day.' Had Unni ever attempted to climb her? I must ask him. But I knew what the answer would be: 'When the dam is finished, not before.'

And Rukmini was praying to her, Dearest said. Praying for Unni's safety. I nearly laughed. I knew the mountain did not like Rukmini, she was too soft, too kind. ...

The Monastery woke, a stir, a yawn, the noise of drums, a chanting, vaguely the boom of bells. Then a triumphant assertion, the great grave voice of the trumpets. They were upon the roofs again, the trumpeters, wearing dark pointed head-dresses with flaps on their ears. Then the click like hens pecking of pails carried half-full of water, the water cluck-clucking at the sides, people calling to each other, the whirr of prayer mills, little boy-acolytes, busy with dark iron pots, the smoky tang of fires; and suddenly a shuffle of lamas, in ranks like an army, booted, swinging out of the Monastery and into the courtyard, droning a chant.

Om Mani Padme Hum. Om Mani Padme Hum. Someone below our hotel was shouting the magic formula which keeps the world existent in the perpetual wheel of illusion. And what was love but formula, words with a sharp, painful, and horrible reality, a gash into heart and brain; to conjure life with, to guard against the menacing night of nothing, the only defence of man against the unreality of death, proof of the reality of existence, but also wounding to death.

Then I saw Rukmini, coming from one of those passages which seemed to issue out of the walls on to the courtyard. Rukmini, wrapped in a soft Nepalese shawl, Biblical, but still Rukmini. I thought I could hear her bangles. Perhaps she had been praying to the goddess again.

My eyes followed the brown mantled form gliding down the courtyard out of the Monastery. There was no prevailing against that marrow-sucking enchantment.

I looked at Mana Mani, the insolent peak. I'll die if Unni doesn't care any more. I must see him again. He will have to choose. With vampire tenacity I clung to the word love and would not give him up.

Mike at breakfast looked jubilant, against my expectations. He was eager to speak to me as we walked out of the Dam View and the quadrangle, still plunged in violet cold, and decided to climb the slope of the hill behind the Monastery. It was a hard, steep climb, between chortens, those Buddhist small monuments like miniature stupas, heaped haphazardly along the roads and among the boulders. I found the accumulated ache of my body irritating, but the inward smart of my spirit was more unbearable, its rage drove me on.

'I'm really very glad. Unni's a great guy.'

'What did he do that was so wonderful?'

'Rukmini's promised to come back to Khatmandu. As soon as there's a plane. And she's going to have a walk with me this morning about ten. It's awfully early, guess she's still asleep, and I don't know where she's staying. Probably with Dearest. It's an awful time to wait till ten.'

I panted as we stepped up, lifting sore legs, pausing for breath. The rarefied cold air went into lungs like icy alcohol. Among the chortens strewing the hillside were grazing goats and mules. At the foot of the ramparts which wound up the slope lines of men and women walked round the Monastery, clockwise, chanting *Om Mani Padme Hum*, and revolving prayer mills.

Mike paused. 'Let's sit down here,' he said, and we sat against a larger chorten stained with dark soot from prayer fires, probably a funeral monument. 'I wasn't very happy last night, I guess. I know Unni doesn't *love* Rukmini, except as a kid sister, but Rukmini does love him, so I wasn't very happy.'

In his halting, simple, fumbling words, sincere and inapt to describe, he relived the scene. In the carpeted room, with the fumes of Tibetan beer, Chinese tea, and oily food about them, the three had come together last night.

I could see it, not only as Mike described it, but as I could see, colour and emotion added, all the baffling, battling contradictions in turmoil there. Unni, Rukmini, facing each other at last. Sitting on the chorten, putting my hand up indifferently to catch the slanting-beamed early sun, feeling my heart knock painfully against my ribs, I knew how Unni had looked at her, looked his full for all the years of turning away, a gaze thoughtful, restrained, holding the man in, holding in also the memory of me, already in the background. Even in my blind rage, sitting with Mike, I knew how Unni must have suffered then. Did Unni see, cold and sharp, the etchings of the past: those spring mornings on the lawn, with his deft long-fingered hands tapping the drum? And here I nearly went mad with jealousy. Suddenly I knew why Isobel hated him too, hated what she felt when she saw him. Looking at mine, I saw his hands, those patient unhurried hands, dallying with hair and limb until the heart's blood rose in sweet roaring tide. Those hands now mine, with all their knowledge of texture and caress, their feel of willing flesh melting resistless in the singleness between man and woman which makes all the difference, the choosing between ecstasy and coitus, between the glory of the positive hour or the slow, indifferent decay. Unni must have known, standing in front of Rukmini, remembering the carefree laughter, the parakeets and sunflowers painted in his room, the sudden separation, the wedding, me. ...

'She'd been here about twelve days, but Unni hadn't come to see her. Didn't want to get her talked about.'

'I see,' I said, letting the sun go through my fingers. One side of the hand was warm, the other cold.

(I see, Mike, I see what you do not see. I see he loves her so much that he will not come to see her. He is eight miles away, at the dam, and he will not, he cannot bear to come. He is so frightened of this love that he must shelter behind you, Mike, *your* presence, when he talks to her.)

'I see,' I repeated aloud. 'Unni did not come to the Monastery. Perhaps he did not know she was here?'

'Oh, he did. They were on the same plane. I was told that in Khatmandu. But I knew,' he said stubbornly, 'it was just coincidence. Why, Unni's in love with you. He'd just come from seeing you at the Hospital.'

(So everybody knew, in Khatmandu. And nobody told me, nobody.)

'Not everybody knew,' said Mike, as if he had heard my silent thought. 'Only a few people. They kept it to themselves. Of course, they all knew it was Rukmini's childish adoration. She's always thought of him as a god. But it's purely platonic. Completely pure,' said Mike, at that moment the typical, candid pure American, who places Purity, on a pedestal, is not perturbed by the thousand faces of love if it wears not also the mask of desire. 'I know it sounds green, thinking Unni's a god reincarnated, but I'm objective about it. It's her cultural background,' said Mike.

'It isn't green,' I replied. Unni had not looked at her at the wedding. What deep, strong roots engendered this negation, this denial, corrupting inwardly, till it had exploded here. 'I fled her, down the arches of the years', and in the self-corrupting flesh, flight from the sensual root and sap of man. Flight to me. And now his every word to me sour, ominous, laden with hypocrisy. 'Believe me, believe me.' Oh, how he wanted me to believe, only to strengthen his own belief

that Rukmini meant nothing, was but a child, that I was all. He was
a liar and a thief, as Ranchit had said. Unni, liar and thief.

'So Unni said to her: "Rukmini, I am asking you to go back to the
Valley," And she said: "My lord, whatever you tell me to do, I will
do." He said to her: "Rukmini, remember, I am not a god, I am a
man." She said: "Yes, now I know it. Now that I see you, I know
it." I know I should have felt terrible,' said Mike, 'but I didn't. Not
at all. It was as if they were singing to each other, and round us all
was singing, too, a singing world, and so many things now I can't
put into words … and I should have been angry, angry and unhappy,
but I wasn't.'

'No,' I said, seeing it all, 'of course not.'

'It was so beautiful,' said Mike reverently. 'Like a kind of glory …
when the world suddenly is so wonderful to live in it hurts with
loveliness.'

'Yes.' Dust in the sunlight, memory in corners.

'He said to her: "Maharani, forgive me." And she replied: "May
your path be tranquil, I shall not see you again but once." And then
she left us, but not before turning to me and saying: "Mike, I want
you to take care of me from now on. I'll see you at ten tomorrow
morning."'

'I see.' I see nothing but my hand, light, cold, numb, waiting for
the death wind that blows with the sun.

Mike picked himself up, to continue our clamber.

'I told her I'd be so happy to look after her, all my life, and she said
yes,' said Mike, flushing and stopping and looking all around him,
'she said: "Yes, you will look after me, Mike." I don't deserve this,'
said Mike. 'I'm so happy. This is the most wonderful day of my life.'

And to confirm, fill the cup of his happiness brim-full, as we
rounded a boulder carved with *Om Mani Padme Hum* and weather-
worn effigies of the Lord of Light, he cried 'Rukmini!', transported
with joy. For Rukmini was there, standing a dark tree against the
wonderful sun, exactly like a transfiguration, behind her the mountain, with the dazzling white of its attendant glaciers rolling down.

Oh, what a wonderful world it was, morning to satiety unfolding
for Mike, with Rukmini coming towards him, and Dearest by her
side. He stood there, foolish with bliss, looking at her gaiety. The
four of us stood on the topmost mound, above us the splendid peaks,

below the brown humps of lower crests flocking to a gather, the green milk of glacier water just become torrent; the Monastery, with but the flat roofs touched with sunlight, and the valley of Bongsor with its boiling river singing away.

'Ah Mrs Ford so wonderful to see you look at all this there is no such thing in other countries it makes one feel like an ant big with passionate meditation,' said Dearest, a poet upon the mountain crest. 'Here the air is so pure it releases the springs and fountains of the mind that is what a friend who came here to see us said only he was not a nice man although a poet always complaining about the food we gave and abusing our hospitality and finally going never to acknowledge gratitude no not even a snapshot.'

'Look over there,' said Mike to Rukmini, 'over there is the dam. They've only started building, can't see much, and most of the work is done in the winter and early spring, when the river's lower of course. See, those two brown humps, with Mana Mani just at the back. ...'

'Yes,' said Rukmini, docile. Of course she knew where the dam was; she's been climbing here every day, to look.

And so while the earth's splendour lay round me my eyes and my ears were blind to it, for I was filled with desolation and anger; a trapped ant in passionate meditation, not of the *Song of God*, but of malevolence. And I clung to malevolence the Comforter, for to lose it now was to relinquish the hard, suspicious but safe shield of myself, to become an unreal self I did not want to become. It meant giving Unni to the world, to everything and everyone, to anyone who'd care to lift a finger. It meant perpetual insecurity, relinquishing. I did not want to relinquish. I wanted Unni, liar and thief.

I must see him. Must fling in his face these words. Must hate. Must. In measure as I was planning to pin him down, to murder him nicely behind the bars of my cage, in that measure I felt love and desire for him well up in me. To have and to hold. I must go to him, somehow, this morning. I had so many things to say. Last night ... I could not remember what foolish, senseless things had been said last night. I had to see Unni, now, now.

A jeep was in the shed where the Rampoche kept his vehicles. It was rather battered, but Tenzin Lama, manager of Happy Drinks, loitering in the courtyard, told me that it could be used by tourists 'for ten rupees an hour. Plus petrol,' he added crisply.

The jeep track wound and unwound itself, steep above the valley, with declivities upon which hung perilous stone houses, and fields of barley meagre and shivering. The sun burnt upon the boulders, a burning-glass brightness, but it was cold in the shade, and one went thus from cold to heat with unpleasant frequency, so that I dreaded going round yet another loop of this tumble-down path with the toppling cliffs above me; the peaks induced a dizziness, a fascination for disaster against which I had to struggle. Loop and loop again, this track had nine lives, more coils than any pool of snakes. Still it climbed, and suddenly it was winter with frost with its teeth fast in the ground, so that I had to stop, put on my sunglasses, with the snow glare so near, and then I was over into the next bend, and before me Mana Mani and the dam, and the people building the dam.

A kingdom of ants, the camp of an ant army, clinging to rock, tilted about it the untidiness of work, with derricks and cranes and bulldozers and great raw platforms scooped out of the brown hills, and shards and grey cinders like untidy wolf-pelts about the slope, the shambles of man's work which this morning had been hidden from us by the tortuous course of the dovetailing ridges.

This was the work of man, disruptive, mapped in this wider gap hollowed by him between the ridges, almost a plain, but narrowing again where some meaningless objects like columns with trenches round them, the dam's beginning, obtruded against the horizon and athwart the tumultuous downfall of green milk waters. Beyond this chaos of activity the next valley could be seen, soon to become a lake, a reservoir of waters held in, already lakewise spreading. Mana Mani stood, a little to one side, surveying it all, glaring down with jutting chisel-carved rock, angular, razor-edged. An impossible mountain, with its bare vertical blade surfaces of granite polished to dazzle by the wind, even worse to look at from here than from the Monastery, a mere elbow-bending eight miles away.

Up and down along the sides of the scooped-out land, huts and huts of Army type, tin roofed, in rows. There was level space now, and I drove on, past more and more people in knots, in groups, past large platforms on which were more rows of half cylindrical Nissen huts. And as I went on I became aware of a curious stillness. People

509

there were, but nobody working. Just ever thickening groups, waiting, staring at my jeep, I could see myself driving towards a kind of amphitheatre scooped out of the cliff edge and crowded with people, at least three to four thousand, with waistcoats of sheepskin with the hair inside, and blankets about them, and earrings, all of them staring at my jeep, stepping backwards to open a passage.

Then I saw the Aid jeep, the same that we had met yesterday going to the airfield, come towards me. In it were three men, two of them with guns, one standing in the vehicle, purple angry, shouting at me: 'What the hell are you doing here, madam? Go away, if you please, go back.'

'I want to see Mr Menon.'

'You can't see Mr Menon. He's busy. Will you please turn back this moment?'

'There's Mr Menon,' I cried. 'I can see him.'

'Please go away,' shouted the man, who looked as if he would burst. 'We're having a demonstration here. It is dangerous.'

But I had seen Unni, walking down a slope, emerging from a row of huts built a little higher than the rest under an overhang.

'Look at that,' said the man who had been so angry with me. 'He's going to talk to that crowd again.'

'Logan's following, he's got a gun.'

'No. Look, he's carrying the loudspeaker.'

Behind him came two men, carrying what is most common perhaps in all crowds everywhere in the world today, a battery, amplifier, and microphone.

'You must go back, madam,' said the man again. 'It is dangerous. The workmen are striking. This is a demonstration.'

Already the voice of Unni was over us, over the amplifier. I could not understand the words, only the sound, the peculiar low vibrations, very deep and low with their curious calming effect, relaxed, reasonable, making one want to sit back and shut one's eyes, the dispassionate warmth, reposeful, a lulling green shade. Lucky man, I thought, bitter and amused, born lucky with this voice and this body. A man to trust. ...

There was a ripple of laughter round me. Unni said a few more sentences, there was another ripple, hesitant, half unwilling. The women especially laughed, holding their sleeves over their mouths.

The angry man in the jeep laughed too. 'That guy,' he said, 'that guy. He's got a tongue like honey.'

'What is he saying?'

'Persuading them to start work again, madam. There's been quite a lot of trouble here recently. There was a riot yesterday, and two of our fellows were beaten up. However, they calmed down, but this morning they started again.' He was now quite loquacious. 'Yesterday our Assistant Engineer gave us firearms, but Mr Menon says he can talk them round. He doesn't believe in guns. He believes in persuasion.'

'But why are they striking?'

'They don't really know why,' said the angry man, his eyes still on the crowd, now swaying uneasily back and forth. 'We've got about twelve thousand people here, counting the porters, the haulage people, and so on. We've had dacoits attacking our food convoys, and a bit of sabotage here and there, with machine-parts stolen, but the worst is the goddess, Mana Mani over there.' He jerked his head towards the mountain. 'These workmen are superstitious.'

Another ripple of laughter. Unni was talking again, I was trying to listen to him and also to the man.

'Hear them laugh now, like children, just because he's talking, telling them stories about themselves. The Rampoche and some of the big landlords round here don't like the dam. For many reasons, but chiefly because of the *tōla*, the free labour. You see, previously every man and woman in the valley had to give a hundred and fifty days' free labour to the Monastery: building, gathering firewood, making butter, breaking stones, carrying for the Rampoche. But money dissolves tradition. Paying the people for each day's work they do is changing their attitude. They don't want to work for free now, and so the Rampoche is telling them there will be plague and famine. I bet he's organized the dacoits to attack our convoys.'

'There are other things too,' said one of the gun-carrying young men. 'The Goddess of Smallpox, for instance. We got round the women here four years ago, vaccinating them and the girl children first, because the men refused, they said it would make them impotent (that's the worst thing that can happen to a hillman). But now we've made a rule: no vaccination, no work (it's easy, because with the floods there are only too many hungry men, walking about, coming here to ask for work). So the Goddess isn't getting any offerings this year, nobody has smallpox, and that means less money for the Rampoche.'

They had forgotten about my going away. They were looking at me with frank admiration, insistently. I understood the rule about no women at the dam. One of them said: 'We very seldom have ladies visiting here, madam. Only very occasionally, a party of tourists.'

'But that's going to change too,' said the angry man. 'We're getting a lady doctor next year. A missionary.' He sighed imperceptibly. 'And we hope we'll be able to bring a friend here occasionally, instead of having to pay a hundred and sixty rupees for the plane to Khatmandu, go and return.'

Laughter was indicated, and not perfunctory. I joined in without false modesty. These men were frank. They went to Khatmandu when they needed a woman ... just as Unni had done, as he did now, with me.

Unni had begun talking again. A small group of men were shouting, obviously threatening, trying to shout him down.

'It's the earthquake,' said one of the youths, picking up his gun again and looking tense.

'There was no earthquake.'

'We all know that, but the Rampoche seems to have persuaded some of the workers that there was ... and an earthquake means a sacrifice. A man must die to propitiate the goddess.'

'Here comes Unni now. I think he's seen you,' said the angry man.

Unni was walking away from the loudspeaker towards us. He wore the same shirt, and sweater present of a woman, as last night. He sauntered towards us, as if he had no care in the world, and I knew the crowd surprised, withheld by astonishment. I did not know whether he was angry or pleased, one could not tell because of this quality of suspended tranquillity which was his, which made me feel that every time I saw him there was a new beginning. He would not presume upon the past to assert himself, so that nothing could ever be taken for granted.

As he came towards me (slowly because of the press of people round him), I felt again that hurt in the chest, as always when he came towards me, and I was helpless and awaiting his will, and somehow glad in my submission. Perhaps it was true what the General said, that when a man is male enough then a woman delights in obedience, because this is pleasure, and a kind of withdrawn domination too, to obey out of sheer love.

As he came towards me my anger was running away from me, exorcized. I must not cage him, erode him away with my doubts and my hurt. Rukmini had been there before me; I had gone to Unni, saying: Help me, help me. Now I saw another Unni, the creative man with *his* work around him. And in this work, another love of his, I did not exist. Yet I had to accept that too. I had to accept the dam and all it meant. The separation, the danger, the days without him to come and go swift as green water, and like water they could not be held back. ...

He was by the jeep, holding out his hand to me, and I came down.

'Walk straight, do not smile too much, don't look afraid. You must help me now.'

We walked side by side, among the crowd. In a courteous, indifferent voice, as if addressing a tourist on a visit, he talked of the dam, for the workers to hear.

'As you see, we've made a start. This is one of the main tributaries of the river, fed by glaciers, in particular one from Mana Mani, the beautiful mountain you see there – no, don't point with your hand, it is disrespectful – she is a haughty sorority of goddesses protecting us, apparently. After the dam is put up, the whole of that area beyond will be one vast lake, with two smaller lakes in two abutting gorges. In this way we'll be able to control at least one-third of the water pouring into the main river ... there are several other tributaries and we'll tackle them in the course of time. Now let us walk to my quarters up that spur. Slowly, or you'll pant.'

He turned to give some orders to the men, waved his hand casually to indicate that the loudspeaker should be taken away, and without another look at the puzzled crowd guided me up the steps, reinforced with wood, going to the huts.

'Please come in.' He held the door of one of them open for me. 'This is where I live.'

It was a comfortable hut, half bedroom, half working room; a desk littered with papers, two hurricane lamps, tarpaulin, lots of rough Tibetan carpets, and a tiger skin on the floor. A Tibetan wood settee covered with fur against the wall. He motioned me to it; and now I knew that he was as near to anger as could be.

It was the way he lit his cigarette which told me. I was ashamed, too proud to plead, to move in such a way as to rouse him, to be tender. I could not avoid what was to come.

'May I know why you came?'

'I was very unhappy. So I came.'

'Why were you unhappy?'

'Because of Rukmini.'

He looked at the floor.

'Unni, I must try to explain. I couldn't bear it this morning. …' And then I found myself telling him everything, meticulously, every shade and change of my feeling, the awakening in rage and despair, the ugliness, climbing the hill, what Mike had said … everything unsparingly.

'It's no use, Unni, I know it is wrong. Oh, it's the mind, not the flesh, which is frail and jealous. Forgive me. I am selfish, and though I know I'm only building a prison for ourselves, a prison in which I shall be more lonely – which is just – and more bereft than ever, yet I cannot help thinking and feeling as I do. I had to tell you. Then I came here … and I saw you. Another you, the you that I did not know. Somehow I'm ashamed of my meanness, yet I know I'll start again. I cannot help it.'

'Anne,' he said, 'there's nothing to be ashamed of. I thought it might be Rukmini.'

And the way he pronounced her name made me angry, bitter, and malicious again. 'You *thought* it might be Rukmini. Or perhaps it might be our baby. What a good thing I lost it. Or perhaps the many times you asked me to believe you. It might be anything, in fact.'

'Anne,' his voice was more smothered than ever, 'what are you doing to us?'

'Us? Did Us ever exist, Unni? Did it? Tell me, was it worth the hundred and sixty rupees every time to Khatmandu and back, was it? Oh,' I said, 'why do I do this?'

'Darling,' he said, 'forgive me.'

'Forgive what? I asked you to help me. I threw myself at you.'

'Forgive me what I am,' he said. 'There is nothing else to forgive.'

'What you are. …' I said. 'Oh, Unni.'

But that was just what I could not accept, the totality of the man. I swallowed hard. This is what we always forgot, in our mania for simple hypotheses at the expense of complicated facts: the fact that he was he, with all the years and the wealth the years had given, and I was I, and neither of us to be moulded by the other entirely, only giving and receiving, strangers on the high road, on a journey, helping each other.

'Have you accepted all that I am, Unni?'

'Yes. The night you asked me to go away, after Eudora's party – remember? You wanted to write. I had to accept everything. Of course it hurt me too. It is hard not to be possessive. Of course.'

'What a small-minded fool I am.'

'I think,' he replied, as always answering beyond my question, 'I think we must live together for a good long stretch now. We have so much to give to each other. I shall try to arrange it. As soon as these silly riots are over.'

'Silly?'

'Yes. The workmen are half persuaded to go back to work, but wish to hold out for the fun of it now. Your arrival too, I turned to advantage. Too clever' – he mimicked me – 'don't you think it my tragedy, dearest, always to be too clever? Yet I cannot help being *too clever*, for I must build this dam with all I am and can use. I used you. I could stun them with your coming, and I did. If they really decided to murder us, there is little we could do. Fight with guns? If we kill one of them, no one will work for us again. I can only hold them by treating them as reasonable, honourable men. By hypnotizing them with my seeming lack of fear. When I saw you in the jeep ... I was even angry at first, for it was risky coming here alone. The road is bad, there may be some of the Rampoche's paid dacoits about.'

'But it was you, Unni, who taught me to drive a jeep on an un-made mountain road, remember?'

He moved from his chair to me, flinging me back in that mixture of ardour and unabashed sensuality which is his. 'So it was, O Anne.' He was laughing hard now, and kissing me, and we could not stop laughing, and I did not wish for anything better.

Unni drove me back at three in the afternoon. I remember the time well because he had waited in case the Rampoche started another earthquake. The news would be relayed by hillmen watching their flocks as they went clutching upon the slopes, it would be sung from hill to hill, would reach the dam within the half-hour.

But nothing happened, except that while we were eating the hot curry and rice lunch (Unni had made me meet the other engineers working at the dam, a half-dozen or so from as many nations), we heard the noise of a plane.

'Airplane,' said the Dane, his face lifted.

'Odd,' said the angry man, from Arkansas.

'Not expecting anything, are we?' asked one of the youngest there, a Welshman.

'I'll find out when I drive Anne back,' Unni had replied.

And now the jeep track went through the golden Himalayan September, with aspens like a tiger coat already autumnal. We drove through alternate showers of icy shadow and sunburn heat. The trees cast long replicas more sombre than themselves, clouds settled like pillows round the snow peaks until they seemed to float, displacing themselves in the breeze. The sky was unflawed turquoise. Mana Mani was slender behind us, neither friend nor foe.

At the bend of the track, where the sun hit the spur of the hill, he stopped. 'Let us lie in the sun for a while.'

The sunbaked boulders were hot, but on their shadowy side the lichen and the moss nestled, blue-damp. I felt both surfaces with my hands, a pleasure inexplicable, flesh other than mine, matter, substance, beautiful to touch without any need of spirit or soul but itself. After all, there never yet was seen function of soul in absence of the body; and this heat, pleasing my palms, was it more immaterial, less spiritual, than the thoughts of my mind?

I woke from my absorption in the stone to find Unni watching me. He had stretched out by my side, pleasure to my eyes lingering over his long lean handsomeness, an excitement similar to that the boulder had given to my touch. The flesh, substance, delight. Delight all about us, held in lovely balance, the poised moment, fallible and mortal. Not the ecstasy of the saint, but the pleasure of the passionate human being, eyes to see, ears to hear.

'I like you when you are away, gone from me completely, having forgotten me, on wings of imagination free.'

'What a poet you are at times, Unni.'

'If it is a poet to learn how to live, perhaps a poet, although a bad one.'

'Poets are people who have no shells; embryos without armour, their flesh emerges, their spirit oozes from them outwards. They're easily hurt.'

'We say that a poet is a man who keeps no secret from God in his heart, and who, in singing his griefs, fears, hopes, and memories, purifies and purges them from all falsehood. His songs are your songs are my songs.'

'But to do that he must have griefs and fears; he must be attached. He cannot be a saint, fulfilled in the love of God alone. He must be imperfect.'

'Yes,' said Unni, 'that is so. He must *want*, to be a poet.'

The grass was coarse and stiff with too much struggle in the wind. The long roar of the rushing river drowned the song of afternoon birds. All this was of earth, magnificent earth, as was our love, guilty, human, not always entirely beautiful.

Not for us the high summit of ecstasy, there reigned beatitude, but not song; apotheosis of the soul, but not the enchantment of its incalculable companion of flesh and blood, the body; grave renouncements, but not the acceptance of joy and woe.

For us the struggle and falterings, the perplexities and doubts, the sordidness and the splendour, the horror lurking behind the commonplace, the torment of love, the squalor of hatred, the magnificence of creation, and the tawdriness of spite. For body was creator, too creating lust and sorrow, and all our virtues grew out of the passions of the body, in that old for ever denied reality of good and evil. At all times we were other than ourselves, and could be someone else than what we were, sure only of our own quicksands.

For us the perfect perishable moments, snatched from deceiving death. Like this one.

'How you cling to life,' he said. 'How voracious you are for living, my beloved.'

'And you?'

'Not as much as you. I am more resigned. Every action inevitable, but not so much my own volition as that of the Prime Mover in me. The dam at present shapes my destiny. But your lust for life is so great, it spills out of you. I love your insatiable demon, with my most unreal self as the Rampoche would say,' he added softly, for never did Unni forget to touch the earth, if only with one finger.

'And Rukmini?' With calm I could pronounce her name.

'If beauty later bear any feature for us, hers will be mingled there.'

For to Rukmini was given straightaway, carried by angelic wings, the true summit, the mountain all at once. But not to us. We had a hard way to go among the paths of men and their self-deludings. Rukmini knew how to love beyond knowledge, and Unni had been right to show her that he loved her, for even she, transported as she was, had needed confirmation before the supreme moment had come to her; confirmation from another human being, a mutuality of acceptance and affirmation. We all needed it, the other one, the human like ourselves, the witness and reactor, to make us reach beyond ourselves. Only through other human beings did we fulfil ourselves. Only human contact created God for us, His Song would remain unsung without the words of man.

To us was given the struggle against uncertainty and imperfection, with needful need and pain, frustration and the inevitable insensibility of forgetting. For us waited work, travail in obscurity, as the mountains still evolving their own landscape. Longing unstilled would lay for us its long hungers, and desire, the endless bounty of tomorrow's thirst.

Bongsor was all purple shadow and smoke as we drove up the main street.

Tenzin Lama stood outside Happy Drinks Unlimited. Unni stopped and hailed him.

'Was there a plane from Khatmandu this afternoon?'

'What do I know of planes, Kushog?' said the Lama, surly, turning his back upon us and re-entering his cave.

The gates were open. I thought Unni hesitated for a moment before he drove in. 'A most unfriendly atmosphere.'

'It's always like that, Unni.'

'Seems worse today.'

We were now in the second courtyard. Then I heard the clang behind me, unmistakable, of the gates being shut.

'Oh, Unni, look, look, they've shut the gates.'

'Yes,' he said. But he had not turned as I had, he was looking straight in front of him.

Standing on the steps of the Dam View Hotel, booted, with a short fur jacket, a kukri in the waistband, and swinging between his hands a large, snake-like, muscular black whip, theatrical and nearly cause'for laughter if not for his cruel face, Ranchit, lifting his upper lip in a frightening smile to show two teeth whiter than the rest.

'Ah, Menon. And you, goddess. Right on time. I was waiting for you.'

There was resistance, of course, a sudden flurry, thuds and hard breaths, and the wildly nonsensical flaying of arms and feet, and I was involved in it because someone hit me and I fell down, and to this day I cannot remember where I was hit, it never hurt at all.

But it ended; into a no-end but ludicrous nightmare finish, pre-figured, scraped out of every legend, with all my senses going numb and Unni like a bundle, tied by the four men who had tackled him (and how difficult it is not to see them a horde, not to add, however slightly, to their number, now that it is over), hands tied, feet tied, thrown on the ground and trying to rise, heaving upon his shoulder, his cheek on the stones, and Ranchit kicking him down.

'Unni,' I cried, 'Unni.'

I could hear my own voice, a strangeness because so astonished and miles away. Someone was holding me, against whom I struggled irrit-ably, not looking, someone whose face I never saw; twist as I might I could not get to Unni.

And there was the Rampoche, ceremonial, with a crowd of sub-dued lamas unwillingly walking out of their stone pyramid, the Ram-poche with hands fluttering like butterflies saying: 'But *Sri* Ranchit, no ... I entreat, *Sri* Ranchit ...' The shuffling lamas, all maroon gowns and butter faces and bald heads, behind him, the henchmen and guards and servants and women collecting about us.

'Ranchit,' I cried, 'Ranchit.'

He looked at me, displaced from his rapt stare at Unni trying to rise and falling again, and by the meditative way he flung his legs, booted, hitting him in the belly, in the crotch, choosing where it hurt, I knew he was inaccessibly mad. Then I thought I was mad too, for next to the Rampoche, unmoved, beautiful in her bright striped robe, was Rukmini, looking down at Unni, and then at me, her face like silk or pearls, luminous and tranquil.

'Rukmini,' I cried, 'Rukmini, stop him. Stop Ranchit.'

But Rukmini only looked on, serene, then drew her woven shawl calmly over her shoulders.

Ranchit laughed, his face came very near to mine, I could not avoid his breath, the close features, his hand stroking me, the high falsetto of his voice, an irrational shriek off at half-pitch.

'Ah, goddess, goddess, now you see who is stronger. Now, now.'

'Rukmini,' I cried, 'please please ...'

But she did not hear, not speak, frozen in some curious dream, smiling almost. I could see her little hands, like a child's, hanging quietly on both sides of her. Ranchit looked back at her and laughed again.

'You see,' he said, 'I am stronger. I will sleep with you tonight, goddess, and teach you many lessons.'

The Rampoche's mouth began shaking, Dearest, stifling her sobs, made a movement towards me but her prudent father held her back.

'Now you see,' said Ranchit, 'now you see ... Bring the others out,' he shouted.

The Rampoche's men brought out, shoving and pushing, Mike Young and Professor Rimskov, the latter gibbering 'But but but ...', trussed with their clothes about them untidily bunched between the thin ropes, and Mike, lips tight, who saw Unni and cried: 'My God, Ranchit, you'll pay for this.'

The Rampoche babbled at the same time: 'Now now, *Sri* Ranchit, I beg of you. By Jove, I mean ...'

And then Unni laughed. It was a small laugh, but prodigious, extraordinary, because he was also groaning a little in pain, lying on his face, laughing.

'You will see, see,' said Ranchit. The black whip cracked in the air, fell with a thud across the laughter. 'Now you will see ... you will see ... I am a Rana, I will whip him, like any slave, this common, low-caste fellow. ...'

Again and again. I could hear someone, but it wasn't Unni, it was me. I, and also Mike shouting, and Dearest sobbing harder at each whip-lash. Crack, crack, I could see the whip go up and down, Ranchit nearly foaming at the mouth, and groaning, groaning with every stroke, huh, huh, until he was tired, and threw the whip away and stood, panting hard, looking round him.

'You see,' he gasped, 'you see. Now see who is stronger.'

'You coward,' I cried, 'you coward.'

'I will emasculate him now,' said Ranchit.

'Rukmini,' I screamed, 'Ranchit's mad, please make him stop.'

Rukmini turned towards the Monastery. She was looking up, and because she looked, I too looked, up at the mountain, Mana Mani, all golden in the sunset.

'No, no,' cried the Rampoche, 'it is forbidden, *Sri* Ranchit.'

Again Ranchit's laugh came out, a croaking sound.

'Old fool, if I did it, all the Valley would think I have been cuckolded.'

'Yes, yes,' babbled the Rampoche, 'I mean no, *Sri* Ranchit, he has not touched the Maharani.'

'I know that. Pity, it would have been pleasant, but a Rana does not dishonour himself. You need a sacrifice for the goddess, Rampoche. She wants a man, I always fulfil women's desires.'

'Oh, but not an engineer, I say,' cried the Rampoche in a paroxysm of terror, '*Sri* Ranchit, please think, the Government, the dam, I did not mean the Engineer ...'

'Anne,' said Ranchit, turning to me, 'tonight your lover's head will watch us make love.'

'Oh no no no no,' shrieked Dearest, 'Daddy stop him stop him.'

'Maharani,' said Ranchit to his wife, 'watch your god die like a slave.'

Two of the four men that had overthrown Unni now held him, one grasping his hair, pulling it like tow out towards himself so that the neck stretched, the other pulling his arms backwards with the taut ropes. Ranchit weighed the kukri in his hand once, a heavy weapon, and took his stance, slashing the air tentatively, then: 'Now,' he said, 'watch,' and swung the blade up.

There was a scream. Perhaps me. I do not know, I shall never know, for I went limp into the arms that held me back and the next thing I was on the courtyard stones, fallen. The pinioning hands that clasped me back from Unni had let me drop. Oh my God, I thought, I will kill Ranchit now. And got up.

But the scream went on and on, a loud, a strenuous clamour, from everyone at once, horrified, horrifying, a texture of screaming, dreadful to hear because it was all the lamas screaming together.

And Dearest's voice, high above the others: 'Rukmini Rukmini Rukmini.'

I was up, standing.

Lying was Rukmini, eyes open still, looking at the sky, with a twisted, sad smile. Round her, all about me, bespattering us all, her bright blood crept over the courtyard stones.

PART FIVE **Return**

> *When you love someone you do not love them all the time, in exactly the same way, from moment to moment. It is an impossibility. It is even a lie to pretend to. And yet this is exactly what most of us demand. We have so little faith in the ebb and flow of life, of love, of relationships.*
>
> ANNE MORROW LINDBERGH

Chapter 1

'IN-CREDIBLE,' said Enoch P.

'Sounds fishy to me,' Pat said, her hands clasped.

'How does *she* feel?' asked Enoch, nearly reverent.

'Anne? Oh, all right,' said Paul Redworth. 'Bit worn out with all this going about. Great strain, you know, planes and all that, but otherwise quite all right.'

'That's strange,' said Enoch, shaking his head slowly. 'I should have thought, finding out ...'

'Finding out what?' Paul looked urbane steel at him.

'Well, some of the folks here do say the other girl went there to meet somebody.'

Paul sat back, in his eyes the twinkle which made his wife call him Tiddlywinks because it flashed in and out so quickly. 'I should have thought, for the sake of the Club, the less said the better. Ranchit was one of your more influential members.'

'I guess that's that.' Pat's voice was bodiless, her restless, twisting hands had dirty nails again after their short-lived post-marital respectability. 'I don't feel very well, darling. I'll go out and paint for a bit.'

'Yes, do, sweetheart.' Enoch was instantly solicitous, getting up and opening the door for Pat. 'I'm glad Pat's painting again,' he said to Paul with mournful admiration. 'So busy myself haven't got much time for creative culture. Lucky Sharma's around to cheer her up ... she's doing a portrait of him.' His face was gaunt with wistful love of Pat.

When Enoch came home Pat was lying down in the darkened bed-room.

'Feel better, sweetheart?'

'Yes thanks.'

'Do any painting?'

'No. Thought I'd lie up a bit.'

'That's right. That's fine.' He paused. 'I've been wondering if they'll send the ... the remains down later. ... Oughtn't our Club to hold some kind of memorial service, I mean ... he was one of our more influential members? A great guy. We'll all miss him.'

Pat buried her face in the pillow, and did not reply.

Father MacCullough had asked Anne and Fred to come with him to the Rain God Festival in Khatmandu. All might not be well with Anne, but a priest should not prejudge. All would be well, in the Lord's own time. Anne going in his jeep to the Rain God ceremony was to him symbolic. Symbolic of what he couldn't say, but he felt that God who moves men invisibly had meant it to be so, and His plans were long-term ones. Meanwhile let All-Khatmandu gossip their tongues out. They'd still be miles off the mark.

The return of Anne, Mike Young, and Professor Rimskov from Bongsor had brought drama to the Valley. News of the tragedy – a totally inaccurate account, fabricated for public consumption and satisfying no one – followed their arrival by plane within the hour. But neither Anne, nor Mike, nor the Professor (who had had a nervous breakdown immediately on arrival and been warded by Fred in the Hospital), had vouchsafed a word to All-Khatmandu, hence malice had it all its own way.

The day after their return, Father MacCullough went to the Point Four Palace to see Mike Young. Mike was packing, going back to work on the American road.

'We're rebuilding that big bit of it the river snatched. Mean to get a lot done this winter, take the road up as far as we can go, maybe reach the dam in another year or two. ...' Mike spoke flatly, automatically, of his work. He would drown himself in work.

'Aye,' said Father MacCullough, 'it's wonderful work you're doing Mike, wonderful work for this country.'

'Yep,' said Mike, locking his suitcase and looking intently at the key in his hand.

Said Father MacCullough, going suddenly scarlet: 'Perhaps you'd like to know, Mike, I'm saying a few masses for ... for her. She was an angel, Mike. An angel of the Lord.'

'Oh, Father,' said Mike, teeth clenched. 'Please. Let's not talk about her ... please.'

'Well, God bless you, son,' said Father MacCullough hoarsely, making the sign of the cross upon him.

Mike shook his head. When the priest had gone he remained staring for a while at the night outside, soft and full of stars. Rukmini, Rukmini, Rukmini. Her name sang in his ears, was in his mouth all the time, until he wished he could die. He wept, unashamed, alone. Nothing of substance was his to remember her by, but a small, dried marigold that she had picked and played with at the Valley Club party, long long ago, in the garden of the Royal Hotel, in the late spring. Her tender fingers had touched the flower, turning and twisting, playing as she played with the bangles round her wrist; she had smiled and the red spot painted on her forehead gleamed in the light, like a ruby ... she had dropped it, he had picked it up after her, hoping no one saw, ashamed and elated and moved. The flower now was a strawy strand, going to dust in the envelope where he had placed it, but it was all he had of her substance, her fingers, and her smile; that and memories, memories to cling to fiercely, dreading the time when they would begin to fade, memories of one day full of joy, up among the mountains of Bongsor. One day radiant with her happy face, one lovely morning when he had dreamt, breathless with happiness and mountain air, of a whole life with Rukmini. He still heard her voice: 'You will look after me, Mike.' Oh, he had known of her love for Unni, he knew ... but it didn't matter, it was Rukmini, part of her, accepted. And in time perhaps she would have liked him a little, for he would have given her everything, done everything to please her. But it was too much, it would have been too good, therefore it could not be. Then so quickly was the horror, the agony, the unendurable quick lurch and spurt of blood, an end, among screaming, an end scarcely to be believed even after he'd seen her burnt, consumed, the ashes, the flowers, the bangles, the gold, gone into the floating river with Rukmini. He would never forget. Not in all his life would he forget. A day, instead of a lifetime, would last him all his life. Fiercely he clung to his memories, wanting the pain, the agony with the joy, rather than the slow forgetting, the indifferent decay. ...

Going down to the market place with Father MacCullough and Fred, body-guards on each side of her, Anne felt will-less, emptied of reaction, possessor of a heap of broken images, haphazard rubble, fear in handfuls of dust, pain inescapable as smell, and withal a deep current of detachment, an aloofness which suffered but remained invulnerable, running as a silent vein of silver winding through the weariness of her spirit. This had been, had been endured, was now sifted, transformed, remoulded, worked upon by the demon of creation, in present stillness, in waiting. She felt enfolded in her own underground travail, the obscure and constant work of the root in her which was to take this chaos of happening and give it shape and meaning, coalesce it into a pattern of words. And she knew now that for this instant of whole vision preparing itself in solitude like a new life, the suffering, the pain and joy, had been merely the necessary raw materials of creation, and all would one day seem inevitable, even august, all fit into place which had merely been unaccountable tragedy, disconnected horror, meaningless hurt.

For seven nights now in Khatmandu, in farewell to the Rain God, there had been dancing on the Durbar Square. Aureoled with lights glowed the golden shell-face of the horrifying Bhairab, an enormous structure of gilt copper seven feet tall from chin to headdress, with a crown of snakes and skulls, and Yama, Lord of Death, upon her brow like a third eye. Fanged, lolling red tongue protruding, her fierce painted eyes moving in the flickering light, she was fed with flowers and sweet-scented herbs, milk and pure water. The Newaris held out their hands to receive, from the stem of a copper tube placed in her open mouth, drops of magic water. The masked dancers of Bhadgaon danced endlessly all through the night the dance of Bhairab, protectress of Khatmandu, slaying the demons, giving their blood to her servants and lesser gods to drink. The dancers had small silver bells tied to their arms and legs, and collars of bells round their necks.

'This is really three festivals rolled up in one.' Thus the knowledgeable Father MacCullough. 'Bhairab slaying the demons, that's the old, primitive, religious festival. On top of that we've got a Buddhist festival and a Hindu one. They used to sacrifice water bullocks too, but it's forbidden now, too cruel.'

In front of Bhairab a lofty pole was being raised, a Maypole, crowned with red flowers, with dependent streamers in ribbons upon which prayers were written. This was the beam to pierce the Heavens, the upthrust phallus, horn of power, snake upon the Pharaoh's brow, salamander of fire, the lingam, symbol of perennial desire, aspiration, sex deified, transfigured, sublimated to prayer, piercing Heaven with invocation, with that passionate attention of soul and body which is love and art. However smothered with niceties, thought Anne, there it was, never forgotten, the priapic design, marvellous monster of life. *Tout tourne autour de cet axe merveilleux* ... everything revolved round it, *poutre qui perce le ciel*, François Luneville had written in his poem. And this too fell into place now, accepted now that reality behind all the self-created conventions and delusions. Life was as simple and as complicated as that erect root reaching for heaven.

The jeep stopped, and Anne slipped away, wishing herself alone, while Father MacCullough innocently took a snap of the flowered upright pole.

The gaudy crowds were there, playful and pliable, the women pyramidally disposed, hiding the pagodas with their conglomerate bodies close-pressed, holding black umbrellas above their heads against the brilliant September sun. Three chariots, with round solid wheels of wood painted with eyes, and canopies of satin topped with gilt copper roofs, lay waiting for the three children-gods who would sit upon them, to be pulled by fifty men-priests round the city of Khatmandu.

In front of the yet empty chariots the priests were sacrificing a kid. They sprinkled the blood in blessing upon the wheels, the shafts, the cocked fronts with the Bhairab face lolling a red tongue out-thrust to lick the blood. The kid lay, oozing blood from its neck upon the cobbled stones.

Anne turned away hastily, a flare of suffering leaping up in her. It would take time for her to look upon blood again.

'Well, well!' said two voices, arch, affectionate. History and Geography, with goggles and cameras, and airs of determined enjoyment aggressive as new hats.

'Well well, we haven't seen you for *ages*.'

'When did you get back from wherever you went to?' asked Geography.

'It must have been terrible,' said History. 'What a dreadful tragedy. Poor, poor, Rukmini. And Ranchit too. Dreadful.'

'Well, it's awfully sad.' Geography was brisk. She dismissed the matter. 'The Institute is getting on very well. We're getting a new teacher, two in fact. I may soon be leaving too, I'm afraid.' She sighed, pertly.

'Miss Potter is going to Bongsor, as nurse for a small hospital there,' said History. 'Isn't it *exciting*?'

'Fancy,' said Geography, 'I never *thought* I'd get that near to Tibet. But the Aid people have been advertising for a doctor and a nurse at the dam. It's Mr Menon's idea, I hear, to get a lady doctor as well as men, and recruit a couple of us nurses.' (She pronounced Unni's name without rancour, watching Anne sparrow-hawk fashion.) 'I thought a change would do me good. Keep changing keeps you young, that's what I always say.'

'You'll like it there,' replied Anne, inane, and not caring to be other than inane.

'Oh, I know I will,' said Geography with conviction. 'I'm looking forward to it.'

They wished to walk about with Anne, both of them friendly and sharp-eyed, hoping that in the course of being together something would escape her, a clue to the entrancing tragedy of Bongsor. But again Anne was gone, losing them easily by losing herself in the crowd.

There was a fracturing blast of trumpets, a sudden shouting like the wind snatching through full fields, as the children-gods, a small girl of four and two boys of eight and eleven, adorned with jewels, with painted eyes and golden head-gear, and the unsmiling solemnity of deities, were carried on the shoulders of priests to their chariots.

'*The Kumar! The Kumar!*' (The virgin.) The crowd's happy shouting was a melody of delight, but it was a crowd noise, too much like that sound still hanging about her ears, the wolf-howl ululation of the maroon lamas, recreating the scene in the icy courtyard with its toppling battlements: the gibbering Rampoche, Ranchit staring downwards at Rukmini upon the courtyard stones, and that glittering wave-ominous tide which came from her, the bright silent blood, with the screaming around it, above it, as, an enveloping octopus, an enormous maroon animal on the rampage, the lamas advancing towards Ranchit.

'Pollution! Pollution! Pollution!' The lamas' clamour rose about Anne, standing in the sunlit afternoon, removed in time and space but transfixed by memory.

'The Kumar, the Kumar,' the beatific crowd watching the marvellous children go by on the shoulders of the priests were singing, but Anne heard them not.

'Aaaaaaaaaaah!' The Rampoche was suddenly immense, swollen with the greatness of his cry. 'Ranchit, Ranchit, you are cursed, you are cursed, Ranchit!'

One of the Rampoche's henchmen was cutting Unni's ropes, and Mike was holding Rukmini, crying: 'Rukmini, Rukmini,' but only the movement of his arms about her made her body move, and Mike could not believe that she was dead though he and Unni were bespattered with her blood from that enormous gash through her shoulder into her breast. Unni stood looking, looking at Rukmini in Mike's arms, her blood was even in his hair.

The lamas did not make an end with Ranchit in the courtyard, for he was fleet, strong with fear. They hunted him through the monastery maze, the crooked passages, the irregular courtyards, the sudden walls; the butter lamps blew in the wind of their running, the contorting goddesses saw them dodge, heard them pant, round the wheeling prayer mills. Up the stairs they ran, raucous, a smelly barbaric horde, ferocious and terrible, to the last flat roof, with its rows of golden-spired chortens, like fluted cuspidors, where the ashy bones of previous Rampoches reposed. There they came upon him at last, a merciless pack. It was a consummation brief and smothered, unquestioned later when there was nothing of Ranchit to send back to the Valley. Nothing that could be burnt in decent burial remained of his handsomeness, and this was also to be accepted, for no one ever raised the subject again, although he was a Class A Rana.

Before Anne's eyes the children-gods were being hoisted upon the chariots. A dozen priests arranged the folds of hand, limb, and garment to perfection. Enormous six-foot gilded trays laden with fruit and grain, baked bread and flowers, were placed round the small central canopies under which sat the gods, and the whole gross machinery, splendid and dangerous, with its grotesque massive primitive wheels with the painted eyes, was set in motion, pulled by the hereditary pullers of the gods' chariots, each in his appointed place; they wore black waistcoats with buttons of silver in the shape of birds and fishes. First went the Kumar's chariot, the four-year-old little girl impassive as if of gold, even when her enormous carriage, tugged too sharply at the start, jerked forward without control into the crowd, the menacing wheels making the pullers scatter quickly for fear of being crushed to death.

Anne was pushed back in the hasty backward motion of the crowd before the Kumar's wheels, upon her were thrown two Newari women, fluttering with laughter like a twinkle of butterflies, and heavier, balance less easily restored, Mariette Valport, glossy with excitement and good health.

'*Ma chère, ah, mais c'est Anne, mais c'est bien vous.*' There were embracings, active on Mariette's part, received by Anne. '*Permettez.*' Mariette snapped her. She never forgot to take a picture. '*Et comment ça va? Et ce cher Unni?* 'Ow is 'e? I 'ear about ze tragedy, *un drame, un véritable drame,* you should write it down, I *wish* I 'ad been there ... *ce beau Ranchit, cette belle petite Rukmini.* ...'

Perhaps Mariette had heard only the idiotic official version, concocted by the Rampoche, Unni, and the officials of Khatmandu, made to be disbelieved: Rukmini playing with her husband's kukri, wounding herself mortally. ... Ranchit, mad with grief, plunging into the river, no corpse retrieved. ...

'Of course,' said Mariette, 'some wicked people think Ranchit killed 'er because she was – 'ow you say? – eloping wiz ... Mike Young.'

But it was another name she was thinking of, not Mike Young.

'Ah,' Mariette went on, looking up, shrugging her shoulders, volatile, relinquishing the tragedy she had not participated in for the one totally hers, her eyes round, glowing earnestly with reminiscence of her own comparable pathos, 'I 'ad my troubles, if you knew. *Une histoire stupide et épouvantable.* 'Ow can I tell you? You know ze little Swiss, my friend? I see you cannot remember 'im ... 'e carried my cameras for me.'

Anne had a disconnected, flitting memory, in hazy black and white like a dream recalled, of a small portly man gazing raptly at Mariette, striving to trundle a mound of gadgets behind her, standing by her side in the courtyard of the Old Palace during the Coronation in May.

'Well, 'e died, 'e is dead also,' cried Mariette, 'and 'ow? 'E took forty-eight sleeping tablets, forty-eight all at once, like zat.' Her round arm made the gesture of pouring forty-eight sleeping tablets between her lips. She looked at Anne. ''Orrible, isn't it? And you know why? *C'est trop rigolo,* too ridiculous. Because 'e say it is love,' cried Mariette, laughing loudly and incredulously. 'In love wiz *me.* 'E leave a letter to say it. I cannot take seriously, 'e is such a funny little man ... so ... *vlan*, the tablets. Imagine, in ze twentieth century, people who still take *love* seriously,' she laughed in great splashes. 'It does not exist, *c'est cocasse*, to kill oneself for love, *voyons.*'

But it was her own drama, possessed by no one else, enhancing her in an inexplicable way, to make her indignantly pleased at the Swiss obsession, to make her feel desired for a long time after the originator of this desire had returned to dust. One day perhaps only the little Swiss would remain, *cocasse*, ridiculous, with a heart so sensitive for such a prosaic little man from such a staid, unsentimental country, his features gradually blurring into that of the adoring bovines, but still he would be there, one way or another, for the rest of her life ... and Mariette laughed to shake his ghost away.

'Oh see, look,' cried Mariette, her attention somersaulting, 'all the flowers, *comme un nuage*, like a cloud.'

From the three chariots, grinding slowly into a halo of dust towards the apotheosis of the gods, the priests threw flower petals in handfuls; they sailed in air with the trembling of birds, settled on clothes and hair and caps, and the Newaris tumbled to reach their many-coloured shower.

Rukmini too had had her rain of flowers. They had taken her down from the plane, Rukmini straight in the straight, narrow coffin, and placed her on a sumptuous pale litter of white silk. She was veiled head to foot in one of Dearest's best saris, she looked of course not dead. They had laid flowers and flowers upon her, camellias and white jasmine and amaranths and roses, and taken her thus covered in flowers to the temple of Pashupatinath, where the pyre was laid for her consummation on the burning ghats; and when it was over, flowers and scented wood and that which had been Rukmini had slid pell-mell into the river, floated with the swift stream away, as the dirge for her and the smoke hung and remained behind in the afternoon air. Returning, gentle, sad, resigned, her family had spoken of her next incarnation. '*Henceforth her spirit becomes perfected and another, her fruit is the untying of bonds. May she, without desire, attain to bliss eternal and immeasurable and therein abide.*' Mike Young had been there, stiff of jaw, paining by the pain he exuded; and Devi, veiled and looking so much like Rukmini. Thus Rukmini's beauty had been dealt out, given far and wide, like fallen rain.

The chariots disappeared in a cloud of petals and dust, the crowds evanesced in that unlingering fluid motion of people who walk away on their own feet. Father MacCullough and Fred became visible again among a sparse remainder of watchers. They were waiting for Anne, and with them the ubiquitous Enoch.

'That's what I call an audience-participation show, the way those crowds seemed to understand everything that went on.'

The jeeps and the official motor cars were going now, honking and grumbling one by one, carrying the Monarch, the officials, the diplomats who had watched from the terrace of the Durbar Hall. In one of the jeeps moving by, Anne saw John with the Irish girl, the one who could not drink champagne of any description. He looked more carefree than she had seen him before. Father MacCullough alone showed unease at sight of John, suggesting a move – as if, thought Anne, there was still something between John and myself. There was, of course, she amended her thought, there was the holy sacrament of marriage, a pronouncement once valid and perhaps for ever so, but it was in another dimension, and at this moment, in the completion of herself, she only knew that she was not feeling one way or the other about John, for she was curiously delivered both of compassion and resentment, of fear and hatred, an implacable withering of the old stems and leaves, while this strong, curious root in her put forth new shoots.

Fred came to her. 'Will you come and have a drink with me, Anne?'

She turned to him gratefully, glad of his companionship. It had been searing hurt to go back to the golden room, her room, Unni's room, Rukmini's room; where every wall looked, whispered, sang, sighed Rukmini, Rukmini, and she and Unni were pale ghosts flitting in the golden radiance of Rukmini's sunflowers and birds. Yet Anne had gone back to it, straight from Rukmini's river dissolution. 'I must now and for ever learn to accept, to understand, to receive.'

And though it was relief to be with Fred, there too were the brambles of memory, the ambushed pricking thorn of recall – a camp bed, pushed in a corner, incomprehensibly empty, evoking not desire but this tireless timeless spreading of pain within, making all sight and sound have meaning now. Sitting smooth-faced and withdrawn, love laid upon her the old twists of tenderness, the curious longing for ever unsatisfied.

Fred, at ease, discoursed of John. Father MacCullough's uneasiness at the sight of John, he told Anne, was due to John's recent adventure into conversion. He was taking catechism lessons from the priest, at the behest of the devout and warm-hearted Irish colleen. 'She's a good shrewd women, she'd make an excellent mother for him. The trouble is, he's now stuck with the pose of never divorcing you and claiming happiness for himself. She *may* make him change his mind; but on the other hand he may be a little too crafty for her. It's a pity. She'd have biffed him one when he went into a tantrum, and he'd have improved no end.'

They sat with the bungalow door open, watching the evening take all colour out of the trees and grass. The General appeared to keep them company, accompanied by his whisky maiden, and began with great directness to speak of his dear enemy, the Rampoche of Bongsor.

'Now His Preciousness is woe-begone and haggard, all his power smithered.' The General looked as wickedly pleased as his saintly face allowed.

The Monastery of Bongsor was drenched with foulness, he told Anne and Fred with great relish, with pollution from Rukmini's blood, the blood of woman, for in all the valleys the female was sacred, whereas the male, the flying seed, expendable, could be scattered by slaughter. And this foulness would last at least one hundred and forty-nine days. There would be no festivals of any kind at Bongsor for a long time. The Rampoche was burning tons of butter in propitiatory lamps, the lamas sluiced and scrubbed the stones of the courtyard and the chortens seven times a day, and all burnt fires, offered prayers, till all the prayer mills went spinning and spinning, endlessly, in a cyclone of prayer, to appease the goddesses for the death of Rukmini.

'Truly the gods are smart. The Rampoche has ripened to his ruin long enough,' said the General contentedly. 'And now he has to pay people to turn the prayer mills. They will not do it without money.'

But to Unni, divinity had come, as a cloak to cling to his frame for ever.

'Truly so,' said the General, 'Unni is now a god. He will have no trouble at the dam, only too many worshippers. Already the legend grows, a tale told from slope to slope to the glory of the goddesses.

The story has now reached the bazaar of Khatmandu, and is become truth incarnate for many of our people. They say the man Unni bears an enchanted life and must be Krishna reborn, the God of Love and Life, since the female deities love him and will let him come to no harm. Did not a goddess come in a jeep to the dam, to warn him of danger? When his enemies tried to kill him, did not a goddess again, in the shape of a woman, throw herself under the kukri? True, she *seemed* to die, as the murderer *seemed* to slay, and the quick cruel blood did *seem* to spurt upon the stones and must seemingly be atoned for, lest it breed fiends, but this was the deathless goddesses' whim, and a miracle. And now the Rampoche weeps and the lamas wail like sad birds, but the people of Bongsor travel to the dam to catch a glimpse of the new Lord, and go back happy, blessed as if by a pilgrimage.'

'An engineer become a god,' said Fred. 'Anachronistic, isn't it?'

'My friend,' said the General, 'you are too conservative in your ideas. Why cannot a god be an engineer in our democracy, if he could be a cowherd, a prince, or a carpenter, in olden days? Unni is very clever at using all things, with his cool head above his understanding heart. He will not contradict this story, because he wants above all to build the dam. And now the dam will be built with great success.'

'Unni is clever,' said Anne, neutral. Something else to accept. His destiny, this cleverness, part of his self-awareness, the product of a constant discipline akin to that of the artist, who observes even as he suffers or enjoys.

But when the General had left, Anne had to say to Fred the taut, single truth which she would also say to Unni, when they met again, for they would have to meet again, although she could only wait now, not knowing when.

'I don't think I could have done what Rukmini did. Not even for Unni.'

'Who knows?' said Fred, 'who knows? Could I have done it, say, for Eudora? Could Unni have done it for you? Rukmini was in ecstasy, I think, from what you told me – for her the wall between the physical and the supernatural had possibly been broken – and the end was swift. It is we who are left alive who must come to terms with our own destiny, we who must accept faltering, decay, the misuse of love, and the slow falling away from perfection. We, Anne, who cannot die upon the mountain top, must take the road back; knowing we could not accomplish the supreme gesture, we must live on.'

There was only one more encounter, obvious nearly, expected surely; Anne walking back to her own bungalow, the prayer-wheeling moon bright in an unflawed heaven, saw behind the rose bush the furtive white shape crouched, to meet with her eyes the bedlam eyes of Isobel.

'Why Isobel, you've got no clothes on!'

They gasped, locked in avid hatred, Isobel growling, groping for throat and eyes, the other pushing back in quenchless horror, attempting to cry out but only half-hearted sound escaping, defence held back by Isobel's nakedness.

But alas for Isobel, for whom all the fountains of life ran dry into arid desolation. Regmi, hearing the scuffle, ran up as Anne lost will to fight. He was not afraid of Isobel's unclad body, promptly tripped her and thus brought her to sobs and a slobbering submission.

Anne returned to consciousness to find Fred bending over her, to wonder why there was always rescue for her, always the trim, lucky ending, to shut her eyes, weary unto death of this conclusion worse than anything else and more bitter. Nothing had come right for Isobel. Nothing ever would. Anne wished that it would not be so, that Isobel's fate should not be so unprofitable, doomed to futility through no fault of her own.

'Knew she'd turned odd ... didn't know she'd become violent.' Fred was muttering, apologetic, giving succour to Anne who needed it least. And Anne, alone, heard Isobel wail as she was led away, knew the monstrous injustice done to Isobel, the primal fault, irreparable.

Isobel's spirit, tangling through the dense thickets of inarticulate, useless suffering, would go on. 'Behold, I kept all Thy commandments,' she cried, bewildered and betrayed, betrayed by all she held to, her very goodness, service to others, the virtues, so strongly kept that they had festered within her. Isobel had ripened to her ruin, and all of them were guilty, each one, subtle or crude, had pushed her further into disaster. Unni, merely by *being* Unni, the sensual sure male, making love to other women but refusing Isobel; Fred, throwing her back to loneliness, unwilling to share, refusing companionship on his walks; Anne, most brutal, taking Isobel's gift, the golden room, and using it for her own purposes – perhaps it was destiny, but at this moment it looked very much like cold-blooded ruthlessness; and finally John, the least to blame, striking a pose and thus bludgeoning Isobel into her final catastrophe ... all, all had contrived to Isobel's undoing. Lost in the maze of righteousness was the vibrant woman, madness holding dominion over the proud spirit, now useless. Such loss, such waste, such desolation, and to what purpose? Oh better, far better be Rukmini. Rukmini had felt her ecstasy and lived her death. Rukmini, of the shining hour and the quick oblivion. To her was not dealt out this long lingering, this insentient waiting for nothing at all.

'Poor Isobel. Paul will be handling the matter, repatriation's the only thing.' Fred's voice, distant as an epitaph.

In time this too would be bereft of grief, but now Anne wept for Isobel as she had wept for no one else, knowing it the greatest tragedy, because of its pointlessness.

Finally, end of October, in the cool delightful North Indian autumn, Anne was back at Agra, this time with Fred Maltby, to meet Eudora.

'It's only an experiment really,' Fred had repeatedly insisted. The unpredictable work of time and absence had made his need for Eudora an accumulation that now dragged him out of the Valley and to the once-hated plain, to meet Eudora in a setting with a palpable touch of comedy. Fred was aware of the ridiculous and comical in the spot chosen for their meeting: Agra, the city of the Taj Mahal, the city hung to the white tomb of a woman whose features none remembered; to a monument evoking the petrifaction of love, a warning to all lovers that marble endures long after its object has partaken of the great ascendancy of dust.

Fred had not actually asked Anne to go with him, but was so obviously in need of her to be by his side in this 'experiment', lest it fail – lest the first sight, glance, word, like the wrong twist to a high precision watch, break the spring of his endeavour – that Anne had said: 'May I come with you, Fred? I'd like to see Agra again.'

Overjoyed, he was careful not to show it. 'Oh Anne, that would be nice, but are you sure you can come? I'm sure Eudora would be awfully happy. ...'

No one dared to ask Anne, no one said to her: 'And what about

Unni? What are you and he going to do now?' No one dared, not even Fred.

Anne merely repeated: 'I'd like to see Agra again.'

It was what she had to do, to repay, not Fred, but the interlocking mutuality of existence which had made Fred run into her on the sacred hill of Pashupatinath, ask her to tea, when she had met the General, who had invited her to the wedding, and at the wedding, by the piano, was the man standing, turning round to her ... she was breathless now, merely to think of it. A chain of circumstance, each trivial link infirm in itself; devolving until it was her turn to add gift of act and gesture to fulfil the design for Fred and Eudora.

They went in the familiar DC.3 from Khatmandu to Patna one morning. As they rose Khatmandu pivoted away below them; its cobbled streets red and gold with great squares of chillies and barley spread out to the sun. They soared and the Valley compacted below, golden and russet with autumn, like a beautiful young leopard, thrown down among brown and gold hills; and then they were up, and Fred said unsteadily: 'Look Anne, all the snow lords are there, in the sky.' And so it was.

They had left the Valley where the gods who live in high places delight to walk in pleasure and harmony. Ensconced in her seat, Anne discovered that all gods were man-inclined, valley-inclined; Divinity always wanted to become Man, incarnate in the frail, fallible flesh; there must be something fascinating in human weakness that it so attracted the majestic, aloof lords of the superhuman. Because it was man, creator of complexity, overflowing fountain of creation, who discovered and gave shape to them.

Safe in the plane, cut off by receding hills from the past, Anne could think with equanimity and a slight mocking sense of the inappropriate of Unni's new divinity. Who knows, one day Unni might be carved in wood and stone in legendary style, striding giant's leagues across the mountains, omnipotent, golden, and tremendous. Unni the Dam-builder, they would call him, Conqueror of Floods. Until now she had held at arm's length knowledge of him, stopping short of him day and night long, not ready yet to face him anew. Now she could rustle his memory too, light as an autumn leaf, and as dry, lightly turning it about and about, feeling the pain with the smoothness of a distance upon it, diluted by an impartiality which might one day turn to indifference. But this also was to be accepted, for nothing was proof against time, nor change, nor decay; time ripened all things to their ruin, for time was the real conqueror of love and woe, ending alert suffering, blunting the edge of joy, until only the inescapable pattern asserted itself, lucid and unbroken as the pellicle over water when all sediment has dropped to bottom.

In Agra the hotel where John, Leo, and Anne had stayed in the spring welcomed them back. Anne knew no other, and her curiosity wanted to re-behold the verandah, the potted palms, the snake charmers, the fortune-tellers, only to find them unchanged. She looked round for the Sikh fortune-teller who had read her palm for six rupees, but did not find him.

Eudora was there, and Eudora's giggle had returned to her, an unfortunate jarring note, so that in the first half-hour together the three perpetrated tedious platitudes, to be saved from rancid gaucherie by no less stale a gadget than Radio India playing the *Dance of Siva*. Eudora's eyes shone with pleasure and recollection, and Fred was moved, and moved towards her, amused, interested, liking her more for her addiction to something beyond herself. Later they went out to see the Red Fort, gentle both, and both without impatience.

A week later Leo Bielfeld also returned to Agra. He was back from Phnompenh and a delicious Cambodian dancer 'exactly like one of those Kmer carvings at Angkor Vat'. 'I am so glad you wrote to say you'd be here, Anne. Of course it's no trouble my dropping in here for a couple of weeks.' He laughed superiorly. 'I have invented a new technique, a unit of *effective goodwill* as opposed to the more theoretical aspect I'd put forward previously. I need some rest from my intensive researches in Cambodia.' All his expenses were paid by the United Nations, and he would stay as long as Anne desired.

Their foursome was pleasantly boring, pleasantly chaste, lethargic. Anne slept long and late, in need of a great deal of hibernation. Then, as November swung on, and it was colder, with crisp delightful mornings, and tourists began to speak of Christmas, Anne woke one morning crying Unni's name, wanting him, his long and muscled body, his taut mind, his deep laughter. His voice rang in her ears all that day.

'Unni, Unni.' As if he could be materialized by calling his name. The days passed and her longing dwelt with her, filling her with its growth.

Together with Leo she watched the golden snail trail of the western sun drag behind the Taj Mahal. The full, bounding river came nearly up to the marble terrace. It had been so low, stagnant and low, in the spring; now it was swollen with the rains of summer. Anne had become silent again, difficult to communicate with, and Leo remembered her laughter in the halcyon May as something delightful, regrettably gone. Though she was more beautiful than ever, he did not attempt to establish himself in a lover's capacity, but lingered on, as if he too were waiting, and made talk, because only talk prevented extinguishment in this pondering waiting pause which was to be with Anne.

'Let me tell you a story about the Taj Mahal, Anne, a romantic tale, to suit your mood. It's about Shah Jehan, the Emperor who built this pale colossal jewel, with its intricate purities, to his love Nur Mahal. She must have been most attractive, since she bore him thirteen children in spite of all the other ladies of the harem. What fascinates me is not this presumptuous pile, but the other Taj, the one on the opposite side of that river, the one which was never built.

'When, after twenty-two years, this Taj was finished, the Emperor's passion for architectural exhibitionism was not slaked. As he gazed on this white perfection, his rheumy old man's stare turned to the empty shore opposite, and suddenly conceived yet another monument, stone for stone the same as this one, but of purest black, an ebony replica to be his own tomb. At once workmen started on the foundations; but the Treasury was empty, the provinces rebellious, and his son, Aurungzeb, stopped his father's ruinous folly by shutting him up in the Red Fort for the remaining seven years of his life. It is that Taj, night-black, dark as Nur Mahal's hair, which I think of. The unaccomplished dream, more fascinating and mysterious than the stony beauty of this grave where we linger now.'

Anne gave him an odd, speculative glance, and made no reply. Then Leo knew it was time for him to go away, to leave her, to leave Agra. He would never see Anne again. He swore to himself he would not. There was no point in it. She could only make him unhappy, remain unattainable for ever. And he was angry with her because he had come at her bidding, and knew that their meeting would be sterile, all possible usefulness exhausted.

'What are your plans?' he asked her.

'To wait here.'

'Wait for Unni? Are you two getting married?'

'I don't know.'

'Has he written to you?'

'No, he does not need to.'

'Tell me,' asked Leo, exasperated, 'tell me, why did you fall for Unni? What did he do to capture you?'

'I don't know,' said Anne. 'The answer to your question is, I suppose, because he trusted me to drive his jeep on an unmade mountain road. It was very mad. Then I asked him to help me. For I was at the end of my tether, humanly speaking. And he did.'

'It worked.' Leo was ironical. 'And that's why you're waiting here? How d'you know he will come?'

'He will come ... when it is time for both of us.'

'How will he guess when it is time, difficult Anne?'

'He will know,' said Anne simply, 'as I know. Meanwhile ...'

She stopped. Once, in the Valley, she had told Leo that she was writing again and he had not listened. Now she would not tell him of this vision, pattern, shaping itself, essential miracle for the artist, for which a life must sometimes be given, for which a lifetime is often too short. She would not tell him that only in solitude could this occur, only to the solitary would be vouchsafed the sure instinct all men craved – and that was why she was alone, at Agra, making no gesture, no movement, intent on completion, the inner travail.

A few days later at dinner Fred said carefully: 'Just had a letter from the General. Wonderful English the old boy writes. All is well with the Valley. There is a move afoot to ask Eudora to take over the Girl's Institute, now that poor Isobel is back in England.' He looked at Eudora. She was calm and happy, as he liked her to be. No obstacle subsisted between them. He wanted to squeeze her hand, but felt shy. It was tremendous, to be in love with one's own wife. What a lucky man he was. And to think he'd run away from her ... but then they had never known each other, never given themselves a chance. ...

Now Fred wanted to help Anne and Unni, as people tidy a room when they leave, for the time must come when he and Eudora must go back to Khatmandu. He added: 'The General writes: "Unni is just back from Bongsor on leave." That must have been, let me see,

three days ago; this letter's only taken three days from Khatmandu.'
He examined the envelope with care.

'I think Unni will be here soon,' said Eudora, bravely. 'Don't you
think so, Anne?'

'Yes,' said Anne. 'I think he will come.'

*

I remember our parting, Unni and I. None of us slept that night at
Bongsor. The lamas had achieved their revenge; all night through the
trumpets and drums and lamentations proclaimed the Monastery's
pollution. All night the Rampoche walked up and down, defeated,
ordering the prayer mills turned as fast as possible, and saying 'Yes,
Sri Menon,' as Unni extracted from him the keys to the weapons'
cache and made his followers disarm. Soon there was a heap of
weapons in the courtyard. Perhaps there would be no more raids now
on the convoys to the dam.

Towards dawn, as Dearest and I sat, open eyed, watching over
Rukmini – we had washed and dressed her, swathing her head to foot
in Dearest's best sari: 'She was much more beautiful than I can ever
be Mrs Ford she should have it' – Unni came to our room and spoke
to Dearest, who got up and went out.

'I have just sent Dearest for some Tibetan balm. Will you apply
some to my back?'

It was stupid to ask: does it hurt? It must have hurt like hell. He
stripped, his back was covered with dark bruises. Dearest made loud
noises of commiseration and pity. I applied the balm, and Dearest
gave him a clean shirt of her father's.

In the courtyard there was hammering, they were putting together
the narrow wooden box in which Rukmini would return to the
Valley. Mike Young, a prerogative no one questioned, placed
Rukmini in it. Unni took the lid and put it on the box, and he and
Mike loaded it in one jeep. Mike sat in the jeep and drove Rukmini,
Unni and I rode in the next jeep, behind us were the Rampoche,
Dearest, and Professor Rimskov. That was Rukmini's funeral proces-
sion from the Monastery to the airfield at Bongsor.

I shall never know what Unni's thoughts were as we drove behind
Rukmini. She must have fallen across his back, throwing herself
under Ranchit's kukri ...

We were at the airfield, in brilliant sun.

Unni turned to me. 'I will come to you. Will you wait?'

'Yes, Unni.'

He would come. Giving us time, essential time, to remake each our own world, our man-made walking circle devoid of supple confusions.

Any hour now he may be here, in Agra, coming to me. I might return from a soporific walk under the gold mohurs to find him sitting on the verandah, throwing his little charm up and down, listening to Fred, or to Leo (if they are still here), waiting for me as he waited, that spring, in the Valley, under the chestnuts. He would come, and be well known yet a stranger unexplored. And for this relationship which we need and want, not the stifling pattern of submission and domination, a limited and mutually exclusive imprisonment, but a live, full freedom for both, he and I must meet as if still unknown to each other. I would pray now, as Unni must have prayed, that love be granted to us, good and clear in binding and also in releasing, love infinitely considerate and courteous, each holding a separate world of being, yet together achieving wholeness.

As all human beings are, so are we solitaries, Unni and I. And this we accept, though others repudiate the thought, for all humans are frightened of their own solitude. Yet only in solitude can man learn to know himself, learn to handle his own eternity of aloneness. And love from one being to another can only be that two solitudes come nearer, recognize and protect and comfort each other.

Unni will come, if not today, then tomorrow. Today is nearly gone, but other todays stir fecund in the word tomorrow, many other todays when this one has lapsed from existence. And because I think of Unni, invoking his name in this for ever recurrent today, already he is here for me.